I0772322

The Hymns of God and Men

A Novel by ERIK DARROW

Preface

The field grew dark around them as the clouds closed the sky above. Lightning struck the darkness of the night, and thunder rumbled the earth on which they stood. Yefimovich spoke; his tongue was tenacious towards his enemy.

"It ends here, Alois!" A hundred yards back was an army behind Yefimovich. To his side, an ally by the name of Tokugawa, and along his right, a young man in fierce metallic armor with a shield donned upon his back that glowed hot white and alluring purple. "Your lust for power and destruction of this land dies tonight!" Yefimovich threatened his enemy. Tokugawa and the knight halted their advance as Yefimovich strode forward, his movement now more aggressive.

"The lust for power never ends; it is only transferred into the next soul who desires it more than its predecessor. If you want to end my reign, it only takes a knife through my heart." Emperor Alois responded as he began walking toward Yefimovich. Clutched in his hand was a sword whose blade gave a glow of rustic orange. His armor screeched a wicked tune, and the sockets of his helmet shone blood red. His pace quickened. Yefimovich, whose armor only covered his joints, saw that Alois's pace has hastened, and he too, began to speed his approach on Alois, he was weaponless.

The lightning struck, and thunder clapped. They seemed to move as fast as light itself. The two were now in striking distance; Alois swung his blade, but Yefimovich, whose foot was planted deep within the ground, moved the ground of the earth and hoisted himself towards the storm above. A pillar of stone and bedrock now stood where Yefimovich once was. He landed forcefully behind Alois, and when Yefimovich landed, by thought alone, he moved the pillared bedrock and hurled it towards his enemy. The column of earth fell upon the emperor, but Alois was mighty, and he was unscathed, and the pillar became nothing more than shattered pieces.

"The ability to manipulate the pitch on which you stand gives you no advantage," Alois spoke ominously. "You are a fool, Yefimovich, and you will lose!" The emperor lunged like a comet heaving itself towards the earth. Almost before Alois made his move, Yefimovich spun from him and struck Alois with the force of a thousand men, striking his back and sending Alois forward to the ground. The emperor rose, removed his helmet, and cast his sword aside. His jaw was clenched, so too his fists, and rain began to fall heavily upon the two men. The sky lit up, but the rumble of the thunder never came. Alois fluttered towards Yefimovich as fast as one could blink. Yefimovich tried to counter his approach. Colonnade after colonnade he created from the earth, but Alois seemed to move as if he teleported from one spot to the next. Yefimovich, nearly in arms reach of Alois, cast another colonnade directly in front of himself, but Alois plunged through the final column and struck Yefimovich squarely in his chest, and the force of the strike knocked him twenty yards and gouged the land as he skidded across it.

The night sky seemed to get darker, almost cimmerian. The thunder roared in the blackness, and the two men began to fight again. Their movements like quicksilver, each blow forceful and destructive, a sound like cannonade they made. Yefimovich pulled back his fist to strike, but Alois leapt skyward, fifty feet into the air. Countering, Yefimovich shot himself upward by creating a pilaster from the earth. He met Alois in the sky and grabbed him by his armor. He clenched his fist as tight as he could and struck the head of his opponent until his arm grew weary. Alois was still in Yefimovich's grasp, and the two began to fall back to the earth, Alois below Yefimovich. The men landed and their impact formed a small crater in the battlefield.

"It's over!" Yefimovich cried as he tried to force himself off Alois, but the battle wasn't over, rather, it continued to rage. Each man was bruised and bloody. Sweat mixed with the rain. Fiercely they fought. The power within both men seemed to grow as they frenzied in the black of night. As the spectacle reigned, Alois took hold of Yefimovich's left arm, caught in his binding might, and slammed him into the ground. Yefimovich cried in pain, the bones in his arm were broken. Alois quickly fell upon his waist and started striking Yefimovich's face with the bones and the muscles of his fists. Yefimovich seemed to be approaching death as he was scraped and battered with punch after punch.

In desperation, with all the strength he had left within his soul, he molded the earth to form a vise around Alois's neck. Alois's hands now reached towards his own throat, but he could not break the stone around it. Yefimovich then encased the rest of Alois from his shoulders down to his feet in the bedrock, binding him to the earth.

Nose and cheekbones broken, blood dripping down his face, Yefimovich now stood before his opponent and spoke, "You are hereby taken into custody for war crimes against humanity. You will be stripped of your title as emperor and will stand trial for the crimes you have committed." He spit the blood out that had amassed inside his mouth. "Do you understand?"

With despair in his eyes, Alois responded, "I do."

The heavy rain began to soften, and the clouds above started to break. Dawn had struck the darkness of the night.

"A new day has come," said the knight, his shield still illuminated with an encryption that read, *This light is our love. May it forever burn bright within our souls, and let it shine brightest when the world has gone dark.*

"It is already better than the day before. Let us go home, Robert," Yefimovich replied to the knight.

The next day came. Alois laid within his cell; its ceiling was of dirt and stone. The ground was of the same. There were no windows or doors, but boulders made of diamonds were on all four sides of him, each wall nearly two feet thick. Alois felt a slight ripple of the earth. One of the diamond walls began to sink into the ground, and as it disappeared into the soil, four guards were seen on the other side of him.

One of the soldiers spoke, "The jury awaits, Emperor Alois." The soldier's uniform was sharp and form fitting. His trousers a dark brown, his coat red with gold lining, a strong ridged officer's hat and leather boots nearly reaching his knees. He bore a patch of a gammadion cross on his left shoulder.

Alois started to speak, "I see you wear the symbol of the sun. You must be an Esh."

The soldier replied, "I am."

"Will you show me a bolt of lightning?" Alois asked.

"No," The Eshan scoffed.

"How about a small flame?" Alois persisted. This time there was no response. The soldier took hold of Alois's collar and shoved him forward.

"Walk," the Eshan commanded. The boots of the soldiers echoed through the halls of the building as they stepped on the marble floors. Hollow tones rang in their ears.

"I can't help but notice that each of you bear a different patch upon your sleeve. One of fire, one of water, another of earth, and one of air. An Eshan, Mahyeem, Adamah, and Avir. I feel honored to be guarded by such soldiers. May I ask, where are we?" Alois questioned them.

"We are in the Citadel," replied the Adamah soldier.

"How far down are we?" Alois inquired further.

"Far enough," replied the soldier. The four guards approached two of their peers standing near a massive slab of bedrock. The two guards wore the symbol of the earth, which was a rooted pyramid; their attire was similar to that of the Eshan, however the Adamah's jackets were forest green and draped with a shoulder cape.

"Take us to Tzedakah," the Mahyeem soldier requested.

"A day of reckoning," replied one of the guards.

"Indeed." The four soldiers and Alois now stood upon the sheet of stone. The Adamah guards widened their stance, both arms at ninety degrees, palms open. They made an upwards motion with their hands, and the massive stone on which the five men stood began to rise. The platform glided to its destination and finally stopped outside the Tzedakah.

"The jury awaits you," said the Eshan with a scolding sound in his voice. Alois stepped forward into the circular court room. The entire building was made from a single piece of glass. A spectacular design in construction and one of great imagination, for the structure itself was more than a building; it was a sun dial. At each hour of the day sat a juror, and the judge was positioned atop the gnomon. Alois stopped at the base from where the judge was seated, looked down at the copper floor, and saw he stood upon a rooted pyramid with an eye in its center. He then spun to look at the entire image that protruded through the copper and noticed the pyramid was a crown worn by a woman whose eyes were blinded by a cloth and who cradled a lamb in her left arm and a sword in her right. At the entrance from where he walked were words that read, *Judged by God and Men, Protector of the Innocent, Punisher of the Guilty, blind to all but the Truth.* The room was silent; there was no audience within it nor any press to write, nor digital recording of the affair. Only a government historian was there to bear witness to the event and the stenographer to write it all down.

The judge addressed the room and spoke in a commanding voice, "Good evening, ladies and gentlemen. We are brought here today to seek out the truth. Calling the case for Alois Bin Hidler whose crimes consists of the use of chemical weapons on his own people, abduction and mass murder of the Telekine people, and the assassination of the Tulku. How do you plead?"

"Guilty," Alois said in a sombre voice. Being he a man who committed guilt, there was no trial. There were only proceedings to administer the punishment for the crimes he had committed and for records to be archived and stored in the dust bins of history. The day would be documented for historians who researched such matters to judge those of the past with the clairvoyance of hindsight. The judge laid down his hammer and administered his sentence.

"Your punishment for these high crimes is death. You will be permitted to see your family once before your sentence is carried out and a day of prayer and fasting if you wish."

"When will I be able to see my family?" Alois asked, concerned, for he desperately wanted to talk to them, to see them before he would perish from the earth.

"We can arrange to bring them here tomorrow," the judge answered.

"Thank you, judge."

"You are dismissed. Guards, please escort Sir Alois back to his cell." The hammer slammed, and in an instant, the case of Alois Bin Hidler was over.

The following day came. For Alois, it was far too quick, yet he welcomed it, nonetheless. The cell wall began to lower into the ground and from behind it, an Adamah guard. "You have visitors," said the soldier. Standing in front of Alois was a woman wearing a black sheer corset and black leather pants as tight as skin. Around her neck rested a black choker, and upon her wrists were midnight bracelets that had sheer dark cloths in the shape of a triangle flowing from them. Her complexion was that of a pale shadow. Beside her was a man near seven feet tall. His skin, a lifeless pale gray. The sclera of his eyes were bloodshot, and his irises fire orange. His teeth were white as pearls and as strong as steel. He wore a form-fitting black body suit; his muscles bulged through it. His eyes met his father's.

"Hello, my son." Alois spoke softly.

"Vater," Alamgeer replied in a melancholy tone.

Alois looked at his wife, "I am sorry Betrub; I have failed you."

She and Alamgeer walked into the cell. Alois embraced his wife.

"There is no need to apologize. It was not you who failed, but our allies, and do not worry about us; we will be fine," she whispered. Alois and his wife broke their embrace, and they sat on the platform Alois used as a bed. "Are you scared?" she asked.

"Scared? No. I am only disappointed in myself. There is so much more left to accomplish. I did not expect the people of Saoirse to enter the war as quickly as they did. I should have gotten their loyalty before I proceeded." Alois spoke honestly, his voice unshaken.

"You should have killed them. They are nothing. Scum, vermin, they are. A horrible people with wicked ideals," Betrub interjected.

"They are more powerful than they appear," Alois said regretfully. He leaned forward toward his son.

"Come closer, son." Alamgeer knelt down so his eyes met his father's. Alois spoke softly, "The flame burns low."

"Then I will make it rage," Alamgeer murmured angrily.

"What I have done wrong, you must make right," his father told him.

"I will, Vater. I promise." Alois rose and wrapped his arms around his son.

"Do not falter, and do not hesitate, for that is where I failed. I did not rid all the poison that lay within the nation. It will be painful to do so, but it must be done," Alois counseled him.

"I will learn to harden my heart so that I may do what is needed," Alamgeer promised his father. Alois looked back to his wife.

"Betrub, help to guide our son."

"I will do all I can, even if it means my life," she replied.

In the hour they had together, none of them reminisced of the past. Their talk was only of the future and how to move forward, to the goal of one Holle. For Alois knew his life was over, and he lived his life and knew what it held; thus, the future was all that mattered now to him. It was for the sake of his son and the sake of a pure, unified country of Holle.

The guard cleared his throat, "I apologize, but this was all the time you have been given." Alois held his wife tightly in his arms once more. Betrub's eyes began to water, yet her voice did not falter. "I love you," she said. She looked up into his eyes and kissed his lips. Their lips separated as did their embrace. Alois turned to his son and folded his arms around him for the last time.

"Goodbye, my son." Alois's heart was broken, but his voice was strong to say the words.

"Goodbye, Vater. The flame looks bright," Alamgeer said back to him. Betrud and Alamgeer walked out of the cell, and the world fell quiet as the diamond wall rose back towards the ceiling. Alois wished he had more time. Not enough words could be spoken in only an hour's time to explain; war and all its facets were complex and webbed in lines hard to connect when executed. He worried for his wife and son and what life held for them after the events of the Great War. He knew that they too would stand trial, and though he ensured his actions never included them and deliberately left them out of meetings and reports to show proof of innocence, he was still afraid. On those thoughts he meditated for all the day and all the night.

The day broke. Alois did not sleep, nor did he pray. Fury burned within his eyes as he sat on his bed made of stone and dirt. The diamond slate began to fall; this time six soldiers were there to greet him. They walked the grand halls of the underground prison. Torches lined the walls, and two Eshan soldiers each had a flaming ball hovering above their palms. They exited the building and walked towards the execution site that was cradled by a mountain, extending out from the Citadel. The site extended a quarter mile past the Citadel walls, and its pathway was of brown and red bricks. It was sword shaped and looked as if it hung a thousand feet in the open air, overlooking the city of Erbil down below.

In front of Alois was a circular scaffold made from the red clay of the land. He walked up the stairs attached to the stage of his execution, turned, and kneeled at the center. He looked up and saw his wife and son along with leaders from other nations. It pained him to see them there. An Adamah soldier approached Alois from behind, and by thought, he began to mold arches around Alois's legs. The soldier slammed the arches into the ground; bounding his legs to the dais. Alois did not react to the pain he felt.

The executioner walked forward onto the stage. He was Heavohen, from the island nation of Heavohe. His skin was bronzed, and his hair was that of blue feathers, and his feathers ruffled in the breeze and fell down to his shoulders. He had markings upon his chest and torso, symbols with meaning behind each inked image. Affixed to his arms and neck was an eclectic mix of bones and gold jewelry. He looked out onto the crowd. His voice was harsh, and he spoke, "Before us is Emperor Alois Bin Hidler. Charged with the crimes of the use of chemical weapons, abduction, and mass murder of the Telekine people and assassination of the Tulku. Do you have any last words?"

Alois looked up, madness still in his eyes, "I believe today that my conduct is in accordance with the will of the Almighty Creator, and that His will, which I have failed to carry out, will one day be fulfilled. So, though I may die today, my soul will rage to finish what I have started. Lange lede der Reich! Lange lede der Reich! Lange lede der Reich!"

The executioner pulled his blade from his sheath, placed the cold metal on the back of Alois's neck as he shouted his final words, pulled back the sword, and swung.

The Treaty

Nearly six months had passed since the execution of Alois Bin Hidler. The leaders from every major nation gathered, from the islands of Heavohe, to the floating continent of Avengler, to the frozen nation of Nihon. They gathered to discuss and bear witness to the Hidler-Nemtsov Agreement. Two men, from the free and diverse nation of Saoirse, mingled amongst one another.

"Ah, Isc! You're finally here." A man by the name of Robert spoke delightedly as his brother, Iscariot, entered the well decorated suite. The walls of the room were of solid white stone with crown molding made of gold. Iscariot's boots percussed on the dark hardwood floors. The two men went to hug one another, to show their brotherly affection, but before they embraced their arms broke away from each other and the men began to wrestle. Iscariot maneuvered to get behind Robert, and when he managed to do so he wrapped his arm around his brother's neck.

"Alright, Isc! You win." Robert chuckled, still coiled in Iscariot's hold.

"Well, that was quick. What's that? Five in a row?" Iscariot said sarcastically to his brother. Iscariot released him and the two men embraced with gladness in their hearts. The brothers were very close and full of love for one another; playful shenanigans were always present between the two, and it seemed as if nothing could separate their bond.

"No, I don't think that's quite right. I think you may have forgotten how to count, Isc." Robert smirked. "You've only won today because I've let you win. I'm just a little tired from battling the Hollen soldiers for the last eleven months," Robert explained, the grin still on his face.

"That was six months ago, and what was I doing? Did I not fight them, too? Did I not help win the war?" asked Iscariot.

"Your words, not mine," Robert said, still smiling. "Have you read this treaty they are about to sign? What do you think of it?" he asked, flipping through some of the pages that had been lying on a mahogany desk within the room.

"To be honest, I feel quite sorry for the Hollen people. Their lands are being taken away, and now, the Telekine control the entire eastern portion of the continent."

"And you think their land shouldn't be taken away? Holle still owns half the continent, and the remainder is to be split into several nations," Robert rebutted.

Iscariot rolled his dark brown eyes, "I'm only saying the Telekine have the meat of the treaty in their favor. That's all."

"Well—I think we can both agree the treaty seems weak. If our country joins this Coalition of Nations, it would be a complete breakdown of how we govern ourselves. It also puts the entire country of Holle in a serious financial dilemma in which they will surely collapse." Robert pointed out just a few of the treaty's errors.

"That's why it needs these other small states to keep afloat. They need to be under the rule of Holle," Iscariot interjected.

"You know we can't do that. Any trace of the old regime will surely bring about an uprising and another war," Robert tried to explain.

"Well, I guess we'll never know, will we? We should get ready. I'm sure Father will be upset if we're late," Iscariot said with frustration in his breath.

Robert was a handsome man. He stood at six feet in height and had piercing green eyes. As he dressed, he threw a white cotton shirt with a high collar over his head. He ran his fingers through his long straight brown hair that almost hit his shoulders. His slacks were trim, of brown tweed, along with his vest and frock coat. He gave himself a look over; satisfied, he was ready for the day. Soon after he was dressed, Iscariot walked out of the room where he had been getting ready. Slightly taller than his brother, his sand blond hair was combed back, his beard was full yet well kept. He wore a dark checkered tweed frock jacket, his waistcoat was a solid color of the same material that match his slacks. Around his neck was an elegant bowtie, and atop his head rested a checkered tweed top hat.

"I still look better," Robert joked.

"You're quite funny. Look in the mirror once more. I think you'll change your mind," Iscariot jested in return.

The two men walked out of the room and into a hallway of Sesom Palace. The palace resided in the city of Erbil. The people of the nation were called the Telekine, and many whom called this new nation home were of the Ivdeyskiy religion. White walls and gold statues lined the halls toward the half landing staircase that was outside the gentlemen's suite. As they strolled through the long anteroom, they saw a behemoth of a man leaving his chambers.

"Tokugawa!" Robert's voice boomed through the corridors of the manor. The creature, nearly eight feet tall with skin like silver, turned. His veins, translucent on his skin, glowed bright white, his eyes the same color only dimmer. His hair was black and styled with a topknot that was held together by a silver band in the form of a dragon. He was dressed in formal Nihon attire, equipped with a black and white hakama, a black haori, traditional open-toed sandals, and a haori himo.

"Boys! It's great to see you. You both look much better without the strain of war on your faces. Where is your father?" Tokugawa asked. His demeanor was kind and lighthearted. He was a gentle soul full of wisdom.

"We are about to meet him downstairs," Iscariot responded. "Join us." So, the man did, and the three of them walked down the staircase discussing matters deep and meaningful.

"We're sorry to hear of your son, Tokugawa," Robert spoke somberly. "He was an incredible warrior."

"Thank you, boys, that is very kind. He always thought of you as brothers."

"As we did him. The news of his passing weighed greatly on my heart," Robert grieved.

"On both of ours," added Iscariot.

"I pray his soul has gone to Elysium," Tokugawa said solemnly.

"I do not doubt it for a second. There is no one more worthy than Oda," Robert said in the same tone of sadness. Tokugawa smiled at them both for their admiration of and kind words for his son.

The gentlemen had reached the bottom of the staircase and continued through the royal residence into a massive ballroom. Inside the room were five stunning crystal chandeliers along with gold-plated pillars which held an astounding balcony overlooking the dance floor. At the rooms entrance were two twelve-foot statues of famous ballet dancers from nearly two centuries ago, embroidered with emeralds, rubies, sapphire, and pearls. Each room seemed more grand than the previous as they walked from room to room to the entrance of the palace.

A white-haired man spoke as the three men walked outside.

"There are my three favorite men. Good to see you're on time for once, Iscariot."

"Well, I didn't want to face your wrath, Father," Iscariot responded slyly.

"Tokugawa, my dear friend. How are you feeling?" the old man inquired.

"As best a man can be after such terrible times. It's good to see your face again, Abraham," Tokugawa replied.

The men paced the grounds and continued their chatter, and as they talked outside, a silver metallic spherical aircraft came booming down from the bright blue cloudless sky.

"What an extraordinary machine, wouldn't you say? Completely powered by air. It's absolutely incredible." Abraham marveled. As the aircraft landed and its doors opened, two Avir soldiers exited to greet them. The soldiers wore pure white slacks with matching jackets that went down to mid-thigh. Their hands were covered by brown leather gloves that complimented their leather boots that rose to just below their kneecaps. Resting on their left shoulders were snow white capes with gold stitching, and sewn upon their opposite shoulders were wings of a windmill with the image of a cyclone at its center, identifying which military branch they belonged to.

"Is this an Orbital One aircraft?" Abraham continued. "Do you mind showing me how this works before we take off?"

"Hop inside, sir, and I shall tell you as we travel to the Arch." The pilots positioned themselves in their seats, and with small hand gestures, the sphere in which they sat began to spin. With gyroscopic precession, the ball began to rise off the ground and into the air. The yellow desert sands began to fly about, encircling the aircraft like a hurricane. Then the air gave a quick snap followed by a heavy boom, and within seconds, they were traveling at the speed of sound. Inside the sphere was an axis suspended by magnets on which the passengers and staff sat. It would counterbalance for any movement the aircraft would make, keeping the people inside the aircraft stationary and protecting them from the forces the sphere endured.

In mere minutes they had reached their destination, and the aircraft now hovered above the 580-meter bow-shaped building. Down below were thousands of people within the town square ready to witness the historic day. The airship glided gently down to the surface. The wind whirled around the spherical craft, and like a feather, it landed, soundless. The craft's door decompressed and rose.

"Antigravity, you say? How fascinating." Abraham spoke in disbelief, continuing the discussion on how the aerial vehicle operated. The men exited Orbital One and headed towards the gates of the Arch. Atop the center of the Arch was a copper sculpture of a woman riding a chariot. They called her the Goddess of Glory, and she rode upon the Chariot of Victory. Abraham looked up and pointed at the statue and told his sons of the woman.

"It is foretold that she will one day return to bring peace to the earth and that the peace she brings will last a thousand years." He told them of her history and how many believed she was the first messenger of God, the Tulku.

As they continued their walk forward to the Arch, Abraham paused every few feet to shake hands and say hello to the people lined in the square. He, his sons, and Tokugawa entered and walked the halls of the gargantuan building to the General Assembly Room, which sat more than 1,000 people. Tokugawa separated from them as they took their seats, which were designated by country. In front of the assembly hall, perched on a wooden platform, sat the signers of the treaty. Center right, facing the assembly audience, sat Yefimovich and the leaders from each military branch of the newly formed nation of Yisra. Center left was Alamgeer and the military leaders of Holle. The session began with formal introductions of the two countries, and then the treaty was read aloud to the assemblage. After months of meetings and deliberation between the countries, it was now finalized. Emotions were high, some delighted, others fueled by anger. Yefimovich, his speech impaired, spoke slowly so as not to stutter.

"Today is the day on which our chains have been broken. We have been beaten and bloodied, but we have prevailed. For centuries, we have looked to call a place our own. For centuries, we have fought through the pits of hell, and today we see the gates of heaven. A promise made to us, three millennia ago, has finally been fulfilled. We have never been more humbled, nor as thankful as we are today. From this day forth, this land will be forever known as Yisra, and may those who died fighting for it never be forgotten!" The crowd roared in applause, boots were stomping on the floor, fists were pounding the tables. The crowd then fell silent as Alamgeer got up to speak his final words to the leaders of the world.

"They say this was the war to end all wars. I say those people are fools. War will never end. It will merely fall dormant like a volcano, and when the world has forgotten about it, it will wreak havoc as it always does. May the world enjoy this time of peace. May you find tranquility after such terrors. May we sleep peacefully and live fully, for I know I will. As I am a fool that believes this is truly the war that ends all wars. Let us rejoice and begin this era of peace by the signing of the Hidler-Nemtsov agreement." Alamgeer scribbled his name on the document, and the room echoed with applause once more.

<u>Robert Chapter One</u>

The crickets were still singing their songs of the night, and the moon had fallen away to the west. The room was dark as Robert quietly put on his clothes. He pulled up his light brown slacks to his waist, buckled his belt, and tossed a beige button-up shirt over his shoulders. He buttoned the shirt, leaving some of his chest exposed, and fitted onto his head a high-crowned, wide brimmed hat. While he dressed, his wife was still wrapped in crisp white cotton sheets, asleep in their massive canopy bed. Robert silently walked on the age-old oak floors towards his wife, and he knelt down and met her face to face. He listened as she breathed, and he marveled at her beauty—her hair a mix of blond and brown, her eyes the color topaz that sparkled like stars in the night sky. She had teeth white as pearls and skin as soft as silk. He kissed her soft pink plump lips. Her beautiful topaz eyes opened, and Robert whispered to her, "Good morning, my love, did I wake you?"

"No." She smiled. "It was this little guy kicking my belly. I don't think he wants you to go." Robert moved down towards Lagertha's belly and placed his hand upon it. He felt two little kicks against his hand and then placed his ear to her stomach.

"Oh, I see," he said.

"What does he say?"

"He says he wants to go with me."

"Tell him he's free to go anytime he likes; he's been cooped up in there for nine months," she told Robert and then looked at her belly and started talking to her son within it. "Ya know, little one, the world is big and beautiful, and bright, and warm, and I can't wait for you to be a part of it." Lagertha spoke warmly to her unborn child. "Don't stay cooped up in there forever. There's so much for you to see."

"You should listen to your mom, little one, but stay in a little longer so I can see the day you're born. Goodbye, my little son, I'll see you in a couple days." Robert kissed his wife's stomach, and his eyes focused back onto hers. He moved the small strands of hair from her face with his fingers and cupped the back of her head. He pulled her forward slightly but gently and kissed her fiercely.

"I sure do love the taste of your morning breath," he said facetiously. Lagertha breathed heavily into his face and smiled at him.

"Just as much as you like the smell of my morning breath?"

"Almost." He grinned. "I'll see you in a couple days and hopefully our little boy, too." Robert kissed her once more, struggling to leave her beauty and the warmth of her heart. Finally, he departed from her love and headed towards the entrance of the house.

In the entryway, Robert began lacing up his leather boots, putting on his final garments before heading out into the day, and while he readied himself, he heard little footsteps echoing through the rooms of the house. He looked up from knotting his boots and saw the light of his life, his little three-year-old girl. She had light brown hair that fell down her back, aquamarine eyes that melted her father's heart, and a voice as charming as any bell.

"Good morning, tiny dancer. What are you doing up so early?" he asked with a beaming grin on his face. She didn't respond to her father but instead ran to him with her arms open ready to receive his love. Robert stopped tying his boots and caught her as she jumped into his arms.

"You're gonna be cold outside, Daddy." Her voice was soft as cotton, as cute as a puppy's whimper, and full of concern that her father might freeze in winter's grip.

"It's okay, Lo. I have my thermal pants on underneath, and I have my sweater sitting right next to me. Are you going to behave for your mother while I'm gone?"

"I will, Dad. I promise," she replied. Her arms wrapped around her father's neck.

"You going to take care of Mom while I'm away, too, and sing to your baby brother?"

"I'll sing Dún do shúil to him every night," Lorena assured her father.

"Oh, I love that one. Can you sing it to me?" Lorena looked at him and nodded her head. She unwrapped her arms around her caring father and left his lap to stand before him and sing the old lullaby:

"Lay down your head,
Lay down your head my chosen one,
Sleep amongst the stars, the spirits of the sky,
Sleep amongst the angels, who stand at your side,
Dream your dreams, your tales of great fortune,
Dream your dreams, of joy and happiness
Let the Spirit manifest your visions,
Let the Spirit lead you in the night,

You are the pelican in the sea,
You are the owl in the tree,
Play amongst the sparrows,
Swim amongst the lilies,
These are the dreams He has for thee." She stopped singing with slight embarrassment in her cheeks and ran back into her father's embrace.

"That was beautiful, Lorena, thank you." Robert encouraged her and kissed her with a tender heart full of fatherly love. "Your little brother is going to love to hear you sing." She beamed at her father's words.

Lorena stayed cozied in her father's warmth, and they sat together talking about what Lorena was going to have for breakfast and about what other songs she could sing to her brother, and she listed everything that she would do until it was time for Robert to leave.

"Well, little earth angel, I've got to get going. I'm sure I have to wake up your Uncle Isc. He's never on time for anything." Robert stood from his seat and placed Lorena upon it. He took the sweater and pulled it over his head and grabbed his jacket off the coat rack. He knelt down to hug and kiss his daughter and then closed the door behind him.

The air bit Robert's cheeks as he walked outside his home. The grass, dead and frozen, crunched as he moved towards the wooden barn. He removed the bolt that locked the massive doors and slowly pulled them open. The yellow lights glowed on the sides of each stall, and the horses stirred towards Robert.

"Good morning, Amsterdam." He kissed the white horse on his face. "We're headed to Uisge Beatha today. What do you want to eat—oats and barley?" Robert asked the horse, pulling the lever that was next to the stall, and the food funneled through into a steel trough. Amsterdam began to eat and then looked back at Robert. "Oh, you're thirsty, too? No need for the death stare, boy." He pushed the blue button that was next to the lever, and water flowed into a separate opening attached to the horses' quarters. He moved over to the next compartment where another horse awaited him. "Hey Beauty, how you doin' girl?" He rubbed her face and fed her a carrot that was stored in a bin next to the stall. "Don't tell Amsterdam I gave ya that; he'll be as stubborn as a mule. You're coming on this trip, too, girl. Unfortunately, you'll be carrying my brother for our journey." Robert spoke to the horse as if it understood him. The horse snorted, and Robert chuckled to himself, "I know, he's just the worst isn't he."

After Robert was done chatting with the giant beasts, he moved to the platform at the back of the barn, kicked a pedal at the base of it from off to on, and the stage floated up to the second floor. The soft yellow light beamed down from the ceiling showcasing five vehicles that were circled on a rotating frame. Robert bypassed the cars, and, tucked away in the back of the barn on the upper level, he pulled out a dark brown wooden sleigh with carbon fiber skis and white trim. He lowered himself back down the shaft and pulled Amsterdam and Beauty from their stalls. He linked the reigns to the horses, attached the sled, and piled his gear onto it. Robert took his position on the sleigh, flicked the switch on the dash, and the sleigh began to float. He snapped his wrist and whistled to the two horses, and in the morning light, they trotted off into the wilderness of the world.

The air was still fiercely cold as Robert approached his brother's massive stone-walled country home. He exited the sleigh and knocked on Iscariot's door. He waited for what seemed like a lifetime and began to get slightly agitated. His brother, still in a daze, pants partially on and a sweater hanging around his neck, opened the door.

"I'm almost ready," Iscariot said tiredly.

"Yes, I can see," Robert said, raising his eyebrows and rolling his bright green eyes.

"I'm really looking forward to not eating anything for the next seven days," Iscariot joked in his scratchy morning voice. "It sounds like a real thrill."

"Stop your crying, Isc. It's the least we can do for our children," Robert spoke of his unborn.

"Not eating shouldn't be one of them. Do you have everything?"

"I think I should be asking you that."

"Of course, I do; let's get going then, shall we?" Iscariot buttoned his jacket, donned a hat to cover his ears, wrapped a gray wool scarf around his neck, and walked out the door. *How laughable*, Robert thought to himself, as if he were the one running late. They piled on the remaining gear they needed for their excursion, and the two men boarded the sled and began their journey to Uisge Beatha, the river of life. It wasn't an hour into their trip when Robert looked to his right and saw his brother sleeping with his arms folded and head back against the sleigh. In his boredom, Robert piled items onto his brother, eventually covering all but his face. He felt rather proud of his playful accomplishment.

The sun had hit its peak and struck its rays upon the earth. Iscariot awoke with countless items upon his body. Robert only knew Iscariot had come up from his slumber when he received some harsh words from his adoring brother, to which he laughed heartily.

"You're a real pain, Robert," Iscariot said while trying not to have the countless items fall off his body.

"What else are brothers for?" Robert chuckled. Slowly and carefully, the items were placed back into their packs, and when all that was upon Iscariot was packed back away, he poured some tea from his thermos.

"Not that you deserve any tea, but would you like any?"

"No, I'm quite alright. How was your sleep? By the sound of it, it seemed like it was very restful," said Robert.

"I was just dreaming of past battles we have fought. How I singlehandedly struck down two anthropoid beasts along with the disgusting Hemitheoi soldiers that rode them. And of when I commanded an entire pride of men at the Battle of Hoffnung and turned the war into our allies' favor. Reminiscing of the glories of the recent past that have made me the fastest ranking general in the history of our country," Iscariot answered boastfully.

"Dreaming of the war sounds more like a nightmare to me. Good men lost, brave till the bitter end. The families these soldiers left behind, fatherless sons and daughters, widowed young women. Parents saying goodbye as they lower their child into the ground. May we never see anything like it again," Robert spoke with sadness.

"No need to get all melancholy, Robert."

"You're right; we have two little boys coming to our families soon. Have you and Anna thought of a name yet?"

"We have. His name is Hanns." Iscariot smiled and stared off as if trying to picture an image of his unborn son.

"A strong name, Isc," Robert smiled as he saw the joy on his brother's face.

"And what of you and Lagertha? Any name?"

"Not as of yet; we are waiting for his birth. I want to see his face, look into his eyes, and see what characteristics he may have so that when we name him, he will be his name, and his name will be him," Robert replied.

"So long as he looks like Lagertha, I'm sure his name will be grand. If he looks like you, well, no need to say anymore." Iscariot japed, and they both laughed at his remark.

The two brothers trekked on, and the day slowly turned into night. They had just gotten over a small hill, and atop the hill was a field of wildflowers as far as the eye could see. Red, blue, yellow, and indigo lay across the great plains—flowers strong enough to withstand the wrath of winter's wind. Robert and Iscariot looked up in awe, a masterpiece come to life. A cloudless sky, the sun setting in the background—it was like living in a picture. It was as if the fields in heaven came to earth to show the people heaven's stunning beauty. The men, dumbfounded by the prairie, decided to rest there for the night. They unloaded their gear, unleashed the horses from the sled, and set up camp. Iscariot dug a small pit to start a fire, while Robert found some kindling to get it burning. The fire was lit, the tents were up, and the night sky draped the earth in darkness. The flames started to die, and the stars began to show their faces. The world was quiet. The crickets only whispered, and the wind hummed a soft tune as Robert and Iscariot looked into the star-spotted empyrean domain. As they gazed upon the celestials, three bright streaks painted the blackness of the night. The first comet colored the sky in crimson; it roared the loudest of the three. The second star glossed the cosmos with an ivory flame. It seemed to sing with the voice of an angel as it fell to the earth. The last of the stars blotted out the richness of the crimson and darkened the earth in oil black. It screeched a horrible cry as it bolted through the midnight sky, leaving fear in the souls of those who heard its dreadful strain. The two brothers looked at one another, both confused and amazed at what they had just seen.

"What the hell was that?" Iscariot asked in disbelief.

"It sounded like an angel's cry, a demon's rage, and a monster's shrill." Robert spoke what he thought. "Do you remember the stories Mother used to tell us? A great war is coming, Iscariot. Nations will rise up against one another, and the earth will rumble beneath our feet. Siblings will betray siblings, and a father his child. The moon shall drink the blood of men and cry it down upon the earth. Constellations will fall from the sky above, for vengeance, for justice, for death, for peace, to conquer. The welkin will trumpet towards the earth, and we will know the end is near." The brothers fell silent and watched the diamonds return to the night sky.

The moon had fallen and gave rise to the morning sun. Robert lay in his tent, groggy, unwilling to get up, and then he felt a small vibration from within the ground. He pressed his ear against the floor and heard a rhythm of percussion. The earth now began to tremble. Robert wondered what it might be: *Is this an earthquake or perhaps more meteors hitting the earth?* He then smiled for he knew now what he heard. He grabbed his hat and burst out of the tent with nothing on except for his sleeping trousers. Iscariot bolted out with far less on his skin. Before their eyes were great beasts, near 40,000 in number. They were twenty feet in length with horns nearly two feet long. Their coats were shaggy and dark, their shoulders broad and heads massive. The heard ran in the morning light across the open plain, impossible not to be heard, impossible not to be seen.

"Thunderbeast!" Iscariot yelled. "Where do you think they're off to?" Small clouds of vapor formed around his mouth as he spoke.

"It seems they are going where we are going. I just hope they are not running away from anything." Robert glanced out onto the field but saw no predator. "Shall we get going soon? We should reach the chapel by nightfall if we leave within the hour."

"I'm ready when you are."

"Oh, really? You and all your clothes?" Robert said to him, pointing out his nakedness.

"Two minutes then," said Iscariot as he walked back into his tent.

The men had packed their equipment, boiled some tea by the fire, and took off. Leaving nothing behind but sand upon the fire that once was. Dew laid on the ground, and a soft layer of fog surrounded them as they continued on their journey. The two trekked for hours, stopping briefly only for water and to stretch their cramped legs.

They had made good time. It was still daylight as they reached the chapel, but the sun was beginning to close the day. Behind the bethel, the men saw a massive rock formation where the water fell from over 2,000 feet, tumbling heavily to the earth. As the setting sun hit the water, it looked as if fire fell from the cataract, hence its given name, Leviathan Falls. Robert's eyes caught the house of worship as he and his brother approached. The brothers disembarked. Robert looked the church up and down in wonder. Its steeple was white as snow, and the door Robert knocked on, red as blood. The sound of the bolt echoed loudly, and the door slowly granted them access.

An elderly man had answered the call of the summoning knock. He spoke in a scratchy, peaceful voice. "Why, hello there. Come, come. It's awfully frigid out there." His silver hair was slightly ruffled, eyes squinted and back slightly hunched. "You two look like the frozen dead. I'll have one of the deacons put your horses in the stables and grab your belongings. Would you all like something to eat? I'll have the cook make you some Thunder-stew. That'll redden your cheeks." He smiled at them.

"Thank you, Aspal Seanan," the brothers replied.

"But we must decline," Robert continued. "We have come to fast and pray."

"Some tea or coffee then?" Seanan asked.

"Thank you, Aspal, you're very kind." Iscariot spoke humbly.

"What is the occasion?" Aspal Seanan looked happily concerned.

"We are both expecting a child." Robert spoke with a grin upon his face.

"Oh, how delightful. I remember when you two were just wee lads yourselves. My, my, I'm getting old, aren't I?" the Apsal said in delight.

"Not a day over thirty-two," Robert joked.

"Plus fifty," Iscariot laughed.

"I can see you both haven't lost your humor. Follow me now, I'll take you to your rooms."

The men walked down the chapel pews. The benches were bleach white and the wood floors a soft gray. The lanterns hung from the high-beamed ceiling; they lined the aisles from door to pulpit. The men walked behind the platform on which the preacher spoke and descended down to the lower floor. Along the walls of the spiral stone staircase was a painting that told a fable of a bird. Robert watched his brother follow the story as his hands touched the painting. The tale began with the bird leaving its nest and flying gracefully into the summer sky. While it flew through the clear skies, it spotted a woman from high above. Snakes coiled her wet legs and arms as the bird rested in the crown atop her head. She stood naked in front of a throne. Further down the staircase it flew with a dragon that burned cities to the ground and men as they ran in fear. The fable became darker as the bird then plucked the eyes from the men who fled the dragon, and it flew over forests that were now burned and without mast. Man began killing man, and children lay dead in the streets as the houses they fled from were engulfed in flames.

"What horrid paintings, Seanan," Iscariot said in distain.

"Very much so. The story of the Badb is not a very pleasant allegory." Aspal Seanan's said sadly in his scratchy voice: "It is so very sad when good people do nothing. The world goes dark as the baneful conquer the light." Neither brother spoke.

The men reached the lower level and arrived at their rooms. "Here you are, lads. Freshen up and meet me back upstairs. We will discuss the Breithtapa when you're ready."

After the men washed and changed, they climbed up the spiral staircase to the sanctuary where Apsal Seanan was waiting for them. The room was quiet and dim, lit only by candles. It gave Robert a sense of calm and peace. The brothers walked to the edge of the platform and grabbed the unlit candlesticks that rested in the candelabra; Seanan slowly approached them. "Kneel," he said in a whisper. They followed his command. In his hand he held a burning feather whose fire gave a soft glow. "What I hold in my hand is the flame of the first phoenix. May its fire grant your children guidance, may it give them courage when there is doubt, and may it forever burn bright in their hearts to be reborn within their children." Seanan lit Robert and Iscariot's candles. "Rise."

The two men rose and walked towards the symbol of their faith, a cross, and resting on each arm of the cross, in a triangle formation, were three unlit pillar candles. Each candle had its own meaning. The top central candle represented the Creator. The candle on the bottom right symbolized life. The final candle stood for death. The triangles themselves betokened strength, and the cross, sacrifice. This symbol is known as the Shamrock, and it is the representation of the Nazar faith. Robert lit each candle and spoke a silent prayer, saying only one word, *Germa.* The brothers turned back to Seanan and were commanded to kneel, facing the candles they had just lit.

Apsal spoke softly, "Let us bow our heads. Our Creator, please guide these men in fatherhood. Grant them wisdom when they lack knowledge. Bless them with patience when they seek urgency, and let them always find you when they are lost. We pray in your name, Germa." Seanan grabbed the chalice that sat on the banister and filled it with wine. He rested it upon Robert's lips. "This is the fire of the Lord; may it burn deep within your soul."

"Germa," Robert whispered. Seanan then repeated the words to Iscariot and the second day of the ceremony was over. The three men walked out of the sanctuary and up the staircase towards the loft. A small golden church organ was the centerpiece of the room.

"Do you still play?" Robert inquired.

"My hands are not made for such things anymore," Apsal replied.

"I'm sorry to hear that. My father said you were quite good."

"Years ago, I had a talent for it, but there is no stopping time. Good things must come to an end, I'm afraid." Seanan spoke, appearing to relive the past in his mind as he leaned over the balcony looking out into the sanctuary. "Now, boys, let's talk about why you are here. The Breithtapa is a very sacred practice in our religion. You have come here as your father did, and as your father's father did, and his father before that. You both have carried on this tradition by coming here today. Today is the second day, and we have performed the lighting ceremony, representing the bond between God, life, and death. Tomorrow at first light, you will set out to climb that massive boulder behind this church, which we all know as Leviathan Falls. Once you reach the top, you will come across a river. There you must make a sacrifice to the Lord by taking something you value and tossing it into the Bealach. From there, you will make your way to the Uisge Beatha, and on the fourth day, you will drink its water and bring a vial back to baptize your child. Before you drink from its water, you must confess all sins to our God. Only then will you be worthy to drink from it. When you are finished, be sure to praise the Father and thank Him."

Seanan paused and looked at the brothers: "Have I lost you yet?"

"I remember this quite fondly," Robert replied, remembering the birth of his daughter.

"Lost?" Iscariot spoke up: "Just tired is all."

"I'll try to be brief; I know it's very late, and you both have a tough journey ahead," said the Apsal in a hoarse voice. "You will return here late on the fourth day. On the fifth day, you will rest, and you will pray to the Lord. On this day, you will recover for you will be weak, as your body will have been without food. It will be the strength of your faith, not your body, that will bring you home as you venture out on the sixth day. And behold lads, the seventh day, you will have sealed your covenant, where you are home amongst your family, and break your fast. That is it, lads. Do you have any questions?"

"No, thank you, Apsal. I'm quite alright." Robert spoke kindly.

"I'm alright myself, Seanan. Thank you," responded Iscariot.

"Very well, then. Goodnight, my boys, and good luck." Seanan smiled back.

The men retreated to their rooms. It was near midnight, and both Robert and Iscariot were exhausted. "Goodnight, Isc," Robert said in a hushed voice.

"Goodnight, Rob." Iscariot slapped Robert on the back. The two separated and went into their rooms.

As Robert undressed and put on his night wear, his thoughts fell on his wife and daughter. He hoped Lorena was listening to her mother and that Lagertha was doing well on her own with only days until their son would be born. He grinned at the thought of Lorena dancing in the living room and singing lullabies to her unborn brother. Robert crept into the bed, his mind still on his family. He laughed as he thought of his daughter playing war in the house and his pregnant wife being an unwilling participant. As his thoughts wandered, his eyes grew tired. Robert turned out the lantern next to his bed. "Goodnight," he whispered. "I love you." His thoughts were still on his family as his eyes grew heavy and closed, and the power of sleep took over.

It was morning. The light had yet to break the night, but Robert forced himself to roll out of bed and start the day. He showered in the bath house that was a few doors down and filled a bucket of water as he left. As he was heading back to change and pack his bag, he stopped at his brother's door. *I guess I should wake him,* Robert thought to himself. He opened the door; he could hear Iscariot still sleeping. He crept inside his room to the edge of his brother's bed and tossed the bucket of water onto it.

"What the hell!" Iscariot leaped from his slumber, but Robert had already left the room, laughing hysterically. "Payback is coming Robert!" Iscariot yelled, still in shock. As the moment was ending, he looked at himself and gave a chuckle. "That bastard," he said with a smirk on his face; Robert could still hear him as he listened through the door.

The two were finally dressed and ready for the climb they had ahead of them. Robert wore clothes of simplicity and practicality. His shoes were flexible so as to grip the stone of the cliff they were set to climb. Iscariot, however, was in gear that was technologically advanced and sport-driven. His gloves had an odd protrusion that seemed counter to climbing, as did his boots. Nonetheless, he seemed eager for the challenge ahead. Apsal Seanan was waiting outside as the sun peaked over the horizon, giving a soft glow to the earth.

"Good morning, lads. I hope you both slept well."

"Very much so, Apsal, and you?" Robert asked.

"I could have done without the wakeup call," Iscariot scolded as he smacked his brother on the back.

"I never get more than a few hours these days," Seanan replied. "When you get to my age, sleep seems like such a waste when there is so much left to do and see." Apsal Seanan looked at the two men in front of him. "Do you both have what you need for the sacrifice?" he questioned the brothers.

They nodded. "Good, now get out of here. One day of you two was plenty for me. I'll see you both in two days' time."

Robert tightened the straps on his bag: "Thanks again, Apsal. We'll see you soon." He embraced Seanan as he said goodbye.

Iscariot wasted no time and dashed past Seanan and Robert: "Thanks Aspal, and see ya Robert!" he yelled as he ran off towards Leviathan Falls.

"He does know it takes nearly twenty-two hours to climb the Leviathan, doesn't he?" Seanan asked with a confused look on his face.

Robert grinned, "I didn't mention that to him." Robert walked off, following his brother's footsteps towards Leviathan. He arrived at the base of the rock formation. He could hear the power of the waterfall as it bounced off the rocks and still water below. The winter breeze filled his lungs as he glided his hand over the stone. He found his line to travel up the behemoth rock. He steadied his foot at the base of the stone and hurled himself up. Iscariot was already 200 feet above him, rushing towards his goal. Robert took the climb slowly, calculating each step, every hand placement, keeping his line towards the peak.

Ten hours had passed since the brothers began their climb. They stopped to rest their muscles and hydrate their overworked bodies. The sun beamed brightly on them.

"I think I have you beat, Robert!" Iscariot yelled down to his brother.

"I'm not too worried; we still have half the day to climb!" he yelled back.

"You seemed to have forgotten to mention that it takes a lifetime to climb this thing."

"Oh, did I? Sorry about that," Robert said with humor. The two continued their climb. The hours had sped by as they rose higher and higher. Twilight now filled the sky, and the stars began to radiate once more.

The path to the summit was one of risk and fright. Foot and hand placement became more difficult as loose stone became more present. Wet rocks soon turned to icy glaciers, for there was no sun to keep their formations at bay. Robert's muscles began to ache, and he knew his brother's must burn and cry with pain just as much as his. It was late in the hours of the night, when not only the muscles were tired, but the mind as well, and in this fatigued state, the unthinkable happened.

Crack! Robert looked up and could see shadows tumbling towards him, and he saw his brother's body fall with them. Robert reached out his hand in vain. "ISCARIOT!" his voice screeched in fear.

BOOM! the sound echoed loudly off the rocks. Robert imagined his brother's death as he could not see below himself. He was paralyzed by such an awful thought, and his mind and body became frozen for he could not process what he had just seen. The wind swirled around Iscariot. It was not his body that slammed upon the jagged stones below that made the wicked percussion, but the whistle of the odd gloves he wore upon his hands. Antigravity gloves pierced the airwaves and echoed in Robert's ears. Iscariot began laughing hysterically: "That was pretty close, wouldn't you say?"

"Are you alright?" Robert yelled with fear still in his eyes. "You scared me half to death, Isc!" he continued with anger and relief in his voice.

"Calm down, Robert; it looks like you won." Iscariot spoke, levitating in the air, as if nothing had happened. "I'll see you up there shortly."

I'm going to kill him, Robert thought to himself, his heart beating in his throat rather than his chest. He took several deep, long, and purposeful breaths. It slowed his heart rate and calmed his nerves. Only then, when he saw his brother start to climb again, did he continue his rise to the peak of Leviathan.

It was past midnight; the only light was from the moon and the temperate rays that came off Iscariot's gloves. Robert sat at the edge at the top of the mountain and shook his head as he pulled up his brother to the top of Leviathan Falls. "You're something else, you know that? One day your luck is going to run out."

"Well, I might as well keep using it while I have it," Iscariot replied.

"I'm glad you're okay, but try to be a little more careful. You have a son on the way, remember?" Robert reminded him. The two looked down from whence they came. Leviathan's flaming fall could only be heard as its water fell towards the earth. The brothers turned from the falls and saw two horses waiting for them at a small stable. Robert looked to see if anyone was near the horses but saw that there was no one. It was then he noticed the horses were his own and kissed each of them upon their noses.

"I'm glad Seanan was nice enough to send up your horses," Iscariot said tiredly.

"As am I. Come, let's finish the ceremony." Robert and Iscariot knelt down, placing three candles in a triangle around them. With the candles lit, they grabbed their offerings from their packs and began praying silently. Robert closed his eyes and lifted his head to the heavens.

Lord, forgive me of my sins for they are many. You have been kind enough to bless me with a son, and for that I am forever grateful. You have given me the gift of life, something I will never be able to repay, however, I ask that you take these heirlooms as these were to be planted for this year's harvest. Please take this sacrifice so that I may honor you, as you have honored me. I thank you, Father, for all that you have given me. I pray on your return. Germa. Robert opened his eyes and sprinkled the heirlooms into the Bealach River. Iscariot had already finished and was standing behind him. Robert turned to him and smiled.

"My eyes are heavy; let's get some sleep."

"I'm too tired to set up a tent," Iscariot complained.

"Let's sleep in the horses' stall; we'll just have to suffer the smell."

"At least we'll be warm." As night had pulled its covers over the light, so too did the sand cover over Robert's eyes. The brothers slept and woke when the light uncovered itself from the darkness.

They washed in the river, mounted the horses, and rode off to Uisge Beatha.

"What did you sacrifice, Robert?" Iscariot asked as he made a tea for the two of them.

"Heirlooms for the harvest."

"Are you mad? The farm is a quarter of all food supply to the city," Iscariot spoke.

"Hence the meaning of sacrifice. We had a bountiful year, and I will rely on the Lord to supply us should there be a shortage," Robert explained. "But what of you? What did you sacrifice?"

"Our father's sword. It is very dear to me. It is what helped shape me." Robert said nothing else on the matter of Iscariot's sacrifice and changed the topic of discussion.

"I can't wait for you to see the river."

"What's it like? You're always vague when I ask you about it," Iscariot said to his brother.

"I'm vague because I don't know how to describe it. It's something to be seen with the eyes rather than to be heard by spoken words."

"My eyes seek to gaze upon it, much like my mouth seeks to drink the tea," said Iscariot.

"Is it ready?"

"Saddle up. I'll pour your cup," Iscariot told him, and then they were off, beginning the fourth day.

Time stood still for no one, and night was almost upon them. Their horses were tired, as were they. Iscariot looked as if he were sleeping on his horse, and Robert's eyes were beginning to close a few seconds at a time and whip back open as he tried not to succumb to the song of dreams. Robert closed his eyes again, and when he opened them, he saw the river. The water was green and radiant. It flickered in the blackness of the night as it flowed from north to south, gliding towards its final destination. Robert felt a calmness over him, the same calmness he felt when his daughter was to be born.

"Isc, we're here," he whispered.

Iscariot struggled to wake and then caught glimpse of Uisge Beatha. Eyes fully opened, he marveled at it as the river gave a heavenly glow. Robert saw that his brother was moved by its sight.

"I told you my words could not do it justice."

"You always were a terrible poet," Iscariot japed. Iscariot kept looking at the river as it shimmered off the trees that surrounded it. Released from his trance, he sought a place to sleep. "Do you see a spot to set up camp?"

"Just over there, about fifty yards downstream."

Vapor came from their breaths as they set up camp for the night. The ground was frozen hard, and the wind was just cold enough to bite their cheeks. A small fire was lit, and the green luminosity of the river reflected off everything in the forest. The two sat outside their tents for a while, not saying much, but enjoying each other's company. The river soothed their souls, and the tea their minds.

As the fire was losing its flames, dark clouds tumbled in the sky, and the wind gave a harsher bite. Robert and Iscariot looked at one another. "I think we should turn in for the night," Robert told his brother.

Iscariot agreed as he shivered. Robert put more wood on the fire to last until dawn, and Iscariot covered the horses in blankets so they would not freeze in winter's grip. As the fire started to rage, so did the night sky above. The wind was forceful, and the black clouds were struck in the darkness with light. Lightning reached across the darkened sky as far as the eye could see, but there was no thunder. The brothers looked up into the heavens. The wind was now screaming, and the lightning began to strike the earth. The bolts struck the ground with loud, thunderous cracks, like a whip snapping the air. The strikes were close, too close for comfort.

Every bolt strikes the same target, Robert thought to himself. "We should get inside, Isc." Iscariot nodded, and they headed in for the night.

Iscariot was soon asleep in his own tent, but Robert's eyes were open as the storm continued its fury. He put on his jacket, strapped his shield to his back, his sword to his waist, and stepped outside. The wind reddened his ears as it blew by him. The lightning had stopped, and flurries began falling from the firmament. Robert thought he could hear a horn playing in the distance, a droning sound. He began to walk to where the bolts battered the ground. Robert was certain now that he was hearing horns play, so he stopped to focus on where the sound was coming from. As he did, the trumpeting fell silent. *I must have been hearing things.* He doubted himself. As he got closer, the snow began to fall faster and heavier. Robert reached the area where the lightning had no mercy. It was a circular clearing about 100 meters in diameter. He tried to peer through the shadow of the night and the heavy snow, but his eyes saw nothing. Robert reached into his pocket and pulled out a clear ball with golden trim, and whispered to it, "Solas." The ball began to spin rapidly and rose into the air, illuminating the space around him. As the light began to glow, it quickly dropped to the ground. In that moment, in the black of night, there was a loud and terrible scream, a shriek that sounded of fear and death. Robert reached for his sword and readied himself for battle, his eyes darting through the coal pitch of night and white flakes of the blizzard. He stepped forward, advancing slowly to where the wicked cry had come from. "Solas!" he yelled. As Robert reached the center of the small clearing of the forest, the light came to him, and with the light, a baby's whimper.

Robert Chapter Two

Robert looked down, and at his feet, lying upon the frozen earth was an infant boy. Without thinking, he dropped his sword and shield, took off his coat and wrapped the child in its fur. "Hello!" he yelled. "Is anybody there? Can anybody hear me!" He listened hard, hoping to hear someone calling back. He waited several moments, but all Robert could hear was the whistle of the wind and the moaning of the trees as they bent back and forth. He held the boy close to his chest, tucked his head down to block his face from the harsh wind and the beating of the heavy snow, and trekked back towards camp.

As Robert reached his tent, the wind began to die as did the heavy snow. The clouds began to shatter, and the wild blue yonder started to show its glorious face as it was freckled with stars as far as the eye could see. Robert placed the boy inside his tent and started up a small heater. He left the child to rest and warm up from the bitterness of the winter that had finally approached. While the infant slept, Robert got the fire roaring back to life and finally was ready to rest himself.

After he had washed himself with a warm wet towel, Robert walked over to the child. "You poor boy," he said to the babe. The newborn boy opened his eyes and stared at Robert. Robert looked back at him and smiled. Raven black, his eyes ran deep, his small soft lips, a pinch of pink, his wisps of hair, blond like the summer's sun. "You're a handsome boy; you're gonna be trouble when you're older." Robert laughed at his words as he wiped dirt off the infant's face. He unwrapped the child from his coat, whose body wore mud and soot like war paint, and began washing the child with a small rag. When the bairn was cleaned, he noticed that the boy had a scar on the left side of his chest. "Seems like you've come into this world fighting, little one. You can rest easy now; there's no need to fight anymore," Robert told the child. He covered the babe in a cotton sweater and then wrapped him back up in the bison fur. Robert was now exhausted himself and laid down to fall asleep with the child at his side. He kissed the boy on his forehead, "Goodnight little warrior, sweet dreams." Robert's thoughts weighed on his wife, his daughter, and his unborn son. He wondered where this child's family was. Were they hurt or separated by the storm? Why would they not search night and day for him? His mind soon fell silent, and sleep finally took him.

Robert woke to the sound of a baby's fuss. He rolled over to look at the small boy. "What's the matter, little one? It smells like you've ruined my sweater," he said with a grin on his face. Robert grabbed the cloth he used the night before and stepped outside to warm some water. The morning sun glistened the snow that crunched below his feet. He poured some water into a small pan and heated it on the coals that remained of the fire. Robert looked around the camp as the embers heated the bath water. The lull of Uisge Beatha gave him a sense of serenity as it trickled downstream. After such a stormy and wicked night, the river's water seemed to put the horses at ease as well. He gathered some grain and some water from the sleigh and made sure Amsterdam and Beauty were fed. He listened to hear if Iscariot was still asleep, then headed back to the tent with water and cloth in hand and cleaned the mystery infant of the night.

Today was supposed to be a full day of prayer, Robert thought to himself. He knelt down and began to pray. "My Creator, I ask your forgiveness, but I cannot pray the whole day. I must unite this boy with his family or at least discover their fates. I pray you find it in your heart to forgive me. In your name, Germa."

He dressed, tied a sling around his shoulder, and nestled the child inside. He noticed his brother was still not yet awake as he headed towards the horses. "Come on boy." He spoke softly to Amsterdam, "Let's go." Robert hopped onto the horse and headed to where he found the child.

The sunlight bent around the trees of the forest and reached the small clearing where Robert had discovered the boy the night before. The rays of light hit the face of the infant, and a small tear streaked down his soft pale cheek. The babe wailed loudly. His cries echoed through the forest, bouncing from tree to tree. It seemed the forest had come to life as he cried. The wind began to blow to the east and rustled the loose snow that was now falling from the oaks and sycamore. As the forest sung its song and carried the baby's cry, Robert took the child in his arms to comfort him. He paused as the child's cry turned to coos and looked at the unusual scene that was before him. The soft light of the sun reflected off the ice that wrapped itself around the trees, and the snow looked like crushed diamonds shining upon the earth. The harshness of the storm had turned the forest into a palace of ice and snow, frozen in time. He then glanced down at his feet. Robert stood upon the spot where he found the baby in the rage of the night. It was a circle of ash and dust, about twelve feet in diameter. There were some embers still flickering from red to orange within the center of the halo. He was dumbstruck. *How can this be?* he wondered. Unable to fully process the scene, Robert called out, "Hello!" There was no response. Again, he shouted, "Hello!" but still no one answered.

He journeyed throughout the forest, a mile in every direction, yet he found and heard no one. In despair, Robert headed back to camp, and as the horse slowly walked through the forest, he saw them, a man and a woman sitting under a giant, old, snow-covered oak tree. Relief struck Robert's face as he approached them. "Dia Dhuit!" he shouted to them. He kicked the horse, and Amsterdam picked up the pace. "I have your boy!" he yelled joyfully. As the horse got closer to them, something seemed the matter. *Did they not hear me?* he wondered, and then he knew. The parents of the babe had fallen to the grip of death's hand.

Robert dismounted the horse with the baby still tucked away in his sling. He looked down into the dark chocolate eyes of the boy; his heart was broken. *I failed you,* he judged himself. Robert picked the child up and cradled him. "I'm sorry," he said to the babe. He looked at the man and his wife and knew he could not give them a proper burial. The snow was too high, and the earth was frozen. He laid the man and woman down, joined their hands together, and covered them in the snow. Robert said a silent prayer and hurried back to the campsite.

"Robert!" Iscariot called out.

"Hey Isc."

"I've prayed and confessed and drank from the river. Where have you been?" his brother queried. Iscariot hadn't noticed the small child in Robert's sling, and then he heard the babe fuss, eager to leave Robert's cramped space.

"A child?" Iscariot spoke in disbelief. "Why do you have a child?" he asked, still baffled.

"I could not sleep last night, and by some miracle, I found him lying in the forest," he told his brother.

"And his parents?" Iscariot questioned.

"I found them, too. Only I was too late to help them." Robert spoke solemnly: "They perished in the storm."

"What do you plan to do with the child?"

"I haven't decided," he said, but Robert's mind was made. "Did you fill your vial, Isc?"

"I have. I am waiting on you for once." Iscariot grinned.

"You're right, I'm sorry. I'll be quick."

Robert knelt beside Uisge Beatha and began to confess of all his wrong doings and asked the Spirit to have mercy upon him. He undressed and entered the mystic river. The water did not rage, nor did it glide downstream with grace, but instead was still, motionless, as if the heart of the river were no longer beating. Robert submerged himself, and when he exited the water, his heart felt full, and his mind was cloudless.

He looked over at the boy, who was snuggled close to Iscariot by the tame fire that was crackling the impurities of the wood. He walked over to him and uncovered the boy from his fur and sweater and walked with him to the river. The pace of the water began to quicken as Robert stepped inside. He submerged himself and the infant under the glow of the holy water, and the river began to frenzy. While Robert and the child were under the roaring of the river, he looked at the child, and the child looked at him. The water raged above, but Robert felt tranquility. He stepped out of the water with the boy and said to him, "You are my son in whom I am well pleased. From this day until your last day, you will be known as Aedus Darroch, son of Robert and Lagertha Darroch, brother to Lorena and my son yet to be." He kissed the child's eyes and clothed him, protecting him from the frigid air.

Iscariot was looking on and could not believe what he had heard. "You're keeping the boy as your own?" He was dumbfounded.

"I am," Robert acknowledged.

"And what will Lagertha say of this Robert?" his brother pressed.

"She will love him as her own."

"Will she?" Iscariot continued.

"I do not doubt it for a second," he asserted.

Robert dressed and filled a vial for his son back home. "Let's pack and get going. It is nearly dark, and I have made us late," he said begrudgingly. The brothers quickly gathered their gear and readied the horses for the night's hike back to the little chapel from which they came. The earth had turned away from the sun, and the moon shined its face upon the earth. Robert told his brother of what had happened the night of the storm and all he had done during the day after it. Iscariot had insisted he give the child to someone who could not bear any children, or to dílleachtlann, as keeping him as his own would seem suspicious.

"Don't be ridiculous, Isc. People know who I am. I would never betray my wife," he told his brother.

"You have been absent quite frequently this past year. It would be easy for someone to assume you unfaithful as they see you coming home with a child that is not Lagertha's," Iscariot voiced his opinion.

"I appreciate your concern, Iscariot, but the boy will be my son, from this day to his last day." He concluded the discussion in a stern manner.

Soon, the moon fell from the sky, and the sun kissed the earth to fill it with its brilliance. It was past noon by the time they had reached the sanctuary. Both men hadn't eaten in five days and barely slept on the voyage from Uisge Beatha to the humble house of worship. Iscariot headed inside to shower and rest for the remainder of the day, as Robert finished caring for the horses with Aedus at his side. Apsal Seanan greeted Iscariot as he entered the church and then proceeded outside to welcome Robert.

Seanan uttered to him, "I see you've brought back a friend." Robert turned, as he had not heard Seanan approach.

"I did, Apsal. It has been quite an interesting two days," he said exhaustedly.

"We welcome all who journey to Tegos Spéire. Go and wash up, lad. Let the caretakers tend to the horses. We can talk of your experience when you have had some rest," Seanan insisted.

"Apsal, do you by chance have mothers' milk here? I've done the best I can to feed the child with what little was available."

"Here, give me the boy. He's in good hands. Now go and rest. I can barely see the whites of your eyes," Seanan told him once more. With his eyes struggling to stay open, Robert went inside to bathe away the sweat and dirt from the ride back from Uisge Beatha. He nearly fell asleep as he laid inside the milky water. Robert left the bath, as his skin was starting to prune. He entered his room, lit a small fire, and fell onto the bed. He shut his deep green eyes and let dream take his mind.

He woke just before the sun rose on the sixth day. Robert wandered the halls of Tegos Speire while the world continued to sleep. He came upon a painting whose tale was that of another bird. The great bird was lost at sea, and everywhere he flew, he could not find his way back home. So, he flapped his wings for miles and miles, but no matter how far he traveled, all he saw was water. The lonely bird called out to his friends, but his cries fell on deaf ears. The feathered creature began to lose hope, thinking that he would never find his home and never see his friends. Fearing this, the bird flew as high as he could, climbing the sky until he saw the bends of the earth. As he looked around the great blue heaven, all he saw was the sea below. In desperation, the bird gave a mighty shriek, hoping someone would hear him, but still, no one came to his cries. His wings began to grow tired for he had been flying day and night. The bird's wings could no longer move the air, and he came falling towards the deep blue sea. As his body hit the water, a monstrous beast consumed him. Inside the massive creature, the bird perished into ashes, as the beast that swallowed him was Leviathan. Three suns rose, and on the third day, the great monster roared thunderously. Fire poured from the creature's mouth like a volcano bursting in anger. From the fire of Leviathan came a bird with feathers the color red, orange, and crimson. Its wings were that of flames, and the bird that had died within the beast was born again. The fowl gave a piercing scream, and all who lived in the world heard its cry. The bird of fire flew day and night once more, but he was no longer lost, for the flames on his wings would always light the way home.

As the story ended, Robert saw that the tunnel he had been walking in led him to Leviathan Falls. Sitting under the waterfall was Seanan with Aedus in his arms.

"I was wondering when you would wake," he said to Robert.

"I didn't think anyone was up. How did the child sleep?" Robert asked.

"He slept as a babe should. Hardly at all," Seanan joked. He placed the boy in Robert's arms. Aedus fussed briefly and then quietly fell back to sleep. Robert told Seanan how he found the boy as he did with Iscariot, and how he decided he was going to raise the child as his own.

"I agree with you, Robert. You should care for the boy. You found him for a reason. What that reason is I do not know, but nothing is coincidence. There is only choice and purpose. You have made your choice; now you must wait to see what the purpose of the choice is. Your actions are truly noble, Robert. I can only see goodness in your decision to raise the boy. With honorable deeds, there are noble outcomes."

"I can only hope that you are right, Apsal," Robert said.

"There are many symbolic meanings in the ceremony of Breithtapa. For example, the Uisge Beatha means river of life. This is why people of our religion come here to baptize their children in this water. The Bealach River that you took to Uisge Beatha, well that literally means, the way. The ceremony's name itself means "fast until birth." With all its symbolism, there is real meaning to what we practice. It is not only a sacrifice you make for your children and wife but a lesson for the man you are and a lesson for the man you need to be. You have come across something unique in this journey. After these past six days, at least to me, it seems you have become the man you need to be.

"But enough of my old man thoughts. Come, let's get back inside. You and your brother should be leaving soon. I'm sure your wives want you home. Ceangal is such a beautiful day, for it is the bond and the last day of the ceremony."

"Thank you, Apsal. I will meditate on all I have seen and all I have experienced these past few days." Robert spoke humbly.

Daylight came. Iscariot finally woke from his slumber and entered the small kitchen nestled underground at the west end of the church. Robert greeted him, "Good morning, Isc. I'm glad you could join us this morning." Iscariot grunted, too tired to say anything. He grabbed the pot of coffee that was sitting on the rustic wooden countertop and poured himself a cup. He took a sip, "Sorry, my brain doesn't work in the morning without coffee."

"Sometimes I wonder if it works at all," Robert jested.

"Funny, I could say the same about you." The two laughed at their childish bickering. "Are we leaving soon?" Iscariot asked.

"I'm waiting on you, Isc," Robert answered.

"Naturally. Give me a few minutes. I think the coffee's working," he told Robert as he exited the kitchen. Robert lightly chuckled at his remark and headed upstairs to the sanctuary to wait for his brother.

It wasn't long before Iscariot had rejoined him. They walked outside the chapel where their horses and sleigh awaited them. The sky was stark blue with small wisps of clouds scattered throughout. The air felt like a spring day rather than a frigid winter morning. Seanan hugged them both and spoke to each of them.

"Robert, as you know, and Iscariot as you now know, Breithtapa is about dedication, sacrifice, and faith. In fatherhood, it is no longer about the self. Instead, everything you do, you do because you are dedicated to your child, their dreams, their future, their success. Through dedication comes sacrifice. This does not mean you have to give up the things you love. Rather, you will someday be given a choice where you must willingly surrender or destroy something you desire for the sake of your child and know that, in the end, it is in their best interest. In this there is faith, for we do not always know if what we sacrifice will benefit our children. I can only tell you to trust in yourself and trust in our God and see that, in faith, your sacrifice is rewarded. I wish you both a safe journey home."

"Slan leat, Apsal, and thank you." Robert hugged Seanan once more and boarded the sleigh. He whistled to Amsterdam and Beauty, waved goodbye to Seanan, and soon the chapel was nothing more than a speck in the distance.

The night stole the light from the day, and then the morning took it back. It was the seventh and final day of Breithtapa. Both Robert and Iscariot were exhausted and famished from the weeklong ceremony.

"Ceangal is upon us, the last day of Breithtapa!" Iscariot said in delight. "I cannot wait to be home to see my wife and baby boy—to have a full belly, a cold pint, and a warm bed."

"I think you have the makings of a song there, Isc. What do you think your little boy will look like?" Robert asked.

"God, I hope he looks like his mother; she has all the best features," his brother replied.

"Ain't that the truth," he said to Iscariot. "God only knows how you got her to marry you."

"Charm, my brother, and some luck," Iscariot smiled. "We can't all be future kings like you, Robert."

"Only God can name a king. I pray he doesn't choose me when the Hoba brings its gift upon our land," Robert said.

The brothers continued talking about their wives, their children, and how great it felt to be back home. They reminisced on the last six days, from the field of flowers and Thunderbeast and the roaring stars that painted the sky, to the majesty of Uisge Beatha and the discovery of a little baby boy. The sun had shut out its light as they came to the pathway that led to Iscariot's home. There was no smoke billowing from the chimney of the massive three story, stone and glass house. The brothers noticed it was pitch black except for a small light in the back entrance on the lower level. They approached slowly up a brick pathway and saw a black figure sitting on the bench under the truss of the stone awning where the light illuminated.

"Who's there?" Iscariot questioned with force. The figure unhooded himself.

"It's me, Antony," he replied. His hair was dark brown, the same color as his eyes. He stood slightly shorter than Iscariot. His face was handsome and clean shaven. "It's good to see you, Iscariot, I have good news."

"Am I a father," he asked impatiently.

"Not yet, she is in labor now," Antony answered.

"Where's your vehicle?" Iscariot asked hurriedly.

"It's just over there," Antony told him.

"Let's go," Iscariot commanded. "You hear that Robert! I'm going to be a father!" he yelled with great joy.

Robert watched as Iscariot and Antony took off to the city, and then he and Aedus finally headed home. The night air was sharp and brisk, and the stars winked from high above. He looked up to see his bedroom light give a golden glow as he got nearer to his house. Robert entered the barn and refreshed the stables with hay and water. He delivered the hovering sleigh to the second floor of the barn, and his tired body took him and Aedus inside his country home. Robert laid the child on the sofa as he took off his winter boots. He hung his jacket on the coat rack and quietly walked across the room with Aedus snug in his arms. He climbed the stairs and heard Lagertha telling a children's story. Robert stood in the hall to listen to her tell the story while Lorena intently listened to the enchanting tale. When the fable ended, he entered the room. Lorena jumped off the bed and bolted to her father.

"Daddy!" she yelled with love and embraced him tightly. "I missed you." Robert wrapped her warmly in his free arm and kissed her on the head.

"I missed you and your warm hugs," he told her. Lorena looked and saw Aedus in his arms.

"He's so cute, Dad. Who is he?" she asked curiously.

"I found him, frozen and alone, next to the river of life. His name is Aedus." Robert looked at Lagertha.

"Where are his parents, Dad?" Lorena wondered.

"His mommy and daddy aren't here anymore. They went up to heaven," he explained to her.

"Did you say a prayer for them?" she questioned. He kissed her on the head again.

"I did. Can you say one for them, too?"

"I will, Dad" she answered. Lagertha got out of bed and locked her arms around Robert's waist. He told her of everything that happened—how he found the boy in the horrid storm the night they arrived at Uisge Beatha. He told her of the morning after, how he searched tirelessly until he found the boy's parents.

"I spoke to Apsal Seanan about raising the child," he told Lagertha.

"Robert," she said, placing her hand on his lap as he fell silent. She then grabbed Robert's hand and walked him over to the bassinet, and inside, sleeping soundlessly, with dark hair and pale skin, was his son. He looked at Lagertha.

"He's beautiful," he said. Lagertha picked him up and placed him in Robert's free arm. While the two infants rested in his arms, Aedus's hand reached over and grasped the hand of the babe that laid next to him and closed his charcoal eyes.

Lagertha locked eyes with her husband, "You have done an honorable thing, Robert. Because of you, this boy has a future, but because of us, this boy has a family. You may have found him cold and alone, but from this day forward, he will be loved with hugs as warm as the sun and with brothers and sisters at his side." She leaned forward and propped herself up on her toes and locked her lips with Robert's.

"You're the most amazing woman I have ever known or ever will know," he said to her.

"And don't you forget it," she grinned back at him.

"Have you named him yet?"

"I had an idea, but I was waiting for you."

"What name did you have in mind?"

"Absolume," she whispered.

"It's a good name," he spoke softly back. The child's eyes started to open, and within them, Robert saw his own. "Hey little Abe, I see you have my eyes. Let me give you to Mom. I bet you're hungry." Lagertha took Absolume and slid her strap off her shoulder, exposing her breast. She sat in a white rocking chair at the end of the canopy bed while her baby boy nursed from her bosom. Robert lowered the shine of the light and crept into bed with Aedus resting on his chest. Lorena quickly snuck into the bed, snuggling close to her dad and new baby brother. While the room was quiet, she began to sing.

"Lay down your head,
Lay down your head, my chosen one,
Sleep amongst the stars, the spirits of the sky,
Sleep amongst the angels, who stand at your side,
Dream your dreams, your tales of great fortune,
Dream your dreams, of joy and happiness
Let the Spirit manifest your visions,
Let the Spirit lead you in the night,
You are the pelican in the sea,
You are the owl in the tree,
Play amongst the sparrows,
Swim amongst the lilies,
These are the dreams He has for thee.
Wake to the day, the glory of His light,
Wake to the day, a blessing He has given thee,
Feel the warm sun on your skin,
Feel the wind at your back,
The road that rises to meet you,
That road, straight and narrow,
Follow it through and through,
Follow it, He'll be there with you,
When the darkness comes, it will fall like the sand,
When the darkness comes, it will not understand,
For you walk in the Father's dreams
For you walk in the light of His plans,
Lay down your head my chosen one,
My pelican in the sea,
My owl in the tree,
My sparrow, I watch over thee."

Iscariot Chapter One

Iscariot left Robert behind as he and Antony raced into the city. Antony's vehicle, like most in Aontu, hovered above the ground. Its body was hot rod red and made from aluminum; it was extremely light and incredibly fast. Its shape was long, sleek, and narrow with a small gap separating the body from the base of the vehicle. Underneath, and at the end of the hovercraft, were cylindric titanium devices that created lift, and in between the gap, these devices generated thrust, making the vehicle float above the ground. Near the butt of the hovercraft was a tinted compact capsule, allowing only two passengers to ride in its cramped quarters. The interior was decorated with soothing blue lights that lit up the dashboard and soft tan leather seats that could warm or chill the body of its passenger. The vehicle was quiet, nearly soundless, so too was it efficient as it was powered not by wind or solar but the purest form of energy known as cold fusion.

The craft purred down the dark and isolated roads with not a soul in sight, and the moon's glow bounced off the snow-dusted fields as the two men cruised through the barren countryside. There was an enchanting aura of cyan luminosity in the scene before the men. The landscape around them was artistically wondrous; a land of beauty; a splendor of the natural world. Even during the dead of winter, it was a sight of great grandeur. The high green grasses upon the hills poked through the snow-covered mounds, and the contrast of the green and white captured the eyes of everyone who traveled through the rural lands. The cliffs to the east looked to cut the ocean below, yet it was the ocean that sharpened the blade of the land. The seaside breeze was strong and twirled the green grasses like braids in a woman's hair. The waves of the ocean, Iscariot could hear its crashing, and the wind carried not only its sound, but the sea with it. As they got further inland, the hills rolled less, and the ocean's voice became faint. Iscariot was elated by the moment and would sear it in his mind forever.

"Is this a new ride?" Iscariot asked Antony.

"Yeah, just came out to market yesterday. It's the new Uriel-One Eleven." Antony replied.

"I love it. I might have to borrow this from you."

"Well, let me show you how fast this baby can go. You'll really want one then," Antony teased excitedly. Pedal to the floor, the speed nearly took the wind out of both Antony and Iscariot, as it accelerated from sixty to 120 in 1.2 seconds. They both screamed in delight at the speed of the craft.

"Woohoo! Yes!" Iscariot screamed at the top of his lungs. "I gotta get me one of these!" He was beaming in absolute joy.

The thrill of the ride died down, and the lonely farm roads fell to the wayside as the two entered the bright and hectic commotion of the city. It was late, near 11 at night, but the city of Buna was alive with blinding lights, a symphony of sounds, and hordes of people from all the cultures in the world. The city looked like a place of magic and myth. The streets were covered in snow while flurries trickled down from the gray clouds above, and along the walkways were streetlights that floated in the air like fireflies giving off a mystical yellow flare. All the roads were made of rustic red bricks, and tracing the outside of the roads were bands of soft white lights. Many of the older buildings were made out of stone and concrete, chiseled and formed in timeless splendor, while the more modern structures were made out of steel and glass but mimicked their ancient counterparts. The city felt as if the past had met the future, and the two eras melded into one.

"God, I love this city," Antony said to Iscariot, looking about the buildings and people like a kid at a candy store marvels at the variety of treats there are to eat.

"It is beautiful, isn't it?" Iscariot asked, falling under its spell much like Antony was. In their drive, the two passed a mammoth colosseum made of stone and concrete. Countless archways lined the circular building with lights of warm purple and gold tones, and beaming out of the center of the colosseum were holographic highlights from games played in the past, of a sport that meant so much to all the peoples of the world, called Cath. "This is where I met her,"

"Who?" Antony looked confused.

"My wife," Iscariot answered. "I can remember every detail. It was a week before Yule, and the Mastodons were playing against the Bearfints to make the playoffs. Robert had gotten tickets for me, and I remember it being cold as the poles and wicked as the devil himself. I thought me ass might get frostbit. So cold I'd thought me nuts had fallen off, so I went to go get some Shockloyd to warm myself up. I was wiggling like a twig in the wind. So, then I get my drink, and as I'm going back to my seat, I see this stunning woman bundled from head to toe, shivering so bad her legs were shaking, and I have no idea what to say to her, but I know I want to say something. Like a gobshite, I'm walking in circles, haven't a bull's notion, trying to find the right words, and then I see her looking at me with this perfect smile, and I'm a deer in the headlights. I'm just standing there like a fool. So, with nothing prepared, I walk up to her and say, 'Here, you looked cold. This'll warm ya up.' She looked at me with her creamy nectar eyes, the snow started falling heavily, and I knew right there, I'd love this woman forever."

Antony poked fun at him when he finished the tale, "What a dreamy story, Loverboy."

"Aw, shut up ya Gobshite and turn right; there's the hospital," he instructed.

Antony turned. The building was modern, consisting of three cylindrical towers reaching forty stories each, and branching out from the primary structures were smaller, similarly shaped buildings about half the size, and at the front of the hospital was a glass sphere near twenty stories in height with a diameter equal to that of the main buildings.

The two entered the hospital, and Iscariot's nerves were on edge, excited, ready for his boy to come into the world. Seconds after they entered the building, a peppy, doe-eyed nurse approached them and directed Iscariot into the birthing room where his wife was calmly in the beginning stages of giving Iscariot a son. His face beamed when he saw her. Her light brown hair waved like the sea, reaching down the small of her back, and her eyes were sweet as honey dripping from the comb. She had a smile that could melt men's souls and a laugh that carried the notes of angels. She looked at him, as he did her, and only love was seen. Iscariot went to her, grasped her left hand, and kissed her soothing peach lips.

"Are you doing okay?" he asked with a concerned expression.

"I'm doing fine, Wonder-boy. I'm happy you're here." She squeezed his hand as she told him. Her voice was smooth as silk, polished, flawless. She loosened her grip and moved her fingers between his, locking them together, and as she did so she heard Iscariot's stomach grumble. "You look thin," she teased him.

"Make all the jokes you want my, Neachtar. I'm not the one about to give birth." He grinned at his wife. She freed her hand from his and slapped his wrist, giving him a scolding, playful look.

"Ouch woman, stop being mean." He spoke lightheartedly. She then wove her fingers into his once more, looking into his eyes with a smile skirting her face.

"Speaking of food, do you know what sounds amazing right now?" she asked, not letting him respond. "Orange and lemon carrageenan pudding—did you bring me any?"

Iscariot looked at her with bemusement, "It's nearly midnight, and Maróg is closed. I think you're out of luck with that."

"Well, I guess that brings you down a point on the husband scale," she mocked.

"Oh, so I went from 100 to ninety-nine?" he played along.

"No dear, that gets you from one to zero. Looks like I'll have to find a new husband after today." She winked at him while he gave her a sour, mischievous stare.

While the labor process was slow, they talked of when they first started dating. "Do you remember our first date at Maróg? It was two weeks after we first met, and to be honest, I don't know what took you so long to ask me out on a date. I would have said yes as soon as you gave me your Shockloyd when I met you at the Cath match."

"How could I forget it? I got ice cream that tasted like toothpaste and fell flat on my ass as we left. It was terrible," he said to her. "I was so nervous the day of the match. I had no clue what I was doing."

"Oh, I could tell. But you were sweet, and the Shockloyd was the best one I've ever had," she told him. "You sure do know how to win a girl's heart. You being in misery—I kinda liked it. I thought it was rather cute, and as I recall, I had some competition that night we went to Marog's."

Iscariot grinned, "You sure did. I was this close to pushing you aside for your smokin' hot Nan." They both laughed at the thought. "That lady was hilarious—I miss her sometimes." As he said the words, the scene abruptly changed.

"Ahh Cac! That friggin' hurt," Iscariot's wife yelled, taking him by surprise.

"Are you alright?" Iscariot embraced her hand with both of his. His wife looked up at him in ecstasy. "He's coming," she told him.

"You're at about seven centimeters," one of the nurses told her. "The contractions are about to get much stronger as we get into active labor," she continued.

"Oh good," she said amused. The pain intensified, from seven to eight and eight to nine centimeters, the contractions were close and intense. Her back and groin began to ache. "I think I'm going to be sick."

"It will pass dear. Husband, give her some water and a damp cloth to place on her forehead," the wide-eyed nurse commanded. Iscariot followed her directions, trying to help as best he could, though he felt like he wasn't helping much at all.

"Okay, we are fully dilated," the doctor noted. "Get ready to start pushing."

The pain became more intense as she started to push in between contractions. Her breathing was slow and methodical, focused. As she pushed, she tightened her grip on Iscariot's hand. He wouldn't admit it, but she was squeezing his hand so tightly it felt like it was inside a vise about to break with the next contraction she had. He ignored his hand. Iscariot was fixated on the moment, a sense of excitement knowing his child was mere minutes from life outside the womb.

An hour had passed, and the infant was close to delivery. The contractions were now thirty second to a minute apart. His wife pushed again, and then once more. She seemed to feel relief with every push she gave. Iscariot encouraged her with every push and every agonizing hand squeeze, "You're doing great, you're almost there." He kissed her vise-like hand.

"We are crowning," the doctor announced. Iscariot's face lit up as did his wife's. She pushed, and seconds later, she pushed once more, and then a third time. With a whimper, she gave her final push, and the cries of a baby boy were heard. All eyes laid upon Hanns as he wailed a healthy bawl. All eyes except for Iscariot's wife, for she lay there unconscious. To Iscariot, the room looked like everyone had panicked. Time froze, but everyone around seemed to move at lightning speed. The infant was cleared from the scene as the doctor and nurses scrambled to tend to her. The vitals on the machine showed the extremes as they beeped and coded for alarms. Iscariot's emotions were no different, from uttermost joy to severe concern, sadness, and helplessness. In his clouded state of mind, a nurse took hold of his arm and guided him into the hallway. She sat him down and took the seat next to him. The lights were bright and disorienting. Iscariot's head began to pound like waves crashing against the shore.

"Mister Darroch, I know you must be a little confused at the moment," she started.

"What's happened to my wife?" he interrupted her.

"You wife is bleeding from within. She has suffered an aortic aneurism," she continued.

"Is she going to be alright? Can you save her?" he interrupted again.

"We have rushed her into immediate surgery to try and stop the bleeding. Once the bleeding has stopped, we will try and repair the aneurysm. I will come by every thirty minutes and update you on the status of your wife."

"What of my son? Is he okay?"

"Your son is doing very well. At the moment, he is being washed and cared for, and you will be able to see him in the nursery shortly. I know this is difficult for you, so if you have any questions or need anything, please let me know," she said sympathetically. Iscariot, still in a state of shock, nodded his head and the bubbly, doe-eyed nurse headed back to tend to his ailing wife.

The sands of time fell slowly for Iscariot. Still in an emotional daze, he began to wander the white halls of the hospital. He stopped by the nursery, but his son was not there, so he let his feet take him to his destination as his mind reflected on memories of the woman he loved. Through the maze of the hospital his mind cerebrated on everything, every moment of their life together. From the first time they met, to their first date, their first kiss, the first time they made love. *All these firsts*, he thought, *and tonight could be our last. Our last kiss, our last laugh, our last life together.*

Without knowing how he arrived, he found himself inside the glass sphere at the front of the hospital. As he stood in the room's center, he saw he was surrounded by symbols of his religion, the marks of the Nazar. Though the building was made of glass surrounded by the light of the city, the room was dark. Its only light was of the Shamrock at the front of the room. The cross had no foundation, as it itself was made of light, suspended in air, as were the daingne that hovered over each arm of the cross. The Shamrock was vivid white, and tails of white light circled around it like the wind, while ivory flakes that twinkled from the daingne fell like snow from the cross and into oblivion. Iscariot knelt before the Shamrock and slammed his fist upon the ground. "Why! Why are you doing this to me?" he yelled without expecting a response. In anger and despair, he bowed his head and prayed. He pleaded to the Lord to save his wife, and if his prayer be answered, he listed all that he would do in return for the grace he was given. *Never will I be envious of others, nor lust for power above my given rank. Lord save her, and I promise I will do all you ask and more of me. Please. I beg you. Save her—save the woman I love. Let her grow old with me and watch our boy grow to become a man. Let her hear his laugh and his cries. Let her hear his first words and see him walk for the first time. Let her tend his heart when it is broken. Please, Lord—let her be a mother—I cannot do this without her.*

His mind grew tired from absence of sleep, his body fatigued from lack of food, and his heart worn from the emotions of the night. He laid himself under the Shamrock, and his eyes began to close. Sleep took hold of his mind, and the power of dreams held him.

The night sky gleamed rich violet with hues of pink and purple, and its face dusted with stars burning billons of miles away. The ground around him was barren and dead, and the wind echoed a hollow, steady note as it swept past his ears. Before him was an amphitheater of stone and concrete benches, and sunken into the ground was a sixty-six ton meteorite. He did not know why, but he felt anger and rage at the sight of it. Iscariot walked down towards the stone and saw its insides swirled like molten. He watched as the substance within the meteor moved like water but looked like sand, and as he gazed upon it longer, he thought he could see dreams, or maybe they were memories; he wasn't sure. He hesitated and then put his hand into the liquid stone. Its surface began to harden, and Iscariot began to panic. He placed his hand upon his wrist, trying to free himself from the clutch of the meteor, but the melted stone consumed his arm and then began to pull him closer. As the watery stone began to grip his body, Iscariot's eyes widened, and he began to struggle for air as he became absorbed by it. He approached closer to the swirling pool within the meteor until he was consumed within it.

Iscariot's body went plummeting towards the earth and landed forcefully upon its surface. The liquid substance that had coated him shielded his fall, yet he still gasped for air. The molten rock cracked from this impact, and as Iscariot gathered his strength, it evaporated into the air. He looked around trying to gather his bearings not knowing where he was, and to his right and left were dark ghostly creatures whose silks were ragged and weathered. Iscariot jumped back and reached for his sword and then saw the army that was before him. The phantom beings rode on the backs of ape-like beasts whose eyes beamed fire red and whose bodies were lined in black scales. Even their teeth and tongue looked like armor as they walked upon the burning ground. It was then Iscariot realized the surface he was standing on was not grass or dirt but a magma floor that spewed from a volcano off into the distance. He ignored his surroundings and readied himself to fight as they approached, but they seemed to pay him no mind, and then, like ghosts, they walked through him. Baffled, Iscariot sheathed his sword and noticed that the apes imbibed the volcanic surfaced they walked on. He had never seen such a sight, nor an army so full of death and darkness.

As the massive army strode forward, Iscariot heard a terrible scream from above, sending chills down his spine and the hairs on his arms to rise. The sky above was full of ash and smoke, but when he looked towards the heavens, he saw the shadow of a beast. Like nails upon a chalkboard, the creature shrieked a horrid sound once more and, breaking the clouds with his wings, it bolted towards the earth and landed violently, shaking the ground around him. The beast was nearly 100 feet tall with spikes of charcoal ivory protruding through its body and on its head were two curved horns nearly twenty feet in length. The creature opened its colossal wings; they spanned 200 feet from end to end. They were torn but looked murderously sharp, and it gave a vicious shrill for the army to hear. The massive military force shouted in unison, "Drachen!

Drachen! Drachen!" Their cries echoed for miles for all to hear. Riding on the back of the drachen was a being that looked just as menacing. His dark metallic armor was jagged and terrifying, his helm was horned and spiked, and his visor pierced the world in orange and red. Iscariot stared at him, and it seemed the man upon the drachen glared right back at him. The armored man grabbed his weapon, a thorned cylindrical hammer taller than he, and pointed it at Iscariot. "Feuer," the knight commanded. The world around Iscariot fell silent, and the great beast broadened his chest, and it began to rumble. Then, with a great roar, the drachen released the fire within.

A blinding light flashed before him, and his body fell into the depths of a dark and deep hole within the earth. His body landed hard, and Iscariot gasped for air to fill his lungs. He lookup up and saw a golden crown covered in blood lying on the dirt floor next to him. His ribs were broken, and his face was matted with earth, blood, and sweat. He crawled towards the crown and reached out his hand to grab it, and as his hand touch the crown, the ground collapsed before him.

His body hit hard once more upon the ground, snapping his head on the cold surface. Disoriented, he heard his name being yelled, "Iscariot!" He struggled to his feet, finding it difficult to stand. He placed his hand on the wall next to him. His eyes blurred. He guided himself towards the call of his name. His name became clearer, but his eyes seemed to worsen with every step. A frigid chill ran down his spine as he came across a figure, and his eyes began to weep. "NOOO!" Iscariot yelled in horror and fright. He looked down upon the figure, his eyes still clouded from tears and concussion; the figure spoke. "Hanns," is all it said, and the body vanished like smoke floating in the wind.

Iscariot opened his eyes and woke within the prayer room. The room was pitch black, and once more he was blinded. He squinted his eyes, trying to see through the darkness. The room lit itself ablaze, and fire consumed it, and through the fire walked a demon, for he himself was made of fire. He looked sharply at Iscariot, his eyes burning red, it lunged at him. Before Iscariot could move, a hand grabbed 'hold of his throat and pinned his back against the wall. The burning beast breathed deep and hollow; its face got closer to his. Its voice void and haunting, it spoke, "Iscariot—Iscariot—Iscariot."

Antony shook him lightly trying to wake him. "Iscariot— Iscariot—wake up!"
His eyes burned, his throat was dry, and his clothes were drenched in sweat.

"Are you alright? You're soaked," Antony told him with a worried look on his face.

"My wife, where is she?" Iscariot asked, still confused from the dream.

"She is still in surgery; there has been no word on her condition," Antony answered. He continued, "You need a change of clothes. Let me give you my sweater." Iscariot removed his wet shirt and put on the sweater Antony gave him. "Come on, let's go see how she's doing."

As they walked through the halls back to the waiting area, a young nurse approached them. "Excuse me, sir. Are you Iscariot Darroch?" she asked.

"Yes, I am. How is my wife doing?" Iscariot asked without hesitation.

"I'm sorry, sir; I do not have an update on your wife. I do, however, have some good news. Come, follow me." The young nurse took his hand and guided him through the hospital and finally to the glass window of the nursery. She put her hand on his back and lightly pushed him forward. The youthful nurse pointed to a brown-haired boy whose name read Hanns Fritz Darroch. Iscariot moved closer to the window; his face was nearly touching the glass.

"Can I hold him?" he asked silently, sounding more like he was making a demand than asking a question.

"Of course, this way." She spoke joyfully, trying to perk up his spirits. She picked the infant up from the small nursery bed and gently placed him into Iscariot's arms.

His face began to glow as he held his son for the first time, snug in his arms. He rocked his child back and forth, humming an old, familiar lullaby. Iscariot held back tears of jubilance as his heart sang a song of bliss, and for a moment he feared nothing. Worry washed away like rain. His smile grew as Hanns's little hand wrapped tightly around his index finger.

There was a knock on the nursery window, and he saw it was the doctor who was caring for his wife. Iscariot's heart sank, expecting the worst. He slowly exited the nursery with Hanns and asked the question he'd been afraid to have answered.

"How is she? How's my wife?" he asked, praying that she was alright. The doctor answered him, and Iscariot's heart shattered. He dropped to his knees with tears streaming down his face. The doctor and Antony helped him up from the ground and sat him down on a chair outside the nursery window.

"If you'd like, you can see her now if you wish." The doctor spoke kindheartedly. Iscariot gathered himself together and made sure Hanns was comfortable within his arms.

"Can I bring my son? I'd like him to meet his mother," he asked with bloodshot, watery eyes.

"That's fine," the surgeon agreed.

The room was dark and eerily quiet with only a single light shining upon his wife. The doctor left Iscariot alone and closed the door behind him. Iscariot stood there for a moment and looked down at his child and then at his wife, not wanting the moment to be real. He walked up to the bed, his voice choked, and his mouth quivered as he spoke to her.

"My Neachtar. Here he is, our baby boy—" Hanns's began to coo. "He's so happy to see you." A tear ran down Iscariot's cheek, "He says, "Hi Mom—I—I love you."" He closed his eyes hard and let the tears wash down his face. "I wish you could see him; he looks just like you, just like I hoped he would."

Iscariot pushed the bars of the bed down and crawled in next to her, placing Hanns in the middle between them. He placed his hand over hers and gazed upon her beauty, "I can't do this without you." His throat tightened like a knotted rope, and his eyes began to water once more. "I'm really gonna miss you." Iscariot kissed her lips for the last time, "I love you, Anna."

Iscariot Chapter Two

Iscariot hadn't slept in days. His eyes were bloodshot, his hair ragged, and his beard unkempt. He stood there naked in the bathroom, gazing at his appearance in the mirror as the water from the sink rushed to fill the bowl only to find its way circling down the drain. The sun hadn't kissed the earth, but winter's freeze found its wrath during the night. Iscariot, still examining himself, stroked his beard and gave a somber sigh. He grabbed the clippers from the double vanity drawer and began snipping away at the bird's nest that decorated his face. As he trimmed and cut the overgrown mess on his cheekbones and chin into something more presentable, he threw on the shower to warm himself up from the bitterness of the cold and begin his day. The steam filled up the room quickly, blotting out the reflections in the mirrors and dampening everything within the room. Iscariot let the water hit his face. His thoughts dwelled on Anna. He imagined her every curve, the long lean muscles of her legs, her toned caressing arms, her plump fruity lips. He missed her honey caramel eyes and her soft wavy hair that always smelled like coconut. He fantasized about her petite, peach bottom and her soft, firm breasts. He began to touch himself as he thought of past memories of them in the shower together. He thought of her arms around his neck and her legs around his back as he held her against the wall of the shower, kissing her lips and thrusting himself inside her as the water fell upon their naked bodies. He thought of the scratches he'd have on his back and the feel of her body as she climaxed. He remembered the bright smile she would have after making love, cute and coy, yet devilishly sexy, and the taste of her lips as she kissed him a thousand times with joy and love.

Iscariot's mind snapped back to reality as he heard the coos of his baby boy. He shut off the water, grabbed the damp towel sitting on the banister, and wrapped it around his waist. He exited the powder room and walked into the blackness of his bedroom. He stopped suddenly; his heart started to race, for his eyes beheld a hooded creature in black whose torn silks waved as if blowing in the wind. Phantom-like it looked, legs apart with one in front of the other, it pointed at Iscariot, and as it did so, it seemed to speak. Its voice like metal rubbing against metal with the pain of a thousand men burning in the depths of hell. The windows in the room shattered, and the wind began to howl. The phantom glided towards the child.

"Get away from him!" Iscariot shouted in fear and rushed towards the wraith. He dashed across the room, jumped on the bed and dived at the hooded creature, but his hands did not grasp the phantom. He hit the ground hard, dislocating his thumb, and when he looked up from the ground, he saw that the room was still dark, the windows were unbroken, and the morning light peaked over the horizon. Hanns's cries still echoed in the room. Iscariot examined his aching thumb and quickly pushed it back into place. Slightly relieved, he picked up Hanns from his bassinet. He looked around his bedroom and saw everything was as it should be. The windows were not broken, the wind was not gusting, and no demon stood before him. Iscariot felt disoriented by what he'd just experienced and turned on the light to comfort his soul and remove his fear.

"Hey bud, are you okay?" he asked his son. "You slept pretty good last night. What do you want to eat today? Do you want milk — or milk?" Hanns made small wiggle movements while Iscariot held him in his hands. "Oh, good choice, Hanns." He praised his son.

Iscariot walked downstairs into his modern kitchen, grabbed a bottle from the fridge and placed it on the kitchen counter. A display appeared on the countertop as it read that a baby's bottle sat atop of it. *Slide right to warm,* the counter read, the diagram around the bottle had lights for indicators, they spun in circles and turned from blue to green, the text on the counter read, *Complete. Bottle is warm.* Iscariot tested the contents on his arm: *Just right,* he thought, and Hanns began to guzzle down the warm milk while Iscariot took a seat at the table with the babe in his arm. Iscariot placed his hand on the table, and another display appeared with options of what to drink and watch. He selected news and coffee. The display moved from the table top and projected as a holographic image, as the coffee he requested was being ground and poured into a mug. Talks were still on the treaty and global economies. Hyperinflation and economic collapse dressed the headlines. Iscariot turned down the stress of the news and tried to ease his mind. He finished his coffee as Hanns finished his milk, and he walked around the house, patting Hanns's back, burping his infant son. As he walked through his home, Iscariot smelled something rather peculiar. He smelled himself first and noticed nothing. He then lifted Hanns's bum to his face and cringed, "Oh boy—Whoa, you stink Hannsie! Let's go upstairs, and I'll change ya."

Hanns was changed and bathed, and Iscariot dressed himself in an all-black suit. The house bell rang, and an image appeared on the wall showing his guests at the front door. "Open," he commanded, and the door slowly came ajar.

"Uncle Isk! Uncle Isk!" Lorena was calling from downstairs; he could hear her prancing as she climbed the stairs.

"I'm right here, Lorena," he hollered back to his niece. Lorena found him and ran to him, hugging his leg tightly, and she began to cry.

"I miss Aunt Anna!" she bawled, tears falling down her cheeks.

Iscariot's throat tightened. "Me too," was all he could let out. He knelt down and hugged her back. "Dry your eyes, little one, and let's go back downstairs. I know little Hanns is going to be glad to see you."

Lorena dried her eyes and gave a smile, and Iscariot scooped up his baby boy as the three of them headed downstairs. Robert, Lagertha, and their two infant boys were all sitting in the great room, dressed in all black, holding one another, with somber expressions on their faces. Iscariot met his brother's eyes, and Robert gave a smile of sympathy.

"Hey, Isc." Robert rose from the couch with Absolume in his hands and embraced his brother as tightly as he could with two babes between them. "How are you doing today?"

"As best I can, I suppose," Iscariot said. "The poulnabrone was finished yesterday, and the women have been Keening all night. As far as I know, the food should arrive as the funeral is taking place, and the beer and whisky should be here around 10 this morning."

"You've done good, Isc. I know Lagertha has the games and pipes set to come around 10 o'clock as well, and I've gotten you something for tonight that might perk your spirits." Robert said.

"Uncle Isk, I've got something special for you, too. Well—it's not really for you, it's kinda for Aunt Anna," Lorena said, trying not to hurt her uncle's feelings.

"Whatever you have for Aunt Anna, I know she is going to love it, Lorena. You were her favorite niece," Iscariot said.

"I know. She told me all the time, Uncle Isk," she said matter of factly. "Can I hold Hanns now?" she asked as sweetly as she could.

Iscariot smiled, "I'll tell ya what. He's a little sleepy right now. Can you sing him a song and rock him softly in the bassinet? He told me he loves your singing voice."

"But Uncle Isk, I never sang to him before."

"Course ya have. When Aunt Anna was pregnant, he always heard you through her tummy."

"Oh yea, Aunt Anna always said he was dancing when she felt his little feet kicking her." She chuckled. Iscariot placed Hanns in the rocking bed, and Lorena started making up songs as she rocked him like he was made of glass and would shatter with the slightest nick.

The morning dragged on for Iscariot. His mind was fogged, and his emotions wavered from sadness to anger. He said little, if anything, to anyone as the morning crept along. The beer and whisky had arrived, along with the games and mala-piopai, and the guests started arriving as well, causing the house to grow louder and louder. Iscariot began feeling irritated with the chatter and all the sounds that had surrounded him, so he had found a moment to slip away upstairs where all he heard was the ringing in his ears. He let himself fall upon his bed. He closed his eyes as his mind began to grow clearer. He grabbed the covers and wrapped them around himself. He could still smell Anna as he breathed in the sheets that had entangled him. His eyes quickly grew heavy, as did his mind, but he did not allow himself to fall asleep. He took a long deep breath and opened his eyes, his body sprung into alertness. Above him, within the ceiling, was the hooded figure. The room grew dark and seemed to fill with smoke as the creature dropped down from above. Iscariot rolled off the bed, pounced back to his feet, and swung his fist at the wraith. The phantom dodged his punch as if Iscariot was swinging his fist underwater. Again, he swung, and once more, he missed. The hooded creature was back against the wall. Iscariot pulled back his fist once more and thrust forward as fast and as fiercely as he could muster. His fist struck the ghostly being, and it vanished like paper in the dancing breeze.

Iscariot heard three loud booms. There was a knock on the door. His heart was racing. "Come in," he said.

The door gave an eerie creak as it swung open. "Is everything alright, Isc? We heard a loud noise downstairs and were concerned," Lagertha wondered sincerely.

"Everything is fine. I had just tripped over my feet," he laughed as he lied.

"Oh, well; be careful. Can I get you anything?"

"No, I'm fine. Thank you. I was just coming back downstairs. Has everyone arrived?"

"I believe so. The food is starting to arrive now. It's nearly 2," she said. "Come on, let's get going. She looks beautiful by the way."

"Who does?"

"Your wife." Iscariot walked towards Lagertha and embraced her.

"I haven't seen her yet. I've been afraid to," he confessed.

"Oh, Isc. I'm so sorry," Lagertha comforted him. "Her beauty can still take your breath away," she said, remembering the story of when Anna and Iscariot had first met. "She loved you so much, Isc, and that love you have for her is never lost. It merely is reborn into new love—love that is just as powerful and just as passionate as it is for Anna right now. Transfer all that love for her into your son, or store it inside until you find someone who needs it."

"You're one hell of a mother, Lagertha. Your kids are incredibly lucky." Iscariot pulled away from their embrace and walked with Lagertha downstairs to the rest of the guests. Iscariot conversed and socialized until the burial ceremony was about to begin. The chattering crowd of his friends and family slowly made their way outside into the vast expanse of his farmland. In the distance was the poulnabrone dolmen with a backdrop of a pink and golden sky as the sun set upon the day. Chairs were lined twenty rows back, each one of them filled, and there were a hundred others who stood to honor and grieve for Anna and with Iscariot.

An elderly man in black robes stood before the gathering. "Please raise your heads," he said in his refined baritone voice. Their faces pointed skyward towards the heavens, and he began to pray aloud.

"Our heavenly Creator, we lift our heads towards your face. May you show us mercy in our time of despair. Our Lord, a child of yours has left the earth and walks in the valley of death. Our Shepherd, please guide her on her path towards your kingdom. Lead her through green pastures and beside still waters. May no evil befall her on her journey, and if she is frightened, please give her comfort. Our Father, wash away her sins like water to the earth. Anoint her, and show her mercy. Our Lord, we humbly request her entrance into your kingdom so that she may dwell within your house, now and forever. Germa."

Iscariot lowered his head back towards the earth, touching his forehead with his forefingers, then his left breast, crossing over his heart to his right breast, and then back to his forehead once more. He then stepped forward to address those who had come to honor his wife.

On the poulnabrone were two torches that hung on each of the eight-foot stone pillars. Iscariot took hold of one of the torches that flickered in the cold air. His throat was heavy; he paused before speaking and cleared his throat.

"In my hands is the light of the first men. It is said that our Messiah was born of this fire, and that one day, he will be born again of this fire. This fire is our light, our guide, and today, it guides my wife towards salvation. Please come forward to light your lampróg."

One by one, the audience came forward. Much like the streetlights, the lampróg floated in the air; only they used wings that buzzed like hummingbirds. The small spherical capsules were opened, and both Iscariot and the Aspal dipped the fire into them. After all the lights were lit, the day had turned to night, and the stars illuminated the sky. The mourners took their seats, and the choir began to sing. They sang in an old tongue whose culture had died from the world. Their voices were celestial, lush in range, and their tone was of majesty and grandeur. Their angelic voices carried in the vast openness of the field as they sang their song of mercy and peace.

> *I lay my head upon the earth*
> *And let my spirit take its flight*
> *To leave this world, a second birth*
> *I am delighted in this sight*
> *Capitis mei ponam super terram*
> *Et accipe spiritum meum, et fugerunt*
> *Ut transeat ex hoc mundo secunda*
> *Et delectatus sum in conspectu tuo*
> *This is my song, a song of life*
> *For my loved ones to hold dear*
> *And in this world, there is no strife*
> *There's no need for you to fear*
> *Hoc canticum vitae*
> *Dilectus meus ad suos*
> *Et in hoc mundo non est pugna*
> *Non opus est quod metuas*

As the choir sang its heavenly tune, the lampróg danced in the night sky. They flew in unison; like a flock of birds they swayed in the wind. Their golden wings hummed as flickers of light darted through the air. Friends and family began to come forward to say their goodbyes to Anna as she lay beneath the poulnabrone. The two stone columns were lined with small sky-blue flowers whose stigmas were snow white and whose ovaries were the sun's yellow. They were known as Blue Beauties, symbolizing a woman's elegance. Resting upon the capstone of the poulnabrone were petite, pure white flowers known as Chamomile flowers, which symbolized an eternal rest. *Lagertha had been right,* Iscariot thought. For Anna's beauty still took one's breath away. For every man and woman that had seen her marveled at her and gasped at her perfection. Her gown was bleach white and strapless, with diamonds that wrapped around her bodice and along the trim of her breast line. Her long wavy hair was swimming with royal blue flowers called Forget-Me-Nots, and as the hymn ended, the flying lights spread across the field, creating a path back to Iscariot's house. Iscariot came forward before the crowd, and addressed them with a single tear falling from his right eye.

"Friends and family, it has been a delight to have you here. To see the love and joy Anna has spread to your hearts. Let us leave tonight in festive sprits and celebrate her life. Let us play games. Let us laugh. Let us cry, and let us never forget the woman we have all loved. Tonight, let us honor my wife with the love and joy she has given to us. Go raibh maith agat!"

Still with mournful hearts, the congregation followed the floating lights back towards Iscariot's house. The smell of food waved in the air as they got closer to the mansion, and the bass of the music could be heard as the beat traveled into the people's ears, attempting to lift the spirits of all who had come to remember Anna. The mood was stagnant. The guests had filled their plates, and when they sat, they spoke quietly and briefly. Iscariot looked at the expressions upon their faces. He couldn't blame them for how they were acting. He felt just as they did, if not more so.

A couple of chuckles crept through the sadness. It was Lorena and some younger children; they seemed to be laughing at an older fellow whose hair was thin yet stuck up in every direction. The children walked on the dance floor to see who had the best dance moves. One of the boys attempted to dance like a machine. Another, a chubbier lad, lifted his shirt above his head and made his stomach dance like the ocean. Lorena was giddy with laughter, and those who had been watching couldn't help but laugh themselves.

"Thank God for children," Robert whispered to his brother. "Without them, I don't think there'd be much to smile about in the world, but they always manage, even in the darkest of times, to show there is light when everyone else sees the darkness."

"Your daughter sure is a pisser," Iscariot laughed as he watched his niece dance wildly, waving her arms like they were noodles. Robert laughed along with him and then joined his daughter on the dance floor, he too waving his arms like strings in the wind. The crowd livened up at the sight of the nonsensical choreography of Robert and the children. Steadily, others began to join the festivities on the dance floor; however, they moved with a bit more elegance than their child counterparts. Folks began telling jokes and embarrassing stories of Anna and of things she had been a part of in their lives. Iscariot was relieved to see people had begun to enjoy themselves, and for a few moments he had forgotten his heartache just long enough to feel a sense of peace before sorrow found its way back into his heart.

The hour had gotten late. Many of the children had already fallen asleep in various parts of the house while drowsy parents went to search for them. As friends and family began to leave, there wasn't a soul that didn't shed a tear as they left to say goodbye and wished Iscariot a mended heart. The smell of the fragrant food had floated off, and the sounds of music played no more. The house was silent as Iscariot walked in from the cold of the night. All that remained were Robert, Lagertha, and their children, all of whom were still awake. Robert was in the kitchen brewing something up, of what, Iscariot wasn't sure, and Lagertha was in the great room with her three children, along with Hanns. Iscariot sighed as he sat on the couch, and before he could make himself comfortable, Robert had called everyone into the kitchen.

It smelled of mint and cocoa as Iscariot walked into the room.

"Hey Isc, I made you something," Robert said. Iscariot grabbed the mug from his hand and smiled. "The first day you met Anna, this was the drink that brought you together; let it bring you together one last time before you say goodbye." They grabbed their children and headed towards Anna's tomb, and guiding their way were the lampróg still humming a silent buzz. When they arrived, Robert built a small fire and laid out some blankets he had been hiding near the site.

"Isc, I wanted this to be like the first time you had met Anna, how you felt when you first saw her and how you acted when you first laid eyes on her. I can't display every emotion, but I know something that can express happiness and wonder," Robert said to Iscariot as he began walking back behind the poulnabrone. He took one of the floating lampróg from the air and began lighting something on fire. Iscariot couldn't quite tell what he was doing until he saw sparks coming from the base of the objects he lit.

Streams of sparkling fire went rocketing into the air and exploded with an array of colors, brightening the dark midnight sky. Iscariot was moved by the gesture. Even if he didn't feel exactly how he felt when he met Anna, he saw the significance. The sound of the booms and whistles of the wicks launching the rockets filled the night sky. Iscariot saw the happiness in his niece's eyes, and she ran to him.

"Uncle Isk," Lorena whispered in his ear, "can I sing you my gift?"

Iscariot hugged her, "Of course you can, ya little nugget."

She stood in the center of the outdoor assembly; the fireworks were still booming in the background. Her little voice began to sing,

Do not stand at my grave and weep
I am not there, I do not sleep
I am a thousand winds that blow
I am the diamond glints of snow
I am the sunlight on ripened grain
I am the gentle autumn rain
When you awaken in the morning's hush
I am the swift uplifting rush
Of quiet birds in circled flight
I am the soft star that shines at night

Iscariot's eyes watered, and his tears fell to the ground. His vision blurred. He cleared them and looked at his wife one last time before he and his brother sealed the tomb. He wished that he could peer into her honey-colored eyes once more or hear the sound of her laugh. His heart felt coiled and bound, his throat vise tight, his eyes clouded. As the final rocket launched into the air, the lampróg followed it skyward and danced around its fiery tail. He bent down and kissed his wife one last time. "I love you," he said as the rocket thundered loud above. He exited the tomb, leaving the shockloyd behind as the lampróg flickered like fireflies falling back down to the earth and finally extinguishing their light.

Iscariot said goodbye to Robert and his family. The house grew dark and the hour late. He took his son upstairs with him and laid him in his bassinet until his son's eyes were closed and the fantasy of dreams consumed him. Iscariot looked at where the hooded figure had been that afternoon and saw a hole in the wall from the punch he had thrown. He undressed and sighed heavily as his head hit the pillow. A new dawn was coming, as was a new man.

Robert Chapter Three

Robert was hiding in the walk-in closet under scores of blankets, trying to be as quiet as possible. He could hear the patter of two little feet echoing throughout the house as he lay there waiting. Into the study the sound of feet went, then into the dining room, and then they stopped in the kitchen. She tried to whisper, but Robert could still hear her speak.

"Hey Ma," Lorena whispered, "have you seen Dad? I can't find him anywhere."

"I don't know where he is, Lolo, but here, take this; it will help you find him." Lagertha handed her daughter a chocolate cupcake with caramel filling, lined with melted frosting.

Lorena's eyes grew wide. "Thanks Ma," she said trying to be as quiet as a mouse. Robert heard the thump of her feet come into the living room. He cracked the closet door to see where she was.

"Boys, boys," she said softly. "If you tell me where Dad is, I'll give you some of this cupcake," she said to her brothers. Aedus and Absolume, being only a few weeks old, said nothing. Lorena squinted at them trying to look intimidating and walked away disappointed as if she expected them to respond.

As Lorena looked around, Robert started scratching the door of the closet and making sounds that would haunt a small child. He watched as his daughter turned nervously in the direction of the eerie noises.

"Dad?" She walked silently towards the door. She picked up a pen that was sitting on the table in the room as if to use it for protection. Robert could see she was scared by the noises he was making, but yet she still walked towards him. On her tiptoes she moved until she reached the closet door and slowly began to open it. The door gave a slight creak, and then with a roar, Robert jumped out at her, grabbing her, and lifting his daughter into the air.

She gave a shriek of fright, followed by uncontrollable giggles as Robert pretended to be a wicked monster. "I found you!" she chuckled out to her father.

"I guess you win then. Did the boys help you out?" Robert asked

"No, they were being little poops. I offered them a muffin and everything," she answered.

"What muffin?" Robert questioned.

"Well, I ate it. Mom said it would help me find you."

"I think we should go back and get another one. What do you think?" he said. Lorena looked at him with a bright smile across her face. Robert placed her on his shoulder and walked into the kitchen, which smelled of all sorts of sweets. Robert gave a slight tap on Lagertha's rear as they entered.

"Dad, don't spank Mom! She isn't being bad," said Lorena. Both Robert and Lagertha hid their laughter from their daughter.

"You're right, Lorena. Mom is being very good today." Lagertha stood on her toes to kiss him and then turned back to finish baking. "Where are these delicious cupcakes our little daughter was talking about?" he asked

"Right in front of you, ya goof," Lagertha mocked him.

"This isn't all for us, is it?" asked Robert.

"No, I'm giving some to your brother and to your father," she said. "Have you talked to Iscariot today?"

"Just briefly over the airwaves. I don't think he was doing much, just entertaining Hanns. I think he'll have to get a nanny soon."

"Why, when does he have to get back to post?"

"Two weeks, maybe a month. It's a difficult situation he is in, and the military understands."

"At least Hanns can give him a little joy while he's in his melancholy state. Will the Leons help him out if he cannot find someone to watch Hanns?" she asked Robert, thinking he might know.

"I'd imagine they would, but I don't think they will have to. I know the church is always willing to help."

"Dad, I'm bored up here. Can you put me down now?" Lorena asked.

"Sure thing, my little cupcake. Can you do me a favor and check on your brothers for me?"

"Can I have another cupcake if I do," Lorena asked, hoping the answer was yes.

"No, you cannot. You have had two already," Lagertha interjected.

"Oh, please, Mom," Lorena pleaded, her wide aquamarines shining brightly. Lagertha knelt down so she was eye to eye with her daughter.

"If you behave for the rest of the day, me, you, and your Dad can all go to the ballet. What do you think about that?" she said to Lorena.

Lorena grinned ear to ear, "I promise, Mom. I'll behave."

"Good. Now go check on the boys." Lagertha gave her a little tap on the bottom as Lorena scurried off to see how her brothers were doing.

"What time does that ballet start?" Robert asked

"Around 7. Your father is watching Aed and Abe. We'll have to leave for the castle at 5:30," said Lagertha.

"Mom!" Lorena yelled from the living room. "Someone pooped their pants! Mom!"

Lagertha looked at Robert. "That's all you, my dear. Have fun."

"Gross." Robert crinkled his nose, and tended to his child.

The afternoon rushed by, and the house still smelled of chocolate and caramel. Robert and his family were upstairs getting ready for the evening's delight. Lorena was waiting patiently as her mother and father still dressed for the night out. She was wearing black stockings and a beige dress with little beige shoes to match, and in her wavy brown hair was a double-strapped hairband with little pearls circling her head.

"Well, don't you look dashing?" Robert said to his daughter. He had just finished getting ready himself, wearing a white turtleneck with a multi-button gray vest and gray blazer. Dashed on his turtleneck was a lapel pin of a purple flower, and his locks were well styled.

"Lagertha, are you almost ready?" he asked, looking at his watch and seeing they were about to be late.

"Just finished." She walked out of her room and instantly caught Robert and Lorena's eyes. She wore a strapless red dress whose waist and collar were lined in gold. Her brown-blond hair was styled in a high bun with a gold Grecian leaf headband. Her lips were plump red, and her makeup was soft and light.

"Are you an Aingeal mom?" Lorena asked in childlike wonder.

"You're so sweet, Lorena, but no I'm not. I wish I was as pretty as you, though. You look so adorable; I could eat you right up." Lagertha gave her daughter a passionate kiss on her cheek, leaving the marks of her lips upon them.

"If Mom's not an Aingeal, Lorena, then I think you might be," Robert said. "Come on, my pretty ladies. Let's grab the boys and head over to the castle." Robert and his family bundled up for the bite of the evening air, as he pushed the buttons on the display at the entrance of the house to summon their carriage from the barn. As the vehicle guided itself to a stop, the family entered a warm and cozy wagon to take them to their destination. Its interior was a rich, dark brown leather, whose seats circled around a holographic multimedia display. At the front was a glossed hardwood steering wheel in case of emergencies or if the driver wanted to pilot the vehicle himself. Its exterior was candy apple red with classical features, giving it an old-fashioned, yet modern look.

The carriage navigated Robert and his family out of the beautiful snow-dusted countryside and into the organized mess that was Bunaitheoir, which the people called Buna. They passed through the traditional part of the city, where the buildings were made of stone and brick, and people would buy vintage clothing or household items, connecting them to roots of the past, which the people of Aontaithe highly respected and valued. The lampróg city lights gave a warm golden glow to the district as people from all over the world shopped and dined within it, especially around Yule time when charity and spirits were high, and all seemed right with the world. As they rode through the city streets, they came upon a great river that cut directly into the city's center, known as Chuthru. It stemmed from the Mor Mountain Range in the north, which seemed to span the earth itself, and its peaks went beyond the clouds as if they reached the stars. As they crossed the bridge made of light, they entered the financial metropolis whose glass buildings were as strong and as lovely as the mightiest lion and his mane. The blinding lights decorated the modern structures as they danced throughout the buildings, giving an ambiance of future successes and the accomplishment of dreams. Though the buildings were modern, they upheld the city's design of gothic architecture. As Robert looked out the window, he could see the many smiling faces of the men and women who walked the city avenues, how they enjoyed the festive atmosphere of the Yule holiday. He could see the eyes of the children grow wide as they gazed upon a gift they were hoping to receive on Ardu-Ceiliúradh. As they left the maze of glass and steel buildings, they came into another borough of Bunaitheoir whose streets were lined with churches and temples of an eclectic mix of religions throughout the world. The carriage had driven past an extraordinary white cathedral. At its entrance was a tower that stood 250 feet and looked to be held in place, on both sides, by ascending stone white pipe organs that spread across like wings. Its pure white steeple was layered like stairways to heaven and capped at its highest point was symbol of the Nazar faith, a Shamrock. The building stretched 350 feet in length, and its end was rounded and dome shaped.

"There's our church," Lorena pointed out to her mother and father.

"It's where me and your mum got married," Robert told her.

"It is?" she asked. "It's so pretty, Dad. It's my favorite building in the city."

"Maybe one day you can get married there," he said.

"I'm only a kid, Dad. I can't get married now. I'm only a kid," she said as if Robert didn't know her age.

At the end of the borough, sitting upon a hill, surrounded by acres of pine trees, was a tremendous stone white castle, whose towers were capped blue as if reflected by the deep blue waters of the harbor and whose backdrop was that of the extraordinary, snow-white mountain range in the north. It looked like a picture on a postcard in a fairytale world, where good and evil were black and white, and truth and love conquered all. Their wagon approached the black gates of the castle where two soldiers, both part of the Liopard branch, greeted them.

Their armor was made of a jet-black metallic alloy as light as aluminum and as strong as diamonds. It had patterns of black and soft gray that mirrored that of a leapord throughout the entire body suit. The warriors looked like gargoyles as they stood as still as stone, but unlike gargoyle's, their eyes glowed forest green. The Liopards' helmets are also made of the same metallic alloy bearing the same camouflage pattern as the rest of the suit. There was no visor for the warriors to peer through, only the lenses of the ominous green glow.

Robert rolled down his window and saluted the soldiers. They gave a salute back, and though they knew him well, asked for Robert's identification so that he would be permitted in.

"Dad—who are they, Dad?" Lorena asked nervously.

"They are called Liopards. They're part of our military and will lay down their lives to protect us. There is no reason to be afraid of them," he told her.

"They look like monsters, Dad," she continued.

"If it helps, think of them as your monsters that scare off the very terrible ones that frighten you at night. Come here and shake his hand; he'll love it," Robert said.

Lorena hesitated and moved towards the window. She looked at the soldier, and the soldier looked back at her. Lorena's eyes grew slightly wider as she put out her hand to say hello. The warrior depressurized the helmet from the suit and removed it. Lorena could not believe what she was seeing.

"You're a girl! Dad, she's a girl—you told me she was a monster," she said in amazement. The soldier laughed as did Robert and Lagertha.

"She must be very brave and very strong to pass the training to become a warrior in our military. Our standards are very high, and we lower them for no one. She is truly one of the best of the best." He informed his daughter.

"Is it true? Are you the best?" She asked the soldier.

"I am not the best, no, but your father is right. I am very brave and very strong, and if ever you are in trouble, I will do my best to protect you, and, if need be, die for you," the Liopard told her.

"She's like a hero in the fables—so cool, Dad," she said dumbfounded.

"Alright, Lorena, we best be going," Robert said.

"Bye Lady Liopard! Bye!" Lorena shouted as she waved goodbye.

The wagon pulled up the long driveway to the castle's entrance where Abraham was there to meet them. Lorena dashed out of the vehicle and sprinted to her grandfather, embracing him with the largest of hugs.

"Grand-daidi! How have you been? Dad said you haven't been feelin' good," she said innocently.

"Your dad is overreacting. You have nothing to worry about; your Gran-di is just fine," he reassured her, as he looked at his son with an expression of guilt. "Let's get inside. It's miserably cold out here."

The castle doors swung open to bleach white marble floors, snow-white pillars, and birch trees that reached the ceiling. Miniature lampróg circled high above, near the skylight, lighting up the entrance when the sun had set.

"Thanks Dad for taking the boys. Are you sure you'll be alright?" Robert asked.

"Oh, we'll be quite fine. To what ballet are you attending tonight?" his father asked.

"We are seeing the Snow Queen," said Robert.

"Aw, a wonderful tale. One of my favorites. You three best be going before you become late." Abraham held out his hands and Lagertha handed over her two boys to him.

"Thank you so much, Abraham. You're such a sweet Grand-daidi," she told him.

"Oh, it's nothing. You all have fun, now."

"We have changing underwear in the bag, along with wipes and milk. They will probably need to eat around 9:30 or so," Lagertha informed him.

"Thanks, Dad. We'll be back around 11 or 11:30."

"Don't worry about me. You all have fun. If you'd like, you're more than welcome to stay the night," Abraham told his son.

"We might take you up on that. We'll see you soon, Dad."

"Bye Gran-di!" said Lorena as she skipped to the carriage.

"Goodbye, dear. I'll see you soon." Abraham closed the massive door behind them as they left with a grin of delight on their faces.

Robert, Lagertha, and Lorena boarded the vehicle and headed towards the art district, which consisted of arenas, theaters, universities, and museums. There were monuments all around the city, honoring great men and women of the past. Some were soldiers, others artists, world leaders, mathematicians; there was even a monument for just a local citizen. Though these people walked different paths in life, they all had one commonality, which was that they all impacted the nation in such a manner that would seem impossible for one man or woman to accomplish on their own. Not only were these people honored with statues and monuments, but the people of the nation strived to be like them, from their moral codes to their passion and willingness to accomplish their dreams. Though the origins of the nation weren't without fault, the people loved it and would come from all over the globe to be a part of it. In front of the most prestigious theater, where the ballet was being held, was a marble statue honoring the country's most influential writer, whose works have gone on to be retold in their original format as well as in ballets, holofilms, plays, and children's stories. The statue was of Christian Andersen who sat atop a bench with a book and cane in hand; his face was turned away as if distracted by something or imagining his next story. To his left was a monument made of light. It honored the country's first ever Prima Ballerina, Pierina Legnani. Like a dream, she twirled and danced all around the courtyard to Andersen's playwright of Ailleacht and the Beast. Further on, to Pierina Legnani's left, was another statue of a great writer, whose tales are synonymous with love and darkness, who goes by the name of Poe. He is deep in thought at his desk, scribbling out his next book on a piece of parchment, and coming from his pen is a beam of light which illuminated the words he was writing, the light refracted into the sky above Poe's head; images of ravens flew all around, sometimes in chaos, other times in unison.

"Who is the dancer made of light, Mom?" Lorena asked.

"That is Pierina Legnani. She is the most famous and greatest ballerina to have ever existed," Lagertha told her.

"When I grow up, I'm gonna be just like her, Mom," Lorena said with certainty.

"It is very hard work. You must give everything you have to become the best, and sometimes you might have to put aside other things you like to do to become the best; would you want to do that?" Lagertha questioned her.

"I can do it, Mom. Dad, tell her I can do it," said Lorena. Robert and Lagertha chuckled silently.

"She can do it, Lagertha," he told his wife and gave her a playful wink.

The carriage pulled up to the entrance of the theater. The air stung their cheeks as they exited the vehicle, and they blushed once they were inside the warmth of the building. Inside, Yule decorations filled the rooms with a festive atmosphere. The people around them were in a joyful mood, smiling and laughing, enjoying champagne and wine as they waited for the show to begin. Robert looked at his daughter who was in awe of the elegance she was surrounded by. She started to twirl and dance as they waited in the lobby for the lights to flicker, signaling the ballet was about to begin.

"LoLo, stay close and watch out for others. We don't want to spill any drinks on their pretty outfits, do we?" said Lagertha.

"I'm right here, Mom. I'll be careful, I promise," she told her mother. Moments passed as Robert enjoyed a glass of champagne, and Lagertha sipped on a mocktail while their daughter danced around them. The lights flickered from on to off, and they scurried off to find their seats. The auditorium of Raidio Ceol Halla was littered with rows of red seats, its stage beamed a sunset yellow as arches seemed to flow like waves down to it. A hand-blown, dazzling and massive crystal chandelier hung high above the auditorium. It looked as if the sun had exploded as the crystal stems reached out in all directions. A morning orange and fire yellow lit the room as its light beamed across the theater. The lights dimmed, the audience fell silent, and the music began to play a soft and beautiful tune. The curtain began to rise and standing in the center of the stage was a little girl, dressed in a ragged fluid dress with torn tights underneath, and a young boy whose boots were new but his jacket tattered and hair ruffled. Above them was an arch of flowers connecting one rooftop to another. They danced and played in the ballet sort of way. Lorena's eyes gleamed wide at the sight, and Robert and Lagertha's hearts were warmed with her joy. Entering the stage in a grand fashion was a stunning woman whose unitard was glove tight and whiter than a swan's feathers. Her hair was blonde and put up in a bun that looked like a crown. Her white sleeves were draped in diamonds, and in her hair were dazzling snowflakes. Lorena looked at her parents with her mouth wide open, mesmerized by the beauty of the Snow Queen.

"Sooo pretty," she mouthed to her father. Robert smiled and nodded in agreement. Wrapped up in the magic of the ballet, with adventure, sadness, heartache, and love, the hour and a half flew by in what seemed like mere minutes. The little boy and the little girl were no longer little but had grown into adults, and the two of them lived a fairy-tale ending, happily ever after. The crowd stood and cheered with thunderous applause as the performers bowed and curtsied to show their gratitude. Finally, the choreographers and director came out onto the stage to thank all who had attended and all who had performed with humble words of kindness.

Robert and his family exited the theater and waited for their coach to arrive.

"Hey, Dad. Can I join a ballet school?" Lorena asked.

"I think it's a great idea. What do you think Lagertha?"

"Please, please, please, Mom!" Lorena pleaded.

"If you really want to do ballet, we can see when classes start up. I will make a few calls tomorrow and see what I can find out," said Lagertha.

"Yes!" exclaimed Lorena as she twirled circles around them. The snow started to fall heavy as the carriage arrived. They climbed in the carriage and watched the snow flurry from the warmth of the vehicle.

"I think the Snow Queen has arrived. Let's see if we can find her," Robert suggested to his daughter.

"I think she's over there, Dad," Lorena said.

"Oh no, I think I see her behind you," Robert told her.

"There she is!" Lagertha teased.

"Where, Mom?" Lorena asked.

"Right here," she said once more as she began to tickle Lorena. She giggled happily, trying to tickle her mother back.

"Dad—help!" Lorena blurted out, chuckling her words as she spoke. Robert squeezed Lagertha's thigh, and she too, started to laugh, and then he tickled her ribs and all her sensitive areas until she was laughing in tears. They had tuckered out, especially Lorena, who now rested her head on her mother's lap. Her eyes were closed, and sleep had taken her. Robert grabbed his wife's hand and kissed it as they rode in silence back to his father's castle.

The snow was falling thick and heavy. Robert could only see a few feet in front of him. It had taken nearly an hour for them to reach the driveway of the castle. Both Lagertha and Lorena were sound asleep as the vehicle parked at the main entrance. Robert picked his daughter up from Lagertha's lap and rested her head on his shoulder.

In the castle, he walked the halls into one of the many spare bedrooms. The entire castle was decorated with Yule decor, and he felt like a child once again at the sight of its beauty. He tucked his own child into bed, and kissed her goodnight and headed back to the carriage to tend to his wife.

"Hey son," Abraham whispered.

"Hey, Dad. What are you doing up?"

"I was just checking to see if you guys had made it back yet. Old habits of a parent die hard, ya know."

"Just got in, Pops. I just put Lorena down to bed in one of the spare rooms. She absolutely loved the ballet."

"Good, I'm glad you guys had a fun time. I'm going to get back to bed. I'll see you in the morning." Abraham wrapped Robert in his arms. "I love you, son. Goodnight." Abraham scuffled off back to his room as

Robert headed back outside to the carriage where Lagertha was still asleep. Gracefully, Robert scooped her up and carried her inside. The snow was chunky and abundant, the night was quiet, almost dead silent. All that was heard was the crack of the snow as he walked upon it. Lightning flowed in the clouds above. *An odd sight, yet it has happened twice this early winter,* Robert thought. He entered the warmth of the castle and closed the door, first with his butt, then with his foot, as carrying his wife made the easy task quite difficult. He walked the quiet halls with his wife in his hands. He felt a coziness within the great structure, though the castle was anything but cozy. It was the effects of the architecture and the festive decorations that set the comforting feeling in his heart.

"Oh, hey, Prince Charming. Thanks for rescuing me." Lagertha chafed as she was being carried in his arms.

"Hey, Princess. I thought I needed to kiss you to wake my sleeping beauty," he bantered back.

"All I needed was your touch, but a kiss wouldn't hurt either," she teased. Robert found the queen's room, though the tradition of the actual queen's room vanished nearly two centuries ago, and he laid Lagertha on the soft king bed. He kissed her ruby red lips and tasted the sweetness of her tongue. He bit her lip as he moved away. Robert caressed her arm and played with her hair as he whispered words of romance in her ear. He kissed her plump lips again and moved down to her neck. A soft moan left her voice. He slid down the straps of her dress, kissing her shoulders and chest, revealing her sheer, rose-colored bra underneath. He slid the red dress down even further, kissing her stomach and the brim of her panties that matched her top. He removed the dress completely, kissing her inner thighs and finding his way back to her labium. As their lips were locked, she began to unbutton his shirt and feel his sculpted body. Robert tossed her on top of him, her baby blues pierced his lively green eyes. She gave a coy grin and shimmied off his trousers, and pulled at the brim of his undergarment. Lagertha slid her body up until they were face to face. Robert breathed her in. He ran his fingers through her hair and gently down her spine to the clasps of her bra and unhooked it. She let the ruby red bra flow off her bodice and tossed it to the side and let her breasts feel his chest as their tongues tasted one another. Robert sat up and took hold of her waist and placed her on her back. Lagertha raised her legs as he glided her panties down her thighs, past her toned calves, and finally finding their way to the end of the bed. He savored her lips once more, circling his finger around her nipple and pinching it as it stiffened. He moved himself down to her bosom, kissing one breast while squeezing the other, and ran his lips down her stomach and across her navel until he found her pink flower. He kissed above and around it as she sighed in bliss. Robert took hold of her legs and slid her towards him, her mouth opened and her eyes closed as she let out a gasp of air in ecstasy. Their bodies moved together. He felt her as she felt him, and the two were bonded as one. Lagertha wrapped her arms around his neck; she panted for air as she was reaching climax. Their tongues were tied. Her hands ran through Robert's hair, and she pulled it as he reached his ecstasy. Robert looked into her deep blue eyes and they beamed at one another.

"I love you," he said as he brushed her hair behind her ear. She pecked his lips and burrowed herself in his arms as they fell asleep in the silence of the night.

The hours of the evening passed and the snow from the storm accumulated outside the castle, building a wall of ice in the darkness of the winter night. The sky began to boom and light the world with bolts of fire. Robert sprang to alertness at the wickedness of the storm. The clouds seemed to gather into one area in the sky as they funneled up higher than the eye could see. He watched as the lightning circled down the massive cloud and struck the same area time and time again. Forty times he counted, and the firebolts were no more. Robert threw on his trousers he wore to the ballet and crept out into the hall as his wife slept, undisturbed by the storm. He walked down the corridor to where his daughter was sleeping and quietly opened the door to her room and walked in. Lorena slept soundlessly, as was no surprise to Robert. She, like her mother, could sleep like a log through the loudest of sounds. Half the covers were off at the end of her bed. He took the sheets and straightened them out, kissed his daughter on the forehead, and tucked her in once more before he left to check on his sons.   Robert walked silently through the halls and inched his way into the nursery rooms where Aedus and Absolume had been sleeping. Both boys were awake. Abe cooed, not from the storm but from hunger, and Aedus was as quiet as a nestled duck. He took the boys in his arms and found his way into the great-room, which was filled with embroidered sofas, restored wooden tables, a massive white brick fireplace and immense arched windows. Robert snuggled the boys into the sofa, gathered some wood, and started a fire. He quickly went to the kitchen and warmed some breast milk that was in the refrigerator and hurried back to his sons. He tested the contents on his arms to make sure the milk wasn't too hot, and headed back to his boys. Abe was still whimpering, and so he held him in his arms and fed him as the fire crackled next to them. Robert could see a shadow coming towards the great-room. It was Lagertha, wearing nothing but the sheets of the bed.

"Hey, babe." She spoke softly as she tucked Aedus into her arms and cozied up next to Robert. She pulled the bed sheet down that was covering her naked body, revealing her teat, and nursed her son. She stroked his head and quietly sang a song Lorena had made up for him.

The sparks flew as the wood splintered in the fire, warming the room with tranquility as they sat in silence. Robert broke the hush with a whispered voice, "I think it has started." Lagertha looked confused, not understanding what he meant by the words.

"What do you mean?"

"A new king is to be named. I was watching the storm through our bedroom window and saw lightning strike near the Hoba site," he explained to her.

"What does that mean for your father?"

"It doesn't mean anything. He could live another fifty years until his reign is over. Until his death, he is God's true king, and only then will his successor take the throne," he said.

"Still, I worry. Your father is a good man, Robert, and I would hate to see him leave so soon. He has done some hard things in his time as king, and dare I say, every action he has taken has led us down the smoothest waters." Lagertha let her feelings be known.

"Those are kind words—words I think he'd like to hear more often. I'll inform him when he wakes. If anything, he'll be delighted to hear of the news. The man is somehow always optimistic. Even when the world seems bleak and full of despair, he's there to say it will be alright, as he often says, 'With every passing second, you can choose a new path with a new fate. You are not bound by one choice alone.'"

The shadows grew longer and the weather colder as the night lingered. Robert and Lagertha brought the boys with them into their room. They bundled them in between themselves and let their eyes rest until the break of day peeked through the window. A beam of sunlight struck Robert in the eyes. He tightened them and hid his face from the day that was before him. He turned his body away from the light and reached over to his wife and sons, but his hand only found the softness of sheets and not a baby's skin. He tilted the pillow that was over his head to glimpse the room around him. The sun's orange and red filled the room with radiance. Robert could hear footsteps approaching, getting closer to his chamber. The door swung open and hit the back of the entryway. He felt the weight of the bed shift and when he opened his eyes, the sweetest face was in front of his own.

"Hey, Dad," said Lorena. "Mom said we're going to Hoba today and that a new king will be crowned."

"Maybe the new king will be you," he told her.

"Girls can't be kings, Dad. Girls can only be queens," she said.

"Oh, how silly of me. Of course," he agreed.

"Hurry up and get out of bed, Dad. I've been waiting to go all morning," she informed him. Robert rubbed the sleep dust from his eyes and slowly rose to greet the day. He rustled through the drawers of the room and put on a pair of cotton bottoms that seemed hadn't been worn in maybe ten years.

"Good morning, family." He addressed them as he entered the dining hall. "I've assumed you heard the news, Pops."

"Indeed. Wonderful isn't it. I have done what the Lord has asked, and soon, my rule will end. I don't know if I have succeeded or if I have failed, but there is no need to worry about that now. I'll find out when I'm dead," said Abraham in a charismatic tone.

"I have not known you to fail at anything, Pops. I'm sure God looks upon you with great favor," Robert praised him.

"Like I said, death will fill my questioning mind with answers. Until then, let's go to Hoba and see what our Maker has given us and who will be my predecessor." His father spoke joyfully as he reached to fill his plate with the morning's breakfast.

The forenoon was served with eggs of all sorts, bacon that was crisp and crunchy, potatoes soft and delightful, pudding sweet to the tongue, and some soda bread. The food filled the room with a delightful air that could be tasted as you breathed it in.

"This is wonderful tea, Pops. Is it from the garden?"

"Unfortunately, no. It's from Tam O'Braan's farm. The man's soil is made of gold. Everything he grows is absolute perfection. Incredible, really," Abraham expressed in an envious sort of way. "Enough chit-chat about tea, lad. Hurry up and eat your meal, and let's get going."

"Yes, my King," Robert said in a joking manner, but underneath the tone was sincerity as he did not know how much longer he could call his father king. He quickly inhaled his meal, trying desperately to enjoy each bite but finding it difficult, as his family was pestering him to be as quick as possible. After hastily eating and showering hurriedly, Robert was finally ready to leave the castle and head towards the Hoba site.

"Ready, honey?" Lagertha asked.

"Yes, dear," he replied. "Do we have everybody?"

"The boys are tucked in their seats, you can obviously hear our daughter, and your father is right behind you," she said as she took his hand and guided him inside the vehicle.

"Finally, Dad! You were like a bearfint this morning. Raawwrrr!" Lorena imitated the animal.

"And you were like a little trumani. Dashing everywhere, faster than the speed of light, but now we need to settle down. Today could be a long day," he said to his daughter. The chariot took them out of the castle grounds, through the boroughs of churches and universities and into the very center of the city. The site was congested with people. Scores of folks came to bear witness of the next king or queen of Saoirse. Some had traveled from other states around the country, while others had traveled from faraway lands, leagues across the sea. The excitement of the people was palpable. The smiling faces and giddy laughter filled the streets of Bunaitheoir as children launched fireworks high into the air and men played and chanted to the song of "Día's Rí." The leather drums percussed through the city avenues, and the chants boomed into the heavens. The clouds above were gray and cold, the breeze soft but bold as it hit the skin with teeth like splinters in the short and dreaded days of winter. The snow sprinkled on the city roads, blotting out the soft white lights that lined them.

Robert and Lagertha made sure their children were bundled tightly from the harshness of winter's menacing air. Lagertha helped Robert put on a harness to hold the two boys and placed them inside it. They sat in soft marten fur, which kept them warm and comfortable and had an outer layer made of nylon to keep the bitterness of the wind away from them. Neither of the two boys fussed. They both just stared out into the world, taking in all the new sounds and smells that came with it. Robert finally stepped out of the hovering carriage and put his hand out to help his beautiful daughter and wife as well as his father, leaving the wagon and entering the hustle and bustle of the magic of the city center. As they walked through the crowds, the citizens stepped out of their way, giving them a passage to walk towards the Hoba meteorite. They did not move for Robert, nor for Lagertha, but out of honor for their king, Abraham. As every person stepped aside, Robert thanked and nodded graciously to them as they got nearer to the stone.

The beat of the drums got louder, the whistle of the fireworks more piercing, the chants more robust. Robert's eyes then became focused on the rock. He could see a man struggling mightily, trying to pull an enormous war hammer from the boulder. Standing in front of Robert was a boy no older than ten. The child, with sandy blonde hair and brown eyes, looked back at him and offered Abraham his spot to pull the weapon from the stone.

"Oh, thank you, lad. You're very kind to let me take your place," said Abraham. Robert's father knelt down to the child and handed him a pocket watch made of gold. The boy beamed at him as Abraham walked towards the meteor. The crowd fell silent, the fireworks too, and the sound of the silence was deafening as Abraham was now face to face with God's decision. Abraham put his hand upon the war hammer. He tightened his grip and gave a wicked pull.

Not a creak nor a crack. The war hammer remained, and a new king was certain to be named. The crowd applauded with respect for the effort their king gave. Abraham put his hands high into the air and then bowed to them all. The ambiance was that of a beloved athlete playing his last game as Robert's father left the stage of the stone.

The blonde boy looked back at Robert.

"Would you like to go, sir?" the boy asked.

"Don't be silly; I think you've waited long enough. Give it a go, and good luck," he said.

The boy was scrawny but handsome and wore a green cape over his formal wear. Robert watched as he approached the rock. He could tell the boy had confidence but was slightly unsure if he would be the next king. The child bent down towards the neck of the hammer and put both hands tightly on it. He took a deep breath and pulled with all his might. He let out a loud scream, using every muscle in his body, but it was not meant to be. The child bowed his head in shame and walked away. As he got closer, Robert stopped him as he was about to pass by and said to him, "Do not fear failure, lad, for in great attempts, it is glorious even to fail." The boy grinned at him as Robert tousled his hair. Robert strode forward with his two children attached to his chest. His buffalo coat twirled in the frosted air as his boots guided him towards the hammer. The drums started beating softly, and a chant picked up in the background. He wrapped his hands over the staff of the hammer. He saw the swirling of the liquid metal as it held the hammer in its place. He closed his eyes and breathed. He heard no one, he saw no one, he only felt the grip of the hammer in his hands. He roared and hauled, and like a knife through butter, the hammer was free from the stone. The people boomed in applause and joy, the fireworks resumed and took the shape of golden crowns, red dragons, and green shamrocks.

Lagertha stepped forward in front of the crowd, "All hail the King that shall be!" she yelled. A chant echoed through the amphitheater, "Hail Robert! Hail Robert! Hail Robert!" The resonance of it was great, and in the clamor, Abraham, Robert's father, was the first to kneel, followed by Lagertha and her daughter. The people took note and did the same, and once again, the theater was quiet. Robert spoke as the crowd was silent,

"There is no need to bow to me. I am only the king of this great country. I am not the king of your soul. Rise with me upon this new day, a time of peace, a time a prosperity. Rejoice in it for the Lord has given me an object of war. Ready your hearts, and ready your minds for our Maker has given us a warning of what is to come. Prepare now, for when this storm hits, you will know, body and soul, you were meant to live another day. God bless all of you, all of you on this good, good earth."

The people erupted with thunderous applause as Robert and his two boys walked towards his family with his war hammer in hand. As he walked back to them, he glanced right and saw Iscariot and his little boy smiling and applauding.

"All hail the king that shall be," Lagertha said gleefully as she greeted her husband back with a kiss.

"All hail the great King Robert," said Iscariot as he joined his brother in celebration. Robert shook his hand and thanked him.

"I would hug you, but we both seem to have weird creatures attached to our chests," Robert said as he and Iscariot laughed. "Today is the day of your ceremony. Do you want to ride together?" Robert asked.

"No, I'm fine, thanks. I have a couple of things left to do before I get ready and go," Iscariot explained.

"We can take baby Hanns if you want," Lagertha offered.

"Thanks, Lagertha, but he's good company even though he's either sleeping, crying, or pooping," Iscariot said with a smile.

"We'll see you at seven, then?" Robert asked, though he wasn't really questioning the time.

"I'll see you all then," Iscariot replied, struggling to get through the crowd of people. Robert and his family waved goodbye, and they too, headed for their carriage. As Robert walked towards the vehicle, every citizen parted before him and looked upon him, not to say hello or words of congratulations, but to say a silent prayer, and every citizen ended their prayers by placing their fingers to their heads, then diagonal to their left breast, across to their right breast and then back to their forehead. As they did so, Robert would look them in the eye and thank them, and reply with Germa as they finished the trinity.

When they made it to their vehicle, the wagon was warm and thawed their frigid skin. The snow did not fall from the sky, but what laid on the ground spun in the wind and gently landed back down to earth. Robert examined the war hammer the Lord had given him. It was long, near as tall as he. Its shaft was a black alien alloy with groves that seemed molded for Robert's fingers, and resting at the end of it was a thick metallic skewer. Dressed along the shaft were four emerald clasps that gave the hammer a look of beauty rather than of fear. The hammer itself was the matte black of an alien stone. Its face was blunt and brutal, and atop it was a piercing metal spike that matched the one opposite the face. Robert placed his hands within its grooves, and as he did so, engraved and glowing were words that read, *Be thou an example of the Believers, in word, in conversation, in charity, in spirit, in faith, in purity. Neglect not the gift that is in thee, which was given to thee by prophecy. For in doing this thou shalt both save thyself, and them that hear thee.*

Iscariot Chapter Three

Iscariot opened his dreary eyes. The morning was still dark, and only the earliest of creatures were stirring. He lay there looking up at his ceiling, his mind void and yet in tangled webs. He removed the covers and went to check on his son who was resting at the foot of his bed. Silent, he slept as Iscariot leaned over him. He watched and listened as his son breathed in and out. It put a rare smile on Iscariot's face to see his son healthy, knowing he had nothing to fear. He watched him sleep a little while longer as he did not want to go back to sleep himself. The nightmares had been wicked the past few nights. Dreams of demons and abominable beasts, others of his wife trying desperately to tell him something but always vanishing before she could speak the words.

He struggled mightily to keep his eyes open as his head bounced up and down, falling in and out of consciousness. He finally rested his head on the back of the chair he had been sitting in, and his mind took him to the Battle of Erbil.

Iscariot looked up in the night sky, examining the stars, wondering what mysteries they held. *Why did God put these in the sky for us to see? What are we to look for, and when we find the answer, what are we to do with it?* he thought. When he looked back down to earth, the night had turned to day; the sky was cloudless and bluer than the purest sea. The desert sands whipped around him as did the bullets of his enemy. His breathing was heavy and rapid, and as he glanced over to his right, Iscariot watched his friend die as he was struck in the head by the speed and the might of a specialized armor-piercing bullet. His friend's body landed hard, and the red sands became richer as they absorbed the blood that seeped through his helmet. Beams of light flashed by him and crumbled the walls that were to his left. Iscariot radioed his team.

"This is Alpha two. The captain is dead. We are outnumbered two to one. Charlie and Delta teams need to engage the enemy head on. What remains of Alpha will flank the enemies right. Charlie-one do you acknowledge?"

"Charlie team confirmed," was the response that came through.

"Delta team, status?" he asked.

"Delta, confirmed. What of Bravo?" questioned the Delta leader.

"Bravo has been eliminated. We are all that is left," Iscariot answered.

"Roger that," the Delta leader responded. Delta and Charlie teams laid down suppressive fire as Iscariot gathered the rest of his comrades. The group had started with twenty men, and only seven remained. Iscariot and his team used the fallen walls and large debris as cover as they moved across the battlefield. The bullets buzzed and lasers seared as the bombs cratered the ground around them. The blue sky turned to purple, pink, and orange, and small lights appeared far in the distance. Among the stars in the sky were Mongnolerian warplanes that spiraled in the heavens with the air force of Saoirse, the Iolars, whose symbol was the eagle—they bore the wings of freedom. He watched as one of the Iolar's struck a Mongnolerian plane with a tracer missile. It fell to the earth in a screaming frenzy, and the smoke tail streaked across the sky, blotting out the beauty of the twilight.

"Take cover!" Iscariot yelled to his troops. The plane was hurtling towards them; the yell of the burning aircraft became deafening as it got closer to his team, and then, like the roar of thunder, it hit the ground and shattered across the small desert town, missing Iscariot and his men by only 100 yards.

The bulk of the enemy force was now in sight, and Iscariot could see the Charlie and Delta teams had had success pushing forward and furthering their advance. In front of him now were soldiers that looked like creatures of the dead, whose helmets were spiked and whose faces looked like skulls. Their eyes were oil black, and their appearance was menacing. Any attack on their body was without effect. To kill them, they had to be struck in the head, and for this reason were given the name Skolastjori, meaning headmaster. Fighting alongside the Skolastjori were Mongnolerian soldiers, whose skin, when exposed, illuminated a golden color. Their eyes were without irises, but when looked upon seemed to penetrate your soul. Their armor, made of a pure alien metal, was tight and form fitting, it seemed almost fluid. Attached on the arms of their armor were guns that fired energy beams generated by their own bodies, some were even equipped to generate shields. Iscariot readied his men to engage the enemy and then gave the order to execute.

Ray cannons and energy rifles echoed through the empty alleys. Bullets rang and thudded as they struck above and below Iscariot and his men. The day was now night, and flashes of light bolted through the black sky. Delta and Charlie teams of forty men were now ten. Iscariot watched as the men he commanded took their final breaths, said their last words, and fired their shots that would ring for their eternity. He took a deep and composed breath. The light from the tracers lit his black and silver metallic armor. He donned his silver helmet, which was of two parts. The faceplate was of a silver man, void of emotion, expressionless. Atop his head, protecting his skull and neck, was the image of a silver lion. It's fearsome two-inch fangs hung from the helm and met at Iscariot's brow. He roared with rage as he ran out into the field of blood and war. His armor gave him speed he wouldn't have without it, and it gave him strength he could only imagine. He charged at speeds like the howling wind as Skolastjori and Mongnolerian soldiers fired upon him. His shots were pure and precise as he battled for his life and for the lives of those he lost. From twelve to eleven, then from eleven to ten, the enemy began to fall. Soon, only five remained, and as he got closer to his foe, his gun was struck from his hands, and then he was hit again, struck on his armored shoulder, which looked like the paw of a lion with three-inch claws.

Iscariot fell to the ground from the impact of the shot. He could see his opposers approaching as he lay there in agony. He waited for them as his soul fell into the desert sands, until finally a Skolastjori soldier hovered over him. His enemy unsheathed his sword that was strapped behind him. His face like death seemed to smile knowing this was going to be Iscariot's final moment. The soldier placed two hands on his sword and angled it down to strike Iscariot from the earth. As he lifted up to add force to his swing, Iscariot uncloaked a dagger from his armor and buried into the Skolastjori's leg. His yell rumbled through the night air, and the soldier fell to his knees, trying to strike Iscariot as he crashed unto the earth. His blade had missed, and Iscariot seized the moment. He rose from certain death. The blood trickled down his armor towards his breastplate that possessed an emblem of the head of a roaring, golden lion. The ember glow in the eyes of Iscariot's helm perforated into the black holes of his enemy's. He pulled his sword from behind his back and quickly struck the neck of the Skolastjori, severing its head from its body. In blood rage, Iscariot pursued the remaining four soldiers. He quickly found his next target and leaped into the air, tackling a Mongnolerian soldier and penetrating its armor with his sword. He briskly removed the sword from the soldier's body and hurled it at another, puncturing its helmet and infiltrating the skull. He picked up the rifle that was next to him and fired the remaining shot, striking another warrior in his throat. Iscariot found his final victim and sprinted towards him, and as fast as his suit made him, he could not help his fellow Leon soldier as he watched him die in the arms of his enemy. The Skolastjori warrior turned to defend himself against Iscariot, but his throat was already clutched by Iscariot's forceful hand. He had him pinned against the debris of a fallen warplane and began applying pressure to the airways of his enemy. The warrior struggled to breathe, kicking and clawing at Iscariot, desperately trying to live. Iscariot pushed harder on the soldier's throat until he heard the sound of his neck collapsing. Iscariot yelled in rage, as he was all that remained of the horrid battle he had just endured.

He collapsed to his knees with tears streaming down his face and thought of all the friends he had just lost. His eyes were blurred, his face a mask of sweat, blood, and dirt. He looked skyward and saw a silver flash speeding towards him. Boom!

Iscariot woke back into the blackness of his room with Hanns sleeping quietly in his bassinet. He looked outside his bedroom window as God painted with streaks of lightning across the night sky. He did not sleep the rest of the night, but instead watched the spectacle of lights dancing in the darkness as the snow coiled in the wind. Iscariot grinned, for he knew the reign of his father was over, and maybe, just maybe, he'd be chosen as king of the free world.

The sun hadn't risen yet, but Iscariot readied himself for the day ahead. His jeans were vintage brown, his sweater porcelain white with amber buttons at the neck. He laced up his brown leather boots and threw a bister stetson over his head. He grabbed his bag, which he prepared during the night and tossed it over his shoulders. He went over to his son, who seemed to stare in amazement at the mobile that spun an eagle, leopard, lion, and wolf above him.

"Hey stud. You and I are going on an early morning trip to Hoba's Meteor," he told him. Iscariot quickly changed his diaper and clothed him in his warmest clothes. The outer shell of Hanns's onesie was a breathable nylon, and comforting him inside the shell was the warmth from the fur of an arctic fox. Iscariot put the smallest of hats over his son's head, gave him a wink, and tucked him pleasantly into the carrier that was strapped across his chest.

He moved his way into his garage. The beige concrete floors were waxed in a gloss; hundreds of bulbs hung down from the ceiling on strings and lit the room with a soft rustic glow. Iscariot walked past his matte black hover bike, then glanced over at his wife's classic carriage, but quickly turned away. Remembering her was like knotting his throat with a tweed rope, tighter and tighter; it collapsed his airways until it would break, releasing the dam of tears he had been holding back and letting them flow down his face. He fixed his eyes on an antique. It did not float like a balloon in the sky, nor project an image on a screen. It had tires made of rubber and was powered by gasoline. The car was hot rod red with white stripes that raced down its sides. On warm days, the roof would fold in, and if he were daring, on the cold days, too. Its leather seats were cracked, its wooden steering wheel weathered. There were no buttons to push or screens to see, only two knobs, one to play music, the other to warm the car on days the world blistered your marrow. Iscariot swiped the key from the dash and ignited the engine, and like an earthquake, it rumbled. He put the car in drive and let the monster bellow.

He rode in the quiet. The low rumble of the engine filled the streets, and the breathing of his son filled the car. Iscariot's mind was blank. His ears heard no notes, nor did his eyes see the road, yet he drove to what he believed would be his destiny. The country roads turned to city streets, the streets to alleys, and the alleys led to a path, and that path led to finality, or so Iscariot thought.

The dark clouds still swarmed and swirled, but the cadence of the thunder had rested, and the crash of the lightning ceased to strike. He left his car running with Hanns inside, and the morning air was still bitter to the bone. The glistening snow was like a wave of sapphires sparkling in the moonlight, and they broke beneath his feet. He came upon the stone and saw the pool of metal swimming within it. It seemed to be alive as it spiraled about, holding a hammer firmly in its place. Iscariot flexed his hands around the staff of the weapon, as did a pair of two black hands. They looked burned by ice, and bits of skin seemed to float away from them like flurries in the desert of the tundra. Iscariot steadied his eyes upon the creature and pulled the hammer menacingly, with fear and anger built inside his soul, yet the hammer did not move. The ghostly figure wrapped his cold, dark, and narrow fingers around Iscariot's wrist with its hooded face intently focused on him. Iscariot reached for the throat of the cloaked eidolon, but like the wind, he could not grasp it. His eyes darted, struggling to find the phantom in the gloom of the early morning sky, then his ears heard it. It sounded like the crackle of the radio, and Iscariot turned toward the sound. The revenant took its long fingers and screeched them across the hood of the car. Iscariot's mind filled with boiling rage.

"Get away from him!" Iscariot's voice was harsh and commanding. He grabbed the sidearm from his thigh and began firing, but as before, the specter drifted in the wind. The click of the trigger sounded until the clip was empty. Iscariot ran to his son whose cries struck his heart and brought him down to earth. He held him in his arms until his cries were soft coos, and dried his tender cheeks.

"I'm sorry, Hanns. I'm so sorry," he told him. The break of day found its way through the thickness of the gray clouds and eerie fog as the people of Buna found their way to the center of the city to see if their destiny, too, might change. Iscariot stayed and watched the citizens of Aontu struggle just as he did, to suffer the agonizing fate of despair. He pitied them, but if it was not he, then who? Who was worthy of such honor? Who was worthy of such grace? Who was worthy of the task to be more than the man they knew they could be. An hour went by, and then another, and as he was about to leave he saw the crowd begin to separate. He caught sight of why the people moved like the parting of the sea when his eyes beheld his father's face. *Surely*, he thought, *if any man is to be king it is the king we see before us.* He watched with a heavy heart. His father failed before him and before all those who admired him. He applauded Abraham because he loved him. Iscariot paid no mind to the boy who followed his father, for if Abraham was not worthy to hold the crown, no man was.

With Hanns in his hands, he tried to move through the cluster of people who swarmed like bees to the honey that was Hoba. Before he could reach his father, the buzz of the crowd hushed as his brother walked towards the hammer of providence. The small beat of a drum could be heard in the distance, and all eyes were focused on Robert, the son of the King. Iscariot's eyes did not leave him, and like so many others, Robert placed his hands upon the hammer and bellowed as he pulled it from its stubborn captor, and like an object hitting still water, the crowd rippled in acclamation. Fire sticks rocketed in the air, illuminating the sky in a blaze of sparkling light, and a chant clamored through the amphitheater: "Hail Robert! Hail Robert! Hail Robert!" Iscariot felt the rage boil in his blood, his eyes sharpened, and his heart grew cold. Jealously consumed him. *How can a man have such good fortune, and I have so little,* he thought.

Iscariot tried to leave without being noticed, his clouded mind was in no mood to praise his brother, but as he tried to move away, the people around him seemed to flow like a current, guiding him closer to Robert, until suddenly, he stood before him. His sly tongue spoke few words of praise to his brother before he slithered back to his car. He sat there in his roadster, with Hanns resting in the back, and set his head against the wheel. It was as if every grain of sand in all the world's deserts was a fracture in his heart. He could accept not being king of the free world just as he could acknowledge a new king to govern over it, but he felt as if no matter how bright he shined, his brother's radiance would steal the gaze of the love and devotion Iscariot so badly desired.

Iscariot put the car in drive, and his frozen heart began to melt. He felt ashamed, embarrassed by his failures, to let his wife die, to have his son grow up motherless, to not be the man she always thought he could be. Iscariot's mind weaved like a web of all his misfortunes, all his struggles, all his grief, and there he vowed as he now sat in his drive, with the grumble of the engine shaking his body, that he would be more the man she dreamt of him, and not a soul would stand in his way. No general would order and no king would command him. There he swore that not even God would dictate his fate.

As the world spun, so too did the hands of a clock, and the hour struck 6. Iscariot dressed his son in the smallest of tuxes, and placed on his head the most adorable top hat. Iscariot's icy heart had melted, and his mind was like simmering water. He took Hanns, and once again, the two boys were on a drive, but this time away from the city. He sparked the craft to life, and it moved through the air as it cruised into the dark agrestic roads. The nuclear reaction gave a minatory blush at the corners of the vessel and propelled them toward Fort Nazar. The open roads were not without life. A herd of 100 fianna pranced and grazed in the open snow-covered fields. Some would look up, doe-eyed, as if they saw an apparition floating by in the hours of the early night.

Nearly an hour had gone by when they reached Fort Nazar. The star-shaped fort was gargantuan. The base was 250 years old. Entirely made of bricks and stone, Iscariot beheld the majesty and the grandeur in its age. He could feel the battles fought. He could see the bullet holes on the walls of the base. He felt as if he were part of something greater than himself. As he and Hanns walked down the stone path to the doors of the assembly building, he could hear the waves of the ocean crashing against the shoreline, and he could smell the salt of the sea and the driftwood as he got nearer to the building.

Two Leon guards stood outside the doorway, dressed in combat attire, and opened the age-old oak doors as they greeted Iscariot. As he entered the ballroom, he had a debonair look and a feeling a confidence within himself. His uniform was dashing, his trousers were golden in color, his jacket was a rich navy blue with gold buttons lined down the stomach. His left breast pocket was adorned with a palette of medals he had accumulated from the war. Resting on his shoulders were two lion paws that held a red cape; it was draped over him and fell down his back. His officer's hat was the same shade as his jacket, lined with red trim, and at its center was the same roaring golden lion that displayed as a chest piece upon the combat uniforms.

The ballroom was beautifully decorated; a red carpet divided the room and stopped as it met the cherry wood dance floor where people were socializing. Eight crystal chandeliers hung from the high ceilings, and there were banners along with works of art that hung from the exposed brick walls. At the head of the assembly room was a long table draped in a table banner of the Leon military branch, and sitting upon the raised platform, in the forefront, were the highest ranking officials of the Leon core. Iscariot's seat was just left of center, and as he and his son walked towards it, Iscariot was greeted by a dear friend.

"Isc!" the voice yelled from a distance. Iscariot turned to see who it was and smiled.

"Antony! It's good to see you."

"I'm glad to see you out of the house. How have you been doing these last few weeks?"

"I'm a little more hopeful tonight then I've been in a while," Iscariot said to him.

"I'm happy to hear it, Isc. I was just talking to your family a moment ago. They are at the first set of tables to the right of your seat. They're very proud of you."

"Thanks Antony, I should go greet them."

"We'll talk more later tonight. I see a damsel in distress whom I must go and save," Antony laughed.

"Of course. It's good to see your face for a celebratory occasion for once. Go rescue that pretty lass, and I'll see you soon." Iscariot smiled and patted Antony's back as he walked away. He found his father and the rest of his family right where Antony said they would be. Robert caught a glimpse of him first.

"If it isn't the man of the hour," Robert beamed at him.

"If it isn't the man of the day," Iscariot replied to him with a grin on his face.

"I'm very proud of you, Isc. This is an amazing honor."

"It's nothing compared to being the King elect."

"I think it more so. You earned your place through bravery and selflessness. I merely was chosen."

"Chosen yes, not by a council of men, but by someone more than a man. This is your day, Robert."

"If this is my day, then let this be your night, and let us share our good fortunes together," Robert said to his brother, handing him a glass of champagne. "To us."

"To us," Iscariot said, raising his glass to sip the sweetness of the drink. A small bell sounded, ringing through the ballroom and grabbing people's attention. The brothers looked up and saw the event was about to begin.

"I guess that means I should take my seat," said Iscariot.

"I'm looking forward to your speech." The brothers departed.

Words of great meaning were said by men of great purpose. No soul was forgotten, living or dead, as they reflected on what they had achieved and what they had endured in a war that had divided one nation into many nations. After several speakers gave words of wisdom and gratitude, Iscariot's name was called. A general, whose jacket was dressed with five stars, whose name was Gaius Marius, called him forward.

"We are gathered here tonight to honor those we have lost, but we are also here to honor those who have fought and lived to tell their tale. To me there is no greater man here than Iscariot Darroch. His stories of battle cannot be seen with an artist's brush, nor with a poet's words; they can only be seen by the picture his words bring when he tells of the battles lost and won. Please welcome to the stage our youngest and fastest ranking general, General Iscariot Darroch." The crowd of decorated soldiers and their families cheered as he approached the podium.

"Friends and family, thank you. Your cries of praise are very kind, and I do not take them lightly. I am very humbled that you would Lionize me here tonight, and I will forever remember this for as long as I live. As many of you know, I have suffered some hardships recently, but I am not here to dwell on my misfortune for nothing can change the past. Like words etched in a stone, they are eternal. Instead, I am here to talk about the future which has been shaped by the roots of our past, but its branches that sprout from the tree are large and abundant. The future of our military and our country are bright. By the grace of God, we have a new king elect in whom I have great faith, as I have had with my father as king. We are now in a time of peace and have been warned that more war and heartache are in our future. I realize that I am newly appointed, and if I am overstepping, please let me know, but I ask that we have additional funds for military expenditures, along with a subset within the Leon Branch which would be tasked with raids and missions of a more precise kind, rather than using an entire squadron for such tasks or requesting assistance from other branches, which is our current process. We are the greatest country this world has ever known. We have achieved more in 300 years than many countries have achieved in a thousand. We are the most free, the most prosperous, and the most charitable of any country in the last hundred years, and I believe that in order to continue our reign as divine liberators, we must reinforce our strength so that when war does come, it will be swift, and peace will rule with an iron fist."

The audience roared in delight at his words, and the general that had introduced him shook his head and whispered into his ear. Iscariot nodded and gave a soft smile.

"Again, thank you all for this Lionization. It means a great deal to me. Thank you," Iscariot closed his remarks as he waved to the audience that was still cheering him on.

The hours of the night moved quicker than the waters of a raging river. The atmosphere was festive in the Yule spirt. Hopes were high, and dreams seemed real. It was as if the sadness of Iscariot's world fell away, down a waterfall, and only joy remained. He danced, he laughed, he drank. *It felt good to live,* he thought. As the night got closer to its end, Iscariot found Antony with a dame whose hair was fire red.

"I see you're having fun," Iscariot said astutely.

"Isc!" Antony yelled in a drunken stupor. "Great speech, my friend—well done."

"Thanks, Antony. You know, if it is agreed upon, I'd like you to join me in setting up the subset Leon branch," he said.

"Isc, you know I'd do anything for ya. You're like a brother to me."

"I was hoping you'd say that. I think General Gaius also enjoyed the idea of a smaller group within the branch," said Iscariot.

"Anything you's needs me to do, just let me know," Antony slurred.

"I'll let you know. Are you going to need a ride home?" he asked. Antony wrapped his arm around Iscariot.

"I think I'll be alright. Me and this beautiful little lady are about to order a hover back to my place." Antony gave him a wet kiss on the cheek, then grabbed the red-headed woman by the waist, kissed her, and began dancing. Iscariot looked delighted by his friend's lighthearted candor.

The minutes ticked by rapidly, and suddenly the room started stirring with a fearsome commotion. Iscariot's eyes darted, scanning the room for the source of the pandemonium.

"Get a doctor!" yelled a voice at the other end of the assembly room. He made haste towards the command, cutting his way through the gathering crowd.

"One—two—three—" he heard a muffled voice say. "One—two—three," he heard once more and realized it was his brother's voice. Iscariot got more aggressive in moving the gathering masses in front of him. His heart began to race, his brow to sweat, and his thoughts languished in fearing the worst. He finally made his way through the crowd of fellow soldiers and their loved ones, only to see the man he loved lying unconscious on the floor. Robert was kneeling beside him, pumping his chest and taking the air within himself and passing it onto his father. It was as if the world slowed down around him; blurred were the faces of the men and woman beside him. He could hear nothing; the mouths would move, but words did not come out.

Iscariot dropped down to the floor with Robert and Abraham and held his father's hand in his. He felt a small pulse on his father's wrist. It pumped once and then again. He could feel his father slipping away as the beat within Abraham's body grew weaker.

"I love you, Dad," he said, and the rhythm of his heart was no more. Iscariot looked up at his brother who was still trying to put life back into him.

"Robert," Iscariot said softly, but his brother either did not hear him or refused to hear what he was about to say.

"Robert," he said again. This time Robert looked up at him. Iscariot could see his brother was holding back the tears he so desperately wanted to let out. The brothers sat there in agony, consumed by confusion, and then, they knew they would never see their father again.

The Leon paramedics soon arrived. Iscariot and Robert stepped aside and watched as they hurriedly cared for Abraham, and just as quick as they had arrived, they vanished. Robert and Iscariot watched their father leave the room, knowing he was gone from the earth.

"Where is my son?" he asked Robert with watery eyes.

"He is with Lagertha. I think they stepped outside," answered Robert. Iscariot quickly found his way to the door to see if she was out there and spotted her instantly.

"Did they say where they were taking him?" he asked briskly.

"I'm so sorry, Isc." she said. "They took a helicopter and flew him to Buna Medical." Iscariot took Hanns into his hands.

"Thanks, Lagertha. I'll meet you and Robert there," Iscariot told her, and he, along with Hanns, sped towards the city.

They didn't wait long when they arrived at the hospital, and when the doctor came out, they already knew the words he was going to speak. Their father had passed, and Robert was now King of Saoirse. In that instant, grief overwhelmed them, and they sobbed as they embraced one another in their hurt.

With a heavy heart, Iscariot made his way home and set his son to rest. He began to wander and found himself in his snow-dusted field, with air colder than ice and a sky darker than death. Acrimony fumed harshly in his mind and in his soul. "I HATE YOU!" he vociferated in heart wrenching pain, screaming to the heaven above. "You are cruel," he said, speaking to his Creator. *This was the day,* he thought. *This was supposed to be the day that I would be the light for the family. This was a day to celebrate after so many weeks of sadness. I just wanted one day to be happy, and you stole it from me.* Iscariot spoke aloud and made a promise, "You are a vile being, and you are no God of mine. Heed my words, for they will ring true. I will destroy you, as you have destroyed me, and if this world burns in my wake, know that it was because of you."

<u>Yefimovich Chapter One</u>

A few months had passed since the Hidler-Nemtsov treaty was signed, and today was a day of equal significance. Yefimovich was nervous as he scribbled some words upon a piece of parchment. As he sat at his desk, he bit his fist as he read the words he had just written and shook his head in indecision. He felt the soft hand of a woman rest upon his shoulder and give a gentle squeeze. The woman's voice whispered in his ear, "Relax."

"I wish that I could. This is more difficult than fighting a war," said Yefimovich in frustration.

"May I suggest to not write what the people may want to hear but to say what is within your heart."

"Viktoriya—I want the people to feel both hope and pride. I want their souls to rejoice. After two and a half years of war, I want them to feel that peace and prosperity are our future," he told her.

"Is that what you feel, Yefi?"

"Deeply."

"Then the words you want are not on your paper; they are in here," Viktoriya said, placing her hand on his heart. Yefimovich looked up from his chair and kissed her pillowy lips.

"Your counsel is wise," he told her. She smiled at his praise and threw the paper he was writing on into the bin beside the desk. "How is our baby girl doing this morning?" he asked his wife.

"She is trying to pick herself up and crawl in the other room. I think she is anxious to see the world." Yefimovich walked out of his study and into the tearoom. He laid on the floor next to his baby daughter.

"Hey, pretty lady, where are you trying to go?" he asked her. His daughter looked up at him and beamed a toothless smile. Her light brown eyes were like the sweetest chocolates, and Yefimovich saw her love, her happiness, and her joy within them that radiated from her innocent soul. He put his hands over his face and quickly moved them away, playing a game of peekaboo.

"Igre v pryatki," he said, and he laughed as his daughter laughed. "Come to dad," he encouraged his little girl. She gave a joyous squeal only a baby would make, excited by her father's affection, and wiggled her little body and gave a yell in frustration as she struggled to get to Yefimovich. "Come on, Yekaterina, you're so close," he said, and with great effort, she moved her hand forward and then her leg. Then she moved the others until she reached the loving arms of her father.

"Well done, Katerina!" Yefimovich picked her up and kissed her forehead. He grinned from ear to ear as he looked at his daughter's face who looked as if she had conquered the tallest mountain. He glanced over at his wife.

"Honey, did you see?" he asked.

"I captured it on holo," Viktoriya beamed happily. For the next half hour, Yefimovich enjoyed himself in the company of his family and cherished it as if it would be his last moment with them. While his family bonded, a knock came on the door.

"Sir, your meeting is in twenty minutes. Should I ready the vehicle?" asked the servant girl.

"Good morning, Rivka. P-please have them swing it towards the entrance. I will be there shortly." He kissed his baby daughter once more on the forehead and let her continue playing with the toys next to her and then took Viktoriya in his arms and kissed her goodbye.

An Avir soldier was gracefully resting the vetervykl vehicle at the entrance of the palace when Yefimovich walked out. The craft was space gray with two large circular propulsion devices on its sides, and underneath the vehicle was another that generated lift. The soldier stepped out of the craft to greet his leader. His slacks and jacket were bleach white. Adorned on the left and right sides of his military coat were eight gold buttons, and stretching across, connecting the buttons with each other, were taut red bands. His black boots and elbow-length gloves accented the white uniform, and giving his attire character was a red cape with gold epaulettes sitting on his shoulders. Resting on his side, attached to his belt, was a black sword sheath whose handle was made of pure gold. The Avi flattened his hand and saluted Yefimovich as he approached. Yefimovich saluted the soldier back and then shook his hand.

"Good morning, Aero. How are you today?"

"Good morning Sir, I'm well. I hope you are doing the same." Aero responded.

"Quite well. Thank you, Aero. Let's get going to the Citadel, shall we?"

"Right away, sir." The airman placed his hand over an opening on the dashboard, and with his body, moved air through the vehicle, lifting it high into the cloudless sky, and then with his free hand upon another opening, propelled the aircraft to its destination.

They quickly reached the walled city of the Citadel. Yefimovich was accosted by generals and members whom he had selected to help him in his interim role as Prime Minister. Press from all over the country and throughout the world were there to behold the historic day. Flashes of light from holocams and holovids bombarded Yefimovich as he was escorted from the vehicle into the stark white, gold-capped capital building. He and his staff hurried their way through the decorated halls and into the capital's briefing room. Yefimovich took a deep breath to calm any nerves that jittered, and he spoke.

"Good afternoon, ladies and gentlemen. It is an honor to have you serving with me as we make a t-transition in establishing our very own country. Please take your seats, and we'll get started, thank you."

The generals of the four newly established military branches took their seats along with the cabinet members Yefimovich chose to help lead the new country. General Iri was the first to speak in his very low and rough voice.

"Good afternoon, Prime Minister. I want to congratulate you on this incredible day. If it weren't for your leadership over the past four years, we would not be where we are today. We would not be a nation today. So, thank you."

"Your words are warmly felt, Iri. What news of domestic threats, if any?" he asked.

"Domestically, the country is rather peaceful, sir. After two and a half years of fighting, I think the people are looking forward to some stability and normalcy in their everyday life. As far as foreign threats are concerned, there is very minimal threat from Mongnolerium as they have been sanctioned for the next ten years for military buildup, and Holle is in near economic collapse. Their country is suffering from hyperinflation, and they are still trying to rebuild from the war. They are very lucky Saoirse is a very generous country; otherwise, I do not think they would exist. There are rumors of a shadow government within Holle which we are investigating but have no real answers on the matter as of yet. Other than that sir, that is the end of my report," said the General.

"For the most part, good news, then. Thank you, General," said Yefimovich.

"If I may, sir," General Dimitre interjected.

"Yes, General, please go ahead." Yefimovich let him speak.

"General Iri is correct on the matter of a shadow government within Holle. However, I just received a brief report about an hour ago that the shadow government is recruiting highly trained military-age men."

"May I ask how we have knowledge of such activities like shadow governments and these secret governments developing militaries of their own?" Yefimovich asked.

"We have a hidden source who is well positioned within the government of Holle. This source has been providing us with what you are hearing today and has been posted there since near the end of the war sir," General Dimitre informed him.

"Is there anything else, generals?" Yefimovich asked broadly. There was no response to his question, leaving him to believe they had nothing left to add. "How do we stand economically? I understand our currency is weak, as it should be. However, we have had talks about backing our money up with either gold or t-tritium. Is there an update on when the meeting is to discuss the matter?"

"Yes, Prime Minister," said a shorter man with ruffled black hair, pale green eyes, and large-frame black bifocals.

"Good morning, Edik," Yefimovich greeted him.

"Good morning, sir. We have scheduled for the meeting to be held two days from now, here at the Citadel, at 11 in the morning," said Edik. "As we discussed earlier in the week, out of the list you had given me, I have chosen the remaining economic advisors who will help us in making a decision on how to make this county economically viable and how to make it grow at a steady rate."

"Thank you, Edik. I'm looking forward to their opinions on the matter with great interest," Yefimovich said with enthusiasm. "Gentlemen and ladies, our very short fifteen minutes is up. We'll meet again tomorrow for a full review. I will see you all outside in about an hour," he said as he gathered his papers and devices.

He headed upstairs to the dome of the capital building. There were a total of five floors within the dome. The bottom floor was contemporary in design and was made from one solid circular piece of polished cement. The room was lined in soft white and blue lights and gave off a calming, yet futuristic ambiance. The floor consisted of countless offices for the elected leadership, and also all things entertainment such as holoreels, virtual reality, digital boardgames, and all delights for a careless youth to enjoy. The floor above was a kitchen built for a king. The all-white cookery was always filled with workers. There were at least two dozen people who worked as part of the kitchen staff. They too dressed in all white from head to toe, and pure white hats were designated to all who worked within the kitchen, which informed others of position and rank. Yefimovich smelled the sweetest of smells as he walked past the floor. The cookatiers were creating a deliciously delicate desert as they meddled with flour, sugar, and caramel. On the third level was an astounding living area. There were three great rooms on the floor. An immaculate dining hall with stunning, eighty-foot oak arches running across the room with dazzling chandeliers hanging from above. Another room within the floor was a great room with fine woven couches and elegant chairs lined throughout, along with stunning paintings from artists all around the world. The focal point, however, was a wall that seemed cracked. Fire ran through it, and as it reached the surface, it ignited the oval shaped fireplace, lighting the entire room with its glow. Just on the other end of the floor was the final room, a ballroom, ideal for hosting military balls, charity events, and ceremonies of all types. Yefimovich liked the idea of having a yearly event celebrating local, everyday people and their accomplishments. He thought it would help unify the country and create less tension between wealthy individuals and those who were less well off. Just above, on the fourth floor of the dome, was the Premier suite. It had the softest of silks and cottons, the finest of linens and a bed that felt more magical than a dream and softer than any cloud. Yefimovich had yet to sleep in the comfortable bed, as he was waiting for this day, the day his country was born. As tempting as the bed seemed, Yefimovich finally found his way to the top floor. From this room Yefimovich could see not just the entire walled city of the Citadel, but its neighboring city as far as the horizon extended. Within this magnificent space, surrounding him were unfinished paintings still on their easels as well as huge pieces of stone and marble of sculpted men and women. The walls were littered with books, a vast library that would take a thousand years to read and you'd still need a thousand more years to finish them all. This is where Yefimovich was most comfortable inside the capital building.

He turned on his favorite composer and had the music fill the room and build him with creative thoughts. He closed his eyes and listened to the vibrations of the strings and the hammering of the drums until his mind was filled with thoughts outside his own world. Yefimovich opened his eyes, gathered his paints and brushes, and began telling a story through the artistic nature of painting.

He had loved to paint ever since he was a small boy. Growing up his family wasn't particularly wealthy, so from time to time, he would improvise. Some water and dirt were always a good base for browns, some spoiled fruits like cherries or avocados would make great pastes and provide rich, full colors. As a child, when he wasn't in school or helping his parents, he would work on a farm, helping to plow the fields and harvest crops, all in the hopes of getting enough money so that he could buy new paints and brushes and create the world the way he saw it.

The full hour had nearly gone by. Yefimovich looked at his work and gave a happy grin of accomplishment as he began to prepare himself for his speech. *Say what is within your heart,* he reminded himself. He briskly made his way out of the dome and into the main part of the capital building. His cabinet members and generals were all waiting for him at the front entrance of the building. They exchanged pleasantries once more, and all had a look of nerves and excitement upon them, as if they were one emotion. It was a feeling of anxiousness, but there were none more anxious than Yefimovich.

The Mahyeem military band began playing a harmonious melody, and the eager crowd outside had gone from loud cheers and great enthusiasm to dramatically calm and attentive. The generals and cabinet members made their way out first and were acclaimed and applauded as they took their positions, and when Yefimovich walked out, the exuberant crowd seemed to fill the entire city with a spirit of overwhelming joy and exultation. There were thousands, if not hundreds of thousands of people outside the capital building. A marvelous ocean of individuals, from the rich to the poor, from the city slicker to the country bumpkin, everyone from all walks of life were gathered as one. They were all gathered by the same ideology, the same moral standards, the same rough and tough grit to get things done in the world. They were all ready to show the world what their new country could be and what it could accomplish.

Yefimovich let the crowd have their moment as their gaieties roared through the city. He then put his hands up into the air, and the crowd, slowly but surely, became silent once more. Yefimovich took a deep breath and clutched the podium with both hands. In his mind, he reminded himself to pause when he felt a stutter about to leave his lips.

"Good evening, ladies and gentlemen. Today is a day of great significance. It is a day that was fought for—a day that was died for—Our sons, our daughters, our brothers and sisters, our mothers and fathers dreamed of this day—and today we live it! We are not here by chance but by providence. Not only were we chosen to be here, we chose ourselves to be here on this day. For all those in this crowd and to all those watching in their homes, know that your life matters and that your service matters. With you, we are strong. With you, we are wise. With you, we are one: one people, one country!

"Together, we will build this nation to honor the ones that were lost, to honor the ones that are living, to honor our God, and to restore us as a people. We have been blessed with abilities that no other people possess, and we will use our en-endowments for the good of our people and for the good of the world. Throughout our time in history, we have been demonized, enslaved, and massacred. I ask you all to forgive those who have wronged you, and where b-b-bitterness and hate once were, to let them be replaced by love—for there is no glory in hate, and there is no honor in—bitterness. Let us mend old rivalries and strengthen the bonds of age-old friendships.

"There is a benevolent country whose leaders have always strived in supporting our cause. They have been our voice when we have had none and our swords when we had too few. As a nation, I ask that we give thanks to our dearest ally, Saoirse. Over the centuries, these people have taken us into their home when we did not have one. They have been our light upon a hill for generations. They have taken us in when we were tired and poor. When our lungs—were shouting for freedom in times of oppression—they lent us their hand and welcomed us with open arms. We owe these people our lives, for without them, we would not exist.

"Therefore, effective immediately, we will send them a gift, a gift made of metal and fire, a gift surrounded by water and air, a statue of liberty she will be! A light, she will shine through the fog of the sea, saying come this way, for here you are free! Her eyes will be soft and kind and yet hold authority. Shouting for all those who are seeking, set your ships towards me.

"This is our mother, a mother of exiles, and as her child, we will make her proud. We will be a country of integrity, a country of law. If her light should ever go dark, we will be here to keep the flame burning. For our country is just like you, Mother. Here we will give hope to those who have lost theirs, and we will be the shield for those who have no sword. We will be a voice for those who have none, and we will ring our sister bell, and it will sing the songs of liberty. We are the country of Yisra! And from this day to the end of days, we will be a beacon upon a hill, shining for all those who are seeking, saying, come this way, for here, too, you are free!"

Tears started streaming from Yefimovich's eyes, and the thousands upon thousands of people roared with thunderous applause. Rocket boomers from all parts of the city launched into the air in jubilation, and as the country's flag rose over the capital building, ovations of hope and of joy echoed from the sea of Yisra to the shores of Saoirse.

Yefimovich thought of his wife and daughter and how relieved he was that his child would not have to suffer the same events which he and his wife had. As the flag rose to full staff, the Avir soldiers gave honor to the flag by maneuvering the air around them to produce the sounds of bombardment. Ten rounds of percussion they rang out into the world to signify their strength, their valor, and their honor. As the city and the country celebrated below, Yefimovich exited the stage, saying goodbye to his fellow colleagues and headed back to his home.

Aero greeted Yefimovich with a salute, but Yefimovich did not salute back. Instead, he squeezed the soldier tightly with jubilance in his heart, slapped him on the shoulder, and said, "Let's go home." Aero laughed at his new Prime Minister for his very unorthodox greeting and readied the vetervykl.

"Aero, would you like to come to the game with me and my family tonight?" Yefimovich asked him.

"I would love to sir, but I cannot," the soldier replied.

"Oh, really. Why is that, if you don't mind me asking?"

"I have a date tonight, sir," Aero explained.

"How wonderful. She must be a real beauty," Yefimovich teased him. "Are you all going to the reels, then?"

"No, sir. I'm taking her to a Premerministr Odin race," Aero replied.

"Premerministr over Dobycha?"

"It wouldn't be my first pick either, but she likes racing."

"Sounds like love to me," Yefimovich teased the young twenty-four year old some more. The Avi soldier dug into his coat pocket, and he showed him a circular band with a large svadkamen gem brightly shining on it. "A wedding ring," Yefimovich said, sounding slightly surprised. "Who is the lucky one in this situation?" he asked.

"Definitely not her," Aero joked.

Yefimovich was finally home and was welcomed with butterfly kisses and coal-burning embraces. Hopes were high, not just for Yefimovich and his family but for all those within the birth of the new nation.

It wasn't long before he and his family were at the Dobycha match. The stadium was filled from top to bottom without a single empty seat. A hoard of purple jerseys painted the stadium, as bits of white and blue from the away team sprinkled themselves among the masses.

The field on which the players played was the most unique of any sport. Water encircled the pitch and weaved like a snake suspended in the air. Floating high and low, at all altitudes, were large pieces of earth about fifteen yards in length and fifteen yards across, plotted across the field. There were four goals in total; one was larger and rectangular in shape, and the other was small and circular, levitating in the open air of the court. The larger goal was worth two points, while the smaller was worth four. All the elements were in play for Dobycha, and each team had to have a manipulator of each element. One Avi, one Ada, an Esh, and a Mahyeem all had to be playing, along with an element of the team's choosing. Each team was allowed three substitutions in a ninety-minute game, and the team with the highest score within those ninety minutes was declared the winner.

A voice spoke over the airwaves, echoing across the stadium while the players and coaches entered onto the pitch.

"Ladies and gentlemen! Welcome to Raqia, home to your Erbil Kleschians!" The crowd hailed them with hoots and hollers followed by resounding applause, and then their eyes gazed upon the challengers. The drums started to roll, and flags started to wave. It seemed 100,000 people became one as they sang a traditional chant to the opposing team.

Shalom Shalom we are the knights of Erbil
We will punish those who enter our field
With stone we will break, and fire we'll burn
Your hopes and your dreams no longer will yearn
With wind we will gust, and water we'll drown
The fight that you had a vanquished renown
We are the knights of Erbil and mighty we are
Enter with caution, or leave with a scar
Klesch
Klesch
Klesch!

The audience cheered with pride at the end of their mantra and quickly began booing the rival team. The rowdiness of the crowd tempered only slightly until they were asked to stand for their national anthem, and like the dead of night, they became silent. The flag flowed in the breeze as the people gazed upon its glory. Its meaning was more significant than ever before, each symbol and color had a purpose and each note in their anthem was a feeling of hope, of pride, and reflection. As the song ended, the blissful euphoria could be felt in the air, infecting each and every person in the stadium. Yefimovich could feel it within himself, as if it were a part of his very being.

The match had begun, and an Avi player for the Kleschians had the ball held snug under his arm as he cut through the air at incredible speeds. He dodged the chunks of earth launched at him by the Adamah player on the opposing team and danced away from the tsunami of water the Mahyeem player had thrown at him until he was met by the Eshan player who had rocketed through the sky, even faster than he, with fire from his feet and hands. He flew towards the Avi and hit him with force, knocking out the ball and securing it himself.

He propelled himself with the power of his flames and barreled through the blocks of earth tossed at him, and scorched the water blasted at his body. He tossed the ball in front of him, suspended high in the air, and kicked the ball a fearsome blow, only to be saved by an even more impressive act.

The game raged on, all in good spirits. Yefimovich felt like a child as he watched the game being played. He sang and he yelled. He acclaimed and he heckled, and by the half, he had nearly lost his voice.

A loud explosion punched the air, signaling the end of the intermission, but something seemed a little different. Yefimovich heard Viktoriya give a loud scream as one of the chairs within the booth had caught fire. The stadium staff was quick to react and hurriedly put out the flame. Then there was another boom, this was less forceful, and the table at which Viktoriya stood had flames flickering from its top. Yefimovich began to laugh for he knew what had happened.

"Our daughter, Yefi," Viktoriya said.

"She's an Esh, I know." He chuckled out the words. "Just like her mother," he stated. Viktoriya smiled at him.

"I am terribly sorry about this," he expressed to the staffer. "Can I please see your manager?"

"Yes, sir." said the young boy who quickly dashed off to get his superior.

"I'll call the driver and meet you out front. I'll have to see what this is going to cost us," he said to his wife. The matter was quickly settled, and Yefimovich was soon in the vehicle with his wife and daughter. "Yekaterina, you have to be careful with this power of yours," he said tapping her nose as if she understood, but all she did was smile a toothless grin.

"She is so young to have abilities like this. What are we going to do, Yefi?" Viktoriya asked.

"I wasn't expecting this until she was two or three. We'll just have to keep a close eye on her. Some rooms will be off limits of course, and we'll have to purchase some ogon to fireproof the walls."

Viktoriya held her daughter out in front of her so they were face to face. "Our little prodigy. I can't wait to teach you all that I know," she said and kissed her daughter's baby lips.

"Our tiny Esh, our baby fire maker," he said, and then a thought hit his mind like the hands on a clock strike the hour. "What if—"

Alamgeer Chapter One

A small rumble shook the foundation of the majestic stone castle nestled in the bedrock of the burning mountain. As the china clicked and clattered and the lights flickered and flashed, a pair of cries echoed in the arms of a woman whose skin was pale white but glistened like diamonds and whose eyes were pink as pixies with a dash of black pepper.

"Shhh jungen. Shhh, Momma is here," she said comforting them. The little boys sniffled back their young tears, and the woman soaked them with her sleeves. "There, there, my boys, no more tears. Let's go see what made you cry, shall we?" she said to them as she wiped their young and vibrant faces. She took the boys by the hand and walked them towards an arched window which gave a view like no other. Peering out, they saw the world, and down below them, lava twisted and turned like a snake in the grass, slithering and sliding until it found its prey. The city was built at the base of a volcano where fire and heat were the people's livelihood. As the volcano erupted and lava flowed, the city planners designed the urban life to guide the magma under its streets and around its boarders.

"It's scary, Mama," said one of the twin boys frightened by its eerie glow.

"It's only scary for a moment, but this beast of destruction is also a giver of life, and without it, we would not exist," she said, comforting her child.

"Is that true, Pa?" asked the boy less frightened.

"Nothing could be truer," Alamgeer said as he watched the liquid fire coast down the mountain side. "How are my boys this morning? Are you behaving for Mom, Almaut?"

"Yes, Vater," said the boy.

"And what about you, Attila?" he asked again.

"Yes, sir," the boy said bashfully.

"These two are always behaving, Alam. Isn't that right boys?" said his wife Hella. The twins shook their heads in agreement. "How did last night's meeting go?" she asked.

"It went well. This is going to be a very long and patient endeavor. I need to make sure I have the right men at my side and to be aware of any leaks."

"I have no doubt you'll succeed. What time are the signings today?"

"They are this afternoon. I'll be leaving here shortly with the publisher. She should be coming within the hour." Alamgeer informed her while still looking out at the flow of coulee as it seeped under the city streets. The lava matched his eyes, as if they were made by the volcanic goo, but nothing mirrored his lifeless pale skin.

"Boys, go play somewhere for a minute I need to talk to your mother," he instructed them.

"Yes, Vater," they said in unison. They quickly scurried off, eager to play and be wild. His molten burning eyes gazed into the vibrant flares of his wife's. His expression was stern and serious, yet it was nothing that seemed to concern Hella. She had seen his many expressions a thousand times over. He grabbed her warm hands and cupped them like a chalice, "Hella, I need you to know—that the next few years will be incredibly difficult. People will go hungry; they will be angry, and the country will be unsafe from its own people. There will be times when I may ask you to do something that seems as if it is wrong. It may betray your conscience, but I beg you to heed my words now. So, when the time does come, when our world seems to be in turmoil, you will not hesitate when I ask you to do something."

He watched as her eyes darted back and forth, looking at his. It was silent for a moment, and then she kissed his masculine hands that held hers.

"Alam, I made an oath to you when we married. My heart is yours; my mind is yours, and my body is yours. Just as you are mine. I am on your side, now and forever. If you're wrong, I will be wrong with you, and if you are right, I will share your glory, but I will let you shine in all of it. I know tough times are here, and they will get worse, but trust me as I trust you, and together, we will fear nothing and achieve everything." She ameliorated the doubts in his heart with her words, and Alamgeer's mind felt less clouded and his path clearer and more direct.

It seemed like only mere moments had passed when their diener entered the large study with a woman who was wildly flamboyant. Her lips were siren red, and her glossy orange hair waved like a flag in the wind as she walked. Her eyes were lined with a dark violet shade, bolding her dark brown eyes with confidence.

"Ala! Ala!" she called him with a voice less seductive than her appearance. "Are you ready, my love, are you excited? You've sold over a million books just in this country alone! It's absolutely astounding," she said charismatically.

"I am thrilled, Francis," Alamgeer answered with a flat tone.

"Don't be such a bore, Ala. Show a little more enthusiasm. These people are coming here to see you! Because of what you have said in your book, you might have started a cultural revolution."

"These are just words on paper. An action must be taken in order to start a revolution."

"And is writing a book to be the voice of the people not an action?" she insisted on arguing.

"This is just a book on how I feel. If others feel as I do, then they should act upon their feelings," he said slightly more aggressively.

"Then why don't you act, Ala?" He did not answer her, but his mind replied, *I will.*

"Where is the car, Francis?"

"Oh, we are not driving my dear, oh no. I have something better, more grand, more exciting, more revolutionary," she said theatrically. As she talked, a black horse with large golden eyes pulling an open aureate carriage stopped in front of them. "I present to you Copenhagen and his auric carriage," Francis said delightedly. Not thrilled with the thought of riding an open wagon, Alamgeer's face was expressionless, but his eyes spoke disdain. He entered and saw there was no place to sit. He looked over at Francis, but said nothing.

"It's more commanding if you're standing. When people look at you, they will see power and strength. Whereas, if you were sitting, they wouldn't think much of you at all," she explained.

The steed was light footed and trotted with an arrogant attitude, which Alamgeer found quite amusing. Copenhagen's hooves clacked on the translucent roads, drawing attention from the people in the city. Francis seemed to be right. The citizens stopped to look at the unique scene. Some were taking pictures, and others videos. They would stop and point in his direction. Some people waved hello, and others yelled out to get his attention. He looked down at Francis and grinned.

"What did I tell you?" she smiled. "I am a sucker for augustness."

Alamgeer could see the newly fallen magma below the streets as his carriage took him to his destination. The sky above was dark and gloomy, as was the city. The skyscrapers seemed old and dated, and the sidewalks cracked and weathered. It was as if all the joy and happiness in the world had vanished, leaving only despair and sadness for those who remained. Since the war, the country had fallen into economically woeful times. Prices of goods and services were rising rapidly; paying bills was getting more difficult for the average citizen. Morale was low, and without a leader to guide the people, only misery would remain. Alamgeer's heart did not ache for the sights he saw. Instead, his heart raged with anger. This was Holle, one of the greatest nations to ever have existed. People would flock from all the corners of the world to learn mathematics, philosophy, and astronomy, but now it was a country of ill repute and tainted scholars.

He and Francis had reached the Atma Library where Alamgeer would be signing books and taking holopics and holovids with his fans. There was already a line of people that seemed to span a hundred yards, waiting to meet and talk with him. Alamgeer felt a sense of pride and dynamism within his soul as he saw all those who were coming to see him and hear more about what he had to say within his book.

After signing countless books and talking to hundreds of admirers, Alamgeer only had a handful of people left in his line. As the next person came up, Alamgeer was delighted by what the man had to say.

"Mein Niza is my struggle too, and your words are my words—If you plan to lead, I will surely follow." Alamgeer hid his smile at hearing the comment.

"You should stay for the speech I have in about an hour and a half. I think you'll like what I have to say," he told the man.

"At 8 o'clock, then?"

"Will I see you there?" Alamgeer asked.

"Absolutely."

The sands of time fell rapidly, and the hour was nearly 8. The room was dimly lit, the carpet a light beige with walls to match its tone. Francis seemed to be holding some clothes as she approached Alamgeer.

"My dear, Alam, I have something for you to wear for your speech," she said. Alamgeer looked at her as if she were telling an unfunny joke.

"Stand up; stand up." She grabbed his muscular arms and tried to pull him from his seat. Alam eventually rose as he knew her persistence would never cease until he obeyed. "Come, come, remove your clothes," she instructed.

"Excuse me?" he said slightly bewildered.

"Don't be such a prude, Ala. What I'm about to give you will be the clothes of a true leader, a man of inspiration and awe."

Alamgeer looked at the clothes she had given him

"These are terrible."

"That's because you lack a sense of style, Ala. If you want to reach the youth, you need more than just words. They are impressionable, so be impressive. Make them feel like you understand them intellectually and culturally," Francis said.

"Leave the room," he commanded her. She smiled and turned away. Alamgeer examined the clothes she had selected for him. The pants were as dark as the midnight sky and fit to showcase Alamgeer's masculine features. The shirt hugged his skin with a fearsome grip and outlined the grooves within his arms and stomach. The outfit was made of a material that was as light as feathers, as breathable as the deepest breath, as strong as the purest diamond. He then came across a black cape, richer than the deepest chocolate and hesitated to put it on. It wasn't an article of clothing a Semideusi would wear as it was associated with the Telekine. He thought for a few moments before putting the cape over himself, and cogitated that if the cape would put at ease the tensions with the Telekine that lived within Holle, then wearing it would be best for him and for the people, but then he thought of those who would oppose it.

"Why should I wear this?" he asked Francis.
She turned to face him and said, "Because it is part of our nation's history. Some of our greatest leaders wore capes. They commanded armies and led entire generations. We must never forget our past as we look towards our future. We can learn quite a lot from it," she said matter of factly. She walked over to him and clipped the cape around his broad shoulders and looked him up and down with satisfaction. "My love, you look marvelous. Just dashing! Oh, I almost forgot. Put this around your arm." She handed him a black armband with a symbol banded in white and red and explained what it meant. "The eight-pointed star symbolizes power, and the elegant double-u character with the crown over it represents God."

"You're a lot smarter than you look, Francis," Alamgeer praised.

"I might be posh, but don't ever think of me as incompetent. A man who does that is no wiser than a child." She gave him a peck on both cheeks. "They are waiting for you."

Alamgeer left the room and started walking down the hall. He could not hear the clicks of his black boots hitting the floor, nor the drumming of his beating heart. He could only hear the echoing cheers of the people that stood outside waiting for him. The rumble of the crowd grew louder as he got closer to the podium.

The sun struggled to strike past the drab of the clouds looming above, but that didn't seem to dampen the spirits of the people in front of him. Before Alamgeer were nearly 500,000 men and women. Both Hemitheoi and Semideusi were standing side by side with a scattered bunch of Telekine. The acclamation of the people amplified and then slowly fell silent as Alamgeer stood on the stage with a stern face and folded arms. His words came out quickly, in a humble manner, and his hands fell, locked together in front of his body.

"Ladies and gentlemen, last month, Lunius 30th, 2046, I and the seven you see seated at my side, formed a new political coalition, and I have been the leader of it. The reasons that have caused me to bring this book to you and to create this movement, bringing a new political party into existence, are known only but to me. You may have read my thoughts, but they are just words on paper. Words that must be spoken from my mouth to say and to your ears to listen." Alamgeer's voice began to rise. His body and arms moved more aggressively as he spoke.

"When the Great War ended, so did the lives of millions of Hollen. These men and women were guiltless of moira, blameless for its start, and without guilt for its leaders. As a nation, we are divided, and we must come together to form a greater union! Divided, we are powerless! And I believe that is what our leaders want us to be! What conceptions! Come this election, we must face an inner battle amongst ourselves and our friends, to sort our differences and be a unified Holle. There is only one way for us to become a nation in high repute and that is by reclaiming a new Holle and tearing down those who lead us at the top, burning our divisions within, and destroying the boarders we have put around ourselves; then will we be able to create a National United Verband!" Alamgeer calmed himself and folded his arms once more.

"Rich and poor, urban and rural, educated and uneducated—the task for our party is not to represent one faction of these people but all of them. Our coalition is the party of unity, and it is not ideal but a reality." His cadence quickened, and his voice spoke passionately. His words began to rumble the earth with the power of his message.

"Today, at this very hour, I declare war! War on our inner strife and political elites. We volk will reclaim the power we have lost! Let us rise up a new Holle—one more grand and promising than the last. No longer will there be class war and class struggle. The ideas and ideals of the Sozialist have failed us for the past thirty years. It is our fight to vanquish it, to rid the rot of the earth and burn it in the depths of hell! Pledge with me today, as a solemn individual, to start this war and to never rest until this poison is exterminated from Hollen life! The Sozi regime has ripped us apart as a country, as a people. In the beginning, it promised us a better life and a prosperous future. The words sounded sweet like honey, but we now know, and we have tasted with our tongues, the bitterness of this sour government.

Alamgeer's voice started to strain slightly, but it did not take away the veracity and the potency of his message.

"Today, we see our wages declining and our debts rising. Inflation is becoming a massive weight upon us all! We are getting to a point when we will have to choose between putting food on the table to feed our children or risk bankruptcy. Our farmers will slave away trying to produce food for the masses while providing very little for themselves. Our miners and our factory workers have all but been forgotten. Our middle class, whom we have ignored for the last three decades, will begin to fall, and then you will know that we no longer have a country to call our own. Let me make this clear, Sozialismus is a war against its own people, and by that a war against its people's culture. From today and until our last, let us fight against them! You have been abandoned, but together in our war, in our struggle, they will know you!" Alamgeer stopped and paused as the hoard of Hollen citizens voiced their approval with resounding applause.

"This treaty, which I was forced to sign, is not my fault, but it is the fault of my fathers. Because of our fathers, we are expected to meet obligations that are unrealistic, and because of these impossible regulations, we are quickly becoming a nation without possibilities for its people. We are becoming a nation in which justice is no longer served. Because of our fathers, we are ashamed of our own country; we are ashamed to say we are Hollen!"

He paused and thought of his father and how much he missed him. How the words he was saying broke his heart—he wanted so badly not to say them, but he knew he needed a united people, a people with purpose.

"There will come a day when our vision and our ideals will rule Holle! There will again be a day when you can proudly say that you are Hollen! It is the time for every Hollen to lift themselves out of the blackness you have fallen into and to be fierce in your new awakening!"

A standard started to rise slowly behind Alamgeer. It was a flag with the same image he bore upon his sleeve. It waved mightily in the stiff breeze of the sunset. The sky became a mix of red and purple and fit the mood of the people—a burning passion and desire for change and a renewed sense of pride and power.

"Let us raise a standard! One of power and glory! Of purpose and the possibility for a future far better than our past. Our standard will be a symbol for the preservation of our soul, our ideals, and our volk. Today! Let them hear your voice! Let it echo down from the highest mountain and into the depths of the soulless monsters who have pressed us! Mark this day, this hour, and know that because of you, those who now despise us will fight against us, and in this fight, we will painfully and honorably acquire a new Hollen "Reich" of greatness and power, fortitude and glory: Amen!"

Once again, Alamgeer could no longer hear the beating of his heart, just the sound of wave upon wave of elated acclamation.

<u>**Seventeen years pass, and the seeds of power and conquest begin to emerge from the depths of the earth, and stemming from its stalk, war.**</u>

Enoch Chapter One

It sat high among the rest, overlooking the world, while still very much a part of it. A land vast and beautiful like fields of flowers on the plains, or rivers gliding down the stream. Pure and without sin is what foreigners called the land, but no nation is without covetousness. The mountain range bordered the entirety of the western coast. Its peaks seemed to scrape the stars as if reaching towards the face of God. The entire continent received all its water from the expanse of the range. Rivers ran like veins across the land, stepping into lakes as clear as crystal, and powering the country to prosperity, before moving onwards until the water reached the eastern coast where it descended down to the earth.

A man walks alone, and the wind whispers quietly in his ear as the falls of water roar to be heard. His face is pale and sharp, with eyes a calming blue. His ears are pointed and arched, and his hair gray and ruffled. His feet fall silent as they hit the ground, his movement like silk, soft and full of grace. The man's heart is heavy and his mind astir. The mountains and cliffs hang high above him as the water moves around him, and he falls to his knees. The man's eyes close and look towards the sky as he whispers to the wind.

"We are a broken people; much like the world, we are lost and cannot find our way. If there be any hope, lead me to it, for what is life without it. We see old patterns of the past, though the characters are new. Help us unveil the fog upon our eyes, and lead us to the truth. My people no longer believe in your divinity, nor your grace. Please shine the light within their hearts, or let me be the instrument who does, for the world is nearly cast in shadow and will soon be consumed by darkness. Hear my prayer, Takk." The wind quickened its pace as if to carry his message to a greater power, though very few still believed in such superstitions.

He opened his eyes, and before him were waterfalls that seemed to fall for miles with glistening crags and reflections of light streaking across the sky in what seemed to be the works of a master painter. The pointed-eared man cupped his hands into the pool of water that sat motionless in front of him and washed his face from the sweat of his walk. Down the expanse he went until he reached his city, which seemed to be hidden from the world as it masked itself within the towering acclivity of stone and earth and water. The buildings and homes were made only from stone and glass, and the glass had no glare in the light. Some were covered with moss from the dampness of the temperate air; others mirrored nature's structure, while a few were bold and prominent like the ministries building, which was molded into the shape of an octagon and rose a thousand feet into the air, though it still looked small next to the mountain range in which it was very much a part of .

The peculiar-eared man arrived home. It smelled of lavender within the quietness of the abode. He did not mind the silence, though he wished from some life of the voices he loved to reverberate within his punktoret. *I hope Uriel is doing alright. How long since I last saw his face, a year? Almost two?* He answered his own question. He missed Uriel deeply but grinned when he thought of his son's successes and how he would be home in a few short weeks. His wife was out teaching ungeengels how to capture light, and once captured, how to bend the light into a physical form using an orb and the Brietwheeler law.

In his silence, the gray-haired man thought he could hear murmuring in the next room over.

"Hello?" he said, but there was no answer. The man walked into the room where the voice had come from and saw no one, nor anything that may have caused a noise. *Strange, must be that time is catching up with me,* he thought.

The blue-eyed Engelelf noticed the hour and dressed in his ministerial robe and put upon his head a woven band made of silver. He stepped out into his entryway and, with an expression of concern, looked about himself and shrugged. The man started walking and then, like fire to water, evaporated out of existence. Not but a second had passed, and he was within the ministries building.

"Good afternoon, Enoch," a fellow minister said while walking by.

"Hello Olav. Ready for today?" he asked.

"Eh," Olav uttered. Enoch gave a grin as his thoughts were the same. Not a single percussive sound was made as hundreds of Engelelf walked the soft, gray, solid stone floors in the halls of the open arid building. Lining the crafted stone halls were vines of elegance with an array of patterns depending on where in the ministry building a person traveled. During different seasons, the vines produced flowers giving off pleasant aromas. Enoch took a deep breath and inhaled the pleasant smell of the vastly colored orchids and continued to walk the halls until he reached his office. His desk was made of pure wood and assembled from an old pine tree, which still seemed to produce its distinguishable scent. His chair was made of the same tree and lined with the vines that outlined the building with a cushion pulled from the cotton fields of Aontaithe. He sat down and saw words written in light, colored in soft pink, spinning in circles within a tiny orb. He tapped the orb and said, "Apen," and the message revealed itself. The messages were notes taken by his assistant for the day's meeting of the ministers. He took the pen resting on his desk and wrote the words, thank you, in the air with light produced from the pen. Enoch gave a small blow to the message, and the lighted words flickered off to his assistant, eventually finding their way to the orb sitting on her desk.

Enoch examined her notes and compared them with his. He noted small discrepancies and bolded consistencies, and when he had finished, it was nearly time for him to attend his meeting. As he arrived in the center of the great octangular building, he quickly noticed there were already some heated discussions taking place amongst his colleagues. He knew the night was going to be long, tiring, full of passion, truths, and untruths, and he took his seat as head of ministers. He took his stone gavel and slammed hard upon its base. The room came to a murmur and finally hushed shortly after. Enoch spoke,

"Good evening ministers. We are here today as we have noted a series of events within Holle, which have given some of us concern. Today we will discuss these concerns. We will listen to our fellow ministers' counterarguments, and legislation will be written if indeed we decide to act on these allegations. Sir Olav, the floor is yours."

Hours passed as deliberations moved back and forth. There were strong moments of frustration, periods of applause, scenes of unity, and, at times, severe division. Awakened eyes at the beginning of the meeting were beginning to squint as the power of sleep tried to grip them. To stay awake, the ministers drank tea and coffee. Catered meals were brought in to sustain them. The night had passed, and the morning light began to rise. The room was silent, but Enoch thought he could hear someone speaking. He glanced around the great hall but saw no lips moving. *It must be the lack of sleep,* he thought to himself, and then someone finally did speak up to break the silence that surrounded them.

"And what do you have to say about this, Enoch? You haven't said a word all night. Why do you hold your tongue?" the minister asked. Enoch was silent for a bit, took a sip of tea that sat to his right, and then gave his answer.

"I am silent because to form a complete and whole conclusion, one must gather all the information about an issue, both its negatives and positives, its origins and the narrative created by those origins to find the truth buried in the web of data about which you all have spoken for the past fourteen hours, and with all the words you have spoken, combined with the notes I have gathered on this issue, this is what I have concluded thus far. There is a nation which was ravaged by a war which they created, and as a result, their economy has suffered greatly. There were elections fifteen years ago, and a new political party was formed by the son of Alois. It was an election he had lost. There was an election just last year in which he had lost again. However, he was appointed Grand Kanzler by the country's current president. During that year of his running, there was a coalition formed of those who called themselves Braunhemd. It is my understanding that they have terrorized its citizens if they did not think a certain way or if they happened to be anything but Hemitheoi or Semideusi. These soldiers, if you want to call them that, bare the mark that Alamgeer wears upon his sleeve, though he himself has not said anything negative about the Braunhemd coalition. At this time, I believe as a people, he poses a significant risk, and I feel, effective immediately, we should cease trading with Holle even though this would be a direct violation of the Hidler-Nemtsov agreement." There was no applause or sounds of discontent as he finished giving voice on the matter. Enoch then called for a vote to take place, needing three quarters of the ministers to pass legislation to halt trading with Holle.

"You have twelve hours to mull over the debates we have had throughout this meeting. When we return after this recess, you will have thirty minutes to place your vote. Go home, get some rest, say hello to your families, and I will see you soon," Enoch told the ministers and then left the ministers great hall, in silence, alone.

His eyes like sand bags pulling down a great weight, he could barely keep them open. He pushed ajar the natural red orange door that led to the entrance of his house. Like before, it was quiet, but there to greet him with warm and loving arms was his wife. She was his angel, his rock, his fire, and his water. For the last 225 years, she was his life, and he knew she would be his life for 225 more. With her, they had three children, Uriel, Erie, and Lagertha, all of whom had become people in high standing throughout the world. From a world-renowned scientist to world-renowned leaders, he was proud of each of them and couldn't image anyone else whom he would have had these amazing children with. Her tender arms embraced his body, but her tight grip was more than just a touch of affection. It was something deeper. It was not the embrace of a wild fire but one of steady embers burning brightly and passionately until the very end when there was nothing left but the cool dark grip of death. She did not say a word to him but instead waited for Enoch to talk.

"The world will one day soon be a place of fallen men, where lives once loved and cherished will be lost to the sands of time. Our vote today may very well be the start of horrors yet to come. Like broken glass upon the ground, so too the families of the world will be. Lightning in the sky we will make, and we will paint our oceans red. Is this the life we'll have to see? What Heilagr, do you counsel me?"

"Enoch." She ran her fingers through his thick gray hair, "I know you have already made your choice, but I will give you words of comfort. There are great men in this world, men who can achieve the unimaginable, men who are selfless and will fight for just the smallest of lights to flicker in a never-ending desert of caliginous. These men will show their face to the world. They will be the lanterns across the open plains and beams of light waving in the rocky sea. They will be the fire on the mountain and the candle in the tenebrous desert. Know that your choice will bring these men to the world, and, in the end, we will be better for it." Enoch kissed her hands that were without imperfection. "Now go get some rest. You look exhausted."

"Thank you, Heilagr," he said with bloodshot eyes, still holding her hands in his. His mind sharply thought of his daughter Erie, realizing he had missed her. "Where is our daughter? I haven't seen her in two days," he asked.

"She has gone out with some friends. She'll be home later tonight," Heilagr told him. "Now scurry off to bed. In a few hours, you will have to be one of those men who light the world in truth."

"The lantern is mighty heavy. You may need to help me carry it," he said to her with a slight grin about his face.

"If you should ever falter, I will be there to help lift you back up. Now go and sleep already."

Enoch stripped himself of his robe and cast his clothes aside and finally laid his head on the soft white feathers of his pillow. The electric bolts fell silent within the storm that was his mind, as the rain fell and cleared the way to consciousness. Tick, tick, tick was the call of the second hand as it moved the minute, which moved the hour, and the hour the day, and the day the night. *Enoch, Enoch, Enoch* was the utter in his ear. The lids of his eyes exposed the iris, but it saw no form to the words that summoned him. *A dream,* he thought—of what he did not know. He inhaled deeply and could smell the sweet scents of honey and cinnamon and knew that his wife was making him breakfast though the hour was late. Enoch quickly washed and readied himself once more to resume his meeting with the ministers. He walked into the kitchen, and much to his delight, it was Erie who had been making him his morning meal. Her hair was like her mothers, radiant as the sun with a smile just as bright—her skin pale and pure and eyes an icy white—a heart of felicity and a mind astute, the soul of innocence, a beauty, cute—with a nectarous voice that heeded your gaze, a talent of tongue more complex than a maze.

"Hello, Pappa," she said with a smile that showed the dimples on her checks.

"My Erie, it smells amazing in here. Is that kanelhonn that strikes my nose?" Enoch asked, knowing the answer.

"Just for you, Pappa. Mamma prepared everything else." The letter to every word she spoke was sugared as it left her mouth. "But I must get to bed. I love you, Pappa." She kissed her father's cheek and skipped down the hall to her bedchamber. "Goodnight!" she yelled as she closed the door to her room.

"Goodnight, Erie!" Enoch hollered back. He turned to his wife, "Thanks for this Heilagr," he said.

"If we didn't make you anything, we know you would have left without eating," she said, knowing his manners. "How long do you think you will be tonight?" she asked.

"Not terribly long. Once the meeting resumes, we have thirty minutes to cast our vote. I'm sure many will leave after they have heard the results. I'll stay for a while to note how we'll proceed should legislation pass, and I should be back before the sun rises. Maybe this time, you'll have breakfast waiting for you when you wake in the morning," he teased.

"I'd like that. I'll see you in the morning, then. I'm off to bed as well." She kissed his lips and strolled off to rest her eyes.

Enoch finished his meal, stuffed a muffin lathered in kanelhonn in his mouth, and visesated back to the ministry. As he arrived, he noticed the clouds above starting to build higher in the sky and their colors turning gray and ominous as the wind began to quicken its pace sending loose flowers tumbling skyward, painting pictures in the open air. He entered the hall, and buzzing about were a cacophony of murmurs, restless men and woman anxious for the fate that awaited them. Some had already cast their vote while others were waiting to the bitter end, still unsure of what to do. Like sand in an hour glass, the minutes fell quickly, and the votes were tallied. Enoch slammed the stone with authority and vigor, all eyes rested upon his face waiting on the words of destiny.

"All votes have been made, and today Mutatio 3rd, 2063, Landavengler will halt all trade." The men and woman of the one fourth minority hissed loudly as Enoch continued onward. "With the country of Holle thus breaking its treaty signed on Purgatio 30th, 2046. I thank you all for deliberating, counseling, and voting on such an issue. This meeting is now adjourned and will be noted in the archives. Thank you." Enoch surceased his speech, but the jeering of the opposition continued.

"This is war!" a man shouted.

"It's economic suicide!" another decried, as others heckled in the background, which sounded like a constant humming from a broken radio. Enoch sat there and listened to them as they quarreled with heavy emotion. *I know. I struggled just as much as you on the choice we made tonight,* he wanted to tell them, but he kept his tongue behind the curtain of his teeth. His mind continued to speak words that did not leave his lips. *If a man does not act in the presence of danger, does he himself not become danger?* Enoch knew that no spoken word from him would convince his disputants to see the path he saw. He sat there a while longer listening to the chorus of antagonism; then he rose from his seat and exited the room. Some followed him down the smooth, stone-floored halls spitting words of reproach at him, but Enoch remained silent as his colleagues berated him. Enoch reached his office arch, turned to his peers, and spoke, "You have nothing yet to fear, for the world will note your candor on this day, and history will show its roll." He said nothing more to them, stepped inside the archway of his office, rubbed his hand over the orb sitting within the wall to the right of the arch, sealing the entryway with waves of light.

He took a seat on his pine wood chair and let his arms rest on his desk that had bits of moss growing about it. He let his mind unravel the hours that had passed. When all the strings of the day had revealed themselves, he pulled the strings that mattered most, noted them with the light of his pen, and cast them in his orb. His notes and summary took him nearly two hours, when he noticed his lighted door begin to pulsate. The opaqueness of the door became clear, revealing the man behind it. Enoch felt a sense of relief when he saw it was Olav. The binds of light fell away from the arch, letting him inside.

"Hello old friend." Enoch greeted him with a smile.

"Who are you calling old?" said the stout Olav with a voice gruff and graveled.

"The man with the cane that stands before me," Enoch responded.

"Ah, I see. Old may be the man, but young is the mind and the heart," Olav said taking a seat across from Enoch.

"Well then, my greeting seems a little misplaced, doesn't it?" He said with a coy manner.

"Very much so, indeed," Olav said, grinning ear to ear, lighting his pipe of minted leaves. "You know," he paused as he blew circles of smoke into the air, "I'm really surprised we got the vote to go as it did. I did what I could to convince the doubters on both sides of the aisle but never felt truly convinced they would follow through. I was waiting to be stabbed in the back. Can't say it was all of me that persuaded the minds of our colleagues; Steinar and Oystein certainly do have a talent of tongue."

"Are Steinar and Oystein on their way? Or is it just you and I tonight, sorting through what needs to be done going forward?" Enoch asked.

"They should be here shortly, I'd say. Give them a few minutes. If they're not hear shortly, we will go on without them," said Olav, inhaling deeply on his pipe.

"We'll be quite handicapped without them. We need Steinar for military strategy should retaliation occur from Holle, and Oystein knows the country's finances like he knows the bends in his ears," Enoch replied.

"Of course, of course. Let's not get too serious; time is on our side at the moment," Olav said, his body relaxed, puffing away, creating figures with the smoke he exhaled. Moments later, the two Engelelves entered the room. Steinar was tall and slender, dressed in all black with an expression of a mythical sphinx. His robes and appearance were always well manicured, but underneath his facade lay tatted ink on his skin and scars that were an art of their own. Oystein was quite the opposite, shorter than most Engelelves with a dark blue robe, tattered hair and glasses that were usually broken. His ears were a bit bigger than most, and his voice was soft and quiet as if dampened by the wet air. He was the first to speak.

"Good evening," was all he said, adjusting his glasses as he took his seat next to Olav.

"Gentlemen," Steinar acknowledged Enoch and Olav in a tone that was clear yet mechanical.

"Boys! How good of you to join us. We were about to start without you," said Olav, giving a punch on the arm of Steinar and tossing the hair of Oystein, somehow giving him a less disheveled appearance. Steinar gave him a bit of an eye roll suggesting it was Olav being his typical boisterous self. Oystein paid him no mind, too focused on examining the lens of his glasses.

Their talks of strategy, both militarily and economically, colored portraits of clarity. The painted fog of doubt was slowly lifted by the heat of faith. Plans of defense dyed the maps of light that showed an image of the world. Splattered red were points of attack and dusted blue marked defense. If war were an art, Steinar was the artist, and his palette of paint was endless.

For centuries, he studied the wars of the world, its heroes and villains, its causes and its outcomes. His mind was a barracks that held the weapon of intelligence.

In order to prepare for war, economic measures had to be taken, and in order to spend the amount that was needed, it first had to be earned. The funds had to hold value and its value was stone, a stone only held in Landavengler, a treasured commodity that was necessary for many industrial practices. It was noted, in the musical harmony of conversation that, some government functions have to be disbanded as money would need to be saved. Oystein distinguished how it would be morally irresponsible to spend the money of the people on frivolous programs when war or economic depression was looming ever closer. Oystein also suggested that war bonds be marketed and sold to the populous in order to generate the support of the people in a cause that they deemed to be in their country's best interests. His mind for money and his genius to predict market movements were well known throughout the world; however, in the divinity of truth, what he hypothesized was subjective, bound by the eternal embrace of uncertainty. For he knew that to predict a certain economic outcome was like predicting the climate. There were hundreds upon hundreds of variables that influenced its direction, and to foresee its patterns was like describing what lies beyond infinity.

An epoch of a grain of sand falling in the boundless compass of space and time crashed upon the surface of its prison, and the night was dark and brooding. A glossy streak of a thousand lights flashed into the wicked sky, and it was no more as it pierced open the clouds and let the waters fall from empyrean. The open structure of the ministries building was tapped by the pressure of rain, and as the water percussed upon the building, like drummers on a snare, its arches formed the liquid falling from the sky into solid sheets of ice, barring any rain from seeping its way into the warmth of its octangular figure, keeping all who dwelled inside dry from the cruel wrath of nature.

Olav's pipe fell smokeless. Oystein's mind closed like a vault. Steinar's mood turned sour, and Enoch's eyes nearly shut as the meeting of the minds neared its end. Enoch said his goodbyes to each of them, but unlike his fellow friends, he did not go home. His mind and heart led him somewhere he did not yet know. He hiked an hour, close to two in the black of night with the rain falling softly on his face. The droplets traced a scar that laid faint about his neck, a wound from a different era, one he'd never forget. The voice inside his mind that chanted quietly his name got ever louder with every step he made and spoke to him one last time saying *visesate, visesate.* Then, like particles floating rapidly in the air, Enoch vanished. He reappeared, and his eyes saw the beauty of the place his messenger had led him. Its river was a calming powdered purple and twinkled with the night sky. The clouds had parted ways, showing its countenance to the charm of the earth. The rocks and snow mirrored the bands of light that reflected off the mystic river. Enoch knew the river as Tilgivelse. It was the river of forgiveness, but he was dumbfounded as he noticed the layers of snow around him. *It was only Mutatio. How can there be snow?* he thought. Enoch looked up and knew now where he was, for there were no mountains when his eyes dashed upwards. There were only the stars and the planets of the undiscovered universe. "It is impossible to be here," he said to himself. "No man or machine is supposed to survive in this place." Enoch looked down below and saw his world as no one had seen it before, and watched the flowing water of the Tilgivelse River slide down the never-ending mountain, from sea to shining sea.

He turned to face the peak on the mountain and saw a monstrous figure, much like a shadow. Enoch could not make out a face, nor the color of its skin. He could only see its outline. Its shoulders were broad and heavy, its waist thin and physique masculine. Beside the shadowy figure was a dark and mysterious hole that stood vertically and whose depth reached for all eternity. Enoch's heart began to flutter like the beating wings of a butterfly. He could feel it knocking on his chest. The acclivity of emotion that swirled within his soul wanted to explore the mysteries that were within the black hole, but his mind felt differently. What lay on the other side he could not see. Was it death? If he were to follow the pull of his heart, would he ever return to the place that he loved? Or would he be lost in the endless bounds of curiosity, never finding his way home? All these things and more, he thought, and he wondered where the voice that called his name was now. Enoch took a step forward, the pace of his beating heart getting ever faster. Another step he took, and then one more. He looked at the cumbersome adumbrate, but he did not fear its unyielding presence of power. Instead, his mind was at ease. Enoch closed his eyes and let the darkness consume him.

Enoch's eyes unhinged from the clasp of fear, but his heart kept its rolling beat. He could see the earth and the heavens, the ways the wind moved, and the pattern of the ocean's flow. Then he gazed upon the expanse that was forever, but he could see its ends. The four winds he could see, which bound the earth to the heaven and the heaven to the earth. The shadow that stood before the endless portal now stood beside Enoch. The shadow strode forward and gestured for him to follow. Enoch was hesitant with nerves snapping like bolts of light, sending signals to his brain—all the signs of caution and prudence. He took a deep breath and followed the towering figure, and the creature told him where he was.

"Steady your heart, Enoch, for this is not your death. You are in the bounds of Empyrean and Terra, see how the two are held together?" Below was the foundation of the earth and the four winds which bear the firmament of heaven. The four pillars of fire, vibrant and glorious, connected the worlds to one another. Enoch's mind marveled at the sights that were before him, and he began to write all that he saw and all that was told to him with the light of his pen. The apparition spoke again, its voice full and imposing.

"See everything that takes place in the Highest, how they do not change their orbits, how they rise and set in the order in which they were destined, and how they never waiver from their purpose. It is the same upon the world in which you live, how the season of the summer comes as it should, so too the winter. Observe the purpose of the oceans, the clouds and even the dew that rest upon the grass on a mild morning of a summer day. Note the trees and how they bear fruit, and see the rivers and clear lakes; observe how they give sustenance and never falter from their design. Hold in mind these are eternal as they do not sin against their cause." The eternal being paused as Enoch scanned the grand design, and then the eidolon continued. "Now behold the people of the world. Their sins vary in severity, and in their transgressions, the world which is for them to do as they will, suffers, and so too they suffer, and thus their days upon the earth are numbered. You can see now, even before you came here, that your home will soon burn bright in reds and orange and then fall dull in gray and be buried in the blackness."

Enoch saw his home. The edifice of the clouds and their dissolving end, the welcoming of the seasons and how they circled one another, being one, but never one. He saw the portals of the sun and the moon, and how the earth waltzed with the moon, and how the earth and the moon danced with the sun like the slow and steady course of a fox-trot. His eyes wept at the beauty of the bond between the heaven and the earth; to him it was the magnum opus—a design pure and exalted, without flaw, eternal and everlasting.

"Do not drip the salted tears within your eyes for there is more for you to see, but now you must go and tell those of what you have witnessed. When you speak the words you have scribbled with your pen, many will hurl imprecations at you, and you will be very much alone. Keep those closest in your heart with a firm grip, for even they may waiver in the howl of the terror in the wind of the storm. Go in peace, Enoch," said the spiring spirit as he opened a portal which was dark and endured forever and ever. Enoch closed his eyes and walked again into the blackness.

When he cracked open the lids of his eyes and absorbed the colors of the world with them, he first glimpsed the massive stone structure of the ministry building. He then moved his eyes across the city, examining every detail of every building, of every drop of water, and of every blade of grass. What he had just encountered, between the meeting of the stars and the earth, transformed him. His mind narrowed and sharpened, like a thread through a needle, and his heart was the bellowing belly of a dormant volcano come to life. It ran full of passion, never to be stopped until he stopped himself.

Dawn had struck the wet and dreary night as Enoch entered his home. The cricketing of the crickets and the ribbiting of the frogs, still sang the song of the night, but the music of the day was slowly and quietly playing its melody. The birds chirped and chattered, the buzz of the bees batted the breeze, and the song of the morning came to life. Enoch heated some water and tossed in some leaves for a cup of tea. He took out the pots and the pans, the sugar and spices and filled the room with the smell of sweet honey and golden cinnamon. He clinked and clattered the glasses and plates and set the table for three. All the while, a creature was stirring. Its hair was mangled and tossed, its voice mumbled and low, and it moved like the walking dead.

"Good morning, Erie," said Enoch with drooping eyes and a grin across his face.

"Morn, Dad," Erie said incomprehensibly and took a seat at the table. Enoch handed her some juice and laid an overflowing plate of food in front of her. With closed eyes, she gave her father a smile and began devouring her breakfast.

Enoch was leaning over the stove, tossing ingredients into the pan when he felt the soft hands of his wife caress him from behind. He could feel her warm body under her silk nightgown, and his mind and soul rose to a gentle but insistent simmer.

"Good morning, and thanks for making me breakfast," Heilagr said to him. Enoch grabbed her hand that laid on his chest and kissed her long and delicate fingers.

"Let me get you some tea. I'm almost done making your breakfast," he said, and handed her a soothing cup of mint green tea with steam that rose in swirls and cavorted around her face. To Enoch, and most others, Heilagr always seemed statuesque. From sun up to sun down her look was flawless and natural. He marveled at her as he reflected upon himself, his hair gray, messy, and without structure; the scar about his neck that would never fade; or the small wrinkles forming around his face. *I love getting old,* he thought to himself and set the plates of food for Heilagr and himself on the table.

As he sat down to eat, Erie had risen from her seat and let out a booming belch. Enoch looked at her, impressed and repulsed at the same time. She cleaned her plate and was back to her perky and loving self. She skipped over to her father and gave his cheek a peck of love.

"Thanks, Daddy. It was sublime!" she said with gratitude. She was about to dismiss herself when the three of them heard a noise coming from the entrance of the house. Enoch got up from his seat to see what was causing the commotion, and his eyes hit the sight of a man.

"Uriel!" Enoch shouted joyously. His son locked eyes with his father's.

"Hi, Dad. It smells great in here—anything left for me?" Uriel asked. With his hands full of bags and luggage, his sister came running down to greet him, jumped on his chest, and held him tightly as if she were climbing a tree.

"Uriel! I've been reading all about you and your travels since you've been gone." She released him and took a bag out of his hands. "I'm so glad you're home."

"Give him some space, Erie; let the boy breathe a bit," said Heilagr. Uriel walked over to his mother and embraced her.

"Hi, Mom," was all he said.

"Welcome home, son." She released her embrace. Enoch grabbed some of his luggage and wrapped his arm around his son as they walked to his room to set the bag there for his stay.

"I wasn't expecting you so soon, son. Is everything okay?" Enoch asked.

"Everything is great. I thought I would surprise you by coming home early. I hope I didn't interrupt anything," said Uriel.

"That's nonsense. Of course you didn't. Come to the kitchen, and I'll cook you up something quick," he said to his son. The family talked briefly and caught up with one another as quickly as they could, never managing to say anything significant as they all had duties to attend to.

Enoch, exhausted and without sleep, steamed the shower room to awaken his body into alertness to take on the struggle of the day. Somewhat refreshed from the steam of the shower, he once more put on his robes to assemble with the ministry for the last time until the new month. Erie had asked to go with him as she was attempting to become a minister herself.

"Erie, are you ready?" Enoch tapped on her door, still waiting for his daughter. The lighted door evaporated.

"All set, Daddy," she said.

"Are you sure you want to go? It's going to be a very difficult few hours," he said to her.

"I'm absolutely sure, dad. If you don't mind, I'd like to shadow you more often if I could."

"If that is what you want, we can arrange that, but we'll discuss that later. We best get going," Enoch said to her. They quickly said their goodbyes and walked out the door. He grabbed his daughter's hand and visesated to the octangular building. Enoch and his daughter sat in his office as he informed her about what would be happening in today's session.

"Now, I know you are an orator of great skill and can debate your case eloquently, but I need you to hold your tongue. Only the future will understand the purpose of today," Enoch said.

"I understand, Daddy. My lips will be sealed." She put her thumb and index finger up to her mouth and made a motion as if to zip them shut. The two left the office and walked the silent halls of the ministry. Enoch watched his daughter watch the blooming of the flowers as they were struck by the beauty of the waves of the sun. They entered the hall of ministers; Enoch took his seat at the forefront of the hall while his daughter took a seat in the back behind the seated ministry. Enoch knocked the stone down onto the surface and called the session to begin. Enoch introduced the session.

"After yesterday's vote, we are here today to lay out a plan of action on events that may occur due to our decision. Olav, Steinar, Oystein and myself will hold the floor today. Each of us will have fifteen minutes to discuss the impacts on our economy, military and culture. Once the hour is up between the four of us, if any minister would like to question or advance the conversation, there will be a thirty-minute window for that. I ask that if there be any discussion after the hour that the minister who is speaking only speak for a minute and a half as we would like to get everyone's concerns or advice. Minister Olav, you have the floor."

Forty-five minutes had quickly gone by with periods of applause, expressions of decry, and moments of deep thought. Enoch rose from his seat to speak to his friends and colleagues. The room was without noise; only the occasional breeze would pass to whisper words.

"No matter how we voted yesterday, the outcome will be the same. I have been told that our waters will run like crimson and splatter the earth in blood. Our lands will burn a fire orange, and the world will fall dark and gray. The grass upon the land will turn to ash, and the trees will hold no roots. All this and more I have been told. I ask you to feel the brush of the wind, the push of the flowing river and see how they never falter from their course. See how the sun and the moon rise and fall, and the seasons come when they are beckoned. They have held true to the Lord, something we have not done for a long time. Sin is a very powerful thing, and the outcomes of our choices are our own. For every decision made, there is a consequence, and for far too long, we have made the wrong decisions. Our great planet is connected to the heaven in a way you cannot see because we have all blinded ourself from the truth. The more we continue to transgress, the more we destroy ourselves and our connection with the stars. I have seen the four winds that hold the worlds together and know that if we do not act and do not correct our course to that which is good, then we and those who come after us will suffer in a lifetime of darkness. Ready your bows, and harness your light, for the world will need them very soon. This is what I warn you. This is the word of Truth."

No one liked the words that rang from the mouth of Enoch. The room of ministers made their emotions heard with a symphony of malice and ill-gotten remarks. Enoch listened to the anger and frustration within their voices.

"You are no prophet, Enoch, and what you speak is heresy," shouted a minister in green robes. Olav, Steinar, and Oystein held their tongues as the jeering continued.

"We as a nation have not fought a war in a thousand years! And if you think the Hollen or any other nation will fight us on the field of battle, in our own land, and defeat us, then you are delusional, Enoch!" shouted another minister.

Enoch locked eyes with his daughter's and motioned her to leave the room. He then pummeled the stone into the base, calling the session to an end and visesated into his office. As he appeared, Erie walked into the room, followed by Olav, Oystein, and Steinar.

"Erie, get what you need; we are going home. Gentlemen, the words I said upon the stand are true. Steinar and Oystein, when we meet next month, we need war game strategies and game theory analytics for the coming storm ahead. Olav, try to win over as much support as you can, and I will see you all in a couple weeks. We may have to look for external sources for help should we be a divided nation as it seems we may be. Thank you all so much for your help and friendship. We'll talk over lightletters." Enoch took the orb from his office that rested on his desk as Erie grabbed his hand, visesating them into the wind.

Lorena Chapter One

The sun shined bits of yellow strings that struck through the open window, drawing silhouettes of dancing bodies shuffling back and forth to the music of the tap and knock of thin silver sabers. Tiptoe, tap, knock the anthem in the air vibrated in the white room with chipped paint and exposed brick bouncing off the cracked wooden hard floors. Tiptoe, tiptoe, tap, knock, a different verse to the same anthem quivered in the room of the swordsmen, one frustrated by the lack of performance, the other composed and well mannered. The duelers held their thin swords vertical in front of their masked faces and then whipped the blade extending it to their sides, bowing to one another. Each of them withdrew their helmets and shook each other's hand. "Five to zero little brother. Try again tomorrow?" Lorena asked, tapping her sword on her brother's shoulder. Her light brown hair ran down her back as she waved it around trying to give it character, waiting for her brother to respond.

"I can't tomorrow. Aedus and I have plans," he said.

"How are you going to get any better if you don't practice Abe?" Lorena asked in a teasing voice, trying to make her brother feel guilty.

"Pout those blue green eyes all you like. I got my butt kicked today, no need to get it kicked tomorrow," said Absolume with sweat dripping down his brow.

Lorena laughed at him. "Fine then, I'll just return your birthday gift, and Ae just became my favorite brother," she said, jokingly whipping her hair into her brother's face as she pranced away.

"Weirdo," he said in a rather hushed voice.

"I heard that!" Lorena yelled back to him.

"Good!" Absolume shouted.

Lorena removed her fencing equipment from her body and rinsed her face in the washroom but didn't bother showering. She brushed out her hair to untangle and smooth it, and then lifted it into a bun, stabbing it with a small sword to hold it in place. She glided into a pink halter tank leotard with matching shorts to go over them and kicked on a pair of white leg warmers and shoes that looked like silk slippers. She quickly stowed away her protective suit and saber into her snow-white fencing bag and waited for her brother outside the mens' shower room.

Absolume finally exited the washroom. His hair was styled, waving to one side with a few strands out of place; his blue eyes swirled like the ocean. His beard was short and rough, and his tall body fit and toned. Lorena was quick to mess the hair on his head.

"Finally. You took forever," she said to him.

"You're really annoying sometimes, you know that?" he said, slightly irked by his sister's nagging love.

"Come on, drive me to ballet, or I'm going to be late," she said, ignoring his statement. The siblings walked outside to the crisp bite of the frigid air and headed to her car. Lorena put her hand on the handle of the door as it read her print and unlocked her vehicle. The hovercraft was a long-bodied automobile with wide, rounded features. Its color was Roman red with white coves on both sides, streaming from the front hover pods to near the back end of the hover pods. It had four silver lights in the front and a menacing grill with silver bars like teeth. They hopped into the all-red interior, and the car rumbled to life. Though the weather was frigid, Absolume decided to drop the top down from the craft.

"What are you doing? It's freezing outside!" Lorena scolded her brother, expecting to be warmed by the hovercraft.

"It's beautiful outside. I thought I'd drive in the open air," said Abe.

"Give me your jacket then."

"Fine. Here." Absolume tossed her his coat.

"Jerk." The two drove off with the wind brushing their faces, a soft red on their cheeks. Lorena's nose began to sniffle from the cold air running across her face. She put on a pair of white fuzzy ear muffs to keep her ears from burning. The lighted soft blue roads were quiet for a weekend, as they traveled down wide roads and narrow streets. As they drove, they saw a cherry red classic car coming from the opposite direction. It had two bold racing stripes down its center and two doe-eyed headlights. Its grill looked like the open mouth of a whale, and its engine roared thunderously through the city. Its top was down as well, and the driver gave a few friendly honks of the horn as it sped down the empty road.

"You two are idiots. Why on earth do you and Aedus think it's a great idea to drive with the tops down when its forty degrees outside?" Lorena said with chattering teeth.

"Cuz were boys, and it's fun. I wonder where he's rushing off to?" Absolume said with a slight smile.

"Who cares, I'm freezing. Take this right; it's a shortcut." Absolume took the right and made a few small turns down side roads, finally arriving at Lorena's ballet studio. "Thanks, Abe. I'm taking your jacket with me," she said.

"That's fine. Am I picking you up?" he asked her.

"No, I have hoplology after this. I'll take the transit home," Lorena answered.

"Alright. See you at home then."

"Don't scratch the car, or I'll kill you," she said as her brother took off, waving his hand in the air to say goodbye. Lorena shook her head in annoyance.

She entered her studio; it wasn't much warmer than it was outside. *At least it's not windy in here,* she thought as she took off her brother's jacket and put on her ballet point shoes. She laid out her bleach white mat and began doing some light stretching exercises for her feet and the muscles and joints around that area. She then moved on to relax the muscles and joints in her quads and hips, raising her leg into the air and then pulling it to the side, then alternating to the other leg. After five minutes of warming up on the mat, she moved over to the ballet barre to finish her exercise routine. Her instructor came in just as she was finishing her warmup with a short and scrawny teenaged boy who had a particularly large and pointy nose, and a few other members of the symphony.

"Good afternoon, Mrs. Pavlova," Lorena greeted her teacher.

"Hello, dear. How are you doing today?" her instructor asked.

"I'm doing great. Ready to get started. How are you doing, Sebastian?"

"Good," he said in a coy and timid manner, avoiding eye contact as he headed towards the grand piano. Lorena smirked at his mannerisms, thinking they were odd but cute. She said hello to the other instrumental players and then readied herself for her performance. The music began to play. The violins were rapid and short-noted, the bells chimed giving an angelic like sound to the majestic dance, and the piano gave the mood of elegance as Lorena turned and kicked in a graceful choreograph. From developpe to balancé, from turn to turn and into a Grande Jeté from one end of the room to the other, she moved exquisitely. Her legs were lean and strong as they flexed and relaxed throughout the routine, and her movements were precise but not without humanity and emotion. Lorena dreamed to be Prima, a title that hadn't been given in nearly a century.

"Lorena, my dear, you are absolutely marvelous today. However, when you are coming down on the Grande Jeté, try to land more softly, like a cat jumping from a tree, soundless almost," said Anna, her instructor. Lorena moved back into position for the movement, and attempted again. "Softer dear, softer," said Anna, and again she tried, and then once more. "There it is Lorena, there it is," her instructor said with gratitude. Lorena, slightly out of breath and a bit tired, smiled as she rested her hands upon her hips. "Now Lorena, let's work on the tempo; you need to be a little faster my dear. Your movements are beautiful, but the pace needs to be quicker. Did you notice sometimes you're a little behind the music? Let's fix that."

Lorena pushed her body until she satisfied herself and her instructor. Her mind focused only on perfection, never believing she couldn't achieve it.

"You did well today, Lorena. If you want the lead for *The Raven*, then you must master this solo piece, and I think you will have it my dear. Good job. I'll see you in two days." Anna kissed her checks and left the room. Lorena's heart was still racing from the dance and fluttered with passion at the thought of lead for *The Raven*. Her heart was filled with fire, as her mind was filled with dreams. Her eyes could see her fate; all she had to do was take it.

Lorena showered off the salt of her sweat that laid on her skin from the movement in her arts, and let her body repose and her mind fall empty. The pitter-patter of the water hit her body and dripped down the delicate lines of her skin as the droplets found their way to the floor and twirled down the drain. The steam of the shower filled the room like fog resting on the dewy plains. She took a few deep breaths, her mind and body refreshed and alert as she listened to the sound of a leaky faucet keeping beat to a song that never played. Lorena quickly put on a fresh pair of clothes, stowed away her ballet attire, and stepped back outside into the chill autumn air. The lighted lines bordering the roads started to glow as the sun began to dip closer to the horizon. She walked a couple blocks, letting the leaves dance at her feet as they rustled in the gentle touch of the breeze and walked inside a coffee shop called The Rabbit Foot. The music played softly a rhythmic blue beat in the dimly lit shop as the customers talked with one another.

"A turtle truffle latte please," Lorena requested. An older man with curly gray hair and a stout belly greeted her.

"Lo-lo, my beautiful Princess. It is an honor to serve you," said the elder man. Lorena gave a chuckle and a smile.

"I'm not really your princess, you know. I don't inherit anything, nor do any of my brothers," she said to the shop keep.

"You are more a princess than anyone in the world Lo-lo. Your family has been chosen not once, but twice by the Lord to serve and to lead. To me and to many, you are our princess," the man said.

"You're always so sweet, Efiac. What do I owe you?" she asked.

"Do not worry about it. You are in here all the time."

"Are you sure?"

"Lorena, I am sure. Just as I am sure I will see you two days from now. Now go on my Princess," he demanded in kindness.

"Thanks, Efiac. I'll see you around."

"Goodbye, my Princess," the old man said as Lorena exited the shop.

As she walked through the city, the streets grew louder with the stomps of feet that percussed from the people and the screeches of tires that berated the ears, and brakes of the cars and hovercrafts that sound like nails on a chalkboard. Bunaitheoir had slowly come to life. Her marbled eyes darted at the sights and sounds around her, and she gathered every detail from them, noting what was happening and where it was happening. She then saw a sign that read "Arc" and turned down the quiet street. The buildings were old and had seen generations come and go. The brick clad in sandstone as well as brick clad in marble structures ran down the entire road, each having a distinct purpose, and all waving the flag of Saoirse. Time had weathered them and the buildings, but their presence was as bold as the tallest skyscrapers. In front of her institute was a bronzed statue of a man named Alexander, who held a sword in his right hand and rode on the back of a lion. Underneath them was a map of the world with writing that read, *Upon the conduct of each depends the fate of all.* She tapped the lion on the head as if to pet it and walked up the stairs for her hoplology lesson.

The rooms were lit with clear bulbs whose filaments burned bright. Inside the historic building were busts of the greatest military strategists from all nations and all eras, and mounted on the walls were paintings twenty to thirty feet in length with a width just as long of battles that changed the tides of war. The cherry oak floors looked untouched, but she could hear their age as they creaked and whined at their points of weakness. She entered a large room with red wooden beams whose walls were dressed in sculpted maps. In the middle of the room was a round table with a large opening at its center. Lorena took her seat and unpacked her study materials. Seconds later, her teacher walked into the war room. He was an older man with dark skin and very short gray hair. His eyes were dark and deep and paralleled his voice. He had a faint but noticeable scar that ran down his lips. The man's appearance, even in old age, was menacing, but his spirit was of humility and extreme kindness.

"General Westmore," she greeted him cordially.

"Good evening, Lorena. How is your day going?" he asked in his sunken baritone voice.

"It's been tough, but productive. Just how I like it. How's your day been?" she asked him.

"Quiet and peaceful. Just how I like it. Are you ready for today's lesson?" Westmore asked.

"Let's get to it," she said optimistically. The general synced a device he wore on his wrist to the table Lorena was sitting at. The edge of the table illuminated a neon blue, signaling the device was paired, and projected a three-dimensional map in the center of the round table. The map quickly narrowed into a city that was barricaded with twenty-foot walls with an army of 30,000 men. Just outside the walls of the great city was an opposing army of only 10,000 men.

"So, Lorena, this is one of the most iconic battles in all of history. This is—" Westmore was cut off.

"The Battle of Jericho," Lorena interrupted.

"Indeed, it is," he said with admiration in his voice. "Now do you know how the Telkinites were able to siege the entire city while only losing a thousand men?"

"I don't know much of the battle at all, except that the sound of their arrival rattled the bones of the enemy, and quickened their hearts and made the mind mad with fear. All the romantic and poetic gestures you see in the reels," she answered.

"Well, I can tell you that there is no romance in battle. There is only the cold blade of tragedy. Nor is their poetry to war, only the prose of reality. The saving grace in war, with all its faults, is truth, for in the end it always rises," General Westmore lectured.

"Sounds like you have a romantic relationship with it," she teased the general.

"We are merely acquaintances in the epic of time," he said with a slight grin on his face. "Now, let's discuss how General Joshua Nun was able to sack a city while outnumbered three to one, and did so in just two days' time." The lesson went on for an hour and a half, and covered several key issues about the battle, from advanced weaponry, to cutting off supply routes, starving the occupants out and ransacking the city at incredible speed with uncanny precision. The neuron pathways within Lorena's mind traveled like lightning moving through the storm of a cloud and struck the prefrontal cortex, welding it to memory.

"Well, our time is up." The general handed her a book. "I want you to read chapters eight and nine. They are not too long, maybe thirty to thirty five pages. We'll talk about them in the next lesson."

"I'll see you in a few days, General." She placed the book in her already full bag. "Have a good night, sir." She leaned into the gentle giant and gave the old man a hug. "Oh, I almost forgot. My dad said he wanted to talk to you and to give him a call, and he also said to give you this." She unzipped a small pocket on the front of her bag and handed him a folded piece of paper in the shape of a star.

"Thank you, Lorena. I'll be sure to call him." The teacher and the student parted ways, and once more Lorena was back in the algid air. She put on a pair of soft pink and white mittens, and pushed on the wrist of the glove, warming them to warm her hands.

The stars were out, but they were barely visible as the buildings and streetlights outshined their glory. She had walked a few blocks and was about to take the stairs leading to the train underground when she heard a familiar honk and howl. She looked up and saw the cherry red convertible glistening in the streetlights.

"Loo-li!!" came a shout from the car. She walked towards the car and rolled her eyes.

"Hey Ae. What are you doing here?" she asked her brother.

"Was just heading home and thought you might need a ride. Hop in," he told her.

"Thanks, Ae," Lorena smiled.

"Anything for my favorite sister," he said as if he had another. The power of the car shook their bodies as it reverberated through Bunaitheoir. Soon, the glimmer of the city lights faded away, and the luminesces of the stars guided them home.

The siblings opened the palace doors of the fabled castle they called home. As they entered the room of seasons, their eyes were drawn to the leaves hanging from the birch trees that filled the entryway as they displayed a rainbow of colors with the dim lights of the lamprog resting on their white branches. Lorena and Aedus walked the ancient and glorious halls and passed rooms the size of houses, until they reached Absolume who was in the dining room setting the table for his family while singing a traditional Saoirse song that struck the drum of the ear in a pitch that was offsetting. Lorena and Aedus looked at each other and laughed at his wretched melody.

"It's better than the lot of you can sing," said Absolume. Aedus and Lorena's stomachs began to ache from the rapid tightening of the ab muscles as they giggled with fervor.

"Aedus, is that you?" yelled a voice from the other room.

"Yes, Mum. Some girl is with me, too. She's a bit weird, but I think you'll like her," he answered back. Lagertha came through the door of the other room with a grand smile on her face that quickly turned to a frown of disappointment.

"I thought you might have actually brought a girl home. Way to get my hopes up, but you are right, I do like the girl next to you very much," she said.

"Were you down stairs helping to cook?" asked Lorena.

"Of course. You know I don't consider myself above anyone. Besides I thought Mrs. Cocaire could use some help in the kitchen," Lagertha said. "Now sit down, dinner is coming up."

"Hey, Dad," Lorena said as Robert walked through the same door his wife had come from.

"Hey Lolo, how was your day?" he asked.

"You know, the usual. Very busy and very productive. How was yours?" she asked.

"About the same. Maybe with a little more stress." The doors to the dining room swung open, and the food smelled of autumn spices as it spun around the dinner table, setting the room in a cozy and relaxing state, full of love and bliss. The evening passed on as they talked about their days and what tomorrow held. They laughed at one another and with one another until their stomachs were full and their minds tired.

"Hey Lo, I have something for you. Good luck with this one." Robert handed her an envelope.

"Is it a riddle?" she asked. "Or a puzzle?"

"You'll see when you open it. Let me know when you solve it," her father answered.

It wasn't long until the family grew weary from the long day and set themselves to bed. As the family slept, Lorena lay awake looking at the envelope her father had given her, and slid her finger across its seal revealing its contents. Inside was a sheet of paper. She looked at it, turned it over, looked at its corners and its boarders, but nothing was there. There was no writing, no drawing; it was blank. She thought it could be some sort of riddle, and in her thoughts, her eyes began to droop, and her mind began to wander. She put the paper back inside the envelope, closed her green blue eyes, and let the subconscious consume the conscious.

Yefimovich Chapter Two

The water floated in the air as a shield around the goal. Held together with his body and mind by a Mahyeem man. Two opposing players were flying towards him, one propelled by fire coming from his fists and feet. The other had hurled himself through the sky by rapidly and aggressively changing the ground below him into a colonnade, causing him to glide through the air like a bullet from a gun. Yefimovich stood on his feet as he saw from the corner of his eye that the time was reaching the final minutes of the game. The Eshan player shot fire from his hands like balls from a cannon, evaporating the water that guarded the net. The Mah player struggled to congeal the liquid, trying desperately to keep his opponent from scoring, gathering droplets within the air and clouds, and piecing back together his wall of water. As the water bower was rebuilding his wall, he saw that the Ada player was losing velocity as he approached the goal, and formed the water into a sphere and hurled it at the player as if it were coming from a siege engine. The massive marble of spinning water struck the earth bower, causing him to lose the ball and fall back down to the earth. "Nooo!" shouted Yefimovich, his heart racing from the excitement.

The fire coming from the fire bower now turned to lightning, and he seemed to move like it as well as he pursued the falling ball. He darted through the open air, like the bends and cuts of a bolt of fulmination, reaching the ball before it hit the ground. He looked like a rocket as he screamed across the sky, being joined by an air bower who seemed as weightless as a feather. The two charged head on, and coming towards them was a Mahyeem who floated on clouds of water, and an earth bower who had created planting stones with the floating boulders in the field.

The Ada player began to toss the stones at the elusive Eshan, as the water bower hurled wave upon wave at the Avi Player. The earth bower then began to form a vice around the fire bower, laying stone upon stone onto his body as the Eshan struggled to fly across the sky. When all seemed lost for the fire bower, the Ada player was grabbed from the ankles by cuffs made of stone and dragged down to the earth, much like a whip snaps the air. At the same time, the air bower moved the wind with the force of a hurricane, causing the water bower to tumble to the earth with his teammate. The Eshan, sweat pouring from his skin, kicked the ball forcefully at the opponent's goal, hitting the back of the net, giving them three points and the victory as the final seconds clicked, and the buzzer sounded. The crowd was elated as they sang, "The Marching Saints," and tossed confetti into the air in joyous celebration. Yefimovich sang along with the crowd.

"We are the Saints, the Marching Saints
We are here for Victory
How you'll want, to be in this number
When the Saints come marching in
Oh, when the Saints, come playing drums
Oh, when the saints sound victory,
How you'll want to be in this number
Oh, when the Saints come marching in
Oh, when the Saints, come burning bright
Oh, when the Saints light up the night
How you'll want to be in this number
Oh, when the Saints come marching in!" Yefimovich sang at the top of his lungs with a surprisingly powerful singing voice. He looked over at his daughter who was cheering and singing alongside her father. Her light strawberry blond hair ran down her back, and her smile was wide and drew the attention of anyone who saw its perfection. Her brown eyes were sweet as chocolates, and her lips like cotton which no man had kissed. Father and daughter embraced in happiness, jumping up and down at their team's championship victory.

Yefimovich and Yekaterina waited in their suite as the people slowly and ecstatically exited the stadium with voices of jubilee. As the stadium noise became a hushed murmur, they left the comforts of the box suite and headed to their vehicle. Like all the transporters in Yisra, it was without tires and hovered in the air. The body was streamlined in a metallic silver color with doors trimmed in copper. Its windows were tinted dark black to keep the beating sun from heating up the car, and its lights beamed a sky blue. Before Yefimovich and his daughter could enter their hovercraft, they were surrounded by their fellow citizens, "Yekaterina! Katerina! Kat!" the people shouted. Though Yefimovich was the most powerful man in the country and the Prime Minister of Yisra, it was his daughter who was rained with all the attention, for she was holy, and could control all the elements of the world. "Tulku! Tulku!" they shouted. Yekaterina stopped and greeted the men, women, and children who adored her. She took holovids and holopics as well as signed autographs on shirts, shorts, and anything the people had available. After fifteen minutes, her hand began to cramp from writing, and her cheeks began to ache from smiling. She waved goodbye to all that treasured her, and left with her father in the quiet comfort of their transporter.

The city was void of brick or cement roads, but was covered in trillions of sand particles that always circuited with the subtle touch of the wind. The earth bowers would flatten and harden the desert sands and pave the way for people to move about the city, which looked as if it were made from confectionary sweets. The buildings were of bright and vivid colors with domes that looked like the buds of flowers or of an upside-down onion; some even resembled that of an ice cream cone. They were striped and multicolored and made the city feel as if the magic of the world was held within it. The roads in which the Adamah formed had designs of their own. Some streets had triangles that intersected one another, forming a star, and the design would flow until the road was no more. Each district had designs ingrained on their roads, and they correlated with the subculture of that district. The main roads, which lead to the Citadel, were crafted in such a way that when they reached the city center, the compositions of those roads formed a complete picture, uniting the city as one people.

Yefimovich loved to see his city full of life. The men and woman gathering in bars after the match, grabbing candies from the local shops, or standing in long lines for pirozhki. His stomach growled at the site of the pirozhki. He could taste the sweet pastry that wafted in the air, filled with potatoes, meat, cabbage and cheese—to him it was the best traditional Yisraian food he could ever have.

"Hey Aero, let's make a quick stop at Vypechka i Pelmeni, I'm absolutely starved," said Yefimovich.

"Yes, sir."

"Dad, that line is forty feet long. We'll be here all night," Yekaterina tried to point out to her father.

"Well, it's a good thing I placed an order thirty minutes ago," he gave a wink at his daughter. "You see that Aero; just because she's the Tulku, she thinks she's smarter than her old man." He wrapped his arm around Katerina as she rolled her calming brown eyes at him. He quickly exited the hovercraft as Aero was quick to follow and quickly came back with a pirozhki stuffed in his mouth.

"It's nice to see you so light hearted, Dad," Yekaterina noted to her father.

"It's nice to not think about running the country for a couple hours," he smiled back. "But when we get back home, reality will set in once again, and all the thoughts of the world will be on my mind once more."

The sun had fallen below the horizon, as they approached Sesom Palace. The lights shined gently on the white and blue building with its gold statues, golden arches, and gold column bases. The country's flag flew proudly in the cool desert breeze, resting high atop the palace Yefimovich and his family called home.

"Home, sweet home, sir," said Aero.

"There is almost no better sight than thee," he said.

"Don't get all teary eyed, Dad. We still have another year here," Yekaterina reminded him as the car stopped and rested at the palace entrance.

"Thanks for the ride, Aero. Tell your beautiful wife we said hello," said Katerina.

"It's a shame she couldn't come. Tell her she is always welcome," Yefimovich said.

"Thank you both. I'll let her know. Goodnight, Ms. Katerina. Goodnight, Prime Minister," said the soldier.

"Goodnight!" Yefimovich and his daughter replied in unison. As the two entered the lavish circular entrance with marbled floors and columns dancing with colors of white, gold, and amber, they were greeted by the kind and subtle voice of Rivka.

"Good evening you two! How was the game? I watched some of it on the Holo. It looked incredible," she said as she took Yefimovich's jacket.

"Ms. Rivka, it was totally amazing! I've never seen such an exciting match," said Katerina.

"You know I'm not into all that. I'm glad you had fun, little Kat," she said.

"Well next time, we're forcing you to come, and my darling wife," Yefimovich said jokingly. "Speaking of my wife, how is she feeling?"

"She's better than she was this morning. She was so upset she couldn't make it to the match," Rivka said with a frown on her face.

"I'd better go check on her," he said, and he left the entryway as his daughter and Rivka continued to chatter.

Yefimovich could hear the harsh coughs from his wife as he quietly entered the grandeur of his bedroom. The light of the room was dim and made him feel at home in the great space of the large palace. He looked at his beautiful wife. Her eyes were red and swollen from lack of sleep. Her bedside was a mountain of tissues and medicine, but even at her weakest, he loved the woman he saw before him.

"Oh, Viktoriya. You look beautifully dreadful." He poked fun at her, and even in her state of misery, she laughed at his terrible jest.

"How was the game?" she asked, her voice rough like gravel.

"I wish you could have been there; your daughter and I had a great time. You would have had a blast, but don't worry about that, how are you feeling?" Yefimovich replied.

"Slightly," she coughed, "better than this morning. I'm hoping the fever wears off by tomorrow morning. I can manage a sore throat."

"Well, don't make it any worse. I'll go—get you some tea and come in to bed. I've got a busy day tomorrow. I'll tell you about it in the morning." Yefi traveled downstairs to the first floor of the marvelous home, heated up some water, gathered some tea leaves into a small tea pod, and headed back upstairs to his adoring wife. As he opened the door, his hands full with scalding tea, he saw Viktoriya had already fallen asleep. He headed back out of his room to see if Yekaterina wanted the cup that was meant for her mother. He knocked on her door with a few faint taps to get her attention.

"Come in," she said, and her father entered. "Hey Dad, what's up?"

"Well, I've made your mother some tea, but by the time I went downstairs and came back up, she had already fallen asleep. So, I was wondering if you wanted it. It's chamomile."

"Thanks, Dad. You off to bed?" she asked as she took the tea setting from him.

"I'm exhausted, so yes. Do you want me to wake you in the morning?"

"No, I'm sure I'll be up before you. Do you want me to wake you?" she asked, knowing her father needed all the sleep he could get.

"Better not. I'm not sure how your mother will be feeling. The more she sleeps the better I think for now."

"If you change your mind, leave a note on the door. Goodnight, Dad. I'll see you in the morning," she said to her father.

"Goodnight, dear." He closed the door behind him and made his way back to his own bedroom. He quickly showered and changed into his nightwear being as quiet as he could, and snuffed out the lights that gave a soothing glow. He placed his head upon his pillow and let the lids of his eyes blot out the world, and what seemed like minutes later, he awoke in the darkness of a new day.

He lay in his bed, letting his body and mind adjust to the awakened state, and swept the dusted crust from his eyes. He looked over at his wife, who was still soundlessly asleep, and kissed her on the cheek. Yefimovich put himself together at a leisurely pace, making himself presentable to the world outside. As he slowly put on his blue suit that Rivka had laid out for him the night before, and laughed at the thought of him heading to the Citadel in nothing but his pajamas as the thought of his helplessness entered his mind.

Yefimovich made his way to the tea room, which was adorned with classical art from masters of years past, some even centuries old. He always took great joy in studying the paintings, the thought behind the picture, the brush strokes used, and the precision and focus to bring the image of the mind into the greatness of the world. Rivka had come into the room with a tray in hand.

"Good morning, sir," she said.

"Good morning, Rivka. I hope you got enough sleep," Yefimovich said with genuine concern.

"That's sweet of you, sir. I'm quite awake, though. I have your coffee here as well as the news of the day. I also brought your holodrive," she answered, presenting him with a small computer chip.

"You're the best, Rivka. I hope you had some coffee yourself."

"I've had a whole pot by now, sir," Rivka replied sarcastically with a smile across her face. "I'm going to check on Yekaterina. Have a good morning, sir." She left the room and left Yefimovich to his thoughts.

He placed the holodrive inside the breast pocket of his vest, and scanned the early news of the day. "Another one," he said to himself as he looked at the headline that read, *Braunhemds Attack Hate Speech*. There was an image under the headline of a man in his early twenties. His left eye was swollen shut, his lip cut and swollen like a balloon as blood ran down his mouth.

"Good morning, Dad." The sweet voice of his daughter shook his mind from the evil of the world.

"Good morning my dear. How did you sleep?" he asked.

"Blissfully," she said, scooping out the contents inside the mason jar she was holding.

"What is that?"

"Breakfast. It's got bananas, strawberries, chia seeds, cottage cheese," Yekaterina started to answer.

"Sounds healthy," Yefimovich interrupted in a dull tone.

"It's good. Want a taste?"

"No, that's alright. I'll pass," he said with a skeptical look on his face.

Moments later, Aero walked into the room. "Good morning, Prime Minister."

"Aero. Good morning chap. We ready to go?" Yefimovich asked.

"Yes, sir."

"Ready, Kat?" he asked.

"Let's go," she said, not fazed by the hour of the morning, nor by the fact that she wasn't finished eating. As they walked out of the augustness of the Sesom Palace, the tingle of desert air crept along their skin, and all that could be heard were the solemn moans of the breeze that flew invisibly around them.

"I've got the vetervykl all warmed up for you, Prime Minister," Aero said as the heat of his breath hit the frigid air, forming small clouds of vapor around him.

"Thank goodness. You'd think it's w-w-winter out here this morning," Yefimovich responded with a shiver down his spine. He and his daughter strapped themselves in the vehicle, and they set off for the city within a city they called the Citadel. The air traffic was light as too was the traffic on the ground. Yefimovich studied the layout of Erbil, how its roads were lined in patterns, how the ancient world gave path to the modern. The artistry of the interconnectedness of buildings and roads and the pipes beneath those roads that made way into the buildings and how they were all separate from one another but together made a structure of growth and prosperity for the people of Erbil and of the Citadel. He looked down at vivid colors of the city, though now, they were covered by the blanket of the darkness of the morning, and saw a large shadow of abandoned buildings that lay in center of the cities, between the Sesom Palace and the Citadel. He examined the structures around the forgotten land and noted the city could use a park—a place for hard working men and women to escape the stresses of the cities and enjoy the nature of the world around them. Before he could finish his designs for the park, Aero had already opened his door for him to exit and brought him back to more pressing matters that weighed heavy upon his people and the world.

He exited the vetervykl in his polished black shoes and trimmed suit with duck tails, and took two stones the size of his fist out of his pockets. He levitated the stones in front of him as they seemed to turn to liquid, and then molded them into an elegant cane bearing the symbol of his people and country.

"Do you really need the cane, Dad?" Yekaterina asked as if it were unfashionable.

"You never know when I might have to bop someone on the head with it," he said playfully.

Father and daughter entered the council chamber. The theme inside the room was of the elements of the world and how man could shape the world to better himself. If man were yin, then the elements were yang. If man were the darkness, then the elements were the light. If man were death, then the elements symbolized life. However, neither held purpose without the other. For what is man without nature except for flesh and bone? And what is nature without man except resources never to be mastered. When one becomes too extreme, its opposite must counter its weight and restore the balance of man and nature. The room was painted to show the extremes of both man and nature and its tranquility when the two are harmonized.

Yefimovich sat down at the head of the long rectangular table; his daughter sat as his counterpart on the other side. Not a single seat was empty; each chair was filled with either generals or council members, all of whom had stern looks upon their faces.

Yefimovich took his cane and reshaped it into a hammer and slammed it on the desk, startling some into alertness. He cleared his throat and spoke, giving himself a cadence so he would not stutter. "Good evening, ladies and gentlemen. We all know why we are here before the rise of the sun, under the soothing presence of the blue moon. Our now sister nation, Holle, is showing grave signs of unrest, and to many of us, is teetering on the edge of a revolution—revolution not of its own nation but of the nations that surround it. We have heard the rhetoric of the country's leaders for over seventeen years, and now they have been able to achieve power, and for the last year, how often have we seen reports of men and women beaten for having a different political opinion? What of the stories of the men and women of Holle who have gone missing, never to be heard from again? We have seen these signs before, and though the words and actions ring from different bells, they still hit the same resounding notes of misery heard long ago. In short, I am here to ask your wisdom on how we should proceed with the trouble we see, from our sister nation. General Iri, what is your opinion on the matter?"

The general stood from his seat and leaned over, placing his fists on the glossed table. His stance was aggressive, but his voice temperate. "This political power that has taken precedence in Holle has been strongly influencing its people for the last ten to twelve years. The schools from the nation have been indoctrinating its students from grade one up to the university level. They have been slowly curving its popular culture through literature, holoreels, and even its music. This political ideology has now been in power for nearly two years, and we can already see how it has influenced its own media in that short time. Though all the signs of tyranny show themselves, they are a free nation that has elected this government, and as long as they do not harm or threaten nations around them, we must be patient and do nothing." General Iri took his seat as the eyes of his peers looked at him in disgust.

General Dimitre stood from his chair, his voice more forceful than General Iri's.

"I must protest, General. For a man who does not act in the face of evil has himself committed evil, and he who tolerates the unjust is himself unjust. We as a people have a duty and moral obligation to smite the seeds of terror when they open from their shells. To not do so, we ourselves then would be committing terror." Dimitre sat down as some tapped their feet on the floor and knocked their fists on the table to show they approved of his statements. Generals Moeshe and Voz stood up at the same time. The twin brothers smiled at one another as Voz gave way to his brother Moeshe.

"Can you two stop playing around?" hollered Dimitre. "Speak!"

"Temper, temper, Dimitre. We all know your heart is made of stone. Let the cooler heads talk for a minute," Moeshe said. Dimitre grunted in frustration.

"Prime Minister. I believe it would be unwise for us to act against a nation that has shown us no immediate harm to our people. To influence or act in any aggressive manner towards them would immediately lead to war. This is something I think we would all like to avoid. I, and I'm sure my brother agrees, believe we should take full measure to ensure the safety of our people, and to do so, I suggest we fortify our borders and prepare defensively should Holle become aggressive towards us or our surrounding nations. I'd think it wise to consult Mr. Edik and our head of defense for strategy and budget." More knocks and thumps echoed in approval, and then the room fell silent, for the Tulku stood from her chair opposite her father.

"Prime Minister, council members, and generals, you all bring a point of view that is incredibly valuable to our success in this unfortunate circumstance. General Iri is right in that we must be patient, but so too is General Dimitre in regards to inaction, and I, too, agree that we should become defensively sound, not only around our borders, but within our towns and cities. However, I think more has to be done. We must not only inform our people of what we see in the near future, but we must warn our neighboring countries. We must form treaties that stipulate guidelines on what must be done should our countries fall into the horror of war, and I nominate myself to be the representative of our nation to travel to each country and negotiate these treaties." The hammering of fists and the stomping a feet was fulminating the room in the abundance of countenance. "What say you, Father?" Katerina asked.

"I say that it is my devoir and that I must go with you," Yefimovich answered.

"When do we leave, Prime Minister?" Yekaterina asked.

"We will leave at weeks end, but first we first must strategize the negotiations, before we approach these countries. Allies they may be, however, in the presence of war, an ally can easily become a distant friend, and sometimes even an enemy. Commander Zash, as secretary of defense, I request that you provide a plan of defense along with Mister Edik and Mr. Gosud. Please have an outline of your plan, with estimation of cost, before my daughter and I set out to strengthen our b-bonds with nearby countries." The commander nodded to Yefimovich that he understood. The meeting was then called to an end, and he and Yekaterina went to the top floor of the dome within the citadel and began engineering treaties for each individual country.

The sun rose and fell six times, circling the earth from east to west as Yefimovich unlocked his eyes to see the bloom of the morning's light. His heart raced at the pace of a snare drum, rolling steady notes of nervousness. He threw on a robe over his plaid pajamas and headed towards the sound of the delicate voices coming from the living room.

"Good morning, Yefi. We were beginning to think you were not waking up today," Viktoriya said kissing him good morning. She and Katerina were wearing courtly white dresses with their hair done up in a bun. Viktoriya's was held up by a thick gold band that had the symbol of the rooted pyramid crested upon it, and Yekaterina's was held by a thin gold band that lined its way up like vines on a tree.

"Ladies, you look absolutely spectacular today. I wish I could say the same about myself at the moment," Yefimovich quipped.

"Thanks, dear," Viktoriya blushed.

"It's two hours till noon, Dad. You might want to present yourself with a little more refinement before we leave. I don't think we'll win any hearts or strengthen any bonds wearing our pajamas," Katerina jested.

"At least I would be comfortable as they turned us away," he joked.

"I wouldn't imagine any of these meetings to be very comfortable, no matter what you are wearing. Now hurry up with your breakfast and get ready. You're already late," Viktoriya said, whipping her husband into shape.

The sands of time sped from the top of the hour glass to the bottom, and when the hour struck twelve, the sand circled within its capsule, neither rising nor falling until the first minute had passed. Outside, Aero was waiting with a fellow Avir soldier. The two men stood next to a large metallic spherical craft known as the Orbital One. Yefimovich stepped outside with his family and greeted the soldiers with a salute.

"Big day, sir," said Aero.

"An even bigger week," Yefimovich responded. "What's our flight time to Arpa?"

"No more than ten minutes—not long at all sir," said Aero as he began to draw lift to the craft. The Sphere began to spin, and the wind began to howl. There was a sharp crack in the air followed by the sonic percussion of the craft breaking the speed of sound. They ascended high into the heavens, traveling through the majesty of the clouds, reaching the ends of the earth, only to be held by the force of gravity from leaving its orbit. The world looked dazzling and brilliant as its blues, browns, whites, and greens pulled the eyes away from the dark and endless blackness of space that surrounded it. They had been in the sky no more than four minutes when a soft yellow light illuminated on the pilot's dashboard.

"Please make sure you are properly fastened as we are about to start our decent," radioed the co-pilot. There was a bright light that flashed white hot as the sphere came whistling down, back to the earth, and it did not seem to slow until it was very near the surface. The sand, dirt, and dust rolled away like a wave crashing on the shore, and the craft landed light as a feather.

"Welcome to Taj, Prime Minister, the capital of Arpa," said Aero.

"Great flying, boys. We'll see you in a few hours," Yefimovich said to them.

Yefimovich and his family, along with two guards, were welcomed by four Arpa diplomats who wore blinding white robes with a headdress they called a Ghandi cap. The four gentlemen bowed their heads forward as they received Yefimovich and his family as guests of the Rajah.

"Welcome, Prime Minister. It is an honor to host you sir," said one of the diplomats.

"Thank you for hosting me. I sincerely appreciate the time you and the Rajah have given me," he replied.

"We are happy to give it," said the man. "And we are incredibly humbled to be in the presence of the Tulku," the attaché said as he and the other three public officials fell to the floor in a bow to honor Yekaterina. She approached the men, stood in front of the diplomat that had been talking, and knelt down to his level.

"You need not worship me, for I am like you, a child of the Divine and a servant to the people. Now rise, and see me eye to eye, Man to Man, equals," Yekaterina said to them. The men rose from their feet.

"Though we both may be the creations of the Creator, your path and your destiny have been foretold and bear a strong and powerful burden; and for that reason, we will always bow in your presence, for the true fate of humanity is within your hands," said the man.

"I am no different than the Tulku who came before me, and though my comings are foretold, it does not mean your story is less significant. Your actions are a choice that interconnect the people and world around you. Your decisions ripple through the world much like a droplet ripples through still water. The initial strike is small, but very intense. It will strike to the very core of yourself and the people you hold most dear to your heart, and then that ripple grows far beyond what you could ever imagine, hitting the hearts and minds of everyone, everywhere because of you. So do not think the burden of the safety of humanity and its fate only rests with me, for you are accountable as well, and will be judged upon your actions."

"My Lady, forgive me, but there are many who believe you are more than just the Tulku of the past. There are great signs that show this to be true. There has never been a Tulku who could bend the light," the middle-aged diplomat said to her, being as polite as possible.

"The Engler's bend the light just as I do. I learned from Heilagr herself."

"The Engler's have always had the gift to manipulate the light into a physical form. Some think you are able to do more." The diplomat expressed his thoughts freely.

"I can only do as they do. I promise you," Yekaterina answered.

"As you say my Lady. I am sorry to have doubted you," said the humbled man.

"Do not be afraid to question, as it leads to reason, and only a fool denies reason," she said in response to the diplomat.

"Yes, my Lady." The man bowed his head. "Please this way. These vehicles will take you and the Prime Minister to see Rajah Harsha."

"What is your name sir? I never got it," Katerina asked.

"It is Sikhna," he told her.

"Thank you, Sikhna," she said as she entered the vehicle with her mother and father already inside.

"You're wise beyond your years, Kat," Yefimovich said to his daughter.

"Well, I learned from you—and books." He laughed, as did Viktoriya.

"I wouldn't give your father so much credit. It will go straight to his head," Viktoriya teased.

"Didn't you know they call me, Yefimovich the Wise?" he played along.

"Oh goodness, what have I done?" Yekaterina put her hand over her face in embarrassment. The transporters drove them through the distinguished city. Every street, every building, and every home was made from either mud bricks or clay. The craftsmanship of the architecture was like no other on earth. Its precision and calculated lines made for an artistic and elegant design which was marveled throughout the world, and at the end of the city was a white palace known as the Mausoleum. At its center was a great dome reaching nearly 250 feet and surrounded by four smaller domes with gold curling spires protruding through them. At the four corners of the stunning structure were four minarets that would beam a solid white light at night towards the center dome, and the dome would reflect the light, giving the structure a halo which the people called the crown of the Tulku. In front of the awe-inspiring building was a reflection pool that was 300 yards in length, lined with people who seemed to be praying or in deep meditation.

"Welcome to the Mausoleum, Prime Minister," Sikhna said.

"What an incredible piece of human ingenuity," Yefimovich said. "I've been here several times, and I am a-al-ways jaw dropped by the site of it."

"It is rumored that the first Tulku is buried in the crypt down below," Sikhna informed them.

"Rumored? It is not true then?" Yekaterina asked.

"The tombs have been searched many, many times, but no one has ever found any evidence that he was buried here," Sikhna answered her. They finally reached the staircase to the building's entrance which rose fifty feet to the building's ivory doors which looked small as it sat underneath an arch 150 feet tall.

As they walked to the throne room, Sikhna told them a story for every room they passed. Yefimovich could see his daughter was drawn to the lore, and then he heard something that he had forgotten entirely.

"Oh yes. Two millennia ago, this palace used to be a temple for our people. The minarets resemble the four elements, and the building itself symbolizes the Tulku. In fact, I believe that is how the myth of the first Tulku being buried here started," Sikhna said as he bowed his head and pointed to the doors of the throne room. "Rajah Harsha will see you now. It was very nice to meet you all." The doors to the room opened slowly, and sitting before them in a chair made of gold was the king of Arpa. The Rajah stood up from his throne and walked towards Yefimovich and his family.

"Prime Minister, welcome. It is great to see you, Yefimovich," said Harsha.

"Thank you for agreeing to meet us." Yefimovich shook the king's hand.

"How could I say no to the great and heroic Yefimovich? Even more, how could I say no to the Tulku? You both are living legends whose stories will last many lifetimes," Harsha replied.

"I think you sit me too high on that pedestal. I do not deserve such high praise. Thank you," Yefimovich said to the Rajah.

"Oh, nonsense. Now let's leave this dreaded throne room and get a little more comfortable," Harsha told his guests.

The four of them talked for hours about their countries, their pasts, and their futures, what dangers they had faced, and how they overcame them.

"It was less than twenty years ago when we were all one nation, Yefimovich, and I do not think Holle would be so reckless as to start another war so soon," said the Rajah

"We were only a single nation for 100 years, and they were never really peaceful, Harsha. I have stories, and you have told me stories of your youth, of the riots and anarchy we would see every ten years. You once told me of a story of your ca-cousin, how his life was cut short, from the terror we would see in the streets. I must ask you, if war does come, will you fight with us?" Yefimovich asked. Rajah Harsha gave a long and inquisitive look as if to reflect on Yefimovich's comments of the past and the wildness of the country when Holle was one large state.

"Hand me the treaty, Prime Minister." Harsha glanced over it a final time. He looked at his advisors that were in the room with him and scribbled his name on the dotted line. "You've got a friend in me, Yefimovich."

"Thank you, Harsha. Let us hope that I am wrong." Yefimovich spoke softly.

"Let us hope indeed," Harsha said back to him.

The day pushed up the night, and the crescent moon hung high as it cut the black silk of the dress of the sky, spilling small beads that twinkled in the darkness. Yefimovich lay in his bed, his wife sleeping beside him, and his mind raced through a maze of possibilities, full of what-ifs and uncertainties. His eyes dashed from side to side, and his heart began to quicken, but then a hand grabbed his, and a voice spoke faintly.

"Close your eyes, my dear, for you have won the day, and do not trouble your heart on tomorrow for it has not happened yet."

Yefimovich looked over at his wife, and her eyes looked back at him. "I love you," he whispered and closed his eyes to let the night give way to day. With the new day came a new country and a treaty was signed with Konstanpol, and then the next day came and stronger bonds were tied with Enuarku. The fourth day arrived with a firmer alliance with Attica, but the fifth day came, and the sun did not shine down to the earth. Truth upon truth Yefimovich gave, but the President of Polsha was blind to it. "Neutrality" was the word the president spoke, neither friend nor foe, neither good nor evil. Yefimovich thought to himself, *An action of inaction, may you have the grace the Lord has given me. I can see you need it more than I.* He left the country in disbelief and ashamed that he had failed, and the sun did not shine on the sixth day, nor on the seventh. Turned away at Danija and shunned from Avstrija, he left for home.

His heart did not rise above the sea. Neither did it sink to its depths, but it sat in the waves, looking for the light of the night from the house on the shore, striking the darkness. Yefimovich sat uncomfortably in his chair, deep in thought about what had transpired throughout the week. Viktoriya, Katerina, and Rivka were gossiping on a story, but all he heard were mumbles. A glare hit his eyes. He winced away and then fell back into thought. Then it struck his eyes again and with it a thought. Not a eureka moment but one of cognizable obviousness. As Yekaterina was moving the light that crossed her father's eyes, he said to his daughter, "Hey Kat. I need you to do me a favor."

"What is it, Dad?" she asked.

"I need you to go to Avengler. We have a treaty to sign with them."

Yekaterina Chapter One

The sun peaked through the windowpane with a light ninety-three million miles away and lit the room an easeful yellow, bouncing off the marble floors and decor within the living room. Yekaterina's eyes gazed out into the world and watched the grains of sand move ever so slightly with a force that never showed its face but made its presence known with a gentle touch across the cheek. As she looked out into the vastness of the earth, she reflected on the last time she was at Avengler. She moved there when she was fifteen, and for three years she was a resident of the land that reached the heavens.

Her daydream blew away as she heard her name called.

"Kat. What are you thinking about?" asked her mother.

"I was just thinking of the last time I was at Avengler," she said.

"How beautiful it must be there now. The change of the season must have the country in a mural of colors."

"I was thinking more of the people and what it was like to live there."

"Oh, I remember hearing your voice when you called the first year there. How upset and frustrated you were. It broke my heart knowing you were hurt," her mother recalled.

"I remember being so angry at myself. I was there an entire year and could not move the light at all. I thought Dad was a fool to send me there. No Tulku had ever manipulated light before, so why should I be able to?" Katerina recollected. It was silent for a moment as they both reflected on the past.

"You were born just after the war, and there was so much anxiety in everyone. When your father suspected that you were the Tulku, he went to great lengths to make sure he could do anything in his power to protect you so that one day you could do everything within your power to protect not only yourself and the ones you love but everyone in every nation." Viktoriya gave light to her husband's reasoning.

"But how did he know? How did he know I would be able to bend light?"

"Well, I believe Tokugawa had a lot of influence on your father."

"What do you mean?"

"Tokugawa is the reason you and I moved to Nihon for three years when you were five years old. He has impacted your father more than anyone I know, even more so than Abraham. We can see the Nihonen's energy flow through them like rivers of light streaming through their bodies, and they have the ability to manipulate that energy. Tokugawa and your father believed that everyone has this spiritual and physical energy that flows through them, and you were the first person that wasn't Nihonen nor Mongnolerian that could do so. When Yefimovich realized you could bend your own energy, he, Tokugawa, and I thought that after you finished studying and mastering the four elements, you could master the bending of light." Viktoriya gave reason to Katerina's wondering mind.

"It was one of the hardest things I've ever done and the most rewarding. When I have the light within my grasp, it's so ethereal and yet so powerful. It's a surreal feeling, moving and controlling it. I feel as though my spirit has fluttered its way to heaven, and I can feel God's presence. I wish you could feel what I feel, Mom."

"It must be truly special." Viktoriya imaged the bliss. "Speaking of light, do you have your orb? You might need it while your there."

"It's packed away already. I'll definitely be needing it," she said. There then came a soft tap at the entry to the living room. "Hey, Rivka."

"Hello, my Princess," Rivka and Yekaterina giggled. "Your transporter just arrived and is waiting for you."

"Thank you, Rivka. Tell them I'll be there shortly."

"I will. I'll start loading your luggage."

"You know you don't have to do that," Kat told her, but Rivka ignored her with a smile and brought down her things. Katerina looked at her mom and wrapped her arms around her.

"Wish me luck, Mom. I'll see you in a couple days. Tell Dad I love him."

"We love you too, Kat. Good luck." Viktoriya spoke with the warm heart of a loving mother.

"Thanks, Mom. I love you, too," she said, leaving her mother's embrace and walking out the door.

Two soldiers stood in front of the airship, an Eshan and an Adamah soldier, who were dressed in warmer attire. Their caps, which they called ushanka, were made of fur with their military insignia sewn on the front. Their pants and jackets were solid in color; there were no capes or elegant designs, but everything about their uniforms was streamlined and tactical. The collars of their jackets were also lined with fur, and their gloves were of the same color as their uniforms, keeping their hands warm as the temperatures began to fall. Both the soldiers bowed as Yekaterina approached them.

"Aren't you boys a little warm in those uniforms? It's not winter just yet," she said as she bowed back to them.

"It's a little warm, but that will change by the end of the week," said the Eshan.

"Oh, the harsh winter months. I can't wait. Nice gloves, by the way," she said, referring to the Eshan gloves that were different from the other military branches as they were designed so that the soldier was able to use their ability to manipulate fire and lightning. "Let's go, boys," she said, waving them inside the ship. Yekaterina entered a room within the airship and took a seat upon a bed within the craft. The vehicle broke free from the clutch of gravity and glided into the gentle wind of the stratosphere, high above the clouds of dust and water and all the creatures of the earth.

She unzipped her luggage and took out the orb she packed away for her weeklong stay at Avengler and placed it in front of her on the bed. Katerina pinched her thumb and forefinger as if she were pulling a thread and pulled out a thin string of light from the orb. The dainty strain of light twirled elegantly, and the letters revealed themselves as she had written them. Yekaterina took a deep breath and began to speak what she had written, practicing her speech, until she felt each paragraph, each sentence, and each word were spoken with the intent in which she had drafted them. Her eyes began to wane, and her mind tired, so she dozed in a docile slumber, and when she awoke, her eyes grew wide to the beauty of Avengler.

The water of the great fall rained down to the earth with sobs of joy, spreading life to the world with its tears so that trees would grow and flowers would bloom, so the clouds could hold the cries and release the water where the earth needed it. "The tears of God," Yekaterina whispered to herself. The glamor of the waterfall stretched 575 miles across, nearly the entire coast of the continent, and as they passed the great fall of Gudsrive, Katerina watched the land below where the rivers moved like snakes on the ground and stopped in great lakes as blue as sapphires. The rivers and lakes never ended but were joined by fields of wheat farther than the eye could see and met with forests denser than the heaviest stone.

The shadow of time grew longer, but her flight ever shorter, and before the day could give way to the night, she was over the city of Krystalvann. The backdrop of the mountain looked painted as it stretched across the rustic sky, and the city down below glistened like diamonds in the rough. The droplets of water from the falls above shined on the stones of the buildings and shimmered on the moss that covered much of the city's hard surfaces. To Katerina, this was a home away from home, and her heart did not patter with fear as it bounced within her chest but instead batted with love and excitement as she could see old friends waiting for her below.

The ship set down like a bird landing on a steady branch, and before the doors of the craft could fully open, Erie came running through with arms stretched wide and a smile brighter than the sun, nearly tackling Katerina to the floor with her embrace.

"I'm guessing you missed me," Yekaterina said with laughter in her voice.

"You're like my second sister. Of course, I missed you," Erie said in her sweet voice, in a matter-of-fact kind of way, finally letting go of her fierce and welcoming grip. "I hope you didn't have anything planned for tonight."

"No, I have nothing. Why?" she asked

"Oh, you'll see," Erie smiled a sly grin. As the girls left the plane, Heilagr was waiting for them. "Hey Mom, look who I have."

"Sweet, Kat, you look beautiful. How was your trip?" Heilagr asked, kissing her on the cheek.

"It was beautiful. We came up from Gudsrive and traveled the entire continent. Every bit of it was picturesque. The falls and rivers, the lakes and forest, the changing of the leaves as you get closer to Krystalvann, it's stunning," she marveled.

"It is wonderful this time of year, isn't it? Shall we get going?" Heilagr asked.

"Let's go," said Erie.

The craft that took them home was shaped like an egg and made from airy materials found underneath the continent. It had an open cockpit with four embroidered seats and was powered by imprisoned light. The energy of the light ran through the body of the car, turning the gears that powered the wings shaped like the feathers on an eagle. The wings kicked the air with a whoosh of a sound. It pumped twice more its wings and glided them to a light in the distance, which Kat remembered as her second home.

The city gave a sense of serenity and peace, almost utopian, but every nation has its struggles. The wet stones of the buildings, and the dew upon the moss twinkled throughout the city in celestial lights with fireflies pulsating the dusk of night. The wings of the carriage began to curve, bending the air and creating drag, making a soft and subtle sound as it slowly descended to the earth, and it landed at the home of Enoch.

The lights of the house shown honey yellow as they gleamed a lovely glow, and when Katerina opened the arched red orange door, she was greeted by old friends with the yell of surprise. Her eyes lit up like a candle in the wind as they flicked and danced across the room until they swelled with tears that never fell but held themselves within the lines of her lashes, fluttering away the drops she never meant to show. She smiled wide with teeth of pearls and put the room a smitten blaze with every bashful laugh that left her darling lips. Her heart felt cozied in their love, as if lying on clouds of cotton nestled by a burning fire, being home, yet far away.

"Yekaterina! Happy birthday!" Enoch said in a gleeful tone, hugging her as if he missed a child of his own.

"But it's not my birthday."

"Oh, we know, but we wanted to throw you a small celebration," he said.

"Well, thank you. I feel at home already," Katerina said gleefully.

"As you should," Enoch smiled. "Where is your mother?"

"She stayed home with my father. She made something for you and the family. She told me not to tell anyone."

"She's darling, your mother. I'd wish she had come with you," Enoch expressed.

"She wanted to. Her eyes and her voice told me."

"Tell your father to take a break and bring your beautiful mother up to visit. We do miss them." Enoch's blue eyes looked like he was reminiscing. Katerina caught his eyes in the trance and let him relive the moments, and then they glimpsed sight of a young man, whose hair was ruffled much like Enoch's but didn't hold the salt and pepper and instead absorbed the yellow of the sun. His eyes nearly matched his hair as they dashed over to Katerina's.

"Uriel!" Enoch shouted through the crowd of people within his abode. His son seemed to be drawing circles with the light of his pen, one within the other, and then washed it away with a wave of his hand, letting the particles of light dart away like sparks popping from a fuse.

"Hello, little Tulku," he said playfully to Yekaterina. She smiled at him with sisterly affection.

"Hey, big brother. Been a while. Didn't know someone so famous was going to be here," she teased.

"Who could be more famous than the Tulku? And don't let my sister hear you call me brother; she might get a little possessive." He gave a wink of his yellow eyes with a smirk across his face.

The house was filled with an orchestra of cachinnates, colored in hues of soft pinks and blues, with faces of merry cheer painted rosy red.

Feet tapped and moved to the beats of music that encircled their ears, and then the sounds began to hush, and the lights started to fade. An angelic voice began to sing a song of birth and life, and Katerina watched in awe as the tunes left the tongue of Erie and reached the drums within her ear, lighting up her heart with sisterly amore. Yekaterina grinned from ear to ear as Heilagr brought out a blue-layered cake, with white frosting tracing its edges in flowers and bows. Holding up each layer was a hollow spire, and attached to the spire, unlit sparklers.

"Happy birthday, dear. You remember how to play don't you?" Heilagr asked.

"A reminder wouldn't hurt," Kat said, slightly embarrassed as she had seen it a few times before.

"In each layer there is a sweet. One is tart and sour, and if you get it, your wish will not come true. The other is sugared and candied, and if you choose this sweet, then your wish will be granted. The last confection is neither sweet nor tart, not bitter nor toothsome, but is without flavor, and if you select this candy, you only discover its true flavor once you see what you desire.

Yekaterina closed her eyes dreaming of what she wanted most in life. She let her emotions consume her heart but did not express them outwardly. Katerina moved the light that was around her, waving its aura around the room, weaving its way through the crowd, much like a needle moves the yarn through fabric. The light found its way into the cake, making the frosting illuminate a blushing pink, as it reached the candy she desired, the light forced it up the spire that held the layers together, lighting the sparklers as it passed them, and as the candy exited the spire, so too did the light, filling the room once more in its delight. Yekaterina grabbed the small treat with her delicate hands and consumed it. She looked about the room as all eyes were on her, looking for her to say something.

"What is it?" someone shouted. "Was it sweet?" another voice asked. "Was it sour, Katerina?" another question rang in the room.

"It was—" Katerina began to say.

"Now, now—you know she cannot tell," Heilagr intervened.

The celebration resounded through the late hours of the night, until the chuckles began to turn to yawns and the smiles made into expressions of exhaustion. Yekaterina hugged and thanked every person that had attended the party as the fire faded with the convivial atmosphere. The long day made for a tired but happy soul as Kat reminisced with the Framsyn family. They talked until nothing in the fire was left but smoldering coals that gave little heat but charming surroundings.

"Well Kat, I'm off to bed. I'm so glad you're here. I'll see you in the morning," said Heilagr in a comatose inflection. "Come on, Enoch. Time for bed." she shook his shoulder as he lay with folded arms pressed against the table with his head nestled comfortably on top of them.

"I wasn't sleeping. I was just resting my eyes," he said groggily.

"You're not fooling anyone," said Heilagr as she and Enoch walked arm in arm to their room.

Uriel stood from his chair and stretched his arms high into the air. "I'm off to bed, too. I've got a lot of work to do this week."

"Goodnight, Uriel," the girls said in harmony.

"Goodnight," he said, leaving the room with a wave of goodbye. Erie and Yekaterina were the only two left at the table and only the flaming hearts of a few candles lit the room.

"So, Kat, what did you wish for?" Erie asked once she was sure everyone was gone. Yekaterina hesitated for an instant. "Oh, come on. It's just me. Pleeeaassee," she begged. Kat looked at her with amusement.

"I wished for the war my father sees to never come," she said, removing the joyous feeling that still enveloped the room. "It's scary to see what is happening, and I don't feel like I can do much to help. I've been training since I was five years old, and still I feel that whatever my destiny is, I am not ready for it." She looked down at her empty mug circling her finger around its edge as the room was void of sound.

"Kat," Erie spoke gently. "I know our fathers have this vision of bleakness that the world cannot yet see, and if what they say is true, then you have no reason not to be scared." She paused to gather her thoughts. "You are an amazing person, and I've never seen someone so skilled in all my life. The things you can do make me feel hopeful, and if this world is to be consumed in a fog of despair, I know you will always be there to push away those clouds of darkness and fill the world with light."

Yekaterina looked up from the table grateful for her friend's kind words. "I couldn't ask for a better friend than you, Erie."

"Nor I you, Kat. Should we head off to bed?" Erie asked with a small yawn escaping her mouth.

"A soft bed and a warm shower sound astounding. I feel in clover just thinking about it." Yekaterina basked in the thought.

"Come on, little Tulku, let's get you to bed." Erie grabbed her hand and walked Yekaterina to her room. "The shower is here across the hall. Of course, you already know that, and here is your lovely, enchanting room." Kat looked inside and saw moonlight shining through the window, spotlighting the bed with soft white sheets and feather down pillows. The foliage within the room let off a soothing bloom of bioluminescence filling the space and giving ambience of dreams and fantasies. Erie gave her a kiss on the cheek, leaving stains of her lips upon them. "Goodnight, Kat. Love you," Erie said with adoration, leaving Katerina to herself.

"Goodnight, Erie. I love you, too."

Katerina walked across the hall, closed the door, and dropped her clothes to the floor. She turned the knob of the shower letting out the water that echoed like rain springing off the firmness of the stones. Kat allowed it run over her, letting the dust of the day descend through the drain as the heat of the shower enveloped her soul and cleared her mind. She turned the knob to cease the water from abrading her body and sat on a stone seat attached to the shower wall. She gathered her hair, pulling it to the back of her head and drew the water out of it. The water she pulled from her hair now sat in her hands in a ball that spun like a slow moving dreidel and let the water slowly flow from her hands like a river moving down the stream and vanishing into the abyss of the conduit. She then waved her hands over her body, collecting the droplets that rested upon her skin, until once more she formed an orb of water, and that too she guided to its destiny.

Relaxed and reposed, she dressed herself for the night in pajamas made of silk and knelt to the ground with folded hands upon her bed and prayed. The moon above seemed to shine brighter as if to give her a stage as she talked to her Creator, and she too seemed to glow like the moon, a light beaming bright white, haloed she was, angelic and content.

She did not ask for her wants and desires, only for the Maker's help—guidance and strength, for light and grace on a future unknown to her, but only known to her Creator. It was not her heart that gave passion to her voice, nor was it her mind that granted reason to her thought, but something within the body—never seen but always felt, a link between dimensions, known to all as the spirit.

"Amin," Yekaterina whispered, unfolding her hands and rising from the floor. She pulled the cotton sheets from the bed and wrapped them tightly around her small frame, placing her head upon the gracious touch of the downy pillows. She shut her eyes, and her mind wandered in the immensity of dreams and fantasy held within the tangled web of light that traveled through the cerebrum.

The sun balanced itself on the line between the earth and sky, bestowing brilliance and life unto the land. Its radiance passed through the droplets that tumbled down the falls and beamed the beads that trickled down the floating boulders, brushing a palette of colors across the canvass of the world. Yekaterina's long strawberry blond hair waved down the trim of her back and shimmered as rays of light reflected from it. Her dress was a powder blue with a white ribbon that circled her waist, highlighting her toned calves that glistened like silk. Swinging from her ears were doves of powder blue that held within their grasp an olive branch, and resting upon her wrist was a bracelet lined with white poppies. She was radiant and elegant, her mind determined, her heart steady, eager for the struggle of the day ahead.

There came a loud thud and the sound of glasses shattering, sliding its way around the floor.

"Are you alright, Uriel?" Katerina asked.

"Oh, he's fine. I think he was too busy looking at you instead of watching what he was doing," Heilagr smirked.

"Mother, please. She is like a sister," he said.

"That does not mean she isn't beautiful."

"That's not what I said," Uriel retorted.

"Do you need any help cleaning up?" Kat asked.

"No, no. I'm fine. Thank you," he said. Katerina could see Uriel's work spread across the table.

"What are you working on? I saw you drawing circles within circles last night. Is it another new invention?" she asked with a bit of wonder in her voice.

"Even better," he said with excitement. "I'm on the verge of discovering the theory of everything." Katerina looked slightly befuddled.

"What does that mean?" she asked.

"It means what it means. This theory could tell you how everything in the universe is made. It is the mathematical formula of nature and the answer to the creation of life," he answered.

"Well, the Spirit created life and the universe," said Katerina.

"Then this will tell you how He did it," he said as he picked up the last sliver of glass from the floor.

"Good morning, family," said Erie as she walked in the room with fluid steps that tapped the floor soundlessly. "My goodness, Katerina. Don't you look spectacular."

"You already saw me this morning."

"I know." she gave a wink. "Your hair is gorgeous by the way," Erie continued.

"This Engler girl styled it for me. She's just the best," Kat played along.

"Oh, what is her name? I should start going to her," Erie said in a coy voice.

"I think she said her name was—Erie. Very talented," Yekaterina giggled.

"Way to pat yourself on the back, Erie," Uriel interjected.

"Be quiet you," Erie hissed in a friendly tone as she sat down at the table. "So, is this your office or the breakfast table?"

"I'm just finishing up, sweet sister." Uriel rolled his sun-kissed eyes at her.

"Where is Dad?"

"He went to bring the floyeg to the front," Uriel informed her.

"I missed flying in those crafts. They're so calming, like floating on clouds," Kat said.

"They could use a design change if you ask me. They are not the best in poor weather conditions." Uriel gave his two cents on the subject.

Katerina and the family heard the front door close, knowing Enoch had just returned from getting the vehicle.

"Brrrrr—It's awfully chilly out there this morning," said Enoch with flushed red cheeks and a cherry nose. "I hope you brought a coat, Kat."

"I did," Yekaterina nodded.

"Son, that was a brilliant idea, adding the orb to produce a cover over the floyeg." There was relief in his voice as he spoke. "We won't be frozen by the time we get to the ministry."

"Any time, Dad."

Katerina and the Framsyns ate a small breakfast at the table before she, Enoch, and Erie headed to the ministry.

As they flew on their brief journey, Enoch sparked the conversation. "How are you feeling, Kat?" The sound of his voice was genuine.

"I'm ready."

"Good. It's going to be a real battle today. I'm ready to sign, but I'm not so sure the ministry is willing to go along."

"I'll do what I can to convince them. Do you have any advice?" she asked.

"Be prepared for a no vote," he said somberly. Katerina didn't say anything but let the words of Enoch sink in. The rest of the flight to the ministry building was silent; only the whispered words of good luck were spoken as Erie separated from Kat and Enoch to take her seat in the hall of ministers.

As the clock sounded the tenth hour of the day, so too did it sound the beginning of deliberation to the echo of the gavel Enoch slammed onto the base, hushing the room into silence. He stood from his seat and greeted his countrymen below, "Good morning ministers. We are gathered here today to negotiate a treaty between Landavengler and Yisra. The Tulku will be representing the Nation of Yisra and is here with the treaty her father and I created. You have had some time to discuss and think heavily on the matter, and now today you must vote. However, before we do so, we will hold a discussion to clarify key issues within the treaty so that when you throw your vote into the ballot box, you can do so with a clear conscience, full of the truth.

Second after second ticked, moving the minute hand until the hour struck eleven. Fuming minds that boiled like water gave heat to the discussion. "We do not want a war, Enoch!" said a minister with a steamed expression. "You will not take our ships, our fleet. This treaty is at the cost of the nation." Drumming fists and feet boomed across the room in agreement.

Olaf, with pipe in mouth, blew clouds of smoke into the room, and as he stood slammed his cane upon the desk that was before him, making sure all eyes were on him. "You're mad; you people are mad! You say this treaty is at the cost of the nation! Pray tell me how, for I know, and I know you know—deep down in that dark soul of yours, to not sign this here today will indeed cost the nation. It will cost us everything." Yekaterina could see Olaf's temper was quite unfriendly to those who challenged him, but she believed in this matter, that he was indeed right. "We have been far too lenient on Holle, and we have watched them break rule after damned rule."

"Shut your mouth, Olaf! You and your foolish friends are warmongers. You got your power from war, and that is how you plan to keep it. By charging in at the cost of our great men and women. Shame on you!" A tall, skinny Engelelf by the name of Democraties gave challenge to Olaf's thunderous voice.

Olaf looked at Democraties as if he could kill him right there in the great hall. "Shame on me? You should mind your pride, Demo. And the lot of ya! You're all weak, every one of yas!" His face now beat read. He took his seat and brewed some more in a low voice.

Ding!—the time struck high noon, and the room was at a hush. A voice yelled from the back, filling up the hall, "Vote!"

"Here, here!" the choir of ministers shouted, knocking their fists onto the desks. Enoch hammered the sound block quieting the minister's great hall. "Ladies and Gentlemen, you have thirty minutes to cast your vote. To pass this treaty, we will need over a three-quarters majority vote. Please choose wisely, for the fate of our nation may very well be in grave danger."

The ministers, one by one, rose from their seats as they scribble words of light and cast them into the ballot box. This room was lit in an array of colors as each minister sent their vote across the room. Shades of reds and blues, a dash of purple and some green, midnight black and snowfall white painted the hall until they rested in their prison as sealers of fate in a nation undecided. Enoch tapped the two small orbs, one to his right, the other to his left, and uttered the word, "Avslore." the lights revealed themselves from both orbs, hovering above their resting place, waving airily until they etched their number in the openness of the air around them. Each light drew the number fifty, and the hall inflated with an assortment of emotion. Many cheered and rejoiced as they believed they saved Avengler from war and destruction, while the others bowed their heads or cursed, for they feared war was to come either way, and to not be unprepared for it seemed foolish and arrogant. Enoch once more slammed his gavel to settle the room, and as the final knock hit the base, Yekaterina gave her mind on the matter.

      "How can you be so blind to the truth?" she yelled. "The signs of war are here, and only your Prime Minister can see this? Be warned, there will come a day when you look into the face of that man," she pointed to Enoch, "and weep because you were too much of a coward to sacrifice everything when the Lord so rightly called for you to stand for good in the face of evil. When you see your friends and family dying in your streets, when you see your great plains turn to ash and your waterfall drip with blood, you will know that you failed not only your God but yourselves. The winds are beginning to howl, sounding the alarm of wickedness that approaches. Go ahead and cover your ears to its sound and ignore the call to war, and hear the howls turn to cries of pain and death with the Hollen army standing at your door." Yekaterina scratched her name on the treaty; the blood in her body ran red hot. "I have signed my name and made my pledge to you," she paused to gather herself. "Heed my words, and know if you summon us for aid, we will not answer your call, but sign this treaty, and Yisra will be your friend, now and forever. May the Lord have mercy on us all." She removed herself from the center of the hall and left the room with a face of sadness and anger, but inside, her emotions swirled with despair and failure. As she stepped outside the ministry, her eyes watered as they hit the frigid icy air, damming the tears she didn't want to shed.

Yefimovich Chapter Three

He sat there in his chair, fist to forehead, pondering the words he wanted to say. The room was dimly lit by the desk lamp that hovered over him, suspended in air, silent. He had grabbed his pen resting on the old rustic desk and scribbled the words he held within his mind, bringing them to life in the world in which he lived.

Yefimovich looked out his window, and his eyes saw winter coming to the desert world of Yisra. The morning air froze the sands, crystallizing them until the heat of the sun broke them free from their prison, once more to roam the desert plains barren to the eye but filled with life beyond imagination. The fire cracked behind him in the early hours as the sun had slowly risen off the horizon. His brain tinkered with words as he thoughtfully and carefully crafted the characters from pen to paper, noting in the end of his letter with sagacious lexeme, *You were born for this time, and in this time you must stand. Love Your Father, Yefimovich.* He closed the letter and sealed it with a wax the color green with the symbol of a rooted pyramid. He switched off the light and waved his hand into the air, as if to say goodbye, choking the fire that burned behind him, letting down a stone wall that fell in front of the fireplace, leaving only the chimney for the blaze to escape.

There was a knock at the office door, and Viktoriya entered the darkened room. "Hello, my dear," said Yefimovich. "I was just finishing up." Without saying a word, Viktoriya placed a sweet and tender morning kiss upon his lips.

"Your ride is on its way, Yefi. You should get ready for the day." She wrapped her arms around him, feeling the warmth of their bodies together.

"When should they be here?" he asked his wife.

"In about twenty minutes," she said, releasing him from her embrace.

Yefimovich smelled underneath his arms. "I suppose I do smell a bit," he laughed, letting his hands slip down Viktoriya's waist, and headed towards the master bath off his bedroom to run the shower a steaming temperature, clearing not only the dirt clogged within his pores and sweat glossed upon his skin, but to wash away all that ever was; the ill and old and dead, both in body and in thought.

Yefimovich was washed and readied for the day, renewed, a new man so to speak, as he headed down to the main floor of the palace. Rivka had laid out his papers and work attire. Viktoriya sat at the table drinking her morning coffee with a bit of toast slathered in a purple gooey jam that smelled sweet and berried.

"My, my, don't you look handsome?" Viktoriya gazed lustfully at him.

"Thank you, dear." He gave a smile and postured himself as if he were a model, giving a series of poses, replicating those in the ads of magazines and holovids. He composed himself as his mind wandered towards the thought of his daughter, knowing that she was coming home today. "What time does Katerina get in today?"

"She should be here this afternoon, around three," his wife replied.

"Good. I have something I want to ask you two together."

"Is it important? What is it Yefi?" her voice was slightly raised.

"Don't stress about it, dear," he said to calm her. She gave him a look only a woman could give and only a man could truly understand. Yefimovich pretended he hadn't noticed the look of looks that says a man is in trouble with the one that he loves as he occupied himself with his work papers, shuffling them, yet keeping them in order. Rivka came into the room, interrupting the awkward air that was floating in the room.

"Excuse me, sir. Your drive is here."

Yefimovich smiled at her. "Thank you, Rivka. I'll be there in a moment." He turned to face his wife. "Please forgive me while I'm away for the morning." He kissed her cheek as he left her to her breakfast.

He stepped outside in the frigid bracing air and was greeted, as he always was, by Aero, holding his salute steady until it was returned.

"Aero, my boy. How have you been? How's the wife?"

"All is well, Prime Minister," Aero said, closing the door behind Yefimovich. "Zima is here sir," said Aero as he entered the driver's seat of the craft, blowing into his hands warm wet air that left his wide mouth.

"Winter is indeed here, in more ways than one I'm afraid." Yefimovich spoke the words, not wanting to say what they implied. As they floated through the vibrant city, Aero continued the conversation about what might happen should war bring its dreadful face to them.

"What is being done—is being done with precaution, but we must show them our power. We must show them our strength should—should they dare cross our lines. Now is the time, when we must walk boldly— and carry a big stick," he smirked as he waved his stone cane in his hand.

"Will you go off to fight, Prime Minister?" Aero asked with grave concern.

"Aero. It's important—that you hear this. I am the prime minister of this country, and as its leader—I believe it is my duty—to lead—by example. All great leaders, whether villain or hero, lead their battles. They are side by side with their men—not above them. If I am to die in war, should I need to fight, then I will die as an equal upon the battlefield, with humility, and above all, honor. It would be unjust of me—to send the sons of mothers and fathers to war—if I am not to sacrifice my life as well. This is my country, as it is yours, and I have already fought for it, and I will be glad to die for it." Yefimovich spoke a true heart. The vehicle was hushed as the moment left Aero speechless until his manners and his thoughts returned to him.

"Well, I thank you for your service, Prime Minister. You are truly the best man I have ever met." The ride fell quiet again as they drove through the city, passing shops with clothes of modern fashion, bakeries with smells of rye and pumpernickel wafting out its chimneys, and delis with meats and cheese slices being readied to eat. The drive at its end, the hover vehicle pulled up to the gate of the city within the city.

"We're here, sir." Yefimovich gathered his things, stacking them neatly to carry. The driver opened the door, letting Yefimovich exit the vehicle, and a spark lit the mind as his face met his drivers. "Say, Aero, would you and your wife like to come over for dinner?"

"I'd like that sir. I'll check with the Missus, but I'm sure she'll be delighted," he said with a lighted face.

"Then it's settled, tomorrow night. What would you like?" he asked.

"I'll have whatever you're having sir," Aero replied.

"Very well." Yefimovich gave him a tap on his shoulder. "I'll see you in a few hours."

"Have a nice day, Prime Minister."

"And you as well."

As always, Yefimovich pulled the two stones from his pocket and flattened them once more with the palm of his hand, forming his walking cane with the stones, as he trotted to the war room, clicking his cane against the hardened ground.

He entered the chamber, and all who were present rose to greet him. Yefimovich took his seat. "Good morning. Shall we get started?" The generals and cabinet members took their respective seats. Yefimovich cradled his cane into a stone and base and called the session to begin. A map of the world lay in front of him, carved and etched on a table made of fine stone and earth. Yefimovich stood, and with a few gentle waves of his hand, he moved the pieces of war into place. "General Dimitre, lead the way, sir." Yefimovich took his seat, giving way to the general to rise and talk of a plan of defense with their newly confirmed allies around the world.

"Thank you, Prime Minister. We believe that Danija and Avstrija will give way to Holle. If that does occur, we will send troops from Enuarku to support Attica, and we will also send troops to assist Konstanpol, though they assure us they are impregnable." Dimitre continued to talk of defensive strategies and ways to maneuver throughout the conflict, moving pieces on the board like a game of chess, and once the room was briefed, he then gave way to Moeshe, general of Yisra's naval fleet, and twin brother of Voz.

"While our ground troops push forward to solidify a defense, the navy will flank the enemy by sea to supply artillery fire prior to a charge on Hollen troops. While this occurs, we do anticipate resistance from the Hollen Naval Fleet. We expect to counter that resistance with battleships we will be posting at Mongnolerium." Moeshe painted the map, adding water and modeled wooden ships to decorate the map.

"Can they be trusted?" came the questioning voice of Iri.

"We have been in talks with them the entire week. They seem willing to cooperate. We have made some economic arrangements with the Mongs that will be highly beneficial to them and should be finishing negotiations by the end of the month." Moeshe assuaged Iri's doubts.

"Yefimovich, I'm surprised you're okay with this. What did Tokugawa have to say about what we plan to do?" Iri insisted. The room was voiceless, still as water on a calm summer morning, until the pebble of his voice rippled through the room. Yefimovich spoke.

"Well—at first, not very happy—but strategically, he sees it as— the right thing to do. I'm actually glad you brought him up. Tokugawa has agreed to send 10,000 men to our aid and will be fighting in Konstanpol, which will enable us to leave many of our men here, to defend our nation—Moeshe, please continue."

"Thank you, sir. Once the Hollen Navy has entrenched themselves, we will pincer them, leaving them the option to either surrender or die."

"Very good, Moeshe. Thank you." Yefimovich's voice rang as the general gave a bow and took his seat. "General Vozduh, we have the largest air fleet in the world, only outnumbered by the Avengler. I like to think we are superior, but that's a personal bias. Please, General, paint us a portrait of our initial defense against the Hollen Air Force."

"Our defense in the North will have two carriers." Voz started twirling his fingers, giving flight to model planes as they buzzed over the location he was discussing. "One facing the Hollen Navy head on and the other at its flank in Mongnolerium. There we will have our elite Avir squadron as support and attack during the initial battle. Our air fleet here in Yisra will support our troops within our country, and we will have a small group in the south with our naval fleet in the Avengler Sea. We are well positioned on all fronts sir," Voz concluded, lowering the mock planes onto the wood ships floating buoyantly on the water Moeshe dumped into the mapped board.

"Generals, I want to thank you—for your candid and vivid descriptions of the battle yet to be. Unfortunately, there is much more to discuss. So, before I arrived, I arranged to have food catered for us. Edik, how are we fairing—on the forecast of cost—on this war?" Yefimovich continued the meeting, letting Edik have the floor to speak.

The sun soon rose from its horizon base to its high point of noon. The sky was cloudless, the air dry, but inside the war room, light was shaded and the air stagnant. Mouths had fallen silent from hours of discussion, and minds turned to mush as they could no longer hold any more information for the times of turbulence ahead.

"Well, ladies and gentlemen, my mind has been burned—to a crisp, and my jaw can no longer speak—an eloquent word. Let us call this meeting to an end. Thank you all for your time and for your service." Yefimovich took his stones and cast his cane, shaking a few hands before leaving the room.

He saw Aero approach him as he walked outside in the cool desert air. His face reddened from its icy nature, as did his nose.

"How did it go, sir?" Aero asked with a salute. Yefimovich returned it.

"It went well. We all seem to be on the same page," he answered tiredly.

"That's good to here."

"It's good to say," he smiled, his eyes drooping from fatigue. Yefimovich shut his eyes, letting the rhythm of the car lull him to sleep.

When he awoke, he sat outside Sesom Palace. Aero was still sitting in the drive with gentle words, trying to wake up the prime minister until his eyes cracked to see the light.

"Prime Minister, we're here, sir," Aero said to him.

"Thank you, Aero. Sorry to have dozed off. I'll see you tomorrow for dinner," said Yefimovich before exiting the hovercraft.

"Yes, sir."

"Very well. Good day, Aero." Yefimovich departed, closing the door and waving goodbye, only to be greeted by Rivka as he left the vehicle.

"Good afternoon, sir." Rivka was there to welcome him home, standing with great posture and full of purpose in her poise.

"Good afternoon, Rivka. Is my family home yet?" he asked.

"No, sir. They should be home within the hour," she replied.

"Wonderful." His voice was slightly chipper after his nap on the ride home. "Did Viktoriya say anything about dinner?"

"No, Prime Minister. You do have a letter though, sir." She handed him a small tube with a crowned top. The contents inside revealed the letter, double waxed, sealed with an image of an eagle whose wings were spread but whose head was bowed. The other stamp was of a charging deer, with antlers big and mighty. Rivka gathered his work materials, and the two entered the great home. While Rivka brought his belongings into his office, Yefimovich cracked the seals and opened the letter.

Yefimovich and the Nemtsov family,

We cordially invite you to a celebration in honor of our two sons, Absolume and Aedus. Come join our festive ceremony as they become men on their eighteenth birthday. We hope to see you and your family here.

Love Always, your dear friend,

-Robert

Yefimovich rolled the parchment up and stowed it away in his back pocket.

It wasn't long before Viktoriya and his daughter arrived home. Yefimovich sat in the library reading a book by an author named Thomas Wolfe. He threw a ribbon in the page he was reading and closed the novel as his wife and daughter walked into the room.

"My beautiful girls, how are you?" he asked them glowingly.

"We're wonderful, Yefi. How was the meeting?" Viktoriya asked.

"Hey, Dad." Yekaterina squeezed in a hello with a blue smile drawn across her face.

"The meeting went quite well. How was your trip, Kat?" Yefimovich asked.

"Somewhat fruitless, but it was nice to see the Framsyns again. Enoch says you should come visit." Kat spoke with a false sense of happiness in her voice.

"I have a feeling we'll see him very soon." Katerina and Viktoriya looked at him quizzically.

"Why do you say that, Yefi?" Viktoriya asked.

"Because—Robert's sons are celebrating their birthdays in two weeks." He pulled out the invitation. "And we've been invited to go."

"That should be fun," Viktoriya said gleefully.

"Speaking of birthdays, mine is next week," Katerina reminded her parents.

"We haven't forgotten, my dear Kat." Yefimovich hugged his daughter tightly.

"What did you get me?" she asked, her tone more delighted than moments ago.

"You'll have to ask your mother if I can tell you that." Yekaterina looked over at her mother who was looking at Yefimovich, a puzzled looked, and nodded her approval.

Yekaterina grabbed her father's hands. "What is it, Dad?" she asked again, eyes beaming with curiosity.

"Well, you should unpack and then pack again. We're going island hopping in the Heavohe Islands." He penciled a smile across his face.

"When do we leave?" Katerina asked with joy in her voice.

"In two days," Yefimovich answered.

"I better get packing then. Thanks Mom and Dad!" She kissed them both upon their cheeks and hurried out of the room with Rivka at her side.

"I think she needs this after such a difficult week," Viktoriya said to her husband. "Is that what you wanted to tell me this morning?"

"It was, and I think we all need this. It may very well be—our last family vacation—that we'll have in a long time," Yefimovich spoke staidly.

The night crept up on the day, and as Yefimovich walked the halls of the palace, he could hear the soft pouts of a young woman, and when her sullen cries hit his heart, it began to slowly crack, lining it with heavy fractures until it shattered into fragments sprinkled on the ground.

He opened the door of his daughter's room. Her face was buried in her pillow as the blue moon shined down upon her cheeks, mourning the same song as she. He rested his hand on her back. "Katerina," was all he said. She didn't respond to her father but instead tried to calm her emotions. "My beautiful girl. Why are you crying?" He knew the answer, but he also knew that the best way to handle failure was to admit failure and to confront failure. Yefimovich moved the hair that was hiding her face. Her eyes were puffy and red. She sat up with her knees to her chest, as she looked to see her father's face.

"Dad, I failed," she said with a tear streaming down her gentle rosy cheek. "I failed you. I failed Enoch, and I failed our people." She struggled to let the words out.

"My dear, Kat. Failure is a part of life. We will fail in the simplest of tasks, and we will fail in our hardest endeavors. Life is about enduring our failures and how we are able to rise above them—a better person, a stronger person. When I was a weaker man, in mind and in body, I was ashamed of my stutter. It crippled me—because I let it cripple me, but when I met your mother—she saw something within me that I never saw. She saw the best me, one not brought down by a stutter, but one who could rise above it. We went all around the world—looking for a cure, and came across a novelist, a poet named Edrick Oak. He lived in Blath and nearly cured me of it," he said to his daughter.

"How did he do that?" she asked, her eyes now dried but still a pinkish red.

"He had me read his poetry, learn it's stanzas, and study its structure. The first poem he had me read was of endurance," Yefimovich told her.

"Do you remember how it goes?" his daughter asked.

"Very much so."

"Can I hear it?" she asked with great interest. Yefimovich cleared his throat, closed his eyes, and when they opened again, the words of rhythm flowed through the river of his tongue.

I have dreamed a dream
Of a place where I belong
And in this dream I am elated
Of all these things my dream created
But how did I get here?
If not by fortune it must be fate
A grand design from heaven's gate?
No
For it was something more
It is the virtue of endurance
A simple word, a common occurrence
But what is it I must endure?
The answer is simple, for it is life
You must brave its struggles and its strife
For life is not a golden road
It is laid by you, brick by brick
And though your road may twist and turn
Each brick you lay, you will earn
So as you lay your yellow block
Take a moment to look back
Of all the things you did once lack
Then look forward at the empty space
And there you'll see your dream awaits
Now you stand where you belong
From the road you built that made you strong

It was silent for a moment, and then Katerina spoke. "That didn't make me happy at all. Why did it end so sadly?" she wondered aloud.

"I asked that very same question, and he told me that—he didn't see it as a cheerless message. He said, "You defeated time, and you defeated hopelessness." Those were his greatest fears, and to conquer them and to achieve his vision as a renowned novelist, it was his utopia, something few get to achieve. I never forgot what he said next though, "Fate can only guide you to your dream, your purpose—But you, you must have the courage to reach out, and take it. For what is life without purpose, and what is man without a dream?"

"They are nothing," Katerina whispered.

"They are nothing," Yefimovich echoed and kissed his daughter on the forehead. "So, chin up. The road you're laying—is more stunning than anyone's I've ever seen."

"Thanks, Dad. I love you." Yefimovich rose from the bed and moved to close the door, and as he was leaving her room, turned to his daughter and said, "Endure—always endure. I love you, Kat." Yekaterina smiled at her father, as he left her to her thoughts.

The world spun into a new day, and then it spun again, like cotton on a gin, and the night dissolved to day. Yefimovich and his family sat aboard the Orbital One; he was studying a speech he had written the day before.

"Sir, we are about to take off. Please stow your belongings until we are in orbit," instructed one of the pilots. The sand around the massive orb defied gravity, hovering in space, rising into the air. The craft gave a noise of low bass that modulated to a lower frequency, a mechanical sound, almost robotic. It was then silent for only a half a second, but to Yefimovich, it always seemed like a lifetime. Then the vehicle gave a whip to the wind as it propelled itself skyward, breaking the sound barrier, only feet from the ground, and howling itself into space.

"Have I told you I hate flying?" he asked his wife.

"Only every time we take the Orbital One." She rolled her eyes at him and grabbed his hand. "We'll be there soon, Yefi." Yefimovich hated traveling in space. The silence was deafening. With no earth beneath his feet, he felt out of his element, almost as if a part of him were missing, and though he always hated the flight, he always loved the views. The blues and browns and greens of the earth, the art of God, painted with snow-covered mountains, vast endless oceans, storms smearing the paint, giving life to the portrait.

"Beautiful, isn't it?" He spoke faintly.

"It's like looking into a fire. No matter how many times you look at it, it's always mesmerizing," Viktoriya said tacitly. Yefimovich didn't say it, but he thought to himself *And soon, a new and sad color will be added to the picture—one only seen when the lives of men are given to the earth.*

The hours slipped through time, just as moments slip through fingers, never to be experienced again. As they reentered the atmosphere, the shuttle hissed to a sound like steam rushing through pipes. It grew louder, and with it came a deep hallowed wain, like a humpback sings its sad song in the lonely seas. There was chatter between the pilots as they discussed the landing in terms Yefimovich had never really understood. He looked out the window, and the earth seemed to move toward him quickly and boldly. His eyes grew wide at the sight, frightened by the rush of the flight. The cacophony became voiceless, and the Orbital One decelerated, the cabin depressurized, and Yefimovich's heart thumped heavy, tickling the cage of his ribs. His hand still held Viktoriya's, locked and unyielding. She ran her free hand across the backside of his hand that held hers, comforting him until he released his tight grip.

Of the nine islands, they landed on the largest; the native people called it Wakan Tanka Island. Yefimovich exited the craft to see the jungle before him. Palms cavorting in the flurry, bent to the might of the gust as it passed; oaks broad and hearty waved their branches as if to guide the wind east, off to distant seas and faraway lands. In the distance, pines climbed mountains, and where the trees could not climb, bedrock patched the steep cliffs a sandy brown. The weather was hot and humid. Yefimovich wiped his brow as sweat was already seeping from his hairline.

An attendant approached the guards that surrounded Yefimovich, "Sir if you will follow me, we will check you and your family in, and you can be on your way."

"Thank you," he said to the young man whose hair was of yellow feathers, mixed with orange and black that spiked upward into the air. The man wore soft leather shoes they called chahunipa and pants made from a similar material with patterns of triangles, stars, and flowers lining the seams of the leggings. The bronzed man did not wear a shirt, but his arms and torso were stamped with tattoos, some ceremonial, others as self-expression. Yefimovich showed his passport to the attendee. She asked a few questions of him, marked his paperwork, and then the Heavohen man came to him again.

"This way, Prime Minister. Your luggage and family are awaiting you at the front." Yefimovich followed the man along with one of his guards, and as he turned the corner to where his family was waiting, standing in front of him was a gigantic deer with massive antlers that glowed in the shadows with patterns that swirled like fallen leaves spinning in the wind. Its coat was dirty brown with spotted white dots that blushed in the shade. The creature stood forty feet tall, standing on all four hooves. It turned its face towards Yefimovich as he approached the beast. It seemed to be looking through him, but its menacing look did not frighten him. His wife and daughter were already seated on the animal. The attendant walked ahead of Yefimovich to assist him up onto the deer. "Let me help you sir," he requested.

"Just a second," Yefimovich said to the native man as he walked to face the towering mammal. "What do you call this?" He looked up and stared the creature in the eyes as the beast looked down and returned the gaze.

"It is called cahnlochan," said the native man. Yefimovich reached up to brush his hand across the face of the deer. The beast moved its weaponized head down towards the outreached hand of Yefimovich and licked his fingers. The gentle giant then knelt down. Katerina and Viktoriya gasped at the movement.

"Dad! What are you doing?" Yekaterina asked a bit nervously.

"He seems to like honey." He smiled as the deer looked at him anxiously for more. Yefimovich stroked the creatures face and then hoisted himself onto his back. "He's beautiful, isn't he?" he asked in admiration of the cahnlochan. The animal rose from the ground and gave a halfhearted grunt as the attendant gave a deafening whistle, signaling the animal to move forward. The Heavohen man rode atop a smaller cahnlochan with one of Yefimovich's guards. There was another cahnlochan behind him, as well as another to his left, both much smaller than the one he rode on. It then struck him that he was riding on the back of the father. "Where is the mother?" he shouted down below.

"Oȟláthe makȟá," the man shouted back.

"I don't understand," said Yefimovich.

"She is no longer with us. Killed by Mahtoh." He spoke with a sadness that spread across his face.

"What is a Mahtoh?" Yefimovich asked with slight concern.

"The gargantuan monster, with claws as tall as me, and teeth shaper than the finest blade, with a roar that rumbles like thunder. You call this a bear. We call it Phankanwita, the master of the forest." His accent made the beast seem mysterious, even more so than the beast was on its own accord.

The forest grew thick with chromatic plants. Their colors seemed animated as they walked past them, a shimmering display of living wavelengths perceived by the naked eyes as color. The expanse of the trees loomed ever skyward, prodigious in their size, mesmerizing in their design. Lines like veins waved up their bodies and through its branches. Yefimovich watched as the water moved from the roots, giving life to the tree that was once a seed buried in the underground, unknown to all, and then sprouting into a sapling until it grew. Fighting off pests, withstanding nature's wrath, holding firm until it was what it became.

The cahnlochan trekked forward with polished hushed steps until it reached a three-story cone structure, molded within a large tree, made of animal hides. Decorated on the sides of the teepee were prancing horses, galloping around the elephantine tent.

Yefimovich looked back at his daughter. She looked at him with a grin and mouthed the words *thank you* to her father. Yefimovich replied with a wink as his wife gave him a small squeeze, expressing her gratitude for the week they planned together.

"How do you get off these wonderful creatures?" Yefimovich spoke aloud.

"Like this." Katerina stood up on the cahnlochan's back and wielded the air around her, guiding her down softly to the forest floor.

"See you down there, Yefi." Viktoriya kissed the back of his neck and leaped off the deer. As she approached the ground, fire came from her hands and feet, propelling her upward to gently slide her down as gravity took over.

"You coming!?" Katerina yelled up to her father. Yefimovich rose to his feet, kissed the head of the elegant beast, and jumped, falling rapidly to the surface until he sunk into the earth, only to be spit out behind his wife and daughter.

Viktoriya slapped him on the shoulder, "Don't ever do that again. I hate when you bury yourself like that," she scolded him.

"Scare you?" he laughed. Viktoriya didn't answer.

"I thought it was rather magnificent," Yekaterina said in amusement. The family paused to look at where they were staying and then walked into the three-story teepee built in a tree.

The teepee was lavished in decor from all nine islands. There were sofas and beds dressed in furs from the jungles of Wakȟáŋ Tȟáŋka, tableware from the volcanic island known as Feváȟn, sanded smooth floors from Čhasmǔ, flowers and plants that lined the tent from Wánaȟeá, as well as tables and furniture from the second largest island,

Čhahnkázepo. The paintings and artifacts within the home came from the remaining islands that enriched the house with cultural splendor.

The humid air of the jungle soon lifted and cooled as the sun hid from the moon. The lunar beauty searched the entire night sky for the sun until it could seek no longer, and when it laid itself below the horizon, the sun peaked from its hiding place, reaching out into the blue sky for its dear friend.

Yefimovich opened his eyes to the new day, and his ears absorbed all the strange and mystic sounds. The harmony of creation vibrated in the thickness of tangled vines and trees as the wilderness was alive both in day as it was in night.

On the floor below, Viktoriya had made a breakfast of grains, fruits, and jellies, and she was preparing snacks of nuts and dried berries for their hike through the thicket of gargantuan trees and kaleidoscopic shrubbery. Yefimovich climbed down the ladder to join her.

"Good morning, Yefi," she said, handing him his plate as it overflowed with the morning's meal.

"Good morning, Vee." He spoke tiredly, still waking his mind and body, reaching out with his hands over his head, stretching his body, letting the blood flow through him, all with a yawn to fill his mind and heart with oxygen. He and his wife sat at the small rounded breakfast table, sitting on air pillows as soft as feathers and as sleek as silk when they heard a noise. A thump blundered from above and then a small frightened scream.

"Katerina!" Yefimovich yelled.

"I'm fine!" she yelled back down to her father. She came down the set of ladders, looking flustered, talking to herself.

"What happened up there?" Viktoriya asked.

"A fox!" she responded, still agitated.

"A fox?" her mother expressed in confusion.

"Yeah. There was a fox sleeping at the end of my bed. It scared me half to death," Katerina explained.

"How did it get in here?" Viktoriya thought aloud.

"It may have been my fault. I think it snuck in through the window flap."

"You left it open?" her mother asked.

"I did," Katerina confessed.

"Oh Kat. At least you're alright. Where is the fox now?" Viktoriya asked.

"When I screamed, I think I startled it, and it jumped out the window."

"Aww. Poor thing. Is it okay?" Viktoriya wondered.

"Poor thing? I thought that thing was going to bite me," Kat continued. "It didn't really jump out. It just walked out onto the branch that sits beside my window."

"Is it still there?" Yefimovich was interested.

"I don't know. I rushed down here after I fell out of bed," she said with little enthusiasm.

Yefimovich climbed the set of ladders to the room where Katerina was sleeping. He lifted the window cover, and to his delight, he saw the furry creature sitting ten yards away on a bulky, bolded branch. The sad blue eyes of the ruby red fox lined with bangled stripes melted Yefimovich's heart. Its ears curved towards Yefimovich, and a fan rose above its head stemming from its neckline, honing in on what Yefimovich was saying. Its fanned mane was colorful and bright, camouflaged with its surroundings.

"Isn't he adorable," Viktoriya sighed.

"He is quite cute," said Yefimovich. The small pup laid down upon the branch, his nose buried forward into his paws with heartbreaking puppy eyes, glancing at Yefimovich and his family. "Do you think he's hungry?" he asked his wife and daughter while tearing a piece of bread he held within his hands. The fox lifted his head slightly in reaction to Yefimovich. He whistled to the gentle creature, holding out a morsel of bread. The furry fox gave a small cry, inching his way over to Yefimovich, crawling steadily, yet cautiously.

"What are you doing, Dad?" Yekaterina asked, the inflection in her tone was of nervousness.

"He's not going to hurt us," he said, trying to settle his daughter's fear. As the small beast was just inches from Yefimovich's hand it ducked its nose back into its paws. Yefi placed the piece of bread down onto the branch at the fox's feet. It sniffed the torn piece of food and looked at Yefimovich, then gracefully consumed it. Its white-tipped bushy red tail wavered with happiness. It sat upward, still looking at him, nuzzling his hand for more.

"Here you go, little guy. Take the rest," he told the wild animal.

"Dad. Don't!" Kat jittered. The red bangled fox looked at her and gave a lovable howl that rang with affection in their ears. Yefimovich ruffled its frizzy head, saying goodbye to the lonely beast.

After a quick shower from the washroom outside, just off the en-suite, Yefimovich dressed from head to toe in hiking gear. When he left his room, he was met with a laugh of mockery.

"What are you wearing, Dad?" Katerina giggled.

"Same as you. It's my hiking gear," he noted the obviousness of it.

"From when? A hundred years ago?" she teased him some more.

"You women and your fashion. Keep it, I say. This is about practicality—not about the poshness of my attire," he said slightly flustered.

"Cheer up, dear." Viktoriya attempted to sway his mood.

"You may be laughing now, but let's see how the day goes, shall we?" He pecked her lips with his own. "Ready?" he asked in higher spirits.

The day moved quickly, but it was not without felicity and satisfaction. They explored the richness of the jungle, the wealth of life, whether animal or plant. It piqued the mind. Yefimovich examined every detail, from the grandeur of a fallen tree to the paltry plainness of the dirt they walked on. The insects scurried to run a society unknown to most. Sweet lullabies and sonnets were sung from birds as bright and colorful as the flowers that perfumed the forest. Howls were heard from high in the canopy and low on the humid floor of the jungle.

Their bodies tired, they stopped to rest, and Yefimovich began chuckling to himself as he noticed he carried almost everything, though most of what he had were for precautionary measures. Flint to start a fire, an axe to chop wood for a fire, a small tent folded into his backpack, and the list went on in his head until he burst out in laughter.

"This is it. Dad's gone mad," Yekaterina joked.

"What's so funny?" Viktoriya asked.

"I do look quite ridiculous, don't I?" he said still giggling at himself.

"You might be a little over prepared," said Viktoriya. "But if I'm honest. I wouldn't want it any other way. I kind of rely on your over-preparation."

"You do?" he asked.

"How many times have we teased you about having little trinkets and devices, only to end up having to need them. Like the time you brought a needle and thread out to dinner, and I ended up tearing a part of my dress," Yekaterina reminded him.

"More times than we would like to admit, but it's something only you would think of," Katerina admitted. Viktoriya wrapped her arms around him as they sat on the body of a fallen TonKali Pine. While they rested their exhausted bodies, there came a ruffle from the copse that hugged the towering fig, maple, and pines, and through the boscage, Yefimovich could spot the steel blue eyes of a familiar acquaintance. The sly red fox revealed itself, keeping his distance, cautious as was his nature.

"Look who it is. Seems our new friend has been following us," said Yefimovich.

"I told you not to feed him, Dad," Kat said, scolding her father.

"I'm sorry little guy. I don't have anything left for you," he told the crimson beast whose ears were tucked down behind his head. The animal took a few steps forward, stopped and sat, still gazing at Yefimovich and his family. He took a few more steps and repeated the pattern until he was just a few paces from Katerina.

"Shoo!" she yelled. "Go away you!" The pup hid its tail between its legs and whimpered. The young fox laid down, his eyes focused on Yekaterina, the time of day getting late. Yefimovich and his family had trekked deep into the forest, and the jungle began to morph as the sun started to drip further down toward the horizon. New sounds emerged, along with new colors and creatures. The vibrant and joyful calls of the day turned to bellows of mystery and sorrow. The palette of painted plants and trees became illuminating light shows as their veins glowed with the water that ran through them. The coy fox that followed them seemed to alter in appearance. The white tip of his tail lit a calm and steady flare, and his fan, when it rose, looked much like embers waving in colors of red and orange.

They soon exited the husk of the forest, and in the distance, they could see their three-story tent high in the steady oak. "We made it," Yefimovich said with fatigue in his speech.

"Good. I can barely stand any longer. I'm completely exhausted," Viktoriya muttered tiredly.

"I can't wait to soak in a hot bath and relax at the beach tomorrow in Chasmu Island," Kat expressed, bone-weary from the day, with the fox still following close behind.

The moon hung, suspended high in the black sky. The night was hushed, harmonious, as Yefimovich and his wife rested comfortably next to the crackle of the fireplace. His eyes were heavy like bags of sand, trying mightily to keep his lids from closing. Viktoriya had already fallen asleep within his arms. He slowly slid out of her embrace, his left arm tingling, feeling heavy as the blood flowed lethargically back through his veins. He climbed the ladder up to the third floor to check on his daughter, and she too was soundly taken from fatigue in the comfort of her bed, and just outside the window was the red fox. The creature's blue eyes darted towards Yefimovich.

He found it odd that the little beast had such a strong connection with Yekaterina. For him, there was no logical explanation, but for the fox, nothing seemed more logical than to follow his daughter. Yefimovich mulled it over in his head, heading back down to the first floor where Viktoriya was still dreaming. He took out the stones he always held with him. He cradled his wife in his arms, and from the stones molded the shape of a flat disc. He stood upon its surface and rose to the second floor, placing his wife on the cottony comforts of the cushiony bed. Yefimovich dissembled the discs back into three stones, and he too let the sandman grant him dreams through the hours of the night.

Time races in the slumber of man until he rises from his coma, and as Yefimovich awoke, he did so to the sound of his daughter screaming once more. His mind went from a groggy goo to a siren alert, and he quickly jumped from his bed and out his room. Forming another disc from his stones, he rose to the third floor, only to see the timid fox, this time sitting on the floor to the side of the bed Katerina had slept on. His bristling tail was sweeping the floor, its eyes never leaving Yekaterina. She floated off her bed, rising from the sheets. The fox looked at her befuddled, tilting his head to one side. The small pup followed her as she glided through the room, giving a chirp like bark as the beast skipped across the floor in a playful manner. Yefimovich was amused by the comical interaction between them, snickering at the two of them.

"I'll see you downstairs, Kat," he said to his daughter without worry of the fox.

"Don't leave me here with this thing!" she spoke apprehensively.

"It looks like you have everything under control," he smiled.

"Dad!" she yelled, but Yefimovich was already lowering himself down to the first floor of the teepee.

When the commotion of the morning had come to a rest and the food of the morning was consumed and the dirt of the early sun was washed down into the drains of the earth that littered their bodies, Yefimovich and his family were finally ready to leave the beautiful tent, the living jungle, and the furry red fox behind. They hopped each day to a new island, exploring volcanos and beaches, small towns and old artifacts, and on their travels, Yefimovich received a letter from the chief of the Heavohe tribe. The letter read as an invitation to a dinner on their final night on the islands. He responded back with a note of his own, humbly accepting the generous gesture. For him, it was an opportunity to see how the Heavohen leaders thought, and what they thought of the events that were taking place around the world as tensions were pulled on thin strings, ready to snap and tear to countless threads.

The sun was setting on the final day as the stars of the universe punched holes through the dark blue and violet sky, but no hole was made larger than by the moon in crescent form with spots upon its face from meteors of a history long ago, slicing the fabric of the night to shine a light across the earth. Yefimovich averted his eyes from the heavens above and turned them to his wife. To him, she was all things cleaver and beautiful—more gorgeous than a starry night and more brilliant than any scholar. She was the stone that stood heavy in place, never faltering. The fire in their love burned like embers, stunning and mesmerizing, and tonight she was that and more to him.

Her dress, jet black, hit the curves of her body in a way women admired and men desired. Her white pearl earrings popped in contrast to her dress. Her neck was bare and so too her wrists, for the eyes of any beholder would be captured by her face. Her makeup was simple, minimal. Her face gave a healthy glow that radiated like the summer sun with cheeks brushed from an ocean breeze. Her hair was braided in the front with a chic messy bun in the back. Viktoriya stunned Yefimovich with her beauty and grace, something he'd seen a million times before, but each time was like the first. Each time he was speechless, though countless thoughts sparked by her glamor ran through his head.

"Wow," he was able to mumble. She smiled at him.

"Wow, yourself," she said, centering his tie.

Moments passed as they waited on their daughter who was still dressing and prepping for the evening. Yefimovich pulled his watch from his breast pocket. "Always pushing the limits, this child of ours," he remarked. Viktoriya gave him a slight nudge. The lovers teased each other with a pinch and a poke as if they were young children caught in the aroma of lustful desire and passionate adulation. They composed themselves when they heard Katerina coming from her room.

"That poor, poor man," said Yefimovich. The girls' faces showed only bafflement at his comment.

"Who are you talking about?" his daughter asked.

"The man whose heart you'll steal. He doesn't stand a chance," he said warmly.

"You look gorgeously magnetic," her mother said with her arm around her husband. Yekaterina walked close to her parents, her black heels hitting the floor in a cadence hidden by a dress that flowered at her feet. Her strapless black gown hugged her hips. Her diamond earrings twinkled with the night sky. Katerina's strawberry-blond hair ribboned as it ran down her back, her lashes fluttered butterflies, her lips like plump peaches, with cheeks bearing a dash of blush. She was a woman fit to be queen but made to be Tulku.

Yefimovich stepped outside into the serenity of the night where three young deer awaited him and his family. Their antlers budded like saplings breaking through a seed to the birth of the spring season, and towed behind the small animals was a carriage shaped like a pyramid with symbols and writings foreign to Yefimovich. He, his wife, and their daughter boarded the indigenous vehicle, talking fondly of the memories they created until, on their brief journey, they got ever closer to the great temple known as Ulama.

Yefimovich looked out the carriage opening and saw the building illuminated in fluorescence that mimicked its surroundings. The base of the temple was shaped like a pyramid, rising eighty feet towards the celestials, then finally molding into a cylindric shape with a coned top. Standing atop the eighty-foot staircase was Nahchah Whay, leader of the Heavohen Islands, and his wife Enah Sica. They, like all Heavohen, have three physical forms. Their natural state, with the body and face of man whose hair is that of feathered birds, light and whimsical, patterned like fingerprints, never matching another's. There is a body form they have for battle and war, where their feathered hair becomes sealed and armored, colored black or silver for all except the chief and his wife. Their final form, their lesser form, is the body of their spirit which mimics that of an animal.

Yefimovich and his family stepped off the carriage and stared in wonder at the majesty of the 130-foot structure. The light from the temple reflected onto the Nemtsovs, consuming them as if to absorb them as part of the building. As Yefimovich stepped onto the first step of the seemingly endless stairway, the pyramid-like structure grabbed hold of his footing and ascended him to Whay and Sica, as it did for Viktoriya and Yekaterina. When he, his wife, and their daughter reached the temple's peak, they were greeted by the Chief.

Nahchah Whay's face was bearded, and the hair on his head was disheveled as it ran down around his neck in all black with few whites mixed into the mane. He wore a solid white robe with a large midnight black belt around his waist.

"Hau," said the chief as he drew his hand from the brow of his eye down to his heart.

"Privet," Yefimovich responded with a hello in his own tongue, extending his hand. Nahchah Whay cupped his hand into Yefimovich's, shaking it in welcome.

"Welcome, Yefimovich. It is an honor to have you," said Whay.

"It is a pleasure to be here," Yefimovich replied.

"This is my wife, Sica." Whay's wife extended her hand with palm facing upward. Yefimovich was slightly unsure of what to do at first until he recalled their custom. He cradled her hand and gently kissed her palm, and then folded his fingers into her hers. Sica smiled at him and drew her now clenched fist to her heart. Her downy feathers ran down her back in pigments of greens, blues, and reds. Her green gown shimmered in the temple light as did her emerald eyes. The skin she had exposed was hairless and tanned a caramel brown.

"I'm so glad you could join us. Please come in," she articulated in a heavy Heavohen accent. Sica and her husband led Yefimovich and his family throughout the sumptuous temple. Inside were dimly lit walls and ceilings made of stone and clay with all their surfaces painted, telling stories of their people, their culture, and their religion. Yefimovich could feel a small breeze running through his hair, a creature drawing breath it seemed to him in this tabernacle, this palace. He ran his hand across a stone statue in a series of statues of Heavohen people. There were letters and symbols behind each stone figure that he could not understand.

"Please, don't touch," Sica scolded him.

"I'm—I'm so sorry," he uttered back. "What do these words say?" his curiosity begged to know.

"Each statue you see here is of a Nahchah, and behind them is a story of their accomplishments. The one in front of us now is Nahchah Ohtakotah. More than 800 years ago, when our islands were divided, he was the one to restore peace with our people. Before him, each island had their own chief, their own customs, always fighting one another for the most desirable territories. He was able to stop the violence of our people; he was able to unite us as one."

"He must have been a truly remarkable person. I can't imagine a more noble and courageous thing to do," said Yefimovich.

"He is our most cherished leader, and to this day, we still celebrate his accomplishment." Sica grabbed his arm and moved him through the labyrinth with his family close behind. They made their way up a long and narrow arching stone staircase that looked as if Yefimovich were walking to the gates of heaven, as lights of sunflower yellow emanated at the end of the tunneled corridor. When they reached its end, it led to a room open and grand. The floors were no longer stone and clay, but marbled. Large columns outlined the room, and at its center, a throne hoisted fifteen feet looked down on those below. The kingly chair had golden wings spreading thirty feet in length. Its arm rests were clawed like eagles, and an image of a raptor protruded above the headrest, its eyes glowing yellow and always appearing as if it were watching the one glaring at its face.

"This is our throne room. Every Soror, I sit here and listen to my people, their fears, doubts, concerns, and once in a great while, some praise," said Nahchah Whay, his accent less harsh than his wife's.

"I'd imagine it would be quite nice to hear and see directly from the people rather than through a representative," Yefimovich continued.

"Sometimes it is easier to hear the truth this way. To hear the real needs of the people, but even they will try to manipulate you if paid the right price. Our Nahpays, our representatives, can lose sight of what is good for the people and be consumed by their own greed," the chief expressed openly.

"I'm afraid—it's the same in every society," said Yefimovich.

He and Whay continued on into the next room where his wife and daughter were waiting for him along with Whay's wife, Sica.

Showcased in the room was a rectangular wooden table from an old willow tree. The inside of the trunk of the tree was exposed as the table's surface. It was sealed and glossed to prevent its aging, so too the bark-covered and rough underside. The rings of the tree covered its center. Yefimovich counted in his mind, 200 of them. The cushioned benches on which they sat were made from the same tree, with branches extending outwards with leaves like vines still green and healthy.

Servants soon filled the room, carrying in dishes of food and filling cups with wine and juices. The attire for both men and women was provocative to Yefimovich. The women appeared to be wearing a single piece of fabric that hung from one shoulder and draped across the breasts, then traveled down the back, running up between the thighs, and finally skirting the waist tightly, scantily covering the woman's posterior. The men's chests and torsos were fully exposed, displaying portraits. They walked with tattoos across their backs, arms, and chests. Covering their bottom half was a white linen loin cloth extending slightly above mid-thigh. Both men and women wore copper bands around their arms signifying rank among the servants.

The spread of the food was copious as it steamed on the table before them. Meats of thunder beasts and craqogate, pined apples and honey pears, all fruits sweet and delicious with vegetables buttered and spiced, giving the taste buds that rested on the muscled tongue a mingled mix of luscious flavors. The two families dined in peace with talk of culture and history, when Yefimovich thought to bring up the topic of current events.

"Whay, are you concerned at all—with what is happening in Holle?" he asked, reading the chief's eyes and body, waiting to see if his words matched what he had already expressed in motion.

"I see a country that was once great and prosperous and now has very little but is now desperately trying to achieve past glories. As leaders, we want our nations to grow and prosper. If you are asking if I approve of the rumored violence and corrupt politics, of course I do not, but to build your nation, to restore it to former glory, who can object to that?" He looked Yefimovich squarely in the eyes as he spoke and then averted his attention to his wife.

"I'm glad to hear it. Violence is quite a terrible thing, but—but what if violence does come? What if war—comes for us again?" Yefimovich asked, his sentence slightly staggered to his speech rhythm.

"We will do as we have done in the past two wars. This, like the others, does not concern us. We are struggling as it is. Our resources are low, as is our morale. I will do what I feel is best for my people, as any good leader should." Whay gave some insight to his thinking.

"Is there anything I can do to convince you otherwise? To join Yisra if a helping hand is needed?" The chief paused a while before answering Yefimovich,

"At this time, my answer must be no. The future, however, is always uncertain," Whay answered.

The mood and the focus shifted back to light-hearted and joyful conversation. Desserts of chocolate cakes and creamy custards came dashing out through the doors with the finest red wine pairings. Viktoriya took a bite of a cream-filled custard. Her eyes grew wide as she chewed the pastry in bliss, giving her husband a bite of the same piece.

"Wow! That's good. How is the wine?" Yefimovich asked as his glass was being poured.

"It may be the best I ever had," she said with surprise in her voice.

"I'm so glad you like it," said Sica, as if relieved. "We have so few wineries here, but this comes from my favorite—" Before she could finish her sentence, there came a ruckus, as an animal came bustling through the room, and not far behind were two male servants chasing it down. The fox jumped onto the willowed table, spoiling the treats as they fell to the floor, spilling the cups of wine that rested on the table's surface, and shattering the decanter that held the sweet contents.

"Kill the rodent!!" Nahchah Whay shouted in Heavohen dialect. The untamed creature ducked and jumped, slid and swerved until he was out of sight while the two servants followed the clever creature back from whence it came.

"Well then—" Yefimovich laughed covered in chocolate and custard with wine stains on his sleeve. They were soon all laughing at the scene that had befallen them. The food and drink now worn, rather than consumed, filled the evening air with buoyancy and sprightliness.

It wasn't long before the sandbags pulled on the eyes of those at the table. The hour was getting ever later with the morning ever closer and another day of travel ahead.

"That fox has been—a most peculiar creature. I swear we saw it every place we went," Yefimovich said to Whay and Sica as they were walking out the great temple, heading towards the eighty-foot staircase that would send them down to the carriage.

"We have been chasing that bangled brute for some time. It is too wise for its own good," said Whay as they exited outside at the top of the stairway.

"Thank you so much—for having my family and I," Yefimovich stuttered.

"Yes. Thank you very much, Sica and Whay. We couldn't have asked for a better stay," Viktoriya expressed sincerely.

"You are all most welcome and are always welcome back," Whay spoke.

The living temple structure grabbed the ankles of the Nemtsovs as they placed their feet onto the first step, and gracefully carried them back to the surface. When they reached the bottom, Yefimovich waved one final goodbye. He thought he could see a hand waving back to him, looking back at Whay and Sica in the soft glow of the pyramid, but the dark of the night left his eyes unsure of what he saw.

With tired eyes and an exasperated mind, Yefimovich's head lay on pillowed dreams and dwelt on the thoughts of the night, the words and bodies of brightless fright. It stirred the tale of two sides of the same coin, twirling in the air, one the light, the other a different sight. Too soon, the rays came crashing down, blotting out the other illuminations, giving call for his eyes to open, for his mind to take on the new day.

Yefimovich was the first to wake. To him it seemed a bit unusual, but he did not weigh too heavily on it. He walked out of his room and headed towards the kitchen to make breakfast for his wife and daughter. Yekaterina was next to wake from her slumber, slowly rubbing the crust of sleep from her eyes.

"Is Mom still sleeping?" she finally asked with a bowl full of fruits and nuts, sinking in a milky paste.

"She is. I'm going to bring this up to her and make sure she feels alright." He spoke quietly to his daughter. Crack and creek, the aged wood staircase sounded as did the floors he walked on. Yefimovich entered the room as his wife was stretching out her arms, opening her veins, letting the blood flow more readily, waking the body. Her deep inhale of the air powered her heart, giving life to her body.

"Good morning, dear." Yefimovich smiled at her with breakfast in his hands. Viktoriya's hair was wild and erratic with her eyes still struggling to open to the morning's blush. "I've never known you to sleep so late."

"I must have been really tired," she yawned.

"Well—your hair doesn't lie," he mocked.

"It's that bad?" she asked, running her fingers though the mangled hair on her head.

"I kind of like it," he said, kissing her lips and handing Viktoriya her breakfast. She took a bite.

"Thanks, Yefi. This is delicious."

"I'm glad you like it. I'll be in the shower—we have to leave in a couple hours."

"Is our daughter getting ready?"

"She was eating breakfast when I came up," Yefimovich replied, walking into the washroom. He let the steam of the shower open his pours and clear his sinuses, like clogged pipes of mud and grime now clear, flowing steady as a river runs down the carved and ancient path to the river's mouth where the sea calls its end. As he let the water drum upon his body, his ears caught the tone of a thud, making his heart race in response to the unknown sound. Yefimovich quickly shut off the water and bolted out naked to where the din had come from. His eyes immediately seized on his wife lying on the ground, holding her foot with tender care.

"Are you alright, Vee?" His voice sounded uneasy as he knelt down next to her.

"I'm fine, just a bit clumsy was all." She shrugged her injury off.

"I nearly stubbed my own foot running out the shower—I wasn't sure what I heard." His wet naked body dripped a puddled pond on the floor.

"Go dry yourself off, silly man. I'm fine." She gave him a slight tap on his bottom.

Ticking time fell steady as it always does; the seconds lead the minutes as the minutes lead the hours. Yefimovich and his family sat in the living area, their belongings packed and ready for flight, and along came the noise of a knocker's fluttered strike. Yefimovich opened the dense wooden door.

"Good morning, Prime Minister. How are you today?" asked one of his personal guards.

"Good morning. I'm just fine, thank you. How are we looking?" he queried.

"We are set to go sir," the guard answered.

"Perfect." Yefimovich grabbed a few bags and gathered his family for the flight to Aontu. He strapped himself into the vetervykl, a book in one hand, his speech in another. He cracked the binding as he opened the novel with the title that read, *Look Homeward Angel*. His mind was absorbed by its context. Its lyrical flow with its southern drawl, charmed from the countryside vibes of Ban-Ros, had inspired his soul for a passioned plea in his open letter, his sonnet he'd sing to King Robert, to aid a worried friend in an age of perplexing complexities. As he read the storied tale, he placed his letter to the side and held his wife's hand, as he always did, in the aircraft before takeoff. The nerves ran wild within his body, a fluttering flicker as quick as a flap from a hummingbird's wings, they ascended into the vacuum of space. The mixing of paints, the blending of words, the earth came together in an emotional blend that both could describe but never truly capture. From the beauty and majesty of the little blue ball in the blackness of space, his eyes watered and fell from the bridge of the ridge of his eyes. He cleared them away before anyone noticed, or so he thought, until his wife hugged his arm and rested her head on his muscled shoulder.

He finished his chapter and gazed out onto the beauty of the world. The ivory clouds swirled against the contrast of the blue oceans, and the brown of the earth struck the iris in a tantalizing trance. Yefimovich's heart, mind, and soul inspired, fired, and bright, finished the speech he'd orate to the people on Saoirse. The ink ran dry, and so too his thoughts. He closed his eyes, letting the cerebrum unwind to a world of fantasy and pleasure.

"Dad—Dad, wake up." Yekaterina softly shook her father into consciousness. His eyes slowly opened to see her face. "We're here, Dad."

"Spasibo, Kat," he thanked her; his voice lethargic as he spoke. He stepped out to the fire burn of the ice-cold air.

"Almost like home," he heard his daughter say in a gleeful tone. Yefimovich shared her delight to be in Aontu. He hadn't seen Robert in what seemed like decades. His family was still young then, when talks of the Great War were painful and sorrowed when it left the mouth of a man or woman, or when the lighted face of a father, brother, or friend jolted the memory of a time more innocent; but grieving had ended years ago, and the presage of another war, one far grander and one far more consequential than the Great War, eighteen years ago, was looming ever closer.

Yefimovich came out of past memories and into reality when his wife yelled a name he hadn't heard in eons, but it was like the sound of a favorite song sung on the radio.

"Robert!" Viktoriya shouted, her hand waving in the air as if to say hello.

"Viktoriya!" Robert hollered back against the sound of hovercrafts and jets landing and taking off for flight. "How do you still look this incredible?" he asked as he got closer.

"Oh, hush Robert. I see you've grown a few gray hairs," she teased him.

"Time seems to do that to us men," he played along, his eyes dancing over to Yefimovich. The two men embraced one another, holding on as if they'd never see each other again.

"My dear friend, how are you?" Yefimovich spoke with deep sincerity.

"Yef, I'm great for a man in constant stress," he grinned.

"I know the feeling—too well." He paused a moment and then continued, "Gosh, you look so much like your father."

"And here I thought we were friends," Robert joked as Yefimovich smiled.

"How—how is your brother?" Yefimovich queried.

"Iscariot? Hot headed, commanding, but he seems happy. His son is no chip off the old block. Surprisingly, he reminds me far more of the mother he never met than he does my brother," Robert answered. "I've got a ride for you and your family. Let's head to the hangar." Yefimovich and Robert walked to it. Viktoriya and Yekaterina were already inside the metal building.

"Where is Lagertha?" Viktoriya asked as he and Yefimovich entered the hangar.

"We are about to meet up with her and my kids. Are you all ready to go?" Robert asked.

"I suppose so. Are we going to the castle?" Yefimovich inquired.

"Someplace a bit more exciting." Robert's tone was unusually giddy.

"What of our luggage?" Katerina asked.

"The carriage behind you will send it to the castle. Do you have what you need? We'll be gone for a few hours," Robert informed them.

"I believe the aides have loaded everything," said Viktoriya. Robert opened the doors to the wheeled vehicle that was styled in beauty, an antique of fine design and craftsmanship. Robert turned on the heat to warm the car, thawing the frozen body of Yefimovich and himself.

"Is this yours?" Yefimovich asked.

"No, unfortunately. It's a gift for today only. You'll see why shortly," Robert told him. Yefimovich admired the upholstery. The intricately hand-stitched leather seats were like sitting on the buoyant softness of a sheep made of cotton. His body melted into its comfort. Its dashboard had a classical appeal, the vehicle's artistry was of the past, but as the band of the nuclear engine sounded its boom, it screamed of the future, jerking Yefimovich into it. Robert put the car into gear and drove north towards the Mor Mountain Range that overlooked the city of Buna.

The lights of the city gleamed bewitchingly as they traced the outskirts of the metropolis while the sun began to creep along the line dividing the land of the known and the space of the unknown, letting the darkness consume the light and the power of the moon reign over the stars.

They had traveled for over an hour, talking of anamneses, the fated future and the moment they were living. Robert slowed the antique craft as he approached an open field track. The echo of a swarm of honeybees perforated the quiet countryside.

"What's that sound?" Viktoriya asked.

"We're at the Pinnacle Eitilte race," Yekaterina concluded.

"Are you a fan of the sport?" Robert asked.

"I've actually never watched it, but our driver Aero is a huge fan of Eitilte," she confessed.

"This is the final race until the holidays are over," Robert began.

"Is your son racing, Robert?" Yefimovich interrupted in some surprise.

"He is. He is doing something in the sport no one has ever done," Robert hinted.

"And what is that?" Viktoriya took the beat before Robert could finish.

"Aedus will be the youngest in the sport to ever hold the driver's lead at holiday end, and if he continues as he is, then he will be the youngest champion in the history of Pinnacle Eitilte.

"That's quite the accomplishment," Viktoriya added as they walked to the grandstand a mile in the distance, filled with Telekine, Saoirse, Nihonen's, Heavohen's, people of every race and culture throughout the world. Admirers of the sport furnished the stands with flags of their nation's driver, banners of their favorite team, and buzzed the track with horns that hummed an annoying inflection into the air. When they arrived at the stands that sat 200,000 people, the growl of the crowd rattled the bones within the body. Yefimovich could feel his muscles wave from the ripple of the congregation.

Robert led them over a bridge that hung over the track a hundred feet into the air. The bridge itself was also the starting line, lighting in colors during the race. Red to stop, yellow for caution, usually resulting in a pace vehicle to guide the racers through the track. Blue signaled slower crafts ahead, and green symbolled go.

Thirty narrow vehicles lined the starting line, each with a slight design change, all using cold fusion engines. Each speeder had front and rear wings, a fusion engine, propulsion jets, and lift discs, along with front and side lasers that would slow and stop the vehicle. The racers were inside an open cockpit with the most advanced technology at their fingertips, ready to push the absolute limits of man and ingenuity. To propel the future through sport and competitiveness.

Yefimovich caught sight of Aedus's speeder, painted metallic silver with a dash of green on its wings, lined with the name Shelby. "He races for Darroll Shelby? I used to know the man back when he created the Cobra."

"I think you and my son might have a lot to talk about then," said Robert as they reached the pits. Staff and crew were reviewing strategy and checking systems to make sure everything was functioning as it should. It was like watching worker ants, each having a purpose and tending to that purpose.

They walked some more, Robert leading them past the pits to an elevator that sprung them 200 feet skyward. The view was breathtaking, even in the darkness of the night. Not but a few miles away was the base of Mor Mountain; the gorge was lit a sunset rustic orange. The sky above was an ocean blue, dark and beautiful, dotted with stars from worlds a millennium away. The moon gave life to the ground as the snow glistened in the magic of the night.

Yefimovich could feel his heart racing, a cadence to the excitement that infused the air. They had reached the top as the elevator dinged its signal to exit, opening the doors to the platform where Lagertha and her two children were there to meet them.

Lagertha's smile was intoxicating, filling the mind and body in the chemical of friendship.

"Hello, Yefimovich." She greeted him with a hug. "It's so great to see your face again."

"As it is to see yours," he replied.

"I see Viktoriya kept you fit." She winked at his wife and began chatting with Viktoriya while he listened in on the conversation. "How were the islands? You look well rested."

"The islands were just what we needed. The culture and the landscape are so exotic. You feel as if you're on a different planet," Viktoriya answered.

"I'm glad you enjoyed yourselves. Is this your daughter? Lagertha asked, looking at Yekaterina. "You're an absolute dove. I remember when you could barely walk; my you've grown to be a beautiful woman and quite powerful from what I hear."

Kat blushed, "Thank you so much, Mrs. Darroch. You're very kind to say so. I've got to spend so much time with your parents and siblings that it's great to finally see you in person. I feel as though I've known you my entire life without ever really seeing you. Your family back in Avengler absolutely loves you and talks of you all the time." Her face reddened some more as she spoke.

"Well, you have the whole week with me. I can't wait to get to know you. And have no doubt, our family bonds will only get tighter after your visit. Now come, take a seat," Lagertha instructed them.

As they took their seats, Robert introduced Absolume and Lorena to the Nemtsovs. Their kids instantly bonded, especially the girls. At first, they talked of fashion and popular culture, but then moved on to topics of more substance. From books to arts, to politics and religion, their dialog was a petri dish of matters of the mind. Yefimovich and Robert looked at each other, pleased with the children they had raised, knowing their kids could form the world in a way they could only hope to.

"Do you remember having these discussions at their age?" Robert asked.

"If I did, I assure you—it wasn't very eloquent," Yefimovich replied, causing the two men to laugh at one another.

The families continued to socialize when a voice protruded through their conversations.

"Ladies and gentlemen. Please give a round of applause to your Pinnacle Eitilte Nukes!" the announcer exclaimed in a hyperbolic pitch. The crowd buzzed and whistled, booed and hollered as the thirty men from all over the world entered the cold and frozen track which would give them immortality whether in fame or infamy. Their names would grace the sport in the dustbins of history. Yefimovich gave a deafening whistle that fifed like a flute. Aedus looked up at them and gave a playful salute.

"I think he heard me," said Yefimovich.

"I think everyone heard you," Robert replied, trying to stop the toll that pealed within his ears.

"What is he wearing?" Katerina questioned aloud.

"It's a pressurized suit that helps to prevent him from blacking out as the blood leaves his brain at Mach speeds," Absolume appraised Katerina.

"How fast exactly?" she queried.

"From 900 to nearly 4,000 miles per hour," Lorena informed them.

"Supersonic?" Kat said with bewilderment.

"That's right," Abe replied.

"Wow." Kat was still in disbelief. "That's incredible. How is that possible?"

"The helmet is programmed with a digital map of the track, giving him visuals of what lies ahead a second and a half before it happens," Robert explained.

"But what of the speeders in front and behind him? How does he pass or avoid them?" Katerina persisted.

"Because traveling faster than the speed of sound generates a longer wavelength, thus resulting in the light taking longer to get to the eye. The helmet takes that data and feeds it to the mind instantaneously, enabling him, in theory, to see a second and a half into the future." The wisdom sprang from Robert's tongue diving into the canal and hitting the drum of the ear, sending the wave of information to the brain of Katerina and Yefimovich.

"What brilliant magician—developed this?" Yefimovich asked.

"I'm not quite sure. Thomas Young I think the name was," Robert said, sounding unsure of himself.

"Edison Young," Absolume corrected his father. Yefimovich looked down at the hovercraft, dumbstruck at what he just heard. He refocused his eyes and mind when the voice of the announcer resonated through the brisk winter air.

"NUKES!—Start Your Engines!" A loud snap and a shrill of static penetrated the world as the speeders were shocked into life with the power of the sun. Yefimovich and his family jumped at the wickedness of the alarming sound. His heart palpitated from the rush of the excitement that enveloped every being in sight. The bridge they had walked across turned an ominous red, and the beat of three-quarter notes resounded through the crowd.

Beep—Beep—Boom. The thrust of the engines exploded, heating the frozen world. The roar rumbled in the openness as the speeders rushed forward in the blink of an eye, faster than the speed of sound, seemingly the speed of light.

Yefimovich could see the entire course from where he sat and had a screen within his booth to see a first-person perspective as well as a third-person perspective. He examined the alacrity of Aedus's movements in the vehicle. He noted his calming breath as he breathed and the steady hand as he directed the rhythm of the race.

Aedus's craft was approaching another. Yefimovich looked to catch his speed and saw him traveling at 2,019 miles per hour. His heart was exhilarated as the two vehicles were side by side, and quickly, without hesitation, Aedus charged ahead, pushing the limits of his craft, reaching 2,200 miles per hour, overtaking the rival racer, pacing him on the outside while he twisted and turned around the bends of the course.

"My God—That was thrilling," his voice quiet. He looked over at his daughter who seemed to be enthralled as much as he was.

"You haven't seen anything yet, Yef." Lagertha spoke as if what had just occurred was a dull event, only to be exceeded by others more intense and with panicked pleasure.

The race proved her right. Each overtake Aedus was a part of was more electrifying and more frantic than the last. The race continued to move in showmanship—absolute masterclass. It was more lyrical than notes played by a symphony and more visually appealing than a moving picture brought to life on a screen. It was truly the pinnacle of sport and art and the peak of invention and innovation. The artistry in the design of the speeder was a manic delineation of rip-roaring spectacle, the racing suit a fashion icon in seeming wonderment, and the fusion engine a kind of scientific madness and engineering marvel, all leading to the world of tomorrow, of creativity in fields that are and fields that will be, propelling the human spirit into what it has always longed for, discovery.

The race was soon half over when a frightful and abhorrent spectacle occurred. There were no flames of combustion or nuclear detonations, just the disintegration of two speeders colliding into one another, decimating each other, leaving only fragments that scattered in the wind. The racers were launched from their crafts, one from the country of Nihon, the other from Mongnolerium. Their bodies hurtled in the winter sky, and just before their soft flesh hit the surface of the solid ground, a blinding light consumed them.

Yefimovich looked over at Viktoriya whose hand was over her mouth and whose eyes were filled with distress. He placed his hand in hers. When the dust of flurries settled back down unto the earth, the two beings rose from what seemed to have been certain death, unharmed from the violent destruction they'd just endured.

"How did they live?" Kat asked what Yefimovich was thinking.

"An Avengler technology. Captured light," Robert said. Absolume continued from where his father left off. "When the body is thrown from a vehicle, or there is an impact of a certain force, each driver wears a band that casts a shield of light that protects the Nukes from any harm outside its protective wall."

"You must be terrified every time your son is in a race, especially a crash," Yefimovich said, still flabbergasted.

"We tried desperately to convince him not to pursue the sport, but he loved it, and unfortunately for us, was quite good at it," Lagertha spoke.

"Pinnacle Eitilte hasn't had a death in over ten years," Robert noted and continued. "Ever since the light shields were adopted into the sport, fatalities have dropped at an unprecedented pace."

"Can there still be deaths?" Katerina asked.

"Regrettably, yes. If your gear isn't checked properly, the results can be disastrous," Lorena admitted as a sonic sound tumbled to their ears with Aedus in the number nine speeder flashing by them in a blur of reflected light.

The race had reached its closing lap with Aedus throttling the back of another nuke. All eyes were on the two men as they flew in the dark of the night, refracting the light that struck their vehicles. The two racers were nearing the final portion of the track, a drop off of a hundred yards. Their speedometers read 3,000 miles per hour, the number nine silver bullet and the number one red rocket were neck and neck. Inside the number one speeder was a racer from Holle, a nuke named Vettel who held the current racing title.

Yefimovich glanced at the speeds again, and the Hollen nuke slowed his craft by 400 miles an hour, controlling his decent as he fell one hundred yards, landing light as a feathered cloud.

Yefimovich's eyes were on Aedus's first-person screen, and all that was seen were the stars, a celestial vision of the pure night sky. Bright red lights darted rapidly on his display. Yefimovich looked up from his screen to see what they were with his own eyes. The laser lights that acted as breaks managed his fall as Aedus descended a hundred yards, still traveling at three thousand miles per hour.

A cheer that rang a thousand bells echoed from the grandstand. Aedus had taken the lead. The boom of his speeder and the call of the engine detonated on the straightaway towards the checkered flag, the bridge coated in black and white checkers launched a celebration of fireworks as Aedus crossed the finish line. The anthem of the crowd was ecstatic in the wild and unbelievable joy and elation in the race of the century.

"Your son made a fan out of me, Robert!" Yefimovich yelled over the wail of the people.

"He'll be glad to hear it!" Robert hollered back, standing in ovation at the accomplishment of his son. "Let's go down and celebrate."

The fans in the stands were in a rousing joy singing mantras and carols of the sport and holiday. There wasn't a frown in the crowd as far as Yefimovich's eyes could see, except for those who had lost the race, and whose heart was sullen by their failure.

They stood outside the winner's square. Aedus's speeder slowly made its way towards them, parking in the position marked first. The crowd was still in high spirits. Aedus jumped from his cockpit, his hand curled in a fist with his index finger pointing skyward, signifying first. He took off his helmet, bellowing, "Woooo!" His grin stretched ear to ear, his hair sweaty and messed, but his face was of angelic bliss. His black eyes were bright in euphoria as he rushed over to his family to embrace their love. Yefimovich and his family joined in on the celebration, jumping up and down in his victory.

After the speeches were made, the awards given, and the hyper excitement began to lull, the Nemtsovs and the Darrochs snuck out from the madness to a small room for each individual driver.

Congratulations were given to Aedus with kisses and bear-strong embraces. The commemoration fell to a simmer, and Robert introduced Aedus to Yefimovich.

"Hello, sir. It's a great honor to meet you," Aedus said formally.

"And to you as well. You're one hell of a racer. I—I hadn't ever really watched the sport before, but today you made me a fan, and I'll be following your career—with great interest." Yefimovich spoke highly of him.

"I've been following yours for quite some time. Your story is almost mythical," Aedus said in high praise.

"I'm sure the stories—are highly exaggerated, but thank you. Let me introduce you to my family. This is my wife, Viktoriya."

"Hello, Mrs. Nemtsov. It's nice to meet you." He shook her hand with grace.

"It's a pleasure to meet you again," she said. "The last time I saw you, you were much smaller. Just a wee boy, I think is what you say here," she winked at him.

"And this is my daughter, Yekaterina." When Yefimovich introduced her, Aedus's cheeks flushed red roses.

"Hello, miss. You look very lovely. Did you enjoy the race?" Aedus asked, his eyes in a chimerical dream, seeming to surprise himself that he had managed to complete three full sentences.

The pupils in her eyes lit up in awe, bomb-shelled light firecrackers in colors of pink and red and all the colors of love and lust.

"Sweet," Yefimovich heard his daughter say under her breath. "Thank you. That's very sweet. I did enjoy it very much. You're quite a talented—nuke? Do you call it?" She flattered him with a compliment of her own.

"Mr. Sanguine. Do you have your things so we can get going?" Robert took Aedus out of his hypnosis.

"I—ummm—Yeah, we can get going," Aedus fumbled a response.

"Come on, lover boy. Drive us home," Lorena teased him.

"Vik and Yef, you can ride with us. We'll let the kids take their own ride," said Robert.

"Wonderful," Yefimovich commented back delightedly.

The hour of the evening was that of early morning, when the souls of men slept and the spirits of the beasts that roamed the night awoke. It wasn't long until Yefimovich's mind was counting sheep, and he soon fell in a slumber to the hum of the engine and the rock of the car. It seemed to him that once his eyes closed, they were forced open by the sound of his wife.

"Yefi—Yefi, wake up. We're at the castle." His blurry vision decried the winsome white castle. "Come on, old man. You and Robert have a big day tomorrow."

Robert and Lagertha walked Viktoriya and Yefimovich to their room.

"The day was long but impeccably sublime. It's great to be around those—I call family." Yefimovich spoke with a heart full of love.

"We're glad you're here, old friend. Now get some rest, and I'll see you in the morning." Robert gave him a small slap on his shoulder.

The door closed, and he dropped his clothes to the floor, entangling himself in the sheets with his wife.

"Goodnight, Viktoriya," he whispered.

"Goodnight, Yefi," she whispered back.

The spinning earth spun at 465 meters per second until the shadows were pulled back from the world and the sun bestowed life on it once again. A subtle knock sounded on the bedroom door.

"Yefimovich." The name was spoken softly and met with no response. "Yef," the voice spoke louder.

"Good morning, Robert." A sleepy tune sung back to him. "I'm awake—I'll be out shortly." Yefimovich woke, showered, and readied himself for the speech that needed ears to hear and minds to understand, and the mind to give thought on to the words, and the thought to lead to an idea, and the idea to transcend into action.

"You're looking dapper this morning." Robert welcomed him in the early sun. Yefimovich was wearing a traditional Adamah winter uniform. Atop his messy crown sat a brown and cream ushanka, covering his ears from the arctic air the winter blew. In the hat's center was the insignia of his military branch; the rooted pyramid was stark and bold. His jacket snug but warm, patched with the emblem of his religion, two triangles to shape a star, and in its center a shin letter. His gloves were fashionable yet practical, much like his belt, which sheathed a blade that gave an image of nobility and power.

"You're not looking so bad yourself," he noted Robert's dress. Robert's top-hat grabbed the attention of anyone that glanced at him. Robert's pinstriped trousers and his solid coat meshed in a cohesive cultivated beauty. His beard was the image of a rugged logger combined with the sophistication of a modern man.

"I should thank my wife later. She picks out all my clothes," Robert laughed, as did Yefimovich.

"It's too bad she can't make you shave that animal—resting on your face." Yefimovich jested.

"Oh, you mean Old Bear? He's pretty tough to get rid of. A fighter this one." Robert stroked his beard as he joked.

"You named your beard?" Yefimovich chuckled.

"Lorena named it when she was a little girl. It's stuck ever since," Robert explained.

"Literally, I see." The two laughed again amongst themselves.

Both Robert and Yefimovich headed to the front of the castle. Yefimovich became quiet, going over his speech within his mind as he sat in the entryway along the bare birch trees and powdered snow that were in the room, and the snow never hitting the floor, but simulating an emanation of the romantic lonely air of wintertide.

"Our carriage is here." Yefimovich didn't hear Robert's words. "Yef," Robert called. "Ready?" Yefimovich nodded as they ventured out into the frosty weather to give voice in which God and God only knew the destiny of the words he'd give to life.

When they arrived at the capital, they were greeted by Robert's brother.

"Yefimovich, you old man! How are ya?" Iscariot greeted him with a gripping embrace.

"A bit out of air—since you squeezed it out of me," he jested. "How are you? How's your boy?"

"Hanns is great. A man soon," Iscariot answered.

"Astonishing how quickly they grow. Isn't it?" he spoke rhetorically.

"He makes me feel ancient. You think two years went by, and then you realize it's been eighteen," Iscariot said figuratively. "Are you ready for today? You know you have mine and Robert's support. I don't think you'll have much to worry about."

"Then my fears have died a bit. Thank you, Isc," Yefimovich said with slight relief.

All 104 members of the Saoirse Comhail were seated in their white seats that looked like balls of cotton or a billowy wave crashing down onto the shore, clashing against the blue carpet on which they stood, surrounded by the red wood walls of the room for friendly meetings and hostile encounters.

Six Ionadai and two Seanads for every state represented the people of the republic. With one king, chosen by the Lord, conscripted to the roll to lead a nation, with all its praises and all its blames.

Iscariot stepped forward onto the risen platform. The lights of the cameras were on for the public forum to witness the session live, to stream across the nation, to give 100 million people scattered across the great expanse of the land of Saoirse an opportunity to see history in the making. He brought the session into being. "Good morning, ladies and gentlemen of the Comhail, and to the people of Saoirse up on the balcony, and to those watching at home, we have an honored guest with us here today—a close ally of the nation and a dear friend to us personally. He calls for your attention, for your full awareness, for your light-filled hearts. Please welcome Prime Minister of Yisra, Yefimovich Nemtsov."

The members of Comhail rose with applause. Yefimovich's whole body was warmed by the introduction and the acceptance of the cheers as he took to the podium. With hurrah and huzzah, the room was engulfed in high hearts that resounded for what seemed a lifetime, putting an end to all the fears and doubts Yefimovich had only moments ago and transforming them into affable confidence. His spirited heart once raced faster than a thumping rabbit but now slowed to the race of a timid tortoise. His hands were still sweaty, though, for he knew his impediment would surely call in the quiet stammer in his mind as it fought the spoken stutter of the words that would soon leave the softness of the muscle of his tongue. His paper was marked with pauses and rests, as if the speech were more like notes of music rather than individual characters creating words. He took a deep, wide breath, swallowing his saliva and fear with closed eyes. His mouth moved without words. Yefimovich opened his eyes and let loose the message inked on the page in front of him.

"In a season of jubilee / there seeps a poison / a leak that was mended / by a broken seal / and for eighteen years / it has slowly / and patiently / infected the hearts of men. / A solemn hour / perhaps the most fateful / in our history / draws near. / I speak / not only to my people / but to those / across the seas / through the threshold / of space / as if to speak / to you / directly. / For some / this is the first / for others the second / time in our lives / in which / the adumbrate / of war looms closer. / We are / once again / forced into conflict / in which / if we prevail / would lighten the world / for all mankind. / We must / in the face of danger / not run from it / but to meet it / with Holy principle / and the highest / of standards / for if cowardice / consume us / our freedom / our Empire / will be fallen / erased / from the existence of the world. / But worse / if those who are good / do not stand / if those who believe / in freedom / justice / and liberty / do not fight / then the nations of the world / will be enslaved / into bondage of fear / where all hope / of peace / would end. / It is with this / I call my people / and to our friends / and allies / to stand calm / to stand firm / united and unafraid / in this / most uncertain of times. / There will be dark days / in which we may feel like giving up / but we must never give up. / Fill your

hearts of the light / of right / of God / and weather the coming storm. /
And with our Creator's help / we will prevail. / May He bless us all."

Enoch Chapter Two

Columns blazed aflame, connecting the heavens and the earth as the four winds tussled in its atmosphere in the expanse that was eternal but whose ends he could see. Uncanny the power and fearsome the image. The cloaked figure walked beside him in the halls between Empyrean and Terra. His heart buzzed in a pitter patter, thumping, bumping, for death was so close, and so too was life. Only the smallest sliver like a blade of grass separates the two forces.

"Steady your heart," the orotund voice of the shadow spoke. "Truly, I tell you, this is not your death." Enoch's heart could not slow, nor did it speed its beat but held the knock of a steady drum.

The walls of the halls were crystals with tongues of fire that ran through their core, smoldering but never melting. In the void of the halls, between the four pillars that connected the blue dot in the darkness of space and the brightness of the beauty of the Kingdom, was a portal circled in flaming red orange crystals, spinning hypnotically. The eyes of Enoch gazed upon its stunning sight. Enoch's beating organ did not accelerate, but it hammered hard against his chest, each rap like a cannon blast in the flesh of the body.

"Soften your heart, Enoch," said the shadowed man. His voice was clear and rich and more powerful than the cannonade inside the bone wall that shielded his heart. He took a deep breath. The apparition took hold of his hand, soothing was his touch that sprung a coiled spring of emotions the greatest of which was love.

Together they walked through the burning door and entered a house of diamonds. Its floors were a tessellation of fire and water, its walls a path of guided lightning with a ceiling of every star in the sky, every galaxy, every dead floating rock, and every massive black hole. All this and more the eyes of Enoch could see, but his mind could not comprehend nor understand all that he saw.

As he walked among the greatness of this unyielding beauty, the man to his side led him to a throne. Enoch's eyes were blinded by its sight, unable to look directly at it for the Great Glory himself sat in the streaming fire of ivory flames that burned white hot. His raiment shone more brightly than that of any sun, and his righteousness was pure as driven snow. Enoch wept. The salted trails of water trickled down his face and neck. His knees bent, resting on the checkered floors of fire and ice.

"Rise," boomed the voice of the shadow. "And weep no more for you are in the presence of God, your Father. It is you, Enoch, and you alone who rediscovered the connection between the worlds, between the Creator and the created."

Enoch rose, and though he could not see the Father, he saw those who stood next to the Father.

"Who are they?" he asked.

"They are those who sit at the hand of the Lord. Tell the children to look for them, for soon, they will travel down to earth. They and seven others will be there. Their hearts are jacinth with the light of fire burning bright for what is right and what is true. Tell the children," said the mammoth ghostly figure, foreign yet familiar. Enoch noted the words with the light of his pen and sealed it in his orb.

"Step forward," the voice of the throne commanded. Almighty was the sound of the call that plucked the strings of the heart like a harp. Enoch moved forward, his face down at the patterned floors. "Open your eyes and see." His sea-blue eyes opened, and he saw. The iris sent electrical signals through a path of nerves to the brain, and his brain interpreted the images. So, too, his curved pointed ears did the same as the eyes as the Maker spoke.

His orbs beheld men and women whose souls were not bound to the light of truth, to the flame of knowledge, to all that was just. They roamed the halls of the celestials, glorious and fair, sent to the blue planet to aid the children who resided on its splendor. A hundred years they helped guide the hand of man, but like that of man, they sinned a great sin and were cast from the sanctity of the High Kingdom.

"Do you see, my son?" The Maker spoke.

"I see," said Enoch, his heart weighed down.

"They are you. The first of you. Angels fallen, expelled from the Highest. I wept for a thousand years, and my tears flooded the earth until they drowned in my sorrow. But see, see those who sinned, raised a land high in the atmosphere, still in the bonds of earth. The father, the mother, your ancestors, and they bore you, but the sins of the parent are not the sins of the child. I have called upon you, for you have called upon me, and I have listened. Through space and time and stone and steel, I have heard your prayers. Now you must listen. For what you will see is written. It is the destiny the world has chosen, and with every choice, there are two paths: one of absolute evil, of rage and hate and all that is unjust, where loathsomeness and fear rule the mind and the heart of men. Yet there is another path: one of absolute virtue where men are led by love and grace, and the hearts of men are noble and just. Stray from one, and it leads to the other. Walk the narrow path, Enoch, tell them." This was His message. "Now step down, my son. They will show you the way." The glory in the music of the Creator's voice ceased, and two towering figures approached him. White as lilies they were, unlike the masked monster behind him. The two stoic beings opened a gate; its appearance was unnerving as it glistened steel blue, spinning rapidly in space.

Thin and statuesque, the angelic figures entered the portal. Enoch looked back at the shadow man whom he once feared, but now he looked to him for guidance. The wraith being moved forward and once more walked through the doors with Enoch.

When he entered the other side, words escaped him, aphonic and voiceless; not a word in any language, in any syntax, nor any form of linguistics could explain the horrifying and devastating scene that pummeled the heart, broke the soul, shattered the mind, and crushed the spirit. A knot in his throat pulled tighter as he tried to swallow it.

"Breathe," said the power of the voice of the apparition.

"Where are we?" Enoch's heart spoke in fractured pieces.

"This is Avengler," said one of the angelic beings in a voice of harmony that did not match the destruction that was before him.

The rivers ran dry, and the mountains crumbled. Homes were aflame in fire that was black and wicked. Men and women lay slaughtered in the streets and in their homes. Children were murdered, limbs severed. Blood and soot and darkness ruled the land. Enoch vomited at the abomination from the consternation he felt with his body, aching deep within the belly of his soul.

"Who could do this?" he spoke with a severed heart.

"This is the work of the sons of Djevelen. They are without mercy. They are without grace. They are the prayers of the wicked," said the other Seraph, his voice as flawless as that of his counterpart.

"What of Saoirse and Yisra and all the countries of the world? Is this terror ruler of all that was once good and bright?" Enoch asked.

"You have asked, so you will see. Come," the Seraphim instructed as if they were one body, and his eyes did see. The world was without hope, godless in a land that was rotted, where eternal sadness and war was everlasting and all the innocence was gone forever, where no light glowed in the murkiness of the night.

"Why? Why do you show me this?" he asked with a heart that hung dead as from a tree, deflated, limp, and broken.

"Because you asked to see. You came to me, Enoch, to be my instrument. This is the song you must play. This is the music you must take with you on your return to earth," said the thundering voice of the obscurity.

"If this is fate, for what purpose?" Enoch inquired.

"You know the purpose. It has been foretold a thousand thousands years, and you are the key to its lock," the ghostly man responded. Those chapters in the Great Book are not fables. They are the path to life, through life, and after life. It is already fated what you will decide and what will be transcribed." The shadow had continued and split the open air that was nothing, creating a portal once more that looked like oil. Enoch no longer trembled at its presence.

"Go and tell them, Enoch, of the Seraphim and the seven. The oblivion of all that is good, of the bond between heaven and earth. Should your words find the ears of men willing to stand, then you and those who have answered the call will burn a thousand suns when the earth has been consumed by the shade of the cimmerian," the bulky beast told him.

"I will do all that is asked of me," he answered.

"Until we meet again," said the phantom.

"Goodbye, my eidolon friend."

"Goodbye, Enoch." And he departed from him.

When he exited the gateway from the center of the mountain, he visesated to the quiet comforts of his home. Mentally he was drained, but he knew the day was young. He opened the red orange door of his house and moved through the halls to his tearoom.

"Pappa." The title of father vibrated in Enoch's ears as it streamed from Uriel's mouth. "Do you have a minute? I want to show you something?"

"Of course," he said. "Is that tea?" He saw his son holding a kettle and cups in his hands.

"Your favorite." His son poured him a cup. The smell of mint cleared his mind. He took a sip, his body refreshed.

"What is it my son?" he asked with a tired look. His gray hair was ruffled, a winded mess in all directions of every axis.

"I've done it, Pappa. I've cracked nature's code, her geometry." Uriel's face was bright with delight as he started drawing with the light of his pen, first a line, then a flat surface, then a three-dimensional cube.

"What are you doing?" Enoch wondered.

"What is a line, Pappa?" Uriel questioned him. Enoch paused at such a simple question and then answered. "A line is a line."

"How many dimensions does it have?" Uriel asked.

"Well—one," Enoch answered.

"Precisely, and what of this flat surface?" Uriel guided him.

"Two, and the cube has three of course."

"What if I told you that you were wrong. That this line has infinite dimensions as does this flat surface and so too this cube?" his son said to him.

"How so?" Enoch played question and answer.

"Fractals," Uriel answered boldly. "Take my shirt, for example. You see it as one solid piece of fabric when we know that is takes thousands of threaded pieces to make it. It's a repetitive pattern, over and over, until we get the finished product. The same is true with a tree. It has millions of fibers that build upon one another until it creates the tree as we see it." Uriel's yellow eyes looked glowingly at his father's mystic blues. "I believe this pattern, this repetition, is true for the creation of everything. From something as simple as salt to the complexity of the eye, to the layout of a forest, to the creation of the entire universe." Uriel's voice was excited as Enoch's mind was reeling from his experience in Empyrean to his son's dramatic dream of calculated reality. He tried mightily to focus.

"Are you with me?" his son asked.

"I'm with you."

"I haven't quite finished the calculations, but I believe within the next few months, I will solve the great, old, enduring question. How was the universe made?" Uriel told Enoch.

"It's revolutionary Uriel." Enoch was merry at his son's achievement, though it was unfinished.

"If I can break down the fractals, I would be able to tell how the universe expands, even how old the universe is. We can discover its structure, where galaxies are located, even where earth-like planets would be, based off this pattern." Uriel spoke with passion in his voice, with drive and determination.

"I'm so happy for you, my son. Of all the genius that is or has been, you are the apex."

"Thank you, Dad." Uriel embraced his father.

"You're welcome, my son. I mean every word of it. Even if half of the time I have not a clue of what you are taking about, I'm glad to be able to share the moment with you." They parted from their embrace. Enoch left the room and took a seat in the isolation of his office.

He dialed the number with a Hololight to contact his friend and minister, Olav. The device scanned his face while a circled ring of light rotated on his desk until a holographic image of the stoutly man with a cigar in his mouth appeared on his desk.

"Good morning, Enoch." Olav's voice was rough.

"Could you put some clothes on?" Enoch shrieked as the three-dimensional image of the minister displayed his nakedness.

"Ah, it's just a boat and a pair a buoys. I thought you had something similar." Olav joked and threw on a towel to cover himself. "Sorry about that, old friend," he snorted.

"You certainly are a man from a different era."

"I'm only a hundred years older. Let's not make any bold statements." He puffed his cigar.

"What about a bold question then?" Enoch asked.

"A bold question shows the heart of a man."

"I can assure you my heart is good." Enoch spoke with humble confidence.

"Of course, of course. Spit out the question." Olav blew rings of smoke as he exhaled.

"Can powers be given to me to declare war without parliament?" he asked brazenly. Olav choked on the smoke that lingered in his throat.

"Don't be absurd," the minister coughed.

"My question could not be more genuine."

"Enoch, you are reaching too far," Olav seemed to warn him.

"Don't mistake me, Olav. I don't mean to declare war now, but I have seen things, terrible atrocities, and I need to know that if our ministers refuse to act in a time of crisis that I have the power to intervene." He spoke boldly what was on his mind.

"You pointy-eared bastard. No matter how good your intentions, the answer is still no—however, there is a skinny fool with the face of a sphinx that may be able to help you."

"Olav, you old fool. Your council is always appreciated," Enoch extolled.

"I told you no, you gray-haired loony. Now, be gone with you, or you can kiss my fat white ass." Olav dropped his towel showing his hams as he left the call.

"Brilliantly senile that man is," Enoch said to himself as he sat alone in his study.

In his solitude, light taps tackled the archway to his office door. "Uriel, come in, son."

Uriel placed a tube on his father's desk. "What is this?" Enoch asked.

"I'm not sure. It looks like it might be from King Robert," Uriel answered. The cylindric container had a crowned top and was sealed shut. Enoch broke the adhesive revealing a rolled-up piece of parchment stamped with an eagle and a deer. He snapped the wax to expose its context.

"What is it?" Uriel pondered aloud to his father.

"An invitation. Robert's sons are becoming men, and we have been invited to celebrate with them," Enoch replied, reading the letter.

"Are you going?"

"I think I will, and I think you should, too. We are going to need allies soon, whether our people believe it or not. I suggest you go, form acquaintances, make friends with the people that are there," Enoch suggested.

"I already have friends and acquaintances there," his son replied.

"Maybe you'll meet someone you wouldn't have expected you'd associate with. I know you enjoy your time alone, but I believe we are beholden to events the world has never seen in all its time of existence," Enoch insisted.

"I suppose it couldn't hurt. When is it?"

"About two weeks from now."

"I'll put it in my schedule then," Uriel said as he left the confines of his father's office.

As Uriel left, Enoch grabbed his pen and began writing. The letter he constructed was brief and to the point. The characters of the words formed in the open air. The light decorated the space with two small paragraphs until he collapsed the note into a small orbiting ball. He gave a blow to raise the words, and they puffed away to the receiver. Moments later, Enoch's orb glowed from navy blue to ivory white with a message that said, *I'm prepared.*

The days trickled by like water dripping from a faucet. A single droplet splatters to its end while another builds to do the same, creating a stream that forms the week, until it is no more. Two times the water ran as it did, and the day was upon them.

Docked at the end of the house of Enoch was a vehicle, winged and graceful, waiting for its passengers. Enoch kissed his wife goodbye. It was a kiss that meant I love you more than it meant farewell; then he turned to his daughter and embraced her with the love of a father. It was full of warmth, comfort, and a familiarity that eased the soul.

"I wish you both were going. Lagertha may be a bit upset, but I will tell her the true purpose of your absence. If anything is to happen to me, the country will hold a special election, and you my dear, Erie, have the best chance at winning. While I am away, trust in Olav, Steinar, and Oystein. Learn from them in the orientation of the leader of this nation, and when I return, tell me what you have booked inside your mind," Enoch told his daughter.

"I will, Daddy. I'll see you soon," she said to her father.

"Build quickly, my love," Enoch said to his wife as he and Uriel boarded the angelic craft. Its wings began to flutter faster than a buzzing bee and more steadily than a hummingbird, and in an instant flew more quickly than a dragon rocketing into space, like the creatures of wings that invaded the sky, escaping its bounds, reaching the stars beyond.

Only a few hours had passed when they arrived at Aontu. The port was a maze of vehicles, chaotically synchronized in a puzzled assortment reminiscent of works by Picasso. He and his son arrived a day before the event. Enoch had a mission, and his mission was the Makers. He and Uriel loaded their things into a hovercraft of a simple design and hurried on their way. The two darted past the wonders of the city that was Buna, getting ever closer to the castle high up on the hill, showcasing world-renowned baked goods from Mia's bakery, meals from master chefs from the CADE Institute and prestigious culinary art schools, cultural treats from immigrants all around the world, who abandon their birth country to become Saoirse citizens, as well as ignoring the historical marvels like the Hoba Meteorite, Raidio Ceol Halla, and the Svoboda Statue, the gift from Yisra during its founding after the Great War. For Enoch, time had become critical, and the sooner he could see Robert, the sooner he could put his mind at ease, for he would know that he did all that he could for the good of his people.

He and his son pulled up to the castle gates at the base of the hill. The pines around them filled the air in an aroma of intoxicating pleasure and joy though his reason for being there was a serious matter. A soldier approached them. His dark gray armor was menacing, giving him bumps like a featherless goose upon the skin. A wolf decorated the center of the warrior's chest, the helmet dark with eyes the color red. The mask came off the soldier and revealed the man. A scar traced across his face from cheek to cheek, but as fearsome as it looked, it did not fool anyone with a good look at his demeanor, as his eyes reflected the beauty of kindness.

"Good morning," said the warrior.

"Good morning, sir," Enoch replied, matching his candor.

"How can I help you two today?"

"My name is Enoch Framsyn, and this is my son Uriel," Enoch replied.

"I thought your faces looked a bit familiar. We've been expecting you. Do you have your credentials?" the uniformed man inquired.

"Of course," Enoch replied, handing over his papers. The soldier looked them over, though he knew Enoch and Uriel spoke honestly.

"I apologize if I am too forward, but do you think I could get an autograph from yas? My little lad loves the sciences and is a huge fan of you, Uriel." Uriel smiled at the man.

"What if I do you one better? How about I give him my pen. I created and designed the balls of light that protect the drivers that race in the Pinnacle Eitilte with this pen, and if you see here, my autograph is etched on the side." Uriel spoke openly and honestly.

"There is no need for that," said the scared man.

"Please, I insist." Uriel handed the pen to his father who passed it to the soldier.

"Thank you both very much. His eyes will light up when he sees this on the morning of Yule." The warrior spoke with joy.

"You are most welcome," Enoch replied, and father and son drove up the drive, parked, and began unloading their luggage from the vehicle when a voice rang behind them, one neither had heard in person for years but one Enoch loved dearly and forever.

"Dad!" the sound like music tickled his punktoret. Enoch turned, but before he could see her face, he was embraced by the power of a daughter's love. Her clasp, just like her mother's, was warm and caring and full of passion.

"Lagertha," he whispered. His blue eyes closed. "I've missed you so much my child."

"I've missed you too, Daddy." Her voice was beginning to break with emotion, holding tears of joy. Enoch released his daughter, and she in turn hugged her brother with a bond of sibling affection. "I'm so glad you're here," she smiled.

"I can't wait to see the family. Are they inside?" Enoch asked.

"Robert and the boys have gone to the capital."

"What for?" Uriel questioned, knowing Absolume and Aedus did not desire the life of a bureaucrat.

"Yefimovich is here giving a speech, his Mordecai to Esther if you will," Lagertha informed the two.

"Does Yefimovich plan to declare war?" Enoch asked.

"It doesn't seem so. At least not yet. It's my understanding he is simply looking for a treaty between Saoirse and Yisra, which shouldn't be an issue. His speech is simply a formality," his daughter answered.

"Do you know when they'll return?" he asked his Lagertha.

"Late, I'm afraid." Lagertha frowned.

"Could you take us to them?"

"Why, Daddy? Is something the matter?" She spoke with slight nervousness.

"I'm afraid so, my dear." Enoch could see his daughter's face turn from pulsing cheerfulness to a state of woe, her eyes hopeful to pallid, her grin effulgent to a dreary frown.

"Tell me everything," she asked her father and then gave a harsh and wicked whistle that seemed to waft in the air for miles, signaling for a carriage to pick up the three of them, and within seconds, a wagon came—a vehicle of unworldly design and nostalgic conception.

The three of them took their seats in the driverless vehicle, and Enoch began to tell Lagertha all that he knew: his visions, the acts of parliament, the failure of Yekaterina, all he knew of what was and what was meant to be. Lagertha listened to him eagerly and intently. Enoch told her why her mother and sister were not attending, which Lagertha understood, and as he talked, she seemed to focus heavily on his experience with the cloaked man and the portals. Enoch's recollection of his encounter with Empyrean was graphic, like how a holomaker frames a scene to display the light which captures the eyes and draws them back to the point in focus.

"Daddy," she said in near disbelief. "No one has had contact with the Creator in three millennia. Are you sure?" Her tone of voice told the truth that she knew her father's story was self-evidently true. She then flicked her wrist, which held a rose gold bracelet of a floral pattern. It scanned her face, and she began to speak, sending a message to Robert that they were on their way to meet him. She then sent another to her daughter, Lorena, informing her they wouldn't arrive home until late in the day.

Enoch, Uriel, and Lagertha stepped out of the vehicle as the craft stopped beneath the snow-white building of the capitol. They walked the massive halls of the underground, climbing their way up to the building itself, finally making their way to the doors where Yefimovich was speaking. They could hear his moving words as they got closer to the chamber in which he stood. Together, they waited, and when the doors of the room were unlocked from their hinges, and as their faces hit the face of Robert, Iscariot, and Yefimovich, Enoch could see that Robert knew that the fate of the world was now in a state in which all that was good teetered on the narrowest of supports, and Robert's first words matched his expression.

"What is the matter?"

Alamgeer Chapter Two

Outside the titanic war chamber of glossed cement and pearly steel, jumping jacks of fire and lava gushed and splashed a summer orange. Dazzling and deadly, it struck the molten-proof window which kept its wrath at bay, lighting the room in a hue of foreboding moods. Alamgeer and his entourage machinated in the burning depths of the belly of the volcanic monster. Talented tongues talked the game of war, of media propaganda, and all the blends of what it took to take a nation of poverty, and help the country undergo a metamorphosis, transforming from the larva that it was into an alluringly colorful creature, soaring with the wind in the blue skies of the earth.

The red flame of Alamgeer's eyes flickered calmly as if a small breeze took hold of his iris, letting those around him know that the fire in his heart reflected within them, and that burning pit of power and fury would raise havoc should he choose to unleash the flames of his passion.

His board of men and two women looked up at him, waiting in a disciplined manner for him to speak as he stood silently against the backdrop of the burning orange goo that ran down the windowpane. His voice sonorous and ominous, he spoke.

"In three months' time, we will reclaim what is ours. Within these fractured nations, our people still reside. They did not consider themselves Danija or Polsha. Heaven forbid they call themselves Yisraian. These men and women are our volk, and we have a duty to these people to free them from the foolish states in which they were forced to live. Not only is it our devoir to free these people, it is our obligation to ensure that they feel, within the deepest depths of their soul, that they are Hollen. But what is Holle? Where is our capitol? Where are our people's hearts? They are not, and it is not, in Atma but in the city within a city. In three months' time, we will begin to reclaim Erbil, for without that city, what is Holle? This is a city that was stolen from us, a history that was stolen from us, vanished at the will of the greedy. Country by country, we will raid and conquer until we are once again restored. Whether it be by force or by treaty, the world will see we are the dominant peoples. The satanic men of Saoirse and its demonic cousin, Yisra, will again bend the knee to the might of this great empire. We will start by land and then by sea, and, too, by air. We will unleash what my father did not and fight with the demons of hell to conquer its domain." Alamgeer paused and let the hammers of feet and fists bang within the room.

"Commander Guderian," he called, and the general rose. "Walk us through the first stage of invasion."

"As you command, sir." Guderian positioned himself for all to see him at the thirty-foot table whose surface was carved in the image of the world, bleeding in a blend of grays and blacks and whites, showcasing the battlements of every nation of the impending war to be.

The commander lacked intonation in his speech. It was stale and of a boring manner.

"The invasion will begin in the early hours on Bellum third. We will strike with speed, using light armaments, dissembling Polsha and Attica at a blinding pace, one not seen in all of history. According to our reports, the Polshan army and navy are deprived of modern military technology, still stuck in a generation long past. The Atticans lack command and leadership, and though they have prominent military technology and weaponry, they fall short in supply."

Guderian stopped abruptly as if all the air from his lungs had left him. He took a sip of water from a clear glass cup that sat at the edge of the table and then resumed speaking.

"At the same time, the Mongnolerians will be invading by sea and blockading any approach from Enuarku. While our navy halts any attempt from the south sea, this will allow our fleet of Skorfleder to invade and overtake Avengler. The leaders of Avengler refuse to believe they will be attacked, and not but a week ago turned down the Tulku to take up arms. They are not prepared for what is coming." After Guderian finished speaking and moving the pieces about the map, he gave way to General Kesselring to speak.

Kesselring's tonality was alto by nature but pitched the scales to reflect the true meaning of his words.

"How many Skorfleder, commander?"

"Five thousand," Guderian answered methodically.

"Led by whom?" Kesselring asked another question.

"The Kreis Inferno." Alamgeer said the words with such ferocity that it tingled the spines of all those within the chamber walls. "What hope they have, they will abandon, and the God of fire will reign over them." He looked over at his two sons as the words left his mouth.

The twins had become men—shoulders broad and torsos thin, chiseled jaws, a serpent's grin. Attila's skin was like his mothers; pale diamonds sparkled from him. His brother was like his father, ghostly white and lifeless. Attila's eyes were coral red, and Almaut's a perfect blend of orange and pink, clashing vividly with his achromatic complexion. Attila's hair was a space gray, in contrast to Almaut who had none, as was his choice.

The room was dead quiet but found its life in Francis. She did not stand, but instead sat with legs crossed, exposing the glistening of her skin—calm, seductive, and authoritative.

"The Hollen people are swayed more and more each day to this cause, Ala. They are tired and hungry and angry and find resolve in your words."

"Then tell me: what do they lack? For they do not act," he said.

"A push." She smiled.

"And what do you recommend?"

"A display," Francis replied.

"Speak clearly, Francis," Alamgeer barked.

"A final act to show the people you are dedicated to them, body and soul, and that you will sacrifice everything for them and for your country," Francis told him bluntly.

Alamgeer weighed her words, teetering back and forth as if children sprung upon a totter. He let the meeting resume while he swished a mix of dark grounds in the chalice of his brain.

He remained mute as the morning sun rose on the string of the pulley that hoisted its rays to the summit of the celestial sphere, and as the burning orb hit its peak, he broke the vault of his mouth.

"Execute order four, two, zero." His words were callously bellowed from his gut. He then rose from his seat and walked from the war chamber with glassy eyes, speaking and acknowledging no one but hearing the whispered words of those who did not know what he had just commanded and the reticent vernacular of those who did.

A military member of the board, Julius Gunther, followed Alamgeer like a duckling trails the mother duck. He was of a heavy-set manner, his mustache trim and proper, his brown eyes slightly squinted, and his head balder than that of a newborn babe. He murmured words of nervousness. "Sir." His brow sweat small droplets like dew on blades of grass. "What shall I command them?"

"Round them up!" Alamgeer spoke ruthlessly.

"But what do I tell the men?" Julius choked on his words. Alamgeer grabbed his collar and pinned Julius to the wall with his forearm to his throat.

"You will tell them to round them up. Do you understand?" His inflection was deep and threatening. He released Julius from his might. "Tell them they are to be moved. They will be provided with proper housing, but their current residence has now fallen under military control due to imminent threats from Yisra and Avengler. Tell them the war has come, and they are the targets."

"I—I will sir. Thank you, sir." Julius uttered the words quietly and with rapid breaths and then quickly scurried away before receiving further reprimand.

Alamgeer, now fuming and irritated, left the steamy depths of the cave inside the volcano. As he rode in the might of his horse-drawn carriage, he reflected on what was to be and grinned, but as the visions in his mind were replaced with the sight of the world before him, his emotions quickly filled the cup of his heart with anger. The crumbling buildings he saw in the distance as he looked beyond at the base of the volcano, the cracked roads and sidewalks struggling to hold back the guts of the boiling rock, the brokenness of the city that had once been a marvel to the world but that was now filth and rot to all who gazed upon it. *This is it,* he thought. *This is the only way.*

The trot of his horse slowed as he arrived at the only gem within the city. The splendor of his castle always amazed him. He felt pride and gaiety at its sight. *This is what is meant to be,* his mind told him. *Not just for me but for those who call themselves Hollen.* Impossible to tell where the castle began and where it ended, it was a structure of superior architecture. It was fitted with immaculate columns, grand towers and with doors that were hand designed in red metal, standing a hundred feet across and a hundred feet high. The behemoth place he called his home connected to a bridge of stone and steel that, with its castle, withstood the rage of men and nature. Through wars and storms, it became known as the Bridge of Meister Mennatur, meaning the master of nature and men.

Alamgeer headed to the room he admired most. Dismissing his servants, he passed the common room, the tearoom, the library, and the main hall. He abandoned the castle's center and climbed the spiral stairs to its highest point, leading him to an oval room, dark and void, with small narrow windows that let in bantam strands of light. The tower's wooden floors were bleak and aged, and at the floor's center, there was a circular stone. He walked past the centered stone surface and headed towards a brick wall on the opposite side of the room. He placed his hand on a single brick, cracking the hinges that opened a door to the world outside, and walked through it. From this point, he could see all of Atma.

The atramentous clouds rose high above his head as the steam of the heat from the mountain of fire rose, letting the water-filled masses blot the light of the sun and the moon and the stars, clouding the hopes of the people for something more beyond the raven-hell city.

He breathed deeply. The red in his eyes sparked and flickered a restless flame. The electrical lines of his mind zipped through the coils of his thoughts to the transformers of his ideas, and as the power of his thoughts reached its conclusion, he fell to his knees and wept. For what he would do would be unforgivable and tear the fabric of his threaded soul.

Alamgeer wiped the tears from his eyes that smoldered the fire within them and lifted his head up to peer beyond the bounds of earth. His eyelids and eyelashes fell over his eyes for what he thought was only a moment, and when they opened again, they looked upon the pink pastels of his wife's eyes. Her cheek to his chest, she ran her nails down the length of his back, causing both pain and pleasure.

"Will you still love me if my heart turns to ash?" he asked his wife, Hella

"I will," she said.

"Will you love me when my soul has frayed away?" he queried.

"I will," she whispered again.

"And will you love me still, when the spirit of the man you love is shattered and lost to the world?" he asked one last time.

"I will love you now, and I will love you forever. If your heart is turned to ash, I will mold it into jet. If your soul is torn and ripped, I will patch it with the threads of my own, and if your spirit is broken, I will mend the shattered wounds." She rested her cheek upon his chest once more and spoke the words, "I love you."

The world was silent as they stood upon the castle's peak. The lull of the air broke as the taps of two pairs of clamorous feet clashed against the spinning staircase. Husband and wife turned to face the percussion and beheld two men they called their sons. The boys glared at the stone center as they walked by to greet their mother and father.

"Is everything alright, vater?" Attila asked Alamgeer.

"Everything is fine, Til," he assured his son. "There is, however, something I'd like you two to do."

"We will do what you command." Attila spoke obediently.

"I want you both to be out of the city while the order is executed," Alamgeer instructed the boys.

"Where shall we go?" asked Attila.

"Fluss in der Nacht, and Zhanheng-he. Go and drink from the river of war, and bathe and pray in the river of the night. I don't want you to return until the night before the invasion," Alamgeer told them.

"Why, vater?" Almaut questioned his father.

"Because I said so." Alamgeer became short-tempered with his rebellious son.

"I want you both gone by tomorrow. Is that understood?" He told them with fatherly authority.

"Vater, I understand why you send us to these places for religious purposes, but help me understand your mind so that when you're gone and we're to lead, our actions will be based on yours." Attila appealed to his father's tactical side.

"The order I gave comes with great risks. Rebellion could occur throughout the city, and coups may be attempted by those who are not loyal," Alamgeer began to explain.

"So why send us away when we can fight for you?" Almaut interrupted.

"If this order fails, the blame is placed on me and me alone. The people will call for my death, but they will not call for yours. The people know of no parts you play, nor do many of those within government, and it is to remain so, for when you both return, you can take the reins of leadership without the stains of your father's sin." Alamgeer gave them clarity in his reason.

Attila took a knee and bowed to Alamgeer, "Thank you, vater."

"You are welcome, my son." Almaut did not bow but instead kissed the cheeks of his father, saying goodbye as he did.

"Ready yourselves, mind and body, and when you return, whether war civil or with the world, know that you are prepared to lead, to conquer, to restore all that was and is broken. Now go, my sons," he commanded in his last words.

"Yes, Father," they said in unison.

"And take Turul and Schatten with you."

The brothers nodded. Attila turned to his mother and embraced her goodbye, as did his brother Almaut.

"Goodbye, my boys. I'll see you soon." The two left Alamgeer and Hella alone once more. "What do you command of me?" Hella asked her husband.

"If you could bring my mother to Hofbrauhaus, I want her to see this speech that I'm to give at the end of the week. It is the turn of the tide of what my father had started, and it would mean a lot to me if she were there," Alamgeer requested of his wife.

"I will make sure it is done. Is there anything else you ask of me?" Hella asked once more.

"Only your love and your loyalty." He kissed her lips, and they both left the tower together. Their feet echoed in the hallowed gray staircase. Alamgeer's mind was on the next step, not of the stair, but of the process of war and rule. As they walked the winding path of the narrow stairs, Alamgeer noted he had to leave to visit Francis to discuss matters of media and appearance for his speech.

Just before they reached the bottom to part ways, Hella spoke, "When should I expect you?"

"Not until the evening. I am going to the temple afterwards to pray."

"I'll be waiting for you." The lovers released each other's lock they had been holding, arm around arm, as their destinations led them along different paths.

As the world turned, so, too, the hands upon the clock, and its face marked the fifteenth hour of the day. Through the red and orange translucent roads, worn and cracked by age and neglect, Alamgeer turned down a side street called Mulhauser Strabes. The buildings down the street climbed three stories, some four and others five, built with bricks, red and white, some a rich and oil black. Each building was a unique character. They told stories of time filled with memories of gladness and, for others, sadness. Alamgeer leapt from his trusted steed to walk the cracked marbled steps to the home of Francis. A pity crossed his mind as he walked upon the stairway. Three thuds unto the door he rapped, and the door opened to the cardinal beauty. Her hair was wrapped in a snow-white towel, her face pure, free of colored lips and eyes. She was her natural self. The gown she wore was short and sheer with daisy frills that lined the straps and whose skirted trim was fine like silk.

"Ala, my love. Come in." Her smile was bright and infectious. Alamgeer tried not to stare as her breasts bounced vividly in her nightgown.

"Will you be putting on something more appropriate?" His tone was slightly flustered.

"Don't be silly. This is my home; I dress how I please," she said to him. Alamgeer clenched his jaw. "Would you like some tea? Perhaps something stronger?" Francis asked, the pitch in her voice high and giddy.

"I'm fine. Thank you." His voice inflected frustration.

"Oh, calm your temper." She spoke as if they were childhood friends. She poured a rich red wine for herself and placed a glass of brandy, neat, as still as a dammed river, or as calm as a glassy lake upon the table.

"We've come a long way, you and I. In just eighteen short years, we have put curricula into our schools, infected our media with biases, corrupted our economy by growing the government. We've even managed to manipulate the free spirits of the entertainment industry—a true bread-and-circus act if you ask me. The youth adore you, and the old have embraced you like a son. Our final steps are our most difficult, both emotionally and physically, and may provide the harshest consequence." She flattered him and warned him as she downed her glass of wine in a gulp that seemed a sip, like water down the drain of an eternal pit, and then she poured another glass. She placed her cup on the oblong white table whose lines of pink lined the vined design around it. She curled herself up in the corner of the silk green couch with floral patterns upon its tapestry. Her cheeks began to blush from the weakness of her vice.

"So, Ala, tell me. What is your spin on four, two, zero?" she asked tenderly, and Alamgeer told her.

"I will tell you what I told Julius. We are at war, and the people who are marked are marked by the enemy as betrayers and are to be evacuated for their protection. I told him to tell them there was nothing to fear and that they would be accommodated appropriately."

"I taught you quite well, but you need just a little more," Frances led him on.

"What is it that is on your mind?"

"Give them papers assuring their belongings and their houses are insured. It will give them more comfort to leave if they have something tangible that says they are insured and secured," she suggested.

"Well done, Francis." Alamgeer was pleased with her idea.

She smiled, "We'll set the time for the conference at six post meridian, this Frater. Do you have a speech written?"

"I have notes. What is written is short and unfinished, but it's effective," Alamgeer said to her.

"I certainly hope so. Do you have an outfit for the day?"

"I was hoping I could leave that to you." His voice was calm and low, in contrast with Francis.

"You're not giving me much notice, but lucky for you, I have something already picked out." She jumped off the sofa, her fit cheeks giving a healthy jiggle as she walked into a small room adjacent to the one they were sitting in. She returned with a binder and a tape measure.

"Stand up," she commanded. Alamgeer did as he was told. Francis stood in the chair he had been sitting in, which matched the sofa she sat in. She drew the tape around his neck, making sure he could feel her breath as she blew onto his neck. Alamgeer rolled his eyes.

"Seventeen and a half," she said. Francis then measured his arms, tickling his pit, causing him to raise it, enabling her to measure the length. Both arms stretched out, she wrapped her arms around Alamgeer, pressing her breast to his back.

"What are you doing?" he asked.

"Measuring your chest of course."

"Well stop." He spoke with agitation in his manner. She smiled and hopped off the chair to measure the length of his legs, running the tape along his inseam. Alamgeer grunted.

"Oh—sorry. Do you want me to kiss it?" She played with him.

"Knock it off, Francis!"

"I'm just teasing you, brute. Besides, what have I gotten from all the help I've given you?" She rose from the ground and grabbed his buttocks and kissed his burning lips.

"Power," he said the words lightly. Alamgeer pulled her apricot locks, drawing a flash of pain on her face, and threw her on the couch. He swallowed the brandy, still sitting full on the table and headed towards the door.

"I love it when you treat me rough," she said rather coyly. Alamgeer turned to look at her, and he spoke: "Go to your friends in the media and tell of the war we've been prophesying. Let them know that it is here. I want panic and chaos in the minds of the weak."

"Anything for you, my love." Francis winked and blew a kiss for him to catch, only for him to turn and close the door behind him as he left.

He breathed as he stepped outside and admired the gallantry of his horse. He walked in front of Copenhagen and bumped his chin with his fist as if to say "chin-up." He climbed upon the horse's back and slowly walked around the solemn-glow of Atma. He looked about its sadness. Statues of great men were now in ruins and distorted. The Copernicus Academy, once the prized school of mathematics, now drained of life, closed to all and abandoned. It's sister school, Kepler University, struggled to keep the lights on as attendance fell dramatically over a quarter century due to the war and economic inflation. He then passed the once architectural splendor to the eyes, the life and soul of the city, visited by millions to see legends play notes of musical masterpieces, but the Beethoven Hall was now nothing more than lost scales and broken keys, where the only note played was at rest.

The clap of the hooves of the horse fell silent as Alamgeer dismounted at the doors of the domed building capped in gold. Etched in the building's side were the words, *The Moschee of the Holy Feniex*. The sun graced the letters as it pulled the shade of the night closer to the horizon. Alamgeer said nothing to no one as he prayed the hour in silence. He felt his heart flow with emotion as he gazed upon his past and looked into the future. The long fight, the hard struggle looming closer to its end, his mind wandered to his father and their final moments together. He wondered if he would smile down upon him now, for what he did, he did for him.

The sound of the bell that hammered the hour uncovered the lambent eyes of Alamgeer. He glanced around the voluminous room of stained glass and columns made of jet. The floor he knelt upon was clear glass, showing the motions of the restless lava below, and the high ceilings dangled golden chandeliers, sharpening the room of the moschee, but nothing drew more attention than the fire that blazed at the front of the room. To the believers, the flighted flaring flames were that of the first reincarnation of the Messiah. As his eyes moved about the place of worship, they caught a glimpse of one of his generals. Alamgeer followed him out of the building of the Lord of Feniex and approached the general as they stepped outside.

"Von-Lewin!" Alamgeer gave a shout. The general's nose was pointed like a sharpened pencil, his face stern, and his eyes dark and serious. He turned to face Alamgeer with a grin across his face.

"Good evening, meine Papst. I hope the fire of the Feniex burns brightly inside you."

"His fire burns within me hot and fierce, more so than the flames that burn inside the moschee," Alamgeer replied in hyperbole.

"So, the flare in your eyes tells me. How can I help you, meine Papst?" the general asked as the two men walked over to Copenhagen.

"I want you to lead the blitz in the north," he told Von-Lewin.

"What of Guderian?" the general thought aloud.

"Guderian will lead the charge to Polsha. I want you to storm through to Attica,"

"I am honored, sir. Thank you." Von-Lewin spoke sincerely.

"And I am grateful to have you lead. We will discuss this further come the end of the week. For now, I must be going. Hella is waiting for me." Alamgeer shook the general's hand and climbed aboard his horse. "Have a lovely evening, Von-Lewin."

"As to you, sir." With a kick, Alamgeer set off to the glory of his castle that the people of Holle called the Magma Krone. He and his horse galloped by the two guards at the front of the Meister Mennatur Bridge. Their armor was dark gray and black with swords like lances hung across their backs. They stood nine and some ten feet tall, their faces of the undead, skull-like and terrifying, and where their eyes should be were sunken holes that traveled in the blackened halls that led to hell itself. The Skolastjori soldiers stood as still as stone gargoyles as Alamgeer rode by them.

The clattered bangs of Copenhagen slowed. Alamgeer dismounted and grabbed the reins to lead him to the stable. He ran his hand across his horse's face and gave him two light taps on his shoulder, saying goodbye to the beautiful creature, and headed towards the tall red doors of his home.

The entryway inside the castle was lit by the glow of luminary stalactite that hung from the cold ceilings above. The floors of the room were flattened stone, yet the walls of the oval entrance bulged and waved in all directions like the facade of a beaten and battered mountain. A servant came to Alamgeer and greeted him. Her face to the floor, she took off his shoes and kissed his feet. "Bless you, meine Papst." Alamgeer noticed her like an ant among men. The girl began to clean his footwear as he walked into the medieval rooms of the ancient and glorious palace.

Exposed stone in every room decorated the walls and ceilings like the tomb of an endless cave, cold and dark, yet mysteriously marvelous in its unique wonder and unknown beauty. He skirted by the dusted library with books an age of old, poems and sonnets scribbled in books next to stories in red to be read of wars and battles that cliffnoted tales of God and gods whose novels touched one another on the shelves, whose covers kissed the books of philosophies and science. He then ignored the tearoom, much like he did his servants, and entered the gallery of the ballroom. Whole walls ran like rivers of fire and lava, and the floors did the same. Its frightening attraction commanded the eyes to behold the natural masterpiece. The algae sprinkled like stars on the ceilings were illuminated a mystic blue to calm the senses in a wrath room of crimson and titian.

In each room he passed, and in each room he entered, within the castle, there stood two armed guards, straight as arrows, ridged and unmoving, armed to defend their Papst to the death if they must. They were a gallant glamor of armor, colored in the comeliness of gold and red, with blades of stunning silver, and to their sides a weapon that was held as a lance and so, too, could be used as one. In its design and function, it was also a firing weapon that shot rounds to kill all who crossed it bearer.

From the great hall, he rose to the solars on a stairway that twisted and turned, rising like a cobra ready to strike its foe, finally making way to his bedchamber. It was a whale of a room marked with the telltale signs of royalty. He entered the splendor of the room. Far to the left was an artist's view of his ruined city. At the forefront a bed of pillowed clouds colored in the setting sun was white algae brushed across the bedposts in cuts and strikes of bolts of lightning. The floors were a slate of midnight black that froze the feet with every step, and the walls were decorated in a painted sensation of God and angels like that seen only in the grandest cathedrals. Far to his right was a natural spring molded in rare gems and stones that steamed in the frigid room.

In the heated water, his wife was waiting for him. Her skin twinkled a tranquil glow of glistening diamond enchantment, with hair wet and smooth as silk, and eyes of passion and desire. She looked at him, a smoldering temptress, and he succumbed. He shed his clothes and joined her in the warmth of the spring and the warmth of her heart. The lovers lounged in the steamy embrace of each other's arms until the heat vanquished the energy within them.

Shimmering in the shine of the water, husband and wife left the comforts of the spring. Their flesh was like new, radiant and bright. They lay upon the softness of their bed, becoming binding bodies, and they slept in the darkness of the blackness of the night.

Whispered words among the people talked of war. The serpent's tongue slipped the lies of propaganda to fool the minds of the weak and warn the minds of the strong. Stories were told of men murdered, women raped, and children missing. Chaos was the name that came upon the muscle of the mouth. Then came the day—the day they called Herde. Families were gone, visesated from their homes, and those whose doors were marked were marked in red with the sign of Zvezda, two triangles in the shape of a star with a shin letter at its center. They were forced to leave, abandon, and flee, struck and shot for those who stood. The night ran waters from the sky caused by bolts that cracked the clouds. Those with faith claimed He wept and that His wrath would meet them soon. The might of the Tulku would destroy those who destroyed them.

Soldiers laughed and mocked their deity. They made gestures of fornication followed with vile words, profane and harsh, to the punktoret. The streets filled with mud and blood, shells from rifles, toys from children, and pictures of loved ones. The neighbors of those marked hid like mice inside their burrows. Not a word they spoke, not an action they made as sheep they became.

Those branded with the mark of Zvezda climbed aboard a train. Chestnut red ran the cars with tinted black windows. Fathers, mothers, daughters, and sons all boarded, cramped, and snugged. Babies cried, and mothers wept. The music of the night sounded in dread.

"Papers, papers to claim what is yours!" yelled the officers. "The war is here! The war is here!" Roars came from the depths in the sinking canals the people never heard. Deep the howl, wicked the sound, it turned faces a frightened frown. The final train left the station. The rain ceased. The booming growl died, and chaos was no more. Only silence lingered, merely to be deadened by white crystals that wafted down from above.

The new day brought a barren sky, fine and clear, the air without fog or soot. The city was like new. The blanket of snow gave the illusion of a city born again, flawless and pure. The volcano they called Drachenatem was of two faces. One side was angelic and glistened like gemstones. The other was a fiendish matte black, and running down its center was an ooze of cantaloupe goo, burning hot and feverous, separating the two sides.

Alamgeer opened those fever eyes to the dawn of the light and stepped outside his balcony in bare bottom to meet its esoteric blaze. His eyes consumed it, and so, too, his lungs consumed the wind, and just as the day was new, so was he. He admired the view a moment longer and stepped back inside the warmth of his castle. He looked upon his wife, her bedazzled back exposed as she slept. He cherished the sight of her as he walked past their bed to the shower at the far right of the room.

Cleaned, he left the steam and water behind and dried the beads of liquid on his skin, and as he did so, the tart tones of a woman called him.

"Good morning." Alamgeer turned, exposed, to see the face not of his wife but of another.

"What are you doing, Francis?" he covered himself.

"Why, I'm here to dress you, my love," she giddily informed him.

"Who let you in here?"

"Hella, of course." Alamgeer looked over to his wife and gave her a look that asked for a reason. She gave none but returned a look of amusement.

Francis walked over to him and swatted the hand that covered his manhood. He heard his wife chuckle, and then he felt a sting upon his derrière.

"Come on now. We haven't got all day," Francis toyed. Alamgeer moved forward to the front of the room as Francis grabbed his attire that hung on a stone.

The uniform was a terrifying atramentous color. It leeched to his body, defining the muscles in his legs, his chest, and his arms. Ethereal, breathable, the fabric was flexible and tenacious. It retarded flames, deadened bullets, repelled lasers. Only but a few materials could penetrate its shell.

The uniform now covered his body. Alamgeer sat at the end of his bed as Francis took a box from the floor that appeared more a present than an ordinary box. Within it were boots of the same material already covering his legs and torso, and they too seized the body tightly, yet were extremely comfortable.

"Rise," Francis ordered him, and he obeyed. She looked him up and down, admiring the shadowed image on his chest of an eight-pointed star and inside it a shin letter with a crown above it. She focused on the symbol, as it seemed to remind her of the band she had him wear the night of the speech at the Atma library.

"Oh, and this." She pulled the black, red, and white arm band from her pocket and slid it onto his bicep. She ran her hands across his body as she circled around him.

"Perfect," she said with gratification.

"Thank you, Francis. You may go," Hella said calmingly from inside the sheets of her bed. As Francis closed the door behind her, Hella stood with the silk covers covering her curvaceous constitution and moved towards the statuesque figure of her husband. She dropped the silky white sheets, letting them hit the floor at her feet. His bloodshot eyes looked into hers with desire and fiery love.

"Meine Papst," she said seductively. "She dressed you with everything you need except for one thing."

"And what am I missing?" he asked.

"Lean in, and I'll show you." The lovers locked lips. Hella's body flickered as the light within the room reflected off her shimmering skin. Their lock released, and she took his hand, leading him to the closet of the master bedroom. "And this." She grabbed an ebony cape, the symbol on its back the same as the one on his chest and bicep. "The cape of a hero. The Great Uniter. Meine Papst, Alamgeer," she whispered in his ear as she snapped the garment onto his shoulders. "Now, my king is ready. Now meine Führer kan Fuhren." Her tongue danced with his once more. He did not want to leave the passion of her mouth nor the hypnosis of her body, but duty called him, and her love adjured him.

He left the room, and standing outside was Francis along with ten girls, young and innocent. Each held jugs of water a vivid stunning blue; he looked at them with confoundment.

"They are helping your wife bathe and ready herself for the day. She is going to look stunning," said Francis. "Let's go, Ala. We have much to do." She grasped his hand and walked him through the halls of the castle, leading him to the entrance. As they walked, he made her release him with a twist of the wrist. The two stepped outside into the cool air of winter to where a carriage hung suspended above the ground, awaiting their arrival. It was square and black with white tinted windows. The corners and the latches on the carriage were capped with pure silver. There was nothing that pulled the vehicle, nor did anyone drive it. It simply moved to the destination desired by its passengers.

They rode the clear streets of Atma, fractured and broken, through narrow lanes, past tattered boulevards, around the bleakness of the shops and gliding past all that had once been glorious until they arrived at Hofbrauhaus.

The building was of a renaissance design, standing at four stories. The floor windows were arched and shaped as long as they were wide, and as the building rose, the windows squared, and at its corner, the building protruded outward a half cylindric shape in stone and of an elegant conception in a city of tumultuous denigration. Yet in its sorry state, it still had an artful charm.

They entered Hofbrauhaus from its backside and through the cellar doors. Its floors were set with unorganized cobblestone. Its setting was dark, lit with light soft and dim. Alamgeer sat in the brew of the atmosphere, concocting the ingredients of his idea within the cozy caliginous. His right leg shook, and his nerves were a misfire of wires, a zap and a shock, or so it felt to him.

"Ala, what's troubling you?" Francis saw his unease.

"It's nothing," he lied. She didn't push the issue, though her facial expressions noted the oddity of his behavior, and then she left him, accounting for those who were to attend. Alamgeer's mind weighed on his mother, wanting her, needing her to be here aboard the stage with him. His daydream traveled back to childhood moments with her—times of merriment and others of anguish.

He recalled a memory in his youth, just a boy of ten in the underground of the underground of the Mausoleum in the city of Taj. He walked among the dead of the great, of heroes sung and written, the fabled and the truth. The white clay walls ran alongside him with every step he took on the sanded clay floor, and within those white walls, the dead rested, a statue next to every soul. The tombs of the dead seemed to rise a hundred feet and circled the cylindric room.

Alamgeer was angry with his mother, more so his father. *You're not to see that boy ever again! Do you understand?* Those were the words that went through his head. The words of his father telling him he could no longer be friends with his only friend, Himmel. He had cried and ran, going through every secret door Himmel had shown him, and doors he had never known and never seen until he found his way into the depths of the crypt. Alone he walked, in the twilight of the room. His nerves began tremble, his heart thumped a bumping beat that rattled the cage of his body he called his ribs. In his startled state of solitude, he came across a face he knew from stories passed down from his father and his father's father, for the man he saw was the face of his great, great, great grandfather, the uniter, Mahatma. Ala touched his statue, and a voice began to speak to him.

"This is the story of Mahatma Bin Hidler, the Great Uniter." The words were spoken in a smooth alto male tone. "Here I lie in the tomb of heroes, an honor few receive. My tale is of many accomplishments, but my legend is of one." His third-great-grandfather continued his story of a series of deeds that led to his position and his final act. "During my final years as king, I united all of the eastern lands, connecting the broken continent into the land of Holle. From east to west, the countries slowly became one, some through war, others through treaties, but the single most uniting factor was our ancestry and how we all came from…" a loud and calamitous rumble shook Alamgeer off his feet. The ground beneath him began to crack and bits of clay the size of his head began to fall from the walls that surrounded him.

His heart raced once more, a galloping trot of a speeding horse; his red eyes watered tears of fears. He forgot his anger towards his mother and called out her name, "Mom!" he screamed in panic. "Mutter! Mutter!" he wailed as he railed through door after door, looking for his way back to her. The door he entered next was a room of darkness, and the world around him still vibrated to the rhythm of ataxia. Rain from his eyes streamed down his face, and calls for his mother soon took on a tone of despair. He ran in the blackness, and as he did, he fell to the ground, a slash to gash the young boy's face. He could not shed another tear as red now swam across his vision, and as the earth roared and thundered in its anger, Alamgeer felt a warm and familiar touch, and his eye beheld his mother in that crepuscule hour.

Betrud tore off her black glove that ran up her elbow and knotted it over her son's eye. She lifted him in her arms and sang to him a song.

Good evening my sweet child
Dressed in the flower rose
I see your petals weeping
Of drooping sadness woes
Oh let me see what they can't see
I'll peep to see your soul
A beauty nectar glistening
A distance pole to pole
Now show the world what I now know
A flower full of fight
The truth is in awakening
To always do what's right

Alamgeer closed his eye that was unharmed, as his mother kissed the one she wrapped, and he dozed to the night of fright. When he awoke, she was by his side, stroking his dark locks. He smiled at his mother as she leaned in to kiss his forehead.

"How are you feeling, my son?"

"Tired." he said to her. He touched his face to wipe the crust from his eyes and remembered the slash that ran across his right. He looked at his mother in a bit of shock.

"It's going to be alright, Ala," she assured him with motherly affection. He rested his hand over the patch that protected it. "You didn't lose it. You'll be able to see again, I promise."

Whispered words came from the room across the way, and then came a shout. He saw his mother look away to see what was the matter.

"The Tulku did this!" came a yell from his father. Betrud looked back at her son.

"I'll be right back," she said, and just as she was leaving the room, Alamgeer needed to tell his mother something. He felt he must.

"I'm sorry, Mom," he told her, and she mouthed the words, *I love you,* and when she was gone, he said the words, "I love you, too."

Alamgeer awoke from the fog that reeled his memory of that time long ago. A percussion of heels slapped the cellar stairs as Francis walked down to fetch him.

"Are you ready?"

Alamgeer rose from his feet, indicating his preparedness. Still not saying a word, he walked up the staircase to the main floor of Hofbrauhaus and strode out the front door of the building to witness the stage where he'd give his speech. Before him was a crowd of thousands, and beyond him, tens of thousands, yet beyond them over 100,000—all lining the streets, peeking through all the windows of every building they could find. The people cheered and roared high praise for their leader.

Standing to Alamgeer's left were his generals, and to his right, his wife, mother, and Francis. He raised his hand to silence the crowd. His heart thumped and bumped a querulous quiver, and it could not be seen, but his skin perspired in his nervousness. He looked to his right to the loving woman beside him and smiled.

"Meine Holle!" he exclaimed, folding his arms, listening to the sound of the people hooting. He stood speechless for longer than necessary, peering out over the Hollen citizens. "Meine Land," he spoke and paused again; his arms still crossed. "My home." the words came out softly.

"In this week, this week of dreaded revulsion, we have had friends, families, brothers, sisters, mothers, fathers, and children moved from their homes. Right in the pitch of night, in the cover of darkness, vanished. They became like ghosts in the shadows. These acts were done on my orders. Cruel and heartless they may seem. I will shed light to brighten the truth." He stood silent, as did the thousands before him, hanging on every syllable of every word.

"We are at war," he said calmly. "In the past few years, we have had the Telekine volk cast a patch aside their sleeves and marked their stores with the sign of their religion. We did this to protect them, for we knew this day could come. The Telekine, who call themselves Hollen, have been labeled traitors, marked for dead by the people of their own religion and by the leaders and thieves of Yisra and the pompous Saoirse.

Last night, there was an attempted attack on our volk to kill them, and in haste, we responded. The Braunhemd and our local police worked side by side to help our friends and family flee their homes from this outside threat." Alamgeer rested his tongue a moment.

"Our Telekine volk have been given papers, assuring them they will be repaid for their losses. Their homes will be restored, possession regained, and memories to be had to hide the pain of the visesated night. However, today, they need our help. Today, your country needs your help. Donate what you can to these families who have lost everything, and give to your country in its time of need to combat the arsenal of evil that has fallen upon our land. One franq or one hundred, it does not matter. So long as you can give what you can, we will come out of this struggle a stronger, more glorious Holle!" The crowd became excited with a hint of nervous energy, but the people seemed optimistic of the outcome that could be. Alamgeer let the voice of the people reverberate as they shouted praises in the area of the square, and then Alamgeer spoke. His voice was serious, his expression fierce.

"Know this! All of what has happened and is to happen could have been avoided. If our fathers and mothers of the socialist ill had not broken this country in war and conquest, we would still be the greatest nation known to man. As the son of Alois, I do not expect you to trust me fully. I hear your words, your grievances, your pains of having me in power. I know you mistrust me, but today, I will right the wrongs of the past and will sacrifice something true and dear to my heart." He paused and breathed deeply. Hella handed him his blade, black and cimmerian. Its hilt was gold and etched with immaculate precision. Red waves of light bounced from the surface of the steel. Alamgeer began to pace the stage.

"What I do, I do for you. I do for my volk! I do for my land! I do for Holle!" His tone was almost one of hatred as it carried through the winds in the cold winter air. As he walked back from the right of the stage to its center, he swung his sword, and the head of a woman rolled. The stage consumed the blood, and the jocundity of the people enveloped the city's center.

Lorena Chapter Two

Her toes tapped rapidly on the surface of the hardwood floor as she spun across the room, waving her arms slowly up and down like a bird flapping its wings in flight. The music was the wind beneath her wings and made the sight of her dance a masterpiece, a masterclass performance. The tempo was allegro, her pageantry a moving picture. She brought the act to life. Sautés, jetés, entrechat, assemblé, her movements rapid yet her wings were adagio. The music fell silent, and so, too, the raven that she was.

Beads of sweat dripped from her forehead as she curtsied the judges with a vivid glowing smile of pride on her face. She floated away off-stage behind the red rippled curtain.

"An-mhaith Lorena! Beautiful, my dear." Her instructor grabbed her face and kissed her cheeks.

"Thank you, Mrs. Pavlova." Lorena spoke graciously in breaths short and choppy, still winded from her performance.

"I'm so proud of you! Now go and change. You won't know your score until tomorrow," Anna happily informed her student. "No matter the score, Lorena, be proud. That was wonderful to watch."

"Thank you, Mrs. Pavlova. Thank you for everything." She spoke with a heart of truth and gratitude, leaving the room to shower the exhaustion from her body.

Lorena rinsed her curves dressed in sweat and impurities that rested on her skin, and refreshed all that was within and without to ready herself for her next dance, one of silver blades and the sounds of war and battle. She felt elated as she left the performing arts center. The brisk air blushed her cheeks a cold and lush raspberry red, making her eyes a stark, spellbinding beauty in which no one could help but stop and stare in wonderment at her fairness and the eminence of her innocence. She walked out, down the stairs of the entrance of the theater, waved goodbye to her instructor, and headed towards her hovercraft.

The nuclear reaction brought the vehicle to life. She turned the heat of the car on, warming her frigid goose bumped body, and drove a few blocks from the theater, turning down Second Street to her favorite coffee shop, The Rabbit Foot. She parked her car in hover mode, above a vehicle that rested below hers, and as the craft rested idly in space, the soft blue lights that lined the roads rose to meet her in the shape of a spiraled staircase. She walked down on the stairs made of light and entered the warmth of the cafe.

"Right on time, my princess. Your turtle truffle is waiting for you." Efiac welcomed her.

"Thank you, Efiac. Do you think I could get a water as well?" Lorena asked kindly.

"Of course, my princess," said the man with gray, curly hair. "Was your big performance today?" he asked with great interest as he went to get Lorena a bottled water.

"It was."

"And how did you do?" He asked, handing her the bottle of water.

"The best I could," she said humbly.

"So modest, Lorena. I bet you wowed the judges in there."

"I certainly tried to. You don't get much reaction from them."

"Men of stone faces, are they? I bet you cracked them and didn't even know it." Efiac spoke flattering words.

"Let's hope so. This is for the role of the Raven."

"Then the raven you will be. I do not doubt it," he said, as if he already knew she had the role.

"Thank you, Efiac." Lorena paid the stout old man and smiled at his praises. "I'll see you in a few days?"

"You will indeed, princess, or should I say, my Raven Princess?" She giggled at the shop owner.

"Goodbye, Efiac."

"Goodbye, dear. Have a great day."

Lorena left the cafe in her roman red craft and headed towards the comely allure of her fencing studio. Her mind wandered to her dance, and she began to think of where the judges could deduct points. She shook the thoughts from her head to remember the words of her instructor on how wonderful it was to watch. She smiled again, turning down River Run Road. Lorena parked her floating carriage and breathed because, for the second time today, should would be tested. It would be a criterion not only of footwork and tempo but one of real-time creativity, where success or failure was not only determined by her but also by her counterpart. Before she exited the craft, she closed her eyes and pictured every foot movement, every stab, and every counter to her action, and when her blue-green eyes opened, 1,200 grains of sand had fallen from the jar of time.

Lorena left her vehicle. The cold air ran through her, but she paid it no mind as she walked out into the crisp and piercing winter and into the cold comforts of the swordsman's temple.

"Welcome, Maid of Aontu. You're just on time," her instructor, Sir Wallace, welcomed her.

"Hello, Sir Wallace." She curtsied to him and headed towards her room to dress, changing into her gear. Her hands shook, and her legs rattled as she donned her armor. She exited the dressing room, her heart still aflutter from the shudder of fear and doubt. Lorena's instructor greeted her as the two walked to the stage of her fate.

"Good luck," Sir Wallace whispered. Lorena's tongue was silent, too focused on the task at hand to speak.

She capped on her helm, the intent of her eyes focused on Sir Wallace. Her blade ran parallel to her face as she honored her counterpart and whipped the blade back to her side. Lorena formed her stance, and the war of destiny began. The ting tang tattle of the silver blades battle-ranted in harmony in the age-old room. Her feet of might were light as she tipped and toed on the mat beneath her. The eyes and mind in sync to guide the hand to seek the points of man found weak. Her blade searched to make the deadly blow only to be countered by her friendly foe, and as the poem of fight raged in steady beats, she felt the point of pain in the first round of defeat.

Round two of combat danced in the struggle of contention of her fate. Mightily and beautifully, she fought only to lose, but she was not distraught. Instead, a flaming soul ignited, engulfing every bone and muscle, every vein and every nerve.

Lorena claimed round three and then round four, leading her to the pinnacle of the engagement, the final bout in which every part of her living being would have to be of utmost perfection, for the slightest of errors in the art of war could cost her life, her hopes, and dreams. A loss would slaughter the details of her desires, and end the elegance and fascination of life, a beginning of nothing but crude drivel and the permanent loss of all substance.

She breathed, taking in the oxygen around her, letting it fill her lungs, feeding the heart and mind, letting all of her become one, focused. Her eyes were dead set on her instructor. She readied her stance for the final time. Her blade skirted his in a frenzy of circles, constantly in touch with his, never letting Sir Wallace strike. Back she stepped and then once more until she neared the edge of the mat—the platform of battle. Sir Wallace struck, but she twirled on the balance of her toes, causing his blow to strike the air around Lorena, and when her rotation was complete, the tip of her saber found the heart of her beloved and worshipped instructor. The battle was over; her fate was sealed. The beating organ inside her still raced as her lungs inhaled and exhaled in a rapid cadence of exhaustion and joy.

She removed her helmet and bowed to her instructor, and then ran to him in an embrace of accomplishment and thanksgiving.

"Congratulation, Lorena," he said.

"I don't know what to say, Sir Wallace. I've trained so hard for this day. Thank you so much for everything you have taught me and will continue to teach me. It is and always will be an honor to be your student. Thank you." Lorena embraced him once more, her voice shaky as she spoke.

"You are most welcome, Lorena." He paused and spoke again. "In the ways of the blade, there is little more I can teach you. You have become a far better swordsman than I could have ever hoped to be. There is no living being on earth that has mastered foil, epec, and saber. You're a true wonder, and I'm very proud of you."

Lorena's tears ran down her cheeks, for she was elated, not only with herself but from the kind and bonhomous words from her instructor. Grace and mercy filled her heart. Her mind was filled with love, and peace invaded every part of her body.

"Go and wash up. If I know you, your day is not done yet." Sir Wallace grinned proudly.

Lorena washed away the grime and sweat that had kept her body cool in the heat of her physical and mental dance with the sword, and when she left the shower, she was refreshed and cleansed. She was clothed and like new for the evening. She met Sir Wallace at the entrance of the temple building and asked for his advice.

"Sir Wallace, what do you recommend for me? How do I better myself with the blade?"

"There are many sword types throughout the world. Practice against not only them but against weaponry of distance as well. Learn their weights, their weaknesses, and their strengths. You're fortunate to have a brother who is one of the best swordsmen in history. Search masters of these weapons, and train with them. Always be a student, even in your mastery." Lorena smiled and bowed to him. Sir Wallace did the same in return.

"Thank you, again, Sir Wallace," she said, and just as she was about to leave, she remembered something her father had given her. "Oh! I nearly forgot." She grabbed a folded piece of parchment from her bag. "My father told me to give this to you." She handed him the paper. "Goodbye, Sir Wallace."

"Goodbye, Mater Darroch." Lorena's face glowed at his farewell as she closed the door behind her and found her way to her hovercraft.

Beaming from the day, she drove in bliss. The blue lights of the street gave a mystic glow, and the lamprog fluttered an enigmatic light as the city glistened in the brilliance. As she drove through the busy streets, she came across a crowd that chanted and hollered, closing down the road parallel to the one she was traveling on. Lorena took note of it but kept driving, not letting anything get in the way of her celebratory mood. She finally made her way to Arch Street, and as always, to Lorena, it felt like one of the greatest streets to drive down in all of Saoirse. The brick clad in sandstone, and the brick clad in marble buildings were timeless in their appearance with the Saoirse' flag hanging from every structure lining the street. Lorena parked her hovercraft near the building she'd be entering and walked to her destination. As she got closer to her institute, the noise of the gathered crowd seemed to grow louder. She focused, trying to interpret what they were saying, but the sound was muffled in her ears. Lorena was at the entryway of her building and ran her hand over the bronzed lion, as she always did, and entered the historic institution.

Lorena took her seat in the red-beamed room, awaiting General Westmore. She placed her books in front of her and turned the pages to a chapter she had marked with a red ribbon, and the title of the chapter read, "The Siege of Orleans." The thud of the footsteps from her instructor became audible, and she looked up as he entered the room.

"Good morning, general," she greeted the tall, dark, and gentle man.

"Good evening, Lorena. Did you enjoy your reading of Ms. Joan?" he asked.

"Very much so. I nearly cried when I found out how she died."

"Tragic, wasn't it?" the general matched her dejected tone. "But let us talk of what made her great, what catapulted her into greatness." Lorena leaned forward and listened. "Starvation, small, coordinated attacks, scouting, brute force, and faith propelled her to extraordinary victories. Her story is a near-fable and everlasting because of these tactics. She is the story man needs, for without stories like hers, hope will fail to blossom in our hearts," the general explained. "Heed the advice of your council as Joan did, trust in your mind's decision, and believe in your heart to execute."

"It seemed to me her faith made her tactics unorthodox, almost foolish," Lorena noted.

"Perhaps that is what made her such a success in the siege. The unexpected is difficult to account for. Turning back to face your enemy in a retreat, scouting along, leading a charge on a whim. Joan believed in the power of the Strong Tower. It gave her strength and victory." Westmore shined a little light on the subject.

"Do you think her devoted faith led to her being shot when leading the charge to Tourelles?" Lorena asked.

"That is simply a part of war." General Westmore stated the obvious, which led to teacher and student discussing the siege in great detail, where improvements could have been made on both sides of the battles, and what ultimately led to the ascendancy of the life of Saint Joan. They talked about her character in words that brightened the imagination, visualizing the scenes of battle and the woman that was sanctified. The hours rushed by in a rhythm of logic and a cadence of conversation.

"Well, Lorena, I believe our session is over." Westmore's voice boomed even when he spoke softly.

"Wow, that was quick." She looked at the time on her watch. "That has to be one of my favorites so far, general. Her unyielding faith and trust in the Deity is something to remember, the way it impacts a person and how they think and act. It can be a great ally in war," Lorena noted while packing up her belongings. "So general, what will you be doing for Yule?"

"I'll be going out west with my wife. We have a cabin in the mountains," he answered.

"Aw, that sounds rather lovely. When will our next session be?"

"Let me check my calendar. Ah yes, as I thought, the third day of the new year," he informed her as he walked with Lorena to the door of the front of the building. "Oh, before I forget. I want you to study some of our own history. Read about the siege of Vickburg, Deonach, and our civil war."

"Any mythic heroes in these?" Lorena asked with wonder.

"Only the author makes a man a hero," the general said.

Lorena looked at the band of her watch, and its face unfolded into a rectangular digital display. She jotted down the siege and the war and folded the band back into place and squeezed the gentle giant Westmore with her arms. He did the same to Lorena but with a softer touch.

"Happy Yuletide," he said.

"Nollaig Shona," Lorena commented back to him as they released their friendly embrace. She opened the door to leave, and when the aperture appeared between the edges, both heard the loud chants of the mob that was at the end of the block. The mob rattled and roared to be heard. "Nua Ri," they cried, "Se Nach Befoil Ar Ri!" Lorena and the General listened to their mantra.

"New king, new king, for he is not our king." She spoke aloud and looked over to General Westmore.

"Would you like a ride to your car, Lorena?" he asked.

"I'm not far. I think I should be alright," she said with slight apprehension.

"Are you sure?" the general asked again.

"I'll call you as soon as I'm inside my vehicle," she assured him.

"Please do." His orotund voice pronounced the words seriously. Lorena grinned and closed the door behind her.

As she walked down the road, she noticed the wail of the crowd grow from an alley on Arc Street. She quickened her steps as her heart quickened its beat to the scatter-shot of nerves that coursed through her body.

Her eyes beheld the crowd, youthful and angry. The first wave walked by her, talking of her father and the meeting with Yefimovich in which a treaty was to be signed.

"I'm not religious. He is not my King," she heard a disgruntled man say.

"His God is not my god. He is no king of mine," she heard another. The crowd now surrounded her, and she was sardined. The assemblage became destructive about her. Cars went up in flames, a fireball fury. Stained glass windows shattered as the mob began destroying the beauty and the artistry of the buildings.

Lorena was still a hundred yards from her hovercraft as the mob began to notice who she was. People started exclaiming, as their attentions turned in her direction, and remarks of ill repute came dashing to her ears. The agitated group began to encircle her in an aggressive manner.

She examined the crowd and its ethnicities, descendants of Holle, Mongnolerium, Heavohen, and obvious Saoirse natives. A hand came over her, large and maddened. Lorena swatted it aside with the brush of rigid fingers. Another grabbed her collar, so she spun like a whirling wind to cause the Heavohen man to released his grip. She swung her bag around her, dropping it to the ground while simultaneously pulling out her saber. Four men came at her, one from every side. The Heavohen man at her forefront, she slashed with her saber, causing him to fall back onto the rough and brutish ground with a brilliant red gash across his cheek, and in the same motion, she sidestepped to her right towards the side of the Hollen man who awaited her and whipped her saber in a fluid motion across the shins of the aggressor. The man knelt down in agonizing pain, and she struck the monster's nose with the hardened bone of her elbow. Lorena quickly turned to face the man behind her and, without hesitation, stabbed him with the tip of her blade, sliding the sword into the flesh of the attacker's shoulder, kicking out his knees, and causing him to buckle to the ground. Elegantly, she moved to face her final foe, and as she did so, in her gracious movement, was struck from behind, catapulting her into the villainy of the angered man. The wicked barbarian grabbed her and slammed her body to the ground and mounted her, but Lorena was not without fight. She took her daggered claws and ran them through his eyes. The man screamed a horrid sound, covering his eyes and rolling off her. Lorena tried to get up only to be knocked back down by the masses. They ripped off her jacket, shredding it in two, and tore the shirt she wore underneath, exposing her violet bra.

She cried for help, but who could hear in the enraged sea of vicious men and women. Then came a growl, hostile, the sound like the warnings of a fearsome beast, and there among the abominable stood a soldier. His metallic armor was a devilish jet black, patterned with dark gray patches to mirror that of a leopard's print. His helmet was faceless, made with the same materials as the body armor, with two eye slits that ignited a brilliant and captivating evergreen. The soldier ripped the man off Lorena and tossed him twenty yards. He fired a shot into the air. The crowd fled in all directions like bees in distress without a queen. The mighty savior removed his helmet.

"Are you alright, my dear?" he asked the damsel.

"I'm fine" Lorena said with a calm voice and tears running down her face. She held the metal waist of the soldier tightly. "Thank you, General Westmore. I'm sorry. I should have had you take me to my car," she admitted, weeping in embarrassment.

"There is no need to apologize, Lorena. You are not at fault for anything here." He spoke with a kind and sincere heart. Lorena grabbed her bag and put on a sweater that was tucked away within it.

"Can you follow me home, general?" she asked with shaking nerves, her cheeks still wet from the tears that had left her eyes.

"Of course, I can," he assured her.

"Thank you." General Westmore opened up her cruiser door for her to take her seat. He glanced about the roadway; the rioting animals kept their distance as Lorena drove to the front of the institute while the General walked beside her vehicle. When she parked the hovercraft, he spoke to those who remained. His voice rumbled a bass, deep and powerful, sounding more fearsome with his helmet upon his head.

"Step any closer than you are now, and it will mean your life!" The general stood at the entryway of the institute for a moment, then entered the building to change, with Lorena following close behind him.

When they returned a few moments later, the car was untouched. Lorena turned on her vehicle with General Westmore in a craft behind her, and the two drove off from the site.

The bundle of fibers within her body that conveyed impulses of sensation and motion were still clattering, but her heart bounced strong and steady. She felt comforted, knowing General Westmore was right behind her. He was with her all the way past the castle gates and into the marvelous castle itself. The extraordinary structure seemed empty as they entered. Lorena called her mother first, then her brothers, and finally her father to no avail. In the midst of the evening hours of the dusky sky, she searched the grand castle for her family. It was only when she was about to give up that she saw a message on her communicator. She wondered how she missed the message before. The narrative read aloud with an image of her mother projecting from her communicator.

"Lo, it's your mother. I hope your performances today were astounding, and I cannot wait to hear all about them. I'm calling to let you know that your grandfather, uncle, and I are heading to the capitol, and we won't be back until later this evening. I'm so sorry I can't be there right now to hear about your day. I love you." The recording ended. Her heart sullen, she headed back to the living area where General Westmore had been patiently waiting.

"They're not here." Her vocal cords spoke in a sad sonnet. "Can you stay a while?"

"I'll stay until you need me, my dear." He calmed her worries. Lorena smiled at his generosity in thankfulness and headed to the kitchen to brew a pot a coffee for the both of them.

When she returned, teacher and student sat across from one another. The seats were cotton soft and immaculate in design. The stitching was superb in every piece of fabric. The paintings that hung from the walls were like the living, frozen in time by the realism of the artists' capture. A small fire soothed the room, and Lorena began to feel at home inside her home.

The big, tall burley man with a deep and mountainous voice began to tell a tale of a little known battle from what the world knew as The Great War. Lorena leaned forward, both hands on her cup of coffee, listening intently to the story Westmore was beginning to tell.

"It was eighteen year ago, when I was a younger man, that I fought in a small but terrible battle during The Great War, inside the beauteous and amicable Red Forest, of what is now Avstrija. It was myself and a fellow, Liopard, my best friend, Major Ardal Iobairt, whom I had known since I was your age now.

The day was new, the ground still wet from the dew. The birds chirped peacefully that summer morning. The leaves on the trees of the Red Forest were still green, and though it was summer, the air was frigid on the skin. We were at the edge of the forest tree line, surrounded by mountains, looking down below at a small town. If your eyes could see the scene, it would be a gorgeous collection of rooftops colored orange and brown, and buildings colored red and white, with a church that stood amongst the rest in the center of the town. The Faithful building was nothing gargantuan, nor anything spectacular, but still, it was the highlight of the quiet village of maybe 5,000 souls.

"While Ardal and I waited in this magical scene for our targets to arrive, we talked about when we were kids, how we grew up, and what the times were like back when we were nine and ten. The world seemed at ease then. There were no wars or battles. People were happy and carefree, or so it seemed anyway. We tend to recall only the best in our youth.

"I remember Ardal was talking about his wife and daughter and comparing his life to his daughter's. It was her birthday that day. She was turning thirteen, I think, and as we talked in whispers, we heard laughter coming from our right. We both turned to see two little boys. They were maybe ten and seven. They hadn't seen us, but they were coming our way and getting closer. The two seemed to have wandered off from the trail. They were maybe 400 yards from the path and having a battle all their own, playing with wooden swords, fighting one another now just feet from us, and then, suddenly, they stopped."

"What happened next?" Lorena asked with great interest.

"Well, their mother yelled at them," he laughed and then continued the story. "She had blond hair, a skinny figure—she seemed a lovely woman. She was carrying a basket in her arms. It looked like she was bringing her sons on a picnic. It was actually a very nice and very real moment. The woman finally caught up to her two rambunctious boys and reprimanded them. The older boy took his punishment with no rebuttal, but the younger one rebelled and ran from his mother, and as he ran, he tripped over Ardal as we were both covered, lying on the ground, camouflaged from the world until we weren't." Westmore paused as he was interrupted by Lorena.

"Oh, no!" her voice soft and sympathetic.

"Our thoughts exactly. The wee lad was immensely frightened, and so too his brother and mother. You could see the dread in the green eyes of the woman. I rose to my knee and tried to help the boy back to his feet, but he wouldn't budge, so Ardal took off his helmet and showed his face to the child. He always carried a few candy bars on our missions, so he helped the boy up and handed him a galaxy bar.

We finally calmed the family down, but now we had a choice to make. Do we let them go? Do we take them hostage? Or do we abort the mission?" Lorena interjected yet again.

"Did you let them go?"

"We did. We watched them head up the mountain to enjoy their day, and it's something we would regret.

From then on, we waited nearly three hours at our post when we saw the vehicle we had been waiting for. Ardal and I peeped for our shot." Westmore stopped again as Lorena asked another question.

"Who was the target?"

"Our mission was to scout a transaction with a shoot-to-kill order if Emperor Alois was present at the meeting," Westmore answered.

"Was he?" she asked.

"He was. The emperor was sitting outside at a bakery called Dreamy Cakes Bakery. Ardal noted the wind, its strength and direction, our position, our angle, and all the things that require a perfect shot, and as we readied our shot, we were ambushed. An ocean of enemy soldiers surrounded us. I slung the sniper around my shoulder while the major started firing at the wave of Hollen men. He cut down three men quickly, and we made our way towards the direction up the mountain, covering our angles from shots fired all around us. North, up the range we went, pausing to fire back, taking out five men of the ten men we knew were pursuing us.

"It was silent a moment, and in that silence, we pulled up our communicator and asked for an extraction from the barrage, receiving an ETA of fifteen minutes. We looked at our map displayed on our wrists and found an area to board the hover plane that was coming for us. It was about a mile up the ridge, and as soon as we mapped our route, another wave from the sea of soldiers fired upon us. Hearing the bullets sprinkle by us and the explosions getting closer in the quiet of the forest was the most vivid and horrific experience in a battle that I had ever been in. Ardal and I trekked up the mountain as quick as we could, pausing every few hundred feet to turn and fire down at our enemy.

"Ten minutes had gone by, and we were only a half mile up the mountain range. We had to stop our movement upward, hunker down, and settle in for a fire fight we weren't prepared for. We struck shields into the ground that extended six feet to block us from the might of the arsenal below. We reloaded and radioed our situation. Our fifteen minutes was up, our plane gone, and another ETA of thirty minutes, this time with a Black Iolar hover plane coming to get us, along with four Mactire soldiers to provide us with assistance.

"The army of enemy combatants now reached thirty, and one by one, we tried to exterminate, and in these thirty minutes of combat and struggle, Ardal was shot in the left arm by an armor piercing bullet, digging its way into the bone. Strong he was. He continued to fight, firing his weapon with his opposite hand while I dug out the bullet as best I could and plugged the wound with a xstat syringe.

"We heard the war plane fly overhead. It concussed the air with the sound of relief, and then we heard the scream of the howling wind from the drop pods the Mactire soldiers were being deployed from. They landed hard in front of us, cratering the earth, and on their approach, the battle intensified. Rockets started flaring towards us. Lasers pierced the air, and bullets still rang loud.

"We were able to manage another quarter mile up the mountain and once more had to position ourselves for a defensive stand. We radioed our position to the pilot of the roaring Iolar, and the metal bird joined the fight, bombarding the battlefield with its own lasers and bullets, laying down suppressive fire in a fight we were losing. Quickly, the beast of a machine killed twenty men, and as it fired in its awe-inspiring display of green lit lasers and red brazen bullets, it received a return barrage. Five rockets were launched towards the plane with one striking the right engine, and together, we watched in disbelief as the sands of time stopped in that instant, and the bird that was to bring us to salvation came thundering down to the hell of the earth."

"How did you get out?" Lorena was pulled into the epic like a leach to the flesh of a man.

"I got out by the grace of God," Westmore replied. The room was silent as the general seemed to reflect on the story, and Lorena was still envisioning the scene he was describing.

"What happened next?" she asked.

"Our mission had now changed. Our goal at that moment was to get to the wreckage to see if the pilot was still alive and to destroy anything of value in the aircraft. So, we traveled a half mile back down to where we had come."

"You had to go back down the mountain?" Lorena couldn't believe the absurdity.

"Back to the darkness, to the death, in the heart of the Red Forest. These men, my friends, fought like myths and legends until, one by one, their stories ended, scribbled in the notebooks of history and silly tales like my own. The pilot was dead, the plane in pieces. Day was now night, and four of the five Mactire soldiers were now with The Almighty. I watched a man fight and saw a laser penetrate his chest and out his back. Bloodless was his death as the burn of the laser clotted the blood but removed his heart. I watched as another was struck in the lens of his helmet by a bullet whose odds of hitting that very spot was infinitesimally small, but the Lord said it was his time to leave the earth based on the choice he had made to come and save my life. I am unsure as to how the other two soldiers lost their lives, as we all became separated in this horrible conflict, trying to position ourselves for the best chance of survival. From what I could tell, it was just myself and Ardal, and we were both so very sad, so very tired, full of sorrow and with little hope left.

"In our despair, in the oily night, water fell from the brooding gray clouds above. With the cover of darkness and the cloak of the rain, Ardal and I sprinted as fast as we possibly could back up the indomitable mountain. In our attempt to flee the wickedness, I was shot in both arms and in my left leg, but Ardal was somehow unscathed. We were finally near the top, close to our extraction point, and the monstrosity of the engagement continued its terror upon us. It flowed like the river of death and breathed the air of fire; the number of men killed was near seventy. It was Ardal and I and another man missing we'd assume dead. From where we stood, forty more men came at us. I was shot once more in the shoulder, but every shot we fired seemed to kill an enemy soldier. Our fortune did not last, however, for soon, grenades had splashed down about our feet. I looked at Ardal, and he looked back at me, and without a thought, with pure instinct and love, my greatest and most cherished friend took his life for mine, shielding me from the shrapnel of the bombs that exploded in his heart. I have never felt such adulation in my beating organ, nor have I ever felt such a sting of heartache, and in my emotional rollercoaster, I wept for him. Tears seeped from my eyes, but still I fought, no longer for myself, but for my dear, dear friend." Lorena's own eyes watered and trickled down her soft white cheeks, sliding down her neck.

"In this agony, I raged against them. I slaughtered them with the power of my weapon and with the honor of my blade. I sent the beings back down to the hell from which they came. Fifteen souls I took until the army of men entrapped me. I took a shot to the chest. Its pain was nothing compared to the loss of my friend, yet it still took me down. Pinned I now was, much like you were today, and the soldier who lay atop of me took a knife from his side. He rested the blade on my lips. It's how I have this scar here, and he ran it down towards my neck, and just as he was about to slit my throat, shots came pouring in from behind those who remained. I watched as this man killed them all. The flash of the muzzle of the gun was like lightning, and it struck fear and death into the hearts of the enemy, and when the bolts of Zeus were no more, the blade of righteousness took over. The sword was nearly as tall as he, and he carried a shield made of light that glowed white hot and purple, and in his hands, it looked as if steam radiated from it. The phosphorescent weapon was circled, and within it there was a triangle and a cross, and etched in light was a letter, and the message on the shield read, 'This light is our love.

May it forever burn bright within our souls, and let it shine brightest when the world has gone dark.'"

"That's—my dad," Lorena whispered.

"That man is your father," the general confirmed. "From that day, I took the love I had in my friendship with Ardal and gave it to your father. He is the greatest warrior I have ever seen and a remarkable and true friend." General Westmore looked at the time on the classical timepiece that rested on his wrist and that only had the time of day. It was dressed in gold trim, and gold marked the hours. He realized the lateness of the hour. "Well, my dear, I must be going," he said, standing from his seat to leave.

"Thank you for staying with me, and thank you for sharing that story. It was a poignant tale I needed to hear." She smiled at him.

"Call if you need anything. I promise I'll answer," he told her. Lorena walked over to him and gave him yet another hug in gratitude.

"My father thinks the same of you, you know." The words carved a grin on the general's face.

"Goodnight Lorena."

"Goodnight, general," she said, and the two departed from each other's sight. Lorena accoutred herself for the evening after showering off the grit and the grime from her body and hair. She dressed in the most comfortable of clothes, of cottons soft and heavy, warm, and cozy. She scrolled through the news of the day, of the riots and the treaty. Hatred filled her heart at the sight of the criminal youths, but that anger was soon washed away by love when her eyes beheld her father as he signed the treaty with Yefimovich, binding the two nations.

Her eyes and body grew tired from the joy and the misery of the day. She wished someone was with her to whom she could talk to as she examined the parchment her father had given her. Blank and empty the paper was, and with still not a clue as to how it might be deciphered. She put the paper to the side and rested her head on the soft down pillows, her body wrapped in the cradle of covers as she snuggled within them. Her eyes were weighted, heavy like iron. Lorena's mind wandered as her baby blue-green eyes closed, and she began to dream a dream of war.

Absolume Chapter One

The night was sparkling in a dazzling display of stars that burned billions of miles away in a sea of blankness that wrapped the orb of the earth. Absolume stood outside the ivory castle with his brother, sister, and Yekaterina, his arm over his brother's shoulder, filled with affinity, admiration, and love. Absolume's ocean blue eyes gazed up at the celestials in wonderment, awe, and simple glamour, and he reflected on when the two of them were just wee boys.

"Do you remember when we were kids, and we would pretend we were Bushi knights?"

"We used to go on hikes by ourselves, and when we got bored, we'd find the nearest stick on the ground or break a branch from a low hanging tree, and we would tell ourselves that they were Bushi energy blades." Aedus drew up the memories with his brother.

"I remember my mean brothers always making me be the bad guy." Lorena joined in on the brotherly conversation. "You called yourselves, The Brother Boys." Aedus and Absolume laughed as they recalled the moments they made together. "You know, I bet I could still beat The Brother Boys," she teased them. Abe and Aed smirked at one another. The brothers broke from each other and began following after their clever sister. The siblings laughed in their light-hearted bickering with one another as they ran about the grounds.

"Come on, Kat! Help us!" Aedus yelled as he pursued Lorena in the woods of the land of the castle they called home.

In his dash to catch his sister, Absolume broke a branch from a nearby tree. He rushed to block his sister's route and held out his broken branch he called a Bushi Blade, but in her grace and elegance, Lorena, as she ran towards Absolume, slid underneath his child-like sword and continued her escape.

The boys once more caught up to her. All of them were armed with branches the size of their arms. "We have you surrounded. Diminish your blade!" Absolume commanded. Lorena chuckled.

"We all know where this goes," she said and leapt at Abe with her wooden sword to strike. He blocked his sister's initial swing and the two began to dual, both laughing in hysteria at their childish manner.

"Aed! Help me!" Absolume cachinnated the words as he spoke.

"Brother Boys!" Aedus yelled as he began to battle against his sister, aiding his brother in the fight. In the choreographed manner they made up as kids, they fought a battle they had fought a hundred times, and in their scripted fight, Lorena lost her sword. Aedus put his fictional blade to his sister's back. "Kneel," he ordered Lorena, and in her defeat, she did so.

"You are hereby sentenced to death for the betrayal of the Bushi order. Your only redemption is forgiveness in death." Absolume spoke in a serious tone, though blithe in demeanor. He pulled back his wooden stick to end her fabricated life, and as he did so, he was struck lightly in the back.

"You are perished, Bushi knight." Yekaterina spoke the words in a monotone calm, and much like a child would, Absolume gave a convincing performance as he played out his death. "Aedus of The Brother Boys, stand aside or meet the fate of your beloved brother," she spoke with authority.

Aedus left his sister's side and prepared to fight the Tulku. "So be it." He smiled at her. With no preplanned sword play, the two tested one another. The imagined blades thudded as they clashed upon one another. Aedus was quick, his strikes precise and to the point. Kat was almost as fast as he, and as they played the game of war, the two became serious as to who was the better warrior. Absolume and Lorena watched intently.

Smack, clack, thud—the sound of fictional blades echoed softly in the forest. Aedus had the upper hand in the fight. His strength and his speed were godlike, his swordsmanship masterful, even with a simple stick. In her slow defeat, Yekaterina began to use her natural abilities, throwing up barriers of earth with a simple hand gesture, floating away to get some distance from Aedus, using the elements she could control to get an advantage. In their play of bladed battle, Absolume could see a connection between the two, strong was the bind if examined with great focus, loose the grip when seen without the bond of family. Their battle stormed until in the end, the dreamt-up blade of Aedus cracked and broke within his hands. Yekaterina grinned at him.

"Behold the kiss of death," she smirked, poking him on the cheek with her lips while poking him in the back with her branch. Aedus's eyes grew wide in surprise, and he too simulated his beautiful demise. "Death to The Brother Boys! Long live The Lost Sisters!" she yelled as she pointed her branch blade at Lorena and smiled.

"Well, that was fun." Absolume spoke a jocund tone.

"Rematch soon?" Aedus canvassed the three of them.

"Without question," said Yekaterina.

"If you want to lose again, little brother," Lorena joked. The evening was late under the twinkling starlit sky.

"I'm calling it a night," Absolume yawned. "I'm exhausted. I'll see you all in the morning."

They all said their goodnights to Absolume. "Congrats on your win tonight, Aed, a true racing Nuke. Don't stay up too late." He spoke jubilantly.

"Thanks, Abe. I'm close behind you," Aedus responded, seeming touched by the events of the night that reflected in his tone as he spoke.

Absolume made way to his room in the maze of the whimsical halls of the castle, walking silently and with only the faintest of clicks coming from the heels of his boots. His room was an alabaster white with trim of solid gold that branched like fire, carving its way through wood. The gold lining decorated the room on the doors and sections made for paintings, of which he had five. One of the paintings was the hand of a man reaching towards the outreached hand of God. Another was the scene of his father's hammer lodged in the liquid living metal at Hoba. One more of the Lady of the Lake who held a sword for a king named Arthur. He had another painting hanging from the walls that displayed the scene of the signing of the Saoirse constitution, and his favorite, the most simple of pieces, yet the most meaningful, was the shamrock, the symbol of his faith, and from the daingne upon both arms, blood dripped, and where the droplets fell, there were puddles of fire and ash. To Absolume, it meant that even in death, the Savior lives and will be born of flesh once more.

He outfitted himself for the night, for which he would sleep for only a few short hours, and when he was washed and his mind and body pure, he prayed at the foot of his bed. He asked for nothing but prayed only to give thanks to the Creator. Absolume kept the fireplace within his room unlit, curled into his soft cotton sheets, and closed his eyes to end the joyous day.

Water, invisible to the naked eye, floating in the open air, froze upon the dead grass and the branches of the trees, crystalizing the world in a still beauty within the quiet hours of the morning before the rising sun awoke from its slumber to rein in the day. Absolume cracked open his sand-filled eyes at the five o'clock hour and prepared himself for the day ahead. Within his room was a safe the size of a large closet, and within his safe was an arsenal of weapons. Of guns, he had twenty, and of swords, he had five, most of which were historic relics. For every treasured weapon, there was a note or a book on the man to whom it belonged, its origin, and the battles and wars the weapon had fought in.

Like his sister, he studied the strategies of war. Absolume was stellar with a sword in his hand and a genius with a gun, as he had trained with the blade since he was three and with guns since he was a wee boy of ten. He packed the items he needed, threw on his winter coat, and headed out the doors of the prodigious frosted chateau. The air outside grabbed him; icebound he was from the sting of its wrath. He blew into his hands to warm them and then pulled brown stitched leather gloves from his right coat pocket. He then rubbed his ears that looked a bit like his mother's and pulled out earmuffs from his left coat pocket. Both hands and head now warm from the thrill of the chill of the caterwauling air, he found a button the size of a coin embedded in the wrist of his glove and pressed its center to summon his car to the front of the keep. In a jiffy, his car guided itself to him, parking only feet from his own. The door opened as if an invisible man catered to Absolume. He climbed in, the feel of it warm as the heated air burned the ice he felt inside his body. The hovercraft was a machine of cultivated beauty and of wild allure. It was a tame beast, white on the outside as well as within, skirted with red trim that accented the lush leather. Absolume took control of the vehicle, releasing it from autonomous drive, put his foot on the pedal, leaving the grounds of his home, and headed towards the arctic countryside.

He drove the narrow winding roads with long green grass pastures, abandoned broken-down castles from a more ancient time, and snow-dusted fields, and on his drive, he listened to the news from a man name Hudson Rush. The words that left the mouth of the radio host fell onto the ears of Absolume and were absorbed by the power of his brain. The canals of his ears caught the story of an event to be held later that day, and the event was called "A Day of Rage," where the youth of Saoirse were gathering to protest his father and Yefimovich and their unity to fight in a war should evil events occur.

At the news of the early morning, he turned down the volume and drove the remainder of his journey in silence, listening to the subtle vibes of the hovercraft until he reached his destination. When he arrived, his eyes beheld the brick ranch home. It had a cobblestone driveway and a stable that was designed into a hill, extending outward from its plateau, leading Absolume away from the country roads and into the loving home. He parked the vehicle and inhaled the bracing country air, walking to the barn of vehicles and a sleigh that was showcased on the second floor, and descended to the stable of horses.

"Hey, old man." He caressed the snout of Amsterdam. "My lady." He bowed to Beauty and ran his hand across the side of her face. He moved along to the next stable, where there was a black horse with a crimson mane plumed in style from his head down his neck and a tail that whipped the same red colors and whose hairs near his hooves were of the same. The silver name plate on his stable read Pendragon.

"Good morning, Pen." The horse stuck out his chest and high-stepped to Absolume. "At ease, soldier," he greeted Pendragon, taking him out of his stable, laying apples on the floor while he brushed the horse's coat. Once the fur was smoothed and groomed, he laid a crimson cape over the back of Pendragon. "Ready boy?" he asked his horse. "You know where we're going." He climbed aboard the gentle beast and gave him a few light kicks with his heels, setting Pendragon trotting off into the field towards the thicket of the woods in the distance.

Six-thirty was the hour, and the minutes continued to tick as Absolume reached a log house in the middle of the forest, isolated from the world in the cover of trees that extended high into the stark blue sky. A man sat outside the home. He was of average height, buzzed gray hair, slender, athletic build, and in his hand, he twirled a sword made of light. His pointed ears and sharp eyes were directed at his student.

"Good morning, my young dalta." The teacher spoke in a pleasing alto voice.

"Good morning, laerer," he greeted his teacher, Myrddin Arthurian.

"It's going to snow heavy tonight," said Myrddin as he looked up at the cloudless sky.

"I'll be sure to drink plenty of shockloyd to prepare for it." Absolume shivered.

"Are you ready for today's lesson?"

"I'm ready." Absolume dismounted from Pendragon and walked with his teacher to a small clearing of stones standing twenty feet high, patterned in a circle. At the center of the circle of rocks was a shamrock carved of stone with lamprogs on the arms of the cross that symbolized the daingne.

"Sit, my student, and let us pray." Together, they sat in silence, each saying their own silent prayer. Absolume focused on wisdom, guidance, and patience. For thirty minutes, they knelt side by side until the time struck seven. "The course is set, Abe. We'll begin the day with your greatest strength, the gun. I'll place your weapons in their preset locations." Absolume handed his instructor his cases of weaponry.

The course was a maze of targets and was a hundred yards in length. Myrddin set up a rifle that shot beams of light, and that light was entrapped in an orb. The weapon was placed at the very beginning of the course for the targets most distant. Then, he placed a small-range rifle further into the course for enemies at midrange and ammo clips for his pistol as he moved along the path of the obstacles. The final weapon, the gunna-grain, was set outside a shack home for close-quarters combat that sprayed bullets when its trigger was pulled.

"There are three targets a hundred yards away that you must take out in order to proceed from your first position. Once complete, you are able to move down the range where you will find your rifle; of enemies here, there are five. Move down the course some more, and here, your sidearm comes into play; for enemies, there will be six. From there, you will advance to the home that you must enter, and awaiting you will be the gunna-grain for which to take out the enemies; another five there will be. When you are ready, you may begin." Myrddin finished his instructions to Absolume. Abe acknowledged with a simple nod of the head and began his test of warfare with the hardware of a gun.

He fell to the floor where Myrddin had positioned the light rifle. He placed his eye in the line of the scope. He calibrated wind, distance, and angle in mere seconds, inhaled deeply, and took his first shot. A beam of light left the gun, penetrating the skull of the enemy. He repeated his action like a needle skipping on a record until all three targets had been eliminated. He left the rifle behind, sprinting to his next location with his sidearm in hand, finding cover along the way. Being exposed for too long could mean his death.

He found the midrange weapon within the labyrinth. His eyes focused, his breathing steady, his pace perfect, he spotted his adversaries. A pull of the trigger, an enemy down, dominoes the lesson became until the fifth foe was vanquished by the rush of the bullet that left his gun. Absolume was relieved he hadn't been shocked, for with every missed shot from his gun, he received a sharp bolt of pain, simulating he had been hit by the enemy.

He checked his sidearm, for he knew he needed it next in the maze of haze and walls of shrubs that became thicker and more narrow the further down the path he went. Pop, pop, pop—the targets flopped, and death consumed them. Pop, pop! Two more dropped as Absolume moved along the course to stop the would-be menace. Pop—that pistol rang once more at the entrance of the small house at the end of the boscage circuit.

Absolume saw the gunna at the doorway, glanced at the windows for tangos—there were none—grabbed the weapon, checked for ammo, breathed once more, then blew the door from its hinges, aimed, click, clatter, the rhythm of the gun scatter. One down and four to go, across the hall another foe he laid to rest. Two steps forward, a steady pace, click, pull, another gone. Two more to act on.

In the room, he noted a hostage. He respirated to stabilize his aim and downed the opponent standing closest to the victim with a shot from his pistol, and in the next millisecond diminished all who meant to harm him to the sounds of a gun whistle.

"Astounding work, Absolume." Praises rang from his teacher's mouth.

"Thank you, laerer," he spoke with grace.

"You know Abe, there isn't much more I can teach you with a gun. I've been training you since you were a small boy, and I'm so very proud. To see an apprentice surpass his master is truly inspiring and quite humbling. It's a wonderful feeling—one I hope you'll get to feel when you train a son or daughter of your own," Myrddin said.

"I've been lucky to have you as my teacher. Your training will leave me indebted to you and linked to you forever." Absolume spoke with gratitude.

"Well, my young dalta, there is still something you can learn from me in the ways of the sword," said Myrddin, patting Absolume on his back as they walked towards a crumbled bastion in which all that remained of the gray brick fortress was an entrance and a tower whose walls had fallen on one side. Myrddin had restored what little was left of the entryway. Many of the gray bricks looked no older than ten years of age. The arches and beams were of fresh oaks, and its floor were four, massive, twenty-yard stone blocks. Decorating the walls were banners from all four military branches as well as others from a different era long ago. Skirting the ceiling and walls were flowers in bloom, an Avengler touch to a Saoirse life. Light from the sun shone above, as a quarter of the roof was still missing. At the end of the main room, the only room, was a display of weaponry, from swords of steel to those of light, to axes and hammers and shields. From an Avengler weapon or Saoirse, even those of Telekine and Heavohe, they littered the room. "I'll let you decide today which type of blade we'll use," his teacher said

"The solaslann, please," Abe requested.

"The swords of light. My specialty." Myrddin turned his lips u-shaped and took his hands and pulled the open air with his thumb and forefinger, as if stringing a needle through thread, capturing the light that was around him and stored the brilliance in a diamond. He then locked the diamond rock into the hilt of the sword and let the imprisoned light release its power in physical matter by nature's law known as Brietwheeler. The color of the solaslann illuminated purple from the optical dispersion of the diamond inside. Myrddin handed the sword to Absolume and then pulled the light from around him once more, generating his own blades, which scintillated blue, and the sound of the two blades vibrated a retro hum of an electromagnetic manner.

Teacher and student took their stances. Their blades were low-lit sabers so that when struck, it would wound a fellow pupil with a soft burn instead of slicing through them. Absolume approached his laerer, and when their blades of illumination collided, it created a sound that resembled a whip snapping the air or of two stars colliding in the vacuum of space. The light of their blades danced in the dimly lit castle. The retro hum of the cracks of the sabers echoed a music of clashing battle until, alas, Absolume was defeated by his teacher.

"Well fought, Absolume. It won't be long until you best me with the blade as well. You and your family are quite the talent."
Abe smirked at the words that came from his instructor's tongue. "Thank you my laerer."

"Come, let us pray." The two knelt once more, and they bowed their heads in prayer. Together they rose in the word of Germa.

"Absolume, before our next session on Spirtus, I want you to read Yishu of Zhanzheng by Tzu Tzu and learn his master strategies. No need to bring any weaponry—our next meeting will be a simple lecture," said Myrddin.

"Thank you for the lesson today, Laerer Arthurian. I will be sure to start the book tonight."

"Have a good day, my young dalta, and happy birthday." Myrddin left Absolume with a friendly embrace, and Absolume mounted his horse outside the home of Myrddin.

"Will I see you tomorrow for my birthday?"

"I wouldn't miss it," his teacher said with pleased eyes.

"Goodbye, Myrddin." Absolume waved with a smile.

"Goodbye, old friend."

Teacher and student separated ways to seize the events of the day. When Absolume arrived back to the lush country home in Buna, he quickly freshened up to wipe the sweat and dirt from his body, hopped back into his vehicle and sped down the narrow country lanes routed to the capitol building in the bustling city. The citizens of Saoirse were out and about early in the morning, gift shopping for the celebration of Yule, picking up last-minute gifts as the holiday was nearly upon them, just a day after the birthdays of Absolume and his brother, Aedus. The city was aglow in light that sparkled and shimmered a hypnotic fancy. Streets and shops were dressed in holiday cheer with decorations that symbolized peace, joy, honor, and above all, the honor of their Maker, the bringer of peace on earth, the man born of fire. Seeing those enraptured and the kindness of so many people filled Absolume's heart with an almost unexplainable emotion of a purpose and meaning greater than himself that could only be seen when the masses of the world come together in a celebration of purity and godliness, which betters the values and morals of all of humanity. He let his heart breathe in the affected air and absorbed the benevolence of others to fill his soul as he drove in the greatness of the city.

Absolume parked his craft outside the capitol building and handed his key to the valet. The resplendent white building played contrast to the stunning blues of the sky. The pillared dome was a tour de force of architectural ingenuity, as it rose four levels to the heaven above, and mounted on the top of the ivory building was the statue of freedom. Its color was blazing bronze. The statue of the man held a sheathed sword on his waist, a shield with an image of an eagle slung across his back, and in his hands, a dove, bleached white, who carried an olive branch of peace within its beak. In the sculptured man's other hand was a staff, and flying from it, the Saoirse flag designed with thirteen stars circled bold and center, colored blue, standing for justice. The red vertical stripes symbolized valor and the white, purity.

Absolume walked the stairs, center right of the building, and entered through the navy blue doors. He passed his way through the stunning halls of the capitol. Skirting the center, and rising, were wooden balconies, carved and studded in an elegant display. Each level was supported by marble pillars whose bases flared like scrolls. The buildings top level was arched and painted in works of art, and each level was lit by lamprogs entangled together to shape chandeliers.

Absolume climbed another set of stairs, and waiting for him at the top were Aedus and Yekaterina. The trio took their seats in the room of red wood walls, sea blue carpet, and snow-white chairs, in a place of friendly meetings and hostile encounters. The comhail members took their seats below in anticipation of the speech Yefimovich was about to deliver.

Absolume listened intently at the words that left the mouth of Yefimovich. His stuttered cadence was like music in words deep and profound that rose above all to set a standard for man to reach and for man to be in a time that was growing ever darker and dreadful—where loved ones could be lost, where all that was once cherished in the light of life could be blotted out by the darkness of death.

Absolume stood in ovation in response to the beauty and the power of the words of Yefimovich, words to a nation seeking another, to help one another as friends, as allies. Aedus and Katerina stood beside him in applause at the might of the speech.

"Let's go join our fathers," said Absolume. The three departed from the room to the halls down onto the stairs, heading towards the chamber doors, and he saw his grandfather, his uncle and his mother. At that moment, the doors opened and out stepped his father, Iscariot and Yefimovich. Absolume could see something was the matter and quickened his pace. Enoch had turned and saw his grandson approaching, and when his eyes laid glimpse of him his demeanor changed.

"Abe! My you've grown. No longer a seedling but a full-grown oak you have become." His grandfather embraced him.

"What brings you here? Why are you at the capitol?" Absolume asked his grandfather.

"We are here for you and your brother, but our stop at the capitol is something, I'm afraid, that is nothing to celebrate," Enoch answered, and it was then Robert interrupted the dialog.

"Enoch, what is the matter?"

"I need to talk to the three of you." Enoch gestured at Robert, Yefimovich, and Iscariot. "I don't believe Yefimovich is being hyperbolic in his words or in his actions."

"Isc, and Yef, do you have time now to meet in the council room?" Robert asked them.

"I don't think I have much say in the matter. After all, you did bring me here, Robert." Yefimovich spoke with a light heart.

"I don't believe I have much of a say either. You are the king, my brother, and if you need me, I will be there," Iscariot responded.

"Good, let us meet in the council room in about thirty minutes," Robert said to them.

"Dad, can I come to this meeting?" Absolume inquired, and he could see his father weighed the choice of yes or no in his mind.

"You may come. Listen and learn," he commanded his son. Absolume nodded.

"May I suggest Yekaterina join us as well," Enoch commented. Kat looked at him, and Enoch gave a smile to the girl he considered a daughter.

"Yes, of course," said Robert, and the group of might and minds, and of love and family dispersed. Absolume departed from Aedus and Yekaterina to tail his father, the king, Robert.

In the majesty of the halls as he walked next to his father, Absolume tried to sense the gravity of the choices his father had to make, to feel what it was like for a noble man, a moral man, to make difficult decisions every day for the rest of his life—decisions that would influence people he would never see and never know, to absorb all the good and all the bad that came from an action he decided was the proper step to make.

"Thank you, daidi," Absolume said to his father.

"What for?" Robert asked.

"For letting me join you in this meeting."

"If Yefimovich and your grandfather are this serious, this afraid, then you must be there. You have become a great man, Absolume, and it seems that great men are going to be needed in the days to come." Robert put his arm around his son as they walked what remained of the journey to the King's study.

Robert grabbed a few things within the room while Absolume took a seat to wait on his father.

"Is Aedus coming?" the king asked his son.

"I don't think so," said Abe.

"Comm your brother and let him know I want him at this meeting as well."

"Yes, father." Absolume flicked his wrist to awaken his communicator to call his brother. His face was scanned by this device, enabling Aedus to see him when he answered the call.

"Hey, Abe." Aedus's face appeared from the device worn on Absolume's wrist.

"Aed, where are you?" he asked his brother.

"I just hopped into my Shelby. I was going to surprise Lorena while you all were at the meeting," Aedus replied.

"Well, don't go anywhere. Father wants you at this meeting."

"Alright, I'll see you up there then," Aedus said without question, not needing a reason other than that his father wanted him there.

"A kind heart your brother is," said Robert. "We'll need that, too."

"Saint-like, that one." Abe poked fun at his absent brother.

"Don't joke about him too much. He is quite good with a sword," his father reminded him. "Let's get going, Abe." Father and son left the study and walked up the flight of stairs to the council chambers.

"Did you know he was bested by Katerina last night?" Abe continued the conversation stemming from the comment about Aedus's swordsmanship.

"Did she really? That's quite impressive, considering he is a master swordsman." Robert's tone struck amusement and wonder.

"Well, he was using a stick as a sword, and it broke. Nonetheless, he did lose," Absolume recounted.

"He must have been embarrassed." Robert seemed to try envisioning the scene.

"I don't think he minded. He got a kiss out of it."

"Smitten those two are. They have quite the chemistry for just meeting one another," Robert observed.

"I'd say that's an understatement."

"If their relationship is going to bring our families closer together, then I can only see that as a wonderful thing for both families. As close of friends as Yefimovich was with my father, I should have made a better effort to keep our families close to one another," Robert reflected.

"At least you remained good friends with Mr. Nemtsov, even though you're not able to see each other often. After all, the both of you are leaders of great countries with heavy responsibilities," Absolume reminded his father, as if he needed reminding, as the two reached the doors of the chamber room.

"After you, son." Robert gestured with his hand for Absolume to walk into the room. He entered. The room was bright with light, the columns blazing golden brown and tan. The only thing within the room was a round, wooden table, large in diameter and nearly 3,000 years old. The table looked its age and so too the seats they sat upon. Of the thirty-two chairs at the table, fourteen had meaning and significance, and in order to occupy those seats, one had to be part of an order and had to be worthy of sitting in a throne of sin or virtue. Of sins, there were seven, and the same held true for virtue. Nine bodies were at this meeting, and of the nine, only one sat in a chair of intention, the king. Robert took his seat on the throne of patience. When selected king by God, it was he, like all kings before him, to take the seat thought needed most of that king. All called to the meeting were present, and when all had seated, the meeting began. In attendance were Robert, his two sons and wife, Yefimovich and his daughter, along with Enoch, his son Uriel, and lastly, Iscariot.

Robert spoke, "Enoch, I have known you a long time and have never seen you act this way. What is troubling you?"

"We all know there is the largest of hints of a great evil approaching, and I am here to tell you, to warn you of what is to come," Enoch replied.

"What do you mean, Enoch? Yef has informed us of the Hollen threat, and we have monitored it closely, and we will act to ensure war does not take place. That was the purpose of Yefimovich's speech today," said king Robert.

"I am here to tell you that war will happen regardless of your treaties and that the destruction is beyond what you can imagine. I know seven angels will come down to the earth as will two seraph and fight among us. My, they were glorious. The Maker told me to tell the people they are coming and that fire will rule the world, and those who remain will be consumed by it." Enoch started to paint a picture for them.

"Enoch, you sound mad," Yefimovich said with concern.

"I know I do. Honestly, lately, I have felt delirious, but I promise you what I say is true." Enoch spoke, his voice sounding tired.

"How do you know this?" Robert asked.

"He has found the bonds between heaven and earth," Lagertha spoke up.

"Is it true?" Robert spoke in disbelief.

"It is," Enoch responded. "It came as a voice, and the whisper told me to visesate, and I found myself at the top of the mountain, where the waters of Tilgivelse begin, and there a figure met me and showed me all that is and all that will be." Enoch rubbed his eyes. Absolume could see the doubt in the eyes of few, and his mind forced his mouth to ask.

"If war and destruction are inevitable, how do we prevail?" Robert nodded at his son.

"I have not been given such answers." Enoch sounded as if he had failed.

"Was there anything else, Enoch?" Robert asked.

"He showed me the spirits of the earth, the water, the moon, the sun, the wind, and how they never faltered. He told me to tell the people. He said he showed me this because I asked to see it." Enoch finished his words, and the room was silent until Yekaterina rose to speak.

"Then, like the elements, we will not falter. We will stay our course, and if death is to greet us, we will welcome him with open arms."

"Here, here," her father resounded.

"Yef, you have battle plans currently in place for an attack. Can we arrange a meeting with your war council?" Robert pondered the question and fed it to the room.

"Consider it done," Yefimovich confirmed.

"Isc, after Yule, I want you to go to Holle as an ambassador. I want you to negotiate and tell me the ongoings of the Hollen leadership as best you can. Report all you know back to me. This mission may last a month or two, until we have enough information to attack. We will work with Yefimovich's timeline," Robert informed his brother.

"Do you mind if I bring my son?" Iscariot asked his king.

"I don't think that would be wise, Isc," Robert responded.

"Robert, should I be gone that long, I will not be able to see my son—please," Iscariot insisted.

"Do you think he will be safe?" Robert asked.

"He will be at my side at all times," Iscariot assured him.

"Will that not hinder negotiations?" the king inquired.

"For meetings of the classified, I will ensure he is nearby yet not a hindrance to our prosperity. Robert, he is a man tomorrow. Graduate of the top military school. This is the perfect time to give him experience," Isc rebutted.

"I will leave the choice to Hanns himself, then." Robert gave his final word on the matter. "Let us reconvene in two days time. Yef, prep your military leaders, and when we return, Tokugawa will be here, and another mind will help guide us to a resolution on this terrible burden." Robert thanked the room of nine and adjourned the meeting.

Absolume left the chamber room with his father, his mother, and his brother. Robert and Lagertha talked amongst themselves as both Aedus and Absolume tried to listen to their murmured speech which seemed to be more about the boys' birthday rather than the topics discussed in the meeting. Robert and his wife parted ways, saying goodbye with a kiss and an I love you. Abe stayed with his father, while Aedus departed from the family with a heartfelt farewell.

Father and son, once more, were in the king's study. Absolume took a seat opposite his father's chair while the king scrolled through documents on his portable device and sifted through papers that rested on his desk. Robert grabbed a pen and a piece of parchment and began to write, and as quickly as the black ink hit the white paper, the words seemed to vanish like a ghost dissolving in a shadow, an apparition of words never to be seen again unless provoked.

"What is that?" Absolume pried.

"It's a letter to Hanns for his birthday," Robert replied.

"What is happening to the letters you write on the page? The ink evaporates before you scribble the next character," he observed and questioned.

"It is an ink that can only been seen when heated at 450 degrees Fahrenheit. Any less and the ink does not show, any more and the paper burns."

"Clever," his tune a quiet curiosity.

"Very much so," his old man grinned.

"But why?"

"Whether I want him to or not, Hanns will choose to go with his father. While he is there, he will be assigned a task of simple reporting. The layout of things, who comes and goes, anything he finds of interest," Robert elucidated.

"You're having him spy?" Absolume tried to clarify the meaning.

"He is merely observing. Nothing more." Robert stamped his statement and sealed his letter in wax, and the seal was of a ring, and upon that ring read, "Culper Ring." Robert stowed the letter in his bag and turned to face his son. "Will you tell him how to read it?"

"If you want me to, I will."

"Thank you. Tell him to burn the letter after he reads it and to remember the seal," the king instructed his son.

"Yes, father," he nodded, and the two of them left the king's study, as well as the capitol, and headed home in Absolume's hovercraft.

For Absolume, the day began early, before the rise of the sun, and ended late, near the twenty-first hour of the day. Robert looked at his son and smiled, and Absolume could see pride and love in his father's eyes.

"Are you ready?" he asked Absolume.

"For what?"

"To fight?"

<u>Aedus Chapter One</u>

The night's algid air reddened his face, numbed his nose, and iced his hands while the lid of the earth was clement in its manner, letting the heavenly bodies of the universe consume his naked eyes in the bravura of the artistry that was above him. It was a night Aedus would not forget. The thrill of the race to place a standard not achieved by someone as young as he filled his humbled heart, and though he was only feeling the fuel of pride in his moment of victory, far more memorable to him was the coupling the instant his eyes locked with Yekaterina's. The pull was magnetic, the emotion unbounded; it was beyond when stars collide, for it was more powerful and more spectacular than any natural phenomenon. The elation was galactic, and it burned a hyper giant luminosity, entangling every fiber, every tissue, every organ, and every nerve, webbing his very being in a spellbound string that wrapped him with just a single look. This and more he reflected on for a mere minute in the endless bound of time.

His dark eyes drooped from fatigue of joyous pleasures shared with the ones he loved.

"Goodnight, Lolo," his voice a tired articulation as he flicked his sister in the arm in a physical display of sibling affection.

"Goodnight, my little brother boy. I'm so proud and so happy for you." She kissed her brother on the cheek while she flicked his arm as he did hers.

"Thanks, Lo. I'll see you in the morning before your trials," he said before she left.

"You better," she teased. "Goodnight, Aed. Goodnight, Kat." Aedus was now alone with the woman who had turned him head over heels, affixed to a fancy, and her name was Yekaterina. Before he could speak to her, she spoke.

"How do you move like that? You're faster than any Saoirse man I've ever seen. You move like a Hemitheoi."

"Well, I'm not your normal Saoirse man," he answered.

"What do you mean?"

"My father found me alone in the woods. My parents he found, too, in the storm of the night that took their lives," Aedus described.

"Oh—I'm so sorry, I didn't—" she began to apologize.

"It's fine. It's a well-kept secret not many people know." Aedus comforted her slight embarrassment.

"I've been training all my life from masters and teachers all around the globe, and never have I come across someone as skilled as you," she complimented him.

"Thank you, Kat, your words are very kind. Like my brother and sister, I have trained with the blade since I was three. Each of us has a different instructor, and we still train with them till this day. Sir Myrddin has schooled Absolume for as long as I can remember, and Lo has been instructed by Sir Wallace since before I was born. Tomorrow, she has a trial in which she will have mastered the three fencing styles. She's quite remarkable." He praised and admired his siblings.

"Who is your blade master?"

"A very old Nihon man whom holds the title, 'Unrivaled Under Heaven.'"

"That's quite the title," Yekaterina remarked with a tone of intrigue.

"He's quite the man."

"I lived in Nihon when I was a little girl to train. How come I have never heard of him?" Kat queried.

"My sensei was quite the swordsman in his day. Of sixty-one opponents faced, he defeated them all, and in his last duel he ended up killing his challenger." Aedus paused his story as he and Katerina began walking back to the castle.

"That's dreadful. Was this not a friendly duel? Who was his challenger?" she asked.

"It was an accident. He and his contester fought with wooden swords they made themselves, and in the battle, his blade struck the back of the head of his opponent, hitting the area just right, killing the man instantly—I guess the reason you don't know my master is because the man he killed was Tokugawa's childhood friend, Master Sasaki Kojiro," Aedus enlightened her.

"That is so sad. What did Tokugawa do?"

"Tokugawa ordered for his arrest. My sensei felt heartbroken, so he fled into exile, isolating himself until my father stumbled upon him one day during a hunting trip. He has been in my life ever since."

"From what I hear, your father and Tokugawa are great friends. Why did he not turn him in?" Katerina asked.

"He did, but as you might know, shame is a powerful weapon in the Nihon society. Miyamoto Musashi's punishment was his exile and still is his exile. He is never to go back to Nihon as long as he lives. His redemption for his actions is to train me until his death or until I defeat him in a duel," Aedus explained.

The affectionate doves stood at the castle doors and though frozen they had become, they lingered longer in its shadow. Aedus enjoyed her company, and it seemed she savored his as she continued the conversation.

"So, have you battled and defeated Miyamoto?"

"I have and in turn have been granted the title of Bushi Masutaa," Aedus replied.

"No wonder you're so skilled. Why doesn't Musashi go back to Nihon if he is redeemed?" she inquired, her teeth starting to jitter.

"I asked him the same thing, and he told me that the shame would kill him. To kill the friend of a friend, even by accident, unthreads the spirit, and to see your beloved friend every day, knowing you had taken the life of his greatest friend, would unravel him until he was no more," Aedus paraphrased to Katerina. "Are you alright?" he noted her shivering.

"I'm fine" she said still chattering her teeth. "Your teacher's story is grief stricken. It pains my heart. I'd very much like to meet him. Will he be at your birthday celebration?"

"I don't believe so. He is too embarrassed to show his face in the presence of Tokugawa," said Aedus.

"A pity—another time then." Yekaterina's voice was disheartened.

"I'm sure he'd be delighted to meet the Tulku." Aedus smiled at her. "Shall we go in? It's awfully cold out here." Aedus opened the door to the birch tree forest the castle called its entryway and what his family called, "the room of seasons," while flurries that never hit the floor fell from the ceiling above, and the lamprog lit the room like stars in the night sky.

"Goodnight, Katerina," he said, departing from her.

"Goodnight, Aedus." Their eyes glistened at one another, telling tales of fleeting hearts, wanting to say words of love and poetry, but holding them behind the walled teeth of their mouths. The two parted to see each other in made-up stories of their dreams.

Temporal hands moved the infinities of every fallen second as Aedus rested his mind and body, restoring his energy, filtering his thoughts, regenerating him body and soul. He awoke before the flare of the abounding sun. Cleansing his physical build while heated water opened his pours, removing the dirt and sweat that rested lightly on his skin. He adorned himself in all white and bedecked over his attire a nacre cloak. Aedus could hear his brother down the hall as he too had an early start to the day, one filled with weaponry and battle, sessions of a warrior and bishop.

Aedus's path, like all others, was different from his brother's. He walked the dark halls of the castle in the shadow of the early morning, leaving the stronghold of his home, and in the lightless ante meridiem, dressed in pearl white, he made a bantam journey to the city by foot, and his destination, a holy place, a sacred place, known to all as Deantore's Cathedral.

The city streets were desolate in the coming of the morning. Lamprogs hung in the air a hushing hue, and the roads were a blushing blue, guiding Aedus to the house of the Devine, and he arrived at the behemoth. The entrance was a tower that kissed the gate of heaven, held by the might of stone white beams that mimicked the look of a pipe organ and spread out like the wings of an angel. The alabaster steeple ascended in a layered display of podiums that lead the eyes of disciples to its pinnacle, and at its peak was the symbol of the Lord.

Aedus took his hand to his head, sent it to his heart, crossing his body and ushering it back to his mind's center while he looked upon the shamrock towering above him. The stained glass overhead the wooden door beamed in beauty as the light that glared from the tile ground ascended the images to life. Aedus unhinged the heavy door that was before him and entered the illustriousness of the sacred house. Inside its glory of the holy sight, the columns curved like arrows melding arched ceilings that led to a silver and gold organ above his head at the entrance of the cathedral, and at the other end an opened domed stage, bleached white where candles flickered, and elongated windows let in the shine of the moon and the sun. He did not linger long in the pews of the church, but instead climbed up the barrow squared staircase, leading him to the bell tower which rang at the top of every hour, booming through the city streets like thunder echoes through the sky.

Ding—Ding—Ding, the bell the people called Ardu rang in the sixth hour of the new day. Its uproar awoke the city, and all who heard its cannon sound looked up and perked up to listen to its mighty roar, and in its steady beat, smaller bells struck a classic tune that carved a metropolis Saoirse groove. Aedus loved its booming sound and watched the 100-ton bell swing on its axis. The stairs he climbed ended at the bell tower, but to Aedus's right was a ladder that rose above it. He climbed until he reached the summit where there was little space for him. There he sat at a razors edge underneath the shamrock that rested at the apex, taking in all that was before him.

Adorned in all white, the head of his cloak hid his face, protecting his ears and keeping him warm from the harshness of the elements. He prayed and meditated. In his prayer, he asked for answers, and in his meditation, he sought them. He did so until, alas, Ardu struck eight notes.

The sun had risen to bask the earth with its light, to give life to everything that inhabited the rock that floated in the dark expanse of space. His stygian eyes opened to meet the shine of the day. He breathed deeply and exhaled all that was consumed in that breath.

"Germa," he susurrated, drawing his hand to his forehead, then to his heart, across his body, and back to his peak. Aedus descended from the belfry to the floor of the sanctuary and was greeted by the Apsal of the hollowed tabernacle.

"Aedus, my dear child, top o' the mornin' to ya." The Apsal spoke. Pint-sized he was, nearly five feet, with gray hair at his temples and no mop atop his head. His eyes were the lightest brown Aedus had ever seen, as if they wanted to be anything but man's most common color. The Apsal's eyes were more beautiful than any blue or green and just as rare as Uriel's yellow peepers.

"Dia dhuit, Apsal Luther," Aedus welcomed him.

"Dia is muire dhuit," Luther responded. "How was prayer?"

"Peaceful."

"Very good, lad. Big day tomorrow; ain't dat right?" said the keeper of the holy house.

"A happy day tomorrow. How's your sermon coming?" Aedus asked genuinely.

"It's a bit topsy-tervsys at the moment. Ya know, gotta find the right word and all," Luther answered.

"I have no doubt you'll find the words. You're the best preacher I know," he praised him.

"Ah, thank ya lad." Apsal lightly tapped Aedus's shoulder with his palm. "I'll see you tomorrow, Aed. I must get going."

"God bless you, Apsal."

"May he bless you as well, Aedus. Goodbye, my boy," Aspal Luther said in his farewell.

"Goodbye, Luther." Aedus stepped out of the chapel doors to the gelid air of the Aontu winter. The streets were a ballyhoo of babbled blokes and lasses, a jabber of bombilation conveyance, and all the sounds that bombarded the organ of hearing and equilibrium, that resided in the world of the metropolis rushed to meet Aedus, bringing him back to the world he had escaped atop the splendor of the indomitable cathedral. He walked in its organized chaos, observing laughs in conversation, cries from upset children and shouts from hurried men and women. Alone he walked in silence upon the effulgent sidewalks until he reached the castle gates, stopping to say hello to the stoic guard.

"Captain Talmidge, is that you?" Aedus asked the warrior. The soldier decompressed the helmet that connected to his armor.

"Hey mate, how are ya tis mornin?" the captain replied. His hair was a nest of red and orange and his eyes a deep forest green. "Happy birt-day to ya."

"Thanks, Cap. You coming tomorrow?" Aedus asked.

"Ah, no mate, sorry. My wife's birt-day is also this weekend. I gotta keep good with the missus, else I get the boot in the backend." The soldier laughed along with Aedus.

"Well, you're more than welcome to come on by, ya know," Aedus insisted.

"Ah, thank ya laddie. I'll let the wife know," Talmidge responded.

"Be sure to do that. It'd be nice to have ya there."

"Thank ya, Aed," the Captain replied. Aedus walked up the paved hill with lampposts that traced its route to the home of him and his family. Inside, he could hear the morning ruckus in the grandiose abode, catching sight of his sister who had trials of mastery in ballet and fencing. Aedus was always in awe of his sister. Her drive was uncanny as she demanded perfection from herself, though it seemed a family trait, but to see it within her always inspired him. To Aedus, she was an example of greatness, a disciple of God, a harbinger of good, he aspired to be like her and to exceed where she may fail, not to diminish her, but to help her. He loved his sister dearly. He loved the songs she'd sing to him, the games they played together and her annoying sisterly affections.

"Morning, Lolo," he accosted her.

"Hey, angel boy, dia dhuit." She tossed his blond hair.

"Good luck today. I wish I could be there to support you."

"No fans allowed," she winked. "I'll tell you all about it when I get home."

"I'll be here waiting to hear it. Have fun today."

"Thanks, Aed. Love you." Lorena grabbed her things and left for the events of her day, looking both excited and nervous.

Aedus had gone to his room to change for the afternoon delights. It was a rather simple day for someone so active and a striver for perfection. His cloak he hung amongst others he had and folded his white slacks along with his ivory shirt and sweater. He dressed himself in an olive tweed suit that fit his form, trimmed and tailored in a fashion of sophistication and courtliness. Its brown red buttons contrasted with his suit, matching his wood bottom shoes. He latched on a simple watch with gold trim and hashes for the hour, with a face a washed silver. Aedus styled his blond hair without product and left his room a proper gentleman.

The door echoed in the hall as he closed it, and then another followed the same cinched clop. He turned to face the sound. His eyes widened, the beat of his heart hit faster, the nerves of his body tingled like shivered clattering teeth, for before him was a woman with strawberry blond hair that fell to the small of her back, styled in a braided crown with a few wisps flirting about her eyes. She was dolled up in a slim black dress that ran down to her ankles, sporting black heels and black gloves that traveled up just above her elbow. The most beautiful thing he had ever seen, she bewitched him once more without a word being spoken.

"Good morning," she smiled at him.

"Good morning," he managed to say.

"Care to join me?" Aedus put out his arm, which she took, and walked her to the courtyard where the others were residing as they waited for their vehicles to take them to the capitol building.

"You look comely this afternoon," Aedus complimented her in a tone soft and affectionate while his cheeks gave a soft blush, her cheeks matching his from his words.

"How suave of you to say so. You look alluring yourself, you know?" She returned the flattery. Aedus couldn't help but grin from ear to ear. No more so could he hide his amorous eyes as they locked with hers. The flirtatious duo walked in silence, arm in arm, until they reached the courtyard. Yekaterina's mother awaited them outside.

"Dobroye utro, mama," Katerina said in her native language.

"Good morning, Kat. Where is your coat, child?" Viktoriya asked her daughter.

"Ay, gluppy devushka," she spoke aloud yet to herself.

"I can run and get it for you if you'd like," Aedus offered his kindly services.

"Thank you, Aed. Here is the key to my room. The coat should be lying across the bed," she described to him.

"I'll be right back." He dashed off to retrieve her anorak, running through the network of halls and rooms, finding his way into his own. He grabbed off his desk a silver fountain pen with a gold tip and a blank sheet of paper. He stuffed the items in his coat pocket and headed toward Yekaterina's room. He entered and draped her winter overcoat on his arm and hurried his way back to her. Katerina's coy manner made her all the more adorable as her doe eyes shimmered into his.

"This the one?" Aedus asked, knowing it was.

"Thank you, Aed," she said, putting her arms through the sleeves of her fur coat that reached her knees. She tied the waist of her anorak and threw the hood up over her head, framing her face in a cocoon of downy fur the color gray. Angelic, she looked to Aedus, but this he only thought and did not say.

A driverless black and gold carriage pulled up to them. Of wheels there were none. Instead, it floated by four devices on the corners of the wagon called gyrolofstot. These devices created gyroscopic precession, lift and thrust, enabling the carriage to defy gravity and move without hindrance. Aedus opened the black and gold decorated doors and put out his hand for Yekaterina and Viktoriya to hold as they stepped up into the tepid transporter.

"Thank you, Aedus. That's very sweet of you." Viktoriya spoke kindly as she entered the carriage.

"You're most welcome, Mrs. Nemtsov," Aedus replied. As his hand became free, he offered it to Yekaterina. She grabbed his hand lightly and then squeezed as if not wanting to let go. She climbed aboard, letting their fingers linger upon one another for as long as possible. Aedus then took his seat across from the two ladies, his bum roasted as the leather cooked it like a ham in the oven.

The three of them made small talk of weather and the events of the day, eventually drifting off to the topic of Aedus's birthday.

"Are you excited for tomorrow, Aedus?" Viktoriya asked.

"Very much so. It's a rather big day for my brother and me, though tomorrow isn't really my birthday."

"It isn't?" Katerina sounded surprised.

"Not really, no. Tomorrow is the day my father found me. It so happens it was the same day my brother was born. So, in a way it is. That day was the start of my new life, and I couldn't be more grateful," Aedus explained.

"We're happy Robert found you. You seem to be growing up into quite the man," Viktoriya praised him.

"That's very kind of you, thank you." He felt more at ease than he had by Viktoriya's tender nature. The trio talked some more, of Aedus and his races, the Nemtsov's vacation to the Heavohe Islands, and the story of the fox. In his short journey to the capitol, Aedus found he rather enjoyed the company of Viktoriya and that his admiration for the Nemtsovs had been worthwhile.

"You know, I have marveled at you and your family since I was a little boy. My father used to tell me and my siblings stories of Yefimovich and how my father was there on the battlefield when he took down Alois and ended the war. I always thought Yefimovich more a myth than a man. Hero to the Telekine people and the Ivdeyskiy religion, father to the Tulku and husband to a beautiful fire bower, but I can see the legend is very true with my own eyes. I'm delighted you all could make it to my brother's and my birthday." Aedus blushed and smiled at them.

"Don't let your father know how much Aedus thinks of him. It'll go straight to his head," Viktoriya jokingly said to her daughter. Katerina laughed at her mother's comment. "You know your grandfather Abraham, as well your father and uncle, are a bit fabled themselves where I live."

"I did. My uncle likes to brag about his stories. I'm sure you'll hear some tomorrow," Aedus said.

"That seems to be the Iscariot I remember. The Great Warrior, and as we call him, Velikiy Voin. The man who killed a hundred souls," Viktoriya stated.

"I know it too well," Aedus chuckled. "I'd assume my father is famous for being King of Saoirse, so too my grandfather."

"Oh no, my dear. Your grandfather is known for giving the people of the Ivdeyskiy religion a country of their own. That treaty, with all its flaws, the Hidler-Nemtsov agreement, it was foretold in our religion. He is the keeper of God's promise to us, and your father is perhaps more famous in our household than our country," Viktoriya described.

"I know my grandfather was influential in the treaty. I didn't realize what it truly meant for your people." Aedus spoke with new understanding.

"He means a great deal, just as your father means a great deal to Yefi. Your father fought in every battle with my husband. He was his left hand and has saved my husband's life more times than any debt could repay. Yefi loves your father, and I have no doubt he would die for him," Viktoriya spoke kindly.

"My father never really tells us stories of himself, only of others," Aedus admitted.

"That's because he is too humble. Yefimovich would be happy to tell you his war stories and the tales of their friendship," Viktoriya confessed.

"I'll have to take him up on that tomorrow."

In the legendary accounts of each other's family, Aedus's hand danced next to Yekaterina's, ever so close to one another yet never touching. He glanced at her, quickly looking away, feeling the gaze of her mother upon him.

His brief look at Yekaterina and their conversation of myths and legends made him realize he was in the presence of a living allegory. Thinking of Yekaterina, he kept his tongue from moving to ask her what it was like to be such a religious icon. The fame, the burden, the pressure of such a task, asked not of by the people, but by that of the Maker. Aedus was reminded of his father as he thought of such responsibility, but Yekaterina was chosen at birth, and it has been her life and will be her life for all eternity. As that notion dwelled in his mind, he changed the topic, keeping the dialog simmering until they reached the capitol.

The gold crowned wagon came to a stop. Aedus hopped out and gallantly assisted the two women in disembarking just as he had helped them in. He gripped Yekaterina's hand, not wanting to let go, enraptured by her beauty, but religion and duty conquered his more natural instinct, dusting off the lustful desire to an emotion more pure and noble, that of genuine care and honor for someone he thought he could one day love. Aedus, Yekaterina, and Viktoriya climbed the white stone staircase of the stunning blanched building.

They entered the glorious halls and were quickly greeted by members of the comhail. Few shook the hand of Aedus. All the attention was on Yekaterina and her mother, and deservedly so. After the commotion of introductions and adulation, the crowd dispersed.

"Well, you two, I have to go meet your fathers. Are you coming with me?" Viktoriya asked.

"I'm very sorry, Mrs. Nemtsov. I'm awaiting my brother," Aedus replied.

"Is it alright if I stay with Aedus?" Katerina asked her mother.

"Of course, dear," Viktoriya replied.

"Do you need help finding them?" Aedus queried.

"They are in your father's office. If you could direct me in the right direction, I'll be able to find them," she said.

"Aedus mapped her the way with directions easy to follow. Viktoriya thanked him, leaving the infatuated duo to play their time in timid love.

An awkward silence lingered like stale air in a closed room, and then a window opened, the silence was swept away as Yekaterina started fiddling her fingers, tossing strands of light between them, weaving the flow from one hand to the other.

"My mom does the same thing." Aedus pointed out her mannerism.

"It's kind of a nervous habit," Katerina confessed.

"For her, too, though she denies it," he grinned. "When I was younger, my mom used to entangle the light between my hands. She'd let me pretend that I could bend the light like her. I remember thinking how amazing it was."

"Like this?" Katerina took the flowing bands she was playing with and guided it around Aedus's right hand. He gave a slight chortle, awed at her gift, as he imagined once more that he was the true son of Lagertha, where her gifts could be transferred to him in nature's law of genetics. He pushed away the thought, knowing she would say to him that it is not the blood and body that connects mother and son, but it is the bond of the spirits that knot their mortal souls, that fills their hearts of unyielding love that cannot be broken. The body will die, and the blood will die with it, but the spirit lives on, and so, too, the immortal connection of mother and son. Aedus brought himself back to the present.

"Of all your gifts, which is your favorite?" he asked. She had no need to give it thought and said to him,

"My favorite would have to be the ability to control the energy that flows within me. I can repress it and guide it to different parts of my body that need it most, or I can build it, and when I do that, it gives me strength and speed beyond what I can do just as a Telekine."

"You're absolutely incredible," he said, thinking of her as a whole. Her elemental abilities, her beauty, her very character he found to be paradisiacal and pulchritudinous. Her face turned a shade of pink from his comment, letting the light she manipulated wave back into the rays from which it came.

The almost lovers mingled at the stairway of the balcony floor of the comhail hall, just outside of where Yefimovich awaited to give his speech. There they waited for Absolume in a colloquy in which both were glued to each other's words only to be broken up by a familiar voice.

"Here so soon?" Absolume's voice came from the stairway.

"Waiting for you, Abe," said Aedus.

"Good afternoon, Kat." Absolume welcomed the Tulku.

"Good afternoon, Absolume," she cordially replied. Absolume put his arm around his brother as the three found their way to their seats to listen to the words of a man whom Aedus held in high regard. Members of the Ionadai and Seances of the comhail detonated in a roaring cheer of applause as Yefimovich took to the podium with the splendid red, white, and blue room of friendly meetings and hostile encounters. Aedus took out the pen and paper from his jacket pocket that he had taken from his room. Like his brother, he listened with great interest, but unlike Absolume, he began to write while the words of Yefimovich danced along the canals of his ears and traveled to his mind. A stir of emotion resided within the mixing bowl of his heart. The heat of the speech baked his thumper to feel the power of the message, one of an admonitory gesture and of a call to aid, underlined in the confectionary elocution that had in it the ingredients of faith, hope, and love, and by all that was true and earnest; the greatest of these was love. In these delicious words that Yefimovich let go from his tickled tongue, Aedus sought to write and note sweet stanzas of his own.

Aedus capped his writing instrument as Yefimovich closed with his final word, and with all in the room, like all who sat within it, he rose and applauded the man who lived a storied life that was a brass-tacks novel of truth. Aedus looked to his left and then to his right. Absolume whistled a punctured note, and Yekaterina called out to her father with a sparkling smile that lit the dark eyes of Aedus into flaming white orbs.

"Hurra, Papa!" She clapped and acclaimed her brilliant father. Though Aedus did not display such animation, he felt what they pronounced as he cheered alongside them.

"That was exemplary." Aedus leaned in to Katerina to flatter her father.

"He's gotten quite good at giving speeches," she said, leaning back into Aedus.

"Are you as good as your father?" he asked her, not wanting to leave this closeness.

"I learned from the best," she gestured toward Yefimovich. The elation of the crowd subdued as the comhail members quickly cast their votes on a treaty with the longstanding ally of Yisra. Tallied the votes were, and the script was signed by King Robert and Yefimovich Nemtsov, and once more, the holler of the room reverberated the capitol walls in joyous celebration.

"Let's go join our fathers," Absolume shouted to Aedus and Katerina.

They left the bird's-eye view of the balcony seats and made their way to the doors of the comhail chambers, and when they arrived, to Aedus's delight, there was his grandfather Enoch and his Uncle Uriel. Absolume had already seen them and dashed to see his family whom he'd not seen in years. Aedus kept his walking pace, in step with Yekaterina, as she, too, was adorned with a smile at the sight of them. When Aedus and Katerina finally reached the reunion, the conversation wasn't what he expected to hear. The tone was serious, as his father hurriedly planned a meeting to convene in the council room above the floor where they stood.

Aedus waited silently, his shoulder grazing the shoulder of Yekaterina until the families dispersed. Absolume went with his father, Yekaterina with Yefimovich and her mother. His uncles, his mother, and grandfather all left together with chatter amongst themselves. Leaving the touch of Yekaterina, he wandered out on his own. He stepped out the blue wooden capitol doors to take in the winter air. He took out the pen and paper he had been scribbling on during Yefimovich's speech and began scratching once more on the parchment. Each word he gave great thought, for every word he used had to truly express what dwelled within his mind.

The pendulum swung 900 seconds as Aedus slowly and meticulously began folding the note he had been scrawling on, turning the papyrus into a delicate, intricate rose, using the tips of his fingers and the tip of his pen until the paper bloomed. In his time alone, his thoughts fell to his sister. He couldn't help but think the best in the trials he knew she'd master. Thinking of Lorena, he had the restless desire to surprise his loving sister and congratulate her. Aedus headed to the black and gold carriage, which he had ridden in to the capitol, and as he entered the vehicle, a call rang through his communicator. Absolume's face appeared before him.

"Aed, where are you?" his brother asked.

"I'm about to leave to surprise Lorena."

"Well, don't leave. Father wants you at this meeting," Absolume told him.

"Alright, I'll be right there," he acknowledged without giving it thought. He carefully put the rose in his pocket and headed back into the snow-white building.

To his surprise, he was the first to enter the council chambers. He looked at the round table and seats of virtue and sin. He did not dare to sit in such seats but instead took his seat on a chair made of stone. Of thirty-two thrones, only fourteen were carved of wood and adorned with red cushioned seats and marked a virtue or a sin. The others were of stone, etched with ogham letters from a far more ancient Saoirse period.

Aedus waited patiently in his cold stone chair, looking up at the stained glass that told a story of peace. The chamber doors opened to the lovely sight of Yekaterina. His eyes dilated as he gazed upon her. Holding the door behind her was her father, Yefimovich.

"The famous thrones of sin and virtue," Yekaterina said aloud as if they were omened. She read the virtued seats one by one as she circled the round table. "Does your father reside in one of these chairs?" she asked Aedus.

"My father's seat is there." He pointed to the throne of patience. Yekaterina knelt down before it and said a silent prayer, kissing the arm of the throne. She then walked toward Aedus and took her seat next to him, draping her coat over the chair she took.

"Do these stone thrones hold any significance?" she asked.

"Some believe they do, but most do not. The history of the seats you and I sit in are lost and now come from vague interpretations based off of what we can piece together from our past," he explained.

"And what do you believe?" she questioned in genuine wonder.

"I believe there is truth to the myths." He spoke honestly. "Will you excuse me a moment?"

"Of course," she said to him. Aedus rose from his seat to welcome a man he admired.

"Dia dhuit, Prime Ministr." Aedus put out his hand to greet Yefimovich.

"Dia is muire dhuit," Yefimovich returned the greeting.

"Your speech was very moving," he extolled.

"Thank you, Aedus. Though you'll have to thank—my wife. She is my—proofreader and advisor," Yefimovich informed him.

"Is she not coming to the meeting?" Aedus noted her absence.

"She isn't feeling well, I'm afraid. She left a few moments ago," Yefimovich said before he changed the subject of the chat. "Aedus—I was wondering—would you mind taking me on a drive in your Shelby tomorrow? I've—I've always wanted to drive one."

"I would love to. How about in the morning, tomorrow?" Aedus asked excitedly.

"That sounds wonderful." Aedus's childhood hero smiled at him. He could not resist the felicity he felt, knowing he'd spend the morning with a man he admired and that his father cherished.

"You're going to have a great time tomorrow," Aedus assured him.

"I'm looking forward to it," he said as the others started walking into the chamber, closing the conversation with Yefimovich, taking his seat once more next to Yekaterina.

"So, you have a date with my papa?" she lightly mocked Aedus as he sat down. He laughed in response to her banter.

"I suppose I do," he said while Uriel took the stone throne to Aedus's right, murmuring something to himself. His sun-kissed eyes were glazed over as if he were off somewhere else but the room he resided in, yet he turned to Aedus and Yekaterina.

"Gratulerer med dagan," he whispered to Aedus.

"Takk skal do he," Aedus responded in his best Avenglarian.

"Donkey's ears, Kat," was his Saoirse hello.

"Donkey's ears?" she said confused.

"It means long time no see." Aedus informed her of the Saoirse phrase. She snickered at the oddity.

"Two weeks is quite a while I suppose." She made merry of the conversation.

The chamber doors opened again. Absolume and Robert walked through them, being the last accounted for. Robert took his seat at the throne of patience. Absolume took his nearest to his father, sitting directly across from Aedus. Robert looked around the round table, seeing all were present, winking at Aedus as he locked eyes with his father's, not knowing what the gesture truly meant, though he had a hunch about what it might entail. Aedus blushed slightly, just barely visible, yet not enough for anyone to notice. Robert addressed the room to receive all who sat within it and then spoke directly to Enoch, asking him what moved his weary heart.

Aedus's grandfather then began to riddle from his tongue a tale of the unimagined that rattled the saddle on which his ticker sat. Vivid was the imagery, his words like poetry with simile and metaphor. An alliteration of words left his mouth so that when he spoke the motion picture of his description reeled in the mind, lighting his story as if his hearers lived it.

His articulate narrative spoke of a shadow—mountainous and fierce was the beast—but truly he'll tell you, his presence when felt, was of divine peace and serenity. Enoch recounted the portals of heaven and earth, the voice that led him to visesate atop the great mountain of Avengler at the start of the Tilgivelse River, where waters of purple flowed from the peak and fueled the continent and country of Avengler. He told of the void that was eternal and how he saw the four winds that bound the earth to heaven and so too heaven to earth. He could see the oceans flow and the pattern they drew across the planet, and of his gaze across the expanse that was forever (yet he could see its end).

Of pillars of fire, he spoke of that which were the portals of the worlds; all this he was told to write and to read to the world. His words sculpted images of horror, of children slaughtered, of men decapitated and of women raped. Fire, he said, would rule the world if man did not act. Seven angels, he cried, would rain from the kingdom and two seraphs would follow, of this he warned and foretold.

Aedus was fully enveloped by what seemed chimerical, and every beaten character of every word his grandfather spoke inked the music sheet of his cerebellum. For deep within his bass beating heart, he knew he'd play on an instrument the song Enoch had written.

In a voice of near defeat, Enoch said to all, "He showed me the spirits of the earth, the water, the moon, the sun, and the wind and how they never faltered. He told me to tell the people. He said he showed me this because I asked to see it."

No one spoke. The room was silent and without the friendly sound of conversation, only the hum drum of nothing and the ringing of ears could be heard. Then the voiceless sound was broken by a tone of beauty.

"Then, like the elements, we will not falter. We will stay our course, and if death is to greet us, we will welcome him with open arms." The words of the Tulku resounded with inspiration. What character,

Aedus thought. Beauty she possessed. Battle she mastered. Grace she gave. In selflessness, she led. She was the sword and the shield for this moment and for which God had so gifted her for this time.

A call to arms came from his father, and Aedus knew he would take up his. Robert planned the next meeting and thanked all those within the room, all of whom he adored in the rooted tree of his blessed spirit. Aedus turned to Yekaterina.

"Can I meet you downstairs?"

"Of course. I'll wait for you where we entered," she said.

"Do you mind if I ride along with you two?" I believe my father and sister are riding together with your father, Kat," Uriel interjected, asking his nephew.

"Fine with me, Uncle U. I'll see you both in a few minutes," Aedus said to them, leaving the chambers with his father, mother, and brother. He, like his brother, listened silently for something more of his father's plans as he talked to his wife, but the topic was not brought up. Instead, it was of family and the boys' birthday celebration the next day. Aedus's eyes glazed over, and he thought of what his grandfather said, of the horrors and the riddles, until the illusion in his mind evaporated from the space where it was held.

Lagertha sealed her goodbye with a kiss to King Robert, saying farewell to Aedus and Absolume, to reunite with Yefimovich and Enoch. Aedus gave a loving goodbye to his family and headed back to rejoin his uncle and Yekaterina. The two were discussing the meeting and what they felt needed to be addressed in the one to follow.

"Coordination is key if countries are to execute simultaneously." Yekaterina seemed to be finishing a point.

"Aed, you ready?" his uncle asked as he was the first to notice Aedus walking down the lamprog lit halls.

"I've been waiting for you two," he joked.

"My apologies." Uriel played the game.

"Fierce weather we're having." Aedus pointed out the obvious.

"It's a bit cold, I'll admit," his uncle agreed.

"I think it's rather nice." Yekaterina gave her two cents.

"Helps to be wearing an anorak," Uriel pointed out.

"I'd say." Aedus ganged up on Katerina.

"Don't take your poor decisions out on me," she lightheartedly reprimanded them, putting her hands in her coat pockets, and as she did so, an "oh" came slipping from her lips.

"Something the matter?" Uriel asked.

"Ummm—no. I just remembered something was all." Both Uriel and Aedus looked at her with puzzlement scattered across their faces. The three of them reached the black and gold carriage Aedus and Yekaterina had arrived in. Once more, Aedus helped Katerina into the driverless wagon.

"No help for me?" his uncle teased.

"Where are my manners?" Aedus jested, and the two laughed at one another.

The seats were warm, heating their bottoms, thawing their frigid bodies from the freeze of the winter air. The hovering transporter led them back to the pearl white castle, slowly driving through the city lights, the nest of people and the chirps and caws of the city atwitter.

"Uriel, how is your fractal theory coming along?" Yekaterina pried.

"The formula is in my mind. I'm almost done with writing it down. It's going to change everything." His uncle spoke in an inspired inflection.

"What is the fractal theory?" Aedus inquired.

"It's the theory of everything. How trees and plants are designed, how the universe was formed, it is the pattern of everything we know and holds the truth to life's oldest questions," Uriel replied.

"What do you plan to do with it?" Aedus spoke with interest.

"Whatever I can. Look for the unknown, create something beyond what my mind can imagine now. I'm not sure. There are endless possibilities for what I can do," his uncle answered. "I'm hoping to achieve interstellar flight—to go beyond this star system faster than any man thought possible."

"Sounds fascinating," said Kat.

"I think so too." Uriel's eyes looked as if they had left the very carriage they rode in and traveled the universe. Their high-minded dialog slowly came to a halt as they approached the gates of Solascnoc, the castle on the hill, Aedus's home, the house of the king, the ivory palace that overlooked the city. The wagon stopped, and once more, a soldier greeted Aedus.

"Hey there, handsome," said the soft and raspy voice of the warrior.

"Good evening, Ann," Aedus responded. The Liopard officer removed her helmet from her suit, exposing her beautiful brown skin, her midnight hair, her smoldering sand-colored eyes, and her dazzling smile. She leaned into the open window of the transporter. "My, my, what beauty resides in this carriage. Is this your date, Aed?" She gestured toward the head turner that was Yekaterina. "Does this mean I have to stop flirting with you?" She winked, and his cheeks glowed soft pink. "No worries, I'm quite taken with this sunflower." Ann looked at Uriel.

"Ann, this is the Tulku, Yekaterina Nemtsov, and this is my uncle, Uriel Framsyn." Aedus introduced them. Ann reached out her hand and welcomed them both.

"Well, you and your lover, Tulku, have a good night, and you, Mr. Framsyn, will I be seeing you tomorrow at the birthday celebration?" She spoke playfully in her creamy tone. Uriel gave a slight chuckle.

"I believe you will," he answered. Ann backed away from the vehicle as it headed up the hill to the bleached castle with stark blue-capped towers that were lit up in gentle luminescence.

The three entered Solascnoc, the ceiling a mix of clouds and stars. The birch trees seemed to shiver from the lights of the lamprog that slowly danced above. They walked out from the entryway and into the tea room where Lagertha, Enoch, and Yefimovich were seated.

"The poor girl. How is she doing?" Enoch asked Lagertha.

"She seems to be alright. I had a small chat with her. She's resting now," his mother answered her grandfather.

"Did Lo's trials not go well?" Aedus wondered, not knowing what the room was truly discussing.

"No—it's not that. Your sister was attacked today by rioters and protesters who stand against your father," Lagertha started to explain. Aedus could feel his heart start to burn at the very notion of his sister under attack. His mother continued, describing the details as she knew them. Like his heart, Aedus's eyes raged in flame as he pictured Lorena pinned on the ground, surrounded by all who wanted nothing more than to hurt someone he loved. He let the fire run through his veins, but then the touch of his hand by the hand of another watered his beating ticker to simmer the flame that roared within him.

"I'm sorry, Aed," she whispered to him. His thumper bumped more gently by her touch and her voice.

"Thank you, Kat. Will you excuse me?" he asked. She nodded yes and let him leave the room to walk the path back to his own. Aedus lit his bedroom with slow pulsing lamprogs, threw his jacket over his desk chair, grabbed a quill and paper, and began to write.

She is the first luminous point in the sky at night, a dancing astonishment to the eyes of the king. Her voice of song enchanted the ears, even those of the unborn. Her love is like the light of the sun, abundant and always giving, a gift she received from her mother. The first link to the bond of family, her brace is forever unbroken. She is a beacon to run to when the waves of the sea were rough and a standard raised to show the way. These things you will always be to me. Let the tears wash away your sadness, and let the Lord strengthen your resolve, and in this time, I will hold your standard, and I will be the lighthouse on stormy seas. I will harden my link and love like the light

Aedus walked out his room to the halls of the castle, leading himself to his sister's bedroom. No light shone underneath the heavy wooden door. He slowly opened it. The fire she had lit was now just coals and burning embers. He placed his letter on her night stand, saying goodnight as he left his sister to rest away the troubles of her day.

Aedus went back to his room of white brick and rustic furniture, entering his stone clad shower to drown away the particles of impurities that resided upon him. He clothed himself in plaid cotton pajama bottoms and tossed himself onto his bed. His muscles relaxed, and his dusky eyes began to close when a knock came at his door. He rose from his restful state to see who was there. He opened the door to find no one, but below him, at his feet, was a rose sculpted from a red stone, petaled with ice, floating on a blue flame. Aedus tested the flame and felt it was cool to the touch. He smiled, bringing the flaming rose into his room and placing it on his night stand. He slid back into his bed, his lids closed, and the flame of his heart beat to the rhythm of the night.

<u>Robert Chapter Four</u>

He stood at the base of the stone, the scene all too familiar, the war hammer lodged in a living breathing liquid metal goop. Robert clutched the hammer's handle and pulled the weapon from the meteorite, only to hear the painful cries of a man. He looked down at his feet, and before him was his father bathed in crimson blood. Robert's eyes grew wide with fear, his heart paced a panic palpitation. The blood that flowed from Abraham and the swirl of liquid metal merged and consumed the hammer. Robert's eyes ran dry for he had nothing left to shed from them; he blinked and before him was a woman, naked, a goddess who radiated a telestic hue of vapor blue. She gripped the handle of the weapon, and the hammer transformed into a blade, gold from hilt to tip with stones coating the blade in reds and greens. The goddess took the bilbo from his hands and ran the blade through Robert's body. He fell to his knees, looking down at the sword that penetrated him. He looked up and saw the face of his son. Absolume pulled the weapon from his father's body while tears streamed from his eyes as they filled with water beyond the brink and funneled through the ducts, finally running down his cheeks. Robert fell to the ground, his back against the shaded surface of the ground. He looked up. His son had vanished like minerals in a chemical reaction, dissolved and unseen. The glowing goddess slowly laid her naked body upon him, stroking the locks of his hair with her fingers, closing his eyes in her strangely comforting way.

He awoke in his canopy bed, the morning sun across his face with his bare-skinned wife upon him, running her thin fingers though his soft flowing mane. Her breasts were against his chest and her legs tangled with his. She looked at him with dilated irises that indicated her affection.

"Good morning, my king." Her blue marbles looked into his green gazers and love consumed fear.

"Good morning, my queen."

"Did you sleep alright?" she asked, seeming to know he had dreamt an unpleasant dream.

"I had the most particular fancy," he began.

"And what was this fancy?" Lagertha buried her face in his neck.

"I died." His wife rose from the comforts of Robert's warmth to meet his gaze.

"That's horrible." She kissed his lips. "I thought you might have had a bit of a nightmare. I could feel your heart race like a scared rabbit." Robert snickered at her description of his beating organ.

"It was just a dream," he said, trying to dismiss it.

"It's no dream of mine," Lagertha said to her husband, kissing his lips once more, feeling her concern within their locked caress. "I love you," she said, holding his body tightly as she curled back into him.

"I love you, too," he smiled. His mind, body, and spirit were relieved by the tenderness of his wife. He laid there a while, letting Lagertha snooze in the early hours of the day.

Just as he thought he could lay there forever with the woman he admired and desired, Robert noted the time, as the eighth hour of the morning had fallen from the sands of the hourglass.

"Lagertha—Lagertha, wake up," he said, trying to move the dead weight of his wife off of himself.

"I'm awake," she lied.

"We need to start our day. It's a rather busy one," he reminded her.

"Can you start the shower for me?"

"Why don't you join me in mine?" Robert suggested. Lagertha's eyes finally opened from her tired state of mind.

"I suppose I could do that, but no funny business. We have an assiduous day today." She rolled her slender yet curvaceous figure from Robert's body, taking all the sheets with her, cocooning herself inside them. Robert walked into the white marbled shower whose pattern matched that of the bark from a birch tree. He tuned the handle of the shower, releasing the water from above like that of a waterfall falling from the peeks of a high mountain to the river base below. He waited a moment as the water warmed, calling out to his wife as it ran hot.

"Lagertha! The shower is ready!" he exclaimed in vain for there was no response from the velvety voice of his wife. "Lagertha!" he yelled once more. Knowing now the sandman had doused her with loose crystals that held the spell of sleep, or she simply, and more accurately was ignoring his calls for her to join him, he walked back to his king sized bed to find his wife awake, nestled tightly within the bedsheets. Robert scooped her up, sheets and all, and carried her to the washroom, where running waters of the shower awaited.

"Robert!" Lagertha screamed and then giggled. "Nooo!" She tried to wiggle but to no avail. Robert stepped inside the steaming shower. Warm and soothing it rapped gently upon his skin. Robert set his wife on her feet, still wrapped in the covers of the bed, now drenched, laying sheer upon her statuesque frame. "You're a jerk," she teased.

"I love you too." He put his arms around her waist, locking his hands behind her, as she put her hands behind his neck and stood on her toes to reach his buoyant lips.

"Can you get the gifts for the boys this morning?" she asked her husband. "I want to spend some time with Lorena before all the attention today falls on Aed and Abe."

"Yea, I can do that. How was she last night when you talked to her?" he asked with concern.

"She seemed fine. Still a little shaken perhaps, but she's strong willed."

"That's my girl." Robert praised the might of her will. "I need to have some alone time with her as well. If I don't see her before the party, tell her I want to see her and that I love her."

"I will," she promised. The mood changed from its more serious state to that of airy weather. Lagertha disrobed from the water-soaked sheets and coiled herself around Robert. Her long, sharp glistening white nails scratched his muscled back.

"Ow! What was that for?" He looked at his wife with stern confusion.

"For throwing me in the shower." She moved behind him to heal the marks she made upon his skin with the healing powers of a lover's kiss.

"You're crazy, woman," he said jokingly.

"You knew that before you married me, crazy old man," she said, not denying his jest.

"Good point," he said, soaping his hair and body, ridding off the unclean that rested on his skin and long locks. "I'm off to get the boys' presents. I'll see you soon." He smooched his wife and lightly tapped her now bare bottom with the back of his hand as he exited the shower.

"Bye, handsome," said Lagertha as she lingered in the falls and steam of the torrid shower.

Robert dressed himself in gray trim cotton slacks whose pockets' insides were a design of purple and gold flowers. The button that latched his pants together mirrored that of the gold flowers. His shirt was pure white except for the inside of the cuff of his sleeves, as they too were decorated purple with golden flowers and were held together by links of the same design. Robert laced his brown pointed shoes and looped his belt around his waist; he looked himself in the mirror near the closet and styled his brown and gray hair, and through the reflected glass, his wife came from the shower bare-bunned and with nothing on except a towel that wrapped around her head to dry her long flowing hair. Her perky bosom bounced while water droplets twinkled on her skin as she made her way over to her husband.

"You're moving slow, old man." She smacked his bottom as if to return the gesture Robert gave her while they bathed together in the heat of the running water.

"Mean and cruel this morning," he said, lusting at her body, grabbing her waist before she walked past him and headed into the closet.

"Don't worry. I'll be nice tonight," she winked.

"I am relieved," he sighed, reaching for his gray coat with silky purple lining within its interior, coated with the same golden flowers throughout its design.

"Let me help you, handsome," she said, offering her assistance. Robert put out his arms, letting Lagertha slide the sleeves over them. He turned to face his wife, and though his mind was filled with concupiscence in response to her thin and barren form, it was her baby blues that captured him, for they screamed with love and ran down into the pit of her soul and consumed all that was her and all that was within her. Robert locked his lips with hers once more.

"Goodbye, earth angel."

"Goodbye, prince charming," she teased him one final time before the two were out of sight of one another.

Robert left his bedroom to walk the maze of halls in the castle, finding his way to his daughter's door. He knocked, but there was no answer, only the hush of the air that would, from time to time, run wild in the tunnels of the castle. He moved his way about the white bricked walled halls to the tea room. There the chairs and tables were set for the purpose of conversation for matters of popular culture or political dialog or even a bit of good advice, or anything that bounced within the mind and found its way to the tongue of the possessor. Much to his dismay, however, she was not to be found within the room. Robert ceased his search and grabbed a croissant with egg and cheese that the cooks from the kitchens made for the family. To wash down his breakfast, he poured himself a cup of tea which smelled of lemon zest. Satisfied with his early meal, he threw on his gray winter coat that hugged his body to mid-thigh, not bothering to button it, as he left Solascnoc. Robert dug his hand into his pocket and pulled out a silver pocket watch. He often called it a pocket ticker as he felt he could always hear the seconds tick and tock whenever he had it on his person. He gave the watch a tap to signal for his vehicle to pick him up at the castle's entrance.

The forest green, two-door coupe arrived at the entryway. Its front end had two bulging headlamps that looked like wandering eyes with two others just below them, and to the side of the bug eyes was the vehicle's bumper with a lined grill cascading downward. The craft seemed to smile, giving a semblance of life, though it was certainly a metal and un-living creature. Its windshield was stout and curved, its wheels white walled. They could fold up into the body of the craft to move with gyrolofstot compressors. The car's soft top was closed, and the ivory interior was warm to the touch from the heat that escaped from the coils hidden within the seats; Robert's muscles relaxed as he sat upon them in complete comfort. He set the car to drive, finally leaving the castle grounds only to enter the bustling horror and madness of the city.

The streets were alive with the sounds of beeps and honks, the yells of the passersby, the smell of syrup breakfasts and gooey pastries, the sights of historic buildings, columned and clad with marble, brick, and stone. The new construction was a kind of modern architecture that modeled itself after the old but with materials of glass and steel and metals light as feathers, more malleable than clay and as durable as marble. Though the old and the new differed in their makeup, the modern architecture held the flare and the structural idea of Buna's past, maintaining its sophistication, its beauty, and its conception, holding the charter of the city, capturing the ideals of those who founded the nation and bringing those ideals forward into the present.

Robert passed the financial district, then the religious roadway, and made his way to the historical district to a shop called The Smiths. He parked his four-wheeled car in an empty spot on the side of the blue-lined street, exited from the green carriage, and stood in front the old brownstone building. The sign on the storefront was made of scrap metals forged in character fonts of elegant cursive and bound to the building's brick facade. Looking up, two smokestacks plumed gray and white and quickly dissolved in the vastness of space. Robert opened the brass door, entering the shop, and a steam whistle blew to signal his arrival. The floors inside were cemented and glossed. Displays of swords, armor, guns, and weapons of war groomed the innards of the shop while two fires burned in the back. The sounds of hammers striking metal was the music of the company and they rang throughout the shop. A broad-shouldered man with hair buzzed to the stubs welcomed him to his keep. His brow was greased with sweat, his face streaked in black, his eyes earth dirt brown, and he had a smile that was perfect except for a stubborn tooth left of center on the bottom row.

"Well shine my boots and fix my hat. If it ain't the king of flowers," said the blacksmith.

"You might want to fix your britches too," Robert jokingly suggested.

"You're not that important now. To me, you're still the same ol' boy I met when we were five. Tossin' in the mud, catching fireflies, causing trouble with your brother," said the man.

"I do miss Blath sometimes. Its southern comforts are so nice, and the winters here in Aontu are awfully cold. How's your day, Dawson?" Robert reflected on his youth as he asked his old friend.

"Tryin' ta round things up round here by four, fore I get cleaned up and start headin' toward that country home of yours." Dawson wiped his hands on his cloth that hung from his waist and then continued to speak. "This gun for your boy, Abe, came out lookin' mighty pretty."

"I can't wait to see it," said Robert.

"Huck Dixie! Bring out Mr. Darroch's fancy new revolver!" he called back to his son. The boy, a year younger than Robert's own, came to the front of the shop with Absolume's gift.

"Here ya' go, Pa." Huck handed his father the weapon that was concealed in a wooden box. "Good mornin', sir," he greeted King Robert. His sandy blond hair laid on his head, disordered and erratic, his brown eyes looked toward the ground, his manner shy, even to those he knew well.

"Ain't she a beaut?" Dawson opened the box and removed the revolver from its silk covers. The handle was handcrafted with hand and finger placements that synced with Absolume's and was striped with gold bands. The gun was equipped with two copper hammers and three silver cylinders. Its barrel was long, and at its end, it had a counter weight that fit over the end of the barrel of the gun. The counter weight was trimmed in gold and made with verdigris, giving it a sky blue color, and burned into it was a white shamrock that stood stark amongst the array of colors.

"Abe is going to love this, Dawson." Robert gaped at its ingenious composition while Dawson explained how the device worked. He stressed the function of the secondary hammer and how it rotates the cylinders after seven shots have emptied the one in use. He also noted the quick pull trigger so that Absolume could fire off shots at a blindingly fast rate. "This is a wonder, Dawson. Thank you for this."

"It ain't me you should be thankin'. My boy did this on his own." He spoke highly of his son with excessive fondness in his tone. Robert looked over at Huck whose head was still looking down at the glossy cement floors.

"Thank you, Huck. It's fine work, son." Robert put out his hand to express his gratitude with a handshake. Huck raised his head to look Robert in the eyes. The boy gave a gentle smile and shook the hand of the king.

"It was my pleasure, sir," he said and then departed to the back of the shop to continue the song of the beating of the hammers.

"He's still shyer than a turtle in his shell," Robert noticed.

"Sure is. I try to crack the boy open, but it's just who he is, I suppose," Dawson agreed, placing the revolver back into the hand carved box, blanketing it in silk, and handing it back to his king. Robert took the gift from his childhood friend.

"Thank you again, Dawson."

"Anytime, Robert. I'll see ya' later on tonight," Dawson said his goodbye.

"See ya' soon." Robert waved goodbye, leaving the shop to go on his way to retrieve Aedus's present. He drove out of the small world of the big city and into the capacious terrain of the humble country folk.

In the middle of nowhere, in the most unassuming of places, Robert parked his car on a hidden back road with tracks of dirt and mud and disembarked from his vehicle. He walked for a few minutes, heading toward and finally into a stand of trees, evergreen, thick, and abundant. The earth was frozen beneath his feet as every step he took was hard and rough.

Snow should stick, he thought, walking through the quiet of the forest, hearing no sound but the steps he took that hit the ground with the breaking of the stiffness of the grass. Robert reached a small clearing, his destination, a most peculiar home in the country of Saoirse. The structure's frame was made of wood with vertical columns, horizontal beams, and diagonal braces. Its roof was made of clay and the walls of bamboo. He walked up the wooden stairs and knocked upon a solid beam.

A man with blue skin and dark hair, styled in a top knot, slid open the door to his home. He was dressed in traditional Nihon wear consisting of a haori, much like a half coat that reached his knees, a culotte-like garment called a hakama, split-toed socks known as tabi and sandals the Nihon people called zori. Though they could not be seen, attached to each wrist were bracelets that punctured his veins. The bracelet on the man's dominant side was called a katana and on his subordinate wrist, the bracelet there was known as the dou. The man's toffee-colored eyes looked at Robert.

"Hello, my king." He bowed to Robert cordially.

"Hello, Miyamoto."

"Come in, come in. It's very cold." Miyamoto welcomed him in.

"Thank you." Robert stepped inside the warmth of the bamboo home.

"Here, sit. Let me get some tea." Miyamoto pointed to a luxurious pillow made of the finest threads and most precise stitch work Robert had seen. It was handsewn. Its pattern was of budding and flowered cherry blossoms on a branch that wrapped the pillow like a vine, searching for the greatest route to the sun's face.

He took off his jacket and sat cross legged on the pillow, placing his coat beside him. In front of Robert was a wooden table surrounded by similar pillows his behind currently occupied. Miyamoto was quick to return with an antique kettle and cups without handles, all painted with images from his home country.

"Lovely tea set," Robert complimented as Miyamoto placed the tableware down on the table's surface. He poured Robert the first cup. The steam twisted and turned as it danced away from his mug.

"Thank you. It was my great-great-grandmother's," Miyamoto informed Robert.

"It's beautiful. How old is it?" he asked with sincere interest. It was not just a question for the sake of small talk.

"It's nearly 400 years old. My great-great-grandmother made these herself." Miyamoto enlightened him as to their source.

"It's quite amazing it has lasted so long in your family. It's nice to have things from the past in our lives. It helps us to remember who we are and what we come from," Robert said.

"It truly does. Each generation will reap from what the former generation has sown. There are parts in the fabric with great beauty, and there are parts of ill repute, yet I am grateful for them both, for both the good and the bad show the way to the light." Miyamoto spoke in proverbs, sipping from the piping hot tea he held in his blue hands, sitting across from Robert.

"How true your words ring."

"What is true will ring for eternity; only the false die and wither away." The two went quiet as they enjoyed the tea they drank, the warmth they felt, and the company they had in each other.

"Miyamoto, will you go back to Edo after this? Truly now your debt has been paid," Robert said.

"I cannot go back, Robert. The sorrow follows me like a shadow. There are times when the shadow is small, and there are times when it is mountainous, yet there it is, always," Miyamoto expressed.

"Why are you so consumed by the shadow? The light is all around you, my friend. Though now, I'm afraid, we are in the beginnings of darker times, but believe me, the world will need a light like you. Tokugawa will need you; I will need you. You have been a dim lantern for too long, Miyamoto." Robert meant every word he said as he spoke. The room was silent once more. Robert could see Miyamoto weighing his words.

"We will see. I will need to meditate on such matters as it waters rooted principles," he continued. "Tokugawa does not want to see me. His disdain for me will last until his death."

"Time changes all things, Miyamoto. What is it you say? Do not fear going forward slowly; fear only to stand still."

"Standing still, am I?" Miyamoto questioned.

"Perhaps."

"More tea?" Miyamoto asked. Robert put out his cup to have some more.

"Yes, please."

"On to another matter. I suppose you will be wanting Aedus's present," said Miyamoto, taking another sip from his tea-filled mug.

"Well, this was your idea," Robert reminded him.

"True, it was. It's about time I part ways with these. They have been nothing but reminders of my past." The Nihon man reflected on the gift.

"Yet, you must be grateful for them."

"Grateful, yes, yet also sorrowful. My road is no different than any others. I have indeed had my trail of trials and so too my paths of peace. I know your son will treasure my katana as he will my duo." Miyamoto removed the bracelets he wore on his wrists, and drops of blood fell onto the floor, but the wood did not absorb their color. Miyamoto sanitized them and rubbed them down in soft downy cotton. "Here you are, Robert."

"Arigatou gozaimasu." Robert gave thanks in the Nihonen tongue, bowing his head as he did so.

"Thank you, Robert, for giving me such a fine student. He has made my life worth living." Miyamoto bowed on his knees. Robert was a bit taken aback as his gesture was of great thanks and humility. He moved beside Miyamoto, kneeling down in front of him.

"You mean the world to him and to me. We are truly thankful for all that you have done for us." Both men rose, giving a quick embrace to one another. "I wish you would come tonight."

"He will not want to see me, Robert." Miyamoto spoke with a saddened voice.

"I understand. The tea was very good by the way." Miyamoto smiled at Robert's praise.

"Thank you, my king." He walked Robert to the bamboo door, sliding it across its tracks to open. "Have fun, and tell your boys I said, 'Happy birthday.'"

"I will. Farewell for now." Robert departed from the man who was saved.

"Goodbye, Robert." Miyamoto closed the door as Robert left the warm comforts of his home. He looked at the time on his watch, neither late nor early, but time perfect for the list of to-dos. He walked back to his car, both gifts now secure, revved his engine, put his vehicle in gear, and drove back toward the wild world of city slickers. He stopped just at the city's outskirts at a place, where machines flew like birds (or more like hurling rocks crashing in the sky), to retrieve a dear friend and his beloved daughter. His arrival read like his departure, perfect. He drove onto the tarmac to the hangar that read Hangar Bay Nine. Robert didn't have to wait long once he parked, for within five minutes of his arrival, an aircraft gently settled down fifty yards in front of him. Its shape was like two sides of a raised cookie. The solid cerulean disc extended its legs out, its curved windows exposed themselves, and rising from the center of the aircraft was the bridge from which the captain commanded. The blue disc was lined in white light, tracing the craft in a luminous display until its humming energy was no more and the landing sequence was complete.

From the bridge walked out a woman. Her skin was a soft blue like that of a setting sun that hasn't painted the sky orange, nor red nor violet, nor the darkness it becomes when it is set below the horizon. Her pale blue skin was flawless. Her irises were like lychee pearls, her dark hair was set in a bun, held in place with two bamboo sticks and decorated with jasmine flowers while strands wisped down her gorgeous face. Her thin figure was clothed in black. Tights covered her legs with boots that cut just before her knees. Her sweater was long and hugged her tiny hips, reaching just above mid-thigh. The neckline of her sweater hung down near above her chest, and her sleeves were tight around her wrists but loose in the arms. Cozy she looked; her fetching eyes quickly caught Robert's. She smiled brightly, waving hello as she walked toward him.

Trailing behind her was her father. Blue silver was the pigment of his skin. His eyes also were like ivory, midnight hair atop his head styled in a top-knot. Fashioned within his hair was a decorative comb with yellow citrine and topaz stones embedded within the accent piece. He stood nearly eight feet tall, dwarfing his daughter who stood five feet two inches. His shoulders were broad, his physique lean. He stole the room wherever he entered. From head to toe, he was dressed in all black. From his boots to his scarf, everything he wore was trim and proper.

"Kon-nich-i-wa," Tokugawa's daughter greeted Robert, articulating the word in syllables.

"Tomoe, it's so good to see you sweet child. How have you been?" Robert embraced her, feeling more an uncle to her than a family friend, perhaps because he and Tokugawa were such great companions, or because she called him Oji, meaning uncle in Nihonen.

"OJI! I've been great. Tired though. Studying and perfecting the arts is arduous work, you know." Robert laughed at her comment as she made both seem simplistic as her artistic talent was savant-like and her mind boldly sharp.

"Your father has told me you've been very meticulous in both pursuits," Robert said.

"The way to perfection is through meticulous effort. There is great beauty in perfection, and I plan to be the most beautiful in all that I do," she said rather stubbornly, as Robert pondered if she was quoting someone or if those were words of her own. He assumed the latter.

"Beauty can only be seen when flaws are present. Do not be so beautiful the world cannot see it." The words of wisdom came from her father who came up from behind her.

"Wise words your father speaks." Robert smiled.

"Aye!" she rolled her eyes, seeming to be playfully annoyed by her father.

"It's always a pleasure to see such as friendly face. It's like finding your favorite fruit for the perfect cider in the midst of a great forest," Tokugawa said as he saw his friend.

"It's always a pleasure to see you, old friend. How was your trip?" Robert asked.

"Short and sweet, just as I like it to be," Tokugawa answered.

"Wonderful."

"Is this our carriage?" Tomoe asked, gesturing to the royal blue hovercraft tall enough to fit Tokugawa's large body comfortably in its seats.

"It is indeed," Robert replied, helping them place their luggage inside the vehicle. Tokugawa and Tomoe sat on the cushioned seats. Robert leaned up against the royal blue carriage with elegant and symbolic gold features upon its exterior, poking his head through the open window on the side of the wagon to speak to Tokugawa and his daughter. "It's already programmed to go to the country home. I'll be right behind you both."

"Thank you for getting a carriage that actually fits me inside," Tokugawa chuckled.

Robert grinned. "Of course, you didn't think I'd stuff you in this little green car of mine, did you?"

"The thought did cross my mind. It wouldn't have been the first time you did that either," Tokugawa reminded him.

"Maybe I will next time then," Robert jeered. "I'll see you soon," he said and hopped back into his car. It rumbled back to life. He set his car to drive, leaving the airport to head to his home and the party that would be there.

Home—the sun hung at the two o'clock hour while busy feet moved about the estate preparing for a grand celebration. The house smelled of sweets and sugars. The outside looked more a circus than a yard, and soon those loved and cherished would come to join in the festivities of boys becoming men, the passing of the torch from the budding child to the ripened fruit of the man they would become. It was an honor necessary, for a society and a people, to make the world a better place for all mankind.

"Tomoe!" Absolume yelled from the second story patio.

"Hey Abe!" Tomoe hollered back.

"Do you need any help?" Aedus asked, standing beside his brother from high above.

Before Robert could answer, Tomoe responded.

"No. We're alright."

Robert laughed and helped Tomoe and Tokugawa with their luggage, carrying the bags inside the three-story brick and wood home. The interior of the house was a mix of stone and wood walls, contrasting with one another yet flowing seamlessly throughout the home.

"Tok, you're on the first floor in the room next to Enoch. Tomoe, do you mind sharing Lorena's room?" said Robert.

"Of course not. I practically sleep in her room every time I'm here to visit," she answered.

"I thought so," he said, knowing her statement was true.

The core of the house was decorated with blooming daphne flowers, white roses, and cyclamen along with clovered vines lined throughout the rooms. In the kitchen were pies and puddings, chocolates and candies, and one towering cake.

Robert helped Tomoe carry her luggage to his daughter's room. He gave a knock on the door, but no one answered.

"I'll let you get set up, and I'll go find Lorena."

"Thank you, Oji!" Tomoe hugged him.

"You're welcome, Toe." Robert left Tomoe to herself, leaving the room and seeing Absolume hurriedly rushing down the hall to welcome the pale blue princess. Robert stopped his son as he got nearer.

"Happy birthday, Abe. Your mother and I have quite the gift for you."

"Thanks, Dad. I can't wait to see what it is. Aed and I have been trying to figure out what it is you got us. Needless to say, we have no idea."

"Good, I'm glad you failed in finding out. I'll tell you this, though. You'll be happy with it. Now go have fun, and behave yourself," he told his son, leaving him to socialize on a day that was his. Robert made his way down the stairs to the hall that connected all the rooms to one another, turning right toward the kitchen and dining area, opening the double doors to the backyard where he saw his wife and daughter setting up lamprog lights for when the day went dark.

"My girls," he called to them.

"My man," Lagertha replied.

"Hey, Daddy," Lorena responded.

"Give us a hand. We're almost done." His wife handed him a lamprog to set.

"Gladly," he smirked at Lagertha. "Lo, can I talk to you when we're done?"

"Yea, sure Dad."

"Did you get the gifts?" Lagertha asked. Robert made a face, squinting his eyes and puckering up his face as if to suggest he didn't.

"Dawson said he wasn't quite finished with Abe's present, and Miyamoto refused to give up his bracelets."

"Robert." Lagertha gave him a sour stare, her tone serious as she spoke his name. He looked at his daughter whose eyes went wide and mouth gaped open, for she knew the look her mother gave her father. Robert laughed,

"Of course, I have the gifts. They're inside." Lagertha bumped him with her hips. "Still being mean, I see," he teased her.

"You guys are cute," his daughter flattered them.

"Thanks, Lo. One day, you'll find a man as great as your father," Lagertha said to her.

"That's not where I was going with this," she replied to her mother.

"Oh, I thought it was," Lagertha bantered in a feel-good manner.

"Did I mention you two were also annoying?" Lorena spoke sarcastically.

"One day you'll be just as annoying as us," her father said.

"I'm not so sure, Dad. You and Mom seemed to have raised the bar quite high."

"You hear that, dear?" Robert asked his wife.

"Very witty, this girl of ours," she said, looking at her daughter.

"I wonder who she gets it from?" As soon as Robert spoke the words, he was shoved once more by his loving wife.

"Like a wild blueberry, isn't she?" said a voice, not of the three, coming from the home. Robert looked to see it was Enoch.

"And what do you mean by that?" Lagertha asked her father.

"Sometimes you are so very sweet, and at times, just a bit sour." Enoch explained his comparison.

"They say the sweet is never as sweet without the sour," Lagertha playfully defended herself.

"Your tickling taste buds would beg to differ," her father slyly responded.

"Shoosh, old man. Is everything ready inside the tent?" she asked Enoch, changing the subject to matters of the festive affair.

"It's going to look spectacular. Uriel and I have captured the light for when the day turns to night, and your tent will shine like the sun in the blackness." He spoke eloquently.

"Thank you, Daddy." She kissed his cheek and set her final lamprog to hover up above from where she stood.

"You're welcome, sweet daughter," Enoch replied.

"Sweet, am I now?" Lagertha asked, still referring to the blueberry comment.

"Both sweet and sour. Let's be honest, no one eats just one blueberry at a time. It's only in the moment when we have our mouth full that we can decide what the mix is. You, my blueberry, are always on the side of sweet."

"I'm not so sure," Robert butted in. His daughter giggled with him while Lagertha gave her husband an acidic look. He moved to her and kissed her on the lips, ending the lighthearted teasing. Robert set up his final lamprog to hover parallel with those his daughter and wife had set up. He turned to Lorena, "Walk with me, Lo?"

"Where to?"

"The skirted path just beyond the tree line," Robert suggested, his inflection almost of that of a question.

"Sounds good to me. I could use some time away from everyone before this place is filled with hundreds of people." Father and daughter walked side by side, passing the two-story tent that bloomed with flowers even in the cold of winter. The ground beneath their feet was getting harder, the air colder, and the light dimmer as the night drew closer. Robert turned his head to look his daughter in the eyes as he walked next to her.

"Are you okay, Lorena?" he asked with the grave concern that comes from a father to a child.

"I am fine, Dad, really." Lorena sounded sincere in her answer.

"I am so sorry I wasn't there to do anything for you and to protect you. Can you forgive me, Lo?" It was quite a moment in the solitude of the woods.

"But Dad, you were there. Your love since my birth has surrounded me with good people and has given me the schooling necessary to defend myself. You were more there in that moment than you know, and because of that, there is nothing to forgive. Sir Westmore was there because of you. I fought off four men because of you. Your love as a father has given me strength within myself, and strength of noblemen and women at my side, always." She spoke with great sincerity.

"Lorena, my tiny dancer. You make me proud every moment of every day, but I feel I must pay a penance. Is there anything you ask of me? Name it, and I will give it to you," Robert said to his daughter. She pondered his question before responding.

"Your penance is paid, though Sir Wallace recommended I start learning other styles of the sword. Would Aed and Abe's instructors take me on as a student?" Lorena asked.

"Sir Myrddin might. I can ask him. He'll be here this evening," said Robert.

"Thank you, Dad." Lorena hugged her father, stopping the walk to show her affection through physical touch to provide more meaning than that of a mere thank-you. Robert could feel her gratitude and the love of his child.

"You're welcome, Lo, but if he says no, will you take me as your teacher?" Lorena looked up at him.

"I would love that." She squeezed her father more tightly before releasing her embrace.

"Me too." They continued walking, going inside the tree line yet still seeing the house, the tent, and all those who socialized outside. "Should we head back? Tomoe is at the house waiting for you."

"She is? Why didn't you say so earlier?" she asked with curiosity, her voice slightly risen from excitement to see one of her greatest friends.

"I wanted time with you before you disappear for the next forty-eight hours." Robert spoke jealously.

"Looks like your time is nearly up then." Lorena grinned at her father.

"I'm afraid so." They walked back toward the house. Some stars began to show in the sky though the sun wasn't set, and so, too, the moon showed its face in the early evening hours. "Have you figured out the puzzle paper I gave you?"

"No," Lorena said with a slight disheartened voice.

"You must be heated about it," Robert tried to hint.

"It's a bit frustrating," she acknowledged.

"Does it fire you up?" he asked, exaggerating the word fire.

"No—oh, is that how I can see what's written on it?"

"You're burning up now," Robert continued to play on words.

"Dad, your puns are terrible." She chuckled at the simplicity of his jests.

"I thought they were quite good." He cheerfully laughed at himself. "Your brother might be able to help you with it also."

"Which one?"

"I'm not sure. You'll have to find out yourself." He played clueless.

"You're weird. Thanks, Dad—for everything." She embraced her father as tight as a coiled snake, trying to squeeze the breath out of him.

"You're welcome, tiny dancer." Lorena departed from her father, leaving Robert alone near the tent that grew luminous as the darkness got closer.

He reflected on the moment he was in, celebrating his sons' birthday, a day on which they would become men. He looked back at his own life and remembered when he was their age, living in the same castle, exploring the same city, recalling the day he became a man and the gift he received from his father and the words his father had given him when the moon ran from the sun and the day was new.

"Life is but a fleeting moment, one full of joy, love, and laughter, yet one full of sadness, hate, and tears. These moments, all of them, are to be cherished for they are what make the person you are and the man you will become. Live life's moments to their fullest. Take in every emotion, every sight, sound, smell, touch, and even taste there is, and relish in the fact that you can. Take not a single breath for granted, for each one could be your last. If every passing breath symbolized your possible end, be sure you did all you could, for yourself and for others. Be noble, be kind, act with great courage, and your last breath may end your physical life, but the spirit you hold within this life will forever be eternal. I love you, my son."

A salty water droplet ran down the cheek of Robert as he did so deeply miss his father. He wished with all his heart that Abraham could be with him today to see his grandsons become men. How passionately he missed his father. Not a single word in any dictionary could truly describe, nor phrase in any language could capture, the emotion of losing someone a person loved with all their heart, for neither words nor phrases can describe all the memories or the bond one has with someone who has left the physical world. No matter how articulate the tongue, it can never fully describe the chemical language of the body and the vehement beating of the human heart. Even now, he begged his father's guidance to provide knowledge as a father, as well as a king. Robert wiped the streaming tears from his eyes and made his way to rejoin his beautiful family and his adored friends.

Inside the sugar-scented home, Tokugawa conversed with Yefimovich. Enoch was in dialog with his daughter and son, as well as his wife. The whereabouts of his children were unknown, though he knew they were close by. He did as his father had told him and took in the happiness and hurrah of the day that was before him, of friends and family together as one, in a time of high charm, without worry, with bliss dressed on their faces, if only for the day until the forces of the world compelled them back to duty where elation and sorrow mixed with one another.

The event of the evening drew nearer as the seconds ticked on the clock, moving the hours. Iscariot arrived with the third man to be, his son, Hanns. He looked a true split of Iscariot and Anna: one eye of honey the other of the blue sky, hair sandy blond, his face soft-featured though it was obstructed by a five o'clock shadow, handsome, quiet, skilled in strategy as well as music, he was perhaps the only thing in Iscariot's life that kept him sane.

The child within Robert that he tried to hide and that his brother so openly displayed awoke in his greeting to him as a clasp of brotherly love turned into who could outmaneuver who in their constant battle of aggressive yet friendly competition. It came to be that Robert had the victory in their playful tussle of hello.

"Got ya brother," he said to Iscariot.

"Ha, I have to let you win sometimes," Isc snickered back. Robert joined in his ha-has. "This place looks great, Robert."

"You should thank the girls. They did most of the work," he said truthfully.

"Ladies." Iscariot bowed in thanks.

"Come, I'll show you the rest of the place." He led his brother through the house to the tent outside. The lights more vivid than just minutes ago, the two-story structure was like a beacon seen from the sea. Its manner of decor, celebratory and magical, was like something from a fairytale or a novel of unworldly bounds beyond the earth. Iscariot put an arm around his brother.

"This is exceptional, Robert. Thank you for this."

"Hanns is like one of my own, and you're my brother, Isc. You both deserve this, especially today." He paused and thought of his brother's wife, Anna. "How was your day, Isc?"

"It was good. I made Hanns breakfast this morning. We spent some time at the poulnabrone. It was probably late morning, and Hanns went out for a bit. When he returned, we came here." Iscariot summarized his day as briefly as he could.

"How's your heart, Isc?" Robert was more specific.

"I miss her, Robert. I look back, and I can't believe I've lived eighteen years without her."

"Nor can I. I miss her, too. I think about you and Hanns a lot when this day comes. It's an odd set of emotions. You want to be happy for Hanns on his birthday, though the sadness does find its way in. I like to think of the times when she was alive and how great a person she was and that you and she had such a full life. For me, it washes the heartache away." Robert revealed his soul in this telling to Iscariot.

"I wish I could say the same. Some years, the pain is too great. The milestone years are the worst, but today, today I feel good. I'm happy, Robert." Robert looked into the depths of the gatekeepers to the soul of his brother to see if the words that left Iscariot's mouth were that of his heart.

"I'm glad to hear it, Isc." He gave a half smile. The brothers headed back inside the warmth of the country home. Hanns was coming from where they were going.

"Uncle Robert," he said.

"Hey, Hanns," Robert replied. Iscariot kept moving forward toward the house, tapping his son's shoulder as he walked by.

"I wanted to thank you for today. You've always treated me like one of your own children, and to be a part of today, to celebrate with my cousins. I'm very grateful." Hanns spoke candidly.

"There's no need to thank me. I love you, Hanns. That's all the reason I need for doing this for you." Robert revealed the truth of his heart in his words.

"Thank you, Uncle. I think my dad needed this more than I did. I caught him teary-eyed this morning at my mother's tomb. Don't tell him this, but seeing him cry for her made me weep as well. I wish I could have met her," Hanns confessed.

"Hanns, your mother was truly amazing. I wish you could have met her, too. She was one of the sweetest women I'd ever known, and she would have loved you more strongly than the bonds that hold the earth in its orbit around the sun and more fiercely than a miracinonyx against any predator. I hope you know that."

"I've been told. Thanks, Uncle." Robert looked at his nephew with sadness in his heart.

"I think you're really going to love the gift Lagertha and I got for you, Hanns." Robert tried to change the subject.

"Aunt Lagertha said the same thing. I can't wait to open it. Thank you, again, Uncle Robert, not just for today, but for everything. Hanns quickly wrapped his arms around him and hurriedly released his grip before Robert could manage to fold his arm around his nephew. He beamed at Hanns's authenticity as he felt the emotion in the tones of his voice.

Mightily the earth turned upon its axis and danced in the darkness of space, tilting the waves of light from the sun to creep upon its surface, moving conceptual time to where the sun no longer kept the hours but where the stars came to take their place as a timepiece for all those who averted their eyes to gaze upon the heavens, the everlasting watch man so frequently relies upon. Crowds of friends soon arrived from country roads that took them to the place where they belonged, in feelings of great merriment and with shared memories for the three boys, thoughts that would be engrained in their minds for eternity.

Mead like champagne filled Robert's cup as he conversed amongst the people. To Westmore he spoke, as well as to Ann, soldier and gate keeper to Solascnoc. He greeted Sir Myrddin Arthurian and once more expressed his thanks to Dawson and Huck. He nodded to Iscariot's closest friend, Antony, later saying hello but not much else. He could have sworn he saw Miyamoto, but he was unable to find the quiet man after searching high and low for him, giving up to talk with others at the party. After a few dialog-filled hours with close friends, he took a seat outside, not knowing that his wife had followed behind him. She sat herself upon his thighs.

"My, my, you're a certain kind of fancy," he said, flattering her as he took in her gorgeous looks. She wore a beige sweater dress that cut past the knees and came up to her neck, keeping her warm from the bite of the winter air. Wrapped around her waist, and showing off her pleasant figure was a thick brown leather belt with a large vertical rectangular buckle. Her hair was worn down, and it flowed like water when a soft breeze grazed past her beauty. She kissed him on his cheek, leaving a stain of her affection upon him.

"And you're the kind of dapper that I like." She gave him a flirtatious wink. Robert looked forward at the two-story, snow-colored, rectangular tent, lit with light from the sun that was captured by his wife and daughter, as well as Enoch and Uriel. It gave a sunset glow that broke up the darkness of the world around them. He looked to the second floor of the tent where two curtains were drawn open. Within the long open windows, he saw his sons laughing with one another, along with their cousin Hanns, and the girls seemed to be gossiping, of what he did not know, but they looked to be in high spirits which put glee on Robert's face.

"Amazing, aren't they?" he spoke.

"Our children? I was just spying on them myself. I swore they were children just yesterday. The boys were always getting hurt, playing with sticks they said were swords. Lorena, I swear, was a grown woman by the time she was three—always curious and driven and a wonderful big sister to her brothers, singing them songs and playing in their boyish games," Lagertha reflected.

"That's our girl." Robert felt pride in the woman he helped create into the person she chose to be.

"Our boys are so grown now—no longer getting dirty or causing trouble, not like they really caused too much to begin with, but now, Absolume has grown up to be just like you, and Aed is the sweetest boy in all the world—always doing things for others, a saint that one." Lagertha spoke with adoration and unbreakable love for her children.

"And somehow, he's an astounding driver," Robert noted.

"I'm not sure how that happened." Both Robert and Lagertha were a little surprised at his hidden talent, though they've seen him race a hundred times over.

"Do you know what you're going to say to Aedus?" Robert asked.

"I do. I've known for quite some time now. Do you know what you're saying to Abe?" Lagertha returned the question.

"I think so." They both lingered just a bit longer in looking at their children.

"We did well, you and I." Lagertha leaned in and kissed him with fervor on his peach-colored lips.

"We sure did," he said, looking deep into her bright blue eyes, knowing neither could have raised them as well as they did without one another.

The lovebird's people watched for a short time until booming footsteps came from behind them, and by the sound of the beating hooves, Robert knew the man behind him was Tokugawa. He took the seat beside him and Lagertha.

"There they are," he spoke aloud.

"We had wondered where they were ourselves." Robert and Tokugawa spoke of their children, who were still talking to one another in front of the exposed second-story window.

"Bright faces and light hearts. True gems they are. If they are as such now, I cannot wait to see them when they are polished," Tokugawa said.

"What do you mean, Tok?" Robert asked.

"A gem cannot be polished without friction, nor man perfected without trials. If they are so beautiful now, how glorious will they be once our children have been polished?" Tokugawa explained his metaphor.

"Their souls will coruscate like luminous points in the sky, and they will be seen like the stars upon the darkest of nights." Lagertha put her thoughts into words and fed the conversation.

"I certainly hope so, Lagertha. With all the things we see coming, I fear we will be the coals of the world—the ones unlit and dead, whose power can no longer produce the light," Tokugawa proclaimed.

"Then have hope our children will be the enlightenment," Lagertha spoke.

"I pray for it. Day and night, I pray for it." Robert could see the hope and the fear within the eyes of his cherished friend. He saw fit to change the subject.

"Tok, come with me to the tent. I've got your favorite winter drink in there."

"And why have you been hiding it from me?" Tokugawa asked.

"I knew you'd drink it all. Come on, let's go. Lagertha, you joining us?"

"To the tent? Yes, once we're inside, I think I'll leave you two to yourselves," she said, raising herself off Robert's lap. The three paced fifty yards toward the two-story structure. Lagertha said her goodbye as she separated from the two once they entered the warmth of the tent. Robert and Tokugawa headed to a display featuring a full palette of drinks, from mochas and teas to meads and ciders. Robert finished his mead in his mug, grabbed a clean cup, and poured a mulled cranberry apple cider into it. He splashed some fresh cranberries into the warm drink and stuck two cinnamon sticks in it. The drink was brownish red, the cranberries floated like buoys in the sea, and the cinnamon sticks shed their sugared coats and spread across the surface of the warm delicacy. Steam circled to the sky like a tornado as the heat clashed with the frozen air.

"Here you go, my friend." Robert handed him the delicious beverage. Tokugawa took a whiff of its sweetness and sipped to taste its delightful pleasure.

"Soul warming." He closed his eyes and smiled as he took another sip from the hot drink. "Thank you, Robert. This is just what I needed."

"I thought so," he smirked. Robert looked about the grandeur of the tent. The dazzling lights glistened like soft morning rays, providing a calming atmosphere. The vines of clovers stretched all over the temporary structure while lilies sat in water inside clear vases with candle lights floating next to them, and circling the vases were wreaths of pine branches covered in white roses. It was only thirty minutes before the ceremony was to begin. The night was filled with friends and family, a true social affair, but time and tradition assured it would end in solitude for Hanns, Absolume, and Aedus.

Robert made a vee shape with his thumb and index finger, placing the tip of the appendages just under his tongue and behind his teeth. He closed his lips over his vee-shaped thumb and index finger, exposing a small opening of the mouth and blew the wind within his body to the opening. The whistled noise grabbed everyone's attention inside the fairytale tent. Robert looked at his boys who were still above him and beamed.

"Everyone! If you would accompany me outside. Our ceremony is about to begin!" he exclaimed for all to hear. Robert, along with all who were in the tent of celebration, exited to the brisk air of the winter night. From the house, Iscariot had gathered everyone within the house and ushered them to where Robert stood. Laughter and smiles were all around. There was not a sad soul in sight. Once all were gathered in the openness of the field under the night-tide celestials, the high voices calmly and graciously fell. Starry, bliss-filled eyes were upon him as he stepped onto the chair that Tokugawa had thought to bring.

"Ladies and gentlemen. It has been a great pleasure to have ya'll here with us tonight. I hope your conversations were full of good cheer and your bellies filled with good drink and food. It is the twenty-third hour of the day. It is the final hour and the start of the rite of passage. We are gathered here this evening for one purpose, for three boys, whom we all love and who have impacted our lives and filled them with blithesome memories. Tonight, you see three boys. Tomorrow, you will see three men. Do not be fooled by their appearance, though young they are in face and mind. Should they survive the night, the experience will evolve both the body and the gray matter, a change so subtle that the eye may not see, though obvious to the one that is changed. Aedus, Absolume, and Hanns—will you please step forward?" The three boys strode toward Robert, stopping before him.

"Three cheers for the boys of Darroch! Hip-hip hurrah! Hip-hip hurrah! Hip-hip hurrah!" The crowd roared with Robert, ending the party and beginning the ceremony. Robert stepped down from the chair and embraced his sons and nephew. "Ready boys?" he asked. The three nodded. He turned them around and put a blindfold around the eyes of Absolume. Lagertha did so for Aedus, and Iscariot did the same for Hanns. The captured light that lit the tent exited in a solid beam to pierce the heavens. The lamprog danced and twirled within the sky and wrapped around the bond of captured light that beamed skyward, coiling it like a vine reaching for the sun until they exploded into stunning colored pictures, as fireworks they became.

Enoch and Yefimovich handed Lagertha, Robert, and Iscariot thick winter fur coats. Robert donned the cloak upon his back, Lagertha slipped into hers, and so too, Iscariot. Robert stood in front of Absolume,

"Listen to my feet and follow," he instructed him. Robert walked forward, leading Absolume into the darkness of the forest, where creatures of the black night waited, where terror and fear were ever-present, for what is unknown is a worry to all.

Silent was the walk to the destination of transformation. Only Robert's footsteps could be heard. Dead was the night, for there was no howl of the wind or wolf, no roar of thunder or bear, all scuttled away in dens and clouds. The sounds of night were silenced, the darkened sky turned inauspicious and formidable even though, just moments ago, it had been the opposite. Four miles into the dense and ominous forest they went, where trees seemed a mile high, and groves of copse and thicket expanded outward. One could be lost within it and spend their days there never knowing of the grasslands that extended into eternity or the oceans that dived the depths of infinity. Four miles in, Robert led Absolume to the butt of a tree that sat a foot above the ground.

"There is a stump just two paces in front of you. That is your post for the night, and here you will sit until the sun peers above the horizon through the burley weald, until it graces the fold over your eyes. Should you remove the fold, your sight will be lost forever, and a child you will remain until your penance is due. Last the night. Evolve yourself to reach your truest potential. Your eyes were closed a child, and like born, new, they will open to the world, the eyes of a man. This you must do alone, my child. May the night be gracious to you. I love you, my son." Robert left Absolume. The wind began to whine. The clouds opened up, and the howl of the wolf cried. The night was alive as snow fell from the heavens, and its purity blessed the earth.

The oiled blackness of the sky mixed with colors of a lighter shade and altered the firmament a powerful purple. A dip of light on the brush of the Maker spread across the canvas to shift the sky a navy blue. The rays of the sun began to caper in the heavens, but they did not bring themselves to the folded cloth of Absolume. A lighter shade mixed with the painted sky and filled the world with reds and oranges. The hour was near as the flare in the vault above rose to reach its apex. The Painter of the night re-formed His composition, and it was day, and the sun consumed all. The fold was lifted by Absolume's hands, and before him was his father who glowed wide-mouthed in happiness.

"Dad?" Absolume was surprised to see his father kneeling before him. "What are you doing here?"

"I never left you, Absolume, just as God will never leave you. Blinded you were, surrounded by darkness. Alone you thought you were. I want you to know that you are never alone my son, and that He will always be here for you. My time will end, where as His is eternal. Look to the Creator for strength within yourself, hope for when none hold it inside themselves, and truth for when its torch is shrouded in darkness." Robert gave these words of wisdom to his son.

"I will, Father."

"I know you will. I heard your prayers through the night. I saw your strength, your ferocity in conditions freezing and miserable. Not once did you lift your hand to your eyes. I am so proud of you, Absolume." Robert spoke with a surfeit of joy.

"Thank you, Father."

"You're welcome, my son." He paused. "I have a gift for you." Robert handed Absolume an intricate wooden box. He opened it. Inside was a letter and a silk cloth that covered his present. Absolume broke the seal that held the paper folded, and he read it aloud.

"Boom, boom, boom
The heart plays a fearsome tune
It cries and screams for its song to be heard
And what a melody it is
Of hope, of fight, of dreams
Do not let the strings stay silent
Or leave the words on paper
Play the music of your soul
Play your song, make your spirit whole
What you play should give you life
Sing your song in times of strife
Carry on in the darkness and in light
And the world will see your gift is bright
Boom, Boom, Boom
The anthem hits another core
This one's young, a blankness score
The harmony is pure and sweet
As it mixes in with your old beat
Play this hymn, hand in hand
And cherish every verse
For one day, this tune will end
Be glad this child's ear did bend
For as you croon your final note

Sing the line held in your throat
I love you, my sweet child
You were my hope when I despaired
And my fight when I was weak
Chase your dreams as I did mine
And sing your tune of life
The kin sang softly back
Its beat is strong, for it is yours
But the melody's my own
My notes will fall, and they will rise
As I chase the dreams held in my eyes
But now your music sheet says rest
And know your song is in my soul
A part of me that's made me whole
And I will revere each note forever
And sing of when we were together
Close your eyes, and you will see
That your life has made a symphony
Boom—Boom—Boom." Absolume moved the wooden box from his lap and wrapped his arms tightly around his father. "The dribbling drums of the snappy snare call us to war, but this song of father and son will stay with me until my dying day, and when I hear my own beating heart, I will think of you, Father. Thank you, thank you for everything. I couldn't image life without the greatest man I've ever known." Absolume let out his heart to the man, to the father that raised him.

"You're most welcome, Absolume. Take another peek in that box. I think you'll like that, too," he told his son. Absolume picked up the handcrafted container, removed the purple silk cloth that covered his gift, revealing the revolver that was hidden. His eyes widened like his smile that painted across his face in excited merriment. Absolume gripped the gun. It melded perfectly with his hand.

"Multiple cylinders, quick pull trigger, multi-hammer functionality. Dad, this is beautiful." Absolume spoke gleefully.

"Thank Dawson's son Huck when you see him."

"Huck did this?" Wow, its better work than his fathers," Absolume said, sounding a bit surprised, his eyes mesmerized.

"Don't tell Dawson that," Robert chuckled.

"If I'd known, I would have thanked Huck and Dawson at the party."

"Thank them today when you're out in town," Robert suggested.

"I'll definitely stop by their shop," Abe said with excitement in his tone.

"Do you want to test it out?"

"You brought bullets?" Absolume asked.

"Your sister, in the middle of the night, came to give me your gift. The bullets are a gift from her, and she thought you'd like to shoot once you saw your gift."

"God, love her," said Abe.

"Load her up." Robert handed his son a box of bullets. Absolume loaded the cylinders while Robert marked a tree as a target. "Ready?" Robert asked, Absolume nodded yes. "Fire!" Seven shots rang out, dressing the target. Absolume pulled the hammer, rotating the cylinder for the next seven. They, too, marked the target. He knocked the hammer once more, striking bullseyes seven more times.

"Amazing," Absolume said joyously, almost dumbfounded while the barrels smoked from the heat against the cold wintertime air.

"Let's head back, shall we?"

"Thanks again, Dad," he said, stowing away his weapon.

"You're welcome, son. Don't forget to thank your mother," Robert reminded him.

"I won't. She won't let me forget, either."

Father and son trekked through the six inches of snow that fell during the night. The four miles went slowly as their steps were deep and fresh in the snow-covered ground. Their spirits were up, their talk was carefree, and the day was good. By late morning, they finally reached the warmth and comforts of the country home. They were the last to arrive from their ceremonial tradition of the Rite of Passage. Before them was a display of breakfast delights. Baked goods and fruits filled their nostrils along with cooked meats that added to the mouthwatering smell.

Together they ate, Robert, his two sons, daughter and wife, Enoch, Uriel, Tokugawa and his daughter, Yefimovich, Viktoriya and Yekaterina, along with Iscariot and his son. The table was full, as were their bellies. The news could be heard and seen in the background, holographic images of events that happened the night prior and in the early morning hours. Robert's jaw dropped at the news on the screen, and the gasps of all that were present spoke volumes.

Absolume Chapter Two

Clink, clatter, tatter—the sound of weapons shatter. Light floats softly in the air. The rays bounce from wall to wall, from eye to eye. The nerves in the iris tell the brain what it sees. The mind guides the hands and feet—where to move—based off the sight of light to dodge or strike the hammer-wielding man who is in front of him. The blows were heavy. His body braced for every bash of the hammer. The weight of every clash felt as if he were holding up a mountain, though he needed only to hold himself up from every pummel, a burden he embraced. Losing the battle, he felt the doubt within himself build, heavy like flat stones piling on one another as he struggled to hold them. Absolume gripped his sword tight, his nerves jolted like branching lightning strikes. He swung his blade, but his beat was batted off. He struck once more; he hit only the air in front of him. He saw the hammer coming to crush his chest. Light glowed from his armor. He cannoned back from the force and might of the boff and landed on his back with the air in his lungs leaving his body.

The armored warrior approached him. From head to toe, his armor was jet black, his hammer tall as he. The emerald handle glistened before him. The face of the man was hidden behind the helm, its front wickedly fierce and fearsome with antlers protruding from the top of it like that of a kingly buck. The man removed his horrid helm. Behold, the face of his father.

"Are you okay, son?" Robert asked Absolume who struggled for air.

"I'm—fine," he gasped.

"Here, let me help you." Robert decompressed the armor his son was wearing. "Better?" Absolume inhaled deeply.

"Thank you," he whispered. He laid there a while, not saying a word, staring up at the ceiling, taking deep, controlled breaths. His eyes watered but did not shed. His heart ached, not from the force of the hit from his father, but from his failure to defeat him. Absolume was angry at himself. Of all in his family, he was the weakest swordsmen and the least strategic. He brooded in silence while lying on the wood floor.

His father knelt down beside him. "What's the matter, Abe?" Robert's voice was soft as he spoke. Absolume didn't want to speak, but his father's concerning face forced him to.

"I'm a failure." He inhaled deeply, his throat tight and arching, pulling tighter like a knotted rope, yet he managed to speak his mind. "I cannot do what you do. In every attempt to be like you, I fail. Who will follow me into battles? Who will see me as a leader if all I do is fail? How will I ever become one if all I am is nothing more than average?"

"Absolume. My son. Never try to be like me. Strive to be more than me by being yourself. Only then will you see how great you are. And do not fear your failures, Abe. There is great wisdom in them if you look for it." Robert paused. "Absolume, average men can do glorious things. Never doubt the common man. They are more gifted than you know, and do not worry about who will follow you into battles. It is the blade of your heart that will bring a warrior to follow your call to arms. Your strength is in your character, Absolume. That is your greatest weapon. That is your brightest light. You have the gift of hand and eye. This sword is not your forte. Trust in your hands the might of the gun. That is your skill, and never doubt, my son, the fortune of luck, as it is so often overlooked. Now, rise and fight another day. You did well, Absolume." He grabbed his father's outreached hand to bring himself back to his feet.

"How do you do it?" he asked.

"Do what?" Robert questioned his question.

"How do you always know what to say?"

"It's something fatherhood teaches you, and they are words my father once told me. Being a dad is a powerful thing. It makes you see beyond yourself and also deep within yourself. It makes you do things beyond what you think you can do and gives you the words of wisdom you never knew you had. You have the gift now, Absolume. You just need the right moment in your life to let it flower," Robert said, removing his armor and helping his son remove his.

"Thanks, Dad," Abe said, comforted by his father's words of wisdom.

"You're welcome, Abe, but know you need to stop doubting yourself, and you'll see that if you use the gifts you have, you can do incredible things. So, stop doubting and start doing."

"From this day forth, I shall. I promise." He hugged his father in his half-armored wear, and they released their affection. Absolume and Robert finished disrobing from their gear.

"Ready to go up?" his father asked. Absolume nodded. The two left the glossed dark wooden floors, the handcrafted stone walls and the weapon decorated armory that laid beneath the castle of their home. They crossed through the tunnel that connected the castle to the armory and took the stone staircase up to the first floor to the warm comforts of home. Both Robert and Absolume entered the living area where most of the family was. Absolume could feel the melancholy vibe—the airwaves in the room.

"What's the matter?" he asked.

"There you two are. Robert, I've been trying to reach you." Lagertha spoke in a brash manner.

"What's wrong, Lagertha?" Robert's expression changed as he heard the tone of his wife.

"Before I set you in a panic, I just want you to know that everything is alright," she started.

"What happened?" Absolume asked again.

"Lorena was attacked by the mob this evening. She's okay, just a few scrapes and bruises, but she is doing alright," his mother answered. Absolume let the news sink in.

"Is she awake?" Robert asked.

"No, she's asleep now," Lagertha responded. Robert took a seat on the couch in front of her. Absolume still stood.

"Who was it? What was the group?" Absolume queried.

"They call themselves the Nua Domhan Ordu," his mother replied.

"The Soisialach?" he questioned some more, his emotions brewing.

"The soisialach," Lagertha confirmed.

"Dad." Absolume turned to his father.

"I know, Abe." Robert stopped his son. "We will need to provide more policing and heavily monitor them. I'll talk to the other branches as soon as I'm able. I'm so sorry, Lagertha."

"Their actions are not yours, Robert," his mother said to his father.

"I should have been there for her," Robert continued.

"Robert Darroch. You are the king of this nation. You have duties as king and orders from God. Do not blame yourself or think you could have stopped this," Lagertha reprimanded her husband. The room was still in its silence.

"Does Aed know?" Absolume asked.

"He does," his mother answered.

"Is he still awake?" he wondered aloud to her.

"I'm not sure, Abe," Lagertha responded. Absolume sat in silence with his family until Enoch broke it.

"Shall we pray?" he asked, latching his hand with his son's until the bond was a full circle with all in the room. "Master of the highest heaven, forgive our sins as we ask you to hear our prayer. A loved one of ours has suffered physically and emotionally by those of wicked thought and action. Please give my granddaughter strength within her soul. Heal her wounds both in body and mind, and continue to guide her now in her time of hurt. Continue to guide her when she has moved beyond it. I, too, ask you to help us against threats internal and external. Give us the light, the fire to see our way as we approach this time of darkness. Lord, hear our prayer. Takk."

"Germa." Absolume opened his eyes and raised his head. "I'm going up for the night."

"Goodnight, Abe," said his father.

"Love you," his mother said.

"Goodnight. Love you both." Absolume departed from the crowded room and headed up the staircase, walking down the hall to his solitude. He entered his alabaster room with trim of solid gold. It was dark, the fire unlit. He moved to the dark end of his room and placed his hand upon his desk. A display appeared before him. On this device he could view, create, and do nearly anything, and so he did. Nua Domhan Ordu was his search, as well as the history of soisialach. He read their creed, their mission, learned of their wants and desires, and studied their story. He filled his mind of the soisialachs and their role in the Hollen war, the global war in which his father fought—how they aimed for a new world order through totalitarianism, how they would shape the world through fire, through chaos, by turning man against man. When the world was consumed in flames, they would mold the glass earth into utopia.

Absolume turned his attention to holovids of demonstrations, rallies, and marches of the Nua Domhan Ordu within the past two years. Their messages were of unity, yet they divided. Their words were of peace, yet they displayed violence. They were the beacons of truth, yet they held the truth of lies. How broken the mind must be to fall for their folly, he thought. The holovids he watched were of the worst displays of man. He watched as a man of Nihon decent was beaten to a bloody pulp as he fought to protect the woman he was with who was of the Ivdeyskiy religion. His ears began to steam at the atrocious sight.

He then watched another, this of a crippled man counter-protesting. He was a man near his father's age who had an artificial leg and arm. Absolume watched in gut-turning disgust as they tore off his leg and arm, smashing his mechanical limbs and abrading the man until his voice was silent.

Then he saw a video that made him rage, that heated his blood and fueled his anger, giving life to the emotion of hatred. A deep loathing cratered in the pit of his loving soul. His eyes bore witness to his darling sister as she fought and struggled against the evil of the crowd, as her clothing was torn from her body, helpless against the masses. He turned off the holovid. *I'm going to kill them. I'm going to make them suffer as they have made my sister suffer. They will rue this day, and when they hear my name, they will fear me.* Absolume yelled this in his beautiful mind that was mission driven, clear without obstruction. Nerves banging like shot fire, he was restless. He lit the fire in his room. The room warmed. Absolume knelt down before it, taking three, deep, air-filled breaths. His heartbeat slowed, his nerves more rigid, his blood at a simmer. He rose in a new state and readied himself for bed as the hour was early morning. His eyes grew heavy, his mind waned, and his body could feel the weight of highs and the lows of the day. Absolume wrapped himself inside the sheets of his bed. He closed his eyes to rest and succumbed to sleep.

He awoke. The day was new, his body sore, and his mind in better spirits. He opened his bedroom door and headed down the hall to his sister's room. The morning light was still new, only the seventh hour of the day, and as Absolume was about to knock on Lorena's door, she opened it.

"Hey, Lo."

"Morning Abe. What's up?"

"Want to go shooting with me after breakfast?" Lorena mulled it over a second or two.

"Yea, I'll go with ya."

"Good. I'm heading down to eat. You coming?"

"Let's go. I'm starving. Is Aed up?" she inquired of her brother.

"I'm not sure. I just woke up myself," he said uncertain. Brother and sister walked down the stairs to the first floor's main hall. Delicious smells tickled their nostrils as they got closer to the dining room. Bacon hit Abe's nose as well as syrups and sweet fruit hams. His stomach rumbled from the fragrant air. His sister laughed at his gargling gut as the sounds seemed hilariously animated. The display of foods was as sweet and satisfying as its smell. Both Lorena and Absolume piled their plates in abundance. The tastes of the food were delightful, quieting Absolume's talkative stomach, generating energy he would need to tackle the day ahead.

"That was great," he said with a bulging belly.

"I'm so full," Lorena commented.

"Me too. I'm going to roll up to my room and get ready. We'll leave at eight."

"I don't think I can move. Can you push me back up to my room?"

"Hurry and I'll buy you a latte," he bribed her.

"Oh well, I'm off to get ready," Lorena said cheerfully. They departed from one another. Abe washed his face, cologned his body, threw on some winter wear, and waited downstairs, sitting on the comfortable couch. His luggage filled with weaponry rested at his feet.

Lorena finally walked down the stairs to meet her brother. Her hair was tied in a ponytail held in place by a band of four-leaf clovers. She wore black athletic joggers, a blinding white hooded sweatshirt, and eggshell colored running shoes. Though a woman of modesty and elegance, her favorite attire was that of comfort, wearing dresses only on occasion or dressing posh when circumstances were necessary.

"Changing it up I see." Abe teased her choice in clothing.

"Yea. I decided to go with the stark white sweatshirt over the vanilla shaded sweatshirt. It was a difficult decision." She rolled her eyes and continued. "I see you chose the white button slacks over your usual brown, you rebel." She spoke lightheartedly. Absolume was filled with joy to see her in good spirits after what she had just gone through the evening prior. He only hoped she wasn't putting on an actor's mask to cover her true feelings.

"The gray turtleneck was the tougher choice, to be honest." Abe continued the banter.

"You chose poorly," she laughed.

"Shut up and let's go," he chuckled. Both he and Lorena left the confines of their home to head to the barn out in the country. When they arrived, Absolume carried his arsenal in a pack over his shoulders. He opened the barley tinted wood barn doors. The horses ruffled about to see who was entering their sanctuary.

"Hey, Pendragon." Abe rubbed his hand over the snout of the horse who seemed to enjoy the soft brushes of Absolume's caress. His red mane was plumed in high fashion. He breathed heavy as if to say he missed his friend. Behind Abe, Lorena opened the door to the stable where her horse resided. His nameplate read Stocai.

"Stock-ee! Hey boy." She wrapped her arms around the neck of the horse. His legs were like milky socks, his body a gorgeous tannish brown. The underside of his face matched his legs, and the top pattern of his head ran in a triangle shape the same color as his body. Stocai's mane was a fair blond shade, and his eyes were like silver.

Absolume took his black horse from the stable and mounted a midnight saddle on his back. He led the beast out of the barn. Lorena was right behind him with her horse. Abe closed the barn doors as they exited.

He mounted his stallion and journeyed off with Lorena in the open range to the woods a mile from their country home.

The blue sky above was dramatic, drawing the eye to His vivid canvas, the air frigid, like breathing ice. The evergreens a half a mile away but still clearly in view were lush and beauteous. Brother and sister began to talk of whatever crossed their minds in the picturesque scene in which they traveled. They teased of their absent brother and his goo-goo eyes for Yekaterina. They switched topics to talk of Lorena's ballet and fencing practices and the trials she had for each.

"Fencing was nerve-wracking. I felt like I needed to vomit during the second duel and after the first bout," she described.

"You lost the first bout?" Abe asked.

"I lost the first two, but after the second loss, something inside me came to life. I had this burning sensation inside my heart, and it charged away my doubts and fears. I felt almost out of body and won the last three rounds of the five I had to endure," she recounted.

"This sounds intense. I wish I could have been there to see it."

"You would have loved the last bout. I was on defense the entire time. Sir Wallace ended up driving me to the edge of the mat," Lorena began to tell her brother.

"Did you win?" he asked anxiously.

"My heels were at the boundaries, and for some reason, I thought of ballet. So, I stood on my toes, and when he struck, I dodged his parry with a twirl and pierced him mid-spin," she said without false elaboration.

"No way. Please tell me this is on holovid."

"Sorry Abe. I don't think so," she said, dashing his hopes. They moved in the quiet of the wind where the voice of the breeze drew reflection. "All this training meant nothing. My victory meant nothing." Lorena's voice fell melancholy.

"What do you mean, Lo?" Abe tried to pull out the meaning of her words.

"I couldn't even fend off four people," she explained. Absolume stopped his horse in front of Stocai.

"Lo, you fought more than four people. The Domhan Ordu posted the video of you. You fought off four but were struck from behind by a man that didn't show himself to you. Then, when you were pinned, four others approached. The holovid ends there, so I'm not sure what happens next, but I know in a battle of honor, based from what I saw and how you have fought against me, I have no doubt you could fight and defeat ten men at once." He tried to embolden her. She cried.

"I was so scared, Abe. I wanted Dad to come and save me." Her eyes ran a steady stream, glossing her aquamarine irises.

"Dad did save you, Lo. It was Dad who taught you to fight by having Sir Wallace as your instructor, and it was Dad who befriended General Westmore, who gifted you on how to strategize. Without Dad, you might not be here today." Abe could see in her eyes that she hadn't thought about it that way. She dried her eyes with her sleeve.

"Thanks, Abe."

"Ready to shoot?" he said, pointing to the targets as they approached the outdoor range surrounded by the abundance of trees. Lorena smiled.

"Show me how it's done, little brother."

Abe hopped off Pendragon and assembled his weaponry on a lengthy oak bench. Lorena sat next to him as Absolume explained the inner workings of all the guns, how they fired, and what best to use them for in combat. As he loaded each weapon, he placed it on the shelving and racks to the right of the bench he sat on.

"What would you like to shoot first?"

"I say we start with the most difficult and go from there," Lorena replied.

"Sniper it is, then. Let me go set up some balloons." He grabbed some loose balloons, climbed aboard his horse, and rushed down a thousand yards to the end of the range. He blew up six multicolored balloons and tied them to three different evergreens, all at different heights, and when he was content with his placements, he left upon his trusted steed and galloped his way back to Lorena. "Ready?" he asked.

"Ready," she answered. Absolume handed her ear protection and readied the rifle, standing it on its legs while its butt sat on the frozen ground.

"Want me to be your spotter?"

"I'll take all the help I can get," she responded and lay on the numbingly solid dirt and dead grass. Lorena put her eye to the scope. Absolume noticed a discrepancy in her positioning and adjusted her legs.

"We have three trees, one to the left, one center, and one far right. Sector one is on the left. Sector two is center, and sector three is the tree on the right," he noted to his sister.

"Roger that," Lorena confirmed.

"All sectors are a thousand yards away from this position. By eye, go to sector one," he told her.

"Contact," she said as she positioned herself to see that sector.

"Go to glass," he commanded.

"Three targets, colors red, yellow, and green. Red is at the highest point, target yellow is below, and target green falls lowest," Lorena described to him.

"Target green. Go to parallax and mill," Abe commanded.

"At one," she stated.

"Confirmed at one," Abe replied and continued. "Check level at five point four."

"Ready." She adjusted.

"Breathe. Wind at point two," he informed his sister. Lorena exhaled.

"Ready," she shouted. The rifle boomed. Its sound ricocheted from tree to tree. The target popped. The green was no more.

"Kill confirmed." Abe's voice sounded his praise. "By eye, sector three."

Lorena turned to the right. "Contact," she confirmed.

"Glass," Abe commanded.

"Two targets colored orange at the highpoint of the tree, second target pink shaded, target low," she described.

"Target orange, parallax and mill," said Abe.

"At one, two, five," she stated.

"At one, two adjust," Absolume instructed.

"At one, two," she confirmed.

"Check level at ten point five," Abe told Lorena.

"Ready." She adjusted once more.

"Wind at point two." Abe gave the final details. Lorena shot, the rifle banged, the barrel steamed, and the bullet hit the target. "Nice shooting," he said, praising her success.

"Nice spotting," she replied, returning the compliment.

"Quick shoot at level two, wind point two." Lorena quickly readied herself and fired. "Miss," said Abe. "Again—breathe." This time, he saw his sister calm herself. She became still like glassy water. She pulled the trigger. The sound of the rifle rang. It echoed its song through the forest. She lifted her head from the scope with a grin stretched cheek to cheek.

"Boom," she beamed with happiness.

"Don't want to see you on the battlefield. Deadly shootin', Lo," he lauded.

"Show me how it's really done."

"Set the stop watch on your communicator," he told his sister.

"It's up," Lorena informed him.

"Name a sector and target."

"Sector two, solo target."

"Ready," he said.

"Go," Lorena commanded. Abe, still standing, held the sniper snug against his shoulder. He put his eye to the scope and pulled the trigger in one solid motion. The white balloon shredded into pieces as the bullet impacted the target.

"No way!" Lorena spoke in disbelief.

"What's the time?"

"Two, flat."

"Boom," he smiled.

"Bet ya can't hit the next two," she dared him. Absolume aimed and hit the second target in sector one. He fired his third shot, but the balloon did not explode. It only floated away as the impact of the bullet severed it from the tree at its connecting point. The small breeze took it, moving it about the forest floor. Absolume put his eye to the glass of the scope, his index finger pressed the trigger, and the balloon was no more.

"Ah-Whooo!" Lorena howled in the mantra of the Mactire. Abe joined her in the bellowed howl. "You're such a good shot Abe. Why don't you join the Liopard branch next year?"

"Because who wants to be alone?" he answered. "Lasevapen next?" he continued.

"My favorite," Lorena beamed. Absolume stored the rifle away and pulled out two guns that harnessed the power of light. One was skinned in black and silver that looked like scales of an alligator. The other was orange, red, and brown and followed the feathered patterns of a tropical bird. Each weapon was about two feet in length and equipped with a scope. Absolume flipped a switch, which turned on the safety, and he, like his mom, bent the light around himself and stored it in the gun's diamond that was hidden inside the weapon's handle. He flipped another switch that produced a note that sounded like an electronic chirping nightingale, and when it was fired, gave a drawn-out, high-pitched squeak at the peak of the nightingale's octave.

They stayed on the range until mid-morning, shooting the small arsenal Absolume had brought with them to get away from the madness of the world, to be alone and meditate through the convivial feeling of firing a weapon and watching a target fall before them.

"Ready to get back?" Lorena enquired.

"Satisfied?"

"Very" she replied. "Thanks for taking me with you, Abe."

"I thought you could use the release. There is only so much ballet and swordplay can do." Absolume organized his weapons and packed them away in the baggage he brought with them. "Race ya home?"

"Is Pendragon up for it?" she asked in sarcasm.

"You hear that boy? She thinks you're gonna lose." Abe rubbed the neck of the beast. It gave a snort as if to dismiss the challenge. Absolume climbed atop the horse's back. Lorena already sat upon Stocai.

He whispered in Pendragon's pointed ear, "Fly, boy." His horse gave a series of nods as if acknowledging his words. "Ready?" he asked his sister.

"Go!" she yelled, and the horses bolted through the greens and browns of the calm and steady forest.

Pendragon sprinted with strong, powerful strides. The ground beneath the horse's feet was the sky, and his feet were the wings of dragons. Absolume leaned far forward, his head near Pendragon's. He whispered again, "Rush, rush," and his speed increased. Stocai was a horse length ahead. The spacing of the trees grew wider, and the clearing of the field ahead approached. They cleared the thicket of the forest, "Roar!" Absolume yelled. Pendragon's hooves moved so quickly it was as if they never touched the ground. There was no distance he could not close and no distance he could not create so long as Absolume rode the steed. He was the Arion, the swiftest horse.

"See ya, Lo!" Absolume shouted from above.

"Ignite!" Lorena yelled to Stocai. Her horse screamed a squeal, shrill and strident. His white socked legs began to glow as the horse focused his energy to empower them. Quicksilver he became. Like a firebolt, he strode a blinding pace that matched the speed of the gliding horse above at half mach. Their finish was the barn. Stocai was the shadow, as he raced directly below Pendragon. Absolume's horse quickened, as he picked up speed on his descent from the welkin, and as he approached the dense and rooted earth, he folded his wings to cause drag, slowing his body so that when he landed, his hooves would not stomp nor stump but move with adroitness on his way to victory.

"Woo!" Abe exclaimed. "Way ta go boy!" Lorena was right at his side as they reached the barn.

"You two got lucky." She stuck her tongue out playfully.

"If we hadn't been in the woods to start, we would have had you beat, but I guess I'll take the tie," he said to Lorena and then spoke to his horse. "Good job, Pen. Nice flyin'." He patted the horse on its right shoulder. Absolume hopped off his noble steed and signaled for him to bow to his opponent. Lorena gestured the same to her horse as she dismounted. Absolume guided Pendragon back to his stable, fed him, and un-dammed the water for his horse to drink. He closed the wooden door behind him as he left the stable. Pendragon turned and walked to the closed barrier that met his chest. He knelt his head down to Absolume's.

"I'll see ya later boy." He rubbed his snout and let Pendragon tend to himself. "I'm off to shower, Lo," he said as he was exiting the barn.

"Wait up. I'm right behind you." Lorena said goodbye to her horse and met Abe at the double doors of the barn's entrance.

"Since we tied, race ya to the house?" Absolume asked. Lorena responded by placing her foot over her brother's, tripping him, and letting him fall to the ground, but on his way down, he entangled his foot with hers to stop her from fleeing.

"Noooo!" she laughed. Absolume stood, and the two picked and poked and cheated their way to their destined goal. They reached the door at the same time, but it was Absolume who claimed victory.

"Beat ya," he said, swinging the door open to a scattering of people, some of whom were eating, others decorating for the lively day ahead. Their mother spotted them in their sibling rivalry.

"There you two are. Where have you been?" Lagertha asked.

"Hey, Mom," they said in unison, but Lorena continued. "Abe took me shooting this morning."

"Oh, that's nice. How did it go?"

"I had fun. It was nice to let off a little steam," Lorena answered.

"Good. Can you help me when you freshen up? We have a lot to set up before the night begins."

"Sure thing. Give me fifteen minutes," Lorena told her mother as she started to leave to clean the sweat and soot from her face and hands. "Oh, Abe, I won the race. You seem to have forgotten something outside," she teased as she walked past her brother, pretending to shoot him with gun fingers.

Absolume let out a sigh, heading back outside to retrieve the arsenal he left behind. He quickly grabbed what he had forgotten, made his way to his room on the second floor, and began disassembling his weaponry to clean and assure everything was as it should be. He removed the impurities from his arms. He oiled the parts which caused friction. He unlit the source from the diamond inside the guns that solidified light and reassembled every bit of the weapon as if it were new, pure, and untouched. He looked at the mess of his hands and the dirt of the cloth he used and thought he must look like a pigsty.

He unclothed himself, signaled the shower on, and set the heat temperature of the water, rinsing away the grit and grime that came from good times, shining himself for more to come. He styled his dark brown hair, shaved his prickled face, sorted the garments he would wear for the night, and dressed himself in shin high, thick black and white colored cotton socks, and a soft relaxed fleece-like pair of pants called allais, patterned salt and pepper, hugging his ankles and hips, along with a thick long-sleeve cotton shirt with embroidered patterns. He slipped on a pair of gray downy shoes whose rubbered bottom felt like walking on a cushioned cloud and whose leather exterior was malleable as it laced from toe to ankle.

In his readiness, his stomach growled. It was nearly high noon, and his belly ached for sustenance. Abe made his way downstairs in the warmth and comfort of his clean clothes and prepared a lunch of meats and cheeses, sliced fruits, and warm apple cider. Then, he made his way back up from where he came and sat himself on the balcony that overlooked the tall trees and the driveway at the front of the country home. He let his mind come to ease as he sat under the cloudless sky, enjoying the pleasantries of the lunch at hand and a hot drink to sip on, and in his comforted state of mind, the brain began to wander. It quickly thought of Lorena and her tussle with the muscle of the Nua Domhan Ordu. His mind connected dots to the past of like events to recall a time when he was a small boy of eleven, when he and his siblings attended the Hubble Academy, a school that focused on math and science. Abe flashed back to a memory of his cousin Hanns. His thought drew a picture. He walked the wooden, hand etched halls of the academy. The day of schooling had ended much to his relief. It was late spring, the air heavy with pollen as trees and flowers bloomed the colors of the rainbow. The feel of the weather was not too hot nor too cold. He recalled it was the start of the weekend, and his family was to head to see the Aontu Bearfints versus the Dearg Antinquea Bisons in a sport man had played for over 500 years. Absolume was ecstatic for the weekend and roamed the halls, looking for Aed and his cousin, Hanns, to share in the excitement.

As he traveled the academy, he came across a crowd of students. He pushed his way through them to see the ruckus they were witnessing, and his eyes bore sight of a clenched fist running its way through his cousin's stomach. Absolume dropped the books and bag he was carrying. His eyes grew wide as the sea, his jaw clenched, and he rushed the three boys who pummeled his cousin.

"Let him go!" he yelled, grabbing the collar of a tubby boy taller than he, slamming him against the wall. The boy fell, and Abe jumped on to him abrading him with his fists. His punches were halted by another boy his size with orange hair and freckles. He locked Absolume in his arms and pulled him off the round, blond-haired child. All the while, a boy of dark skin kept Hanns in his grasp, watching his wicked friends fight Absolume. The chunky lad gutted Abe with a loaded punch to the belly. Absolume began to rage and headbutt the kid that held him locked in place. Released, he fought the two boys, but his freedom was short-lived, for the black child whom held Hanns, knocked him to the ground, pinning him to the marble floors. Absolume was now defenseless. The black boy's fist pulled back to swing, and then, from the corner of Abe's blue eyes, he saw a foot clash into the face of the boy that laid atop of him. The bully flew off his body. His azure gazers looked up and saw the outstretched hand of his brother. Absolume looked around. The three punks laid on the ground, two in tears. Then, suddenly, the group of children that had assembled for the spectacle dispersed like loose cattle.

"Hey! What's going on over there?" The voice of an adult echoed in the halls. Abe, Aed, and Hanns gathered their things and sprinted toward the doors of freedom, answering the call of the weekend.

Safe from reprimand, the three boys walked outside. Abe looked about and spotted his mother's vehicle: a rich royal blue titanium carriage with molded gold decor lining the roof of the wagon and an interior plush and pearl white. They bolted to her as soon as the hovering carriage was seen by Abe.

"Hey boys. How was—Hanns! What happened to your eye?" Lagertha asked with a shocked expression.

"Hanns was bullied again, Mom!" Absolume quickly tried to explain.

"Abe, shush. Hanns, tell me what happened," Lagertha urged him to explain.

"Mom, I swear," Abe began.

"Absolume, I want to hear from Hanns. You can tell me why your lip is cut after Hanns tells me why this happened," his mother said. Absolume put his hand on his mouth not knowing the skin of his lip had cracked open. Hanns spoke up in timid tones.

"They called me the devil because of my eyes and said only the devil would kill his mother." Hanns recalled what was said to him.

"Who were these boys, Hanns?" Lagertha's voice was sweet and tender, calming and caring as a mother's voice should be.

"Geebags!" Absolume spoke once more out of turn.

"Absolume Darroch!" His mother's eyes daggered at him.

"They are," Abe affirmed.

"Not another word, young man."

The clouds of his thought lifted, and his mind brought him back to the present as it mapped the faces of one of the holovids he had watched earlier. Absolume brooded, for the enemies of his past were still his enemies today. *I'll make them atone for their depravity*, he thought to himself. How could they do that to the poor man? What monsters! He felt sorrow as he re-imagined the tearing of artificial limbs by these monsters of men.

Absolume fanned away the gray-clouded thoughts and focused on the peace that was in front of him. In his newly found tranquility, he heard the sound of his brother approaching.

"There you are. How was shooting?" Aedus asked as he walked out onto the balcony.

"Lo and I had a good time. I think she needed it."

"Heard she beat ya in a race," his brother continued.

"She leave out the race to the barn?" Abe didn't sound surprised.

"Seems she did," Aed winked. Absolume's eye sought Katerina as she sat down next to Aedus.

"Hey, Kat."

"Hey, Abe," she replied with a smile.

"What have you two been up to this morning?"

"Your brother woke me at five this morning to go to the frosted Fields of Diamonds," Yekaterina answered.

"Oh, what did you think?"

"I was stupefied. It was so beautiful. It was amazing to see that, just as the sun hits the horizon, the ice on the grass glistens and gleams like the stone itself. The only thing I can compare it to in Yisra is the Sparkling Cacti Forest, when the needles of the plants blush a milky vanilla. If you stand on top of the Hill of Zion and look down onto the forest, it's like looking at the stars."

"That sounds quite alluring. Does that happen all year long?" Abe asked in wonder.

"No, the display happens two months from now, right before spring. The cacti forest will shine for about six weeks before the flowers bloom, which is also very bewitching," she answered.

"Sounds like Aed and I have a trip to make soon."

"Of course! I told Aed the same thing," she said matter of factly. Absolume smiled at the thought of exploring and seeing new places and going on such adventures with his brother. In his mode of being in good cheer, he caught a glimpse of his father's car pulling up the driveway with a large carriage behind him.

Out of the wagon stepped Tokugawa and his dazzling daughter, Tomoe. Absolume yelled to her. His heart raced, his eyes were emboldened, and his mind was a tizzy frizzy electrical firework, but the explosion within his body never left bounds of his bones, and to those who looked upon him, they would never know the emotions he felt for her.

"I'm going downstairs to put these dishes away. Do either of you want anything while I'm down there?" he inquired.

"No, I'm alright." Aedus pointed to his clear glass of brewed sweet tea.

"I'm fine, too," Yekaterina replied. Absolume quickly made his way down the stairs and into the kitchen. He cleaned the dishes he had dirtied and made his way back from whence he came, passing his father with a short conversation to say hello to a woman to whom he was attached like a prickled vine embedded in his heart. But it was a love he left fettered, caged in his ribs for him to feel but none to see.

"Tu." His voice pastoral and tender, he said her name. Tomoe turned from her bags with a radiating smile whose glow flashed into the eyes of Absolume, making its way to his heart where his beating bumper basked in the warmth of her beauty. The happy expression on her visage screamed of a heartfelt adoration for the person in front of her—one of a deep burning, yearning blaze of wanting something more than the magnetic bind of friendship she had with Absolume. In his foolhardy ways of honor and high value, and with all his might, he restrained the emotion she wanted him to display. It was from the wishes of her father that he dared not free his beating heart from the prison of his body to hand the love within to Tomoe. It was the Nihon custom for a woman, as well as a man, to be self-sufficient before pursuing a partner. For if a woman could not care for herself, or a man himself, then how could they care for another and the children they would create together?

The tradition was something Absolume admired, as it not only made the person a better individual by honing their skills and craft, but it also improved the collective, for it gave society the best of oneself to produce a product and a service superior because the individual was made superior, because they strived to perfect themselves.

A love worth waiting for is worth fighting for, and what it means to fight signifies the importance of the love desired.

"Hey, Abe. Here to help me unpack?" Tomoe asked.

"I didn't think you'd need any luggage. You've been here so many times, I thought you had your own room," he joked.

"I should mention that to your mom." Tomoe played on the idea of her own room.

"Lo will have your back," he assured her.

"Where is she?"

"She's downstairs setting up."

"Do they need my help?" Tomoe wondered to him.

"I don't think so. They seemed almost finished, but let's go down and get her."

"Let me finish unpacking, and then let's go," she said. A tap on the arch of the door was heard. "Hey, Aed." Tomoe waved as Aedus approached from behind Absolume with Yekaterina near his side.

"Hi, Tomoe. What are you all up to?" Aedus asked.

"We are going down to steal your sister. Is that the Tulku?" She looked at Yekaterina with a curious expression. Katerina stepped forward to shake her hand.

"You can call me Kat."

"I'm Tomoe. It's—it's nice to meet you." Tomoe spoke with a slightly tangled tongue.

"It's nice to meet you, too. Our dads see each other all the time. It's a shame we haven't met sooner. My father tells me you're quite the cellist. I'd love to hear you play sometime." Yekaterina expressed her interest, seeming delighted to meet someone she heard so much about from Yefimovich.

"Your father is very kind. I've met him a few times. He always speaks very highly of you," Tomoe replied. "I've brought my cello with me. Maybe I'll play something tonight."

"Looks like you two are going to miss a good show," Katerina teased Aedus and Absolume and then changed the topic. "Aed and I were just about to go to a pond nearby to skate. Do you and Absolume want to join us?" she asked.

"I don't think we can. I was hoping we all could go into the city quickly to pick up Abe's gift," Tomoe said.

"Oh, no gift for me?" Aedus spoke lightheartedly.

"Yours is right in this bag here, Aed. Don't worry, I didn't forget about you," she comforted him.

"Well see you back here then," said Kat.

"Hai." Saying okay in her native tongue, Tomoe replied, "Have fun skating, you two."

"We'll see you in an hour or so." Aedus said goodbye. Katerina was behind him and said farewell.

"Where we going in the city?" Absolume turned from the door, asking Tomoe with great interest.

"Don't worry about it. You'll see when we get there," Tomoe told him with a soft chuckle almost unheard.

"I'm worrying," Abe smirked.

"Let's go find Lo." She grabbed Absolume's hand to guide him out the room and released before they exited. His heart was storming from her touch, and his mind was a whirlwind, calm and then explosive. He followed her to find his sister, making their way down to the first floor and searching the grounds outside until they ran into Lagertha.

"Tomoe, my second daughter. How are you, beautiful?"

"Haku!" She wrapped her arms tightly around Lagertha's waist. "Where is Lo?" Lagertha pointed out to the field where two dots were off in the distance, heading for the trees.

"Aww." Tomoe's expression was the sound of adoration and shucks. "Well, Abe and I are heading into the city quickly. His present awaits."

"Don't be long," Lagertha told them. "Abe, have you seen your brother?"

"He went to the lake with Yekaterina," Absolume answered.

"Dial him and let him know he has to be back in an hour."

"I'll call him," Tomoe insisted.

"Thanks, dear. See you both soon. Hurry back and drive safe." Lagertha said her goodbye. Tomoe gave her a peck on the cheek, and the two headed to the upper floor of the barn in the collective gallery of vehicles that was as broad as the River Canyon and as unique as the intricate print of the human finger.

"The gluaisrothai?" Absolume asked, knowing what she was looking for. Tomoe found her treasure in her search, quickly dusted it off and climbed aboard the hoverbike. It rested soft on three gyrolofstots, one large and at the rear of the bike, the other two at the front, attached to two titanium spring forks that connected the pieces together and were much smaller. The cyclops eye of the nukebike was bold, bright, and unblinking. The handles for steering were of a vintage design, as were the mirrors that were attached to them. The body was slim and melanoid in color with nuclear power running through its core. The seat was elongated polished black leather, the back lights blood red, and its undercarriage radiated like an angel. Tomoe brought the beast to life. Absolume flicked the pedal to open the barn doors of the second floor. He hopped on the back seat, his body pressed against Tomoe's. She steadied her way out of the barn as she drove the gluaisrothai, and when she was clear of the doors, she took to the sky with Absolume holding on for dear life.

"Close your eyes, and no peeking!" Tomoe yelled as the rush of the wind tried to hush her voice. Absolume obeyed her command, closing his eyes to the world before him. He leaned into Tomoe. The smell of her hair was the same scent as the jasmine flower she wore atop her head. His hands could feel the heat of her body as they gripped her little hips. Absolume's mind was not erratic, nor did his heart skip any beats. He felt bliss, as if wrapped up in a blanket next to the crackling fire, listening to the roll of thunder and the taps of rain. Only now, the warmth was of her body next to his body, the sounds of the call of the wind, the comfort of the smell of her hair and the embrace he gave her as he rode with closed eyes to a destination unknown.

The gluaisrothai coasted to a stop.

"Don't open them," Tomoe told him once more.

"They're closed," he assured her.

"Good, we're here," she said. Absolume released his embrace, letting Tomoe free to dismount from the nukebike. "Here, take my hand." She grabbed Absolume to assist him.

"Can I look yet?"

"No," Tomoe was quick to respond. Absolume could hear the sliding of a door opening. The floor he stood upon sounded hard when his shoes knocked onto the surface, yet it felt soft when contact was made. The air around him was perfumed with the scent of a natural flower blossom.

"Hello, can I help you?" Absolume heard a voice ask. It was quiet and pleasant to the ear.

"Kon'nichiwa, Tokugawa no chūmon o tori ni kimashita." She spoke her Nihonen tongue.

"Ah! Un. One moment." The footsteps of the shopkeeper deadened as he walked further from Absolume and Tomoe. A moment later, the steps became louder in the canals of Absolume's ear.

"Okay, Abe. You can open your eyes now." He did so. His vision was blurred. He blinked rapidly to better his vision. The walls were beaten bricks, and the ceiling was covered with ume blossoms of whites, yellow and bright red. The floor was made of thick green bamboos. Absolume's eyes finally looked at the elegantly wrapped black box with red ribbon tied around it in a bow.

"Open it," Tomoe insisted. Abe untied the bow and opened the black box. Inside the compact vessel laid two rings. One was made of a viscoelastic and the other aluminum. Their design was debonair, their craftsmanship immaculate. He slid the aluminum ring onto his index finger.

"It's perfect," he said, examining the silver color with two coiled lines running through the metal.

"Put this one on your thumb." Tomoe handed him a piceous ring, fitting it onto his finger.

"What is this made of?"

"It's a viscoelastic material. Its properties are very unique. It's soft and compliant, but strike it, it becomes hard. This ring is a concealer of energy," said the shopkeep, his skin similar to that of Tomoe's yet much older in appearance. The merchant had his sleeves rolled up, exposing his arms, giving Absolume sight to the energy that flowed within the old man. Tomoe leaned into Abe to whisper in his ear.

"Oh, wow!"

"Shh!" Tomoe put her index finger to her mouth.

"Thanks, Tomoe. I love it." He squeezed her body tightly, and she wrapped her arms around him in return.

"You're welcome, Abe," she replied "Otsukaresama!" she smiled at the storekeeper. His humble face with squinted eyes smiled back as he bowed. Tomoe bowed back. She took Absolume by the arm, intertwining hers and his together.

"Ready?"

"I'm ready," he answered and continued. "Thank you," he said to the shopkeep as Tomoe dragged him to the doors of the shop.

"Bye now!" the vendor hollered with a wave of his hand. Tomoe and Absolume stepped back out into the city streets.

"I'm driving," he said with an amused look skirting across his face. Tomoe didn't respond but climbed on the back of the hoverbike folding her arms around Absolume, pressing her body against his, and laying her head on his back as if it were a pillow.

Push to start, and the vehicle came to life, floating above the concrete surface. Tomoe's grip tightened, and Absolume bolted through the air, buzzing through the streets, leaving the center of the city to arrive at a place that was the center of his life. Home. He was surrounded by the sweet smells of cakes, pies, candies, and the mouthwatering scents of honey-glazed ham and oven roasted turkey. His eyes were enveloped by the scene of flowered decor and the emanation of merry making. He thanked Tomoe once more, leaving her side to ready himself for the ceremonial events ahead.

Upstairs in his room, he became naked and rinsed his athletic figure with running water. He dressed himself from head to toe in snow white. His hair was styled in a messy look, and he was refreshed. He put back onto his fingers the rings that were gifted from Tomoe and wandered back down the stairs to enjoy the festivities that were for him with people that were there for him. He was excited for the night ahead. Absolume draped across him the final piece of his ensemble, a hooded, wool, royal blue cloak with vivid gold buttons that latched to looped holes from the neck to just under his chest and so, too, at the cuffs of the sleeves. He walked out the door of his room. His brother was in the hall heading to his own.

"How was skating?" Abe asked.

"Perfect. What did Tomoe get you?" Aedus spoke with interest. Absolume showed him the rings and whispered something in his ear.

"Whoa. That's wicked," he said, a stunned tone to his voice. "I'm going to go get ready. You look good."

"Thanks, Aed." The brothers departed from one another.

Downstairs, everyone socialized. Absolume found his way next to Tokugawa and Yefimovich who were talking of a scientific matter. Words of the lively tongues rambled of celestials and travels beyond their star system. Uriel joined the conversation in the free thought of the meeting of minds to provide influence and knowledge of what was soon to come. Absolume listened with great interest as the vocabulary sank inside the depth of the ears as sound to which the body responded, encoding and converting the message into electrical energy, sending it through the pathways of the body to the brain where it would project an image from the music of the spoken words. He pictured the moon and stars and what laid beyond them—the solitude of the blackness of space, infinity and beyond. From what his mind could picture and decipher, the daydream imagery of spoken pictures, like a flash of light, for the faintest of seconds, he saw Tomoe in the imagery of celestials, and his mind returned to earth.

"Sir, Tokugawa," he said while there was a pause in the conversation.

"Absolume, happy birthday and congratulations."

"Thank you, sir, I'll accept your congratulations once the ceremony is over. I wanted to thank you for the gift." He spoke with gratitude.

"You're very welcome, Absolume, but to be honest I have not the slightest idea what I got for you. Tomoe said she wanted to do something special, so I let her do as she pleased." Tokugawa spoke honestly.

"Well, see for yourself." Absolume put out his hands, displaying the rings.

"Oh! Most interesting." He sounded a bit surprised when he saw them. Tomoe, Lorena, and Katerina walked over as Tokugawa examined the rings.

"Outousan, what do you think?" Tomoe asked her father.

"I think they make quite the couple. One full of energy and drive, the other calm and patient but with the ability to produce wonderful things. Keep them safe Absolume, for one is useless without the other." Tokugawa spoke seemingly symbolically.

"They're on safe hands." Absolume tried to calm his doubts.

"I do not doubt it. By the way, since you have been listening quite astutely, do you have anything to add to our wild thoughts of spacetime and the future?" Tokugawa asked.

"I'll let those of a different mind fly amongst the stars. My mind is rooted to the earth. But the future is something that everyone dreams of, and it is for those who fear to fail but have the courage enough to leap time and time again who see their dreams come to life, if not now, then surely in the future," he said with certain wisdom.

"Truly spoken," Tokugawa praised.

"Here, here," Yefimovich agreed.

"They are the words I heard once from my father. I'll have to thank him later."

"You used his wise words well," Tokugawa noted.

"Abe, we're going to the tent. Do you want to join us?" Tomoe asked.

"Yea, I just wanted to thank your father."

"Happy birthday, Absolume" Tokugawa said as Abe departed, echoed by Yefimovich and Uriel.

Inside the two-story tent of conjuring lights, vines of luck, perfume of flowers and sights of food and cheer, Abe and the girls found their way up to the upper level to chat, feast on meats, and sip on tasty pleasures. Absolume had noticed all the girls had changed from what they had on earlier. Tomoe wore an ornate hairpin the Nihon called kanzashi. It flowered a powerful purple that pollenated the nostrils. Her dress was a kimono, lavender in color, embroidered with patterns of blossoms, and wrapped around her, just under her bust, was a white string she called obijime that had a sash clip of a lavender flower worn over it. Her feet were slipped into socks called tabi, and she walked upon sandals called zori with violet straps and white flowers. Absolume's blue eyes fell into a trance at her beauty, and if the spirit of man is found through the window of the eyes, she most assuredly captured his and let it rest within her tranquil stare.

"Abe, where is Aed?" Lorena took him out of his daze. She was changed from relaxing and comfortable clothes to a full-skirted white dress with regal copper Versailles print and with a long-sleeved ivory top with a sultry sweetheart neckline, revealing a hint of skin. Her pearl white heals kept her calves flexing, showcasing her stunning legs.

"Last I saw he was getting ready," Abe answered.

"Here he comes." Yekaterina spotted him from a distance. He was dressed in reds of crimson and rome, and he, too, was adorned in a cloak, but his was the color of blood. His eyes dark as ever and hair a sandy desert blond was short in style though it still waved like dunes formed by the winds. When Aedus joined the group, Lorena had the five of them gather together to capture their image in time to save until it withered away a hundred years after their deaths. Abe looked at the holopic and admired it. *We all look so happy*, he thought to himself, and the thought filled him and uplifted him, putting him into an emotional state that was beyond the thought of himself but for that of those he was around and their very well being.

They all talked of their dreams and the goals they set for themselves. For Lorena, ballet was everything. It was her art, her expression, her athleticism. Her dream was Prima, her goals were solos and to perfect every movement when she danced—a mathematical art, from the arc of her foot to the angle of her arms and the height of her kicks. Her desire was to be so artistic, so mathematical in every movement, that writers would make performances with her in mind. If her name could twirl amongst the lighted name of Pierina Legnani, she would have a name that would tip-toe the tongues of history. Absolume had no doubt she would achieve such ambitions.

Tomoe expressed her dream of painting ceilings of cathedrals and bowing strings upon her cello in tempos and with notes that, when they struck the human ear, would be undeniably beautiful. Absolume already thought that of her cello playing and knew within his heart her dream was just a stone's throw away.

When it came 'round for Absolume to voice his dreams, he felt somewhat ashamed and embarrassed, for his dream was to fight in battles of great peril and lead men on the battlefield to victory. But *what a horrible dream*, he thought to himself, *for the world to be so broken they are willing to kill one another for their beliefs. Yet he also thought how great an honor it would be to lead men of like minds into battle for the might of goodness and truth against the skewed mind of perceived goodness and untruth.* Just as he was to release this thought from his mouth, his cousin Hanns joined the quintet.

"Cousin Hanns!" Lorena cheered him a welcome. In his shy demeanor, he smiled, barely whispering the words hello.

"Happy birthday, Hanns," Absolume greeted him. "We were just discussing our futures. What do you want for yours?"

"Well—" Hanns's face reddened. "I'd love to be a famous sculptor one day, like Donte or Michel or Auguste and have my work displayed throughout the city." His face was cherry red in extreme contrast to the white cloak he wore.

"Are you working on anything now?" Yekaterina asked.

"I—I've been working on a piece for the last two years," Hanns answered.

"Is it almost done? You haven't let any of us see it yet," Absolume asked.

"It—I, I'm still learning new techniques. It will be a little longer, but you'll see it soon. I promise," he continued. "What about you Abe, what do you want?" Absolume hesitated before answering.

"We all know of Winston Church. All his life, he thought of war and prepared for war. War wasn't something he wanted, but it was something he was prepared for. It's said he was put on this earth for war as the savior of the state of Konstanpol. Without his foresight, without his bravery, his talent of tongue, or his cunning mind of strategy, Konstanpol would have surely been consumed by the Hollen Army. I want to be like Church, hated by my enemies, loved by my friends, and revered by the tellers of history." Abe shared his dream.

"He was brilliant. It's unfortunate he passed away when we were little," Aed chimed in.

"My father was good friends with him. 'A sourpuss with a big heart,' my father used to say of him," Katerina added.

"Here's to our dreams." Absolume raised his glass of hot cider and hoorayed to their futures.

The jocund air of the evening delights rang through the night. Songs were sung in gladness for the boys and also of the holiday cheer, as Yule was just a day away, and the people of Saoirse and those who shared in the Nazar religion would celebrate its significance.

Bellies became full as well as hearts, and the celebration was nearly over. Absolume heard his father's call as the eleventh hour of the night was upon them.

"Ready?" he asked his brother and cousin.

"Let's go," Aedus answered. Absolume and his party walked outside the tent into the frigid air. His father was at the front of the crowd, announcing the beginning of the ceremony. Absolume was called forward. A call for hurrahs was given, and his eyes were blinded by the cloth his father put over them. Through the darkness of the fabric came a blinding light and then with it, the booms and cracks of fireworks. Absolume pictured the scene in his mind. The dancing of lamprog, the beam of light, and the explosions of cannonade.

"Listen to my feet, and follow," his father spoke within his ear. Absolume could feel the energy of the crowd slip away as he intently listened to the sound of his father's footsteps as they walked out into the wilderness where fear of darkness lingered and the monsters of the night roamed. The beating drum within his body picked up in tempo. His hands were cold as ice. He blew on them and then slid each hand into the opposite sleeve of his cloak. As he walked in nervousness, he found it odd the only sound he heard came from his father. The cry of the wind did not wail. There were no cracks or snaps of branches from the beasts of the night, nor were there songs of any creature, large or small, that sang the notes that rang ominously in the blackness. The night was dead, but Absolume was very much alive. Unknown was the distance he traveled. The sound of his father's footsteps stopped, and so did he. Robert spoke.

"There is a stump just two paces in front of you. That is your post for the night until the sun peers above the horizon through the burly weald, until it graces the fold over your eyes. Should you remove the fold, your sight will be lost forever, and a child you will remain until your penance is paid. Last the night. Evolve oneself to reach your truest potential. Your eyes were closed a child and like born, new, they will open to the world, the eyes of a man. This you must do alone my child. May the night be gracious to you. I love you, my son." Absolume could hear his father's footsteps fade away until all that he heard was the death of the night.

As the hour hit midnight, the wind began to whistle a harsh shrill, like screams of a frightened child. He could feel the flakes of snow fall upon him, and every minute the snow seemed to be heavier. Absolume shivered from its ferocity. His heart beat faster, and as the night went on, the harsher it became. The howl of a wolf sounded just yards away. The branches of the trees collided like the antlers of two bucks in battle. The trees could be heard crying as the stresses of the wind and snow came upon them. The dead forest was teeming with a life of horrors his eyes could not see, and in his fear, he began to pray.

"Father, keep me safe through the wickedness of the night. Give me strength against my fear, and see me through until the morning light. Keep me warm though my body is cold. Let me see the light. Let it pierce the fold." The sounds around him seemed more intense than the hour before. The cold air with the power of the wind made it hard to breathe. He felt as if death were before him. Absolume prayed once more.

"My Maker, fill my lungs with your breath, for mine are fainting. Keep me from the grip of death, but if it should come for me, place a sword within my hands so that I may fight to live. I'm so cold, Father, and so tired. Please let your sun shine soon. Germa." Absolume finished his prayer, and in that instant, the wind fell silent. The snow stopped falling. The depravity of fear fell from his heart and mind. The world around him was still, almost lifeless. It was quiet once more.

A vicious snap—it penetrated Absolume's heart. A thunderous boom rattled his bones. He prayed once more.

"Lord, save me."

Aedus Chapter Two

Oh, how the moon hovered over the horizon, how it lit the earth a bonnebell blue of beauty and allure. It softened the appearance of the world and showered its luminescence in humble glory. Aedus was awoken, his room a wall of books, the fireplace a solacing simmer of coals, the hard floor cold to the touch. Shirtless, he walked in the brisk air of his room. The moonlight struck his body. It glistened like marble, and his eyes refracted the light as he gazed out the open, stained-glass windows of Solascnoc.

He opened a book with the daingne on its hard cover and flipped to a page he marked. He read, and when he finished, he spoke of great faith, Germa. Aedus walked to his washroom to freshen himself for the day ahead and draped himself in slacks dyed blue that were not loose, but hugged snugly to his body. On his feet, boots of cowhide with laces of the same material and whose bottoms were white rubbered, and when he walked in the boots he adorned, it was as if he walked on the air itself. His upper body sported a luscious white sweater of thick cotton, soft and warm upon his skin. He wrapped a scarf around his neck and donned a leather coat, waist length and with a high collar.

Charmed with his fresh appearance, he quickly closed the four-inch thick, heavy wooden door of his room and strolled down the marble hall to tap on the entry door of the room where Katerina slept. Aedus waited, but there was no answer. He knocked once more and waited for what seemed an eternity. The door cracked, and his eyes caught hers.

"Good morning." Yekaterina's voice, soft and dazed, greeted Aedus.

"Good mornin'" he paused, dumbstruck by the beauty of her eyes. "Are your things packed to be moved to the farmhouse today?" he asked.

"They are."

"Well, I was heading out to see the sun rise this morning, and—I was wondering if you'd like to join me?" Aedus asked, shaking in his boots. Kat seemed to give it thought, putting Aedus's nerves on edge.

"Oh, that's so sweet, Aed. Sure, I'll join you. It sounds nice. Just give me a few minutes," she told him. Aedus was quietly ecstatic, like fireworks without the bang, to hear the simple word "yes" slip from her lucid tongue.

"Meet me down in the room of seasons."

"Where is that?" Katerina asked, still just peaking from behind the bulky door. Aedus grinned.

"It's the main entrance to the castle, where the snow falls amongst the birch trees," he explained.

"Oh," she smirked. "I'll meet you there." Katerina closed the door, her face beaming. Aedus's heart fluttered with the rush of endorphins and emotion, filling his soul with the treasured wonder of young love.

Waiting in the room of winter, he stood with a calm expression and erratic nerves. She walked into the room. The snow that fell seemed to freeze in midair. The glow of the moon beheld her, an angel. She radiated in the gentle light of the milky sphere that hung above the earth. Black were the pants that wrapped tight upon her body. Effulgent her ivory sweater with black bands at the wrist of the sleeves and skirting her neckline. Her strawberry blond hair was down and waved like the mane of a male lion in its prime.

He had never seen such beauty, and if there were anything more beautiful than she, he could not see, for he, the beholder, was blinded by her light.

"Where we off to?" she asked with a honeysuckle voice that sounded elated even in the early hours of the morning.

"A place called the Field of Diamonds."

"Sounds very enchanting." Katerina seemed amused.

"Truly, I tell you, it's quite stunning," he admitted. "You might want to put on your coat," Aedus suggested, looking at the white fur that hung from her left arm. In a devil-may-care attitude, she responded flirtatiously.

"No need to worry about me, Mr. Aedus Darroch. I can handle myself just fine."

"Yes, ma'am," he snickered. The two of them stepped out into the boreal air. The chill of the morning sprung Aedus into a status of high alert, and the sky above was so vivid that he could see the stars twinkle and pulsate millions and billons of miles away with the nakedness of his eyes. The mood was quiet and peaceful, the silence ataractic, beautiful.

"Where's your vehicle?" she inquired, expecting it to be at the front door as they walked out, and as she asked the question a copper-colored bike, powered by nuclear energy, came before them. "We're not taking your car?" Her faced was confounded, her tone one of confusion, her voice slightly higher in pitch.

"I'm afraid not," he answered. "I think you might want to reconsider your coat," he teased. Her eyes squinted at him, and her lips turned up in a grin. She put on her soft and snug overcoat, throwing the fluffy hood over her head, swaddling her ears and face from the sting and numbing wind as they rode the open roads on the motorbike that very much exposed them to the brutality of nature.

The city was empty in the newborn babe hours, though the city lights still shone mightily in the darkness. They soon escaped the glitz and glam of the metropolis and entered the serene backwoods of winding roads, deep green grass, and celestials that burned far brighter than any city lights could ever dare dream to beam. Aedus drove the two-wheeled vehicle that balanced on wheels of grooved rubber to grip the streets and dirt of the terrain, to an open field miles long that fell shadowed to a great mountain expanse, which rose high above the cotton ball clouds and seemed to expand from bounding main to bounding main. Though the morning was still dark, the range was ever visible, and as the sun slowly rose higher and higher, the mountain began to glimmer a pleasant melting gold, capped with pure driven snow.

He parked the motorbike in the sea of green grass and pulled a blanket from a pouch on the side of his vehicle. He laid the plaid fabric out onto the hard-beaten earth and sat on its cushioned comfort. Side by side, hand to hand, Aedus and Yekaterina sat next to one another. They listened to the number being played by the small creatures that endured the freezing weather, but they soon stopped and only the constant of the subtle wind could be heard in their ears. Aedus broke the sound of the wind with his voice.

"They call this mountain range Mor, meaning the great range. It's rumored to have once spanned past the bounds of earth and to have traveled so high into the sky that it tore a hole into the blackness of space and let loose a million suns." He looked at Kat as she looked at the mountains.

"Are you sure that's a rumor?" she asked jokingly.

"Who's to say? Though it is taller than Mount Tilgivelse in Avengler, and if Saoirse sat as high as Avengler, it would be 3,000 feet taller at its peak." He offered facts to support the myth.

"That I know to be true, even though it's hard to believe," Katerina admitted. "Those peaks are terrifyingly beautiful."

"The floating boulders of the range of Tilgivelse are quite breathtaking, though I prefer the mountains of my home," Aedus said.

"One day, I'll have to climb this mountain to see if I like it more than Tilgivelse."

"Maybe next time you're here, we'll climb the cliffs of Mor together," Aedus suggested.

"It's a date." She smiled at him and he at her. The young hearts fell silent and watched as the sun crowned the mountain range with the halo of an angel, and as the rays bent over its great barrier, the frozen grass with frosted tips began to sprinkle sparkles of light, capturing the sun and shining like diamonds far beyond what the eye could see. Katerina stood to look at what was before her. Aedus stood with her and looked at the woman next to him, her eyes glowing from the beauty of the scene, her smile wider than the mountain range in front of them. Yekaterina turned to him,

"It beckons the heart to flee, Aed. Thank you for showing me this." She embraced him warmly.

"You're welcome, Kat." The two lingered in the charm of the vibrant field until the diamond grass was no more, and the rich green of its true color took over. Unleashed from their embrace, she asked Aedus, "Is your date with my dad going to be this romantic?"
Aedus laughed at her jest. "If I'm to remain in your company, how else am I going to win his heart?"

"Good point. Take him on one of those country roads, and go as fast as you can. Afterward, stop by a pastry shop. He's a sucker for sweets and baked goods," she suggested.

"Oh, we'll go fast, and as far as pastries go, I might know a spot or two," he assured her as he thought aloud.

The sun climbed up half the mountain, or rather the mountain only covered half the sun. Its warmth felt brilliant as it struck Aedus with its luster. He and Katerina enjoyed the majesty of the landscape that was before them, and in its heavenly beauty, they talked a great deal of their education, their training, and their families. They discussed their similarities and their differences, and as their untied tongues talked of many things, Aedus sought to chat of religious differences, as it was often the root of why people act and how they act. It is their compass in life and their sextant in reason, or so it was for him.

"If you don't mind me asking, what is it like?" Aedus asked coyly.

"Being the Tulku?" she questioned him.

"To so many people you are their spiritual leader, their teacher. To some, you are even the Phoenix, the light bringer. I want to know what is in the mind of the Tulku, what is in the mind of the prophet?" Aedus asked of her, and he looked at her as she thought of her words before sharing them.

"Well, I will tell you I am never alone, that there is a voice that dwells inside me, who is talking to me at this very moment. I do not see my responsibilities as a burden but very much a blessing to guide my people to a higher purpose. I do not see myself as the Phoenix, as I am flesh and bone and not a spirit, even though the very word Tulku means high priest who is reborn, so I can see how people will interpret the book that way. What of you? I've studied the Nazar, but tell me what it is you believe."

Enjoying the conversation, Aedus spoke. "I believe the Phoenix and the Tulku are two separate spirits. The Tulku is the word, my prophet, and the Phoenix is my savior. I believe you are here to guide all peoples, and the Lord, who sacrificed himself for us, will rise from the ashes of the burnt world to bring a thousand years of peace, to absolve us of our sins, and to banish the ill of the earth, but I very well could be wrong, and you may very well be the last Tulku, the Phoenix, the Goddess of Glory, the bringer of a thousand years of peace."

Katerina gave him a friendly nudge. "It's funny, isn't it?" she asked.

"What is?"

"How the original text, due to human language, has taken the same book and interpreted it ever so slightly to generate two beliefs."

"More than two," Aedus added. "The four major religions vary greatly, though yours and mine do not vary on morals or values, but as you said, lie in different interpretations based off the translations of man due to language."

"The truth is there, somewhere in the blend," Kat said to him.

In their rhapsodies, they began quoting verses and listened with great intensity. Aedus weighed on the scale of his mind every word Yekaterina spoke, for he thought so surely that God would want man to fix reason firmly in its place. For if there be a God, he must assuredly want man to come to know him by questioning his very existence, not to follow blindly with fear words written on paper. And if reason came to show that God did not exist, then it be so, but if reason lit the path to Him as truth, then only a fool would look the other way to see the darkness.

As they spoke of spiritual bonds and connected links, they began discussing the two other prominent religions, the Califfe and the Shin Michi. The Califfe held a god called Ulama and believed the Nazar Phoenix was a false savior and the Tulku a false prophet. They believed Ulama would descend to earth and emerge from the flames of man to smite the Phoenix of the Nazar and cleanse the earth of its believers, and upon his return, the Tulku would bow to him and serve him as the true god of men. Those of the Califfe belief followed only a quarter of the holy book of the Nazar. A dominant portion of their practice came from two other sources, known as the Ťhunkášila Wóopȟe, and the Akhiya.

In their dialog, Aedus pointed out key differences, "I've been studying their books and listening to their holy teachers, and it seems to me, because of those two sources, the religion is of an extreme. Even now, as those of the Califfe have swept into Holle and neighboring countries like Avstrija and Danija the past twenty years, their open borders have invited their radical ideology, and as a result, we've seen horrifying attacks on the peoples of those countries and major changes in their country's culture."

"That's why we are preparing. That is why we are ready to fight." Katerina paused. "There is hope for them. The reformers are rising in the Heavohen Islands, and when we fight in this horrid war to come, we must think of them. They will need us, and we them." Kat spoke of what she had seen.

"Perhaps they are the new enlightenment, like the one the Heavohen's had under Nahchah Ohtakotah. It's sad how quickly the enlightenment perished. The islands made one by Ohtakotah are now divided once more, and 800 years of growth and understanding are now lost," Aedus noted.

"I was just at the islands before I came here, and outwardly, all seemed fine, but there was something underneath the façade. Nahchah Whey seemed distracted when we had dinner with him and his wife. I'm not sure if the resistance had encroached within their regime, but something seemed to have happened recently. When we asked if he would join us in the fight to come, he was quite standoffish," Katerina mentioned. "Maybe when—no, I'm not sure," she started to think out loud. They talked a bit more of the religion that was almost foreign, except for what the reformers believed, and their discussion naturally led them to the Shin Michi religion.

In Shin Michi, the Tulku was and is the spirit of many forms in which they call the Kami, and though the Kami had many embodiments, it was and is a singular divinity, who could manifest in rocks, trees, rivers, fire, air, animals, and all the elements known and unknown. To them, the living Tulku had a dominant form, and when the Tulku died, they would be reborn with a new dominant power, and the powers of the Tulku ran in cycles. The start of the cycle started with the sun, then the moon. From there, the earth, water, fire, air, eagle, dragon, wolf, yin, yang, and spirit. From this cycle, a calendar was made that followed the order of the Tulku's reincarnation. They believed a person's fate was intertwined with the Tulku based on the month a person was born, as well as the year. The practitioners of Shin Michi were predominantly from Nihon and Mongnolerium. Aedus was reminded of his father's good friend

Tokugawa, and how even though he and his father's beliefs were quite different, they were the best of friends.

Aedus looked at Kat who seemed to be in deep thought.

"What's circling through your mind?" he asked.

"I was just—it's silly. I'll tell you another time. Shall we get going? I don't want you to be late for your hot date. He's quite the catch you know," she giggled the words she spoke.

"I suppose we should." He drew a smile across his charmed face. They folded up the quilted blanket and hopped back onto the motorbike. Aedus kicked the pedal of the vehicle, and it rumbled back to life. It rattled lightly, shaking his body, as it did Yekaterina. He gave a rev to the engine, and they left the rich emerald fields with a backdrop of a golden high mountain and headed toward the bright castle atop a hill, which Aedus called home. The hour was still early, only the eighth hour of the day. They passed the gates, rode up the hillside, and parked outside the great white home.

Inside, Solascnoc bustled with people Aedus loved. The seasons room they entered glared a bright and brilliant sun. The mood was exuberant in the castle home. Aedus and Kat walked into the living area where a fire was roaring, and as they came into the comfortable room, his uncle thought to greet him with a solid beam of manipulated light. Before he had time to react, Yekaterina had shielded him with the light of her own. Taken aback, Aedus looked at both Katerina and his uncle, Uriel.

"Nice reactions, Kat." Uriel gave her praise.

"What was that for?" Aedus asked, knowing the light was not meant to harm him.

"You're lucky I didn't send something your way." Katerina spoke back to Uriel.

"That was for not inviting me to see the Field of Diamonds," he answered Aedus then looked at Yekaterina. "Maybe a duel later?"

"You're insane, Uncle." Aedus continued to walk into the now-hostile room and sat next to his uncle who had tried to shoot him.

"Aren't all scientists?" Uriel replied with a rhetorical question. Katerina took a seat next to her father who seemed to be enjoying the family camaraderie. Kat looked at Uriel and finally answered.

"I'll accept your challenge." Yekaterina turned to her father. "Good morning, Dad. Where's Mom?"

"Good morning, my girl. Your mother is still in bed. She still isn't feeling all that well," said Yefimovich.

"Aw, poor Mom. I'm going to see if she needs anything. Have fun on your date with Aedus." She kissed her father on the cheek and exited the room.

“Thank you, dear. I’ll see you up at the farm,” Yefimovich said, saying goodbye to his daughter.

“Have you eaten yet, Mister Nemtsov?” Aedus asked.

“No, not yet. I’ve just this cup of tea is all.”

“I know of a really good bakery called Chez Jacqueline’s. The tastiest croissants and crepes in the state,” Aedus told him.

“That sounds wonderful.”

“I was thinking you could drive the country roads to the country home on the way from the bakery. You’ll really get to enjoy the Shelby then,” Aedus told him, and happiness painted itself across Yefimovich’s face.

“I’m ready when you’re ready,” Yefimovich let Aedus know.

“Let’s go, then. Uncle, see you up at the house later.” Uriel smiled at Aedus and blinded him with a flash of light. “Is that for leaving you here?” he asked his uncle.

“Maybe it was, or maybe it was because I’m your uncle, and I like to annoy you,” Uriel jested with his nephew.

“You’re a madman.” Aedus spoke jokingly as he and Yefimovich left the room.

As Aedus and Yefimovich walked side by side, Yefimovich commented on Uriel.

“I’ve only ever known Uriel to be a quiet—and reserved person.”

“To those he doesn’t know, he is. He keeps to himself mostly, but when he’s with family, he’s rather good fun.” Aedus filled in the gaps in Yefimovich’s knowledge of his uncle, Uriel.

“That’s good to know—that he isn’t always serious and consumed by his work. Laughter is what makes a man happy ever after,” said Yefimovich as the two stepped outside and walked toward the garage that looked more like a small mansion in the same likeness as Solascnoc Castle. Draped was the car, and Aedus unveiled it. A crimson two-seater, ravishingly glossy—the sight of the vehicle captured the eyes of any who beheld it and saw the thrill of man in its curves, its muscles, its style, and its deafening sound when the engine exploded from shrill death to blaring sentience. They sat in the heated comforts of its leather seats and fastened their safety harnesses.

“Ready?” Aedus asked, putting on his leather gloves to protect his hands from the icy temperatures and the wicked wind as they drove with an open roof.

“Ready.” Aedus let the car roll down the hill, soft and subtle, until they were past the castle gates. He pressed his foot to the metal petal, and like a deep brooding moody thunder that suppressed its emotions, it revealed them with the vociferation it made, letting all know he was here, letting all know he was powerful. Yefimovich put his hands to his ears while Aedus laughed in amusement at his gesture. Naught to one hundred in three seconds—Aedus looked at Yefimovich who clutched the side of the door.

"High heaven!" Yefimovich yelled. Aedus began to slow the four-wheeled vehicle down.

"What do you think of that?"

"My word—that is something else."

"This old thing can take just about any of these new hover vehicles in a race." Aedus spoke loudly as the wind tried to take his voice as he drove. "Have you ever driven stick before?"

"Do you know how old I am?" Yefimovich asked as if to answer his question with a yes. Aedus gave a smirk.

"Good. So, I won't have to teach you much." The two men hushed themselves for a bit on their short journey to the bakery, enjoying the hymn-like purr of the nuclear powered engine. On their drive, they passed over the Chuthru River on the bridge known as Castle Bridge, which was eighty-six feet long and thirty-two feet wide with lacy arches and prominent spires. It added a romantic and classic presence to the City Beautiful, as it connected not only lands but two sides of the metropolis. One side was of homes in an abundant amount of architectural styles, yet they flowed seamlessly with one another. The other side of the city was filled with churches and theaters, buildings of historic significance and others yet to make history. Once more, the city sidewalks were packed with holiday cheer as those who walked them dashed to pick up gifts of meaning and value to celebrate the promise of the return of their Savior. The Yule spirit flowed through the people, and though Yefimovich immortalized this time of year in a different manner than Aedus, he was charmed by the chipper faces, the decoration in the streets, and on and in the buildings, the gayly songs and the great heartedness it brought forth in people.

On the corner of Rue de Passy, an intersection where five streets connect, lay a white, three-sided storefront, where smells of churned butter, rising bread, brewed coffee, and the delights of breakfast wafted through the air in the streets to guide passersby into the wonder of the bakery. Lining the storefront like a crown, in black and gold, read the name Chez Jacqueline's. Outside the bakery were tables for two, and each one of the ten tables that surrounded the bakery were taken by people with full mouths and conversation.

"My mouth waters already," Yefimovich said, breathing in the aroma of the air around him.

"Your tastebuds will love you after this," Aedus told him as he parked his muscled transporter, and both he and Yefimovich walked into the pastry shop. Their eyes were arrested by the delicacies that were before them. Croissants that melted on the tongue, buttered, soft and airy, yet of fullness when consumed. Quiche, warm and savory, that filled the belly with content. Crepes, thin, sweet, and pleasing to the soul as well as the stomach.

"There's no place better for breakfast pastries than this spot right here. Isn't that right, Adalene?" Aedus asked the owner of the bakery his rhetorical question. She was petite in stature with short gray blond hair. She was nearly fifty and with an accent from a different land within Saoirse. Her words ran like chopped water and as rapid as a river flows downstream. Her R's rolled, words that began with a TH sounded more like Z's, and her I's left her tongue in the sound of double E's. A snarky lass she was, yet always kind of heart.

"Hallo Eadus, of course eet's dee best. How are you doing zis morning? You luke beautiful. Your face eet's like a glowing star, just beautiful," she spoke spiritedly.

"Good morning, Adalene. I'm doing well."

"Who ees zis? My new husband?" she asked. Aedus chuckled.

"This is the prime minister of Yisra, Yefimovich Nemtsov," Aedus answered.

"Ouy vay. Hallo, Meester Nemtsov," she curtsied.

"Hello, Ms. Adalene," Yefimovich greeted her cordially.

"What ees eet I can get you both?"

"I'll have a chocolate croissant and a bichon au citron," Yefimovich replied.

"And for you, Eadus?" she asked again.

"I'll have a banana crepe with hazelnut cocoa spread and an orange juice, please."

"Take your seats. I'll serve you soon," she instructed them.

They found two seats outside, at the corner of the entryway, to have their breakfast and juice. The chairs were of classic wicker with curves that featured a posh gray and white pattern with a table that matched its chic design. On clear glass plates, their breakfast was served. Aedus's crepe covered the entirety of its surface. Golden was the breading with a light dusting of powdered sugar on top. He cut the first piece. Banana and hazelnut spread oozed out of the full pastry. He consumed its ooey goodness. His mouth full of toothsome tranquility, he enjoyed every sweet bite. While they enjoyed and ate the bounty that was before them, Aedus asked to hear stories from the Great War.

"Of course, I'll tell you a story," Yefimovich began. Aedus leaned forward, ready to hear of tales that sounded more make-believe than stubborn fact. The cool morning air, the sweet smells of the bakery, and the constant of the busy sidewalks set the mood for a fairytale. "I don't think this story—is one your father would ever tell you. It's a very sad account, one I wish wasn't true. It was at the start of the war—in a midsize town—called Amor in Attica. The sky was cloudy and dreary, the summer air was stale. In a town of fifty—50,000, your father and I were on the ground when we heard them. Sirens for a bombing raid sounded. Their cries were delayed, and then it rained both water—and bombardment. It rattled the streets we stood on, and concussed the ears, ringing a monotone. Those—on the avenues screamed and cried—and ran for their lives, but your father, he stood—and he looked to help those in need. In the clouds of explosions, he saw a woman, and—and in her arms a baby, and the baby wailed. The mother of the child sat up against a building—wall. Robert ran toward her and scooped the babe from her arms amongst the horrid quakes—of bombs at his feet. When he—when he grabbed the babe, he and I ran to the cellar of a nearby shop—until the raid was over."

"What happened to the woman? Why didn't my father pull her from the raid?" Aedus asked.

"Well—the mother of the child—was already dead. A piece of metal from a sign—severed her head. This was the first person—your father saved—and yet, he thought he failed," Yefimovich explained.

"What happened to the child?" Aedus insisted to know.

"That same day, during another raid—in the underground of the streets, we waited—we waited for the bombs to end, and while we waited, we came across a man, and the man was the father—of the young and helpless child. It was then—I saw your father weep—and I could see how much it meant to him, to reunite the baby girl with her father." Yefimovich finished the bitter sweet tale of his and Aedus's father's first experience with the war.

"My father told me that story once before, but he had never mentioned that it was he whom saved the child or that the mother perished holding her little girl. He always ended it with the whole family united together," Aedus mentioned. Yefimovich then told another story of Aedus's father's heroism on how he saved him under siege in the field of battle.

"Sometimes, I think your father—was born from selflessness. I— I can see you were made of the same strings," Yefimovich told Aedus.

"I think I'll have to do a lot more to be compared to my father. I have never fought in wars, led a nation, or saved a child in the smoke of fire and death, but thank you, Mister Nemtsov. Those words mean a great deal to me, especially coming from you."

"You're most welcome, my boy. You truly are your father's son," Yefimovich noted without stutter.

Their bellies bulged, their hunger satisfied. They thanked Adalene for the breakfast they consumed and parted from the salivating smells of the quaint bakery on the corner of Rue de Passy. Aedus and Yefimovich found their way to the muscled mechanical beast. Aedus unlocked the vehicle and opened the driver's side door.

"After you, sir." He handed Yefimovich the key to its life. He could see Yefimovich's eyes widen with thrill and excitement.

"This is going to be great." Yefimovich took the key from the hands of Aedus. They sat in the comforts of the leatherbound seats. Key to ignition, the gas flowed through the system, the air intake not too much or too little, a spark to bring the metal monster to life. It bellowed like thunder and ran like a rolling drum.

Minds still on war, Yefimovich brought up modern events and asked Aedus what he thought of them, which led to him asking a serious question.

"Aedus, when war breaks out, I have no doubt it will. What do you plan to do?"

"I'd hope—I'd like to finish the racing season for myself and for the people to turn to when the world is dark and dead, to bring some joy for them to see, a break from all the sadness and all the worry. But this I know, the Saoirse culture has a strong current, and it flows like a river, and any man that walks into it is carried downstream. If the nation is to fight, the river will lead us there, and like the river, we will travel to its end. Forceful when necessary, calm when permitted. We will never quit until the journey is over. It is our way," Aedus answered.

"Do all Saoirse men answer in prose?" Yefimovich wondered aloud to him.

"We all have our expressions. The south relies on a backwoods narrative, while we northerners speak of fanciful wonders. The midwest always utilizes a straightforward explanation, and the west—well, they're something else, let's just say," Aedus described.

"What military branch do you favor?" Yefimovich spoke with curiosity.

"The Iolar draw my fancy. The freedom of flight, the thrill of the speed, the view of the heavens. It's right up my alley. Why do you ask?"

"Just so I know where to—where to find you on the field of battle," Yefimovich responded.

"Is there no escaping war?"

"Your uncle's intel will be the decider in that. I—I will surely pray for him," said Yefimovich.

"As will I." It became quiet again. The city hustle was becoming distant as the countryside slowed the pace as it approached. The air was cooler, sharper, more alive to the senses. The hair on Aedus's skin rose; bumps like pulled goose feathers revealed themselves. The water vapor from his exhaled breaths clouded the face for a fraction of a second, and then Yefimovich broke the silence.

"I've noted you've—you've been spending considerable time with my daughter," Aedus answered with a hard swallow.

"We get along quite well. She's a very impressive girl."

"She makes me marvel every day. I'm glad she's made a friend in you," Yefimovich expressed.

"I'm happy to have made a friend in her and in you. My family holds you all in such high regard. There is a lot to aspire to and admire in your family, and you live up to every story told of you. Like I said before, your family is nearly mythical, the hero of the Great War and the Tulku. It's like a book come to life."

"I'm flattered to hear such high praises," Yefimovich thanked him. "May I ask a favor of you, Aedus?"

"Anything."

"If tragedy should befall me, seek her out. I—I would ask your father, but his role is far greater than to—to look after just one family," Yefimovich requested.

"You have my word," Aedus answered. Yefimovich smiled at him, and when he turned back to face the road, Aedus and he were launched back into their seats. Yefimovich had put his foot to the floor. He shifted rapidly the gears of the vehicle until he reached 120 miles per hour. They both laughed as the frigid air danced around their faces.

"Happy Birthday!" Yefimovich yelled as they cruised the silent roads. The coupe fulminated deep and mightily, concussing the air for ears to hear miles away in the quiet land of the boonies, where one was more likely to hear the moo of a cow or the bah of a lamb than the sonic booms of a machine built for speed. Their hair whipped at their faces as they moved about places in a vehicle that traveled through spaces in the land of the free, in the land of the brave, settling at a place called home, where the mind rests, the heart beats slow, and the soul fills with love. Yefimovich reigned in the hot rod racer, slowing its wheels to a halt as he guided the vessel into a small spot on the second floor in the barn of the country estate.

"Well, I'll be—that was a wicked time, Aedus. Thank you." Yefimovich spoke in praise.

"It was my pleasure. Maybe sometime we can take the coastal drive and take in some scenic views. The drive is quite beautiful."

"I'd like that," Yefimovich said, unfastening his seatbelt and exiting the vehicle.

They departed from the barn to enter the nestled comforts of the large ranch home. Like a hive, the nest was stirring with friends and family who baked, decorated, and did all the little things it took to get the party and ceremony ready for the evening. Aedus could hear his mother instructing others as to where things should be. The home was nearly half complete in décor, and already, the house smelled of savory salivating splendor and sweet saporous satisfaction. He caught sight of his sister who ran to him and wrapped her arms around his body.

"Happy birthday, baby brother, and thank you for my poem. It was just what I needed." She kissed his cheek. "Now go relax and enjoy yourself before mother sees you and makes you cater your own birthday."

"Thanks, Lo. I'll duck out of here then. Just so you know, I meant every word in that poem. You're truly amazing," he said to her, and she smiled at his words.

"Your bleeding heart is too kind my sweet, sweet brother." She kissed his other cheek and turned to leave but quickly turned back around with a grin on her face as if she had thought of something particularly humorous. "Oh, and be easy on Abe. I beat him in a race this morning. He may be licking his wounds.

"I'll be sure to tease him about it," Aedus joked.

"Please do. I'll join you all in a bit. We're almost done here." Aedus left her and headed toward his room to be alone, away from the noise, for there was soon to be more.

His room here was much simpler than his room in the castle. Brick walls surrounded him with a large single piece window nearly twenty feet wide and ten feet tall. The floors were large, bold wood panels, his dresser a rustic red, and the lighting included just four floating lamprog, which he controlled with a dial on his dresser, moving them in different locations and adjusting the brightness of the light. He laid on his cushioned king-size bed, and the gears in his mind began to move. He thought of the stories Yefimovich told him of his father, and he contemplated a great depth of what Yefimovich asked of him and the war. What is my duty? What is my purpose? What is my destiny? he asked himself—the son of a king chosen by God, and a young international cynosure. Of all that has ever been, he held a position few ever hold in life, but his mind was all his own, something no other person would ever have in any time period. Was it the thoughts in his mind that drew conclusions of what he must do, or was it already decided by others past and present, or yet was it designed to be by a Maker, the Sculptor of man? If God were to plan it, why create consciousness at all? If decided by others through reactions of the very first choice made by man, then what reason was there for logic? The thoughts of his mind he sealed as truth until and unless he was provided with evidence to change his thinking, and this is what he knew. God laid the paths, intersecting, encircling so frequently that the roads that were built by Him were like a blank slate to the naked eye. Men walk these paths by the choices they make, which cross the paths of others, all leading to a single destiny, for there be only one, and the destiny is death. Man's future and purpose is what he decides it to be, though the Divine has laid a path of righteousness. The thought of man is his own, his choices his own, and judged man will be when the door of death leads to a new path, to a labyrinth so unfathomable that the intricacies and complexities of it the human mind would never be able to comprehend. For man alone cannot handle such wonder. Only when reborn in the spirit, and by the gift of the Holy Spirit, can man truly understand the greatness, the power, and the love of God.

His very electric mind now knew what he must do. An hour had passed since he first deliberated on the tasks that were before him.

Knock, knock came the soft percussion on the quaking aspen wood door. His eyes drew to a focus to the beat of the drum.

"Come in."

"Hey, Aed." Katerina entered. "How was your date with my dad?" she jested.

"It was quite nice. Thought-provoking," he answered. "It looks great downstairs," he noted, as if to draw away the attention on his thoughts.

"It smells great downstairs. I can't wait to start eating," Katerina remarked. "The decorating is all finished now. It's going to look amazing when the sun goes down and the lights we assembled start to glow."

"Oh, I believe it. What do you have there?" he asked, looking at the drink she was holding.

"I thought I'd bring you some tea."

"Thanks, Kat." His heart was warmed by her thoughtfulness, and he took the glass she handed him. "What do you want to do until the celebration begins?"

"What did you have in mind?"

"There's a pond not too far from here. Want to go ice skating?"

Her eyes lit up, "That sounds great. Should we ask your sister and brother?"

"Yeah, let's go find them."

Aedus closed the door to his room as he and Yekaterina left to search for his siblings. As they walked down the hall of the second floor, Aedus noticed the double doors of the balcony were ajar. He peered through the glass windowed entryway and saw his brother with lunch in his hands, enjoying the brisk cloudless day, basking in the sun's rays. Aedus teased him just as he had promised his sister, and the two talked of their early-morning adventures. He was just about to ask his brother if he wanted to join them to skate on the pond when he saw his father pull up in the driveway with a carriage close behind him. Exiting from the carriage was a giant with blue skin and whose veins glowed. Beside him was his daughter who was more beautiful than the most vivid blue sky on a perfect summer's day.

"Tokugawa! Tomoe!" Aedus yelled to them. "Do you need any help?"

"No, we're alright," Tomoe hollered back to Aedus. His brother Absolume turned to him.

"I'm going downstairs to put these dishes away. Do either of you want anything while I'm down there?" he asked. Aedus pointed to his glass of iced tea.

"No, I'm alright."

"I'm fine too," Kat replied. Absolume left them, and they were alone once more.

"Should we let them get settled before we go and greet them?" Aedus inquired.

"I suppose we can give them five minutes."

"While we wait, let's go grab some skates," Aedus said, leaving the balcony with Yekaterina at his side. The two went to the opposite end of the long hall and down another until they reached a stairway that brought them down to the house's side entrance, to a room they called the mudroom. It was filled with outerwear, accessories, and gadgets for activities more atone to nature's groove.

"Here, try these on." Aedus handed Yekaterina a pair of white leather, white laced skates. She knotted one on her foot.

"It's a bit loose." Aedus kept looking and handed her another. She tried it on with little luck. "This doesn't fit either, but I have an idea," Kat told Aedus.

"What is it?"

"You'll see," she said. "Let's go get the others and say hello to Tokugawa and his daughter." Both Aedus and Yekaterina walked out the room and down the long hall that led to the great room. The seven-foot tall, blue-skinned man walked into the room just as they did. Aedus approached him.

"Tokugawa!" His voice high with joy, Aedus opened his arms to embrace Tokugawa's tall frame.

"Little Bushi boy," Tokugawa greeted him with a friendly appellation and a soft and gentle expression on his face. He opened his arms to receive Aedus's embrace. "I watched your race the other day. Your move was as elegant as a flock of birds in flight and as deadly as the poison from the fangs of a cobra," Tokugawa praised him, releasing Aedus from his kind welcome.

"That was by far my best race. I was so full of pride that night. To win at my home track was something I always dreamed of doing," Aedus recounted the thrill of the evening.

"Congratulations, Aedus. Really well done, little Bushi boy." Tokugawa smiled at him and then set his eyes on Yekaterina. "Kami." He bowed, knee to floor, his head down. Yekaterina walked into him, locking her arms around his neck. Her affectionate clasp was heartfelt and loving.

"It's so good to see you again, my master." She let go her clutch, letting Tokugawa rise.

"It's good to see you, sunflower. Happy belated birthday to you." Tokugawa spoke as if she were his niece.

"Thank you," she said and then asked, "Where is Tomoe? I finally get to meet her after all these years."

"Shame on me and your father for not introducing you both when you were younger. If you're looking for her, I believe she went upstairs to unpack."

"I'm so happy you're here. Do you mind if I go introduce myself to her?" Katerina asked.

"You are the Kami. You have no need to ask such things," said Tokugawa.

"I'll go with you. She's likely in my sister's room," Aedus said. "My mother should be outside, Tokugawa. Be wary. She may ask you to help decorate." Tokugawa laughed at the warning.

"You mean they aren't done? This place looks as beautiful as a flower in bloom and smells as beautiful as one, too."

"Your answer lies that way." Aedus pointed toward the back patio.

"An answer I shall receive." Tokugawa started heading toward the back entrance while Aedus and Katerina walked up the flight of stairs to say hello to Tokugawa's daughter.

Up the stairs and down the hall on the north side of the house was Lorena's room, and as anticipated, Tomoe was there along with Absolume, conversing and unpacking. Introduced they were, and like peas in a pod, Katerina and Tomoe began talking like old friends. Aedus listened as they quickly talked of their fathers, their interests and plans they had until the celebration of the night began. Aedus and Kat's plans to skate led in a different direction from that of Absolume and Tomoe, who were heading into the city to pick up a birthday gift for Aedus's brother. The gratifying moment of introduction and hellos passed, leaving Aedus and Yekaterina by themselves.

"I hope you don't mind it being just you and I," Aedus said to her.

"Don't be silly. Of course, I don't mind."

They walked out of the house of brick and stone to the barn of heavy wood with two mammoth doors. He pulled them open, and as always, the horses stirred to see who had entered. They were all very interested in Yekaterina who was genial to them, stopping to say hello to each and every horse, giving them gentle brushes with her hand. Lorena's horse, Stocai, was entranced with Katerina, nuzzling her with his snout as if to say, "Give me attention," much like a dog who craves its owners love.

"Easy, Socks, you attention harlot," Aedus said to the mighty horse. Aedus moved a few stalls over to Amsterdam. Hey boy, you up for a short trip?" Aedus let him out of the stable and draped him with a blanket and saddle. "This is my father's horse. Don't let his size intimidate you. He's probably the most gentle of them all."

"Hey, boy." Katerina caressed the side of the horse's face. Amsterdam closed his eyes, relaxed by her touch. "Where's your trusted steed?" she wondered to Aedus.

From the back of the barn, in the last stall, Aedus appeared with a long-eared, blond-and-brown-patterned, adorable donkey.

"A donkey?" Katerina's voice spoke with a surprised inflection.

"His name is Hephaestus." He acquainted her with him.

"He looks so happy."

"Heph is always in good spirits," he said and looked at the size difference between Yekaterina and the horse she'd be riding. "Do you need a step up?"

"That's alright," she answered, lifting herself up, using only the air around her. Aedus smirked and climbed aboard Hephaestus and trotted out of the barn. "Come on, Amsterdam." He gave the horse a tap as his donkey walked past him.

They strode along the woods and the fields, reaching the frozen pond. Only fifteen minutes had passed. They spoke of little things, simple things, on the small journey to the pond.

They reached the water and dismounted from their living carriers. They walked to the edge where the ice met the earth. Aedus walked toward the frozen water's center and gave a frown.

"I'm not sure it's skatable. To me it's on the fringe of pass or fail."

"Here, let me help make up your mind." Katerina placed her hand on the icy pond, and the water began to harden even more. New ice crystals were formed, and the thickness of the ice grew.

"That's amazing," Aedus said in astonishment. He thought of how incredible it would be to have such abilities, but he did not envy it, for what use was envy for something he couldn't attain. He sat his bottom on the hard surface of the dead ground and slipped on his ice skates. He looked over at Yekaterina who took moisture from the air and froze it, molding it to the bottom of her shoes in the shape of a blade.

Aedus stepped onto the ice and put out his hand to help Yekaterina. "That's very clever." He looked down at her improvised skates.

"Maybe I'll get you a pair for your birthday," she winked.

The two skated a bit without saying much of anything, and on their quiet skate, Katerina asked him of his donkey.

"How come you don't have a horse? Why the donkey?"

"I was maybe six years old. I was too young for a horse at the time, and when Heph was born, I thought he was the most adorable creature I'd ever seen. He was this little fur ball with giant ears. You couldn't help but laugh at him. In the summer, when we were up at the farm, wherever I went, he followed me. He helped me with my chores and was always a good companion to talk to when Abe and Lorena weren't around. As odd as it sounds, he's been one of my best friends my entire life, and when it came time for me to get a horse, I told my parents that Hephaestus was as good a horse as any." Aedus recalled his childhood memories.

"That's cute. You'll have to show me some holopics of when he was younger," Katerina insisted.

"I'm sure I have a few lying around in my room somewhere. I'll show you when we get back," he said and continued the conversation by changing the subject. "So, I have a question for you. What does it feel like?"

"What do you mean?" Kat asked, a bit confused by the broad question.

"What does it feel like when you use your abilities? Is there a sensation of sorts, or is it like reaching for a cup resting on a table?"

"Well, they're all a little different. Each has its own mark, its own print, its own sensation. For example, when I froze the lake just now, I could feel my whole body turn to ice, and when I reach out to freeze something at a distance, it's like water droplets forming an icicle, and when I move water itself, my body feels like waves in the ocean," she elucidated.

"That's fascinating," he said as both he and Katerina's pace of skating had slowed to a crawl. "What of fire?"

"With fire, as you might expect, I feel my body warm, and my nerves move like the flicker of a flame that dances on the wick of a candle, and depending on how bold I make the flame, the release is either like the explosion of a volcano, or it's like a soft kiss, where the heat and oxygen in my body whirl, and the spark ignites the passion," Katerina explained, the two no longer skating, but standing on the ice, facing one another. "Kind of like this." She pulled him by his jacket, bringing his face down to hers. She leaned into him, and her lips pressed against his. Aedus didn't know what to think, fire wire, his heart desire. He felt the softness of her lips, the heat within them. He breathed her in, and the spark ignited within his very soul. The feeling he had inside him was not of lust, nor did he feel sinful. Rather, it was as if he filled the whole of the hole he had within himself. Like gears on a watch or keys to a lock, he felt his spirit fall in place, and where his beating heart once raced, there was only calm. He opened his eyes and peered within her earthy browns and smiled.

"That was—unexpected," he said.

"Well, that's fire. It can be unpredictable." She spoke of the element and of the metaphorical flame within every human spirit. Aedus took her hands, his eyes still staring into hers and asked, "And what of air?" And she answered, and of earth she answered, of light and of the energy within herself, she gave clarity to all.

"And when used all at once?" he persisted.

"Scary," she said. "Brilliant, terrifying, exhilarating, passionate, humbling."

"What makes it scary?"

"The power." Katerina did not hesitate.

"And humbling?"

"The power." She fielded his question once more. "Would you like me to show you?" she inquired, while moving him to where the ground of the earth met the ice of the pond. Katerina walked to the center of the ice and closed her eyes. Under her ivory sweater, where her heart would lie, began to glow, glorious as the sun, and when she opened her eyes, the brilliance refracted through them. Like leaves in the wind, she propelled herself to the sky, and there she floated, the air beneath her feet. She reached out, and chunks of earth ran toward her and encircled her like orbit. She reached out again, and the ice turned to water and did as the earth, and then she created fire, and it too moved around her. Katerina inhaled deeply, and like a bang with no sound, she shone like an angel. Her description of how it felt to control all the elements at once was the same for Aedus as he watched the magnificent marvel. She then let the earth fall back toward the ground, the water spray away, the fire extinguish, and the light within her heart and around her body fade away. She landed softly in front of Aedus.

"It's as you said. Brilliant and terrifying."

"As it should," she said back to him.

Aedus glanced at the time on his wrist. "Should we get going? Mother will be furious if I'm late to my own party," he said, whistling over the horse and donkey they rode here, summoning to take them home.

Upon arriving at the brick and stone country ranch, Katerina and Aedus parted from one another, both to ready themselves for the evening's ceremony. Aedus met his brother in the upstairs hall and complimented his good looks. In his excitement for the night, Absolume showed Aedus the gift Tomoe took him to get. Fair in appearance and impressed by the gift, Aedus was happy that his brother found joy in them. After his brief moment with Absolume, Aedus showered himself clean. The oils removed from his hair and body by the ingredients within the soaps that ran counter in battle to them. Peppermint the smell of his hair, mint the smell of his body—he was cleansed. His pants were blood red, his sweater pure as the lamb it was taken from, and over his shoulders, a hooded rose cloak with buttons of twenty-four carat. His hair was styled in a classic finish. He was fashioned for the night. Aedus closed the door behind him as he left his room and headed down the stairs to galivant amongst those loved and cherished.

He entered the main room, bold in its size, decorated with vines of clovers linking the ceiling and walls with flowers of the winter in reds, blues, and whites. Hands of the men and women held full plates or drinks of courage and pleasure. Aedus surveyed the room and heard a familiar voice come from his blind side and into his ear.

"Happy birthday there, handsome." his arm was taken by the hands of Ann, the gate keeper, the Liopard soldier. Her raspy voice was sweet yet tart like marmalade.

"Hey, Ann. Enjoying yourself?"

"My date is quite entertaining, so yes, birthday boy, I am," she answered, taking Uriel by the arm.

"Uncle U, if she finds you entertaining, you might want to hold on to her," Aedus joked and was quickly dealt a fist to his bicep from Ann, numbing his arm after the impact.

"You're too kind, Ann," Uriel said, smiling at Aedus.

"So kind," Aedus said, rubbing his arm with his hand. "Have you all seen Absolume?"

"I think he's with the others out in the tent," Uriel answered, his eyes near highlighted yellow, more vivid than Aedus had remembered them to be.

"Thanks, Uncle U. I hope you two have a nice evening."

"Happy birthday, Aed," said his uncle.

"Happy birthday handsome." Ann planted a red lipped kiss on his cheek. "That's the only one you'll get from me. Have fun, Aed."

Aedus left Ann and Uriel to their night, a fresh sight. He thought of them together and how they complemented each other quite well. Aedus made his way through the crowd and was stopped by Tokugawa, looking commanding as he dwarfed those around him.

"Saber master." Another nickname he gave Aedus.

"Master Ieyasu." They embraced one another.

"Happy birthday, Bushi soldier. Here, I have a gift for you." Tokugawa was dressed in blue slacks with brown boots on his feet. Over his body, he sported a gray sweater. About his waist were two swords, as was the custom for Bushi knights. His hair was styled in a traditional topknot. His veins of energy were hidden except for those on his hands. Tokugawa reached into his pocket for the gift he had and presented it to Aedus. "Keep these with you always, and you may find they hold many purposes." Aedus put out his hand to receive the gift Tokugawa was handing him. "These are two, five-colored jewels of Ryou. They hold great power if you know when to use them." Aedus's eyes lit up with thankfulness and blessing. He examined them in his hands with attentiveness. He then closed his hands, looked Tokugawa in the eyes, and bowed with admiration and honor.

"Arigatou gozaimasu," he pronounced in the Nihon language to thank Tokugawa.

"You are most welcome, Aedus." His deep voice was cottony soft in accepting Aedus's thanks. "Tomoe and I got you something else that goes with the jewels. I suggest you read it."

"I'll be sure to do so. Thank you, again, Tokugawa," he said and sought confirmation that Absolume was indeed in the tent as Uriel had told him.

"I saw him maybe twenty minutes ago. He was here with me and a few others, talking about what lies beyond the plane on which we live. I believe he stepped outside with Tomoe," Tokugawa admitted.

Aedus thanked him once more and walked about the room. He saw people he'd not seen in some time, and they'd stop him to say hello and greet him with festive hearts. In his reception of good wishes, he'd overhear conversations. Many talked of the war to come. Some were anticipating a speech from Alamgeer the next day, the day of Yule. Others talked of the holiday, past memories, and the thrill of life. Aedus neared the exit of his home at the back of the house where the celebration was very much alive, both inside and outside the tent, but just before he could escape his home through the double doors, he saw his uncle, Iscariot, talking with his friend, Antony.

"Hey, Uncle Isc."

"Nephew, how's the evening?"

"It's quite nice. I've gotten some incredible gifts already, and it's nice to have everyone here to celebrate. It makes tomorrow seem even more bewitching than it already is," Aedus said and then wondered what his uncle had gotten Hanns for his birthday.

"Uncle Isc, you never told me what you got Hanns." Iscariot leaned into Aedus and whispered.

"It's a secret."

"Not even a hint?"

"He'll die by it," Iscariot answered.

"Who, Hanns?" Aedus pressed. Iscariot looked at his nephew but said nothing more about the issue. "If you're looking for him, he's outside with your brother and sister. I believe they are inside the tent."

"Thanks, Uncle."

"Happy birthday, Aed," Iscariot said with his farewell.

Aedus finally escaped the confines of the house and stepped out to the starry sky that hung above him. The luminous structure that was in front of Aedus drew the eye like a moth to a flame, entranced in its sparkling splendor. The lamprog floated like suns in the night sky, burning billons of miles away, faint enough to provide light but not too bright that it blinded those from its beauty. Bioluminescent plants and flowers dressed themselves around the structure and about the tent's windows. Aedus could see his siblings and friends on the second floor through one of the open window frames, and he entered the structure to join them.

Alive it was inside as songs of Yule were sung. Colors of the holiday filled the rooms in blues, reds, greens, and whites. The green symbolized the praise of eternal life, and the reds stood for sacrifice, like that of the Savior. The two colors were often combined, so those of the Nazar faith remembered that it was and is by the sacrifice of the Phoenix that eternal life is possible. The blue symbolized the winter season itself, the frost of the cold dreary days, and the humbling hue of the hardships the winter season brought to those who had to endure its tribulations when the comforts of the modern world had yet to be, where death was frequent, and every day was a struggle. The final color, the simplest color, white, emblemized the purity of new beginnings, the blanket slate of a sinless soul or one of true repentance. The meaning in the colors is why people of the Nazar love the season as they do, and even those who do not follow the faith fall victim to its infectious cheer.

The captured light inside the tent was shaded blue, and like the castle of Solascnoc, images of snow seemed to fall from the top of the structure. An evergreen tree was at the center of the tent, touching the ceiling, and in between the branches were red roses of which there must have been over a thousand. Magic was in the air, exultation the spirit, and the two formed a feeling in the belly of man that warmed the heart like a fire on a cold winter night.

When Aedus reached the second floor, like magnets their eyes connected. He saw her and she him. The group, now a quintet, talked of the future and all it beheld in its possibilities of failure and success, of heaven's highs and hell's lows, of everything the mind could dream, and more.

Aedus was the first to say what he saw within himself of what he could achieve. He spoke of his desire in Pinnacle Eitilte, to be the best there ever was, to one day build his own team and surpass those he looked up to all his life, and before he finished articulating his lofty dreams, he ended in a but.

"But if the horrors of the world continue to manifest, if our time of peace is over, then my dreams I must set aside, and the call to duty will bring me forward to take on new dreams and new desires, most not my own, but of others I will never know nor ever see."

After Aedus spoke of what might be, the others followed suit, and how beautiful it was to imagine what could be. To paint things not of this world, to sculpt the very wrinkles on the human body, to play a series of notes so spellbinding it would bring the world to tears, or to be so honorable in life that man would hold you up to aspire to be what you became. In the end, he thought, they are just dreams. It's what happens on the ground and in the sea that truly matters. For once man has conquered them, only then can a person live amongst the stars.

The call of the eleventh hour came from the mountain voice of his father. The time of boyhood was over. The age of manhood was to begin for Aedus, and as he realized this, his heart felt sadness, for how wonderful it was to live the life of a child. He and all within the tent found their way outside it. The night air, now fierce and bitter as ever, made the hairs on Aedus's arms rise even though they were covered in layers of clothes. He looked upon his father, who stood upon a chair, as he concluded the celebration of his sons' births, and thanked all who surrounded him for attending and honoring such a celebration. Aedus heard his father call him forward, and he walked to him. His eyes were then blinded by a fold his mother put around him, and she whispered in his ear.

"Are you ready, my child?"

"I'm ready, Mother."

"Then lead the way," she told him, and as the words left her mouth, there was a magnificent glow that pierced the blindfold around his eyes, and, with it, the sound of cannonade echoed in the air. The bumping timer in his chest was steady, a drummer keeping tempo while the notes of others played. His nerves were steady like that of a boulder—he was unshakable. Aedus stepped forward. The presence of the crowd vanished. Only his mother could be felt by his senses. In the midnight field, he trekked and turned right as he approached the forest's edge.

It was quiet, haunting in its quiescent state. The wind did not speak; the branches of the trees did not wave hello. There was no animal that scurried on the ground; the void was almost maddening. Aedus walked nearly three miles inside the dead forest he was in until his foot kicked a stump that rested, bolted to the ground with roots that reached the core of the earth.

"We're here."

"We are," his mother confirmed. Aedus sat upon where a tree once stood. He could feel his mother kneel down in front of him. She grabbed his right hand with both of hers. "Cocooned you are by the shadow of the night, just a boy. You must brave the loss of light until it knocks upon the cloth that blinds you. Let the radiance enter, and you will be reborn a man, and though a man you will become, you will always be my child. Good luck, my son. I will see you when you return to me. I cannot wait to see the man you'll be."

Aedus could hear his mother leave him in the darkness, alone. He called out to her.

"Mom!" Her footsteps stopped. "I love you." Aedus did not hear the words said back to him, but instead he felt the peck of a kiss upon his cheek. He knew the sensation as he had felt it so many times before as a child. It was the kiss of light, heart-shaped the rays were bent, and stemming from its base, a string like loose thread. And when it made contact with any solid object, it vanished with the sound of a soft and comforting sizzle. Of all the loving gestures his mother could give, this was by far his favorite. Being unable to bend the light around him like his mother, brother, and sister, he felt unequal, and when he received the kiss of light from his mother, it made Aedus feel warm like the sun because, for him, it was his mother's sacrifice to take the light she had and to give that light to him. How blessed and how loved he felt that his mother would use her power to bend light to show how much she cared for him.

The sound of Lagertha's footsteps were no longer heard in his ears. Aedus was truly alone, and in his desolation, nature became cruel. Wicked was the wind that whirled a wailing cry. It burned the ears numb with every gust it gave. The atmosphere that surrounded him became colder. Like hell frozen over, it was mean as it bit the skin of Aedus and froze him where he sat. The trees around him began to riot, yelling in creeks and cracks, some even thundered in their madness. Snow soon consumed him. Aedus wrapped himself tight within his crimson cloak, trying to keep from freezing. For an eternity, it seemed to last until he heard the cry of a lost wolf. He almost pulled his blind to look to see if it was as close as it sounded.

The snow died with the first yowl of the wolf, and as it howled again, the trees calmed their brutish ways, and on the third cry, the wind was still. All that remained was the glacier air. Even in its hyper boreal state, Aedus could hear the sounds of morning. The call of the early birds, the scuffle muffles of the rodents who braved to venture from their burrow, and the pouncing fox who listened for them.

Alas, like flame to the wax on a letter, Aedus could break the seal that blinded him, and though now his blindfold was off, all he could see was the light, and he thought himself blind. Aedus wept.

"Why do you weep my child?" said a voice. He looked up to where the vocal tones were spoken and saw that he could see. He rose from the stump he sat upon and embraced his mother who was before him.

"That was cruel," he said.

"That was necessary," Lagertha replied. "You did well, Aedus."

Confused he asked, "You were here?"

"The whole night, just as the Lord was with you. Let it be a lesson for you, Aedus, that you are never alone, that God is always with you, and will be here for you when I no longer can be." His mother said this to him and tightened her already wrapped arms. "Happy Yule, Aedus."

"Happy Yule, Mom." They released their lock, and Lagertha handed him a silk maroon cloth that was in the shape of a triangle and knotted at the top. It seemed to hold a gift within it, and attached to the knot of the cloth was a letter. Aedus removed the letter and opened it. He read the words aloud.

Time
A dimension all its own
A quantity most treasured

An idea most feared
If you are lucky
You will have two point five billion of these
And every one of them counts
These are seconds
These are infinities
Each second is like sand through an hourglass
And each grain of sand is a choice
Now imagine you are a single speck of sand
And you are falling from the top of the glass to the bottom
That one second is a lifetime
And with that one eternity
You create your destiny
Cherish this granule
For it may be your last
Or, it may be your first
There are none better
And there are none worse
It is the action you make in that one second that decides for you
It can be an act of good
It can unite people in times of struggle
This action can inspire those who have lost hope
It can bring light to the world when it is consumed by darkness
Though sometimes
You lose your way
And you help shade the light from burning
Know that in this shadow you will suffer
And it will become a moment you wish you had back
But you should not fear this one infinity
For you have two point five billion of these
And with every particle that falls
You have the opportunity to reshape your life
To mold the world around you
Choose wisely and act nobly
Be thankful for the time you have
For even the longest infinity must end.

Aedus was inspired by the words of the letter. "Mom, this is beautiful. Thank you. I promise to keep these words with me, always."

"You're welcome, my son. Keep them safe."

"I will," he said and then asked, "Do you mind if I open this?"

"Go ahead, my dear," she insisted. Aedus untied the knot and was taken aback when the cloth let down its cover. Tears welled up within him.

"He gave this to me?" He looked at the sacrifice of his sensei. The bracelet bands of his master's katana and dou. "Has he left? Has he gone back to Edo?" Aedus asked, his voice in shock.

"I do not know, Aed. I do know that he loves you. To have given you such a gift does not come from a man who would abandon you."

"I'll miss him." Aedus's heart had sunk.

"Lift your heart, my son. It is what he would want." Lagertha spoke true words as she lassoed him in light to ease the pain with her motherly embrace. "Ready?" she asked. "Let's go celebrate with the others."

Iscariot Chapter Four

Caw! Caw! was the coming of the morning. Harsh the cry of the raven that sat beside the windowsill. Black its wings, wicked its words, as it mocked Iscariot whose eyes were opened to the bird's call. The light of the sun had not yet shone its face to the earth as Iscariot removed the covers from his naked body. His room was dark, and he was a shadow in it. He approached the cawing fowl, his temper flaring from its speech, and as Iscariot was mere inches away from the raucous raven, it spoke once more to ridicule before it flapped its wings and vanished in the night, for the light of day had broken the egg of the night it nested in.

A brewed mood now tempered within Iscariot. For eighteen years, the bird taunted travesty every morning before the early light of day. At first, he thought the tapping rapping at the window glass was just a lonely bird that would surely pass. The night became a week, a week a month, a month a year, and years to years came the raven knocking on his window glass, and every day, he would harass. The call that left his bill was shrill. Of ghost and phantoms it would speak, the name of Anna left its beak, to enrage the soul of a man whose heart was a cratered hole.

A haunted man he had become. Anger was always within him, deep in the crevasse of his heart. Iscariot rose in the blackness and dressed in its likeness, for it was a day of darkness for him. His thoughts were of his wife from the minute he awoke and opened his eyes to the second he closed them to end the slumber of the night. He dwelled on her, and though it was his son's birthday, it did not brighten the murky oil of feelings past that swirled thick and harrowed inside his troubled core.

Iscariot left the gloom of his room and traveled outside his home. He walked in the lonely field he owned to the poulnabrone where his wife rested all alone. Hanging from its stone columns were two torches, and their flames never ceased. Only when the name be forgotten of the person who rested in the mausoleum would the fire lose its burning glory. Iscariot knelt down at the burial site of his wife. He put his hand to the base of the stone that encapsulated her in her eternal rest, and he prayed, not to God but to Anna. Of power, he asked to halt the coming war, and though he did not voice it, he thought Robert and the like were wrong to prep so highly from rumors and accusations of the Hollen nation. Though

Iscariot loved the thrill of battle, he always thought Holle was given the short end of the stick that was the Hidler Nemtsov Agreement. He thought, a people broken by war, with a treaty that imprisoned the people of the State, had the right to rise above the tyranny of its oppressors. He looked for clairvoyance to see what might be in his months he'd spend with Alamgeer. Iscariot then talked to God directly.

"Surely, Father, you have made a mistake. My brother, Robert, takes that hammer as a symbol of war, and as the lies of the world grow, he is more certain that it is inevitable. That weapon has blinded him, and the crown has clouded his mind. Misery is the path of the nation should we ride into battle. Free him of the forces that keep him in the dark, or help me to do so for him." Iscariot fell silent, his back now against the coffin stone. He looked to the east, out to the rising sun, and the night was no more, for the sun had fully risen.

His mind began to wander over the days of his past. The memories hurt the spirit inside his broken clock. The loss of his friends in battle, the loss of his father on a day of joy, the loss of his wife on the day of his son's birth, the lack of favor the Maker showed to him—his remembrances brought about a twisting, turning, gut wrenching anguish that squeezed the light from him to only leave the horrid darkness. Iscariot's mind brought about a scene, a memory of a request for a subset branch within the Leon military core. Through law it was granted, and he, the designer, the bearer of the idea, was not selected to lead it. Infuriated he became at the thought for he still did not hold primacy. Iscariot believed misfortune followed him. He did not know the feel of the sun. He'd forgotten the warmth of love. Lost he had become.

"I hate him," he said aloud, yet to no one. Though before him was a masked creature, cloaked in charcoal rags, that waved in the wind that did not blow. In static radio tones, he heard the wraith say, "Kill him."

"Shut—up!" Iscariot yelled, his fists clutched with eyes like the devil, evil and full of fury. He brought himself to stand to meet the lowly phantom and swung his fist at the ghostly image.

"Dad!" a voice brought him out to see his son's face.

"Sorry Hanns, I—I'm sorry." Iscariot's voice sounded ashamed, his eyes wide with fear. He hugged his son, his grip tight as if he would never let go.

"Are you okay?"

I'm fine. Just a daydream was all," Iscariot told him. "Do you want to be alone with her?"

"No, your company is welcome. Could you tell me a story of her? She's more alive to me when you're here," Hanns requested of him.

"Sure," Iscariot spoke softly, and he thought of all the times he had with Anna and tried to find one he had not told his son. It took a moment, until it finally struck him.

"Your mother and I were in Criostaiocht for vacation. The days there were beautiful. The weather was mild, the humidity low, the sky was always blue. The hills were so fried that the grass looked like desert sands. It's part of the reason they call it the Golden State. Your mother and I were in the city. She was wearing this white, long-sleeved dress that stopped just above the knee. I think it had black bows on the wrists and one that sat on the waist. Her hair was down at her shoulders. My, she was mesmerizing, like a stunning statue come to life, perfect lines and far too good for me, but that's another story.

"While we were walking through the city, we came across this small boy of maybe five. His eyes were watering, and he had a fresh scrape near his elbow. Your mother ran to him as if he were her own. She knelt down in front of the boy and began talking to him. Hanns, I wish you could have heard your mother's voice. If you were feeling down, it was the medicine and the sugar to lift your spirits. If you were happy, it was the brightest breath of light, and so, instantly, she calmed the child. She searched her purse for a bandage, because for some reason she had everything in this tiny bag of hers. She patched the poor lad up and kissed his little scrape, mending not the wound but his heart. I think he may have fallen in love. Then she took the boy's hand, and together, we walked to search for his parents. This was the moment I knew I wanted to have a child with your mother, the moment I knew I wanted her to have my son.

"She was my life, Hanns, and I'm so glad she gave me you before she passed through this life." Both father and son were quiet as they took in the scene Iscariot described.

"Thanks, Dad. Thanks for telling me your stories of mom. It makes me love her though I've never met her, and it makes me feel as though she has been in my life and has loved me and still loves me," Hanns expressed to his father. Iscariot put his open palm on the side of his son's face and looked him in the eyes.

"From the moment you were conceived, she loved you. She loved how her belly grew, how she craved food, how little feet and hands kicked and punched inside her even though she couldn't see you. She loved those things because they came from you, her son, her baby boy, and I think, when your mother died, before she did, she took all the love she had and gave it all to you. So, when you hear my stories and feel your beating heart fill with emotions, you feel your mother's love inside of you." Iscariot's mouth spoke the words of his heart.

"Should we pray, Dad?"

"Lead the prayer." The two bowed their heads, and Hanns gave thanks and sought blessings, kissing the stone where his mother rested as they ended the prayer.

"We heading up?"

"Let's go, my boy. I'll make us a nice breakfast. How does sugar bread sound?" Iscariot asked.

"Sounds sweet."

They entered the three-story stone house and walked into the kitchen. The countertops were a solid polished concrete with display technology embedded in it. Iscariot pulled out eggs and milk from the refrigerator and placed them on the counter. A display appeared listing the ingredients as Iscariot placed them on the countertop. He selected the type of meal, breakfast, and then the meal itself, sugar bread. The display checked off the ingredients for the meal as they were laid upon the counter. Vanilla, cinnamon, and sugar were blended into a mix, a thick bread was selected for the meal and was dunked into the toothsome blend until it became saturated. Iscariot buttered a part of the surface of his counter that was blended into the natural surface but worked more like a skillet. He placed the soaked bread onto it until it became a golden brown.

Hanns had pulled out two plates, tableware, and poured two glasses of orange juice. He handed his father the plates, and Iscariot placed the sugar bread on top of them. He then sprinkled powdered sugar onto the sweet bread, piled whipped cream as high as a mountain, doused it in syrup, and decorated it with fruits. Iscariot placed the plates on the table where his son already sat.

"Happy birthday, son." He put the plate with sugar bread in front of him.

"Thanks, Dad." The two gorged themselves until their bellies were full like melons. "Wow, that was phenomenal," Hanns spoke in praise.

"It's your mother's recipe. She would make it for me at least once a week."

"Lucky." Hanns said the word as if he was genuinely disappointed he'd missed the weekly breakfast. Iscariot winked at his son. "Do you mind if I go out this afternoon?" Hanns asked his father.

"No, I don't mind. Just be home on time for your party."

"Of course." His tone expressed confidence as he picked up the dirty dishes from the table.

"I've got them. Go do what you plan to do. Happy birthday, my boy," Iscariot said.

Hanns left his father, and Iscariot was alone. The dishes were rinsed to be washed and placed inside the machine. The button was pushed, and the dishwasher came to life without a sound. Iscariot then headed to his room to shower and ready himself for the day. He undressed, but he did not turn on the shower. Instead, he lay atop his bed. His eyes quickly grew heavy, like weights on ankles as a bound man tried to reach the surface of the sea. For Iscariot, the weight drowned him into slumber, and his mind brought him an ocean's wrath of dreams. One of great violence, of dead men, and the art of battle, and war in its most animalistic form.

Iscariot's face was painted in dirt, his helmet lost in the battle that raged for seven days. Nearly 700 men lost, a hundred of his own. His armor was scratched, chipped, and worn from the harshness of the fight. Entrenched they became, he and his men, like rabbits in their holes, frightened of the hawk that watched them as prey. Just outside the city of München, in the valley of country fields, they fought for a strategic strong point where a castle base overlooked the fields below. He, his brother, and their men waited seven days for reinforcements.

The sun had been up nearly an hour when the first shots of the day rang in their ears. Advancing were men of the dead, or so they looked. Skolastjori soldiers pushed toward Iscariot and Robert a hundred strong, while the brother's forces dug deep. The bullets flooded their base as they tried to hold off the enemy combatants, as they battled for their very lives.

"Aim for their heads!" Iscariot screamed to his men in the concussion of gun fire. Slowly, his men began to fall. The rate of death for men was greater than that of the Skolastjori.

"Fall back!" he heard Robert yell.

"No!" he shouted to him, making his way toward his brother.

"Iscariot, we must turn back. We cannot hold this position any longer."

"Take fifty men back to our retreat point. I'll take twenty of our best. We need to hold." Iscariot was adamant as he spoke.

"Fight smart; fight brave," his brother said.

"Come with reinforcements," he pleaded to Robert. Iscariot called the twenty best men within the unit and scripted a plan. Ten men to stand tall, two groups of five to flank in a pincer motion. Iscariot sent the details to all seventy men who were in the unit so that if reinforcements were to come, friendly fire would not occur.

Robert's men fell back while Iscariot's executed the plan. "Godspeed," was the departing words from brother to brother, and their final stand began.

Iscariot and four others went right on to the battlefield. Trenches, haystacks, and metal shields were the decorations on the field of the fight. The men of ten stood tall, suppressing fire, so Iscariot and his men could move without detection.

Antony, Iscariot's trusted friend, took another set of men to move left of the Skolastjori soldiers. No men were lost as they transitioned, preparing for their last attack. The standing men of ten took down thirty, giving them odds of just over three to one. Iscariot radioed his team.

"On my mark," he said. Iscariot took a deep breath, feeling his lungs fill full of air, as if it were his last breath. He could feel his ribs expand, the soothing air go through his nasal cavity, down the windpipe, and into the bags that were now full of oxygen for his heart to pump out the energy needed for the swan song of the seven-day battle.

Engaged the men of ten had been, then the men of five from the left flank attacked, spreading out the seventy Skolastjori, and their ranks became thin as Iscariot and his lot of four fired on the enemy.

Five Hollen men had fallen, then ten as the battle raged for hours. Three of the ten Saoirse men who stood their ground perished, along with one man from Iscariot's group and another from Antony's. The firefight went into the fourth hour. The Skolastjori warriors were down to fifty soldiers while Iscariot's squad was holding on to thirteen. He could sense the pressure mounting on his men. Their tactic was failing, their fancy fool's folly of hope was dimming. Iscariot's group came back to one. The shots of gunfire rained upon them. Thirteen was quickly ten. The end was near for Iscariot.

The earth beneath his feet rumbled, not from trembling fear but by a force of a great scale. His ears heard high screams, but not from the mouths of his men. Then he saw them, Robert and his merry men of 500 strong. They came from the heavens above. Some fell from pods of airships; others flew in battle suits. Jets whistled in the sky, tanks and battle jeeps concussed the earth as they landed. Two balls of fire exploded in front of Iscariot and his men, and the Skolastjori were no more.

After the dust of the dirt and the blood and the sweat settled, Iscariot sought out his brother, and when he found him, he grabbed his shoulders and tossed him to the ground, jumping on top of him with a fist pulled back to punch.

"You should have stayed!" Iscariot shouted at Robert with ferocity and malice in his voice. "They died because of you!" Before Robert could respond, Iscariot opened his eyes. He was back in his home, naked on his bed. His heart thumped and bumped in a rush from the nightmare.

Iscariot walked into his lavatory and turned the lever to the shower that quickly ran like water falling from a mountain on high. The water, hot, soon fogged the room. When cleaned, he dressed. On his feet, black ankle boots, his trousers dark like the night. His shirt was white, crisp and sharp. His waistcoat hung snug on his body and matched the shade of his pants. He put a bow tie around his neck but did not tie it, and he placed his top-hat and frock coat on top his bed. His beard was already cut neat. He stood in front of the mirror and styled his blond locks, his hair pushed back with volume to its flow. Tapered to his design, he was ready for the day ahead. Iscariot picked up his coat and top-hat and headed down the stairs to his living room, draping the frock coat on a coat hanger near the door and also placing his cap on another arm of the rack.

Iscariot flicked the communicator on his wrist and scrolled, and images displayed in three dimensions. His finger on the band of the device, he scrolled to the name Antony. It dialed out, and Antony's appearance displayed in holographic form from the communicator that dressed his wrist.

"Hey Isc," Antony answered.

"Hey Ant, we still on for this afternoon?"

"We are. I'm just picking up Major Andre. We'll be at Imperial in twenty, thirty minutes," Antony informed him.

"Sounds good, my friend. I'll see you both soon." Iscariot closed the communicator interface with another twist of the wrist. He looked at the time on the same device and decided he'd leave the house and arrive early.

Iscariot put on his knee-length frock coat, latched its golden buttons, picked up his top-hat, and headed out of his home in a small hall that connected to his garage. The lights hung down from the ceiling above, glowing like the rising sun. His once antique car now gone, he rested his bottom on seats of black leather with black stitching that molded to his body. The steering wheel was of the same hide, as was all the interior that required elegant composition rather than unfitted beauty. He grabbed his ebony gloves from the glovebox on the passenger side of the vehicle, and then he brought the craft to life. It roared like the deep bellow of a male lion in the victory of battle over golden fields on a foggy winter morning. The vehicle's exterior color was livid and ink-like. Its curves were flagrant and drew the eyes to their boldness. The interior lights were honey yellow and ran in high contrast to its dark appearance. Iscariot threw the car in drive and left his mansion ranch to drive the winding roads that led to his destination.

From cold green fields to the frozen city streets, he arrived at Imperial, and he sat himself in a secluded spot. Iscariot ordered a drink from the short, skinny, bald bartender. He sipped on the sweet sauce of scotch that slithered down his slender belly. He hadn't waited long when he saw Antony, as his friend entered the rustic bar. The lounge was lined in refurbished woods from around the world. It was not too light nor too dark in the establishment. The music was at a quiet hum and could only be heard if closely and intently the ear focused to the beating sound. Iscariot was sitting at a table made of handcrafted wood from Holle. The rectangular table was held up by wood columns ending in bear paws. Etched across the tabletop were marks that looked like a bear had clawed its surface. The chairs around the Hollen table had long backs that curved over the sitter's head, and atop the chair's arching design was the carved face of a grizzly.

Inside the bar, Iscariot hailed them over to him.

"My friends." Iscariot stood to welcome them.

"General." Antony and Andre spoke in unison, and the three of them took their seats. As they sat, the bartender came over to them, welcoming the two arrivals and took their orders.

"Brandy for me, please," Andre requested.

"Whisky," was all Antony said. The slender man left them to retrieve their drinks, and the three men began to talk.

"You always said it would come to this," Antony spoke, addressing Iscariot.

"The treaty was a disaster. Truly, what were they thinking?" said Iscariot.

"To keep a country yet to make them powerless on all accounts. To be at the mercy of other countries. I agree, it was and is madness," Andre chimed in. His slacks were tan and tight fitting, his boots polished, his shirt pressed, and his jacket decorated with medals of all his many honors. Andre's hair was brown and pulled back into a taut, well-held ponytail, wrapped in a silk blue ribbon. Andre's facial features were sharp and narrowed, yet he was not unattractive.

"Fools, our fathers were. To drop us in a hole, they dug with their hands, leaving it for this generation to one day fill or be buried in it." Iscariot spoke a certain truth.

"Your drinks." The tiny bartender handed Antony and Andre their liquor. Antony grabbed his and hollered, "Here, here," to concur with Iscariot's verbiage.

"So, what are you proposing, Iscariot? What is your plan?" Andre asked of him.

"This war Robert seeks will cost hundreds of thousands, maybe millions of lives. Is it not our duty to prevent such a thing? We may be men of war, but that does not mean we should rush to battle," Iscariot averred.

"Where do we start? When do we start?" Antony inquired.

"We start the day after tomorrow, and I will begin the first stage of the plan when I arrive at Holle. If we are to stop the coming war, we must know what Alamgeer is thinking. What are his intentions and why? There, I will offer my help and my counsel. I will draw up a proposal of a new treaty to prevent aggression, better trading opportunities, and some stability for him and his country." Iscariot laid out step one of the plan's timeline. Andre was quick to speak.

"And if you fail?"

"Then war cannot be stopped," Iscariot answered.

"And if you succeed?" Antony wondered.

"Then we proceed to phase two. The Leon coalition within the Leon Pride must take over all military branches and arrest the high generals. I, myself, will arrest my brother, and all will be charged with high treason," Iscariot described.

"High treason?" Andre questioned.

"How is it not? A man set for war, willing to sacrifice men and women of the State, to bring about economic uncertainty, all with the possibility of losing their great nation. I see no other explanation." Iscariot spoke with reason, speaking to Andre directly. "Andre, with you as chief of staff to the Leon coalition it makes you the perfect person to execute such an order."

"What happens after the arrests are made?" Antony asked, leaning in to the dialog between the men.

"We must act quickly. We will need to send out a radio and holovision transmission, letting people know my brother has committed such a horrid act. We must also seal off the castle and any government buildings. After these events take place, they must be confirmed with me that the coup was successful. We will then invite Alamgeer over to our country and sign the treaty I will draw up with him while I am over in Holle for the next few months." Iscariot detailed the third act.

"I'm at your side," Antony asserted.

"I am on board, so long as your return from Holle brings a valid treaty between us and the Hollens," Andre stated.

"So little faith in Iscariot?" Antony asked slyly.

"Just the thoughts of a realist, Antony. Something you wouldn't understand," Andre answered.

"You will have it," Iscariot reassured him. He then raised his glass for a toast. "To Saoirse!"

"Saoirse!" Antony and Andre raised their cups and spoke in unison.

"Who else is involved with this?" Andre queried.

"Us three, ten men of the Comhail, a few lieutenants, and a few other officers in other branches of the military," Iscariot replied, his mind on what he was about to do. He began to talk about his brother once more. "I have argued my case to Robert from the very end of the war, and when he became king and spoke his words of caution, I knew that I might one day need to act. I'm sorry to say that the day has come. Today, I will either be known as a brother betrayer or a hero of the kingly republic."

"Let us hope for the latter," said Antony.

The bar started to fill in with more patrons as the minutes moved the day.

"Shall we discuss this more later?" Andre suggested.

"I'd think that best," Iscariot answered.

"How is your boy?" Andre asked, moving to a different topic.

"He's well. He's excited for today."

"As he should be. It's a big day for him," Antony said.

"One of sadness, too, I'm sure," Andre noted.

"Hanns manages just fine. If I'm honest, I think I upset him more than anything on this day."

"Anna was a hard loss, Isc. You have every reason to have a tender heart on this day." Antony comforted him with kind words. Andre remained silent.

"I've grieved this morning. Only cheers of celebration are in order for the remainder of the day." Iscariot spoke with optimism.

"I look forward to its splendor." Antony smiled, then gulped down the last of his whisky, letting the glass hit hard on the table. Iscariot and Andre finished their drinks as well but with much less vigor.

"Shall we, gentlemen?" asked Iscariot as he rose from his seat. The others followed suit, leaving money on the table and then walking out of the bar with a wave to the bartender. Iscariot shook Andre's hand and embraced Antony in departing gestures. "See you both tonight."

"See you then, brother," Antony replied.

"Farewell, Antony, Iscariot," were the goodbye words of Andre.

Iscariot got into his hyper car, and with the sound of the engine, he growled away with an ear-to-ear grin on his face. His spirits risen, he was home, and shortly after he arrived, Hanns came following through the door he'd just entered. Hanns was a bit disheveled in his appearance with gray dust on his hands, face, and clothes. Iscariot greeted his dirty son.

"Hanns," Iscariot looked at him with only a slight confounded expression. "I thought you were going out."

"I did. I needed to pick up some supplies. Then Oscar and I met for a quick bite to eat. I've been home for about two hours, chiseling away."

"Oh, I hadn't noticed the time. You off to get ready?"

"Yea, just a quick shower. I'll be back down in about twenty, twenty-five minutes," Hanns approximated.

"Alright, son. We'll leave when you're ready then."

While he waited for his boy, Iscariot brewed a cup of coffee, dark was the roast, strong the flavor. He drank it black and walked outside and looked out past the fields to the setting sun. He thought of what his time would hold while he was in Holle. His mind weighed on his son and how Hanns would handle the situation he was putting him in. He wondered how Hanns would react to the possibility of Robert's arrest should events lead to it. He knew a talk would need to be had—a dialog of loyalty and honor. A discussion on how to act even if the world saw his actions as wrong, and how history and time would be the true writer when he, the man, was long gone from the earth and all the events he suffered through had transpired.

Tick-tock, the minutes ran like rolling rock down the rugged hills of time on father clock. Inside he went, and his son awaited him, ready for the night, dressed in a blinding white from head to toe, with a cloak bleached white like new snow.

"Ready, my boy?"

"Ready," Hanns responded.

"Let's go." He slapped his son's back in good tidings, and together, they drove the lowly fields of Aontu's back roads to a place of gaiety and exuberance.

They arrived, and so had many others. The attendees were of a melting pot. Some of high society, others of country bumpkin origins, some of war, and others from the cloth of peace. Iscariot walked in the welcoming doors of his brother's home. The smells and the sights were magnificent to the senses. He took them in and harbored the sensations within his beating heart. He loved it, for he knew his son deserved such an affair, and he loved it because he knew Anna would have adored such an event for her son. Iscariot sought out Robert to express his gratitude, though only hours ago, he thought to jail him for the good of the country.

Odd, he thought, to have such swings in ideas. How family ties and kind gestures of good men with good intentions could also lead to heartache for that person of good character, as parts of their beliefs would lead to horrors and whom people would deem as wicked men.

He found his brother out in the field, next to a two-story tent that looked like it was made of magic from wizard hands and make-believe. Even in the light, it glittered like pixie dust from fairies the size of a human thumb. Iscariot smiled at Robert as he approached him, and he greeted him in their usual rustle and tussle manner, as if they were still boys at the age of six. Iscariot loved his brother. He admired him in many ways. Though he knew that if needed, he would act against him for the good of the country. To save not only the republic but his brother in his misguided ways. They talked briefly of their day, of Anna and Iscariot's emotional state. Iscariot twisted the narrative in a positive manner as the brothers made their way back to Robert's country home, only to be interrupted by his son, Hanns. Iscariot looked back at Robert, tapping his boy's shoulder as he passed him, and headed inside the house while Hanns talked to his uncle.

Dwelling within the estate, Iscariot mingled with those he knew, and filled his belly with savory meats, cold drinks, and delicate desserts. The memories of his wife faded as the night went on, and the heartbreak faded with those memories. As Iscariot talked amongst friends, he noticed a moment in the night of Hanns and Lagertha. He watched closely, though he could not make out the words that slipped their tongues and left their lips. In their interaction, there was a physical exchange. Lagertha handed Hanns a gift which he did not open, but put inside his pasty cloak. She kissed his cheek and hugged him with a mother's love. In their interplay, the faded memories returned to Iscariot and so, too, the pain, leaving him to seek out another drink. In his search, he found what he was looking for, along with his most trusted friend, Antony.

"Isc!" he called to him with a stein in one hand and a lady in the other, a woman who was not invited, but whom he brought with him.

"Ant, I see you're enjoying the evening as you always do."

"And I see you're sipping on memory chasers. Why don't you switch to something that brings about new memories instead of chasing old ones away?" Antony replied.

"What do you suggest, old friend?" Antony handed him his half drunken stein and then poured a sweet alcoholic beverage into it.

"This will make you right as rain," Antony assured him. Iscariot sipped from it, and then once more, and indeed his mood did swing. Their chat turned toward the future rather than the past, and in their conversation, he glanced about the room. The lights were like fire. The people became shades, and the aura around him fell to a most peculiar reality—one where he could not tell if what and whom was around him was there, but that small speck of time soon finished, and he saw with his eyes a man in red come his way, and the two talked.

He was asked of Hanns and what he got him for his birthday. Iscariot answered in a drunken manner, which did not reveal the gift, but instead answered in a manner obscure, that he'd die by what he sees. Iscariot blinked his dry eyes. His nephew looked at him in confusion. Not knowing what to say, he left him in a flummoxed state. Iscariot changed the topic and let Aedus know where Hanns was, and set him off to enjoy the remaining hours of the celebration for the ceremony was soon at hand.

Like passing clouds or changing tides, time moved along to its own cadence, never one moment truly the same, whether cumulous in its build or rapid in its junction, the minute would pass the hour and day, ever different, a je ne sais quoi in its display.

A call came from outside the house as the minute hand hit the twelve and the hour struck eleven. The gleeful people in attendance made their way out into the yard near the tent that shone like a starry sun. Iscariot could see and hear his brother as he called the celebration to an end. He now stood among the crowd, and his son and nephews were brought forward. Lagertha grabbed Iscariot by the arm, and together, they walked up to the boys who stood in front of Robert, who was elevated on a chair.

Iscariot's mind became sober as the importance of the honor hit him. Lagertha handed him a blindfold to place over his son's eyes. Nerves began to shake within Iscariot, for happiness was upon his soul. The party ended with a bang. The lamprog that hung about and twirled in the air like dancers on a stage were synchronized and rhythmic in their movements. The twinkling light that radiated in the tent beamed to the heavens, and the lamprog danced up the rod of light and exploded with a blast and a boom. The lamprog burst into color of erupting flames, and fireworks they became. Iscariot smiled in the moment, wrapping his arm around his son.

Side by side, they walked into the darkness of the field and into the lightless forest where trees grew high, and beasts of all shapes and sizes roamed the night on the forest floor and in its treetops. Miles they walked in the blackness until they reached a stump that sat alone, almost encircled by other trees that grew near to it. Iscariot helped Hanns onto the butt of the tree.

"Good luck, my son," he said, and he departed from Hanns. He walked fifty meters back from where he came and perched himself under a blind to watch his son throughout the night and to bear witness to his transformation.

The world around him was hushed. Dead were the sounds of the forest. Deceased was the frozen ground he walked upon. Breathless was the wind. His surroundings were lifeless, and in its mortified state, he peered through the blackness, and he saw a being. Cadaverous it was; it glided toward Iscariot. Unbent in its course, the wraith was upon him. Faceless the creature, wearing ragged cloths, its tall lean figure was unsightly yet fearsome to look upon. The winds began to beckon in shrill calls and whistles. The trees swung with anger. The air ran cold and pricked the skin like bee stingers. The black sky became darker, and the clouds bemoaned snow so dense the eyes could not see but a foot in the distance. With the frozen vapor a freezing blizzard, the ghostly creature seemed to grow.

The banshee was face to face with Iscariot. They were just inches from one another, and then the haunted being spoke. Its voice was harsh like static, ominous its tone, its pitch was hollow. Its elongated fingers reached for Iscariot. Afraid Iscariot became. His eyes widened. His heart panicked. He sweat in the cold. His nerves rattled on edge. Iscariot reached inside his jacket.

"Kill him," scrambled the sound of the phantom's voice.

"Get away from me!" Iscariot yelled, but the wraith persisted. Anxiety fell onto Iscariot's troubled spirit, and he rushed out of the blind he was in. The poltergeist was right at his back. No matter how quickly he ran, the specter was always an arm's reach from him.

Iscariot was distressed, as if the next moment would be his death. To him it felt a nightmare, where no matter how fast he ran, the murderer who chased him was just feet away, ready to end his life. His mind was in absolute terror, a hysteria of emotions. He was scared.

He had run, how far he did not know. Now in a small opening, he thought himself free. Iscariot turned to the center of the circle he was in, and there he stood. Faceless the ghost, it stared into him, and the beast screamed as if it were being skinned alive, its pitch was hair-raising— chilling to the bone as if it were the yells of a person just before a murderous death.

Heart sunken from the creature's sound, Iscariot drew a dagger from his coat. A warm tear fell from his eye as he ran at the pale figure. His hand up to strike, just inches from the phantom, it yelled to him.

"Dad!" Iscariot dropped the dagger before he came down with it. He fell to his knees and wept, for before him was his son. Hanns cradled his father as he lamented in his fear and sorrow.

The wind spoke no more. The trees fell still as statues. The air no longer stung, and the night sky got lighter. Iscariot gathered himself and looked at his son.

"I'm sorry, Hanns."

"It's okay, Dad. I know you'd never hurt me," Hanns spoke softly.

"Thank you. Thank you for always being at my side. The sun may not be risen, but I have no doubt you are a man. After our duty in Holle, I think I'll escape for a while. A vacation to someplace warm. I need to be away from the world, my son," Iscariot told him.

"I think that's a great idea, Dad."

"Please don't tell anyone of this. I'll go and seek help. I promise."

"So long as you do," Hanns replied.

"I hope I have your loyalty forever. I'd be lost without you, Hanns."

"You'll have it always. I promise." His son smiled at him. Though Iscariot was ashamed of himself, he smiled back at his son. He turned back to grab the dagger held just moments ago and rested it on his palms.

"This was and is my gift to you, Hanns. It was my father's and my father's father's, and his father's father's. It has been in our family for many generations. I hope that it is as loyal now to you as it was for them in the past." Iscariot handed the dagger to his son. Hanns examined it carefully. Its handle jeweled with emeralds and diamonds, engraved in pure silver, it read, Darroch. His son looked back at him.

"Thank you, Dad. Dia linn." Hanns embraced his father.

"You're welcome, son." When they detached from their lock, Hanns opened his cloak to set the dagger inside his pocket, which caused Iscariot to remember that his son had placed something in that same pocket earlier that Lagertha had given him.

"Hey Hanns, what was it Lagertha gave you at the party?"

"Oh, I'm not sure. She said to watch it when I miss her," Hanns answered.

"When you miss Lagertha?"

"I don't know. I was confused by it as well."

"Here, let me see it." Iscariot reached out his hand. Hanns placed the chip that Lagertha had given him into his father's palm. He implanted it in the band of his communicator and a holographic video appeared in front of them. The words of an angel could be heard. A voice, Iscariot perceived the sound many times before. It was of Anna. She lay on a bed of soft linen sheets. Her belly was huge, yet she looked magnificent, glowing in a glorious bliss. Escaping her lips were words of a beautiful song, a lullaby to her unborn child. She looked so happy. Her smile was vibrant, and her eyes were sparkling. There was nothing more beckoning or more enchanting to Iscariot than the sight and sound of his wife. He looked at his son who was wiping tears from his eyes. Both men were beaming from ear to ear.

Anna's song had ended, and the camera came close to her face, and she stared with great intent, and then she spoke. "I love you, Hanns. I love you with all my heart."

The holovid dissolved back to its source, and together, father and son walked out of the woods into the snow-covered field and headed to the ranch to rest within the warm walls of Robert's estate.

Robert Chapter Five

Robert's jaw had dropped as a head of a woman rolled. The scene projected through the hologram. It disturbed his mind, and grief filled his stricken heart. Speechless he was, for now he knew, evil was upon him, and it would stop at nothing to smite the light of lady liberty, whose flame danced in the fog at sea and whose voice beckoned those to come to the land of the free. A shiver down his spine, he looked at his wife whose eyes watered in sadness. Robert grabbed her hand and glanced about the room of stunned faces and worried hearts.

A day of joy it was meant to be. A day of remembrance, a day of life, a day to rejoice as it was the Savior's day. It was Yule, the day of the Phoenix, and in the day's morning hours, it became a paradox. Robert rose to turn off the projection and called the room to prayer.

"Our Lord, forgive this world and all its sinners. A day of good tidings and humble blessings has been corrupted by hatred, by a dark heart of a man broken. On this day, the day of your birth, we must ask of you strength, we must ask of you guidance. Above all, we must ask of you love—love of the things that bind us together, for the world has pulled the shade of darkness upon itself, and it is only the light of love which binds us, that will lead us out of the darkness. We will cherish this day, for it is still your day, but when the morrow comes, give us the courage and wisdom to act and plan for the coming storm. In Phoenix name, we pray. Germa."

To rid their minds of what they had witnessed, Robert walked to the piano in the great room of the country home. He sat down at the bench in front of the instrument, putting his fingers on the white keys. He closed his eyes and struck a note and then began to play a song. A four-four tempo, the notes etched into his memory, its title, "Auld Lang Syne." As Robert played the soft sounds of the heart-gripping song, the harmonic voice of his wife began to sing. In the stunning glamour of her voice and the hammer and string of the piano, Robert saw the mood lifted. In higher spirits, if only slightly, Robert played another tune, one more upbeat. It was titled "Joy to the World." In a merrier state, Tomoe came into the room, cello in tow and bow in hand. She played the strings to match Robert's play, improvising where she saw fit, and in their vital spark, they started to forget the horrors of the morning and began to truly remember what the day was about.

Of canticles they caroled, and songs of humor they sang. They let the wickedness of the morning's news fall to the rise of pleasantry, and though most in the room did not share Robert's faith, they sang along with him and his family to share in his memory. Gifts from parents to children, spouse to spouse, children to parents, and children to children were given. Robert and Lagertha didn't want their guests to be left out of the exchanging of presents, so in their festive shopping, they got small but meaningful gifts for Tomoe and Tokugawa, as well as for Katerina, Yefimovich, and Viktoriya. In the giving and receiving, they became humbled as the thought put into each gift showed meaning and purpose.

Morning was soon noon. The snow that laid upon the ground was bright and pure. The blue sky was magnificent in its stark appeal. Snow birds whistled in the trees and danced along the snow-covered ground. Lunch was served, but the meal resembled more of an early supper. The food that was served was not the dishes of leftovers from the meal they had from the night prior, as it had been already been donated to the poor. Rather, it was a meal of thanksgiving. A turkey—large, lean, and golden— sat on a great serving plate. There were sweet potatoes, stuffing, gravy, raspberry jams, buttered croissants, green beans, corned beef hash, colcannon, and for dessert, candied sweet potatoes, apple pie, and apple barley pudding, all to be washed down with sweet mead, wine, coffee, and tea. Robert cherished every minute of this day, for he knew soon he'd be in battle, and those at his table, he might never see again. He looked at each of their faces and memorized the details—how they laughed, how they smiled, how they looked when they thought no one else was looking at them. He peered into their eyes to try seeing their blessed souls and how beautiful they were.

The day went on. His children went off into the snow to enjoy what sunlight remained. Others watched a movholo about a group of kids who try to capture the meaning of Yule by making a digital reel of their own. The tale was of a little boy who is desperately trying to buy his mother a Yule gift. He worked and he worked as hard as he could, and before the day of Yule, he goes to buy the present he's been so mightily trying to get. The cashier tells him that he doesn't have enough money to pay for the gift. He pleads to him but to no avail. As the story comes to a close, the child sits outside on the ledge of the store's windowsill, and he weeps tears of tremendous pain brought from the hurt in his heart. A man who walks by the storefront sees the weeping child.

"What's the matter, boy?" asks the man. The boy looked up and was confused to see the owner of the shop in front of him.

"I've worked so hard, Mister Smith, and I can't do it. I can't buy my mom a gift. She's been so good to me, when I've always given her trouble. I wanted to show her how much she means to me." The boy cried as he spoke.

"Come on." Mr. Smith put out his hand and walked the child back inside the store. "What is it you wanted?" he asked. The boy pointed out the gift. "Oh, that's very lovely. I think she'll love it." Together they walked to the counter with the item in hand.

"Mr. Smith. I can't pay for this," the child reminded him.

"Give the cashier what you have. Whatever you are short, I will pay the difference," the owner told him.

"Mr. Smith." The child beamed, overjoyed by his kindness. He wrapped his arms around the man he had been working for. He cried once more, but with a full heart of happiness.

"You have been a big help to me, my child. You have worked hard, and this is just a small thank you. Now, run along before it gets too late," Mr. Smith told the boy. The child scampered off to the hospital just down the road. His mother lay in the hospital bed.

"Hi, Mama. I have a gift for you," he told his mother. She smiled at her son with warmth in her heart and surprise in her eyes. The child put a necklace around his mother's neck. It was of a cross and daingne, the shamrock of the Nazar religion. The boy held his mother's hand. They were happy as they got to spend the eve of Yule together, and in the night, he slept in the chair beside his mother. Their hands still tightly together, she parted from her beloved son to touch the face of God.

The movholo always stirred the emotions of those who watched it, and though it held great sadness, the meaning of Yule was so vividly captured.

The sun soon was no more, and the radiance of the moon and stars took its place. All gathered once more in the great room to watch a sporting game the people called Footer. While the game was on, they played simple board and card games and enjoyed each other's company with conversation of lighthearted things.

As the evening came to a close, Robert called Enoch, Yefimovich, and Tokugawa into his office. Robert called the room, the soldier's room. It was adorned with the decor of warriors from around the world—armor of all four military branches as well as armor of Bushi knights. Symbols of the fallen were placed at the entrance to the office—a pair of boots at attention and a rifle at its center with a helmet atop the barrel of the gun. The nation's flag was draped behind his handmade wooden desk, which had carved images of an eagle, a wolf, a leopard, and a lion. Known only to Robert and his immediate family, the desk had hidden compartments which his children would find, and frequently hide in when trying to escape their parents. It was used often by Lorena during hide and seek. The desk was a high contrast, and the immediate attention of the eyes, as the walls of the office were white stone and the floors a washed gray wood.

"Gents, I hope your day has been pleasant. I rather enjoyed it, except for this morning, of course. But the events of this morning are why I have called you in here. I want to know if we are ready for tomorrow. Are your advisors on their way?" Robert asked them all, and one by one, they answered, confirming they would be ready for tomorrow's meeting. "A shame it's come to this." He let the mourning words leave his breath.

"A shame indeed, but the past is the past. It's time to act so that our future is brighter than what shines upon the world today," said Enoch. Yefimovich responded with a "Here, here" in confirmation.

"We'll meet late in the afternoon so that those who arrive in the morning have some rest and are relaxed before the meeting begins. I'll make sure we're fed that evening. I'm sure this will be a long discussion," said Robert. "Who's the latest arrival for tomorrow?"

"Olav won't be arriving until around the ten o'clock hour," Enoch answered.

Robert look at each man individually.

"Papa." He stared at Enoch with his green eyes. "Thank you for all that you do for me and my family. You've been in my life since I was a boy, and though my father has passed away, I still have you here on the earth with me."

"My boy, you are most welcome. I, like your father, am very proud of you, and will be here to support you until my dying day," Enoch said back to him, and the two embraced one another.

"Yef, once more, we battle, my friend. If there is anything you need of me during any time of the war, do not hesitate to ask. They will seek you until you are dead, until the city of cities is captured. Be safe, old friend." Robert spoke with care and warning.

"As goes for you, Robert. As old as we three are, it is you, the youngest of us that we will look to end this war. So sad it is, in your young life, that you must experience two world wars. I pray that when this one is over, peace consumes you." Yefimovich's kind words touched the emotions of the heart. Robert embraced him in his arms, fierce like a bear, and then released him from his clutches of deep devotion.

"Tok, my dear friend. I'm glad that, once again, I do not have to fight you on the battlefield. You truly are a menace to any enemy. How happy I am that our nations are so close and how lucky I am to call you my friend. I hope our relationship is always this strong and that our nations' bonds become unbreakable, bonded not only between us but between all our peoples. Robert expressed to him the importance of their relationship.

"So long as we're alive, I think our nations will just be just fine. A rare thing, isn't it? Almost like providence to have four nations so close, so bonded. Cherish this, we must, for this grain of sand will one day fall, and a new time will begin." Tokugawa gave promise and warning.

"How true that is. How wise the words. Let us hope our children keep the bond firm and harden it with their resolve." Robert put out his fist. Tokugawa knocked it down with a fist of his own. Robert copied and knocked Tokugawa's fist down. They then collided their closed hands together, and after the impact of their clenched hands, they separated them, their fingers spread and danced in the air, all the while creating a sound from their mouths of an explosion. They then bowed to one another, and ended their handshake in an embrace.

Robert took a step back to look at them collectively.

"I love you all so very much. Fight bravely, fight indomitably, and may God be always at your side." The men walked out of the soldier's room except for Yefimovich as Robert called for him to stay, and alone the two men had become.

"You're a wonderful friend, Robert. Whenever we talk about you, no matter what policy we may disagree with, it's always with kind words," Yefimovich flattered him.

"Thanks, Yef. The same holds true for you, you know."

"Oh, I know. I can tell by how your children talk to me and of me," Yefimovich laughed.

"I hope they haven't bothered you too much."

"Contrary really. I had a wonderful morning with your son, Aedus. A great boy you've raised," Yefimovich continued to compliment. "He took me out to a bakery. H-he even let me drive the Shelby."

"Is that right? He must be really trying to impress you. He doesn't even let me drive the thing." Robert was lightheartedly jealous.

"If there was anyone to be jealous of, it would be my daughter. Your children, eh-eh-especially Aedus, have made her feel right at home. I guess he's taken her ice skating and to a Field of Diamonds. I think is what she told me," Yefimovich expressed and questioned the name of the field.

"Tongue tied and stupefied Aedus is around Yekaterina. But I'll tell ya, there ain't a kid more sweet than Aed. Ask him for help, and he'll give it. Sometimes, you don't even have to ask. He just knows. Bewildering sometimes," he reflected on his son.

"Young love is a funny thing. You've raised some good kids, Robert," Yefimovich reaffirmed.

"Don't sell yourself short, Yef. You've got quite the daughter. Speaking of our families, how is your wife doing? I noticed she's been a little under the weather." He spoke with concern in his tone.

"I think the change of climates may be affecting her. From Yisra to the Islands—to here. They're all quite different this time of year. Yisra will pra-pra-practically be a tundra. The Islands are all a bit different but all very hot, and here in Buna, winter has come," Yefimovich explained.

"She seemed a little better this evening."

"I'm hoping she's alright by the morning. Some of her symptoms, dare I say, seem like she might be pregnant." Yefimovich spoke with some hesitation. Robert chuckled and grinned as his friend's equivocation.

"Well, if that's the case, congratulations, and good luck, old man," he joked.

"Old man, indeed." Yefimovich seemed to reflect on his age, as if he wasn't up to the task of taking on a kid at his age.

"Yef, before we go back out with the others, I just want to say, be careful. Like I said, I do not think they will rest until your death, and I'm afraid they may not stop their battle until they capture or kill your daughter. If you feel she needs protection, please let me know, and I will send what you demand." Robert gave caution and aid in his words.

"Thank you for your concern, Robert, I know you have my interest at heart. I guess we'll see how things progress—but we know the stakes. We know our roles, and if it is our time, then we will go out doing—what we were meant to do, what we were called to do. I will fight in this war, Robert, but rest your heart, knowing this. The country is not me; I am only a small piece of it. Should I die, you need not fear, for the might of the Yisraian spirit burns in all—all who call it home." Yefimovich stood steadfast in his words, and the two embraced once more.

"God bless you." Robert spoke warmly and genuinely.

"May He bless us all," Yefimovich replied, and the two left the soldier's room, knowing they each would give everything within the fiber of their being for the good of the cause in the trouble that lay ahead.

It was the twenty-third hour in the day of Yule, and tired eyes consumed all, and one by one, those who stood in the late hour, drifted off into their rooms to dream dreams of tomorrow. Robert and his sons were the last to call it a night. They resided in the kitchen. Robert sat at one of the stools where the island set in the middle of the room. Aedus stood near the countertop, and Absolume was seated next to his father.

"Aed, come sit," Robert told his son. Aedus took a seat across from Absolume. "You boys know what is coming. I want you to know that, whatever your choice, I will always love you. I do not want to see you go into battle, and I would stop you if I could, but I was only slightly older than you are now when I went off to war. Give this choice some heavy thought."

"I'll be with you, Father. My place is on the battlefield," Absolume interrupted Robert.

"To not use our training—how shameful it would be if we did not fight. You've prepared us for this father. It is our duty. It is the fate we chose," said Aedus.

"Are you certain?" Robert asked.

"As certain as the sun will shine in the morning," Aedus responded. Absolume nodded.

"So be it," Robert reluctantly said to them. "Get some rest, boys. It'll be a long meeting tomorrow," he told his sons as they stood from their seats. He hugged them both, a powerful embrace of father to son, as if to transfer all his power he had into them. "Goodnight, boys, happy birthday, and merry Yule."

"Goodnight, Dad," said Absolume.

"Night, Pops," Aedus said his goodbye, and alone, Robert felt heavy weights upon his lids, as he struggled to keep his eyes open. He made his way upstairs into his great master bedroom. The room, dark, silhouetted the objects that were in it. He disrobed and wore nothing but his naked flesh. Robert crawled into the soft, wool sheets. Lagertha shuffled over to him. He consumed her in his arms, and together, they slept.

Only three and a half hours had ticked by. Robert had risen from his bed, leaving Lagertha to rest soundly. He moved toward the giant window in the room and looked out to the world. The night was a picture from the hands of the Greatest Painter. The shades of black were just right. The fall of the flurried snow was pure. The soft blow of the wind was ideal, and the cold touch of the air an ace to the senses. Robert thought of the day ahead and the days to come. He looked back at his wife. He reflected on his children, and he knew that he must end the conflict before their lives should fall ever closer to the danger that lingered in the world, where the dreams they had would fall to ashes and their lives would wane in the fire of survival.

Robert was ready for the day. He kissed his wife goodbye and left the room she slept in. For breakfast, he had only a pear and a coffee he brewed in a traveling mug. He was out the door in brown leather dress shoes where the tips were pointed, in light blue debonair wool pants, a soft, off-white, cotton button-up, pressed on his shoulders was a slim-fitted jacket that coordinated with his pants. Robert left his country home. The world was still, and he could feel that the world around him was asleep. It set his mind at peace, and in his state of calmness, he was able to think clearly, precisely, and abundantly. Inside his green, classic, bug-eyed vehicle, he made notes for himself, whom to talk to, and why, recommended strategies for state-side during the war, and what he should say to his wife and children before the day of the battle of Holle.

Robert was out of the hillside boonies and deep within the sophistication of the metropolis. He parked his car underneath the capitol building and was greeted at the gates by two Liopard guards. He shook both their hands and offered them a good morning before striding off to his office to jot down all that he conjured on the drive over.

The sun rose, but Robert didn't know the hour. Occupied, his mind was focused on matters of importance, of substance, of true life or death. His desk was covered in papers and texts, consumed like a worm inside a book, eating the pages of sustenance. Robert finally glanced at the clock and looked at the time, noting the hour of the day. He sent out two messages from his communicator and buried himself back into loose papers and novels like bricks.

Nine o'clock, the bells of the clock rung to echo in his ears, chiming the time of day. Knocks, the square root of the hour, percussed on his office door.

"Come in," he spoke. The door opened.

"Good morning, Uncle."

"Hanns," said Robert with a smile. "Top of the mornin' lad."

"Dia dhuit." Hanns spoke the familiar greeting, and the two began to chat. Hanns sat across from his uncle. Robert asked of his life, what he was working on, what he was pursuing. He asked of his wellbeing and how his morning had gone.

"How is your heart?" Robert asked his nephew.

"My heart?"

"How strong is your resolve? How controlled are your emotions? The world is about to undergo a radical transformation should we fail to stop the coming war, or worse, should we lose the war and all that we are. Have you looked inside yourself and asked your heart and mind if you are prepared for such change?" Odd questions Robert asked, but it was all with a purpose.

"Son to a dead mother, son of a widowed father, I have known heartache since the day I was born. I am loved by my father, blessed with an uncle who cares for me. I am loved by an aunt who is like my mother, grateful for cousins who I see as siblings. I am not crippled in body or mind. I can tell you my heart is strong, my emotions abundant but stable. I am part of a family who has known war their whole lives, and though my father may have tried to keep me from it, he always let its influence slip the cracks of his wall and trickle down to me. It's his life, his mission, and it was impossible to shield me from it," Hanns responded.

"Wow. Seems you've given this quite some thought," Robert spoke, surprised by Hanns lengthy and thorough answer.

"I have a lot of alone time when I'm sculpting. My chisels are in the details."

"It's far more than I expected to hear, but your answer lets me know you're ready because I have a mission for you while you're away in Holle," Robert began. "First thing I need you to do is to note your surroundings, the lay of the land, where civilians live, and where key government and military buildings lie within the city. I need you to observe the people, listen to their thoughts, look at their actions, how they move." Robert paused a moment. "I want you to start today, at this meeting."

"You want me there?" Hanns was taken aback.

"I do. I want you to look around at the people in the room. I want to see how well you can read them, both their words and body language. They are not always one and the same," Robert explained.

"I understand, Uncle." Hanns's ears and eyes were intent on what Robert was telling him.

"When you're in Holle, if you can, monitor who comes and goes to see Alamgeer. You should be in close proximity to him since you'll be shadowing your father. If it is difficult for you to get to Alamgeer, find and talk to people who seem to be close to him and to those who seem distant," Robert instructed. Hanns nodded his head, still focused on the words that left his uncle's mouth. Robert shifted in his seat. He leaned forward, his green eyes unblinking, as he looked into the multicolored irises of his nephew. "Did Lorena or Abe talk to you about a burning flame and the properties of paper?" Robert asked. Hanns seemed to search his mind and gave a grunted laugh. "Lorena was talking about a message she was going to crack. About a letter with no words. Abe seemed to know of it as well. Why do you ask?" Hanns looked confused by the question.

"And do you remember your birthday?" Robert asked another unusual question.

"Uncle, what are you asking?" Hanns was nearly baffled, and in his bewilderment, there came a knock on Robert's office door.

"Uriel, come in." Robert rose from his seat, coming around his desk. Hanns had stood with his uncle. Robert faced his nephew, placing his right hand on Hanns's left shoulder. "Remember me," he said. "I'll see you at the meeting." Robert could tell his vagary had flummoxed his nephew, but Hanns nodded as if he seemed to know what Robert meant. "I love you, Hanns." He made sure he said the words before his nephew left the room.

"And I, you." Hanns left the office. Uriel stood near Robert's desk.

"Morning, U," Robert said.

"Hey Robert, how's your morning?"

"Eventful. How did you sleep?" Robert continued the pleasant small talk.

"Quite well," Uriel answered. "What was Hanns doing here so early in the morning?"

"I just wanted to get him up to speed on what to expect over in Holle. He's like a son to me, you know," Robert responded and gestured for Uriel to take a seat. He opened a drawer from his desk and pulled out a large, red, leather-bound book.

"What is this?" Uriel was intrigued.

"This is a secret." Robert turned the cover to reveal this first page. It was an image of a ring, and inscribed in the ring were the words, The Culper Ring, and the outer part of the bend of the ring read, A light concealed in the shadow. Robert then closed the crimson book and spoke. "Inside this book is a list of names and numbers. Those are to be memorized, inscribed in your mind like chiseled stone tablets that mark the common laws of man. From this day forward, you are its keeper. If you should ever feel that danger is too close to you, burn it."

"But what is it, Robert?" Uriel asked. Robert pulled a letter from his drawer and handed it to Uriel.

"When you arrive home, open it. It will tell you all you need to know. The main reason I called you here today is because I know you've been working on something quite big. A theory," Robert began.

"Yes, when done, I'd call it a law. I have yet to find any error in my arithmetic." Uriel spoke with certainty.

"Be it law or theory, I know your meticulous nature, and I know it is destined for something great, but I must ask this of you," Robert started; Uriel leaned forward in his seat. "I must ask you to burn your work as well."

"Don't be absurd," Uriel said with a dumbfounded tone.

"Uriel, if the enemy were to get their hands on your plans," he began to explain but was cut off by his brother-in-law.

"Might I suggest something else? Something that could give us an advantage, and put the enemy further behind," Uriel queried.

"What do you have in mind?"

"What if I write a belied set. If you believe my work to be valuable enough for the enemy to want to steal it, then why not lead them with breadcrumbs away from the truth," Uriel suggested. Robert thought it over for a few minutes, his mind working through multiple scenarios before accepting the idea.

"I'll agree to it. Might I suggest coding your work as well, for even a fool can be a hero." Robert spoke prudently.

"Do you have a recommendation for the best method?"

"The letter has what you need." Robert pointed to the folded paper.

While secluded in Robert's office, the two heard the grumblings of a sour man who seemed to be arguing with a woman of the staff of the capitol building. The voice was harsh, grating the words as they left the man's mouth. So, too, was his speech low and mumbled. Robert opened his office door to see the commotion that was outside it. His eyes took in a man with pointed ears, a rounded belly, average in height. He puffed a pipe that smelled like mint and walked with a cane, though he did not need it. His steps were light, so soft they were not heard as they clashed against the floor, contrary to his loud mouth.

"Sir, you cannot smoke in here!" the woman scolded the man.

"It is not I who smoke, but rather the leaves that burn, which create the smoke you see," the bellied man replied. The woman was visibly agitated at the man's manner. "Ah! There he is!" the man said with a gleeful smile on his face. "Thank you so much, my dear. You've been a big help," the Engelelf spoke. The woman was confounded by the outlandish man. Robert approached the over-the-top, unique gentleman. Robert snatched the pipe from his mouth. The loud-mouthed brute gave a sourpuss face and then a hearty laugh, embracing Robert with a hard slap on his back.

"Good morning, Olav," Robert greeted him.

"God murgen, god murgen," Olav said back to him.

"Do you have to be so mean to the girl?" Robert asked rhetorically.

"Mean? Sorry, my dear, if I offended you. I'm a bit of a lost cause, I'm afraid." Olav turned to the young woman who couldn't seem to make heads or tails of the eccentric man. His apology put a bewildered face on the girl. She thanked him, not seeming to know why she did, and then headed off down the long hall from Robert's office.

"Uriel! Korleis har du det?" Olav asked of his wellbeing.

"I'm very well. Thank you, Olav. Yourself?" Uriel returned the question.

"I'm old, and I'm fat. Whatever you want to make of that," said Olav, unabashed by his answer. "Some light reading, I see." He poked his cane at the red book in Uriel's hand.

"A bit of homework," Uriel responded back.

"I did some studying myself on the way here," said Olav, who then changed the subject matter. "What time is this meeting? I have a three o'clock nap that I cannot miss."

Robert looked at his wrist for the time.

"It's in ten minutes. Uriel and I were headed there now," Robert informed him.

"Good. Lead the way, my king." Olav gestured forward with his cane. The three men walked the columned halls of golden lights, traveling up the marble stairs to the council chambers, whose stained-glass ceilings of gold and purple shone with the peaceful rays of the stories the glass projected onto the council round table. Robert's sons were sitting in the room, across from one another as before. All who needed to be present resided in the chamber. None sat on the thrones of virtue or sin, as the myth of the chairs and the events of those who sat in them seemed far too coincidental. They blended fact and fiction, just enough to make even the most skeptical or the most intelligent mind to keep from testing their fate.

Robert took his seat at the throne of patience. The dark oak wood was carved in a floral vined pattern. The base of the seat was a square, box shape. The back of the throne rose six feet and curved to form a rectangular roof with spires of the Nazar faith on each corner. The red seat cushion was plush, its stitching precise, its embroidery superb.

"Lady and gentlemen, please take a seat. We will be in this room for quite some time. I promise, nothing shall happen to you if you should choose to sit upon the chairs of sin and virtue," Robert paused. "Except maybe that one," he expressed some doubt and tittered at his own comment. The men and woman slowly moved forward, still hesitant to sit.

"That one that he is referring to is the throne I currently reside in." Iscariot winked at his brother. Robert mouthed the words "thank you" as the guests were still spooked by the rumors. Cautiously, the attendees began to sit at the seats of the round table. Twenty-nine bodies sat around the 3,000-year-old wooden piece of furniture, and as the last person sat, Robert stood, addressing the twenty-eight men and one woman in the open-columned room.

"After today, there will be no more talking of planning and executing by one's self. After today, we will leave this room of one mind, of one goal, of one purpose. Our course will drive straight and true. After yesterday's events in Holle, there can be no doubt that evil is upon us. The leaders of Holle have made their intentions clear. They do not mean to restore what was lost, but instead, they seek to improve upon what they never achieved. Alois saw a threat with the Ivdeyskiy people and challenged them openly. I believe today, the goal is the same for his son. If you listened to his rhetoric, Alamgeer claims he is protecting the Ivdeyskiy people. He does this by branding them; he does this by segregating them. He talks of a united Holle where the capitol lies at Erbil, in the heart of modern day Yisra. If we are truly good men and women, then we must not stand idly by, for that is how tyranny grows, that is how man drowns in the black water of the sea of death. In a vivid and horrifying display, Alamgeer sent a message to the world, that those who do not see his way will die by his blade. To cast down one's own mother, surely his mind must be deluded, corrupted by the illness of hatred." Robert stopped his opening speech to the room and took a moment to breathe, trying not to think of the death the world witnessed on the Lord's day.

"Out of nobility, out of honor, out of our very lives and the lives of those we love, we will try to negotiate with Alamgeer. At the conclusion of this meeting, my brother Iscariot will leave for the Hollen nation. Two months he will stay, and if nothing fruitful comes from it, I suggest we attack the second week of Bellum. Let us pray we do not need to and hope for my brother's success in his duty. However, we are not here to discuss if negotiations succeed. Today, we are here to discuss our plan should we fail. Prime Minister Nemtsov, you have the floor as you have planned for such a thing for quite some time." Robert took his seat, conceding to Yefimovich who rose before those at the table.

Yefimovich swallowed hard, then took a sip of water from the glass to his right. He closed his eyes for longer than a standard blink and then began to speak to the room.

"We have watched them, carefully, year by year, encroaching on the Ivdeyskiy people, who call Holle their home. Indoctrination through schools, the media, even their entertainment. I have been warning my people for years and the world for months. I—I have found mouths that will speak the truth, and I believe, I have found those who will act in the face of danger, who will look evil in its blood-red eyes and will meet the challenge, even if their life be forfeited, to uphold the good in this world. The men and the woman I have brought here today have pledged to do such things." Yefimovich took his seat, taking another sip of water.

Robert rose once more from his throne of patience. "Enoch, would you like to address the room?" Enoch rose, but Robert did not sit.

"I have painted a mural with the words that left my tongue, but my own people do not believe such images are possible. Even the Tulku they shun and shame and claim falsities. I will only say that I am grateful to be in the presence of men and women who have taken the paintings I have made, even if they do not see the picture fully, and seek to move the painter's brush to design a scene of peace rather than the art of war." Enoch sat back down. Robert looked over to Tokugawa.

"Anything to add in an opening statement?"

"Only that I am here to listen and to give aid where needed," said Tokugawa.

"Very well. Yefimovich, I leave the floor to you once more. Robert sat back down, but Yefimovich did not rise.

"I will concede my time to General Dimitre," Yefimovich informed the room.

"Thank you, Prime Minister. I will be as brief and as descriptive as I can," Dimitre started. "The first thing we must note, in order to build a better tomorrow, is our future negotiation tactics with the countries of Danija and Avstrija. Our failed attempts, and other nations' lack of attempts, has drawn them to the side of Holle, and both of them have great military forces. In order to move forward, we must also take note of our failure to maintain and keep Holle in check with the Hidler Nemtsov agreement. Our lack of fortitude, from year after year, from broken promise after broken promise, has made us blind to what was happening before our very eyes. Now, because of our lack of attention and firmness to keep to what was agreed to, Holle has raised a vast standing army.

"We, Yisra, have taken precautionary measures by creating treaties with Enuarku, Attica, Konstanpol, and Arpa. Intelligence reports have concluded that the first attacks will fall on Attica and Konstanpol. Enuarku will supply its support to Attica, while Yisra supplies forces to assist Konstanpol." General Dimitre then went on to discuss defensive measures within Yisra and defensive tactics to abed other countries upon the war's onset. On his conclusion, he sat, and General Moeshe of the Yisra Naval Fleet detailed the lay of the sea and the tactics they currently had in place. Moeshe talked of bringing the navy to the North, supplying artillery for when the Attican and Enuarku troops begin to counterattack the Hollen might. He described how they would encounter Hollen resistance by having a flank at Mongnolerian ports to pincer the enemy ships. He continued to inform the room of what would happen in the southern seas and the oceans to their east. After thoroughly explaining the details of the naval formations, Moeshe passed the torch of speaker on to his twin brother, Vozduh, the general of the Yisraian Air Force.

General Voz had two paper air-carriers he set afloat in the room, twirling his fingers to move them in the air around those in the room, using them as a visual. In his preamble, he talked of an airship already based in Mongnolerium and another that would travel with the naval ships heading north. Voz vaguely described details to the south and within his home country, seeming to blatantly withhold such information. Robert saw it as understandable though unfortunate. "Prime Minister, the room is yours once more," Vozduh yielded.

"I have not much to say, except that, we need your help in this fight. We will fail without our brothers from across the oceans," Yefimovich said, circling three stones above his palm, seeming to do so out of anxiousness. Robert could only guess due to the days of war that were getting nearer for him.

"I can provide you with aid, Yefimovich." The towering blue-steeled man with veins of light rose. His voice was kind and calm, and tender was his tone. Tokugawa spoke to Yefimovich and addressed the room. "Prime Minister Nemtsov, I will expand our previous agreement. On the day your troops push forward, a million men will come your way. From the west, we will rise to take on Holle, landing on their shores, preventing any type of reinforcements. You already have 10,000 of my men to help on the Konstanpol front. Here, our paths will cross through the Dead Sea and land in a small town called Emden. We will continue east until our forces meet at Atma." The sterling man had war-gamed his thoughts to the leaders in the room.

Tactics were the tale of the tongue, tenacious to the mind were those of sturdy thought. Strategy of faulty foundations were argued upon until solidified. Like the markings of a sword, they hammered out impurities until the blade was sharp and strong. The slightest weakness in its make could break the steel in half, but here the lives of men would die should the weapon of their minds fail in the art of war.

One post meridiem, the hour struck. The arguments of war swung like the pendulum on a grandfather clock, and their powers of thought were dwindling with the passage of time. The mouths of the council no longer fed the ears in the room. Only the grumbling of stomachs voiced their needs and wants, and in this lull, they ate to replenish their minds and their bodies.

Rice and bread, fruits and meats—their bellies became full, and their brains were restored to think critically and creatively. Be it his lack of sleep or just his personality, in their reprieve, Robert watched as Olav popped his pipe, blowing pillars of smoke. The scent of the plume was a sweet mint. He voiced his mind with his graveled grumbles. His words traveled to the ears of those in the room, even if they did not care to listen. His words could not be unheard.

"The negotiations with Holle are a fool's dream. Nothing will come of it, I tell you, nothing."

"Your people and those with the Avengler council seem to disagree, Olav," Iscariot spoke his mind.

"Don't be silly, Iscariot. The Avenglers know very well the threat," Olav began to rebut.

"If that is true, why did you and your wise men turn down the Tulku's call? Is your council a council of eejits? Come off it." Iscariot got slightly louder as he talked.

"You're quite right. They are idiotic. For a month, I tried to show them their errors in thinking, but truthfully, they are thick in the head, dopes, numbskulls, eejits. No matter the word, they are wrong, and negotiations are nonsensical. Alamgeer must face the wrath of the sword, for the blade of the word is dull," Olav replied.

"I'd love for your council members to hear this," said Iscariot.

"If they didn't already know, then they are dumber than I thought," Olav responded.

"You're an asshole, Olav," Iscariot cursed him.

"Hey! Knock it off!" Robert interjected.

"Piss off, Robert!" Iscariot snarled. "Look at you twits. So steadfast, so narrow-minded, your only thought is war. Think of all the people who are to die by your command, your citizens, Robert, your soldiers."

"Do you think I have not thought of this? Do you not think this guts me, that it breaks my heart?" Robert asked trying to repress his fury.

"Yet you send them!" Iscariot yelled.

"And I, on the field with them, Iscariot." Robert raised his voice.

"In the back, upon your high horse, you mean," Iscariot antagonized.

"Stuff your mouths, boys!" Yekaterina demanded. Robert looked around the room, realizing his kingly behavior had devolved into a boyish quarrel. A brother's bond and a brother's love—each knew well the other's mind, and each knew the other's heart so well that habits of their past as bickering boys still persisted, though they were now men in their forties. Robert looked at Yekaterina, and then at all within the room.

"My apologies, and thank you, Yekaterina, for putting two children in their place," Robert spoke, composed, and in kingly fashion. The brothers held their tongues until their meals were finished. Iscariot was the first to speak.

"What do we offer, Robert? Of the Leon, the Liopard, the Mactire, and the Iolar, what do the branches offer? What do our branches sacrifice?"

"Two weeks prior to the main attack, we will send 2,000 Mactire soldiers along with 100 Liopard soldiers in reconnaissance. They will land on the eastern border of Holle and be involved in high tactics, quick-strike missions.

The day of the main attack, we will send 100,000 Leon warriors and 10,000 Iolar airmen to the shores of western Holle at Dusseldorf. The airmen will strike prior to the pride landing on the beaches." Robert looked at his brother. "What say you, Iscariot?"

"I think the plan is solid. We will need to discuss if the troops are discovered prior to invasion," Iscariot mentioned.

"We shall. You, Antony, myself, General Lance Sijan of the Iolar, and General Toyle of the Liopard branch will need to discuss multiple scenarios. We will relay such war games to our allies here in the room," Robert informed his brother.

The sun now crossed the sky three post meridiem, and the meeting of the world's future continued. Another hour passed in detailed discussion, one of fresh thought, and in this hour, all hearts and minds became one. The goal was clear; the blueprints of attack and defense were etched in stone. The plan was sanded and polished; flaws vanished in its making. They were now of one spirit. Stop the coming of the war, and if failure brings about the coming battle, the animus to execute was vivid, unyielding, and powerful. Robert rose from his throne of patience once more.

"Lady and gentlemen, thank you all for coming. I know the hour is late, our minds weary, and our hearts full of emotion, but tonight, we leave here knowing we are giving all we have. Tonight, we leave here with a vow to give our lives, our fortune, and our sacred honor. May God be with us all."

"Here! Here!" shouted Olav, and the twenty-eight other members in the room followed his cry.

Robert walked to the door and opened it, holding it to let all those who resided in the council chamber out, to exit before him. As each individual left, they each said the following words. "Mercy unto you, Darroch, and peace and love be multiplied."
To each, Robert replied, "Beloved, we give all to attain such things." Robert's sons were the last to leave the chamber, and he repeated the same line to them, but he stopped the boys before they left and told them, "Like your eyes, open your mind to see, and of closed mouths you'll find the secrets that will be. I love you boys." The brothers responded with

love of their own, and then Robert was alone. He closed the council doors.

In his solitude, he admired the walls of the capitol as he walked through the halls to his vehicle, taking notes of the designs and the artistry in them. In his car, his green craft rumbled down the city streets leading him to Deantore's Cathedral. Its entryway tower climbed high into the heavens, playing music as the wind rushed into the pipes. At the steeple's pinnacle, enshrined in golden light, the shamrock beamed. The lamprog that acted as the deinign and hovered over the arms of the cross glowed sparkling white and danced around the shamrocks' limbs like the building blocks of an atom dancing around the nucleus. He parked in front of the great structure and walked toward the place of worship. He drew his right hand to his forehead, moved it to his heart, and then across his chest, and uttered the word, "Germa."

Inside, the sacred house was warm and inviting. The open-dome stage, where the Apsal would give his sermon, was bleach white in stone and marble. The candles on the pulpit waved him forward, and the elongated windows let in the shine of the moon, enveloping the stage where the preacher preached, highlighting the symbol of the Nazar. Robert knelt before it, and in his silence, he prayed. As with every prayer, he asked for forgiveness, for he was a man, flawed, a sinner. He prayed for the success of his brother. He prayed for the hearts of the men and women in the council. He did not ask for items to possess, only that good people prevail against the looming darkness, and should the darkening clouds of destruction rain upon the earth, that man might be able to seek the lantern of light in the shade of night.

When he finished speaking to the Lord, he turned and saw he was not alone, and the man before him spoke.

"He plans for such things, should the good men you speak of seek his plans. 'For I know the plans I have for you, declares the Lord, plans to prosper you and not to harm you, plans to give you hope.'"

"And a future." Robert finished the Apsal's message as was written in the Holy Book.

"I will say a prayer for you Robert, as I do every day. You will need them, for your success is the preservation of this great united country," Apsal Luther spoke to him.

"It becomes more divided every day, Apsal. Religion is lost in the heart of men. Only secular ideas reign within it now. Feeble is the mind of those who believe in the faith, they say." Robert spoke the words of his soul, as he had continued to see religion's decline.

"Funny, it is, how once science was a way of discovering the Maker. Now it is to discover how He is not. Their theories can only travel so far, till once again they see da truth, me lad," Luther said to Robert.

"It will take a great mind or a great event to sway such thought."

"It seems we may have such an event on the way. The Spirit lies in all of us lad. It'll awaken when its vessel aims to explore it," said the short man, who was balding and with gray hair at his temples.

"Pray for them, too, Apsal. They shall need it more than I."

"I shall, me boy. Now go off to ya loved ones. Tis the days now most cherished," the holy man said to him.

"Goodnight, Apsal."

"God bless, me son," the Apsal replied.

The soft honey-blue lights kissed the curbs of the streets, guiding Robert home to the castle upon a hill, in the city Buna, yet seeming so far removed from it. The golden gates of Solascnoc were upon him. A salute given, a salute returned. He traveled up the lighted path of the castle's driveway to the top of the mound, and before him was his abode. It kindled softly in the light hue emanating from the bulbs, heavenly to behold with his eyes, whimsical to feel in his heart. Robert's mind could rest just for a moment, knowing he was in the comfort of those he called his family, a place where the roots of his life were buried in his heart's core, never to be severed, always and everlasting.

He entered the snow-white room of birch trees, the crescent moon above with burning balls of gas twinkling in the clear night sky. He removed his heavy winter jacket and roamed the castle halls. Those who had stayed with Robert the past few days had not returned yet from the meeting of the minds, which allowed him to rest, if only for the briefest moment.

Solascnoc was empty. What little servants there were, who worked within the walls, were nowhere to be found. Away they were with their own loved ones, still enjoying the Yuletide spirit. Robert, in his wandering of the castle, found himself beneath it. The floors he now walked on were a deep, rich, dark wood, glossy, fair, and royal. The walls of stone around him were carved with a mural of battles and events throughout history, telling the tales of Saoirse. The soothing lamprog lights hovered in the air, their wings beating ever so lightly, showering rays upon the woman who was in the armory.

Center stage of the practice hall, she wielded a saber in hand, her dance with the blade a graceful, toe-tapping wonder. She moved like the wind, fierce and mighty. She flowed like the ocean, constant and rhythmic. She was adroit. She was lithesome. She was beautiful. Her shoes, a soft slipper, were soundless against the hard wood. Her white pants hugged her hips. Her ivory shirt gripped her body, covering her arms and wrapping her neck for warmth. Her aquamarine eyes were sharp and focused. Robert watched his daughter dance with the blade in silence until her performance was over.

He was in awe of her swordsmanship, how she used her dancer's mind in her sword play. It was artful, but more than that, it was strategic. It was not beauty in motion for the sake of beauty; it was purposeful. Each movement had a true intent. Robert had never seen such perfect motion. The ocean and the wind stopped, and Robert moved forward into the room.

"That was magical, Lorena," he praised his daughter. Lorena nearly jumped, as if surprised to see her father. "Art in motion, my tiny dancer. Mind if I join you?" Robert asked his daughter. Lorena nodded her head yes. From the armory, Robert suited himself in his gear. His armor was different from all other branches of the military. Pitch black, like a moonless night, his armor was strong and light. His hammer was tall as a man, its pommel embellished with emeralds. His helmet was a horrid beauty with two-foot antlers branching out from it. In full guard, he was as breathtaking to behold as he was dreadful. His armor was a sight of hope for many, despair for others, and hostile to some. Robert detached the shield of light from his back. Its rays glowed hot white and smoldering purple. The illusion of steam hovered from the shield. The transcription from his wife was dim but not unnoticed.

"Are the area shields on?" Robert questioned Lorena.

"They are," she confirmed. "Best of three?"

"I'll make a deal with you. If you get three kills on me, I'll give you my shield," Robert challenged her. Lorena removed her helmet and looked at her father.

"But, Dad. This is the shield Mom gave you. It's blessed for you by her." Her tone was in disbelief, hesitant to take the offer because she knew the shield's significance.

"And if you win, to be blessed by both your mother and me. Imagine how much brighter it can glow. Imagine how much power it can hold," he spoke genuinely. Lorena put down her mask. Robert closed his helm, and the two began to battle.

Robert's technique was patience. He let Lorena barrage with strike, swing, and thrust with her duel blades. Robert's shield was attached to his left forearm. It blocked and deflected any attack she tried to lay, while he waited for his opportunity to strike. He bid his time until, finally, his daughter had the smallest imperfection in her sword play. Robert moved swiftly, sweeping her legs. She collapsed to the floor, and Robert threw the thirty-pound hammer over his head and pulled it down to strike his daughter. The hammer hit, but she was not there. Like a gust of wind, she pushed herself away from the blow. She came at him like a whirlwind. She spun as she moved to attack, and it looked, to her own surprise, that she had struck the first strike.

"Quick little bird." Robert smiled.

"You have my heart pounding." She sounded out of breath from the fight yet excited from the first victory.

"Try to calm it. This will be more intense," Robert warned his daughter.

The next bout was quick. She came at her father with both swords coming from the same direction at the same time, giving long and powerful blows, but on her upswing, Robert noticed it was the weakness in her attack. As she lifted her arms back, Robert lunged forward. His shield struck her jaw, and her head jerked back, but before Lorena could bring her head back to center, Robert's pointed metal spike atop his hammer was at her throat, his other hand on her chin. "One, one my dancer."

Reset, the tango began again. Lorena tapped her toes on the floor, as her blades tapped her father's shield. Agile, flexible, creative with every attack, Robert looked for the weakness, waiting for the fault in her dance to come. Her form was too perfect. There was no break, no pause. Collision after collision, Lorena was relentless. With no flaw in her attack, Robert had to switch from a patient guard to an aggressive warmonger. He pushed back with his shield, using only his daughter's momentum, trying to throw her off balance, but it was in vain. Lorena did not seem to tire. As his daughter twirled, he tried to sweep her legs, but she danced away the brush of his hammer, and as she did so, Robert found her blade at his neck.

"That was magnificent, Lorena. Not a single mistake in that entire attack. Brilliant, my child." He was filled with pride as he said the words to her.

Poised, they began once more. However, Robert no longer played the game of willing endurer, but rather took on the role of impatient agitator. His swings were powerful and mighty as they came toward Lorena. Though the hammer was a heavy weapon, Robert swung the great mallet with ease. Lorena dodged and darted away from every blow Robert tried to strike. The roles were turned, as it was Lorena who now needed the moxie backbone of longanimity. Robert swung, stabbed, and twirled his hammer, each attempt a miss, until, alas, he struck. Yet, much to his astonishment and his delight, Lorena's blade was also at a kill point.

"Well, my tiny dancer, a deal is a deal. The shield is yours." Robert removed his antlered helmet and smiled. Lorena removed hers as well, dropping her swords and embraced her father. "Your mother and I will get it blessed, and from that day forth, it is yours," he said with gladness.

"Thank you, Dad!" Lorena was ecstatic and courteous.

"You're most welcome, my dear. I do have one more thing for you as well." He walked over to where he had suited in his armor, and there lay a book, much like the book he gave to Uriel. Before he handed her the red-covered leatherbound book, he made sure their eyes were locked with one another. "Keep this secret, my sweet child, and commit it to memory. Your life may very well depend on it one day." His voice was serious.

"Yes, Father," she replied, looking intently in her father's eyes.

"And read that letter if you haven't already done so."

"Yes, Father," she said once more.

"You fought beautifully, earnestly, and honorably, my precious child. I'm very proud of you." Robert pulled his daughter into his arms once more. He wept, but he made sure his daughter did not see the tears fall from his eyes.

"Thank you, Dad."

Iscariot Chapter Five

The night tried to rush away the day with the fairy lights of stars shining in the late hours of midday. Iscariot walked in the field away from his wife's place of rest to a solemn sanctuary of his own. A black arched door in front of him, the shamrock shone a heavenly white, as did the door's edges. It was as if the light were trying to escape its entrapment to illuminate far beyond its confines, to expand across the whole of the world.

As Iscariot opened the door, the light retreated, scared to free itself from the space in which it dwelt, and the room became aphotic. Only burnished strings ran panic in the air, like strands of molasses lightning, it moved with a timid spark around a small floating symbol of the Nazar. Iscariot closed the door, and the light ran wild in the room. Its radiance was blinding. It was as if he walked upon the surface of the sun, and the source of the light was the Light. A 100,000 spheres made the mirrored room glow, and the glass surface of the floor was illuminated in its hue.

Iscariot knelt on the floor and prayed.

"Lord, you have failed me time and time again. I call to you, but you do not answer. If I were to sing to You, You would not hear my voice. I hold my faith on the thinnest of threads and ask one last time for Your favor. I beg you, my Lord, help me stop this coming war. I do not wish good men to die, but above all, I do not wish my son to fall to the perils of battle. He is all I have left. He is the only thing that keeps me sane, the only light in my life of darkness. I have said it before, my King, but fail me now, and your son will forever turn his back to you. Please, Father, do not fail me. I ask this in the name of the Phoenix. Germa."

Iscariot stood, his prayer finished, and opened the door that was behind him. The glory of the Light hid once more in the shadows until he closed the door to leave. Iscariot turned to face the entryway, his hand on its surface. He closed his eyes as if to feel the light that tried to free itself from the room it was within.

Please, Lord, he said in thought. He opened his ocean eyes and headed toward the front of the house. His bags were packed. Hanns was sitting on the steps, waiting for his father.

"Ready, my boy?"

"Waiting on you," Hanns smiled.

Not but a minute later, Antony arrived in a heavy, titan-like vehicle. Its boxy body filled the road, its windows straight, curve-less, untiled from the roads it traveled on. The interior components were exposed. Raw and rugged, the vehicle was a behemoth, a savage set in civility. The matte gray finish gave an even more masculine appeal than it already had. The growl of the hovercraft was a low graveling bass.

Antony stepped out of the hovering militaristic truck. His brown hair was short and trim. His brown eyes looked out into the world with a satisfied glint. His skin was a light tan, and his teeth were egg white.

"How was the meeting?"

"Informative. I'll fill you in on the drive." Iscariot grabbed a bag and began loading the truck with his luggage.

"Hanns, you looking forward to this trip? The Hollen girls are quite pretty," Antony asked playfully.

"Very much so. It's a great opportunity for me to experience a culture other than my own and for such a long period of time."

"The beer and food are quite good, too, and don't forget the Hollen motto," Antony told Hanns.

"What motto?" Hanns inquired.

"Hollen titten got me smitten. Hollen bier, I'm in good cheer, drink and dance with your heart stricken, but don't grab her titten for you'll be bitten." Antony sung the rhyme. Iscariot chuckled at the lyrics.

"And how many times were you bitten to memorize the rhyme?" Iscariot asked.

"One too many I'm afraid. You see this scar here." Antony pointed to a faint mark on his lip. "A Hollen wench tried to bite my lip off. That crazy lass."

"I'm sure you deserved it," Hanns chimed. Antony laughed and scoffed at Hanns's comment.

"Maybe so. Last time it happened, I was with some lads, and they wouldn't stop singing that song to me. And well, it's stuck ever since."

All the luggage was now packed as Hanns loaded the final piece inside the utility vehicle. Iscariot sat inside the front passenger seat, his son in the row behind him. On their way to the airport, their talk was casual of places to visit, what foods they wanted to eat, and how Iscariot and Hanns would spend their leisure time.

"I'd love to see Nymphenburgh and Charlottenburg. The sculpting and artistry, I hear, is a very wonderful sight," said Hanns.

"Are you going to Volkfest?" Antony asked with curiosity.

"You'll be missing out my friend," Iscariot teased with a grin from cheek to cheek.

"Quit smirkin' at me, ya bastard. I'm a bit jealous now." Antony cracked a smile back at his friend.

"I'll bring ya back somethin' nice." Iscariot gave a wink.

"Like what?"

"A bottle opener perhaps?" Iscariot jested. Antony gave Iscariot a playful punch in his arm.

"Good thing we're about there. It's getting hostile in here." Iscariot poked some more in fun at Antony.

They arrived at the port. Antony drove his hovercraft onto the tarmac and parked his vehicle in a hangar next to a private jet that flew at Mach two. The plane was sleek and narrow. Its body was almost a golden color, and the nose of the plane closely resembled an arrow at the tip of a spear.

"Want to come in for a drink before I take off?" Iscariot asked.

"I'd love to. However, I have a previous engagement, Isc," Antony replied.

"Who's the lucky lass?"

"Just a Seanades member is all," Antony winked.

"Well, I hope she finds favor in your request," Iscariot joked.

"I think we'll see eye to eye, at the very least lips to lips." Antony laughed at his own words.

"Get out of here, you mutt. We'll talk more later. Good luck." Iscariot gave a brotherly hug to his dearest friend and boarded the golden jet.

The luggage was stowed away. Hanns had already taken his seat, and the stewardesses were already preparing drinks and a meal for the two of them. Inside the elegant cabin were two king-sized beds, a bath and shower, a full kitchen, and a common area. It was a home in the sky. The wood paneling was polished and hand-carved with decorative designs. The balsa wood flowers were stained and polished. The tan leather seats were plush and comforting. The windows of the plane were large and unobstructed for astounding views during the flight.

The pilot made an announcement that they were about to lift off and to prepare to take to the skies. The jet rose into the air, hovering like hummingbirds to a flower but with wings still and unmoving. The plane rose to an altitude of a thousand feet, and as it reached its max hovering height, the thrusters ignited, and within a few seconds, they reached the speed of sound, and but a moment later, exceeded it by traveling at twice the speed.

The stewardesses came to both Iscariot and Hanns with drinks in hand.

"Thanks for helping us load the plane," one of the stewardesses said, addressing Hanns. She was young and beautiful. In her uniform, she was adorned in a red, long-sleeved dress, equipped with white gloves and a red and gold flight cap. Her smile was charming, and her eyes spoke with generosity. Her black hair was tied in a simple but stylish bun to look like a blooming flower in the spring sun. Her name tag read, Natalia.

"It was no trouble, really," Hanns replied politely as he was handed a flute of orange juice.

"Here you are, sir." A stewardess by the name of Matilda handed Iscariot a drink of his own, a scotch whisky, straight up. Iscariot looked at her name tag. Her bust was noticeable. Iscariot smiled at her.

"Thank you, Matilda. Just what I wanted."

"You're welcome, sir," she beamed at him.

"So, where are you from, Matilda?"

"I'm from Anozria, in a small town near the desert," she answered.

"I've only been there a handful of times. Never really got to visit as a vacation destination." Iscariot relaxed and continued the conversation.

"Well, if you ever get a chance, I'd say you must stay at Oasis. It's such a unique and gorgeous city. The Anozria River pools right in the city center before it flows west into the ocean. The water is crystal clear and surrounds the entire city. The palms there are decorated throughout the entire landscape, and the mix of sand and grass brings a mesmerizing color into the city like none other." The woman seemed to fantasize of her home.

"Seems like you miss it." Iscariot noted her tone and eyes of wonder.

"Very much so. The adobe like architecture, the brick flooring, the flat roofs drained by canals, and the viga beams that support the homes. The people are always shocked by how pretty the desert life can be." She praised her home state in Saoirse.

"You know, I've been talking about getting away after my visit here to Holle. A trip to Oasis sounds like the perfect place to free my mind and clear out any demons that are housed within it," Iscariot said, tempted by the stewardess' description of her state. "Maybe, when I'm there, you can show me around."

"I'd be happy to. I plan to move back there myself next month."

"Well, before we part ways, give me your number. We'll make a date of it." They both smiled. Iscariot gazed into her brown eyes and moved downward to her peach lips, her large bosoms, her lengthy bare legs, then back up to her eyes.

"Sounds lovely," she said and then seemed to realize the time. "Oh! Let me go get your meal. It should be nearly ready."

"Thank you, Matilda," Iscariot spoke kindly. Matilda gave him another smile and turned to leave.

On her return with Iscariot's food in hand, they conversed some more, and the three-hour flight rushed by as if it were three minutes. Iscariot thanked her for her warm hospitality. They exchanged numbers and parted ways.

The port in Holle was lit in blue as the city glowed an orange-red from the volcano it was founded on. The night was dark and moonless, as the clouds above blotted out its luminescence. A pale figure awaited them in the hangar they walked into. If he weren't so slender, Iscariot thought he could be the moon itself. He was a tall comely fellow with thin but abundant gray shining hair. He dressed in military wear and greeted Iscariot and Hanns cordially.

"Guten nocht."

"Good evening." Iscariot put out his hand to shake.

"Pleasure to meet you, sir Iscariot." His accent was harsh but understandable.

"It's a pleasure to meet you as well, Mister Bormann," Iscariot replied. "This is my son, Hanns Darroch."

"Hallo," Said Bormann.

"Hello, sir."

"Let me help you with your luggage." Bormann took two bags and placed them in the trunk of his midnight colored vehicle. Even the windows were tinted a deep oily black.

The vehicle stuffed with luggage and the three men, they left the airport. The ride was quiet, except for Bormann pointing out landmarks as they drove. The streets were silent as was most of the city. The only lively sight was the lava that flowed beneath the clear roads of Atma. They passed schools once great and libraries once grand and places of historical significance. All were beyond their days of glory, for the might of Holle was lost twenty years ago, and in its loss, the eyes could see its suffering. Iscariot could hear the pain in the back of Bormann's throat, its hold getting tighter the more he spoke.

"It's a lovely city," Iscariot commented.

"It was a lovely city. Maybe, one day soon, it shall be again," Bormann said to him with hope. They then came upon a great castle, and Bormann's tone was chipper at its sight. Iscariot had seen the view twice before. Once before the Great War, the other during it. He watched as his son gazed upon the tallest columns he'd ever seen—stunning towers that fit with the rock of the volcano. They traveled across the great Bridge of Meister Mennatur. Its old gothic look was hauntingly spellbinding as it crossed over the volcanic river below. At the entrance of the bridge were two demonic looking men. Dark gray and black was their armor—swords as long as lances, giant in size. The faces of the dead they had, horrid creatures to set one's eyes upon, for their eyes were the sunken depths of a wicked darkness. Skolastjori soldiers they were, statuesque in their demeanor.

Iscariot's mind had flashed back to a point in the war, where he alone slaughtered ten Skolastjori men so that his team could advance forward in their mission. He quickly snapped back to the present. The fingers on his right hand shook, and his right leg bounced up and down like a jack rabbit running from the predator that chased it. Iscariot's son grabbed his hand from the back of the vehicle. Bormann didn't seem to notice, too distracted by the sight in front of him. Iscariot turned back to his son and thanked him. Their small moment passed when Bormann voiced their arrival.

"We are here." They exited the vehicle a distance away from the castle doors.

"Whoa." Hanns was impressed with the behemoth structure in front of him melded into the volcanic rock. "That's a big door," said Hanns as they stopped at the feet of a 100-foot red steel door. A bang at the edges of the door rang out, and the steel curtain began to open to the castle's interior. Just as impressive as the castle's exterior was the natural and unnatural design within it.

The entry was lit by luminous stalactites that hung from the ceiling above. The flattened gray stone they walked upon was cold, though just feet below them was the hot boiling liquid of magma. The walls around them flowed like waves in the ocean. Beaten and battered was its appearance, yet its natural architecture was the art of God in the eyes of men.

Martin Bormann parted from Iscariot and Hanns as they waited in the cave-like entrance, and as the crimson doors closed, a servant approached them. She was young, just sixteen years of age, or so it seemed. Her hair was a light blond, her eyes dark like pools of swirling mud. She was short in stature, petite in waist. A cute young woman, she was dressed in black, four-inch, closed-toe heels. Her pants were a binding matte leather, and she wore a sheer charcoal top with a deep V-neck, and it flared away at the belly button, parting down her legs to just past her knees.

"Willkommen." The young woman welcomed them with a simple
smile. "The Bin-Hidlers regret that they cannot welcome you themselves.
Both are at rest for the evening."

"We understand," said Iscariot.

"Please, come this way. I will show you to your rooms." The
teenaged girl grabbed two pieces of luggage and walked them through the
labyrinth. Through many darkened halls they walked. The caverned
castled was grooved and carved by the might of the men who mimicked
the design of the natural tunneling of the lava that created it. At every
doorway entrance stood two soldiers at pin-straight attention. Their armor
was a gorgeous gold and red with blades of stunning silver—holding in
their hands a weapon that resembled the look of a lance, and to be used as
such. However, it was more than just a weapon of hand-to-hand combat.
It also functioned as a weapon with great firing power against all who
crossed its bearer's wrath.

"Here you are, young sir." The young woman opened a door for
Hanns that led to a room of copper-colored light. She walked inside with
him as Iscariot stood back and observed from the entrance of the room.
The girl turned back to Iscariot and guided him to a room of his own.

"Goodnight, son," he said to Hanns.

"Goodnight, Dad." A few doors down the hall was Iscariot's
suite. The blond servant opened his chamber door.

"Here you are, Mister Darroch."

"Thank you, child," he said, looking into her eyes. "May I ask your
name?"

"My name is Alwine, sir," the young woman answered.

"Thank you for your kind welcome. I'll be sure to sing my praises
of you to Mister Bin-Hidler," Iscariot told the young woman who beamed
at his words.

"Thank you, kindly sir. Thank you." Alwine grabbed his hand and
kissed it. "Sleep well. Guten nocht, Sir Darroch."

"Goodnight, Alwine," he said to the young lass. Iscariot closed
the door behind her as she left the room and looked about his lodgings.
His suite was much different from his sons. Hanns's room was dark, but
the ceilings glowed a brilliant dark blue from the algae that covered the
ceilings. Hanns's room was like that of a tranquil starry night, where one
looked up to the stars and wondered of age-old unanswered questions. In
contrast, Iscariot's room was larger than his son's. The luminescent light
was sparse compared to Hanns's chambers. The most significant
difference was that within Iscariot's room was a view to the magma down
below that whorled in the belly of the beast they were in. A windowpane,
fifteen feet in length and seven feet in height, gave a view to the lava's

glow. Iscariot's room glistened a mellow orange, and as the light receded, the algae's light let off a blush of soft purple.

Iscariot looked out the pane at the stew of burning fire down below his chamber. He watched its power and its might, letting his eyes grow tired in its phosphorescence. He disrobed, letting his garments fall onto the stone floor, and walked toward the chamber's shower. The stone walls of the bath curved into a cylindric shape. The surface was smooth. He ran the water. It flowed hot, and he stepped into it. The water warmed his body, easing his muscles, relaxing his mind. Iscariot succumbed to fatigue. He toweled off his soaked body and walked toward the bed of soft silk sheets and cottony fluffed pillows. His eyes gazed at a folded piece of paper sealed in wax. He broke its casing and read what was within.

It was an invitation to breakfast at Alamgeer's request. Both he and his son were to attend at the eight o'clock hour. They would be awakened by a servant of the castle, who would assist with any need they may have, and they would be escorted by this same servant to the dining hall. Iscariot finished reading the letter and placed it on the bedside table. He bound himself within the caressing embrace of the silken sheets. He closed his heavy eyes and let the sand within them draw his mind to sleep in the foreign land of Holle.

Day came, and there came a tapping at is chamber door, but this was no raven rapping. Instead, it was the young servant, Alwine, who lightly knocked to wake him of his slumber.

"Good morning, Sir Darroch," Alwine said, as she closed the door behind her. Iscariot, still naked under the silk covers, returned her greeting.

"Good morning, Alwine."

"I'm here to be your servant for the length of your stay and here to treat your every need. Her attire was different from the night before. Alwine was dressed in dark black leather, thigh-high boots, a black body suit with a sheer vee that extended down her breasts, past her belly button, stopping just above the pubic bone. Atop her body suit was a light sheer cape with a collar that was thick at her neck. "Is there anything I can tend to for you at the moment?" she asked, eager to help.

"If you could just—turn around," Iscariot requested, slightly embarrassed for a brash man.

"Oh! Of course." Alwine seemed to realize the reason for the request. Her face blushed a soft pink. Iscariot rose from the bed and walked into the shower to rinse off his body and wake himself to the morning. He yelled to her while the water ran across his body.

"You are free to leave, Alwine! I don't think I'll need anything! Thank you for waking me!" Unable to hear anything except for the splash of the water, he assumed she left at his behest.

Iscariot departed from the confines of the warm water. Towel wrapped across his figure, he walked back into his room, and to his incredulity, Alwine was still there, waiting patiently for him.

"Alwine?" He said her name in shock.

"Hello," she said nonchalantly.

"I thought you'd left."

"It is customary to dress the guests within the castle," she explained.

"That isn't necessary, really." Iscariot insisted.

"Sir, please," she seemed to beg. "It is my duty to serve. It is my job. I may only be a servant, but there is great honor in it. There is an art to fine caretaking. You must know this from your travels, as there are similar customs elsewhere," Alwine expressed. Iscariot thought a moment and then agreed to her plea.

"Fine," he said. She smiled brightly. "But let me at least put on my undergarments," he told her. She stared at him and nodded but did not look away from him. Iscariot laughed at the situation he was in. He took his pointer finger, pointed it down toward the floor and spun it around, as if to tell her to face the other way.

"Oh, sorry," she said, flushed. Spinning to face away from him. "Do you have your wardrobe laid out?" she asked.

"I do not. Sorry," he said with sympathy.

"It's quite alright. May I turn?" she said cheerfully.

"Yes, I'm covered. Thank you."

"Do you mind if I ruffle through your clothes?"

"Go ahead." He gave her permission. Quick and precise, she chose an outfit within two minutes. Black ankle boots that came to a point, midnight slacks that drew thinner as they ran toward the ankle. A suprima cotton black rollback sweater, with a slim fit sports jacket equipped with golden clasps in the shape of a male lion's face. "Smart yet casual. You'll be quite the looker for her," Alwine said.

"For whom?" he questioned curiously.

"You'll see," she smirked at him. Alwine made sure all his clothes were without wrinkle, all lines flowed as they should, and not a hair was out of place. "Gut aussahand." Alwine looked Iscariot up and down.

"What does that mean?"

"You look very handsome," she blushed. "Now come, I'll take you to the dining area." Before they left, Iscariot fussed with his hair, assuring everything was in place. It was slicked back in a professional fashion, and when he was satisfied, he walked out the door with the comely young servant.

They walked the cave-like halls, side by side. Alwine would indicate each hall by a marking, which Iscariot noted, and she would also point to where they led. As they passed a major room, they would stop briefly to observe it. All she said and showed him, he kept within his vaulted cerebrum as best he could.

Alas, Iscariot reached the dining room where his host was already present. The room was lit with blushing stalagmites and stalactites. The walls appeared to be ever flowing like a painter's brush washing across its surface. The floors were of the same stone only sanded and ground down for a smoother walking platform. The stalagmites rose from the ground, a tender blossom of soft white light, almost blue in its hue. The stalactites hung like bats in the cavern, but unlike the creature, they radiated a light of the sun's orange, warm to the eyes, it could calm a wild mind. Gathered together, almost on top of one another, a chandelier of stalactite hung over a wooden table that bent and curled a similar pattern as the walls in the halls so beautifully rippled in its design. The room was radiantly stunning and decorated to match the cave's natural attraction, never contrasting with harsh angles or stark colors.

Once he had taken time to admire the room, Iscariot stopped to look at the people within it. His eyes were drawn to a man of pale gray skin, whose physique was a sculpture of muscle that could be seen through the tight attire he was wearing. His eyes were like burning flames from the depths of hell, yet he was handsome, even with such dark and menacing features. The man rose with a bright ivory smile and welcomed Iscariot.

"Good morning, Iscariot."

"Good morning." Iscariot returned the greeting to the man who towered over him, standing at seven feet.

"You look well. Did you sleep well?"

"Thank you, and yes, very much so. It's a lovely home you have here, Alamgeer," Iscariot praised the führer.

"Well, thank you. We've worked hard to keep it so." Alamgeer looked over to his wife. "Let me introduce you to everyone. This is my wife, Hella." She put out her hand. Iscariot cupped it with both of his.

"It's a pleasure to meet you." He let his eyes gaze upon her face. Her skin glistened like diamonds. Her lips, a subtle plumpness, did not shine like the rest of her, but were nonetheless attractive to the eyes, yet it was her eyes that were her most stunning attribute. Pink, like a flowering phlox, they pollinated the senses in a state of marvel. Dusted with specks of pepper black, her eyes were hard to turn one's head from. Hella curved her lips in delight.

"Welcome, Master Darroch. It is our pleasure to have you here," she said to him. "I am very much happy to have you here and your son." Hella seemed to take control of the introductions, connecting everyone at the table with Iscariot. "Across from me is General Helfen of Avstrija. Very smart and a great friend of ours. Next to him is General Forradare of Danija. Iscariot walked over to the two gentlemen and shook their hands. Helfen, though he looked youthful, had already lived half a century. The mix of Hollen lineage that dwelled within his blood took on the characteristics of a Semideusi and Hemitheoi, including a longer life span and slower aging process after the adolescent years. Forradare, though a similar heritage, did not luck out in terms of slow aging. The man was close to the age of seventy and looked it, too. He had wrinkled skin, gray hair, and was shorter in stature. He welcomed Iscariot with what seemed like genuine pleasure. Helfen, on the other hand, was far more standoffish in his demeanor.

Hella continued with the greetings.

"At the far end of the table is Möngke Khagan. He just arrived yesterday himself," she noted. He had the physique of a man built like a tank. Large, burly, muscular, he stood up slowly. His eyes glowed a soft white light, his face a blushing gold color. His scalp was devoid of hair. He, like Tokugawa, had energy bands that ran like veins across his body. Unlike those of the Nihon, his face was marked with energy pathways. They decorated his cheekbones and the temples of his skull, and his exposed dome shone like the moon in the night sky. His attire was rich in color and in quality. His morning wear was a set of elaborate gold silk pajamas. The trousers around his waist went down to his ankles and fell loosely before reaching his feet, and his silk shirt was a solid blue with wide arms. It hung loosely upon his body. Around his body was a silk terlig, which was like a robe, and sewn into the fabric was a golden dragon. At the tapered end of his terlig was an embroidered story of the dragon's life from birth to death, and upon the arms of the terlig, at its folded seams, was a story of the dragon's power. Upon Khagan's feet were leather shoes with rabbit fur inside, and the tips curled upward. He looked to be a man of elegance and power, and he took the attention of everyone in the room.

"Hello, Master Darroch. Welcome, welcome." Despite his dominant appearance, he was cheerful and quite a joyous fellow, surprisingly likable for a man of great power, both in body and position.

"It's a great honor to meet the Khan," Iscariot said. Möngke took Iscariot's hands, folding them together and placing his own hands over Iscariot's. He looked Iscariot in the eyes.

"No, the honor is mine. You are the Great Warrior, are you not?" Möngke's voice was quiet, smoky, deep, and came from the bellows of his throat. Before Iscariot could answer, the voice of a woman came up behind him. Her silvery tone was pleasant to the ear.

"He is the man you speak of." Iscariot turned to the woman who spoke of him. Her feathered hair was thick and black and shone a healthy, glossy radiance, running to the small of her back. Her waist was thin, her bottom small and tight, her bosoms large for such a tiny frame. Her eyes were bold, dark, and spellbinding, her lashes long as a summer's day, her skin a seductive confection of caramelized wonder. Of all the beauty and glamor within the room, she was what Iscariot was most drawn to.

"Hello miss." Iscariot put out his hand, his mouth slightly open in awe of the woman before him. She took his hand, raised it to chest level, and placed hers on his, palm to palm.

"Good morning, Mister Iscariot. My name is Yuskita. Yuski, if you'd like. I am very thrilled to meet you." Her smile was like the morning sun, warm, radiant, a filler of the human spirit, beautiful. Their hands locked together, and he looked deep into her chocolate eyes. His drumming heart skipped a note in the beat it played. It was as if he had died and then was revived by her very sight. Iscariot beamed. He was dumbstruck, almost without words.

"A pleasure to meet you." He let out the words.

They dropped their hands back to their sides. Affixed to her, he looked at Yuskita's dress. She wore copper armlets on both her right and left side. Her head was adorned in what looked like a dazzling tiara with gems, emeralds, and diamonds. Around her waist was a copper shimmering skirt that halted at mid-thigh. Covering her breasts was a copper chained bralette that strapped at her back and hung from her shoulders. A sequence of copper coins covered her bosoms, her cleavage exposed by the open chain links that squared across her chest, and at the neckline the same sequence of copper coins.

"Here, come sit next to me," Yuskita instructed him.

Iscariot took his seat to the right of Alamgeer who sat at the head of the table. Hella sat across from Iscariot and Yuskita on Iscariot's right hand. As Iscariot began to sit, Hanns entered the dining room. Iscariot made the introductions to his son, who took his seat to the left of Hella, and just as he sat, the food began to be run out by servants and placed atop the table's wooden surface. From tea to applesaft, bread rolls with various spreads and toppings, quark and cheeses, eggs and musli—they consumed the bounty that was in front of them, talking of lighter topics, getting to know one another.

Iscariot noticed the comings and goings of the servants, the guards unwavering at their posts outside the room, and the interactions between the three classes. He examined his mind for any sign of abnormalities between the three groups and the guests that sat before him. He noted what servants talked to what guards, the body language between the servants and the higher class, as well as between the guards and those of the elite. This and more he examined in his silence. He wondered if his son was doing the same thing. Iscariot turned to Hanns, who was conversing with the gold clad man of Mongnolerium lineage, Möngke. *Perhaps not*, he thought.

Iscariot's observances were fanned away from his mind when Alamgeer addressed him.

"Iscariot, what brings you here?" The question was basic but blunt and direct.

"Well, sir," he started, gathering his thoughts. "I'm here because there is a great tension between our nations. We see hostilities growing within all countries, and I am here to remedy the uneasiness between our two countries."

"Mr. Darroch, I do appreciate your candor, but Saoirse seems to have made it clear that Holle is the enemy. The alliance with Yisra and the greedy Yefimovich indicates to me that your brother seeks his war," Alamgeer stated.

"Well, that is why I'm here, Mister Hidler. My brother is simply weighing all options, even an alliance with you, if you'll have it." Iscariot slid in the words for Alamgeer to wrap around his mind.

"I'm sorry, Iscariot. I'm finding it difficult to believe. Your king has never once suggested siding with us. He has not acknowledged our strife; he has not given a hand to pull us out of our ill. We were great! Now look at us, abandoned, like our buildings, broken like our roads, uncelebrated, infamous, left to cure our own disease." Alamgeer spoke from a solemn heart.

"Mister Hidler, I do not want this war either. I have seen too many people pass in my life, and to see anyone else leave this earth before me would surely rip what bits of the soul I have left within my flesh. I alone, convinced my brother to be here with you today, to draw out a plan together, to rebuild together, to halt the coming storm that has been brewing over our two nations." Iscariot spoke an honest tongue.

"His words are true. His tone admits it. His eyes behold it." Hella gave council to her husband.

"His words may hold no lies, but I do not see how you can get me what I want, what my people desire," Alamgeer admitted. "Can you abolish the Hidler Nemtsov agreement? Can you pull us out of hyperinflation? Can you restore our borders? Can you bring back the allure of what made us a country adored by the world?" His voice grew louder with every question uttered.

Iscariot looked around at the faces in the room. Eyes were locked on him; his next words were sought after. He thought quickly and rationally and gave a response to Alamgeer's questions.

"The Hidler Nemtsov treaty can most certainly be abolished; quite frankly, I never liked it to begin with. I felt it gave too much power to Yisra and buried Holle too deep in the grave it was already in. You asked of aid for your economy and the wellbeing of your people, and to this I tell you, it is dependent on the policies you implement once the treaty is terminated. In regard to your borders, I believe there is always room for negotiation."

Alamgeer smirked at Iscariot's remarks. He rose from the breakfast table and bid farewell to all who sat at it. Alamgeer then walked over to Iscariot and whispered in his ear.

"Your brother is the devil, Iscariot. He carries the instrument of death." Alamgeer pulled away. "Hella will be entertaining you this afternoon. I, unfortunately, will be tending to other matters, but I am very interested in continuing our talk, Iscariot. You offer some promise, some hope." Alamgeer walked out of the room, and the mood within it changed. It became less structured, less ruled, more free.

Hella came to Iscariot, took his arm and locked it in hers. She wore a one-piece, skintight leather suit. The sleeves of the suit stopped just past the elbow, the collar flared around her neck and clasped around her throat. The hidden zipper that ran up the suit halted at her breast, exposing her cleavage and neckline. They twinkled like water in a summer's morning light, refracting the rays to dazzle the eyes of man. Laying in the cavity of her breasts was a silver pendant of a holy cross, different than that of the shamrock, which was the symbol of Iscariot's faith. This cross she bared on the bare of her chest did not have the diengne. Instead of two solid beams that ran north and south and east and west, her cross's northern beam flared like a flame in the wind. Hella looked over at Hanns, who stood next to his father and addressed him.

"Dear Hanns, your father and I have matters of state to discuss. Feel free to explore the castle grounds. Should you feel the need to travel outside into the city, I suggest taking your servant with you. Make yourself at home. I won't keep your father too long."

"Thank you, Mrs. Hidler. If I were to venture outside, would you happen to have any recommendations?" he queried.

"The memorial of the Great War is a good start, as well as our museum of science and mathematics," Hella suggested.

"Thank you for the proposals. I'll be sure to heed them," Hanns spoke courteously.

"You're very welcome. We'll be back shortly." Hella turned to Iscariot, arms still locked with one another. "Shall we?"

"Lead the way." Hella's black heels clicked as they walked the stone halls of the volcanic castle's caverns. "So where are we going?" asked Iscariot.

"We are just going to tour the grounds. I wanted to talk privately as well. 'Tis why I wanted Hanns to stay behind."

"I understand. He will still need to join me in some meetings as he is here for secretarial duties," Iscariot briefed her.

"I don't think it should be a problem. It's reasonable, and I think Alamgeer will understand."

The two talked of their families in their walk to their destination— Iscariot of his son, Hella of her twins. Iscariot noted their absence, Hella letting let slip a hint of where they might be. As they gullied down into the beast of the belly of the active volcano, Iscariot noticed the cavern went from a soft frosty chill to a melting steady warmth. He removed his coat and draped it over his arm. Iscariot looked over at Hella who didn't seem to mind the heat, but he noticed that her exposed forearms and bosoms sparkled more vividly, like pulsating stars burning in the night sky.

As they traveled down the rabbit hole of the depths of the halls, they came upon an entryway of a stairwell. It seemed to run a mile deep, and it dwelled within a vast open room where stalactites, twenty to thirty feet in length, hung from the cavern ceiling. Down below, the swirling and bubbling of the molten magma jumped from its source, trying to free itself from the slumber it nested in. The stairway was narrow, hugging the stone walls. Iscariot quickly noticed there was no railing for support as he walked along the edge, just behind Hella, who kept her hand on the walled side of the staircase.

"Well, this'll get the nerves going." Iscariot spoke in a joking manner, yet the words were very much serious in his mind.

"You've walked through worse, I'm sure," Hella replied.

It's true, though it's still very nerve-wracking, he thought to himself. His uneasiness began to grow on the stairwell when they traveled through a tunnel on their descent. It was a new type of darkness for Iscariot: a darkness like death, where there was no beginning and no end, where man was truly blind of sight—a blackness so rich, man would draw up images of what his surroundings looked like. It was truly terrifying to the senses and horrific to the mind if lingered on too long.

Finally, a light at the end of the tunnel. Relief consumed him, but it was short-lived, for as they reached their final steps, his eyes beheld them—a thousand rows for 20,000 men. Soldiers of Hemitheoi and Semideusi stood at attention. Black banners with a red, eight-pointed star and a white shin letter with a cap of a crown. The images and the soldiers filled the massive underground room. Gooey magma flowed like water around them. Iscariot's eyes gazed upward to see Alamgeer perched high above his army. They erupted "Hagel Ala! Hagel Ala!" Down on bended knee with their right arms extended outward and a stiff straightened hand, they saluted their führer. Alamgeer returned the salute by raising his arm upward with an open palm and then closing it into a fist, saying to those who served him, in the Hollen tongue, "Loben sie den diener!"

Iscariot was flabbergasted. In all his military life, he had never seen such a display of surrender to one man. He saw the petrifying might, but more, he saw its power, the strength in one sole person. He was envious, as he was pusillanimous. Iscariot turned to Hella.

"Impressive, isn't it?" she asked. Her face looked flush with lust.

"Very much so," Iscariot confirmed with a voice of awe. "What are they saying?"

"When the soldiers kneel and raise their hand in salute, they say 'Hail Ala,' and in turn, Ala raises his hand, then clutches it to signify solidarity and says back to them, 'Praise those who serve.'"

"It's a very powerful scene," Iscariot admitted. Hella grinned, saying nothing more.

"Meine Holle!" Iscariot heard Alamgeer yell from above. His ears now attuned to the flapping muscle inside the mouth of Alamgeer, he listened and watched. Alamgeer folded his arms as he began his speech.

"The new Reich, the symbol of unification, the monument to the volk of Holle. That is what you are. You are the standard of the Hollen people. You are its shield. You are its sword. You are the dreams we once had of a Holle now awakened!" Alamgeer's arms unfolded, and he used them like a conductor to a symphony. Precise and purposeful, he continued. "It has begun, the coming of a great time, the coming of the power of Holle! We have won over the Hollen people. Now we must win over the world! We have had difficult times, but you are its solution. You are the savior of our struggles! No longer do you obey the wills of others who have chained us for more than two scores. You are the conqueror, the rule breaker, the rule maker!" Alamgeer paused. The military force chanted in praise, hands raised in clutched fists.

"Machtig Holle! Machtig Holle!" The force of the army yelled in unity. The volume in Alamgeer's voice rose and fell to words like notes to music.

"As the symbol of the people, as the standard of the Hollen volk, for the sake of all who call Holle home, we will struggle and fight and never slacken, never tire, never lose courage, and never ever will we lose faith!" Alamgeer enchanted his soldiers. He brought life to the whole of Holle. Its people had purpose, desire, and love for their home. Alamgeer's speech lasted only ten minutes, but Iscariot had never felt so uplifted. The power of spoken word, the power of a united people, it was intoxicating in every way, from the flickering shocks of the nerves to the muscles, from the lightning bolts of stimulus to the brain to the chemical feel inside his very spirit.

"It's quite spectacular," he said to Hella.

"I still have more to show you," she said, taking his arm and locking it with hers once more. She walked with him amongst the soldiers who all knelt before her. With a soft spoken word, they muttered "Guttin" to which she said back to them, "Schutz." Goddess and protector, that was their relationship. Iscariot could see that this was truly a movement that ran deep in the core of the Hollen people.

Now, at the other end of the open room of the cavern, they approached a darkened corner, and to Iscariot's surprise, it was another stairwell. The stairway was lined in luminescent mosses, green and blue their hue. It was dark, yet the flow made the stairway safely visible to the naked eye. The stairwell was eminently warmer. Iscariot looked at Hella. She was her own light. Her diamond skin shined brighter, and the light that beamed from her projected onto the stone walls like the heavenly bodies that were affixed in the night sky, calming and wondrous.

Sweat began to bead on his forehead, and the temperature climbed the lower they went into the underground until, once more, they came upon another open dwelling within the cavern. His eyes were set upon them, the beasts born of fire and darkness. His heart raced a quick thumping, bumping pitter-patter. He became ever more certain he needed to do all he could to prevent the coming war. Fear once more struck his beating heart. It became anchored, falling to the depths of the sea.

The chained beasts had skin of cooled, cracked black magma, and visible within the crevasses of the monsters' skin was the lava that flowed through them. Ape-like their appearance, they towered at twenty-five feet, their teeth made of jet, their canines five inches long. The semi-quadruped behemoths had mammoth cuspidated claws upon their paws, and their roar shocked the body as it passed through the air. The creatures in front of him were unlike the anthropoids he had fought twenty years ago.

Those in the past were flesh and bone. What stood before him now were monstrosities, forged in the belly of hell. War and death were in the eyes of their soul. Who could control such titans? Iscariot thought. Who was the master of rage? His blue globes scanned the cavern of a thousand brutes until they found the tamer of the beasts.

"Who is that, there?" Iscariot pointed to a woman in a black veil with midnight hair and whose eyes sunk forever into the blackness. Her lips were like onyx, and her skin was a pasty white. Her arms, stomach, and legs were exposed. Her bust was modest, and freshly carved into her chest was the image of an eight-pointed star. This symbol was for a religion, an ideology, that was increasingly becoming the counter symbol to the Nazar, and more so to the Ivdeyskiy peoples. It was and still is a symbol of the power of God, but popular culture was swaying the symbol's meaning to that of anti-Ivdeyskiy. Extremist thought without tolerance of others was consuming the Califfe religion. She was a frightful fiend of ferocious dreams, a terror of torments in the dead of night. Her voice was quiet and seemed to ache, as if the wind had stolen her sound.

"My queen." The pasty woman bowed her head and put out her hand, palm up. Hella kissed her open hand.

"Iscariot, this is one of seven commanders of the anthropoid you see before you. Amber Bin-Amburgh, this is Iscariot Darroch." Iscariot politely put out his hand. Amber clasped his in a formal handshake.

"Nice to meet you," he said. Her eyes were stone cold, her face emotionless. She stared deep within his livid blues.

"Do you like them?" Amber asked of him.

"They're much different from what I remember," he answered.

"Some eugenics and gene splicing can go quite a long way," Amber answered. She walked over to one of the chained creatures, jumped upon its neck, and freed the beast from its collar. The titan roared, pounding his chest, declaring its dominance. Its yell immersed the cavern, tunneling into the crevasse of the ear. An animal it was, wild in its manner. Then, as a sudden shock, there came a spine tingling noise like metal grinding against metal. Eerie the sound that raised the hair on the skin. It came from the pale woman atop the monster's back, and the titan was calmed. Amber looked over toward Iscariot with a deadly expression.

"Kill him." The beast's molten red eyes glared at Iscariot. It pounded the ground below its feet. Petrifying was its growl, daunting its howl. Iscariot was stricken still as it charged at him. It was close enough to strike, its massive paw swung back, but then another sound came from its master. Hollow the voice, like the haunting tones of the whistling wind in the chill dark of a nightmarish horror. Iscariot could see the anger in the brute. Its eyes were a richer red. The cracks exposing the magma within it seemed to flow quickly inside its body. The beast got face down with Iscariot and boomed a blustering bellow of aggression toward him. Both the monster and the monster's tamer were grisly: a jolt to the nerves, a rattling of the senses.

"You look as pale as I do, Iscariot," Hella commented.

"That was ghoulishly unpleasant."

"Now imagine them on the battlefield. There are a thousand of them, all with the same anger and rage. Make sure your king knows of their presence," Hella instructed Iscariot. "Thank you for the presentation, Amber." Hella took Iscariot by the arm. "Come," she commanded, and the two walked away from the anthropoid animals.

"What are they?"

"They're called Affe. All their organs are grown. Their bodies are born from the lava that flows within this cavern, and as the body forms, we surgically implant the organs into the beasts," she answered.

"How do the organs survive?"

"We seal them with Ogon," Hella replied.

"They are like something out of Victor's lab. They're monsters."

"Victor's lab? As in the gothic novel?" she inquired.

"Yes, Victor Epstein's creation," he confirmed. Hella grinned.

"We started creating these, as you say, monsters, shortly after Alamgeer was put into office. We found a scientist named Prometheus Bin Deucalion. He is the father of the Affe, and its mother, the tamer, Margret bin Sanger. We've applied their ideologies throughout various species. We are quite happy with the results," she beamed.

They ascended up the cavern, traveling through the dim castle with guards at every door. High into the tower they went until they overlooked the city of Atma. "Do you remember what the city was like?" she asked Iscariot as they entered the room of the tower. Dark and vivid was the space, but glaring in from the small narrow windows were hands of light that circled the room.

"I do," he answered. They walked across the wood floors and the stone center piece. Hella placed her hand on a loose stone, and a hidden door came ajar. They stepped out to the world that was in front of them.

"Look at it now, Iscariot. The policies of that treaty have ruined us. Would you not do all you could to rise above this? Would you not sacrifice everything to get your people out of misery? Would you not go to war, Iscariot? We were once a land of hope and glory. Now we are the graveyard of an empire." Hella spoke with concern.

"Believe me when I tell you, I do not want this war to come. I have argued with my brother on this issue, and as I said before, I am here to ensure war does not happen. I have said from the beginning that the treaty is too harsh, and I can see with my eyes the truth in those words," Iscariot declared.

"The day after tomorrow, I will take you down into the streets of the city, and you can hear the words of the people, and you can see how they live. It is a true struggle for them. They do not live the lives of your people. In two days, you will see the truth of my words," Hella assured him. Iscariot's eyes crossed the length of the city. He saw its rot from above. The moody clouds in the sky matched the gloom of the city down below. Gray and dreary the clouds, so too the city, and as the clouds cried, Hella cried in words of anguish and sympathy for the Hollen volk.

The two talked a while until it was near time for lunch. They left the eagle's eye view of the city. Iscariot swore he could hear the room howl in a frenzy as he left the oval space with Hella. Descending the stairwell into the halls of the castle, together they entered the tea room. Its floors were of slate, the ceiling a painted masterpiece framed in elegant white clay that twisted and turned around the images with molded gold that accentuated the feathery flow of the white-framed design. Crystal chandeliers enveloped the hanging stalactites, giving sophistication to the rustic natural structure.

Iscariot took a seat in a wooden chair with blue seat cushions, flowing with gold and red stitched symbolic images of the country's past. The chair on which he sat had golden lion pommels whose faces roared. Hella took her seat in a similar chair. A small wooden table was between them, circular in shape with a painted image of the volcanic castle they resided in. Just as they had sat their bottoms on the elegant chairs, Alwine appeared with a silver tray, and atop it, a white teapot top with a golden cap painted with green and purple abstract images. The cups and saucers mirrored the teapot's design.

"Hallo, Queen Führer." Alwine greeted Hella as she placed the settings down onto the table. She poured the tea into the hand painted cups. "Enjoy Queen Führer, Master Darroch." She expressed her honor by kneeling and then exited with the silver plate in hand. Hella then began the afternoon's conversation.

"Tell me your history, Iscariot, your childhood, the summed story of your life."

"It's quite a long story."

"Just the highlights then. I'll start if you'd like," Hella offered.

"By all means." He gestured for her to tell her tale. Hella took a sip of her hot tea that steamed into the air.

"I was born and lived most of my life in Nikolaiviertel. I come from a wealthy family. I am the daughter of Albert and Mary Bathoryspeer. My father was an architect, my mother a caretaker for my brother and me. I am highly educated, a graduate from Kepler University. I had a very easy childhood. I met Alamgeer at a dinner party at my father's palace, and within two years' time, we married. My mother, brother, and father all died in the Great War. I became pregnant with my two sons at the end of the war, and shortly after, gave birth to them here in Atma. Nearly twenty years have passed as I have watched my husband struggle to move this country forward, to get it out of the dirt his and my father put it in. Most of my life has been easy and carefree, but these past twenty years have given me a new perspective on people and the world. I have, perhaps, become a little more cruel as I've seen what struggle is." Hella paused a moment.

"I'm sorry to hear of your parents and brother," Iscariot sympathized, knowing the pain of losing the people you love.

"Thank you, Iscariot. My brother died in battle. He was crushed by two boulders from an Adamah soldier." Her eyes began to swell as she spoke. "My parents—" her voice broke. "We were inside the castle walls when the raid began. The bombardment was horrifying. We—we were eating lunch when it happened. I remember looking out the window, a perfect view of the Speer River, and," her voice knotted, "in an instant, an explosion. I watched my father shred apart before me. I flew back into the white stone walls. I dug through the rubble, hoping my eyes deceived me, yet all I found was my mother who was caved in by the weight of the castle." She let drop a few tears from her eyes onto her cheeks.

"It was a Saoirse raid, wasn't it?" Iscariot asked, knowing it was, knowing the very raid that hadn't left her mouth, knowing the raid because his father was the one who organized it. Hella nodded

"It was the raid on Niko. It was the worst day of my life," she cried but quickly hid what tears had fallen. "I'm sorry. I didn't mean to cry."

"It's quite alright," Iscariot assured her. He was so taken by her story that he hadn't noticed Alwine had delivered meats, cheeses, and breads to the table. To ease her mind, he began to tell his tale. "Let me tell you my story, Hella. I was born of a poor family. My mother and father were farmers in the southern state of Blath. My mother died when I was ten. My father became king that same year she died. I hated that year. I missed my mother. I missed the simple life on the farm. I missed my friends when we moved to Aontu. I missed what I would never have again.

My father ended up sending my brother and me to separate schools in separate countries for two years, and when we came back, we were instructed to join the military. My brother and I never really had a say in what we did once our father became king. I loathed Aontu until the day I met my wife, Anna. She was my light; she was my phoenix. She pulled me from the ashes of the hellfire I burned in, and then, the day my son was born was the day she was taken from me, and back to the inferno I went. Soon after, my father died, and I was nothing but coals.

When I'm done here in Holle, I'm taking my son to Blath and living my days as I always wanted to, on the farm, selling crops and living a hard but simple life. Maybe, then, I'll be born again. Maybe, then, I'll have a phoenix story of my own." Iscariot fantasized aloud about his newfound dream.

"That sounds like a welcomed pleasantry, Iscariot. I hope that you continue to follow that path, and if it wavers, let it waver to a happy life," Hella expressed to him.

Guest and host talked a while longer until their meal was complete. Iscariot separated from Hella, thanking her for her hospitality. Iscariot, still tired from his late journey to Holle, went to his room. Alwine was close behind him. The room, a tangerine color from the light of the volcanic goo below him, was calming to the mind. A restful peace struck him. He draped his coat over an accent chair, slipped off his shoes, placing them next to the chair his coat hung on.

"May I help you sir?" Alwine asked.

"No, that's quite alright. I'm just going to rest my eyes for a bit. Can you wake me in an hour?"

"Of course, sir. Sleep well," Alwine said, leaving the room for Iscariot to slumber. In this hour he dreamt the words Enoch had spoken. He dreamed of the Affe. He dreamed of monsters that hadn't been seen for a hundred years—of the wicked and the damned. His mind dwelled on their fates. He remembered the Badb and his story, the darkness of the world, the words of Seanan. "It is so very sad when good people do nothing. The world goes dark as the baneful conquer the light."

Iscariot awoke. His heart raced from the delusion his mind conjured up at his time of rest. The door opened. He expected to see Alwine, but to his delight, his son entered the room.

"Hey Dad, Alwine told me you were in here. Is everything alright?" Hanns asked with concern.

"Yes, everything is fine, just relaxing for a moment."

"I'd wish I'd done the same. I'll sleep well tonight, as long as they don't have anything planned too early in the morning," said Hanns, already thinking of tomorrow.

"Don't hold your breath," Iscariot grinned. "Come in. Let's chat. How was your day?"

"It was interesting to say the least. I had an interesting conversation with the Khan," Hanns started.

"I did find his presence here, peculiar," Iscariot admitted.

"He said he was here to discuss aiding Holle, on how he wanted to rebuild his empire. He said he came to settle an agreement with Alamgeer. He never got into specific details, unfortunately."

"Intriguing—he didn't say what he expected out of Holle?" Iscariot asked, trying to answer his own question.

"Sorry, Dad, he did not," Hanns replied. "On another note, I met the strangest man, a stout fellow named Julius Gunther."

"I vaguely know him. He's on Alamgeer's board. What did you discuss with him?" Iscariot pried.

"Not much, really. He said he was the protector of the Ivdeyskiy. He seemed like a nervous chap."

"We might see him at some meetings we're invited to. Keep him close," Iscariot instructed.

"Yes, Father," Hanns replied and continued. "How was your day? What did you and Hella do? I don't think she has a true concept of time," he laughed.

"It was very eye-opening—frightening, really. They are prepared for war, son, and we must stop it at all costs. I so desperately don't want you to fight, Hanns. I don't want you to be like me, to lose friends, to see the brutality of man the way I have. They are not pleasant images to have captured in your mind." Iscariot's words sounded weary as he spoke to his son.

They talked some more of their day, and then the subject matter changed to family, sports, and even the weather, and in the father-son dialog, there came a tapping on the door. Alwine walked through the entryway.

"Master Darroch, Master Hanns, dinner will be served shortly. When you are both ready, I will guide you there." Hanns and Iscariot tidied themselves for the evening's meal and walked out the door together. They walked alongside Alwine and Hanns's servant girl whose name was Mallory.

They entered the same room they began in earlier in the day. The table was adorned with pure silver plates, spoons, knives, and forks. Pear-shaped wine decanters lined the table, sitting upon their own silver plates. The table settings were of silver elephants with obelisks on their backs, and etched into them was a history of those who resided in the Magma Krone. Along with them, white roses were at the seat of each person. In between the elephant decorative pieces were candelabrum that held six candles each and rose a foot and a half. Iscariot once more took his seat next to the führer. The meal before them was called the King's Feast: plates of Eisbein, bratwurst, weisswurst, leberkase, nornburger, knockwurst kessler, heaven on earth potatoes, kasespatzle, and sauerkraut. The sight of the savory meal was mouthwatering. The aroma filled the nostrils, sending pleasing signals to the brain. Iscariot's belly began to rumble, calling for the food to be consumed. The attendees at the supper were the same as those at the morning's meal.

They ate, and while they dined, they talked. Alamgeer had the ear of Iscariot.

"Did you think of my parting words to you from this morning?" Alamgeer inquired.

"I've had quite a bit to think about, Hidler."

"I'm sure you have," Alamgeer agreed.

"But to your question, I don't think my brother is the devil. He is only misguided," Iscariot gave answer.

"Have you thought about a vote, then? Impeachment? A vote of no-confidence?" Alamgeer insisted.

"We have no such votes since our leader is chosen by God," Iscariot informed him.

"Have you thought of a coup d'état?" Alamgeer persisted. Iscariot did not answer. "So, you have? Interesting." Alamgeer's fire eyes burned bold at his discovery. "We'll talk more of this another time. Let's enjoy our meal, shall we?" Alamgeer took a bite of the bratwurst that was skewered on his fork. Iscariot held Alamgeer's question in his mind, something to ponder in solitude while he finished eating the meal before him.

Minds devoured words for thought. Mouths ingested food for sustenance. The feast for a king concluded with a slice of chocolate cake and a hot cup of coffee. While eating dessert, Iscariot approached General Helfen of Avstrija and General Forradare of Danija. He asked how long they'd been at Magma Krone, how they enjoyed their time, and what their purpose was for their stay. Both replied similarly. Helfen and Forradare arrived on the same day, four days prior to Iscariot. Both seemed to have enjoyed their time at Holle. They viewed only parts of the city for informal lunch meetings or evening drinks with one another to discuss topics of the day or discussions they had earlier with Alamgeer. Both men were there for the same reason; both resided in Holle for a trade deal. They sought peaceful terms yet were of the mindset that they were child countries of Holle and owed the country a tremendous favor, as it was the mother country.

An interesting perception to hear, Iscariot thought. *Twenty years of independence, and the nations have fallen back into old ideologies, or was it corrupted from the start of the Hidler Nemtsov agreement?* His mind spoke, but his mouth never talked.

The hour was late—the coffee cups emptied, the plates of food cleaned. Iscariot rose to excuse himself from the attendees of the dinner. Alwine was quick to move to his side. Iscariot said his farewell and thanked the host and hostess for another delicious and bountiful meal. Iscariot turned to leave, and he was stopped by Alamgeer. The towering man placed his hand on Iscariot's shoulder. Fire met water, yet the water did not evaporate, and the flame did not extinguish.

"Before you leave for the evening, I wanted to give you something more to think about. Is Robert your true king? Perhaps the hammer wasn't placed at Hoba by your Creator. Think of your brother's actions, Iscariot. These questions and thoughts are my gift to you this evening. May your mind think on them with clarity, and may you find revelations into the questions I ask. Sleep well."

"Thank you, Mister Hidler. I will weigh your concerns in the balance of truth and righteousness. May they lean toward peace. Goodnight." Iscariot departed from the dining room and headed back to his room for a proper sleep and for his mind to rest and his body to restore much needed energy.

Just as Alwine helped Iscariot dress in the morning, she also undressed him for the evening—down to his underwear. He dismissed her.

"Thank you, Alwine. Go and rest yourself. I'm sure you have a busy day tomorrow." Iscariot discharged her. Alwine took his hand and kissed it before departing for the night.

"Goodnight, Master Darroch."

"Goodnight, Alwine." She left, and Iscariot showered to wash himself from the day's events. Cleaned, he dried himself with a warm towel. As he pulled the covers back to lay within his bed, there was a knock upon his door. *Alwine*, he thought. He grabbed his towel to hide himself. "Yes, Alwine?" he said in the tone to form a question, not opening the door.

"You have a delivery." The voice of a man was heard. Iscariot scanned the room for anything that could be used as a weapon. He grabbed a stone statue of a Hollen leader of the past and opened the door slowly.

"Can I help you?" he asked a burly man of tan skin and little clothes upon his body. The man was bald, and his body hair was shaven. There was another like him, both holding a rug.

Like bees to a hive, the alarm bells buzzed within his mind. Iscariot was ready to sting should those men be an enemy to him.

"We are here to deliver this rug," said the unclothed man.

"A rug? Why would I want a rug?" Iscariot asked, perplexed and cautious.

"A gift from the Führer," the man tried to explain. Iscariot let them proceed and watched as the two men unrolled the carpet. The rug was beautifully stitched of greens and purples with lines of gold within it. It had a flower or snowflake-like pattern. Iscariot wasn't certain, for his eyes were fixed on something else—something that was hidden within the rolled carpet and that now came to light.

Iscariot Chapter Six

Behold, thy woman fair, thou hast kitten eyes within thy looks, deep they traveled like spiraling hands of a galaxy with swirls of melted confection. Her feathered hair, an integument pattern of interlocking downy barbs that flowed like a river down an endless fall. Her Teeth of a color swan, that were an even shorn. Lips like scarlet thread, her voice was comely. Her neck a slender tower, built for an armory, a thick golden band shined around its elegance. Her cheeks, two halves of a pomegranate, thy breasts soft as cotton and firm as ripe fruit upon on tree. Bonny as the painted art, there was not a blemish to see. From first sight she ravished his heart. Behold Yuskita, woman of thine eye.

Awestruck he was. No voice left his larynx. *Who was she?* he thought. Iscariot heard the door close behind him. They were alone. He gazed upon her, still with confusion. Clothed in a tight garment, a kalasiris, her feet were bare, yet clasped around her ankles were two golden bracelets, and so, too, her wrists. As he looked at her eyes, he noticed they too were lined in gold. A smoldering glamor, an aureate composition, he had never been more entranced, and then she spoke. Drops of honeycomb were her words—honey and milk that left her tongue.

"Hello," she said to him, her cheeks turned red as cherries.

"Hello." Iscariot muscled out the word.

"I'm sorry to disturb you. Please forgive me, but I had to see you." Iscariot began to laugh. "What is so funny?" she asked him.

"Well, the very scene itself," he answered. Yuskita pursed her face. "What are you doing here?" he finally asked. Iscariot noticed her gaze did not meet his.

"Could you please put on something—more formal," she requested. Iscariot was still wrapped in a wet towel. He grinned.

"Of course." He met her request, letting his towel fall to the floor, gazing at her reaction, noting the shielding of her eyes. Gingham bottoms and shirt he put upon his body. "You may open," he said to her, and so she did. Seeing she was comfortable, her blushed cheeks of innocence soon vanished. "So, what is it you need to discuss with me? It seems you have taken great lengths to have these meetings discreetly. For what reason?"

"I mustn't be seen, for my actions are treasonous, and I am here to tell you that you've come here to negotiate with the wrong person," Yuskita began. Her words caught like a fly in a web. Iscariot listened. "Alamgeer seeks the east, the walled city, the Citadel," she stated.

"I am aware," replied Iscariot.

"Then I'm sure you have seen what I have seen: the assembly of his forces, the monsters that hide beneath us."

"I have," Iscariot answered.

"Where does Saoirse lie from here?" she asked.

"West."

"And who are the allies of Holle?" She asked another question.

"Danija and Avstrija."

"And where do they lie?"

"East of Holle, Saoirse to the west. What of it? Speak your point." Iscariot was looking for the purpose in the questions.

"I'll ask again, who are the allies of Holle?" She pointed to herself.

"The Islands?" He said with a hint of surprise. "We have no such intelligence."

"What I tell you is true. Your enemy is not to the east. Rather, your foe lies south. In secret, they wait for the signal to strike," she told him.

"Why do you tell me this? If I am your enemy, why let slip the secret of your nation?"

"What do you know of me, Iscariot?" Yuskita inquired.

"Very little," he replied. The two of them now sat in chairs at the far side of the room, overlooking the volcanic goop bubbling below, protected by the glass shield that gave boundary.

The narration of her tale she told.

"I am the child of the late Ahpay Nahchah, like my brother and current chief, Whey Nahchah. As you may know, my father died at the start of the war. Our country chose to remain neutral, a decision he and the elder members of our society agreed upon. Before my father died, he and the elders decided who should lead the future Heavohe. My brother was wild, stubborn, and paid no mind to authority. I was quite the opposite. They came to a decision, that should anything happen to my father, I would take up the chiefdom. No one thought my father would pass away so suddenly. He seemed in good health. He was active. Nor was he all that aged. His death came as a shock to all the islanders."

"I remember hearing of his passing. My father was rather concerned from what I recall," Iscariot noted and let her continue.

"When my father died, I was to take the seat, but being only ten, I was too young. My brother, five years my elder, held an interim role with the elders as his guide.

They thought they could control him, but one by one, the elders began to perish, and as I reached the age to lead, at fifteen, my brother denied me. It was then I was usurped. There were no elders to pull away his authority." She paused as Iscariot questioned her.

"What happened to them?"

"They died, presumably by natural causes, but I have come to suspect he killed them, and as they died, he replaced them with elders of his own. So, when I was of age, no elder questioned him or relinquished his reign."

"So how do I fit into this? What is your reason for visiting me at such an hour and in discretion?"

"If Heavohe is your enemy, let me be your friend," Yuskita said to Iscariot.

"And does my friend propose an action?"

"To me, your negotiations with Alamgeer have already failed."

"They have yet to begin," he informed her.

"When you realize they have failed and war is inevitable, what do you plan to do?" Yuskita inquired. Iscariot hesitated to answer. The boat of truth and lies rocked back and forth within his mind. The waves of truth would surely sway the boat to tilt upon its edge, yet would not falsities swing the boat onto its edge as well? He decided to ask a counter question.

"What do you know that you're not telling me?"

"Two weeks after your return, Heavohe will bomb Saoirse." She did not stutter. She did not hesitate. She answered with clarity and intent. Iscariot looked at her with grave concern. "If you want to save your people, if you want to prevent this war, tell me what you plan to do," she nearly demanded of him.

"With this information, why wouldn't I just inform my brother of your nation's intent?"

"Because it still leads to the very thing you are so desperately trying to keep from happening, and only I have a solution," she said matter of factly.

"And what is your solution?"

"I cannot tell you until you tell me of your intentions should you fail here with Alamgeer," she answered. He gave great thought to the words she spoke, and in his pensive mind, the crashing waves of truth calmed and righted the ship to sail on steady seas.

"Martial law will be declared, and my brother will be arrested." Iscariot let out the truth. Relief seemed to rise from Yuskita's eyes.

"I had to be sure," she said.

"Of what?"

"How far you were willing to go for your cause."

"So, what is it that you propose?"

"My proposal is this," Yuskita began. "If you plan to follow through with your coup, then let me help."

"And how are you to help? Will you stop your nation from attacking?"

"No, deception is everything for this to work," she informed him.

"Then what is your strategy?" Iscariot sought an answer.

"The invasion will occur, but I am its leader. No harm shall come to you or your people. We will arrive peacefully. Once we discuss your coup further, we can decide where we should be and how we can be of value in that matter. What I would like is for when I arrive with my soldiers in our mock invasion, my men and I will go back to Heavohe with your men at our side and dethrone the wicked chief I call my brother. There would be little risk when we return to Heavohe. It would be something truly unexpected for Whey," Yuskita concluded.

"So, none of my people die, and war with Alamgeer will cease from happening?" he asked.

Iscariot's grinding gears inside his mind turned with vigor. The gears connected to a single needle that moved upon a scale of right and wrong. Undecided on his choice, the needle stayed neutral, but in his manic thought, it swayed drastically from right and wrong. *Yuskita's words struck a bell of truth*, he thought to himself. Iscariot looked into her big doe eyes, and they struck him with sadness. She was a woman, lost, a woman whose destiny had been stripped away. In her eyes, he could see the slightest flame of hope, the smallest ray of light, the slimmest glint of happiness.

For just a second's time, his mind fell from the topic of discussion, and his eyes looked at her, her totality, her heart, her mind, her body. If this sad woman were so beautiful now, how might happiness make her glow like a thousand suns. Iscariot let the thought hex his very being.

"What say you?" Yuskita inquired, snapping Iscariot from his brief but very wonderful trance.

"I—I—" he fumbled with his words.

"Yes?" she said.

"I need some time. I'm sorry."

"I understand, I can give you until the end of the month."

"Thank you." He spoke genuinely.

"Well, I must be going. You have a lot to think about and little time to do so." Yuskita walked over to Iscariot, who still sat in his chair, overlooking the magma below. She knelt down before him, extending her hand with her palm facing upward. Iscariot kissed her palm as was the Heavohen way of both hello and goodbye. They locked fingers, their hands now clutched together. She moved the bond to her chest. Iscariot could feel her heart beat. Yuskita smiled at him.

"Goodnight, Iscariot."

"Goodnight, Yuskita," he said back to her. They rose together, hands still locked. They walked to the bedroom door. He opened it, and Yuskita walked through the doorway, breaking their bond. Her guards now beside her, she stepped into a large sack, as if it were laundry, and they went away to her room. Iscariot closed the door when the guards turned the corner, and he could no longer see them.

Alone in the sunset room, his eyes were once again weary. He removed the shirt he had put upon himself for the sake of Yuskita and left the soft trousers to linger on his legs. Iscariot pulled back the sheets and slid into them. Tucked into bed, he closed his eyes, for they were weighted. Like anchors on a ship, it sails in the sea of the day, hoisted to the sky, but as the night falls, so, too, the anchor of his eyes. The ship, he Iscariot, lay in the ocean of his bed and slept.

While he slumbered, he heard a tapping, rapping—he thought it might be the Raven on the windowsill. The anchors of his eyes pulled up to start the day, his ocean blues awoke to a charming face.

"Sorry to wake you, sir, but I have come to inform you that you have a lunch today with the generals of Danija and Avstrija." Alwine spoke softly to his freshly awakened ears.

"Why wasn't I informed about this yesterday?" Iscariot spoke with the raspy broken tones of a voice that slumbered in the night behind the cave of his mouth.

"Alamgeer only thought of the meeting this morning, and wanted me to inform you," she answered.

"What time is it, Alwine?"

"Eight in the morning," she responded. If you're rising for the day, I can have breakfast prepared for you." Now fully awake like the sun exposed above the horizon, he rose from his bed.

"That would be great, Alwine. Thank you."

"Will you be dining in your pajamas, or will your attire be different?" she queried.

"What do you recommend?" Iscariot sought her thought.

"It is probably best to change."

"Alwine, am I able to have breakfast here in my room instead?"

"Of course, sir."

"Is my son up?"

"I believe he is."

"Can you see if he'd like to have breakfast with me, here?" Iscariot requested.

"Certainly." Alwine quickly left, and as quickly has she had left, she returned. "He will be here shortly. The breakfast this morning is sausage, musli, and spätzle with applesaft, coffee, or tea." Alwine listed the menu.

"It sounds delicious. Thank you, again, Alwine."

"You are most welcome, Iscariot. I will be back shortly with your meals." She left Iscariot to himself.

Entering through the doorway was a man, who, to Iscariot's eyes, was made of light. The man, his son, he loved like the warmth of day. Iscariot welcomed him delightedly, embracing his body to feel and share his affection, from one heart to another. Then, another knock to the door arrived with fragrances to make the mouth salivate. They conversed as they ate of aromatic meats, luscious sweets, and pleasant drinks. They talked of the day's events to come—a city tour, a meeting of minds, one seeming more interested than the other. They enjoyed each other's company and devoured the food. They parted with one another in the love of father and son, a farewell till when the sun had set and the meal of the evening was served.

Iscariot showered, and Alwine helped him dress once more in black trousers that grew tighter down the legs, tapering as they traveled. She put on his torso a white oxford of the softest cotton, tucked and pressed. There was no tie around his neck, but atop his head of long locks rested a top-hat. It was a signature style of the Saoirse culture. His black shoes clicked as they struck the stone floors of the cavern, and they were patterned with blooming flowers daisied on its edges. His black belt was simple and clasped in silver.

"What of a jacket?" Iscariot asked, knowing the nip of the air was frigid as it stung the skin.

"You brought a topcoat, did you not?" Alwine asked, knowing he did. Iscariot didn't answer, as Alwine was already retrieving the jacket for him. "I'll carry this until it's time to leave the castle." With the topcoat in hand, she handed him a red scarf. "You can carry this." He looked at the scarf with some confusion.

"This isn't mine."

"I know, but it goes well with the outfit I chose for you. You are dressed in all black. You will see you are surrounded by a world of gray.

This will make you stand out amongst those you are with." Iscariot took her advice, and together, they left the warmth of the room, then the heat of the castle, only to be embraced by the harsh cold grip of winter's frightful freeze.

A carriage pulled by two horses approached. It was bulbous in shape. It was all black with red accent lines, handles made of silver, candle lantern of the same metal and small decorative pieces that crowned the wagon. The valet opened the carriage door, and much to Iscariot's delight, the cabin was invitingly warm.

"So where are we off to? I never asked," Iscariot questioned Alwine.

"The Orlando Hauz," she said.

"Have you eaten there before?"

"I have."

"What do you recommend, or rather what is their best dish?"

"The kase-burger is my favorite."

"Really? Such a simple thing." He had expected something of more sophistication.

"It's world changing. You won't be disappointed," she guaranteed.

"Kase-burger it is, then." He smiled and realized how beautiful she was for the afternoon. Though she was only a servant, her dining wear was quite ingratiating: a floral lace, long-sleeved black cocktail dress with a boat neck adorned her body. Alwine's lips were painted black as was the shadowing of her eyes. The black dress contrasted magically with her pale skin and bleach-blond hair. "You look very nice, Alwine."

"Thank you, Master Darroch. It was a gift from the Queen Führer," she mentioned as she examined herself. Iscariot could see the slightest hint of a bashful beauty, holding back a witty remark, and looked out the carriage windows.

The scene was not a pleasure to the eye. Buildings were worn and tattered—broken stone and brick. Streets were a littered mess, and the city showed its distress. A frown across his face, he turned back to something more pleasing and far more enchanting.

"Sad, is it not?" Alwine asked.

"I have never seen a city fall so quickly."

"I have never known anything else." The comment from Alwine caught Iscariot off guard, and the statement was obvious. *How unfortunate,* he thought.

The horse and carriage soon came to a stop in front of a six-story building of white, gray, and maroon. It, like few others, still had gold letters and pieces of art on its facade. The front of the building had three arching entryways. At the building's center, from the second to the fourth floor, was a small stone balcony, and above it in golden letters read the name of the restaurant, Orlando Hauz. Their carriage door was opened. Alwine exited first with Iscariot at her tail.

"How does the restaurant still exist?" Iscariot asked.

"Almost all the restaurants and shops that are still open are because of the wealthy who can still afford to go to them. Otherwise, shops and restaurants would be just an idea, nonexistent to the Hollen culture," Alwine informed him. Iscariot and Alwine walked through the arches and into the restaurant. It was charming inside the haus. White, gold, and soft blues were the primary colors of the building's interior. Fine tables and chairs were spread throughout the rooms. Chandeliers hung high from every ceiling in every room. It became ever more clear that only the prestigious could dine in such a place.

Iscariot and Alwine were guided by a hostess to a table marked reserved. As they took their seats, Helfen and Forradare approached the table. Iscariot quickly rose to greet them. They sat once more, and drinks were ordered. Beer, auriferous in color, rested in glass chalices. Bubbles rose from the bottom of the glass, aired in the light, uniquely hypnotizing. Iscariot sipped the golden drink. His taste buds absorbed its flavor of pine and florals as it filled his mouth. The drinks helped loosen tongues, and chatter made its way about the table.

Helfen began telling tales of war, of blood and dirt and sweat, of moments of extreme stress and absolute boredom, of beautiful streets turned to rubble, of great pastures transformed to mud and ash and unsightly colors. Forradare talked of the reasons to fight, the reasons to give life for life, to give life for ideals. Of the Great War their voices articulated the clearest memories. Iscariot listened to hear their words and imagined their spoken words on a reel within his mind, and he came to realize he fought in the very battle Helfen commanded. It was just prior to the Battle of Erbil in the Yisra city called Iveysalem.

It was a three-day battle, both armies stuck in their positions. For if the enemy advanced, they would have a clear path to the Citadel, and if Iscariot's allied army succeeded, they would surely push the enemy outside of modern-day Yisra. Iscariot held his tongue as they talked about his friends being slaughtered, as they laughed about the fourth deadliest battle of the war. Iscariot could no longer take their arrogance and sought to advance the conversation to its true purpose. Their meals came rushing out and were set before them, and he asked them in the transition what it was they sought.

"We seek treaty with Saoirse," said Forradare.

"I don't understand. We are nations in good standing with one another. We have fair trade agreements and have been at peace. For what reason do you seek this?" Iscariot asked with concern but held back his judgment.

"That is true, and that is why we seek to continue those terms. We are in agreement that Alamgeer will seek peace with Saoirse. However, to us, it seems Yisra will still be a target for him. We seek a treaty of no interference while this occurs and a continuation of our trade deal," said Helfen.

"This is a request that requires the King of Saoirse. If you were to draw up a treaty for me to give to King Robert, we might be able to come to a compromise. But I do say that it is rather bold." Though he increasingly disliked the men in front of him, he thought it best to keep the peace if peace could be had with a stroke of a pen rather than the stroke of a blade.

The afternoon soon slipped into the evening. The sun lowered and the temperature with it. Those at the table said their goodbyes. Out into the frigid air and streets of glowing fire they went where the carriage waited for Iscariot and Alwine. Inside the comforts of the carriage, they talked of the morrow and what it would hold.

"A day of celebration," said Alwine. "A feast for the volk, of bier and food and game and song," she continued. "A place where the stranger becomes family if only for a night." She then looked at Iscariot with speculation in her eyes. "Do you have lederhosen?"

"Those leather shorts?" he asked for confirmation.

"Yeah, those are it."

"I do not."

"Well then, I shall go and get you a pair."

"That isn't necessary."

"If you don't want to look ridiculous, then you will have me get you a pair," Alwine smiled. Iscariot smirked at the young girl.

"Here then." He gave her money from his wallet.

"I already have your measurements. I will have it for you in the morning." Such innocence in a corrupt world, in a broken city. To Iscariot, it was pleasant to see it in such a place as Holle.

They approached the Magma Krone. Iscariot shuddered as the carriage went past the guards who stood tall and were like death at the ends of the Bridge of Meister. Iscariot went inside the castle alone. In his room, he disrobed. He declined the call for tea. Hours later, he shooed away the call for dinner. Instead, he sat at a small desk inside the room and wrote of all that had occurred in just two short days. He closed his journal and then penned a digital letter. In an encrypted nature were the contents. The addressees of the message were Antony and Andre: "We have more friends than you may think...."

Iscariot Chapter Seven

'Round the axis, 'round the sun—it spun at 1,040 miles per hour
as it hurtled through space and time. Slung by a trebuchet and held in
orbit by the mighty hand of the yellow orb of fire, the days and nights
moved with gusto. 86,400 seconds moved at the speed of light, while the
power of the sun swung the ball of the earth at a velocity of 67,000 miles
inside a given hour. It was almost mechanical, as if designed, ever
constant.

The earth had spun from the shadows of space to bask in the
warmth of the light of the sun. It was morning, and Iscariot rose to greet
it. A knock on his door, and Alwine entered in a dress called a dirndl. The
ensemble was a light purple close-fitted bodice with a soft purple and gold
ribbon crossing up her torso. Under her breastline and pulling over her
shoulder was a rumpled design strap with yellow flowers and white polka
dots. A lavender bow was wrapped around her waist and seated on her
left side. The skirt was the color lilac and a rich forest green that was
patterned with vines and flowers. Her bosoms were lifted by the outfit,
her bleach-blond hair like rolling hills, her lips a soft peach. If beauty were
held in the eye of man, then every man held her, for not one dared glance
away. Alwine smiled at Iscariot, for he gaped at her fairness.

Noticing that he had been staring, he greeted her good morning.
"You look lovely."

"Thank you," Alwine blushed. "I have your outfit here. You'll
look just like a Hollen man."

"I don't doubt it," he remarked, heading to the restroom to
quickly wash himself.

He entered the room with nothing but his underwear on his
behind. Alwine showed him a pressed ivory long-sleeved shirt with brown
and red buttons. "Put out your arms," she instructed, helping him put on
the garment.

Soft and airy, Iscariot thought.

"Now are the lederhosen." Alwine knelt down, holding the leather
shorts open for Iscariot's legs to go through. She ensured his shirt was
tucked into the leather shorts and his belt with a holden buckle, properly
clipped. She then handed him thick brown shin-high socks with two

crimson stripes at the top and put them on his leg. "Put out your arms again," she told Iscariot, and he did so. She put on him a fitted vest, the color of oxblood. Lined down the vest's center were eight golden buttons and stitched cardinal red pockets, one on the right breast, the other two down toward the hips. Alwine then tied the laces of the worn boots Iscariot wore and topped his head with an alpine hat that had a red rope wrapped around it.

"So schon," she blushed. "You look like us Hollen volk now."

"Thank you, Alwine." Iscariot looked at himself in the mirror, stunned that he looked as sharp as he did.

"Ready for breakfast?"

"Very much so. I'm starved."

Out the door they walked. They ran into Hanns and his servant girl, Mallory. His son looked wickedly swank. His leather shorts were charcoal in color with light yellow trim of patterned leaves. A light, soft yellow, long-sleeved floral shirt and a dark, blood-red vest with blinding gold buttons pressed to his chest. He did not wear a hat but instead had styled his hair in a traditional Hollen way, which resembled that of a pompadour.

"Lookin' good, my son." Iscariot wrapped his arm around Hanns's shoulder. Hanns smirked at his father.

"You don't look half bad yourself," Hanns joked.

"Yea, Alwine fixed me up real nice. Made me look like a real gentleman," Iscariot grinned, then turned to Alwine and gave a wink. Bashful she was, rosy turned her cheeks.

They entered the dining room. All the young servant girls were dressed in traditional dirndls, all fair in their own way, yet the fairest of them all was Hella. Her skin glistened like rays of the morning sun in the rippled lens of water waving on the surface of a lake. The flats she wore on her feet were as dark as the moonless sky, her dirndl of the same blackness; it bounced and swayed as she moved. The magic of her white dazzling skin was hypnotizing to the human eye. Under her dirndl, she wore a sheer lace, black floral top. Hella's hair was pulled back into a bun with her hair braided, crowning her head. Inside her braided crown were pink flowers, the color of her eyes. She had two strands of hair that fell to the left and right of her face as if to draw each person's eyes to meet hers. The hairstyle almost reminded Iscariot of a popular hairdo back home.

To Hella's right, her husband, Alamgeer. His lederhosen were of gray and silver. His shirt was not visible to the eye, as he wore a gray wool Bavarian jacket that was stitched in the shape of diamond on its front and back. Eight leather buttons lined the front of his stylish jacket. He too wore a slate-colored Alpine hat—only his had a red feather fanned from it. His calves exposed, the muscles were flexed, defined, and powerful. They looked like sculpted stone and as strong as stone themselves. His eyes were a softer flame. He welcomed Iscariot and his son.

"It's a very nice jacket you're wearing," Iscariot complimented him.

"Thank you, it was hand stitched for this festival. It's quite soft, as the wool was just taken off the sheep's back." Alamgeer praised its quality.

"Hella, you look magical this morning," Iscariot said with flirtatious eyes.

"Thank you, Iscariot. You look handsome yourself." She returned the compliment. "The meal will be rather light this morning. I hope you don't mind. We'll be sure to overindulge at the festival," she informed him. All within the room conversed, but Iscariot's tongue was still when he was struck by such majesty.

She entered. Her sable feathered hair surrounded her like a mane, shaping and framing her astonishingly facial symmetry. In her ebony locks were the tiniest of white sunflowers and roses. Around her forehead there was a golden headband. Her eyes were lined in gold, her lips painted gilt to compliment both her eyeliner and circlet. Her dirndl was a royal violet with gold buttons under her bodice. She wore no blouse. Instead, to cover her bristols, she wore a revealing armored bra of gold that twirled like coiled springs, leaving part of the breast exposed but covering the mammilla, accentuating the embonpoint of her bust. The flats on her feet were black with white ribboned lace.

Stupefied by the radiance of her ravishing splendor, he was inaudible, immobile, subdued by the curves of her frame and the lines of her face. She approached him, putting out her right hand, her palm open. Unconsciously, Iscariot mimicked the movement. Their hands connected; their fingers locked together. She pulled their bonded hands to her chest, to feel her beating heart.

"Hau. Good morning, Iscariot."

"Dia dhuit, Yuskita." He spoke his native tongue, too entranced by her beauty. His mind did not connect that she would not understand the words that came from his mouth.

"Does that mean good morning?" Yuskita asked. Slowly coming back from his hypnosis, he answered.

"I'm sorry. It's a formal greeting in Saoirse. It means hello." Iscariot paused and grinned. "Its full translation means, God be with you."

"Wakan takan kici un." Yuskita brought their hands to meet Iscariot's chest.

"What does that mean?" he whispered, and she answered.

"May the Maker bless you." Yuskita released her grip.

All within the room sat at the table, same as the day before, with the same people in the same seats. Not much of substance was discussed. Hella was teaching Iscariot popular songs that were sung at Volkfest. Iscariot's singing voice was not the fairest at the table, which made for some jesting, bringing laughs to all watching his failure. He himself laughed at his own struggle.

While at breakfast, Iscariot would glance over at Yuskita, and her eyes would flirt back with his. The meal was light. Hearts were light. Iscariot rather enjoyed the morning and looked forward to a carefree day and learning more of the country and culture at the biggest, oldest, and most celebrated festival of the Hollen people. Stomachs content, they departed from the dining area.

Iscariot found his way over to the library inside the Magma Krone. It was one of the most bizarre, the most unique, and one of the most gorgeous personal libraries he had ever seen. The walls waved like the sea and rolled like the hills. Carved into its rocky surface were stories of stars. It was as if the designers of the room etched the walls and ceilings in such a way that the luminescent algae fell into the crevasses the artist created. So, when the eyes befell the room, it would click in the mind in awe and wonder, and the mind would yearn to seek truth. The heart would covet poetry, and the spirit would long for discovery and adventure. This and more sparked within Iscariot. His feet stood on stone floors that were an image of the earth, and where the ocean should be, mirrors, and the mirrors reflected the tales of the heavens from the ceiling above.

His heart excited, his peepers peered onto a book of poems and prose. He opened the leatherbound book he held within his hands. The title read The Kernel of a Helicoid Heart, and his eyes saw, his mind thought, his heart felt, and his body reacted with hair-raising chills. There was an ecstasy prompted from the words in the text, striking a feeling so complex, so bewildering, an emotion that builds other mental states to their highest potential, a sensation that brings out the very best in man, to make him go beyond what he believes he can achieve, an emotion so magical and whimsical that people sacrifice all they have for it.

This emotion is the seed, and as it grows, branches of the tree create kindness, sympathy, charity, patience, diligence, humility, chastity, selflessness, faith, and hope. This feeling of man is the root of man, his very core. It is his very being, and as Iscariot read those heartfelt words, water fell from his sky blue eyes. He had never been so moved. He had never felt such sadness, such beauty, nor such joy or happiness as he felt from the enchanted words that marked the pages of the book within his hands. It was music to the human heart, truth to the human spirit. It was love.

A hand touched his shoulder in the dim light of the algae-starred room of knowledge. He dried his eyes and turned, and once more, he wept. For the woman before him was his wife. Falling to his knees, he was stricken in disbelief. She knelt down beside him.

"Iscariot, why do you weep?" she asked him.

"I weep with gladness to see your face," he answered. "How are you here? How is this possible?"

"I am here because you willed it so."

"A dream then?" His words were filled with grief. He rose, as did she, and he looked at her with longing eyes. He put his hand upon her cheek and leaned in to kiss her lips. His heart raged in fire; their lock was broken. He looked deep into her honey-colored eyes and brought her into his chest. He could feel her arms wrapped around him. The clouds burst, and it rained once more.

"Goodbye, Anna. I love you." His chest ached as he spoke those solemn words. Iscariot closed his eyes, and Anna was no more.

His oculus blues opened once more, stunning the woman in his view. With concern in her eyes, she asked him a question.

"Iscariot, are you alright?"

"I am fine. Just remembering a life I once had, and is now time for me to let go of the hold I had upon it." There was a sorrow in his tone.

"Can I help ease the pain?" Yuskita asked with sincerity.

"Your presence is healing enough." Iscariot could see her caramel skin flush as he said the words. His heart could feel her warmth from the look in her eyes, and he smiled, for bliss was upon him when he was with her.

"I'm glad I am able to help. If you need an ear to talk to, I will listen." Her kindness reminded Iscariot of Anna.

"Yuski," he said her name softly.

"Yes?"

"Would you meet me here after the festival today? I'd like to get to know you better." Iscariot could see glee in her brown eyes.

"What time?"

"Does nine post meridiem sound alright?"

"It sounds perfect," she replied. Iscariot felt some solace in her answer.

"Shall we get going?" He put out his arm, which Yuskita took, and they walked the halls of the volcanic cavern to the entrance of the castle.

Horse-drawn carriages trotted in front of the Magma Krone, a total of four. One was a coach of black and gold, another of purple and gold, the third of red and gold, and the last a buggy of all white. Outside the crimson doors, already waiting, were two generals, Hanns and Möngke Khagan, along with their servants. After only a moment had passed, Alamgeer and his wife came to the front of the castle.

"Good afternoon." Hella greeted them with a curtsy. The valets dismounted from their stage and opened the doors to their carriages upon the führer and the queen führer's arrival. The servant girls, without instruction, entered the ivory carriage, sitting all six comfortably.

"Generals, Hanns, why don't you three take the black and gold wagon? Yuskita and I will ride together in the violet coach; and Möngke, Iscariot, and Ala can ride together in the red carriage," Hella instructed, rather than suggesting.

With slight disappointment, Iscariot released Yuskita from his arm and entered the elegant carriage of red and gold. The outer appearance of the coach was that of scales of a dragon, and the bottom of the carriage doors were gold-plated wings that were used as footsteps to get into the wagon. The wings were drawn back and partly wrapped around the back wheels. The top was crowned with a trim of gold and decorated with gems and rubies. The coachmen sat, pitched on the coach box, and in front of him was the head of the golden dragon whose eyes were fire lanterns with flames eight inches high. The breed of horse that pulled the carriage was called a Breton. They were broad of shoulder, chestnut in color—strong, muscular, a flaxen mane and tail, and a short neck well tucked into its muscular withers. Its legs were well feathered. It was a horse that spoke of power and wealth. The interior was of cherry wood with a red and black patterned print rug. Its seats were of the finest brown leather and its ceiling of fine crystals. The whip of the rope struck the horses, and the coach began to move. The clattering of the wheels and of the heels hitting the surface of the streets echoed down to the gates and into the city.

Unlike the day before, outside the castle gates and over the Meister Mennatur Bridge, the rumored city of ruin did not strike Iscariot. The homes and shops looked pleasant to the eye. Minor blemishes that could easily be concealed, cracked sidewalks, overgrown plants, flaky paint work—there was nothing that spoke of a depression or a struggle of a people. The citizens that roamed the streets were dolled up in their best dress to attend Volkfest. They looked ecstatic and overjoyed with laughter and smiles on their faces. Iscariot's spirits rose at their sight, getting ever more excited for the thrills of the festival.

"Hidler" Iscariot began, "Do my eyes deceive me? This is my third venture into the city, yet I do not see your signs of struggle, where are your crumbling buildings, your broken people. Were my eyes fooled?"

"That is because you have not yet traveled into the city. We are still within two miles of Magma Krone. Here, people of government, corporations, and churches reside. Here live the men and women that keep Holle from sinking into hell. Here are the people that keep Holle from being a footnote in the tales of history. Here are the people that keep this nation on its feet to fight for a new day, a new Holle. What you seek you will find, Mister Darroch. Then, you will see your eyes did not deceive and why it is we are willing to sacrifice everything and fight for our survival," Alamgeer explained.

It wasn't long before Ala's words were true. Iscariot's eyes did not lie from what he saw in days past. How abandoned the city looked. It was weathered and worn, covered in soot that rain could not wash away. There was no green of trees or colored blossoms hanging in flower boxes. The world was brown, gray, and black. It was lifeless. How dreadful was the thought of Iscariot. They rode further into the city and began to see the people of Atma. The people seemed to stand in line a mile long. Eyes dead and hallowed, some still held some lingering hope while others showed the grit and grind of the struggle. The sign over the store they passed read Suppe, Brot un Kartoffels.

"What does that banner say?" Iscariot asked.

"The sign reads, 'Soup, bread and potatoes,'" Alamgeer replied. Iscariot looked at the queue of people standing, waiting to be fed. His heart was a mix of sadness and anger, for in the line, in tattered clothes and unwashed faces, were men, women, and children—some as young as two. Iscariot swore he even saw an infant in such tragic circumstances. As they rode by the distressing scene, the men, women, and even the children saluted the coach as it went by. On bended knee with an outreached hand, they praised him.

Suddenly, to Iscariot's surprise, Alamgeer rose from his seat and opened the carriage door. Still in motion, he saluted back to them with a raised clutched hand, saying, "Praise those who serve!" Alamgeer then closed the door of the carriage, and they headed deeper into the city, and here his eyes saw grief, and his beating thumper felt heartbreak for those he did not know and would never know, for before him were acres of tents—makeshift homes and families living in boxes. Those who were out of their would-be homes and saw the coach, saluted.

"Stop the carriage," Alamgeer commanded the coachman, and the driver followed his order. Alamgeer exited the wagon and walked into the dirt and mud and trash and into the borough of box homes. He found a platform to stand upon. He cleared his throat and began to speak.

"Meine Holle!" Alamgeer yelled.

"Unser Holle!" the people hollered back.

"Come and feast with me this day! Come and fill your bellies. Come and drink to our future! Your meal and your drink will come from me, your Führer and your Queen Führer. We will hand you a ticket. Please, do not lose it. Come and fill your bodies with sustenance. Come and ease your minds, for we must be ready. We must be strong, for we must change the world, and that change begins with you. The time is close, my fellow Hollen volk. Will you fight with me?" Alamgeer called to the crowd.

"Kempf!" the people yelled.

"In this struggle, in this rubble, we will rise like the Phoenix, and once more, the Hollen people will be praised. Once more, Holle will be the light of civilization. Ick liebe dich!" he shouted, and the people responded, "Haben Ala!"

Hella came from her carriage and handed out the promised tickets. All the people knelt in salute. Back to the coach the führer and queen went. Alamgeer raised his hand once more with a clutched fist, and the people hollered, "Hail Hidler!" The carriage door closed to the chants, and the wagons once more headed to the festival.

The difference from where they were to where they stood was night and day—from the ashes of despair to the lights of prosperity—one a lifeless death, void of color, and the other a spirited life, full of pigments blushed with colors of the rainbow, stretched across the bare blue sky. Iscariot walked through the archway of green shrubs and colorful flowers and a banner that read Willkomenen Zum Volkfest. Carriages of barreled beer were scattered throughout the grounds. The tents were forty feet tall and forty meters wide and as deep as fifty meters. The tents were vivid and variegated, each different than the one before it. They flashed with windows and toppers and over-the-top decor. Their interiors were just as stunning. Some mirrored the sky with walls like the towns of old Holle. Others had chandeliers made of flowers with glass ceilings to make visible the stars outside. Another was as green as the thickest forest with golden lights high upon its ceilings, traveling down every row. Every tent was filled with food and drinks and song and laughter. The atmosphere was intoxicating with jubilant peoples escaping the strife, grateful for a day to forget their worries and live carefree, if only for a day.

Outside the magnificent tents were rides that soared to the sky with blinking jazzy lights, and there were games of all sorts. From shooting to tossing, there were prizes to be won and fun to be had.

Iscariot took a seat at a table inside of a tent of yellow and blue ribbons that looped and crossed the entire ceiling. Möngke took a seat next to him, and on the seats across from him sat Hella, Yuskita, and a woman he did not recognize.

Her lips were like tangerine, her hair the shade of sunset, her eyes lined in shades of green, deep and rich like moss on a tree—confident they were when gazed upon. Her dirndl was the same shade as her eyeliner, patterned in white ribboned stripes. The heels she wore were also moss in color. Her neck was lined in pearls; so too her wrists. A dashing, perky woman, she introduced herself. Her voice was a sharp contrast to her appearance.

"Hello. Meine name is Francis. You must be the handsome Saoirse man, Iscariot."

"You presume correctly. You're quite the chipper lass," said Iscariot.

"Look here, warrior man. I may be ostentatious and perhaps a bit charismatic, but I assure you, my dear, I am, by no means, chipper." Francis corrected him as only she could do. Taken aback by such fortitude, he couldn't help but laugh and grin.

"I have been rectified. I apologize," said Iscariot.

"To make it up to me, a beer would be nice," she teased.

"A beer it is, then."

"I see I do not need to make introductions," Hella chimed.

"Of course not, beautiful. I have no trouble speaking for myself." Francis spoke with great charisma.

After just two minutes with a bombastic personality, Iscariot turned to a person of a very different manner. A man, quiet and calm, though he shared the same resplendent fashion style as Francis—the two could not be more different. To Iscariot's amazement, the Khan was dressed in traditional Hollen wear, though he added a flare of his own to the costume. The boots on his feet had upturned toes, and he wore a hat with a brim folded up, encircling his head. His legs exposed, they radiated a rustic gold. The patterns on his legs from which the energy within him shined, was as if God had carved upon his skin the art within heaven. His forearms bare, they glimmered of the same design. Resting on the right of his hip was a golden band that locked with the band wrapped around his wrist. When the two bonds connected with one another, it formed a curved sword made of the energy that came from Möngke's body, mind, and spirit.

When the two men talked, Iscariot learned what his son had told him was true. Möngke talked of strengthening his country with an agreement with Holle, Danija, and Avstrija. They had just signed the paperwork yesterday, and today was a day of celebration for their future relationship with one another. He made it clear that should either side abuse his people or abuse his kinds that they would surely suffer the Mongnolerium might. Iscariot knew of their power and abilities all too well from firsthand accounts from the Great War.

A full pint down, Iscariot moved his conversation from Möngke Khagan to Francis and Yuskita. Neither he nor Yuskita were able to get much of their own words in, though he didn't mind listening to looser tongues, for they sometimes had more information than intended. To his dismay, he did not get such lucid details from Francis, or so he thought. She merely praised Alamgeer's efforts the past few years. How he was able to bring together people of all walks of life for a common goal, a restored Holle—a nation of one people, a pure people, a standard for the world to strive and uphold. When she was done singing of Ala's glory, she turned to film and fashion, and the stories they told and the symbolism behind some of Holle's designers. Francis then combined all the topics together saying, "Can you imagine? Can you see it? Such a wonderful place of art, power, and sophistication—a place I now faintly remember, a place my parents and their generation ruined for the Great War." Her voice held both hope and woe.

Another pint down the gullet, he soon found his gracious host, who was in song as the band played at the center of the tent they resided in. Knowing the words to the song, he joined in the carol. The music changed, and they sang to the changing tune. Their cantillating voices ceased, and they began to talk, and their chat turned to politics and war and what they would like to see from each other's nations. Of leadership they spoke—of treaties and trade, of the past and the people who led it into the present—the flaws of its commanders and how to change the flaws to bring about a brighter future, a new order, one that is vastly different from that of their fathers. They talked about their fathers—how they loved them and hated them, how they never felt like what they did was ever good enough. The enemies bonded, and their night was coming to a close.

Iscariot made his way to the carriages that were awaiting him and those he came with. He opened the buggy door, and to his eyes' delight, an angel was before him.

"Yuskita," he beamed.

"Iscariot," she glowed. "You seemed to have had a good time."

"Very much so," he answered. "Are we moving?" he was slightly startled. Yuskita glanced out the window.

"It appears so."

"Our private coach. How nice." The two sat side by side, thigh to thigh. Eye to eye they communed in the night. They shared their likes and dislikes. Tongues rattled of customs of their own, which led to talks of their home. His heart felt at ease with her. A misplaced hand to adjust his position—it fell on top of hers. She did not shoo it away or pull hers from below his. She displayed only the slightest grin and the gentlest of tint on her cheeks.

As they went through the city, they spoke of the horrid living standards of the people of Holle. He admitted in a roundabout way that he was becoming swayed by her proposal. They planned what they could do, but before much detail was shared, they were at the gates of the Magma Krone. Unconsciously, Iscariot grabbed her hand and helped her from the carriage. Their hands locked together, they walked into the castle through the dark and mystic cavern halls, to the foot of the doorway to Yuskita's room. She looked up to him and he down to her. Their bodies pushed close together. Iscariot's heart pounded in his chest with fervor. He brought his head down to her, and she raised herself up to him, standing on her toes. Their lips met and held.

Upon release, Iscariot's mind flew to seventh heaven and landed on cloud nine. His muscles were shocked and struck with nerves of joy. He was beside himself. He had not felt such happiness in nearly twenty years. Blood rushed to his cheeks; he could see it rushed to hers as well. His mouth grew wide with glee. Their hands untangled from each other's. Yuskita looked into his baby blues.

"Goodnight, Iscariot."

"Goodnight, Yuskita." She entered through the door and closed it behind her. Iscariot made his way to his room, stripped himself of his clothes, and let sleep overtake his waking mind.

Days of meetings passed—negotiations, discussions, and work to finish a war before it began. Information was relayed every week to the king, Robert. In the data given, they included ways of new strategy, new discoveries of who could help and how. Months had passed of proposals and painstaking work of long days and sleepless nights, but in the ten weeks, Iscariot, in all his servitude to his country, found time of peace and relaxation. A relationship formed, one of dalliance with subtle touches, coquetry, gentle words, and amorous actions.

Upon an evening, in a weary state of mind and body, he lay across his bed in thought of sleep and needed rest. There came a gentle tapping on his door. The hour was late and the moon at its peak. He rose to meet the call of the drum upon his door. He opened it, and his eyes looked upon a woman. Before he could speak, she spoke.

"I have a gift for you," she told him. "You need but answer my question," she continued and asked, "What say you?"

Hanns Chapter One

Arriving home on a midnight dreary, he pondered acts that made him wary—over many curious days and weeks of voluminous lore. While he bobbed and nodded, eyes hung nearly napping, his mind was steady in its wrapping. He snapped together mapping, capping truth inside his cerebral core. "It is an axiom," he whispered. "It must be spoken on council floor, for this is knowledge of pre-war."

"Hanns, wake up. We're nearly home," said his father's tongue, and in alertness, his eyes were sprung. Wind and rain and lightning flashing—it came and roared, bashing, crashing. They found cover from the thrashing, under brick and stone to cease the lashing.

"Wicked weather," said Hanns under the veranda of his home

"I'm soaked." Iscariot dripped from head to toe.

"I managed okay," Hanns joked as he pressed his foot down onto the floor, making a squishing noise with his waterlogged shoes. They laughed at themselves, tired but in good cheer.

"What did we run? Ten feet?"

"Give or take. Looks like winter is over, and spring has sprung." Hanns noted the drastic change from whence they left. Three months had passed, and more than just the weather had shown vicissitude. "I'm off to shower and sleep. I'm exhausted," said Hanns, his eyes ever evident of his words. "I'm leaving the luggage here in the mudroom."

"That's fine. So am I. I'll see you in the morning, chap." Iscariot slapped his son's back as a farewell for the evening.

"Goodnight, Dad."

"Goodnight, Hanns."

The night raged in its madness—a tantrum of wrath brewed in sadness. The earth wept through the darkened hours with screaming gusts of wind, slamming drums of thunder, horrid breaks of jagged lights piercing the blackened sky. In this mania of frightening sounds and daunting sights, Hanns slept. His mind closed him from the fearsome storm outside his door. He dreamt of an angel and of a demon. He dreamed of his youth and of days recent past. He dreamt of fact and of fiction until his mind, in friction, awakened in thought.

He broke the seal of his eyes as the sun broke away the knockings of the storm. The spring birds chirped, and the early morning flowers bloomed. The busy bees buzzed. Life stirred a peaceful pattern. Hanns woke with a full heart. The hour was half past eight. He left the comforts of his room and walked down to the kitchen. Iscariot was nowhere to be found as he wandered the course toward the pantry door. He quickly realized there wasn't any food inside the house. They'd been gone for three months, and if there were anything, it would be spoiled.

Hanns's stomach sounded a rumble-grumble, calling to be fed. He tapped the head of a cubed electronic device. It quickly scanned him to generate a holographic projection for his receiver.

"Call Dad," he told the machine. The communicator rang, but the line was not answered. Hanns took a look out back to see if his father was at the poulnabrone, and with regret, he was not seen. Hanns proceeded down to the garage to see if his father's car was there. He noted its absence and assumed he was either out shopping for groceries or already hard at work. His stomach grew louder as if yelling at his mind to feed him, and so he acted.

Back in his room, he showered and dressed. The weather was still chilly, and he wore blue fitted slacks, a white collared shirt, and a blue sweater. The collar of the undershirt fell over the sweater. His hair slicked back, brown shoes knotted, he traveled back down to the garage and unwrapped the cover of his vehicle. He smiled at his ride—a red truck with highly stylish features, a flashy glossed exterior, a small squared bed, two doors, and a rounded front. He loved its farm-look flare, its fine shining grill with bulbous headlamps, its black footsteps that ran just after the front tire and just before the rear tire. He admired its narrow but raised hood that looked like a cartoonish nose with two vents at the front of it. He adored the simplicity of the interior—a single brown leather seat that spread from door to door, the handcrafted instruments on the front panel. It seemed very much a family trait to laud simplicity and elegance, as he, his uncle, and two of his three cousins drove similar vehicles with like aesthetics.

He turned the key, and with it, ignition. A hum and a purr, and the truck came to life. The truck rolled in reverse, and his phone rang before he left the driveway. Hanns set the vehicle in park and answered. It was his uncle, Robert.

"Uncle Robert," he answered the call.

"Nephew Hanns," Robert answered back. Hanns chuckled at the greeting. "Good morning, lad. I didn't wake you, did I?"

"No," he replied and continued. "I was just heading out the door. There's nothing in the house to eat, so I'm running out to pick something up."

"Feel free to stop by Solascnoc. I know it's out of the way, but it's an option," Robert told him.

"I think I'm going to head to Knightly's. It's much closer."

"That sounds nice. They have such great food there. I'm sure the fire is burning, too," his uncle commented. "Anywho, lad, I was wonderin' if you'd like to come over tomorrow? Have a chat about your trip?"

"A'course uncle. What time were ya' thinkin'?"

"Say around nine, nine thirty."

"Morning, right?" Hanns sought confirmation.

"Yea, we'll do a full Saoirse breakfast."

"Fine by me."

"Alright then, I'll see ya tomorrow mornin'. Rest up today, lad, and good eats to ya at Knightly's," Robert said to him.

"Thanks, Uncle. Slan." Hanns said goodbye.

"Slan, lad." The call ended. Hanns put the truck back in gear and drove down to the small pub on Castlemaine Road.

It had a stone facade, maroon window frames, and a maroon-colored sign that read Knightly over the building's doorway. Hanns entered.

"Dia Dhuit!" the keep behind the bar yelled to him as he entered.

"Dia es muire dhuit," Hanns replied back.

The man behind the bar was always cordial. He'd regularly bring up topics of insignificance, keeping the conversation light, so anyone could chime in. Though, at least once a week, he'd spit out a poem, a sonnet, a hymn, or a stumper of a thought, which would bring a stir of debate or marriage of agreement. He was a man in his mid to late fifties. His hair was of medium length, every inch of it gray. He had a crooked smile, kind eyes, and a nose that had to have been broken at least once or twice—a man of modest stature, never seeming weak or strong. He asked Hanns how his trip had gone. Hanns responded, "I certainly learned a lot, and I quite enjoyed myself, but I'll tell you more later, Mister Boyle. I'm going to mind myself for a bit."

"Go about yourself, lad. You'll be eaten, I assume?" Mister Boyle asked.

"I'm starved."

"I'll send Thomas to ya, and don't call me Mister Boyle. I've known ya your whole life," said the keep.

"Sorry Brian. You know how my southern dad raised me. I'm thinkin' yer lucky I aren't talkin' like this," Hanns joked with a southern accent. Brian tossed the towel that hung over his shoulder to dry cups at Hanns, hitting him and settling on Hanns's own shoulder as he walked to a table set up for two in the far corner of the room. Hanns tossed it back at Brian. The towel fell in the most comical manner, and the two blurted out with laughter.

"It's war now, laddie," Brian winked.

Hanns sat. The small fire to his right cracked and popped. It smelled of buttered walnuts and sweet syrup. The scent of hickory and maple filled the room as the bark roasted in the small blaze. Thomas came over with a cup of coffee and a glass of water and sat down across from him.

Sixteen years old with soft blond hair, gentle eyes, and a soft spoken voice, he began to talk.

"Mornin' Hanns. How ya been?"

"I've been well. Long time away, just taking the day to relax and adjust. How about yourself?" Hanns asked politely.

"I've been good, mate. Really focused on my studies. What can I get ya?" Thomas was casually professional. He was an honest, gentle soul, a driven person who was very much a person of solitude, but if a friend be found in him, he was extremely loyal and reliable. Hanns thought himself lucky to be called a friend, and Thomas frequently confided in him.

"I'll have two eggs, sunny side, some toast, sausage, and a chocolate drizzled, chocolate-chip scone."

"Oh, those scones are quare good. Still in the oven, actually. They'll be fresh for ya." Thomas seemed to salivate thinking about the pastry. "Let me get this to the kitchen. You want company?"

"Sure, mate. Come back if you're not busy." Thomas left, leaving Hanns to himself. He thought of what to do while the light of the sun shone down to the earth.

Like pen to paper, his mind drew images, and in the lines and curves, a face appeared to him. He smiled at her brilliance. He longed for such beauty and such grace.

"Here you are, Hanns," said a voice that unclouded his mind. He saw Thomas sitting before him with a drink called a hot toddy. Thomas slid the hot beverage over to Hanns. He took a sip of the splendor. The tongue danced on honey, jived on whisky, tingled with cloves, frolicked with cinnamon, jumped with lemon, and leapt with nutmeg. While his tastebuds ran wild, his mind was relaxed and his body calm, for he was home in the company of friends, next to a crackling fire, awaiting a meal fit for a prince. He felt at ease, comforted by things familiar.

"That toddy will really put ya back at home," said Thomas.

"It's perfect mate," Hanns complimented. "What's your day like?"

"A bit full. Workin' here till two. Then off to my apprenticeship at the garden. Not sure what the night holds, but that's my day," Thomas answered.

"Take that free time at night for yourself. Everyone needs a de-stressor after a long day's work."

"That's not a bad idea, mate. I haven't played the piano in a while, or maybe I'll do some reading. Escape in some fantasy. What's the day bringing you, mate?"

"I think I'm going to finish that sculpture I've been working on. It'll give me time to myself, and I'll get back to doing something I love."

"Wicked! I can't wait to see it."

"I've been working on it long enough. I think my skills are as good as they can get for now, and I think the timing is right." Changing the subject and getting back to his duties, Thomas spoke. "Well, I better go get your breakfast. I'll be right back."

Upon his return, there came a breakfast that sizzled with sound, fumed with smell, dazzled in sight, and when consumed, it bloomed with taste to touch the senses with satisfaction. Thomas let Hanns be while he enjoyed his savory meal. As he ate, he thought some more of his sculpture and what he thought needed to be added or improved since last he worked on the piece. Hanns took some mental notes and stuck them in his cerebellum to reference upon his return home.

His meal was quickly gone, his plate cleaned, and his belly rounded. Filled with food, his body said to his mind that he was full. Thomas came back and took his plate away and then returned once more. Sitting across from Hanns, he spoke, his voice slightly hushed.

"It's getting worse, you know." His words were cryptic.

"What do you mean?" Hanns spoke with confusion at Thomas's vague approach.

"You must have heard while you were away."

"Of what, Thomas?" Hanns asked.

"The attacks. They've been happening all over the country."

"I heard there was a demonstration when I left, much larger than the one when Prime Minister Nemtsov was here," Hanns began. "My uncle told me about an attack in Criostaiocht and then a week later in Morcnoc."

"And one just last week in Ban-Ros. Rumor has it, there's to be one every week," Thomas interjected.

"Where did you hear that?"

"Your cousin. Abe came in yesterday for a pint. Showed me a holo of the group saying as much," Thomas explained.

"Show me."

"Mmmmm—come with me," he told Hanns. "Brian, I'll be right back; just taking five, ten minutes."

"Hurray back, laddie," he commanded Thomas.

Hanns and Thomas stepped outside and entered Hanns's truck. Thomas flicked his wrist to activate his communicator, and the holovid appeared in front of them. The hologram was tightly framed and focused. The image before them was of a man who was slightly heavyset with a round face and dark unkempt hair. He was bound hand and foot on the cold concrete surface. The hostage wore a hat that read God save the King. He looked abused, afraid, and his eyes searched for hope. Then a voice came on the holograph, but the man behind the voice was unseen. His tone was serious and crude. The camera approached the captured man.

"What's your name, King Saver?" The bound man's mouth was taped, unable to answer his captor's question. Suddenly, violently, a hand came across the projected particles, striking the detained man. The imprisoner ripped the tape off the captive's gate of speech. He asked the hostage again. His voice was threatening, barbaric, inhuman.

"What is your name!?" The aggressor sat the hologram device down, and he came into the image. The lighting in the room was dim, crude, and withered.

"Ca—Conall." The beaten man stuttered with fear to answer the wicked man who held him against his will.

The ghastly man had dark black circles under his eyes, his skin ghostly white, his iris taupe and glossy, his head shaved, his body muscular. His appearance was indicative of Hollen decent. Even in his emotionless eyes, Hanns could see evil within them. The wicked man had a cross engraved on his arm, and the head of the cross was a dancing flame. The daingne that were to rest on the arms of the cross were fallen at the base.

"You think God can save the King, Conall?" he asked menacingly, dangling the hat his captive wore.

"Yes, I—I do," the repressed man answered, holding back tears.

"And what about you, Conall? Is God going to save you?" asked the dreadful man, grazing a sharpened knife on his hostage's cheek, letting blood drop down to his chin and hit the floor.

"Is the King going to save you?" he berated the fallen man. Conall was now in tears.

"The King already has, and the Lord surely will," the bound man answered. The appalling man whipped his captive with his own hat.

"The King is not saving you, Conall, and neither is the Phoenix. They will both let you perish into the dust. Now, let's watch. Let's watch as you die and they do nothing." The camera went out of view, but the screams were shrill, hair-raising, and severe. It was as if the spirit suffered and wailed as fearful as the stormy winds on the blackest of nights, as if the power of the human heart felt all the pain of all the people in the world, and then his screams stopped. The hologram came back to focus. Only the face of the murderer could be seen, and he spoke.

"Robert Darroch. Disband your power or have a citizen die on your account every day for seven days. If you do not relieve yourself of power, prepare for the deaths of a thousand men." The hologram faded out to a deep, booming, demon-like laugh. The particles of the holovid perished. Hanns felt his gut was knotted, twisted, and uneasy.

"I wish you hadn't shown me that," he told Thomas.

"Why not? You're on my side, aren't you?"

"And what side is that?" Hanns questioned him.

"The side of men and women who believe in what is true and right, the side that believes man is the maker of his own destiny, the side that sees violence as a last resort but is well trained in it, the side that believes there is honor and righteousness in this world and that it's worth fighting for." Thomas spoke with passion.

"There are those who believe exactly what you believe but whom you would call your enemy," said Hanns. It was quiet for longer than a standard pause in a conversation.

"No—Hanns, you're wrong. Those whom I call my enemies believe in what they call 'their truth,' who believe that only a select few can govern man, who restrict your full potential and halt your true destiny. They may believe in honor and righteousness, but they have corrupted its meaning. If you think that man on that holovid believes what I believe, and what I know you to believe, then my friend, you are lost, and if you be lost, though it would sink my floating heart, I will disband this friendship." Thomas spoke with temper.

"Thank you, Thomas."

"For what?"

"For letting me know where you reside," Hanns explained. "Can you give this to Brian? Your tip is there, too." Hanns handed Thomas the money for his meal.

"I won't take this tip," Thomas told him. It caught Hanns off guard.

"Why not?"

"Not until you tell me what side you're on." Thomas gave the ultimatum.

"You already know, and if you don't, you'll know soon enough," Hanns answered. Thomas left the truck with a blank stare at his friend.

His mood changed from the hologram he had just seen. He traveled back home and went to a spot that only he knew about, a place where he was free from everyone but himself, a place where his mind could think past the bounds of earth, a place he frequented for clarity. Off road his truck took him on his desired course, an open field with nothing but tall grass and snow-capped mountains in the background, and off in the distance, not so far as the mountains, was an abandoned shack or so it looked to the naked eye. Hanns flicked a hidden switch underneath his steering wheel, and the barn doors of the shack opened, and he drove inside the structure.

Ignition off. He stepped out of his classic truck. The walls were of sculpted stone and marble, plastered in place. Chiseled, etched and painted, the walls were sculpted pieces of a vast and beautiful landscape. Some pieces were as large as ten feet, others as small as six inches, yet they all came together in a masterpiece of genius sculpting. The ceiling above was different only in that it was of the heavens with blues and golds and sculpted images of celestial beings. It was a master stroke of the renaissance, but he did not linger on its beauty. Hidden by hay and grass was a latched door, and its entryway led to a room of scrap pieces, unfinished slabs and dozens of lanterns, along with a fireplace.

Hanns sat his behind on a weathered leather chair. Putting his hand inside his jacket pocket, his fingers danced on a piece of what felt like folded paper. He pulled out the parchment and saw that it was blank. He thought only for a moment, and his mind suddenly rushed to the meeting with his uncle the day he left for Holle, and then it jumped to a scene where Abe and Lorena were talking about solving a blank puzzle. Inquisitive, his curiosity got the best of him, and so he built a fire. As the fire roared, he put the paper up to his face to see if he lay sight to any hidden words, but it was to no avail. Hanns thought some more, and remembered a distinct temperature. He started moving the parchment closer to the flame, but nerves struck him, and he withdrew the paper he clutched in his hands. *If this message is for me and me alone, I cannot be hasty. When I talk to my uncle, I'll ask him how it's done. Then its secrets will be revealed,* he thought.

Hanns sat back down in the leather chair. The fire crackling before him, his eyes peered into it, and all afternoon he thought, recalling memories and piecing them together. In his thought, he began to move his hands, and his hands began to sculpt bits of stone, and when he completed the small fragment, he walked back upstairs to his masterclass work and put the small piece of art in a very inconspicuous place.

Hanns walked back down the hidden stairwell and cut the air from the fire until it died out. He turned off all the lanterns and then left his room of isolation. He started his truck to venture home, and so he drove in the green country fields of Aontu. Hanns took in nature's view and admired the Maker's work, clearing his mind from the morning and afternoon events. His cerebrum now blank, a canvas new, he arrived home.

His father was still nowhere to be seen. He walked into the kitchen, washed his hands, and made a small meal. He consumed it quickly, and upon completion, put his plate and glass into the washer. His mind still bare, he made way to his studio inside the house. He entered the room, and as he did, his unfilled mind began to drip in works of art of lines and curvatures he thought of in the morning light, and he regained the peaceful bliss he had when he awoke in the early hours of the day.

Hanns looked upon the structure he had built. He examined it for imperfections and chiseled them away. From that moment on, he thought of nothing else but of the work before him. He worked tirelessly without food or water, without break, until a knock came upon the door of his studio. It cracked opened. He quickly covered his work.

"Hello?" asked Hanns. His father walked through the doorway.

"Hey, son. You've been in here all day. Aren't you tired?" Iscariot wondered aloud to him. Suddenly, it hit him. He hadn't noticed until his father said the words.

"What time is it?"

"It's just past two in the morning."

"Are you just getting home?"

"No, I've been home for a while now. Today was a long day. Let's go get some rest, and we can talk about our day tomorrow," his father suggested. Hanns put his tools back into place and walked out with his father. His eyes heavy and his mind exhausted, he said goodnight to his father and walked into his room. He undressed and showered. His muscles relaxed, as did his thoughts, and in its comfort, he grew ever more fatigued. Washed, he slothed into soft pajama bottoms, untucked the sheets on his bed, and wrapped himself up in their comforts. Just as his head hit the pillow, his brain hit on chiseled dreams.

A new day rang to the sounds of falling water coming high from the powdery gray skies above. The droplets played a peculiar song as it struck the tiled roof, one without a thundering beat. Hanns rose from his slumber, making his bed, drawing the sheets tight without wrinkle. He dressed in brown slacks, fitted and tapered at the ankles. He tucked in his pants, his white, long-sleeved oxford shirt. On his feet, he slipped on brown leather ankle-strapped boots and then threw on a knee-length brown frock coat with folded wrist cuffs. He walked out of his room and closed his bedroom door behind him.

Hanns walked into the kitchen. His father was looking at the news that was digitally displayed on the counter. He was drinking coffee. There was no cream or sugar in his glass. The hot beverage steamed swirls into the air, rising high and then coiling as the cool air pressed it downward.

"Good morning, son." Iscariot welcomed him to the day.

"Good morning, Dad. Are you going to Uncle Robert's? They're having a Saoirse breakfast at the castle," Hanns asked.

"Sadly, no. Your aunt insisted that I come, but I've got to meet with a few people this morning."

"You'll be missin' out."

"Oh, I'm sure. My stomach is already growling for it."

"I'll have seconds just for you," Hanns joked. They both chuckled.

"Let's do dinner tonight," his father suggested.

"Going out, you mean?"

"Yea, what do you think?"

"I could really go for some pasta. I've been craving it these past few days," said Hanns.

"How does Terra Mia sound?"

"It sounds perfect."

"It's a date, then."

"It's a date. I'll see you then, Dad. I'm off to Solascnoc," Hanns told him, hugging his father goodbye.

He grabbed an umbrella from the mudroom and hopped in his truck to head to his uncle's castle. As he drove the slithering roads of the countryside, his mind slipped into a trance. It fell on reflections of yesterday's memories and the egregious hologram Thomas had made him watch. From there, his mind slid to the conversation he had with Thomas. Then his thoughts traveled to the meeting with his uncle. His mind wandered further to all he would tell him of Holle. Before Hanns knew it, he was out of the lonely lanes of hills and dips and grass as bright as spring and into the mathematical lines and edges of city avenues, where shades of cream stone and brick built buildings stood as grand as the folds in the mind and as artistic as radiolarians.

Over the castle bridge, Solascnoc was in sight. The beacon on the hill that overlooked Buna was like radium in the moody atmosphere of dreary skies and the tears that fell from them. If Buna was the core of Aontu, then Solascnoc was the mantle. In all the darkened times in the country of Saoirse, the Maker sent a light to the castle on the hill and burned a fire in the spirit of its host, and their actions, throughout history, gave rise to a new day, to pull not only the city of Buna out of the darkness but the entire country.

He stopped at the gate of Solascnoc to be greeted by a familiar face.

"Hannsie!" Captain Talmidge greeted him.

"Captain Talmidge," Hanns smiled. There came a knock on his passenger window. Hanns turned to look and saw the face of a scarred man with a wolf at the center of his armor. The man beamed a brilliant smile. "Good morning, Niall."

"Dia Dhuit," Niall greeted him. "Here for breakfast?"

"Saoirse breakfast," Hanns answered.

"Ooohh," Niall said with enthusiasm.

"Bring us lads down a plate," Ben told him.

"I'll be sure to have them send a plate down to you both," Hanns said assuredly, though his uncle had likely requested it already.

"Good eats, mate. Up ya go," said Niall. The golden gates opened, and Hanns drove through and up the hill of the driveway. Surrounded by dense evergreens, the lanterns that traced the driveway guided him to the castle doors. Aedus was sitting on the staircase of the castle entrance and rose when he saw Hanns's vehicle, giving him a wave and a smile.

Hanns turned the engine off and exited the truck. Aedus greeted him with a hug.

"Welcome home, Hanns."

"Thank you, Aed. How ya been these past three months?"

"I've been good. I've joined the Iolars and started flight school while you were away," Aedus answered. The two walked through the castle doors into the room of seasons.

"What happened to racing?"

"Do you remember our conversation about our hopes and dreams and what we saw for ourselves?"

"Of course," said Hanns.

"Well, I had to put what I love to do to the side and do what's most needed for those I love. What happened to my sister is unforgivable, and the Soisialach have only gotten worse since you've been away," Aedus explained.

"I've seen."

"And I made a promise to myself and to someone who has become dear to me," Aedus further explained.

"I wouldn't expect anything less from you."

"Breakfast should be about ready." They walked through the great halls of the castle, their feet beating the ground and giving a knock with each step. The walls gave echo, signaling their arrival as they made their way to the dining room.

The family sat together, all in their pajamas. Abe and his mother were laughing together. Lorena was half asleep but was grinning at the remark Hanns and Aedus had missed. The food was being brought out onto the table by the servers of Solascnoc. Some of the servers must have overheard or were part of the conversation, as some of them beamed by what was said.

"What's so funny, Mom?" Aedus asked.

"We were just talking about your father," Lagertha began.

"Oh, what about me?" Robert came from behind Hanns and Aedus, putting his hands on their shoulders while a smirk played across his face.

"Just saying how handsome you are," Lagertha lied in a tease.

"I didn't know my good looks were so funny." Robert played along.

"Your appearance is quite funny, Dad." Abe poked fun at his father.

"Weird, because I get a lot of people telling me you look just like me, Abe," Robert said slyly.

"Well, at least I didn't fall in some, how should I put this, horse droppings yesterday," Abe rebutted.

"Funny lad this morning, are we?" Robert grinned. "Come on, boys, let's sit and eat."

Hanns sat down next to Aedus. The meal before him was beautiful, and he was ever grateful for it—a plate of bacon a mile high, sausage fat and juicy, a bounty of eggs, delicious mushrooms, ripe pan-seared tomatoes, a sloppy bowl of beans, and three plates of potato bread.

In their gorging on food and drink, they talked of what their day held, and they caught up on the most recent events in one another's lives. Hanns talked of Holle but spared details of events he saw as sensitive and meant only for his uncle. He talked of customs he enjoyed and those he didn't. He reflected on Volkfest. He described the city's appearance and talked of surface topics about the Führer and his queen. He made no mention of Möngke or Yuskita. Aedus had asked about the twin sons of Alamgeer, but Hanns only replied that they were not there during his stay.

"What was it like to see a man who murdered his mother on a worldwide stage for all to see?" The striking question left the mouth of Lorena. Hanns paused, gathering the words he needed to convey his emotion.

"Chilling," he answered. "Striking in fear, staggering in power. Eyes of burning flames shown within him, his hellish heart. His mind is masterful. The man is statuesque, and we should all be very much rattled by such a being so magnificent." His words changed the mood in the room. A feeling of good tidings became one of displeasure. It was quiet but only for a brief moment. The sound of a belch resounded in the room.

"Lorena!" Her mother looked at her with shock and disgust. Abe and Aed laughed, as did his uncle.

"It got weird, so I made it more weird in a different way," she blushed slightly.

"You're gross." Lagertha began to crack a smile.

"On that note, I'm getting ready for the day," said Abe, excusing himself from the table.

"I should do the same," Aedus said. "Hanns, you sticking around? Maybe we'll go out later."

"I should be here a while," Hanns informed him.

The servers came back into the room to clear the dishes.

"Here, let me help," Lagertha told one of the servants.

"I'll help, too." Lorena joined her mother. Robert and Hanns were alone.

"Well, shall we?" asked his uncle. Hanns knew he meant to be debriefed.

"Let's do it," Hanns agreed. They left the dining room and traveled through the castle to Robert's office. In the castle they walked, through the arching hall a hundred yards long and forty yards wide, letting in the natural light from the world outside. This was the hall of Kings and Queens, and in this great hall, statues were erected in the king or queen's image, and most were buried underneath their sculpted images. The walls were beige but were not without color. On the beams and arches were symbols and stories of the lives of the kings and queens of Saoirse. As the stone arches approached the center of the ceiling, they formed a triangle shape, and in this triangle frame were paintings of angels high in the wondrous heavens. Running down the center of the hall, where the ceiling flattened, were individual paintings of the kings and queens being taken in to meet the Father of the Most High. These images were alternated in rectangular and circular shapes and were lined in bands of gold. The checkered marble floor was brilliantly waxed, and it gave a stunning shine. Hanns and Robert passed the statue of Abraham.

"Do you visit your father's statue often, Uncle?" Hanns asked as they walked by it.

"In the beginning, yes. As years went on, a little less. But now, perhaps, I visit more than ever. He may not be able to talk to me, but coming here helps me remember the lessons he taught me when he still roamed this wonderful world," Robert answered.

"Do you ever think about the day you'll be here?" Hanns asked, stopping at the end of the Hall of Kings and Queens.

"All too often, I'm afraid. Speaking of which, would you like to be my sculptor?"

"Seriously?" Hanns said with stunned amazement in his voice.

"I can't think of anyone better. You know my face better than any other sculptor out there. Who else would be able to capture me more than my nephew?" His uncle spoke with authenticity in his voice.

"But Uncle, you've never seen any of my works."

"That's because you never show anybody. If you have something for me to see, I'll gladly go to view it." Hanns weighed his words. They walked through the doorway at the end of the great hall and entered into a new one. The floors were of tiled stone, and the walls still rose to an arching ceiling, but here, there were no paintings or statues. To their left were thin, tan and black stone columns. They ran up the wall and arched like bows as they touched the ceiling. To their right, every two feet, were artfully constructed windows that arched to meld into the ceiling, rising twenty feet high and ten feet across. The windows were three panes across, separated by two columns that flared as they reached ten feet in height. The stone work at the upper half of the window carved out three, four-leafed clovers set in a diamond shape. The clovers were encircled by protruding stonework, and in the clover's frames were glass. The segment of the castle they walked in was called The Halls of Light due to its westward direction. The sun shone fiercely, illuminating the stone walls and floors, giving the passage a glorious glow.

In this walkway, his uncle asked him about his wellbeing. It was a common question of his, and every time he asked it of Hanns, it seemed as if it was the most sincere question his uncle could ask of him. Hanns answered him truthfully.

"I'm nervous, Uncle."

"Me too," Robert replied. Hanns was confounded by his response.

They walked into his uncle's office. The small room was consumed by the light of the sun. The five windows, framed by brick and stone, let the rays pass through. The triangle columns at the corners and the squared columns in between the windows were also laid in brick and stone. Curved beams rose from the columns, giving the square room a round ceiling. The floors were of old but well-kept wood. The room itself looked aged, not quite medieval, but not as recent as the renaissance, either. It was a design somewhere in the middle of the two eras. Hanns sat down on a wooden chair with a thick, tanned cushion, with arms pommeled with antlers for one's hands to rest on. Each finger had its designated spot. The desk in front of him seemed to be more a part of the architecture of the room rather than furniture. The body of the desk looked like the same brick as the walls within the room, and the top of the desk appeared to be carved from the same stone. His uncle's chair matched the design of the bending beams and arched window frames of the office.

"Would you like any tea or coffee, Hanns? I can send for some if you'd like."

"No, I'm alright," he replied. Robert grabbed two glasses resting on a small table at the corner of the room. He walked over to one of the curved beams that resided in the column. He lifted a stone piece on the beam, and behind the piece, water flowed. He filled the glasses.

His uncle sat down in his chair, placed one cup in front of Hanns and one in front of himself. Robert then grabbed a leather journal and a fountain pen. He opened up to a blank page and looked at Hanns.

"Ready?" Robert asked. Hanns nodded. "Shoot," said his uncle. "I'm all ears."

"I guess I'll start from the beginning."

"It's a good place to start," his uncle joked and smiled.

"Day one was fascinating, really. I was awakened by a servant girl, though she may have been more a spy than a servant."

"Why is that?" Robert asked.

"I wasn't really able to travel without her. Almost everywhere I went, she was."

"I see," Robert noted. "Continue."

"After I dressed, we had a great Hollen breakfast, and the attendees were very peculiar," said Hanns. His uncle was leaning forward, pen to paper, awaiting his next word. "In the room was the Führer, his queen, and two generals, one from Avstrija and the other from Danija. There was this gorgeous woman from the Heavohe Islands. She said her name was Yuskita."

"Was wondering where she was hiding," his uncle said while writing down those in attendance. "Anyone else, lad?"

Hanns nodded his head yes, saying the name "Khan."

"Do you know what he was there for, Hanns? The news outlets said he was there for trade negotiations." Robert seemed keen on the Khan.

"It seemed they all were, uncle. The Khan seemed to genuinely want to help Holle and talked of its rebuilding."

"Rebuild in what way?"

"It seemed to me like infrastructure. Anything outside the castle and upper ring of the city—it's nightmarish," said Hanns.

"Anything else on Möngke?" Hanns thought a moment of the only meeting the Khan was in.

"He was there only a short period of time. In a meeting that was held, he talked of sending a ship and an aircraft in exchange for property and igneous stone," Hanns detailed.

"Granite and diorite are used for construction. There is some validity in the trade. Do you know what was being shipped and flown over for the trade?"

"Mostly food, from what I remember."

"We'll have to check some other reports and see where this leads. It's imperative Mongnolerium remain neutral." His uncle looked concerned. "How were the meetings? Did you learn from them?"

"I did. I learned the most from the trade negotiations with my father and Alamgeer. It was interesting to see the micro and macro implications of trade," Hanns reflected.

"Game theory at its finest. Your father is surprisingly good at it, considering his mind for war, and battle is his strong suit."

"Oh, he definitely seemed to use our military to give weight to his offers," Hanns told his uncle.

"Naturally,"

"I was in another meeting with the generals of Avstrija and Danija, the Khan, Yuskita, the Führer, my father, and a few others, though most of what they discussed seemed to be finalized information where they were tying up loose ends to current deals. This meeting did talk of treaties."

"How were the people in the room?"

"What do you mean?" Hanns didn't quite understand the question.

"What spoke the truth? Their mouths or their eyes?"

"I believe what left the mouth of everyone was the truth. You will not find allegiance in Avstrija and Danija. The Khan seemed firm on his trade deals and no interference if war breaks out."

"What of your father, Hanns?"

"I thought you had weekly reports with him?" Hanns spoke carefully.

"We did, but I'm looking at events from your perspective."

"Just as the Khan, my father offered food and infrastructure materials in exchange for a summit meeting of leaders around the world and a delay to any invasive movement," Hanns informed Robert.

"Do you believe him?"

"Who? My father or Alamgeer?"

"Both," Robert replied.

"My father's words, I believe. The Führer's? It's difficult to read his flickering eyes. I cannot truly say," Hanns responded. Robert finished writing down words in his notebook and looked up at Hanns.

"Sure you don't want that coffee?"

"What's the brew?" Hanns inquired.

"A Gaoth roast."

"The best comes from the mid-west. Topeka Pete's?"

"You guessed it," said his uncle, while sliding a stone on his desk.

"Good morning, my king! How can I help you?" asked an ornate voice of the servant through a telecom system. With a chuckle in his tone, Robert answered.

"Good morning, Gilchrist. It's getting close to noon, isn't it?" Robert greeted the man.

"Nonsense. Two hours still, my king," replied the servant.

"Feels later. Can I get two cups of the Gaoth blend?"

"For the king, anything," Gilchrist replied. "I'll brew a pot now. It'll be up shortly."

"Thank you, Gilchrist."

"Anytime." The conversation ended, and Hanns and Robert picked back up from where they left off.

"Let's pick your brain a little more, shall we?" Robert suggested.

"Let's."

"What was it like in the castle? What were the servants like when you were out? What were the attitudes of the people?"

"Driven, inside and out. The people want change, Uncle. Alamgeer is that change. When people see him, they see a leader, one that will guide them to prosperity, one that will bring about a revolution. With him, they see a life that will be changed forever," Hanns paused. "But there is also great fear—fear that they may never see the light of day again. If we go to war, we must not think that we are fighting men that have nothing to fight for. Most of them may have little, but they crave change. They desire for something new, and they are willing to fight. From what I understand, they have been in such despair for so long that they finally have something they can look forward to," Hanns briefed Robert.

"There is brief hope in tyranny. If he succeeds, they will surely suffer far greater than they do now," Robert noted and let Hanns continue.

"While I watched the people, I also watched my surroundings. If we go to war, there is a weakness in the city of Atma," Hanns grinned.

"Is that so?" Robert grinned back. "How do you know this?"

"It's true. I don't know entirely, but from my observances, west of Atma is the river Oder. A forest leads to the river. There are garrisons on the other side, but it holds the fewest troops," Hanns explained.

"How do you know it holds the fewest men?"

"The Führer said so himself."

"Nice work, Hanns."

Breaking their conversation, there was a knock on the door of the office. It cracked open, and a man walked through it.

"Good morning, King Robert, sir Hanns. Two cups of Gaoth blend," said the slender dark-skinned man with a joyous smile and kind eyes. He held a tray of condiments and the two coffees. He handed Robert his cup first and then handed the second cup to Hanns.

"Any cream or sugar?" he asked Hanns.

"No, thank you, Gilchrist," Hanns politely said. "I like your shoes, by the way. Very sharp." They were polished brown leather shoes with squared tips, strong laces, and a wooden bottom.

"Thank you, Hanns—a gift from your uncle during Yule," Gilchrist answered.

"I might have to get myself a pair. I like them a lot. Uncle, where did you get them?"

"If I recall, they're from Henry Sands," Robert answered. Gilchrist smiled and then spoke to the two men.

"I'm very grateful for them. It is a very comfortable shoe." He seemed to know matters of importance were being discussed. Gilchrist slowly made his way to the door as he talked. "I see you men have business to attend to. Please continue."

"Goodbye, Gilchrist," said Hanns.

"See ya, Gilly," Robert smirked. Gilchrist laughed as he left the room, closing the door behind him.

Hanns took a sip of his black coffee. "Sets you right at ease, doesn't it?" he said. Robert took a sip from the hot cup.

"Delicious."

"Back to the discussion?" Hanns suggested in question.

"Have at it, lad."

"Back to the castle, then. The movement of the guards—they are literally at every entryway within the castle. You know the weapons, the saber cannons? They hold them at their sides. They rotate at their positions at every hour, on the hour. They seem to interact with the help quite a bit. I'd overhear them talking about everything from what they were doing later that day, talk of side bets they had made, gossip of others. Some even seemed to be in relationships," Hanns recollected.

"Any out-of-the-ordinary topics?" Hanns gave the question thought.

"Some girls had gone missing, which was a topic for the entirety of my stay. They also brought up a word. It must have been code for something. I could never figure it out." Hanns spoke of what he remembered.

"What was the word?"

"Gorlab was the word. Any idea what it means?" Hanns asked, looking at his uncle, hoping he would know the answer.

"I don't. Sorry, lad." Robert answered his question, still looking stumped by what the word might represent. After throwing back and forth possibilities of what Gorlab might stand for, from the logical to the absurd, they found themselves talking of Volkfest, the outfits at the festival, and the customs they celebrated during it. Of pretty girls they spoke, and even those of the oddest demeanor.

In that exchange, Hanns mentioned the charismatic flare of Francis, the trembling fear of a man, Julius, the helpful manner of Alwine, the quiet personality of Mallory, the hospitable candor of Hella, and the ever menacing yet esteemed Alamgeer. The dialog revived a moment on the first day of his stay in Holle.

"Uncle," he paused, his voice more serious. "The Führer seemed adamant that you be dethroned. He kept talking of your heart and how the hammer from the rock from which you pulled upon the Hill of Hoba was poisoning you—how the hammer made you mad, how it was the weapon of the devil and you held its curse. I see his words as folly, but I must know, is there any truth to his words?"

Robert bowed his head, stroked his face with his hand, and let out a soft sigh. He looked at Hanns with worried deep blue eyes.

"There is truth within them." His uncle's voice was low; forlorn it seemed to ring. Hanns's heart was stricken with shock that there was any semblance of truth within Alamgeer's words.

"Uncle, it can't be," Hanns began, but Robert interrupted him.

"You mustn't tell anyone this, Hanns. It is critical to the war. What I am about to tell you, no one knows of except your Aunt Lagertha. My children don't even know what I'm about to tell you. You must promise me that what I say next will never leave this room and that your mouth will be sealed to all but me on the matter." Robert made Hanns look him in the eyes and swear to him. Hanns became afraid. His heart pumped a rapid rhythm, and chills consumed his body. His uncle told him the truth, and with stormy eyes, Hanns wept.

Iscariot Chapter Eight

In the black and cloudy sky, nature played its song. The drumroll of the droplets on the windowpane rumbled like the falling beats on a tom-tom. The thunder was the foot upon the bass, and it boomed a steady beat. The wind was the strings that whined in worry and doubt. The concert played, and he was awakened, not from the rainstorm, but from the deluge in his mind. His body trembled with pricked nerves; his heart slowly unthreaded as his mind unraveled the flood of thoughts he had sewn together these past four months. His conscience weaved with threads of righteousness and vulgarity. For every stitch, there were two tears, and with every rip, a spate, only stopped by a makeshift patch. He was a man torn in the early hours of the day, where the sun did not shine and the night was at its most nightmarish. The turmoil that dwelled within him made him mad. He showered to wash away his thoughts, to clear his mind, to seek clarity, yet only his body was clean, and like his mind, the room was now clouded.

The weather outside softened its rage, but Iscariot's own storm ran rancor. Feeling the urge to flee, he dressed in dark boots, black slacks, and a coal-colored henley. His hair was slicked back. He tossed on a jacket and hopped into his car. He pulled out from his drive, and with not a thought of where he was going, he drove.

The barren roads were soaked from the showers of the night and glistened as the light from his craft beamed onto the beads that rested on the blackened concrete surface. He felt the desperate need to talk to someone to help him reason. Iscariot's mind could only think of his brother, but it was his brother who gave his mind the strife he felt within his very spirit. He needed an open-aired space to free his mind, to release his tongue, to liberate his burden if only for a day.

He did not know it until he stopped his car, and turned off its engine. His eyes left the mind's eyes, and he could faintly see that he was in the Field of Diamonds. The morning was still dark. The sun did not yawn its brightened face to create the day. It still rested under the covers of the night. Iscariot gazed out onto the field searching for blooming spring flowers, seeking for beauty to penetrate the grunge inside his head.

Movement his eyes beheld. *An animal*, he thought. He checked the hour and saw it read six. Aedus perhaps. He liked to wander in these fields to watch the sun peek from the mountains of Mor, his mind surmised. He stepped out from his vehicle. He focused on the shadow, still unable to make out the image. He started to walk toward it. Three steps he took, and the obscurity halted its movement.

"No." Iscariot spoke to himself, knowing now the entity before him, hearing the static crackling within his ears. He took a step back, but the shadow was upon him. Its ragged robes waved like tattered sails riding in the wind. The faceless hooded creature, tall and slender, a horrifying figure, spoke in percolating tones. "Kill," said the phantom. Like a waterfall in the harsh winter months, he could not move. The wraith took Iscariot by the shoulders, and if it had eyes, it would peer into the depths of Iscariot's blue bulbs. The creature pulled back his right hand, bringing it up to its shoulder, and it let out a cry as grim and as gory as a gruesome gallery of sanguinary murders, where the blood ran cold, and the shrill of the screech raised the hairs on his arms. It was a wail so hideous that it hid Iscariot's handsome eyes from the harmonic beauty of the world. It made a place of light and color and wonder and turned it into a place of solemn darkness, where flowers never bloomed and the sun never shined—a place where all that was good and righteous is gone from the harboring heart of humanity.

The raised hand of the golem creature traveled swiftly through the air. Its index finger, like a daggered spear, pierced the flesh of Iscariot's chest. Iscariot let out a grunt of terrible anguish while the apparition billowed like smoke. A hole in his chest, it began to close, but the smog of the spirit slid like a snake in the air into the void of his body. Iscariot's mind began to tire, and his eyes began to droop. He fell to the floor of the earth like a tree in the forest, crashing his body and his mind.

A rising sun, a cracked window, a door ajar, the slits of his eyes slowly sprung to the call of the world. The burning ball atop the mountains gave light upon the earth, and in its basking glow, it gave sustenance and life. Iscariot sat up in the patch of green grass, and his eyes peered into the expanse, and he saw the piercing blue sky, the sharp and jagged mountains that rose to meet the ocean above it. He beheld the colors of the world, of pinks and yellows and blues. The flowers in the Field of Diamonds reigned the planes in bright and uplifting complexion, and he was consumed by its majesty. It brought his spirit to rise.

He walked in the field of blooms and inhaled its perfumed scents. His mind began to cerebrate. The gears spun, the pullies rolled, the crankshaft turned, and the machine generated an idea. He flicked his wrist, and his communicator beckoned for an action. In the picturesque plain, he gave call to Andre and Antony, to two Comhail members and three officers of other military branches. He called for a time and a place to meet and discuss high volumes of significant matters which needed immediate resolution and urgent response before events of others ill will could occur. He gave one last look at the beauty before him. Iscariot turned back to his vehicle. It ignited, and he drove off. His destination, Imperial; his motive, the coup; the discussion, the day and the signal.

The bar was not too dark or too bright. The furniture was all handmade and refurbished with masterclass perfection. The music was soft to the ear. Iscariot took his seat at the bear clawed table in a chair that had a sculpted bear head atop it. In his secluded dwellings, the bartender welcomed him.

"Hello, General."

"Hey, Tim. Can I get a scotch, please."

"You bet. I wasn't sure if you wanted to change it up."

"Why set aside a good thing? Why push away a steady constant?" Iscariot asked.

"You never know what fruit may bare when you wander from the known path," the barkeep remarked.

"Better to stick with what I know rather than what I do not."

"Scotch it is then," Tim replied with a smile on his face.

Slowly, inconspicuously, those Iscariot sought to meet arrived. In total, there were two Comhail members, a male and female named Ainbheartach and Bedelia. Ain was a stoutly man, big of belly and little of hair. His face was stern, almost in anger or as though severely frustrated. His dress was comely. He was a man who gave the appearance of basking in wealth and delicacies. Ain was a Seanad from Criostaiocht, who held very unusual policy beliefs such as open borders and a universal basic income—ideals most Saoirse peoples objected to.

Bedelia was neither thin nor thick, just above average height for a woman at five feet seven inches. She had sharp dark eyes; her nose was just slightly too big for her face. She was neither ugly nor beautiful. Bedelia, like Ainbheartach, dressed in fine clothing. She was the minority leader in the Ionadai house, and her district was from counties residing in BanRos. She too hosted beliefs unusual to most Saoirse citizens.

To her right sat a man from the Iolar military branch. From head to toe, he was dressed in light blue. His clothes were tapered and pressed. He wore a pin on his chest, and the pin was the spread wings of an eagle. The man stood around six feet and was of modest build. His hair was brushed to the side, and atop his head was a sky-blue flight cap. The man's name was Arnold.

To Arnold's side was another man by the name of Harold Cole, a brigadier general in the Liopard branch of the Saoirse military. He was a cunning man, forty-seven years of age. He was notorious for never smiling and was dubbed with the nickname Harold Coldheart. Beside Harold, there was another man. He was a two-star general of the Mactire. His hair was that of a great gray wolf, his eyes a daggering blue. The man was fit, though he was nearer to fifty than he was twenty, but he had a youthful appearance. His face was without wrinkled flaws, and his teeth were aligned in symmetry. His voice was cool, as were his mannerisms. He sipped on a glass of Mahogany, which was a creamy vodka liquor, stirred with coconut milk and redemption rye, poured into a glass with a single cube of ice. It balanced the combination of sweet delights and the bitter sting of hard liquor. Hints of coffee and notes of cocoa tickled the tongue to a tantalizing satisfaction. He went by the name of Sidney and was as cunning as he was brilliant.

To Sidney's right were Andre and Antony, and next to them sat Iscariot.

"Lady, gentlemen," Iscariot began, "Thank you all for coming here this afternoon. The time to execute is near. Alamgeer made it very clear that he will not cease his actions unless Robert signs the treaty that I have brought back to Saoirse."

"What are the terms?" Bedelia interrupted with her inquiry.

"Patience, Comhail woman," Antony scolded her.

"Come tomorrow, I will present this document to Robert, and if he fails to sign, we will move our first piece and execute his removal of office, installing martial law until a new government is formed," Iscariot explained.

"Here, here!" Antony banged his fist upon the wooden table.

"While I've been away, Andre and Antony have instructed you all on what to do and how to perform your duties. Each of you was given a manifest. Each of you has the Pamphlet of the Sleeping Bear. Each of you has a mission in its message. Watch for the signals," Iscariot informed those before him. "We have all waited for this day. For some, it has been many years coming. For others, it has been months." Iscariot glanced at Andre, "But alas, the stars align; alas, our fated night has come. One way or another, the fate of Saoirse will succumb to our will." Iscariot creased his lips. It was quiet for a moment until Andre wiggled his tongue to express his thoughts.

"I want to thank you all for awakening me from the slumbering spell I resided in. A sacrifice of the few to save the many is the just way, the noble way. The faith I had in my king is now perished, gone to float in the wind with the ash and dust. Robert has always sought war. It is time we halt what he has welcomed from the time of his reign. Our plan is solid. The use of the Soisialach has given us a great advantage and swayed thoughts of the people who find our current structure inferior to what it could be." Andre finished his thought.

"The system is flawed, indeed. I mean you no disrespect, Iscariot, but your family has lost my trust since your father entered the Great War," Ainbheartach expressed himself. "Warmongers, the lot of them!" his voice spoke harshly, both in tone and in manner. "I say we boot Robert out of office, even if he does sign the treaty."

"He's a terrible leader, wouldn't you say, Iscariot?" Bedelia commented.

"On the contrary. I think he's quite brilliant. Only a fool would undermine the ability of their opponent. You make me skeptical to even include you in this plan, Bedelia." Iscariot spoke with contempt of her thought.

"The signal, Iscariot," reminded Arnold.

"Enough of this folly," spoke a frustrated Harold.

"Thank you, Arnold. I will meet with my brother at five tomorrow evening. Should the treaty be signed, look for the head of a lion in the window of Robert's office. This will signify the objective is off, and we can proceed with project B. If my brother doesn't sign the treaty, look for the head of a bear within the window. From there, we need to act quickly. We must be confident; we must be precise. The arrest of the high generals is key. Bedelia and Ain, make sure your contacts are prepared to send out the message. Andre, you know your way at the castle. It's imperative we are all on the correct frequencies for the final act to happen. After we leave here today, make contact with those who need it, and prep for all possibilities. Good luck to us all," Iscariot bespoke.

"Beware the bear within the den," Antony started. "For its roar is loudest and its might most deadly." Those around the table echoed his words.

Iscariot began to talk about his trip to Holle—the monsters he saw, the army vast and menacing, its leader strong and willful, its people with nothing to lose, and their commitment to a new Holle—a drive to end their suffering of twenty years and a restoration of their nation. He talked about how their minds were made, that the ideals of the Soisialach of the past had ruined them and how the Ivdeyskiy peoples corrupted their country and led them to a civil war which began the Great War.

Iscariot whispered secrets to those at the table, of those aiding Alamgeer, what their mindsets were, and how they would act when they were in Saoirse.

"Alamgeer proved to his people that absolute sacrifice was needed to achieve their glory. The slaying of his mother at his hands was not evil; it was justice." Antony spoke with vivacious candor.

"To justice." Iscariot raised his glass, and those around him followed, repeating his words.

After these remarks, those with Iscariot began to dine on cheeses and wine, their tongues becoming looser and their topics of hobby and ease. Antony, in his hyperbolic idealism, spouted poems and quotes of those from a distant past, but one in particular stood out for Iscariot. "The new world, with all its power and might, step forth to rescue the liberation of the old."

"To the new world." Iscariot raised his glass again, and his plotters followed once more. "Lady, gentlemen, the hour is late, and I must be going. Cheers and good tidings to you all." Iscariot's comrades said goodbye to him, and he exited the Imperial. It was an hour later than he had intended. He set his vehicle to self drive while in his drunken state, and he made his way home. Of all the things he and the others talked of through the afternoon and evening, Iscariot 's mind was focused on only one thing. Home he now was, and he exited the craft that brought him to his abode. He walked to her. Long has she rested in the poulnabrone in the fields of his home. Iscariot sat next to her tomb. The sky was now dark. How fast the hours ran in the day, and he talked to her underneath the starlight.

"I'm sorry, Anna," he began. "You would not be happy with me if you were still here. Tomorrow, if need be, I will betray my brother." His eyes began to fill with water, building high between the folds of his eyes. "I have no choice. If you can help me—please—show me the way. This is the only path I see," he begged. He pleaded for something to happen.

The night was still, motionless, as if time and space had ceased, and it was only he, in the moment, amongst his thoughts with his wife who had long passed.

"Do you not hear me, anymore?" Iscariot asked Anna. "You do not blow the wind. You do not break the clouds with thunder or light the world with lightning. Have you left me here, alone?" The balls of water in his eyes finally fell. "Is this goodbye, my love?" Still, he heard nothing. Still, he saw nothing.

"Forgive me Anna—this is our end. Tonight, my love for you must perish." His voice was steady as he spoke, though the rain from his eyes still fell down his cheeks. He rose from her grave, his hand on the mausoleum. "Goodbye, my Neachtar." His hand slipped off the marble as he said the words, his heart depressed, his mind and spirit full of great sadness. He slid his hand off her stone. He rose his head, pulled his heart, and freed his mind of her. He did not kiss her stone or tell her he loved her. His eyes were focused to the front, and he walked through the fields to his home, never looking back.

Iscariot did not know the hour, but the hour was late. Not a soul stirred. The town slept. His son slept, or so he thought. He hardened his heart. Like stone, it was solid, impenetrable. His eyes, once fogged, now evaporated as he looked toward the future with his view reborn. It was a world with no king. It was a world with a new hope for Iscariot. It was a world where he saw himself loving again. As he walked throughout his home, a soft light beamed through his son's studio door. He knocked and waited for an answer. There was none, and Iscariot cracked the door open and entered.

"Hello?" said Hanns

"Hey son. You've been in here all day. Aren't you tired?"

"What time is it?"

"Just past two in the morning. Let's get some rest, and we can talk about our day, tomorrow," he suggested to his son, who looked as tired as he felt. They walked out of the room together and to their beds that awaited them.

Iscariot showered, and in his shower, he was cleansed, free from all negatives. In his bed, he did not stir. He had only just shut his eyes, and the world he lived in vanished. The world he dreamed arrived. Iscariot saw a life of perfect bliss, a life free of his demons, free of his past. He was dreaming of the world he had wanted for so long.

A mirage of a woman entered his dream. Beautiful she was. His heart was afloat in her presence. He felt a whirl of emotions he had not felt since his time with Anna. As he walked within this dream of his, he was adored by all around him. He had never received such praise. As his fabled dream continued, the sun was setting upon the horizon's crest, and there before him, a face. 'Twas his brother there in front of him. He smiled at Iscariot. Iscariot put his hand to his brother's cheek and smiled back, but in a sudden change, his brother's eyes grew wide with pain and fear and shock. A grunt left Robert's voice and blood began to drip from Robert's face.

"Robert, no!" Iscariot yelled. "Not you. Not you, too, brother!" They fell to the floor together, onto their knees. Iscariot looked into his brother's eyes as Robert looked into his. He laid Robert onto the ground. He wept, and Robert vanished before him.

Iscariot awoke, his cheeks damp from the water from his eyes, and he rose. The day felt odd, ominous, as if the fruition of something horrid to come. It seemed he slept a lifetime, but the time was not yet seven. Dressed in only a pair of black joggers, soft and comforting to his body, he walked out of his darkened room and into his kitchen. He tapped his countertop, and a display appeared on its surface.

To clear his mind of the peculiar dream, he thumbed a tab that read sports. Surprisingly, his nephew's image covered the front of the digital page. The title above the picture of his nephew, Aedus, read: "Team Haas struggles after rookie departure." The image of Aedus played a trailer of highlights and lowlights of Aedus's racing team in a very sophisticated fashion. He then moved on to another sport and scrolled through its news. While he read, he tapped the counter surface, and a side display appeared with the word "Brew," and a moment later, the smell of coffee filled the kitchen. A message popped up on his display when his cup was filled, but before even reading the message, he swiped it away. He grabbed the cup from the surface of the coffee maker. The contents steamed a spiral staircase, climbing high into the air.

Iscariot could hear Hanns walking toward the kitchen. The hour was still early as he looked at the time.

"Good morning, son," Iscariot said warmly.

"Good morning, Dad. Are you going to Uncle Robert's? They're having a Saoirse breakfast at the castle."

"Sadly no. Your aunt insisted I come, but I've got to meet with a few people this morning."

"You'll be missing out."

"Oh, I'm sure. My stomach is already growling for it." Iscariot put his hand on his stomach as if to comfort it.

"I'll have seconds just for you," Hanns jested with a light laugh. Iscariot found it amusing and grinned alongside his son.

"Let's do dinner tonight," Iscariot suggested.

"Going out, you mean?"

"Yea, what do you think?" He left the choice for Hanns to make. His son seemed to be thinking of where to go.

"I could really go for some pasta. I've been craving it these past few days." Hanns expressed his thought.

"How does Terra Mia sound?"

"It sounds perfect." Hanns voice spoke with joy in the morning hours.

"It's a date, then."

"It's a date. I'll see you then, Dad. I'm off to Solascnoc." Hanns smiled, hugging his father goodbye. Iscariot watched his son leave the room to head to the castle. He loved his son. He worried for his son. He was afraid his mind might be swayed against him should the night of the event go way of the coup. *At dinner*, he thought. *That's when I will know if he is fully with me.*

Iscariot continued to read the news of the day. From sports, he went to local affairs, from local to national and national to global. Information was his friend, knowledge only half his power. Like many around him, to be informed was to be influential, powerful, and looked upon with favor. When Robert became king, he saw what being informed could do. So, Robert, two years into his kingship, made it ever easier for the common man to have the same power. Iscariot's brother opened up communication by the very source Iscariot received all his news.

Sixteen years ago, there was a competition in which private news outlets created a model interface to provide the news that impacted the individual from most significant to least significant. Of the fifty companies that entered, two would be prized the victor. The highest voted application sorted the news by where an individual lived, providing the user with all local news from state and local papers. The news would become broader as the user moved about the tabs of the interface. Of the five tabs, one of the tabs on the interface was a user-edited tab, customized to the individual's needs.

The second highest application for news provided the individual with a feed of where they were located. The user also had the option to select what states or countries they also wanted news on. This provided the user up-to-date news related to wherever they were at a given moment as well as around the world. Both companies received grants for winning the competition and have since been ranked in the top five for most used news applications.

His mind was filled with knowledge, and his body was filled with the sustenance of coffee and a croissant with egg inside its flaky crust. Iscariot closed the digital image on the counter surface with the touch of a button. He went to his room to shower and dress. Black dyed jeans, custom made for him, covered his lower half. On his feet were black suede boots with a tan trim at the sole. Molded onto his torso was a charcoal colored henley. Upon his left bicep, he wore a band with the image of a burning oak. His light hair slicked back and his blue eyes sharp, he left his abode with a sport jacket in hand.

In his car, he sat for a moment as the vehicle rumbled. He made a call to his mates.

"Antony, prepare your men. Alert the others," Iscariot told him without a greeting.

"Understood. When do you meet?" Antony asked for confirmation.

"The time is unchanged."

"I'll look for the symbol."

"Don the bands. Be ready," Iscariot instructed and then hung up from the call. His communicator then dialed for Andre. At the sound of the answered call, Iscariot spoke.

"Be ready. Don the bear," 'twas all he said. Andre never said a word, and the conversation ceased.

His craft now in drive, he cruised just outside the city of Buna to a town called Nemetunim. It was a city known for its gargantuan conifer trees that rose high on every city block, towering over the brick-clad buildings. It was a charming town of 30,000 folks and beautiful with its mix of natural allure and manmade designs. Iscariot parked his vehicle on the city streets in front of a bar that only served cream-based liqueurs. "Brady's" was the sign burned into the glass window.

Iscariot entered the building. Its lighting was a soft yellow, its furniture cheery wood with dark rich leather cushions. High above, beating in the hidden speakers, traditional Saoirse tones played softly to set the mood. The hour still early, not yet noon, the bar was lively as many came to drink their coffees with cream liqueur and breakfast pastries. Iscariot sat next to a tanned man with tatted arms. He had multiple piercings on his left ear and on his oval head, a gray fedora with a black band.

"Good morning," Iscariot said to the rugged man who now sat across from him. The tattooed fellow drank a warm alcoholic beverage called a hot chara mudslide made with coffee, chocolate syrup, cream liqueur, vodka, and sweet whipped cream that concaved and melted within the steamy contents.

"Good morning," replied the man. His voice quiet, a tenor tone, his tongue and mouth moved in a deliberate fashion as he spoke the greeting, giving him an accent, for the man's native language was not the Saoirse Gael.

A waitress came over to the table where Iscariot had just sat. She greeted him.

"Hello, welcome to Brady's. My name is Nishi. Do you know what you'd like?" she asked Iscariot. Her blouse was short-sleeved, her arms exposed. They flowed like rivers of light.

"Dia Dhuit, Nishi. I'll have the white Saoirse mocha with a chocolate croissant."

"Dia murre-dhuit," she smiled. "I'll get that right out to you." Nishi spoke with a kind voice.

"Thank you," Iscariot smiled back. The waitress left, and Iscariot turned to the man that sat across from him.

"When did you arrive?"

"This morning," he answered, taking a sip of the beverage before him. "Some late last night, and more to arrive within the next two hours." His words were long and drawn out as he spoke them quietly.

"Has she given you your instructions?"

"She has," said the tanned man.

"And you and your comrades know the signal?" Iscariot investigated for answers.

"We do. You should have no fear. We will be where we are needed." The man paused. "Should we agree how long we wait? We were told six months."

"That is my best estimate. It would take some time to convince many of the Comhail," Iscariot informed the rugged man.

"I do not like that. So much time wasted," the foreigner spoke, sharing his thoughts.

"We need to be strong on both fronts, internally and externally. Unfortunately, I see no faster way, unless of course, my brother doesn't sign."

"Then let us hope he doesn't sign. My people need a new hope," said the man from a faraway land.

"For all our sakes, let us hope he does sign. Solidarity is the key to success," Iscariot retorted. The painted body man grunted at the comment. Iscariot swung the conversation back to the plan. "To be clear, castle, bases, capital."

"Like I said, have no fear," the man smiled.

The two drank and bonded with one another, learning about each other and discovering a new friendship. The sun tilted in the sky at 220 degrees on the spring day on the second day of the month of Bellum. Iscariot looked at the time on the band upon his wrist.

"Thasuka, I really enjoyed my time with you today. One more drink, and I'd be here all day." Iscariot spoke with contented tones. Thasuka smiled.

"I will see you soon." His accent became heavier as the three drinks weighted his words and drove them to a more native tongue.

Iscariot departed from the brick-clad building, driving home to sober his mind, polish his argument, and prepare his soul for what lay ahead of him. In his drive, he arrived at his house where the light from the sun penetrated through the fifty windows that wrapped the abode, bringing radiance and organic elegance to the rooms scattered throughout his country dwellings. Iscariot did not bask in the abundance of the light but wandered to a place where it did not exist. To the fields of his yard, he walked in the lime green spring grass until he reached his land's edge. A shrouded hidden place before him, an onyx arched door at his arm's reach, the symbol of the Nazar beamed upon the door. His hand to the knob, the light was no more. Iscariot entered; the room was black like the vastness of space with fleeting strands of the smallest rays of light scattering about the empty room. The shamrock at the opposite end of where he stood was frighteningly bright. The emblem surrounded him as he walked in the center of the room of mirrors. Iscariot knelt before the magnetic symbol.

"Today is the day, my Lord. Are you with me, or are you my enemy?" he asked the Maker. "Silence once more. It is the only language I know from you. In this desperate hour, you do not speak nor act. In this hour of darkness, you stay silent. In the hour of need, you lay motionless. As I said to you, if you do not bring my brother to reason, then you are no longer my Lord. You are no longer my Father. Disowned. I will abandon you forever. Hear these words, for they may be the last you ever hear from me." Iscariot rose, and the glorious light of the shamrock was blinding, more radiant than a thousand suns, more vivid than lightning on the darkest of nights. Iscariot covered his eyes to shield them from its brilliance. Consumed he became by the might of the light. Afraid he became from its power. Doubt pierced his mind as if the scintillant bands hammered the cave his mind resided in, cracking the wall he had been building for twenty years. Iscariot panicked, searching for the door, looking to flee from the Glorious Gleam that enveloped him. Iscariot's hand found the knob of the door, but the light did not retreat as it did all the times before. Painful it was to twist the knob. Mightily he turned. His muscles flexed. He used both his hands for more power and strength and put all the force of his body into it. He yelled in frightful desperation. The knob turned, and he bowled out into the field of his yard. His hand felt of fire, but there were no burns. His body ached in soreness, but there was no bruise. He looked back from whence he came, and he saw the darkened door, but so, too, the symbol of his faith was lit in the light no longer.

He had only been inside the hideaway for what felt like a few minutes, but hours had passed. Iscariot looked to the sky; the sun arched at the angle of half past five as he moved forward to his country home. Inside, his heart still raced; he breathed deep to calm it. He splashed water on his face to see more clearly and changed his clothes from the soils of the world. Steady he became to leave his house once more, for now the hour of his fate was truly at hand, tipped on the scales of an action of another, hoping for balance, prepared for the scale to weigh against him.

His mind was empty as he drove. He did not see the road nor the people on the city sidewalks. He did not see the green grass or the cattle that roamed them, and in the blink of an eye, he was before the might of the white castle. Another deep breath he inhaled. He closed the door of his craft and walked through the doors of Solascnoc.

The room of seasons bloomed of flowers—roses red with love, ivory calla as pure as fine silk, sunflowers golden as the yellow fire in the sky. The birch trees were no longer barren. They sprung spring-green leaves, bringing a darker color into the room of vibrant shades. While there were sounds inside the cyclopean fortress, there was no one to be found, no servant attending, no welcomed greeting, no songs to skip from wall to wall. There was not a soul in sight. Through hall after hall, he wandered in the king's castle. No worm squirmed inside the library; no warrior danced in the armory. There was no glutton to be found in the dining room. Subconsciously, he avoided the room he knew his brother would be in. Up and down he paced the open hall whose windowless arches gave view to the north of the Mor Mountain Range. Sensing his nerves, he stopped. Iscariot leaned over the balcony with stone columns at his side, and looked out over the scenic view before him. Again, he breathed deeply, his eyes closed. He exhaled, eyes open, and he walked to his brother's office.

Three knocks upon the chamber door. It opened. His brother stood before him. Robert smiled at him with open arms and embraced Iscariot.

"Welcome home, Isc."

"Good to be home."

"Are you tired?"

"I don't sleep much anyway. I'm always tired these days."

"You and me both. You look good, Isc. More youthful."

"Beauty secretes from Holle," Iscariot joked.

"You letting me in on that secret?"

"And risk you looking better than me? Not a chance brother," Iscariot grinned.

"That's a good point. I guess I can't blame you," Robert jested. The brothers walked into Robert's office. The sun was at the twilight hour, the room lit by candlelight, and the soft glow of a gothic chandelier whose light source was that of a flame from a candle. Beauty in its dark design, elegance in its meticulous craft, it gave the room a picturesque phosphorescence. The fulgor of the room seemed to slow time, open thought, and drive the spirit. Robert sat in his arching chair behind his brick-clad desk. Iscariot rested his behind on the seat his son sat in hours before.

"I always liked these chairs," Iscariot praised.

"Surprisingly comfortable, right?"

"My bum is quite satisfied," Iscariot smirked.

"Speaking of satisfied, Gilchrist is on his way up with your favorite scotch."

"Always the perfect host, brother."

"I do my best," Robert replied, and just as the remark was made, a knock came upon the office door.

"Come in," Robert answered with a beaming smile. Gilchrist came through the door.

"Gilchrist, how have you been?" Iscariot asked.

"General, I've been quite good. I'm a happy man. That's all we can ask for in this world, isn't it?"

"Hold on to that happiness. It's a rare thing, Gil. I struggle to find it nearly every day," said Iscariot.

"Well, don't lose hope. There is always tomorrow, General," the servant remarked, placing the drinks down beside Iscariot.

"Tomorrow might be the day. We shall see," he agreed.

"I pray that it is." Gilchrist voiced a genuine, comforting tone as he said the words.

"Me too, Gil, me too." Iscariot spoke softly in agreement.

"My king, General, I must be going. God with you both." Gilchrist left the room in good cheer and high spirits.

"Goodnight, Gil," said Iscariot.

"God with you, Gilchrist," Robert expressed as he departed.

Alone the brothers were. With a sip of scotch, Iscariot began to voice his thought. Eloquent were his words, passioned his plea. He spoke of all that could be. In his hands, a treaty brought—a new order to be sought. Words on paper to cease a war, thy characters in page, in sacrifice it bore. 'Twas a clash of ideas and ideals, the moral argument to anneal. Iscariot spoke of the monstrous perils; he described the army of imperils. His articulate tongue sprung of great command. Alamgeer was the might, the hand. The Führer's path laid east. "Why trifle with the manic beast? Think of all the children, should we fight, all the women in their fright. Should they die, blood is on thy hands. Can't you see?" he asked. "So much death in all the lands."

Iscariot looked at his brother, gazing at his face for a reaction, a change of mind, a change of heart. Robert did not speak. Instead, he peered out the window, eyes glossed as if his mind were elsewhere, and then he broke his silence.

"Iscariot, brother. Have you lost your reason? Have you lost your way? Do you not remember why we fight?"

"Robert, I have been fighting my whole life. I no longer have the heart for combat."

"That is not the heart I ask from you," Robert told him. "I seek only the brave heart that will stand against the poisoned principles that threaten all that is just," his brother said to him.

"I am standing, brother."

"Am I thine enemy?" his king asked.

"Robert, you asked me if I've lost my reason, my way, but it is you who should consider why we fight," said Iscariot. Robert glared at his brother.

"Let me tell you the reason. Let me tell you the way. Let me tell you why we fight." Robert's voice rose with every sentence.

"The simple laugh from child's breath. The glinted glare of eyes shone love. The heaven's Maker from above. Doth the things that freedom breadth.

"Of bright green fields that farmers sow. The potter, the welder, of masonries with drove. Of the small business owner and the oil man who interwove. 'Tis this country, which we sew.

"The unborn baby in thy womb. For thy mother, thy father who raise thy dove. With nurture and care inside thy glove. We fight for life until thy swoon.

"My brother, we fight for thy neighbor whose down on their luck. We fight for those of other class. No regard for race nor creed, we fight for those, so they are freed. The beauty of thine spirit be thunderstruck.

"We fight for our friends in the east. From Attica to Yisra, our brethren are in worry. A flurried, hurried mind is anxious to scurry. 'Tis ingredient of fear, we must hold the yeast. 'Tis our fight, too—the lion, the beast.

"A man threatens those I hold dear. He slayed his mother, a heart like no other. 'Tis conquest he wants, while the un-pure he will smother. On dying breath, I will not veer. I will stand tall, so those I love can have no fear.

"Is it so hard to see, Iscariot?" Robert asked. "There is real evil in the world—a force so fierce, so vile, that it will destroy all I hold within my heart. It will break the bell of liberty should we let it. It will drown the hopes and dreams inside the galaxies of our wondrous minds. Should we not fight, I will assuredly lose all that I love. Saoirse will be forever lost, my friends, particles in the wind. My wife and kids would be left with no future, with only tyranny to beat them through a dreaded life. My brother, I will lose you, and how terrible that sting if that string should unweave from my heart.

"Can you bare to watch Yefimovich die, knowing you could do something, brother? Could you live with yourself when you see them turn west? Can your beating heart still pump should you lose your son when they do?”

Iscariot detested the answer, just as he despised the questions. His mind like a furnace, his tongue a whip, he lashed at his brother.

“How dare you, Robert.” Iscariot spoke softly. “How dare you!” he shouted, pushing his brother. His palms struck Robert’s chest. “We can stop all of that. A stroke of a pen, not the sword, is all that is needed. There will be no death of our friends in the east; there will be no tyranny upon the west. A restructuring of the treaty, Robert! That is all that is asked of you and Yefimovich. This is why we don’t fight, my brother! The mighty pen can save far more lives than the strength of the sword, and all that need be spilled is ink on paper. Why is this so hard for you, Robert?” Iscariot exclaimed. “Can’t you see that I’m trying to save you, brother?” His voice was more at ease. “Can’t you see that I’m trying to save us all? If we go to war, we will surely know the men and women that will die, but should we halt the deadly storm, there is far more a chance that the rain of death never comes, and all our desires become fulfilled.”

The room a hush, both men had retreated inside their own heads, and a rattle of words and emotions filled Iscariot’s mind and body. Robert pulled a brick from the wall of silence, and it crumbled to the floor.

“Iscariot, you asked why this is so hard for me. I can tell you, it isn’t,” his brother began. Iscariot was slightly confused, a bit shocked, but what his brother said next burned his very soul. “It is you who struggles with this choice,” Robert continued. Iscariot clenched his jaw. “We have gone to Alamgeer many times in the past. In fact, we have gone to Holle five times in the past twenty years. You have been with me for two of those visits. We searched and struggled to find a resolution, but he and the Hollen government have been steadfast in their narrow ways. They speak of reason and compromise. Yet, they are unwilling to achieve either. The time to talk is over. The time to risk my life, my fortune, and my sacred honor has risen to the peak of this twenty-year climb. My choice is clear, free from the fog of doubt, but I can see your mind is clouded.”

His body was like fire, and his spirit raged in the blaze of indignation.

“A fool’s errand you sent me on. For months, I researched. I pried. I did everything you asked! What was it for, Robert? If you planned to fight all this time, why send me away? Why lie to me brother?” The king opened his mouth to speak, but Iscariot’s speech kept the words from bouncing off his tongue. “You betrayed me, Robert. You have shown no faith in me.” Iscariot composed himself. “It’s clear I am no value to you, just your puppet.” Iscariot turned to walk out the door.

"Oh, I almost forgot. A present for you." From his jacket pocket, he pulled out a jet stone figurine in the image of a bear. He placed it on the windowsill behind Robert's desk. "It's the last gift I'll ever give you." Iscariot left his brother's office. His nerves snapped inside his body like mis-wired bands, breaking from their source. He was rotting in fury, blighted in sadness. His heart pained him, for now he knew what he must do. His action was the symbol, the first piece to move on the board. The sun blotted from the sky; the players of the game began to execute the coup.

His mind was in such a fury, he knew not how he got home, only that he was there. In the back of the field of his house, next to the poulnabrone was where his wife rested for all the days and nights left upon the earth. The uneven pillars and slated stone ceiling were decorated in moss and blooming flowers. His mind wandered in time; far into the past it traveled. Every memory pained his heart and broke his spirit. So much loss, so much suffering—he was broken as he fell to his knees and wept. Iscariot didn't want to feel the torment of his troubled soul a moment longer. He wanted a slate that was clean, a spirit new, wanting to be filled, not one to drain all the happiness from his life. *I must rid myself of all sadness*, he thought to himself. His eyes like a river, his hands shook like the quaking earth. With a match between his fingers, he set the stick to fire. He placed the burning match between the white blooming flowers and walked away from all the things that made him suffer, all the things that wrecked his soul. All the memories of his past burned. He moved forward to embrace the future.

<u>Yefimovich Chapter Four</u>

High rises the sun as it peeks above the curtain of the horizon where the land and sky collide. Rays like the blade of a sword pierce the world in glorious light. The sun-kissed sands of the Rossija Desert spin in the soft breeze, rolling down the dunes that seem the size of mountains. Eyes open of a man, and they gaze upon the sight of a beauteous sensation. Though she slept, she was as fair as she'd ever been to the beholder. Her blond hair spread across the pillow her head rested upon. Her arms stretched wide. The bed she lay upon was disheveled. The straps of her nightgown had fallen off her shoulders, though her bodice still covered her. She basked in the morning glow of the desert sun; it ran brilliant through the window. Her brown eyes opened, and he became entranced in them.

"Good morning, Viktoriya." Yefimovich kissed his wife to welcome her to the new day.

"Good morning, Yefi." She smiled at her husband.

"How—how did you sleep?"

"Too well it seems. I've taken up the entire bed," she grinned.

"And how is that different from any other night?"

"You make a good argument, Yefi." She rolled onto her husband, hip upon hip, face to face. She beamed at him and kissed him with great passion. She fell upon his body and closed her eyes as her head rested on his shoulder. "I love you."

"As I love you," Yefimovich said back to her. They stayed there a while, silent in each other's arms. "Viki," he called his wife. She groaned at her husband. "I—I need to get going. My briefing is in an hour."

"Just a few minutes longer," Viktoriya begged.

"Five more minutes, then." Yefimovich let her stay rested on top of him. The minutes trickled by, neutrinos the speed, frozen the memory. She was still atop of him, but Yefimovich began to rise. Viktoriya clung to him, wrapping her arms around his neck and her legs around his waist.

"Nooo," she moaned in a whisper in his ear. He stood with his wife's embrace, still holding her up with the strength of his core. Yefimovich laid back down, though now he was atop his wife. Viktoriya's gown had shimmied down to her waist, leaving her breasts exposed, but

Yefimovich's eyes only gazed into hers as he towered over the beauty that was before him.

"Sleep a little longer, love. I'll—I'll be back soon." He bent down to kiss her lips, his chest upon her breasts, his lips upon her lips. Eyes closed, the love and bond caused by that moment palpated his heart, making it stronger than it was before, making their love for one another run deeper than any tunnel could travel.

Released from the grip of the love of his wife, he showered and was clean. He dressed and was made civil. He looked back to his wife who squirmed under the covers of the bed. He walked toward her. "I love you."

"As I love you," she said back to him. The lovers parted with a kiss, and Yefimovich's day had begun.

Out the doors of his bedroom, he walked the Sesom palace. Hit with the sight of white walls with gold moldings and painted pictures, he traveled in the splendor of the palace. Statues of golden women from eras past sat atop ivory stone pillars. The wood floors his feet percussed across were a washed beige color. Bright was the palace as the sun radiated its majesty through the countless window panes. Down the winding L-shaped staircase he walked to a room of brown and alabaster columns with copper bottoms. The room had painted marble floors of the landscape of the country. Bleach-white stone statues decorated the open space, each displaying some holy significance. In this open space, a copper door to his right with mirrors on its facade was trimmed in gold with flare and elegance. Yefimovich pulled the copper handle and entered the briefing room.

His staff was seated at the rectangular table, awaiting his arrival. Yefimovich smiled at them.

"Brothers and sisters, good morning." Yefimovich spoke with charm in his voice.

"You're nearly late," General Iri jested with him.

"Nearly, but not." Yefimovich smiled. Commander Zash, the head of defense chuckled at the remark.

"Something amusing, Zashhitnik?" Iri seemed quite irritable in this early morning hour.

"Temper, temper, General. Did the night treat you so poorly?" General Dimitre pointed to his disgruntled friend with mockery in his tone.

"Dimitre, pisavek," Iri brooded.

"I—I—I see we're all in good cheer this morning," Yefimovich said sarcastically, sitting at the head of the table. "Down to business, then?"

"Yes, sir," said Zash. His look was peculiar. His dark hair was slicked back like a rolling wave, his beard thick, trimmed, and full. His mustache was pronounced with pointed ends. His appearance was serious, but his mind was light and quick to make remarks. He rose to speak with sober words, and the room was alert to his manner.

"We received word from Saoirse about negotiations with Holle. Currently, they run stale, but there has been news of trade deals offered to Holle from Saoirse and other countries that have the potential of reprieve and a dampening of Hollen threats."

"What are the rumored agreements?" Yefimovich was keen to know.

"From what we gather, it is trade for food and construction materials. Some seem to be of hired contractors from Mongnolerium to help Holle in their exaggerated state of disaster," Zash informed.

"Sounds like an investment plan from Möngke. Rare materials and construction contracts—seems like he's buying in low should Holle ever get out of its current economic state," the head of treasury, Edik, commented.

"Or invasion," Moeshe spoke.

"Or worse, alliance," his twin brother Voz observed.

"What—what is confirmed in these agreements?" Yefimovich asked.

"The Möngke reconstruction and aid program is confirmed and signed. Danija and Avstrija have already committed to wartime treaties with Holle and have a similar reconstruction program for the country. The leaders of Danija and Avstrija seem to want a union formed between the three nations," Zashhitnik affirmed.

"We play a risky game, trusting the Mongnolerians," Iri expressed.

"Tokugawa is ever vigilant. His eyes ever watchful," Yefimovich replied.

"Even the most watchful eye must close to rest," Iri commented.

"Iri, we are very aware of your concerns. But this is the way." Yefimovich explained. There was no further comment from the general of fire. "What further news?" Yefimovich asked.

"The size of the army is significant," Zash informed them.

"How large?"

"In Atma alone, 250,000 men, easily," Zash remarked. "Without question, a million men."

"What ha-have we been doing all this time? How is it that Holle has developed defenses on a scale equal to ours? And worse, right under our very nose?" The room had no answer. It was hushed. Not even the inhale or exhale of a person could be heard. A voice feminine and fair came from the end of the table, opposite Yefimovich. She was quiet, almost unobserved until she spoke.

"This is it, right here. We held our tongues. We did not call out every broken promise of the treaty. We did not act the wolf and bite when our enemy snipped at us. We became a wolf who laid in the sun but never howled at the moon." His daughter, the Tulku, spoke honest words.

"Too true, your words," Yefimovich acknowledged. He glanced around the room. Heads were down, eyes averted. "Don't all look so gloomy this beautiful morning. We-we may have failed to call out Hollen transgressions, but we must not fret it. We must now look forward. We must now trust in our allies. We must now trust in ourselves. Our call may be late, but our pack slowly gathers, and when the howl of war sounds, we will be confident. We will be fierce, and the enemy will fear the wolf, for our call is horrid, our jaws vehement, and our assemblage tumultuous."

"Who-ra!" yelled the general of earth in agreement with the prime minister's words. Others around him tapped the table in affirmation. "Might be the best thing you've said all year, Dimitre," General Iri commented in response to his "Who-ra." Dimitre laughed at the candid statement.

"Settle down; settle down." The voice of the head of the state department tried to calm the room. "Rallying the words may be, but now is not the time to cheer," Gosudarstvo warned the audience.

"What's on your mind, Gosund?" Yefimovich asked.

"Erbil, we know to be secure, but there are still weaknesses at our borders, particularly at northeastern Yisra."

"Explain," said Yefimovich.

"I would suggest an additional garrison where Yisra and Enuarku meet," Gosund suggested.

"What be the reason?" asked Zash.

"Enuarku is the smallest country of our allied forces. Should they fall or Holle find ways over water to attack, then their invasion into our home will be swift. I believe additional troops are needed should this instance occur." Yefimovich considered his motion and looked about the men and women before him, looking for a reaction of avowal or opposition. He saw General Voz adjust and then the man spoke.

"Mister Gosund, I am in agreement, and I believe I can help. A small fleet could be sent. If I'm not mistaken, I can send twenty Avir airmen to supply air support—ten with vehicle and ten without. We can discuss the tactics in our next council meeting."

"Co-commander Zash, could you please note that for further discussion?" Yefimovich queried.

"Already done, sir." Zash offered a wink and a nod.

"Thank you, commander." The prime minister nodded back. "Doctor Rachamim, you're awfully quiet over there. Ho-how do you fair on supplies, on beds, on blood—heaven forbid we need it?" The head of health had bright, lime-green eyes—like candy they looked. Her voice was soft, her mind sharp. Locks of sun, skin like snow, lips of a plump peach—she spoke.

"It is impossible, as you know, to prepare for such a horror. I believe we are suited as best we can for such a cataclysm. We have popup sites at the ready, and we have an additional 50,000 beds ready throughout the state. In total we have near 200,000 beds. Doctors are on standby, as are all appropriate staff. At month's end, we will have letters going out to all households and a nationwide meeting. Of medicine and supplies, we have a full list here of what is currently in storage." She slid a sheet over to Yefimovich. "As far as blood goes, we will issue a campaign to give until resourced at capacity. Knowing our people, it should not be a problem." She went on to discuss logistics of the matter in her field should such events take a turn for the worst. She was confident in her ability yet very much honest about how things could be. Her report was sealed tight, without error.

The morning briefing concluded with points to dwell over for upcoming meetings involving war-time state processes and war-time offensive and defensive strategies as further discoveries of enemy findings bubbled to the surface, findings of facts that had been buried far under the dark sea of secrecy.

"Thank you all very much—I—I hope you enjoy your Solisdies." Yefimovich rose from the comfort of his seat, and those around him followed his lead. They departed from the room, back out to the grand, open, brilliant, silo-shaped hall. He shook the hands of all who exited and waited for his daughter, who was always the last to leave.

She had her hair in a slipshod bun, the pants upon her legs a faded black, the blouse upon her torso thin white cotton with cut sewn cuffs and neckline. She was gorgeous in the ante meridiem rays. Though her bright brown eyes looked tired, her smile beamed joy.

"Good morning, Papa."

"Good morning, Kat." Yefimovich brightly smiled back at his daughter, as if her beam were infectious. He could not help but express delight at her appearance. "You were awfully quiet in there, this morning," he noted.

"I was tired and didn't have much to add to the discussion."

"You seem rather lively now," Yefimovich pointed out.

"Do I?" she played coy.

"You do."

"I'm just happy is all, Papa."

"Well, I'm quite glad of that—since most of our talks are of trouble and—and fear," he said to her. "Anything that has vivified your gaiety?" His daughter looked forward, as if to think about whether to respond.

"I suppose I'll tell you if you don't already know. But I've been talking to someone," she confessed.

"Oh, is that so?" Yefimovich said with interest. "A boy?" Katerina nudged her father with her hips and shoulder.

"Yes," she admitted abashed, cheeks of rose, and a grin of shyness expressed upon her face.

"Who is this poor soul, whose, whose heart you've captured?" Yefimovich could guess who it was, but he waited to see if his daughter would tell him.

"It's your favorite Saoirse boy."

"The boy whose tongue is tied more than mine? Who-whose eyes grow wide, and the crease of his lips expands the length of the earth when he sees my beautiful daughter? That boy?" Yefimovich teased Yekaterina, who laughed at her father's description of Aedus.

"Don't be mean," she barked in jest.

"I, I think Aedus would be fond of my description of him," Yefimovich smirked.

"It's nothing serious of course. We know what might come to be in this world, but he offers me a place to escape. We talk about silly things, of topics that don't matter, and it's nice to just forget the world, if only for a moment." She expressed her thought. Both father and daughter stopped walking through the palace as Yefimovich was escorting his daughter back to her room. He turned to look at her, and she turned to face him. "My precious daughter. Should he fill your heart with honeyed ardor, ease your mind like a summer's breeze. Should he uplift your spirit to higher mountains, if trust be found within his heart, and should it speak to yours, then do not waiver from its call. In life, it is so very hard to find the song that beckons thee, but if you think you've found a beat you love, keep it close and treasure every minute with your soul's mate. For it is what makes life so winsomely grand."

"Thank you, Papa." Yekaterina wrapped her arms around her father tightly.

"I'll see you outside, my dear."

"Okay, Dad," she said and diverged from her father and Yefimovich from her.

His bedroom was bathed in light when he entered to the sight of his wife and Rivka. Her brown eyes were as bright as the room that basked in the sun. She had a frame small and slender with rolling hair, xanthous in the early morning sun. Her bust was small, her bottom petite and rounded like the crescent moon. Upon her svelte figure was a loose navy blue, long-sleeved floral print dress. Her feet were inside white and tan leather, flowered sandals. Youthful she looked, and she locked eyes with her husband.

"Ravishing, my love." Yefimovich was overwhelmed by her appearance.

"Thanks, Yefi." She radiated a smile, teeth stark and bleached, void of stain, but in her charm, a slight and pestering cough left her larynx and exited her mouth and into the world in a wearing way.

"Viktoriya, it's back again?" Yefimovich asked with grief in his tone.

"It is," she answered, her voice a grinding rasp. "But it's not too bad, Yefi. I called Doctor Bolnoy. He said it was likely lingering effects from meningitis, perhaps the common cold from travel and fatigue."

"I hope it's nothing more. Ha-have you called Doctor Diamond? He might be able to see what Bolnoy can't." Yefimovich was growing concerned as his wife's health had been an issue for what seemed far too long in his opinion.

"If it doesn't improve by Tyedias, I'll give Doctor Diamond a call. I promise." Her voice resounded with the sound of swollen glands. "Come, get ready, and let's go get some lunch." Listening to his wife and seeking to match her style, he threw on a long-sleeved navy floral cotton shirt, and dark solid slacks, as not to clash with the patterned shirt.

"Doesn't he look handsome, Rivka?" Viktoriya asked her friend and servant.

"He's looked better." Rivka laughed, and so, too, did Viktoriya. Playfully abashed, Yefimovich spoke of his heart. "My heart, that of a broken twig, snapped and shattered," he said with a hand to his chest where his thumper laid.

"I think I have something that will make him look much better," said Viktoriya. She leaned in with a kiss. Yefimovich puckered his lips and sealed the kiss.

"Much better," Rivka giggled.

"Are—are you sure you don't want to come, Rivka?" Yefimovich asked.

"I appreciate the offer. Thank you, both. But I think I'll go for a walk and enjoy some time alone."

"We'll bring you back dessert then," Viktoriya insisted.

"You really don't have to," said Rivka.

"We know, but you're family; also the desserts at Mattie's are just too spectacular not to get," Viktoriya asserted.

"Surprise me, then."

"Surprise you, we will," Yefimovich responded.

"Have fun, you two," Rivka told them as they walked out of the room together.

The makeshift cane in his left hand and his wife's hand in his other, husband and wife walked together, side by side, meeting their daughter at the front of the palace, awaiting Aero to greet them.

Proper and timely, with doors to the vehicle open and an outreached hand to take Viktoriya into the craft, Aero said hello with a bow and salute and guided Yefimovich's wife, helping her inside. He did the same for Yekaterina, who had changed into a light blossoming dress herself, in a style similar to her mother's but with colors far brighter and more lively. While Aero tended to Viktoriya and Katerina, Yefimovich walked himself to the front of the craft and sat his bottom in the cushioned seat.

"I'm sorry, sir," said Aero.

"A, you've been at my side for how long now? I—I'm not so feeble nor so superior to anyone," said Yefimovich. Aero grinned at the truth. "How's the wife and daughter?" he asked.

"They're very good, Prime Minister. They've been asking of you as well," Aero replied.

"Aw, I love your wife. She is always so sweet when we see her," Viktoriya remarked.

"Thank you, Missus Nemtsov. She prays for you often."

"As we do for you, Aero," Viktoriya assured him.

"Thank you, Missus Nemtsov. Your prayers are always welcome and much appreciated." Aero's tone was one of pleasant gratitude.

From park—shift to drive—and they were off. Yefimovich and Aero talked of the upcoming Dobycha season, what players were transferring where, and how well the Knights of Erbil would do with a new Avi-player who looked promising in the under-twenty-one league. In the back of the vehicle, the women talked of wanting to see Tomoe play the cello in Edo. She was holding a small performance in an open-stage theater. It was a very small but very prominent venue in Edo called the Noh Theater. It had stood in the city for nearly a thousand years. The small stage had bamboo floors, four solid bamboo posts, and a traditional Nihonen roof, with triangular sloping curved eaves, extending beyond the pillars that held it in place; it was the dominant feature of the structure. The four corners of the stage were lit with small flames, and hanging from the ceiling's center, a large chandelier engulfed in fire spotlighted the performer.

"She was terrific when she played at the Darroch's," Katerina noted.

"Let's look for tickets when we get home," Viktoriya suggested. The foursome conversed some more as they traveled through the bustling desert roads.

They arrived. Yefimovich's stomach rumbled with a growl of hunger, audible for all to hear within the craft. Embarrassed, he poked fun at himself to hide his nervousness.

"Round the belly must become; round the belly will be." He slapped his gut, which gave a hollow thud.

"Yefi," Viktoriya started.

"You see, it's hollow and needs to be filled," the prime minister informed his wife and daughter in jest. Viktoriya shook her head in dismay, while Yekaterina let out a chuckle of pleasure from the actions of her silly father.

The vehicle parked, Aero stepped out of the vehicle and opened the door to let out Viktoriya. Naturally, Yefimovich let himself out while Aero tended to the two ladies.

"Are you sure you don't want to join us?" Viktoriya asked, her voice sounding a bit unusual.

"No, really, I'm quite alright, but thank you very much." Aero spoke with a humble manner.

"Well, when we stop at Mattie's, we are getting you something. We won't take no for an answer," Katerina told him.

"Yes, ma'am," Aero grinned.

The restaurant was quaint and simple in design. There were no lavish chandeliers, no golden crowned ceilings, no sculpted statues. There were only two wooden tables to rest one's plate and drink and wooden chairs to rest one's fanny. Its noted features were the high ceilings, large green framed windows, and an atmosphere that made everyone feel like family. The Nemtsov's opened the restaurant door and carved into the body of the door was the name BakeChop. Greeted as they entered, they sat in the center of the small room. The tables were shared, and though Yefimovich sat next to a stranger, he did not feel unease. He rather enjoyed the company of strangers, to hear their ideas, the dreams they dreamed, and he was always curious about the day-to-day life of the Yisra citizen. It made him feel connected to the people he served.

"Zdravstvujtye," Yefimovich greeted the man to his right. As if abashed to see Yefimovich, the man had an expression of amazement.

"Prime Minister, hello sir. Boker tov."

"Shalom, my friend. H-How are you?" Yefimovich acknowledged the man with peace and kindness, taking the stranger's hand in his, staring into his eyes with genuine care. To nearly all in Yisra, Yefimovich was a hero, a godsend, a bringer of promise.

"Anything we have is yours, sir," said the stranger.

"Come now. What's yours is yours. There is n-no reason to treat me different."

"Please sir, I insist," the fellow persisted.

"If you insist, I'll oblige. Would you like a drink?" Still seeming surprised, almost unworthy, the man declined the offer.

"Oh, declining your prime minister, I see." Yefimovich played with words to fool the man, as if he felt slighted.

"Oh, no, sir! I just." The stranger fumbled for words as nothing coherent left his tongue. Yefimovich laughed.

"I'm joking. What is your name?" he inquired.

"Artyum," the man replied.

"Artyum, it is a pleasure. I'm Yefimovich. When you're r-ready for your drink, just let me know." Yefimovich turned back to his family who were talking amongst themselves and stopped as the waitress approached the table they sat at and put her bottom in a spare seat next to them.

"Shalom." She greeted them and bowed at Yekaterina, who rose from her seat and bowed back to the girl. "It's an honor to serve you," the waitress said.

"And it is our honor to serve you and be served by you," Katerina replied to the woman with a smile as she sat back down into the wooden chair.

"I am very grateful," the servant replied. "My name is Annika. Can I start you off with drinks?"

"Hi, Annika," Viktoriya greeted her. "Can I have a glass of water, please?"

"Of course."

"May I have the same?" Katerina asked.

"Yes, Tulku," the waitress bowed. "And for you, Prime Minister?"

"A water is fine for me, too," he smiled. Annika smiled back.

"I'll be right back with those."

"Thank you," said Yefimovich, and then, quickly remembering something: "Oh, can you also get this gentleman a ma-Mango Yerusha Sunrise?" The man next to Yefimovich looked at him with eyes of wonder.

"Todah Rabah," Artyum said.

"My pleasure," Yefimovich replied.

"Right away, sir," Annika acknowledged the order. It was only a sliver of time that had passed when Annika returned to Yefimovich and his family.

"Do you know what you would like to order?"

"We," Viktoriya began, and then started a fit of harsh coughs that sounded like sand in a storm, pushing its coarse particles through the soft walls of her throat. "I'm so sorry," her voice craggy and ill sounding. "I'll take the soup and the veggie flat bread."

"Sure thing." Annika seemed to note the order in her mind. She then looked at Yekaterina who ordered meatballs on a grilled baguette, and then to Yefimovich who decided on the grilled chicken. The waitress left to put in their order. Yefimovich stared at his wife with worry.

"Viktoriya, my dear. After lunch le-let's go home to rest, and I'll call Doctor Diamond."

"Okay, Yefi."

"When we get home, I'll put on a kettle for some tea, and we'll watch a holoseret," Yekaterina told her mother. Viktoriya perked up at the kind thoughts of her daughter.

The meal came, and the meal was consumed, and during the feast, Viktoriya's cough worsened. The friendly stranger to Yefimovich's right left with thoughtful parting words for Viktoriya, and grateful verbiage left his tongue as he said goodbye to Yefimovich. Yefimovich and Viktoriya thanked the man at his departure. Viktoriya's cough continued as the waitress approached with water and the bill for the meal she served them.

Yefimovich felt terrible, a tremendous heartache at his lover's ailing. He reached for the check while looking at his wife who removed the cloth napkin from her face, and there came an anguish, a binding around his beating vessel. Heavy it became, an anchor in the raging sea, pulling down the broken ship. His eyes looked upon the red that soaked into the fibers of the cloth that left Viktoriya's lips.

"Viki." Her name left his mouth in silence. "Kat, take your mother to the car. I'll be right there." Katerina took her mother's hand and led her out of the restaurant. Yefimovich stayed behind to pay the bill.

"I'll say a prayer for her." Annika spoke somberly as she handed the check back to her prime minister.

"Thank you, Ann. Yo-You were fantastic." Yefimovich smiled at her before he exited the shop, and the smile left his face when he turned to the door.

Outside in the light of the day, he walked. Blinded by the sun for only a moment, he became focused. His heart was not broken or shattered; it became dust. For his eyes captured a sight of tremendous agony. A scene he hoped he'd never see. The love of his life was gasping for air. Her eyes were flickering in fear. Viktoriya lay upon the sandy brick-clad road. Yefimovich rushed to her side and held her hand. Aero was on his communicator, calling for an emergency vehicle to their location. Yekaterina locked her fingers with her mother's and set her hand in her lap.

"It-it-it will be-be okay, Viki." His stutter severe in his panic and fear, Yefimovich held her tight. His eyes pierced hers. Helpless, weak, and terrified he felt, knowing he had no power to help his wife, to relieve her from her struggle. Her attempts to breathe were short and convulsed, as if you could hear her throat lock up, closing off life from her soul. Viktoriya's eyes widened; no air escaped her, and none entered. She peered at her husband, as if she knew it was the end. Tears fell from her husband's eyes.

"Don't go," Yefimovich cried. "Please." He gripped her hand with both of his. "I-I-I love you."

Her body started to shake. Yefimovich sat her up, knowing she was in her final moments. He held her body tightly as the rain fell from his eyes. Her body stopped its tremble, but Yefimovich did not let his embrace release. His mind and body felt nothing but pain and sorrow. The woman he gave his life to and who gave her life to him died in his arms. He would never hear her laugh nor see her smile. He would never hear another scolding or playful words of love. He would never feel her touch, taste her tongue, or see the beauty in her eyes. He would never hear his name leave her mouth again. She died before him, and the two who had became one broke and became two again. One was left in life, the other in death.

He did not know how long he wept outside upon the streets, but he was awakened by the touch of his daughter who gripped her loving arms around his waist and whose tears soaked his floral shirt.

"Come on, Dad. They need to take her," she told him. Confused, he did not know what she meant until he saw the flashing lights and two men with a stretcher to their side. With quaking hands, he let go of his wife. He turned to face his daughter, and together, they wept in the open air around them with all the world to see.

The brilliance of the sun glistened upon the earth in all its glory three times, but Yefimovich remained in darkness. Though he walked in the light, he was a shadow on the ground, and though the world saw him, he could not see the world. Three days had passed since his wife left the bounty of this globe—three days of wretched blackness, hades of the earth—his heart was buried in it. In a bleak and somber mind and within those three days of hell, he and his daughter made arrangements for

Viktoriya's funeral. The Ivdeyskiy religion prohibited the practice of autopsy unless foul play were somehow evident in the case of death. However, due to Viktoriya's position in the State of Yisra, it was necessary for such an action to be performed, and so it was on the first day.

Upon day two of Yefimovich's dreadful nightmare, Viktoriya's body was cleansed in a process the religion calls Taharah. She was washed, perfumed, and dressed in plain white clothing, pure and unsoiled in order to meet her Maker, and from the moment of her passing, a family member tended to her and had always been at her side, even during the practice of Taharah, as was religious law for Ivdeyskiy.

'Twas the third day. The sky was blue as ripe berries with clouds like wisps of hair flowing in the gentle breeze. Desert birds chirped. The dazzling waters of the Peka Cbeta ran from west to east into the Adom Sea. Yefimovich sat upon a red rock in the open desert, outside the city of Shalom. Boulders high and wide as metropolis buildings surrounded him. Before him was his wife inside a closed pine casket. Her vessel sat underneath a lone desert tree with yellow blossoms blooming brightly, bringing beauty to his bereaved life.

Behind Yefimovich, a crowd 100,000 strong, dressed in mourning black—the people of Yisra were there to share in his grief. To his left, in a black dress and midnight vale, his daughter sat quietly. To his right was his most cherished friend, Tokugawa, and the dear wife of Robert Darroch. Support they were for him, a crutch to help him keep moving forward, a jester to keep him laughing, a gentle voice to prompt him to reflect, and a friend for him to cry with. He looked at Yekaterina and did something he had not done in three days. Yefimovich smiled. He thought of how strong his daughter was, how she kept her chin above her shoulders, how she spoke without a crack in her dampened state, how she continued to strive forward, for forward was the only way out of hell. *What character*, Yefimovich thought, for not once had she given into despair. Only the road of faith did she travel, never surrendering to her lowest self, always looking for the path of hope. He looked at her and saw the embodiment of inner strength. He gripped his daughter's hand and gave it a squeeze.

"I think I'm ready," he said.

Yefimovich pulled from his coat pocket a lock of braided hair, his wife's, a token, a piece of her he kept to keep her passing on from generation to generation. He rose from the stone seat and walked forward to his wife's casket. He took a deep breath and turned to face his friends, his family, and the people of his nation. Together, they remembered his Viktoriya. Yefimovich spoke in praise of his wife, her duty during the Great War, and the role she played in it. He talked of her as a mother and as a wife. He spoke highly of her courage, her intelligence, but more importantly, her love—her love for the country, her friends, her family, her God; how many she had mothered in the Ivdeyskiy religion. At the end of remembrance, he prayed, and the crowed of 100,000 prayed with him.

"Here I lie, my life in green pastures—He who led me here from flowing river to still waters. The Lord restores my soul and prepares me for a new journey. He readies me for the path of righteousness. Though, now, I travel in the shadow of death, its valley deep, its expanse wide, I shall have no fear, for the Tulku is with me. The elements, they comfort me. Thy Lord has given me the feast of life, and my cup runneth over. Surely, the path I travel is of goodness, truth, and mercy, and I will walk upon its bricks to the house of the Lord, where I will forever dwell all the days of my life. Amen."

Yefimovich's daughter joined him, opposite of where he stood. Together, they shot through the air stones the size of fists. At least 200 stones rose from the earth under their power. They flew like birds in motion at the setting of the sun. Images they made in the sky with the floating rocks. Under their spell, they would break them down to dust and re-form them, creating works of art under the blue backdrop of the heavens: symbols of love, a story of life and death and what was to come, according to their faith. It was ceremonial and known as the dance of life, and while the stones they controlled in the sky told the story of life, they drew into the earth the symbol of their faith and etched into the ground words of remembrance. When they finished the dance and their commemoration of words, they slammed the stones back down into the world, as if to stamp its end. Clouds of dust burst from the impact, and when the wind cleared their fog, her resting place could be seen once more, but her casket was now six feet into the earth, invisible to the naked eye.

The image now before the people created oohs and aahs from the crowd that had come to say goodbye to Viktoriya. A flaming wreath etched into the dry desert sand, it protruded out from the earth in a two-dimensional arch. In the arch of the stone wreath was his wife's name, Viktoriya Elizabeth Nemtsov. Twenty feet its diameter, within the wreath the Ivdeyskiy star, and in the star's center, the shin letter, and beneath the letter, she slept her eternal slumber. The words written in the ground inside the Ivdeyskiy star read: "Here rests the mother of the Tulku, wife to Yefimovich Nemtsov, Captain in the Eshan Army and leader of men and women in The Great War. She was the Mother of Yisra and will be forever remembered, now and forever after."

Yefimovich and Katrina went back to their seats and took the hands of Tokugawa, Lagertha, and Heilagr. Together they each laid a single rose upon the mark of the shin. Each said a silent prayer and sat back down upon the rocky pillared seats, and then those who came— friends, family, acquaintances and strangers—100,000 people mimicked their actions.

Hours passed; they sat in the living room of an old castle in Shalom. The historic place was known as the Castle of Ester. It was a place, according to the known tales of history, where Ester, daughter of a peasant, and of Ivdeyskiy beliefs, forged a bond and marriage to King Alaric of Ancient Holle. Their sacrament was the origin of the binding of the two countries and would forever shape the world into what it was today. At the middle of the room was a coffee table that had a small fire burning in its center. Yefimovich reflected on his life with the woman he loved and talked about their adventures together. He talked of when they first met, of her hometown of Nazar. He talked of how they wrote each other during the Great War, how they fought alongside one another at the battle of Nebuchadnezzar, how before the war in their playful youth, they traveled the world which led to the meetings of everyone in the room he was with. From Tokugawa to Heilagr, to Heilagr's daughter Lagertha, he described their meetings. He reminisced of the day his daughter was born and all the years that followed. *Such a full life*, he thought, *and such a short one, too*, were the words that followed.

"It's because of her that I've met all of you. It's because of her that my people have our own nation. Wh-what webs form in life—how beautiful the silky strings that m-make it whole."

"That reminds me," Heilagr began. "I have something for you, Yefimovich."

"Oh? What is it?"

"Do you remember the day you met Enoch and me?" she asked, pulling out a small wooden box with green moss on its top from the sleeve of her waving silk ebony dress. "It was the first time you had ever seen Fangetiys, our process of capturing light and using it to create something." She handed him the ornate box. Yefimovich held it in his hands. "Do you remember what I used?"

"A ring," he answered as he opened the gift Heilagr gave to him.

"But not just any ring," Heilagr began, "This is one of the Seven," she hinted, and Yefimovich knew exactly what she meant. His eyes expanded into a state of stupor.

"Flott Ringe," he whispered. "Wh-Who would sacrifice a ring, for me?" The timbre of his words sounded of shock.

"The one you hold now is mine." Yefimovich's head sprung up from the ring to look upon Heilagr's face.

"Heilagr—you can't."

"Mister Nemtsov, Prime Minister, my friend, do not tell me what I can and cannot do. In fact, I should have done this twenty-three years ago. The ring is yours. Keep it safe, Yefi, I fear you may need to use it sooner than you think." Stern but sincere, she spoke to Yefimovich. He looked back down at the stone ring. Clear like crystal, the stone that made the ring was called Engleaktig. Brilliant it was, beautiful its appearance, strong was its structure. As he gazed upon it, a hand not his own took it out from its bedding.

"Your hand," Heilagr instructed him. He obeyed and gave her his right. She held his hand with her left and slipped the ring onto his finger closest to his pinky. "Come, let's step outside." The two of them, along with Yekaterina, Tokugawa, and Lagertha, walked out into the twilight. The stars were faintly vivid, the moon cut in half—low it hung in the purple sky.

"What are we doing out here?" Tokugawa asked.

"Teaching," Lagertha answered.

In a field behind the Castle of Ester, Heilagr stood behind Yefimovich, almost in an embrace. Lagertha, Tokugawa, and Yekaterina stood ten yards in front of the two. Heilagr spoke silently in Yefimovich's ear.

"Within this ring is the waters of Hira-Kawa, the light of the sun in the summer sky, and blood shed from my own body. The water gives the ring a power to form structures of its nature. As the waters of the ring are from Hira Kawa, it possesses healing properties. It can mend wounds in battle, produce cells to fight illness, and provide light to shield you from all that might cause you harm," Heilagr explained. Yefimovich was about to speak, but she stopped him with a shush. Still whispering, she continued.

"Now, the light used can be in three forms: the light of the sun, the shine of the moon, or that of a shadow. Since you are Telekine, the source of the light does not matter; rather, the water used is what impacts its power. Since this water is from the Hira Kawa, it is light of weight but of mid-elemental properties. Since you are a natural Adamah, the mixture of your power and the waters will double your power."

Yefimovich's mouth opened slightly as if to let out a slight gasp. Heilagr continued. "However, in order for you to command this ring, it requires a sacrifice from you."

Before Yefimovich could ask what it was, Heilagr activated the ring, making it shine a magical blue, and while she did so, she took from the light of the moon and formed a blade, cutting Yefimovich's finger that carried the ring he wore. Yefimovich looked at the others in front of him. Tokugawa looked like he was trying to get to Yefimovich but was being held back by his daughter and Lagertha. Yefimovich looked back down at his cut finger. The blood ran down it, and the ring consumed it. The power of the ring healed his wound, and the blue hue slowly faded.

"My stars," he said

"The ring has fused with you—bonded together by blood. So long as you wear this ring, it will protect you with a shield of light. However, to use the light as a shield, you must not only think of it. Your thought must lead it to action," Heilagr explained.

"What do you mean?"

"Let me show you." Heilagr wrapped her arms around Yefimovich. "Now, I want you to think of a domed shield," she instructed him.

"Okay."

"You see how nothing happens?"

"I-I do," he stuttered a bit nervous about what might happen next.

"Now, call it to action. Say the word," she commanded of him.

"Shield." He spoke with the image in his mind, and in an instant, faster than the eye could see, light consumed his body, and a domed shield was put around him. "Heilagr!" he yelled. The light retreated back to the ring upon his urgent notice. Heilagr was lying in the grass, ten yards from where he stood. "Are you alright?" Yefimovich asked in a panic.

"I'm fine," she answered. The others were gathered around, concerned for her wellbeing. "It did exactly what it should have. Though, if I'm honest, I'm surprised that it did," Heilagr confessed.

"What do you mean, Mom?" Lagertha asked.

"Since my blood is also fused with the ring, I wasn't sure if it would harm me." She made clear her reason.

"Seems its loyalty is to its bearer," Tokugawa chimed.

"Seems so," Heilagr admitted.

"I-I'm so sorry, Heilagr." Yefimovich helped her to her feet.

"Really, Yefi, it's alright. I had known it might happen." She tried to ease his worry. "But now you understand its use." Only slightly comforted by her words, more so by the fact she wasn't hurt, Yefimovich guided the group back inside.

The flame was lower around the coffee table. It made for a more relaxed setting as the hour became late. Family and friends took their seats, resting their bums on the soft cushions of the sofa that wrapped around the fireplace table. Yefimovich examined the ring that rested on his finger.

"This is some ring," he commented. He looked toward Heilagr, who smiled slightly.

"Wait until tomorrow. Before I leave, I'll show you its power and what you are capable of." She hinted at more than could be seen. It became silent for a moment, and then Tokugawa broke the peace.

"The hour is late, but would you all like some Hojicha tea?" The ears perked up to the sound of his words, agreeing to the pleasantry. "Where is the kitchen? I'll go and set it," he said, grabbing the bag sitting in front of him.

"Come, my friend. I'll show you." Yefimovich guided Tokugawa through the castle. The room they left was on the east wing of the stronghold. They traveled west, down the yellow stone-walled hall that led to a staircase of large, sand-colored slabs. Down they went until they were directly in the center of the castle.

The kitchen was quiet. No workers were seen, only the pots and pans that hung on display over the long rectangular countertop. Yefimovich spotted a tea kettle and cups on the shelving next to an area of the kitchen that looked like a cafe.

"Yef, thank you," Tokugawa said, grabbing a pot and filling it with water. He turned on the stove and set the kettle on its surface. As the water heated, he tossed in the leaves that were roasted over charcoal at high temperature. While the tea brewed, he looked over at Yefimovich. "Be careful with that ring, old friend. Should it fall into the hands of the enemy, who knows what atrocities those who wish us harm will conjure up."

"My dear friend, we have been through a lot, you and I. I-if the ring consumes me, kill me. Be sure it falls into the hands of no other. Should I die with it, return it to Heilagr."

"Of course, Yef. I will do as you ask."

"The storm is here. The clouds, they band over us. We are just waiting for the light to strike and to break the billowed plumes. For soon, the waters will come crashing down."

"Then let it rain. The storm may be fierce, but from it comes clear sky," Tokugawa revealed. The teapot howled as steam escaped it. "Tea is ready," he smiled. "We'll let this simmer for five minutes."

Cups and tea in hand, the two walked back upstairs to the warm room they had left, and there the girls talked of simple things. Yefimovich and Tokugawa sat back down to join them. Tokugawa arranged the cups in front of each person and looked at the time. Yefimovich noted it as well, and in doing so, looked upon his wrist, and onto his hand, and he noticed the wedding ring that dressed his finger. He thought of his wife and the day they were married, and then looked at the ring that Heilagr had given him. He cogitated for a brief moment, if his wife could have had the ring. Then the horrors of the last three days could be no more, and the world he knew could continue onward. He quickly brushed away the thought for there was no time for fairytales or what-ifs. There was only time for what is and pragmatic thought, because deep within his heart, though it ached in such despair and such sadness, he knew that, in the end, when his time should come to leave this earth, he would once again be reunited and would assuredly live happily ever after. As his mind came back to reality, he wondered aloud a question to Heilagr. "Heilagr, I have one of the seven. Where are the others? What do they do?"

"Surely you most know the poem, Yefi. Six rings to guide the hearts of men, two to the men who ring the gates of heaven, two to the men whose bodies fill with spirit, one to the men who feel the planets core, one for the men who protect the world from war," she quoted the verses.

"But I only know of two," Yefimovich admitted. "If I-I didn't know of yours and Steinar's, I'd think they were a myth."

"Deliberately so. There was a time, long ago, when the world came to war because of the Flott Ringe, and in the War of the Rings, there was a seventh ring made. The Avengler claimed the Maker created it himself, and its bearer was the Phoenix. It was the counter and the abettor to the six, and when the Phoenix perished from the earth, so, too, did the Maker's ring," Heilagr answered.

"Why didn't the Phoenix destroy the other six?" Yekaterina asked.

"No one truly knows, I'm afraid. Some say it was to show grace to the men of the earth, for men to seek redemption and repent of their grievous ways. Some say he didn't have the power to do so. Others claim the seventh ring is but a fable, never to have happened," Heilagr answered.

"Do you know of any others?" Yefimovich asked.

"Of two more I know. The Ring of Life is with a man who travels the world and goes by the name Nagi. The other, I'm sure, Tokugawa could tell you." Heilagr looked at the Nihonen. He gave a sour look back at her. Yefimovich was astounded to hear Heilagr suggest that his great friend would know of the ring's location, and more, that he had never told him.

"Musashi," Tokugawa said with grit and snarl.

"Aedus's teacher?" Yekaterina's voice was high with disbelief. "How did he come to own the ring?" she asked.

"He earned it," said Tokugawa. "Generation to generation, the Ring of Faith is passed down to the greatest Bushi Knight—" He paused, his voice lowered: "He was the best among us," Tokugawa quickly explained.

"Those are all I know of. The Ring of Darkness and the Ring of War are unknown," Heilagr confessed.

"What do they all do, Heilagr?" Yefimovich asked.

"The Healer's Ring you already know, as it now belongs to you. The bearer of the Ring of Light can command all light and shadows and, with it, conjure up anything the wearer desires: a sword, a teapot, a cup. Whatever it may be, the light will make it, and with this ring, for any user, their power increases five times their original strength.

The Ring of Life can control the minds of weak-minded animals, but its primary function is what it's named for. It can save a life; however, it costs the bearer's own life to save a life.

The Ring of Faith uses the bearer's energy, chakra, and faith to use light magic. Depending on these three factors, the mage's magic and strength increases so long as their heart is pure and honorable. The Ring of Darkness is its opposite, as it uses only energy and chakra and grants the user the power of dark magic. Like the Ring of Faith, the user's strength and magic are based off their energy and chakra.

Lastly, the Ring of War can summon any offensive or defensive weapon. It can generate armor, and every bearer's strength increases ten times that of its user's natural ability. Its enduring quality is that it provides the wearer with exactly what it needs when the bearer needs it," Heilagr finished.

"What about the Maker's Ring?" Katerina pried.

"There really isn't much known about it, except for what I already told you. It is, however, also known as the Ring of Fortune, and it is sometimes called the Lucky Ring," Heilagr replied.

The room was silent, the tea cups empty. Yefimovich's eyes weighed heavy, and in the lull, just as he sought to seek the comfort of his bed and depart from his friends and daughter, a tap came on the wall of the entrance of the room. He and the others looked in the direction of the sound. Rivka stood before them, her eyes a sappy mess. Katerina quickly rose to comfort her.

"Rivy," she said in a soothing tone. Yefimovich approached her, wondering of her tears.

"Rivka, my dear, what's wrong?" he asked.

"The holophone rang," Rivka began. "A message for you, sir." She turned the device on her wrist, and the hologram appeared.

"Yefimovich, prime minister. I'm so sorry to tell you this and at such a dreadful hour, but it is a matter of the state," the message started. "The autopsy results are back, and with a heavy heart, I regret to tell you, your wife, the mother of our nation—we believe she may have been poisoned. Please call me as soon as you can. I'm so sorry." The message from the pathologist ended, and the room was dead.

Heads hung, and tears fell. Yefimovich was in a state of confusion, for he could not process what he heard.

"P-poisoned," he muttered. He did not know what to think, but slowly, the realization hit him. *Someone whom I call my friend killed my wife.* "I—I need to leave. Ka-Kat, I'll be right back," he said.

"Let me come with you," Katerina told him.

"No, stay here with Rivka and the others. I need to talk—to Doctor Drogee myself," he told his daughter.

"Dad," Katerina started.

"Kat, please." He looked at her with eyes of serious strength. He turned and left the room and headed to his own. The jagged gray walls seemed cold and lifeless. He dialed the pathologist; it beeped twice, signifying the signal was dialing out.

"Hello?" said the man. "Prime Minister?"

"Dd-Doctor, it's me," Yefimovich answered.

"I'm sorry, Yefimovich. I thought it best to tell you right away," Drogee explained to him.

"I understand. Do we know what the poison is and where it came from?" He spoke without stutter.

"Not at this time, but after looking over the organs in your wife's body, it was all too unusual. If I work at it, I can find what the substance was and its lineage."

"How long until we know?"

"Best case, a month," Drogee replied. Yefimovich felt like he had been punched in the gut, knowing he'd have to be patient and wait.

"Do you have any leads?"

"Not at the moment, Prime Minister."

"Thank you, Doctor Drogee, for the information."

"You're welcome. I'm sorry, Yefimovich. I'm sorry you have a life of such heavy burden." Drogee sympathized with him.

"It is the life I chose, and though there are times of pain and anguish, even today, I would not trade a single moment," Yefimovich stated.

"God bless you, sir," Drogee prayed.

"And he you, doctor," he replied.

"Good night, Prime Minister." Drogee spoke parting words.

"Good night." Yefimovich ended the call. He now lay in his bed and began to look back at the last year, but before he wandered too far in his memory bank, he rose from his bed and headed back out to call it an evening with his daughter and friends. His mind still in thought as he said parting words for the night, it conjured up something he didn't intend to think of.

At the Prima Minstar? his thoughts began. *The dobycha match? Was it someone here at the castle?* His mind asked the questions as he walked the dimly lit halls.

"Dad." He heard his daughter's voice. He looked up and brushed away the web of thoughts. "Are you okay?"

"I am what I am, dear," he answered.

"What did Doctor Drogee say?"

"We'll talk about it later, Kat. I just wanted to thank you all. You—You've been my greatest friends. I need to be alone for a while." He spoke to all within the room. His heart was pained to think that one of them could have plotted or committed the act of killing Viktoriya. It felt like needles struck his nerves; numbed he became. He turned back to head to his room, his mind heavy in thought, for he thought he knew where the act took place.

"Solascnoc," he whispered to himself. His body was depleted from excitement and the hardship of the night, his head rested softly on the pillow, sleep held him, and so, he dreamt.

Alamgeer Chapter Three

His darkened mind ran wild as he dreamed of things he'd never seen. A man, his face familiar, perhaps seen in a picture, a painting, a story—Alamgeer did not know. The familiar fellow his mind dreamed of held a man up from his collar and over his head. A crown of gold and jewels rested on the hoisted man's pate, and the man who held up his foe had a painted face of dirt and blood and sweat. He spoke to the man he gripped with the might of an outstretched arm, his hand holding the kingly man's collar.

"The bondage of slavery from your tyranny is over. By the grace of God, we conquered it, for we spoke to Him of freedom, and we called out for the world to hear: give us liberty, or give us death. Alas, liberty is here," he spoke to the man with a golden crown. He pulled back his right arm, and a sword appeared in his hand. It pierced the belly of the jeweled man he held with his fist. Limp went the king, and the crown fell.

Alamgeer's dream was clouded, like the building of a cumulonimbus. Lightning struck, and vivid was the scene of a man he knew well. 'Twas his great, great, great grandfather. He stood in a hall of independent nations. He looked about the room at all the separate flags; his great-great-great grandfather sturdied his stance, and he spoke.

"Three score years have passed us since that time. We were more united then; we were stronger then. We were a nation of one mind, one heart. Today, we cast our independent flags aside and hoist from the pole a binding and eternal flag—one we all call to, one we all pledge to, all for one people, one nation. Let us battle one another no longer but stand together in our struggles and rise together in our successes. Today, we united nations come together as we once did. Today, we are no longer men of a different name. Today, we are all Hollen." Alamgeer watched from the perspective of his grandfather, how the members in the room of nations tossed their flags aside that sat upon their desks and raised in their hands the Hollen flag he knew today.

The waving flags got bigger as the scene became more narrow, until his eyes were blinded by it, and when the flag was moved aside, he was a child deep in the depths of a forbidden place, a mausoleum.

"Come on Ala! Auf geht es!" said the voice of a boy. He looked at the child and saw his friend, Himmel. Alamgeer was happy that his only friend was before him once more. A heart filled with joy, he felt free and mirthful. He smiled in his bliss. He ran to Himmel, and together, they traveled through the forbidden halls. Door after door they walked through. Every room was something new. The door they entered next was stark white, nearly blinding to the eyes from the dark and gloomy walls they had come from of the blue-hued mausoleum.

"Ready?" Himmel asked him. A bit of fear in his heart, Alamgeer nodded yes. They opened the door and entered a room. The room was octagon in shape, each wall an image of a man or woman, except on the wall they entered from. The floors were marble with crevasses of circular patterns made of light. The light streamed through the cracks, giving clear boundaries for each marble slab. The walls around them were of a similar pattern, but the light that ran through the grooves protruded like holograms. The dull white lighting gave the room a sense of mystic wonder.

At the base of each stone wall was a square slate boulder with shattered diamond dust within its body. Six feet in height and six feet in width, the stone cubes stood. On the top of each square block was a cylindrical shaped chasm and fit perfectly into it, a scroll. Alamgeer climbed atop the slab and grabbed the scroll that rested within. He unrolled the paper, and words he could not read were written on the parchment. At the bottom was an image of a ring.

"What is it?" Himmel asked.

"I don't know. I can't read it," Alamgeer answered.

"Here, let me see." Himmel reached out for the scroll.

Boom! the sound startled the boys.

"Put it back!" Himmel panicked. Alamgeer quickly rolled it up and placed the scroll back into its chasm, and the boys ran off. As they ran, the light ran with them, and the light blurred Alamgeer's vision, and a flash came to them, a snap image of his father face, another of a boy in tears, the chest of a woman and the feel of her embrace, and then darkness.

The darkness broke, and the sun shone down upon him. Alamgeer stood upon a stage and looked out over thousands upon thousands of people. He could hear his heart pounding loudly, forcefully. It was strong but filled with fear. His eyes looked to his feet. Red, in blood, they were covered—so, too, the stage on which he stood. The body of his mother was before him, her head ten feet from her corpse. He looked to his hands, a blood stained sword in one, the other gripping his chest where his heart thumped. The rapid beats persisted. 'Twas all his ears could hear. Blind he was from shock. His pumper stopped its beat. A hand touched his shoulder, and he was awakened from his blindness, and his heart beat once more. He turned to see his wife. She stood atop her toes and whispered in his ear, "It's over." A tear streamed down her pixie eyes. Alamgeer could hear again, and he heard the raining swoon of cheers. His eyes still gazed into his wife's and he spoke to her.

"It has just begun." The roaring sounds of joy became a visual display, and he drowned in it.

His eyes darted open. He awoke to the dark day. His pupils waved like a flame in the wind, and when they saw his wife, they became calm as static air. Her white hair shined as did her skin. Like diamonds in the light, it glistened in beauty. He looked away from his wife. The city was framed in his opened balcony view. He could see the dark clouds of the storm approaching. He could hear the calling of the rolling thunder. There was no rain or flashes of brilliant light. Alamgeer removed the covers from his body, and his feet stepped onto the cold slate surface of his room—a far different feel from the warmth and pillowed bed he rested in. The stone walls in his room were covered in a mural of angels amongst God. The air was warm around him as he leaned over the balcony. He sat high above Atma and looked down onto his people, his Hollen volk. In a few hours' time, the clear streets, where lava flowed beneath them, would be filled with Hemitheoi and Semideusi, a united people, looking up to him to hear his spoken words. He closed his eyes to picture the scene that would be before him.

His lids opened when the familiar touch of the woman he loved caressed him from behind. Her hands were warm to his chest as her arms bound him and her face rested on the muscles of his back.

"Guten morgen," she said in a tired voice. Alamgeer grabbed her hand and kissed it with the softness of his lips. "Get ready, meine Papst. You have a full day ahead of you." She pecked his back with a kiss and released him. He stood there a moment longer. He breathed and turned to his room to prepare himself for the path that laid ahead of him.

He bathed himself, and when he dried his body, his wife was before him. Hands locked, she walked him to his closet. She dressed him like a squire dresses a knight. Adorned he was in his uniform. First his legs and hips, then his chest and arms—boots struck his feet; bare were his hands. The clothing fit tightly onto his body—breathable it was, flexible and hardy. Hella put the band of red, white, and black upon him, the eight-pointed star with a shin letter and crown. She skirted behind him and commanded him to kneel. She clasped a dark cape upon his neck and ordered him to continue kneeling.

"What for?" Alamgeer asked. He looked up at her, and in her hands was his sword. The color of the night was his blade, his hilt etched in gold. She locked the blade into its sheath as red waves of light spewed like mist from the steel. Alamgeer grabbed the weapon and rose. Hella let go the blade and knelt.

"Meine Führer." She gave the Hollen salute.

"My majesty." Alamgeer put out a hand to lift her up. Their lips smacked one another.

"Be off, meine Papst," Hella told him.

"I'm off," he replied and turned to leave her and the room they were in.

"Wait," she said as if he had forgotten something. Alamgeer stopped to turn. Up she was on her toes, arms around his neck. "One more," she said and kissed him again. "See you tonight," she smiled, and they parted once again.

Down the cold and windowless staircase, he walked. Through the tunneled halls, a mile it seemed he went until he arrived deep within the babbling burning blaze of the volcano in which he dwelled, to the chamber of his staff. Within the gloom of the room, sitting at the stone table, were Commander Rommel, General Kesselring, Julius Gunther, Major Speidel, Captain Montgomery, and three others. Displayed in the seats, in holographic form, were Von Lewinski, who was in Avstrija, General Guderian, who was the spearman, the ice breaker, the bell to the war. He and his troops sat in south Avstrija, ready and waiting to fight. Alamgeer's two sons also sat via hologram. Strapping, tank-built men, with eyes of war, they sat quietly, awaiting command.

"This meeting will be short," Alamgeer began. "We have prepared, not for days or weeks or months but for the last eighteen years. We have planned, educated, and led our people to this moment. Today, we fight for our volk, our nation, our very lives. Today, we begin our war to secure our dream and our lost worth. To the men in this room, I ask: are you prepared to give me your life? Are you prepared for the course? You have seen, first hand, what I have sacrificed. I intend for you to do the same. If you are ready, bend the knee. If you are not, this will be the only moment you have to leave without repercussion, for if you betray me, death will surely follow."

One by one, those at the table rose and then knelt to give salute to Alamgeer. Those on the hologram mimicked the motions of those in the room.

"Lewinski, are your men ready? They may not fight today, but their time is close at hand," Alamgeer called him out.

"Yes, Führer. Upon the signal of Guderian, we are ready," Lewinski answered.

"Guderian, you have become so dear to me. How are you, my friend?" Alamgeer asked of him.

"I am in high spirits. I am confident in our men. On your go, we will blitz the Polshans and begin our path to freedom," the general replied with drive.

"And I shall meet you on the morrow." Alamgeer showed his pearl daggers.

"Hagel Ala," Guderian acclaimed.

"Praise to those who serve," Alamgeer replied with a clenched fist held out in front of him. The rest of the room did as Guderian did. Still kneeling, they chanted, "Hagel Ala! Hagel Ala! Hagel Ala!" Warmed his heart was with their loyalty, their devotion. Pride filled him.

"Praise those who serve," he said back to them. "You all know the signal. Is there any amongst us who have questions before you part? If so, please speak. So long as the strategy is kept, victory is assured." No one questioned the plan. "Go in peace, and may this war bring amity among us," he said as those in the room rose to their feet. They were dismissed except for two; his sons he commanded to stay behind.

The room was now empty except for Attila, Almaut, and him. He spoke to them.

"My boys, meine jungen. How is your beating heart?"

"It beats strong," Attila answered.

"It is hardened and prepared," Almaut replied.

"There is no need for you to talk to me as the Führer here. Are those your honest words?"

"We speak truly." Almaut spoke for him and Attila. Alamgeer looked over to his more timid son.

"Is it true, Attila?"

"It is true, Vater," Attila responded.

"Good, my sons. I'm glad to hear it. How was your journey to the rivers?"

"Pleasant and fulfilling. It was what I needed before the fight begins," said Attila.

"Boring." Almaut offered his thoughts.

"Tisk." Attila sounded the word of disappointment.

"That is the response I expected. Though you are twins of the same womb, you are feathers of a different bird. One is of stone and steel, the other of fire and water. Tell me, my sons, what were the people like in the nearby towns? Were their outposts in your stays when you ventured to Mongnolerium?"

"What people we saw paid us no mind. A passing glance at our size, perhaps, nothing more," Almaut informed his father.

"We stayed in rural areas. There were no outposts where we stayed. It was quite peaceful," Attila remarked.

"And what of the people, here, on the day I sacrificed everything for them?" Alamgeer inquired further.

"We were in the Black Forest at Fluss in der Nacht. We saw no one that day and did not go to town for three days more," Attila began. "When we did go back to town, either none spoke of it, or they spoke with praise."

"What did their eyes and body say when they talked of it?" Alamgeer persisted.

"For most, they matched their words. For some, maybe fear harbored in them or uncertainty. The eyes read similarly for both," Attila answered.

"Almaut, did you notice anything?"

"Hmph, I paid no mind to them. They are nothing to me," Almaut responded.

"Stupid boy. That's the action of someone who doesn't care about their own death," Alamgeer scolded him. Almaut snarled, deflecting his father's words.

"My death means nothing, nor could anyone kill me if they tried." Almaut spoke with arrogance.

"Almaut!" Alamgeer raised his voice. "If you were here, I'd grab you by the neck and throw you to the wall. Do you not know what you mean to me and your mother? When Ulama sent you down from heaven and into our arms, I knew his time was coming to reign once more. Answered prayers you boys are. Instruments of our God to bring on a new era. Feel the fire within you. You boys are not like the others; feel its rage, its burn. Do you hear the flames call to you? Let it consume you, and absorb its power, so you, in turn, become empowered. Almaut, your death would mean everything to me and to the peoples of this nation. So close we are to becoming more than we ever were, and it's all because of you. I know this, your mother knows this, and soon, the world will know this."

"Thank you, Vater." Almaut spoke in softer tones.

"Set your saddles, my sons. The hour pulls closer." Alamgeer rose from his seat. "Show the world the might of Holle." His sons rose from their chairs as well, and in unison, they spoke.

"We will burn it to ashes, and from it, Ulama will rise and, with him, a new Holle."

"Good luck," Alamgeer wished them.

"Goodbye, Father," the boys said together. The holograms that displayed Attila and Almaut evaporated, and Alamgeer was alone.

In his lonesome thoughts, he pondered his religion. He, of Califfe faith, prayed to Ulama, his god. Inside the belly of the volcanic ash and lava, he bent the knee to a ring of fire that circled in a dark and cylindrical caved room.

"Ulama, my God. Please tell me the time is here. Please tell me it's time to end the rumors of the savior, the Phoenix. Please, my Lord, bring word to my ears, that the false prophet, the Tulku, will be vanquished by my sword. Lord, is it time to kill the Phoenix of the Nazar and smite the non-believers? Will you show yourself upon the earth and make pay the Ivdeyskiy for all their sins? Will you prove to the people of this earth, the blasphemies of the Nazar, and will you convert those of the Shin Michi? Lord, it must be time. I can see the signs. The heavens have been chanting your name. They claim they see your rebirth. They say your coming is at hand. Lord, I reach out my own as your instrument to abolish those who call you by the name, "Devil bird." Ulama, I ask for a sign. Should we win the battle of Polsha, I will know you march to us and that aid is on the way. Before I part, I wish your blessing and your protection until your coming. Ratif." Alamgeer ended his prayer with a solemn amen.

The morning sun had burned to bring the coming of high noon and, in turn, blazed through the clouded sky to fall victim to the night. The burning globe hovered just above the horizon, ceasing to put the flame out, to look upon the volcanic city and gaze upon the city's glow. The orange and red and purple hues fell upon the metropolis. Atma basked in the evening light, both of nature and men. The city held an eerie calm. The air was filled with the nervous energy of fright and excitement. Outside, the people gathered around radios and moving picture boxes. The few with enough money to do so set their eyes to a holoset, yet all Hollen waited for the call to war to leave the lips of the Führer, Alamgeer.

Once more, he was before the people. He showed no sign of anxious jitters or weakened manner. The beat of his heart was slow and steady. The breaths he took were calm, not heavy but light. He was at equilibrium. Alamgeer could feel the buzz in the air as he sat underneath an open stage of an outdoor auditorium that sat 50,000 volk. He bathed in their call to him as they chanted his name.

"Hagel Alamgeer! Hagel Alamgeer!" The crowd was loud and filled with energy. They hushed a bit. Alamgeer could hear Francis's voice as it bounced from the mic on the stage to the speakers hidden around the auditorium. The people applauded his name as she called Alamgeer to the platform, but Alamgeer did not show his face. He waited, alone, underground, until they became silent. It was then that he came from underneath the hidden door below the stage—when he showed himself. The crowd roared in a detonation of his name, "Ioben Ala, Praise Ala!" The words rang, bouncing off the columns and stone surfaces of the amphitheater. Alamgeer looked out unto the people. All gave the Hollen salute; red and black banners of the eight-pointed star hung from the towering columns thirty feet in height. Skolastjori soldiers stood at attention. Cutthroat and terrorizing they looked, men of skull faces with red and gold armor resting on their bodies. On their backs, there were wicked blades five feet long, and in their hands, a golden flagstaff with the Hollen banner and a golden bird, and eagle-owl, a symbol of Ulama. To his right were scores of children from the Hollen youth program that Francis and he initiated fifteen years prior. Behind them were soldiers, and to his left, the Braunhemd. Front and center and littered throughout the amphitheater was the common man, his volk.

Alamgeer did not grin or smile at their presence. His eyes saw beyond to the world he imagined, and his eyes saw behind to the world that had once been. His pupils came to focus. He admired the grandeur of it all. *Everything was set as it should be*, he thought. On the stage, sitting at his left, was his wife. It was she and she alone. If it weren't for his size or his power to command, Hella could take the room with a single look—a muse she was for portraits and poetry.

The people became silent. They sat at the edge of their seats, forward and attentive, ready to capture in their ears all the words the Führer had to tell them. Alamgeer's arms were folded as he observed all that was before him.

"Diejenigen, die dienen zu loben!" Praise those who serve. These were the words that became the motto of the Hollen volk, which he exclaimed, and in turn, they responded, "Hegel Ala!" and then, quickly, they hushed, waiting for the oration to leave his pale lips.

"Holle! Meine volk! Today—today is our declaration!" Alamgeer spoke with vital exuberance, and the people applauded and roared, responding to his words. He let the crowd grow quiet once more.

"On this third day of Bellum, in the crisp spring night, we march. We march because of the sins of our forefathers. We march to battle our oppressors. We march on this night to break the chains we have been enslaved by. We march to take back our lands. We march for our freedom, for our liberty. Today, with gun and sword and shield, we march for a new life. Tonight, we march for Holle!" Alamgeer's fist hammered the podium he stood at. He took a breath, and calmly, he began again. With every sentenced uttered, he expressed its meaning in his tone and in his body language. With the swing of his arms, his gaveled fist—every movement had a purpose; every rise and fall of his words spoken were driving to a point.

"How long have we waited? How long have we waited for the foolish ways of Yisra to end? We have been treated like sheep and cattle, and they have herded us to the slaughter. Do they not think us human? Are we not men? No, I tell you we are men, but they—they are the devil. They are evil in flesh. They are the widow makers, the death eaters. They are our enemy!" Both fists concussed the surface of the pulpit. Alamgeer composed himself and began again.

"Today, we sacrifice more than just our money and more than just our time. Today, we sacrifice more than not seeing our friends or our families daily or weekly. Today, we forgo the simple pleasantries of life because, this day, we sacrifice our very lives! We put our hearts and our souls into our beliefs for the life we know that we deserve. We put our life on the line of death, ready to be cut by our enemy, in order for our children to have a life far greater than our own. We fight to relinquish ourselves from this poverty and rise as the bird of fire, renewed and reborn." He paused again and gathered his thoughts.

"The Ivdeyskiy have poisoned us, my Hollen volk. For twenty years, they have slipped us the pill of promises, of compromise, but have never healed Holle. Every trade deal, every economic policy—they have undermined the Hollen people and led us into this squalor. They were the people, them and the socialitze, who brought about the Great War. They preached for years of their independence, and our forefathers were too weak, too narrow-minded, to stop them. They have soiled this land and have stolen from us a part of our home. Erbil will be ours once more. The Holle of the Great Uniter before me will be restored! There will be no force that stops us! There will be no body of water too wide for us to cross. There will be no mountain too high for us to climb. There will be no battle to out-toughen our might. There will be nothing that breaks our resolve!"

"Hagel Ala, Hagel Ala!" The words engulfed his ears and came from all directions. Alamgeer raised his hand for silence.

"At this very moment, we are at war. At this very instance, we have stormed the border of Polsha. At this very second, our men fight! They are fighting for you, for me, for those yet to be!" Alamgeer hollered to the crowd. As he spoke his final word, a percussion, a series of explosions out in the distance could be heard. Alamgeer could see the blast, and he pointed to the sound. The people turned to look, and their eyes beheld the highest tower of Magma Krone and the volcano it rested upon. They saw the ash and dust, the red balls of flame hurtling skyward, and from all the madness in the darkness, the fright of the power of the volcanic mountain brought forth a creature. It looked like a streak of fire burning through the night sky. Plumes of black smoke tumbled off its body, and then the beast let out an odious screech. The sound pierced not just the ears but went through the body and made the very spirit of man to tremble. It was as if a man's fingernails were being pulled from his body, and his scream brought terror and pain. The monster in the sky plummeted to the earth and landed behind Alamgeer with the force of 10,000 men.

A hundred feet from tail to head and with spikes of charcoal ivory protruding from its body, donning on its crown two curved horns nearly twenty feet in length, the beast expanded its astronomical wings, spanning 200 feet from tip to tip. They were torn and murderously sharp. The monster broadened its shoulders and let out a staggering roar that rattled the bones and muscles of all men.

Alamgeer looked upon the dragon, and the beast looked down upon him. Alamgeer looked over to his wife who marveled at him and the creature. He mounted the dragon, sitting at the base of its neck, where it was void of any spikes. Alamgeer looked at the frozen crowd below, who hadn't seen a beast of the kind in over 200 years. He yelled down to them: "Tonight! I fight for you! Tonight! The world will once again fear our might. Diejenigen die dienen zu loben!" He cried out to his people, and all who saw him knelt before him and praised his name: "Hagel Ala, Hagel Ala!"

"Gehen!" he commanded the dragon. Its wings flapped like the whirlwinds they created. Gusts of air came from the beast, and it became airborne with Alamgeer on its back as its master. Alamgeer looked down at the people below. Thousands upon thousands looked up to him, their hands raised toward him, their voices loud and in unison as they hollered, "Long live Holle!"

"Schall fliegen!" he yelled at the beast, and in an instant, it was at Mach, heading toward the country's border, toward Polsha and the spear of the Hollen army.

The world was different as he traveled through the clouds of the night sky. The moon glistened and shone upon him and the monster he rode. It was quiet: just the whistle of the wind, the hardened breaths of the dragon, and the sounds of his thoughts. For twenty years, he had waited for this moment—twenty years of pain, hatred, and longing. He had waited. His heart pounded in his chest. He reveled at the moment before him. A more perfect world he was to build, and today was the first brick laid in its construction. As he got closer to the border, he did not think of his children or his wife, nor did he think of his people. Only the battle was on his mind and how to win it.

He soon crossed the barrier of Holle and Avstrija and sped ever faster in the early morning sky to where Avstrija meets Polsha. There, in combat, in the dead of night, Guderian and his men fought. Alamgeer raced to see his men in action, to see the massacre of the feeble Polshans. Alamgeer approached his targeted destination, and much to his disbelief, with heated anger brewing, he saw his blitz had not already pierced the heart of the Polsha capital. His men were still 200 miles from their objective.

"Sturz!" He demanded the beast fall back down to earth, and so it did as it was commanded. It wailed in its descent and cratered the earth as it landed. There was a morning fog across the land. The sun had crept above the surface and beamed its rays upon the world. Guderian had rushed from his luxurious tent. Alamgeer looked fiercely at him. He could see the fear and regret in his general's eyes. Alamgeer jumped from the dragon he rode.

"I'm disappointed, Guderian. Why do we halt here?" Alamgeer spoke with a scolding voice. His general was still stricken by the sight of the monster behind Alamgeer. "It is not him that you should fear, Guderian." He grabbed his general's collar, and his eyes became focused on him.

"I'm sorry, sir. There has been an unexpected resistance." He finally spoke to Alamgeer.

"Explain." Alamgeer was harsh.

"Yisra, sir. Yefimovich—he fights for them," Guderian answered.

"He's here?"

"Yes, sir."

"Tent." The Führer pointed, and they walked in to quickly strategize a new tactic. He sat down in a folding chair with a cloth back decorated with the Hollen symbol that had been printed on it. A board of a map was in front of him and sat upon the table. Placed on the map were metal pieces that indicated strongholds and the types of troops that held those points. "Where are we failing and why?" The Führer demanded to know.

"They hold strong at Plock, along the river. At Lodz, Radom, they are well fortified, and at the other river entry of Pulawy," the general informed him.

"Our men attack from the rivers, the flanks?" Alamgeer questioned.

"Yes, sir."

"No Skolastjori at those positions?" Alamgeer inquired further.

"No, sir."

"They are held here, correct?" He pointed at the map. Alamgeer spun the wheels in his mind, strategizing as the information rolled into his cerebellum. "How many?"

"About 300, Führer," Guderian responded. Alamgeer looked at the time on his device. It was the eighth hour of the morning. The sun was slightly higher, slighter hotter. He realized every minute lost could mean a loss to the first battle of the war. "Where is Yefimovich?"

"He is in Plock, sir," the general answered. Weaving all he knew within his mind, Alamgeer sewed a plan together.

"Guderian, send out all 300 Skolastjori, 150 to each flank. Leave Yefimovich to me. I'm leaving Sieradz. You will not see me until you finish this campaign here. Expect reinforcements to Lodz and Radom. Make sure the Skolastjori make haste. They need to be at their locations by ten ante meridiem. Send half of your 5,000 men here to Lodz and Radom. My reinforcements will head to those locations.

"Yes, Führer," Guderian acknowledged.

"We strike at high noon, when the fire of the sun is at its peak," Alamgeer instructed.

"We will be ready, sir."

"Don't fail me." Alamgeer turned away and strode out the tent. He leapt up onto his dragon. Guderian was close behind Alamgeer.

"Hagel Ala!" He knelt at the führer with a salute. Alamgeer saluted back.

"Machzahl!" He yelled the command to the beast he sat on. The dragon raised its 200 foot wings, giving shade to where Guderian stood. The wings crashed down at a stunning pace, and he catapulted into the heavens.

Robert Chapter Six

"Ten, thirty, forty, and twenty. Location, riders, location." Robert gave Uriel the information.

"I'll make sure he is aware Robert," Uriel replied.

"Thank you, Uriel. The sooner the better. It's nearing time." Uriel nodded.

"I noticed that you are not in it." Uriel waved a book in his hand. "May I ask why?"

"I had to be sure of your diligence."

"What do you mean?" Uriel sounded doubtful.

"Let me see the book," Robert told him, taking a pen as Uriel handed him the red leatherbound journal, and he jotted the number seven-one-one onto the parchment. "There we are," sliding the book back. "How do you think we look?"

"You didn't answer my question, but to answer yours, attack is imminent—no later than the end of the week. You sure you're ready?" Robert thought for a moment.

"Yes."

"Is your boy ready?" Uriel questioned. Robert pondered further.

"It's a difficult mission. If he succeeds, I'd say we have the advantage," Robert responded. Uriel gave a long, drawn-out yawn.

"We need to make these visits later in the day. Four in the morning is far too early," Uriel complained.

"I thought it rather nice. It's quiet. I can hear myself think. Plus, I thought you liked this time with your favorite brother-in-law," Robert grinned.

"I'll admit, though our conversations are thought-provoking and with real purpose and consequence, it is a nice bonding experience." Robert smiled and turned to look out his office window inside Solascnoc. The daylight hadn't quite come to the land of Saoirse. The sky was a very dark shade of the midnight black. It was just at the moment before the sun punctured the shell of the egg it was hidden in to bring about the striking world of light to shine across the sky an exquisite blue that conquered the heavens.

"Will you stay for breakfast?" Robert turned from the window and asked Uriel.

"I'm afraid not. Time is of the essence now."

"Both an ally and foe to us all. You know you're missing a Saoirse breakfast?" He tried to bribe his brother-in-law.

"Precisely why I must go. If I were to eat, I'd not move the rest of the day," Uriel joked.

Robert chuckled at his remark. "Fair point. Not sure how I'll manage myself."

"So, our hope lies in seven-two-two for our first mission," Uriel stated, though it seemed more a question to Robert.

"For this and many more," Robert confirmed as a look of sadness crossed his face. To draw away the worry, he thought about his past. "Do you remember when we met?"

"Of course. You were a stubborn kid of eight or nine," Uriel laughed. "Strange how your personality has changed as you've aged. In your youth, you were far more outspoken, and your brother was the quiet one. Seems now the roles have switched. But yes, the first time I met you, you were yelling at my father. It was quite funny, really."

"Looking back at that—probably not wise, knowing the power of Enoch."

"I don't recall what it was that you were shouting at him for," Uriel conceded.

"If I remember right, it was because your sister had taken me to the forbidden forest, and your father was scolding her quite harshly," he reflected.

"He has rather a talent of tongue in all forms of speech, but I don't think it was that she took you to the forest. I believe it was what lies within it," Uriel reminded him.

"Looking back, there is no doubt. I remember seeing the four guards that stood around the temple—the reason its call the Forbidden Forest, or as your folk call it, the Forbudt Skog."

"The four pillars are quite scary guards at that—all as tall as Tokugawa and just as broad if not broader," Uriel reflected.

"I remember them fondly. Seeing the guards for the first time— my mind's call to flee never screamed so loud. Even to this day, they are most menacing in their look." Robert recalled the sensation. "Your sister had no fear—not a stutter in her strut and no stammer in her speech. I remember admiring the sturdy spine of courage, and as she talked to those eight-foot guards, my angst and timid heart began to embolden, and I became unafraid."

"Lagertha has never been one to cower. It's not surprising you two got along so quickly, considering your personalities are strongly similar," his brother-in-law remarked. Robert looked at Uriel who had glanced at the book on the table. "So back to the book before I leave. Seven-two-five," Uriel began.

"Will be here. A primary source with ample connections. Our go-between," Robert interrupted. If you are the needle point of a drawing compass, then seven-two-five is the legs of the instrument, to be sent as a rider and act as an informant. Seven-two-five is to fall under your command, just as all others will," Robert told him.

"Seven-two-five can be surprisingly bold."

"It is why I'm the hinge. I hold the two legs in place of the compass. The tighter the screw, the better the compass performs," said Robert.

"Interesting analogy."

"On to a different matter: How goes the project?" Robert asked.

"Well, so far. In the beginning stages still, of only men and women I trust."

"How were they chosen?"

"A test."

"Curious?" Robert sought clarity.

"A really complicated test. Those who could solve it were qualified to take another test," Uriel began.

"And what was this test?" Robert asked in between Uriel's explanation.

"A series of very high-level mathematics."

"Mmh." Robert was interested in his method.

"It brought about quite an interesting crowd: teachers, engineers, students, schlubs on the streets," Uriel continued.

"And because of this test you believe them qualified?"

"Well, as I said, it was rather difficult. So yes."

"So, what was the other test?" Robert's curiosity led him down the rabbit hole of Uriel's complex mind.

"For the other test, for those who qualified, they had only a few minutes to finish. Impossible to get the correct answer, of course, but it was a good way to test their resolve as well as their way of thinking. The test was on a piece of paper, and within the paper was additional information needed in order for the questions to be solved, and you would only know this if you put the paper up to a light, and you would see what information was missing," Uriel informed him.

"So, what was the outcome?"

"Eight, highly qualified and extremely intelligent candidates," Uriel smiled. "Though I think I scared them quite a bit when I told them that if they should disclose any information, they'd be killed for high treason. None backed down, so I think I've got strong-spined men and women," Uriel's grin grew wider in delight.

"These schlubs, these men and women, you're sure of them?" Robert sought for one last strand of certainty.

"Well, Robert, you say it all the time yourself to never underestimate the common man. I find it all too true myself that the people we imagine not amounting to anything are those, when given the chance, who do the things that no one can imagine," Uriel responded.

"How bright the heart of the hidden gem locked inside the common man. Brilliant it is when the world sees its glory." Robert smiled and knew full well that he had chosen perfectly the man to lead his hidden soldiers.

"Here comes the sun. I'd best be off," Uriel said to Robert.

"Safe travels, and thank you, Uriel." Uriel rose from his seat inside Robert's office and opened the door to leave.

"Farewell, my friend."

"Godspeed." Robert spoke parting words and turned to look out his office window to the world outside. He started to think of his children and the moments he had with them. He then tried to recall his favorite memories of each child.

His mind fell on Absolume. So much like Robert as a youth. Unafraid to voice his opinion, constantly seeking to better himself, kind of heart. A man of honor he'd quickly grown to be. As Robert's eyes gazed upon 843 acres of pines that surrounded the castle, he spotted a white-tailed deer. A lovely doe and its fawn grazed in between the strong sturdy trees of the small forest the castle nestled in. The corners of his mouth turned with happiness as he reflected on a memory he had with his son. He let the picture of his mind consume him, no longer seeing what was in front of him but seeing instead what had once been before him.

It was the first chilly day of fall. The leaves ceased photosynthesizing, creating photogenic colors, like a painter dabbing on a canvas. The leaves were marked in a palette of colors, warm they were, as if all the rays of the summer sun melted into the veins of the leaves, turning them into the sunsets and sunrises they once enjoyed.

Absolume, only eight years of age, was bundled in comfortable fall clothes—a gray sweater and blue hunting slacks, ear muffs, light gloves, and on his feet were thick and sturdy boots. He purposely breathed heavily through his mouth to see the hot air of man battling the cold air of nature.

"Look, Dad. I'm a brooding dragon," he said, making an angry face and huffing and puffing to cause the clouds of condensation to pour from the depths of his body.

"Oh! Pretty scary there, bud, but did you know your dad is Oighear-ean?"

"Oh no." Absolume spoke as if his father was the mythical creature and he a dragon. Robert scooped him up and spun him around. "Dad! Dad! I'm getting dizzy." Absolume laughed as he yelled. Robert slowed his spin until he was stopped and a little wobbly himself. "You're funny, Dad," Absolume said happily, trying to catch his balance. Robert noticed his expression changed. He seemed to be pondering something now that he had his bearing.

"Dad, do dragons and oighear-ean really exist? I don't think they do."

"And why is that?" Robert asked.

"Because I've never seen one."

"Just because you haven't seen one doesn't mean it isn't real."

"Then how would I know?" His son pressed him for answers.

"Well, there are books about them, describing them in great detail."

"So, are mermaids real? There are books about them," Absolume questioned further.

Robert chuckled. "You're a sharp kid. You know that?"

"You and Mom tell me to always ask questions, so I do. I don't think Lorena likes it. She seems to get annoyed sometimes," Absolume expressed.

"Don't worry about your sister. She'll love you no matter how much you annoy her."

"Well, I'm relieved, 'cuz I really like Lo. But Dad, what about the mermaids and dragons and Oighear-ean?" Absolume seemed desperate for an answer.

"Well, Abe, we know there were dragons because we have fossils of them. Remember when we took you and your brother and sister to the natural history museum? Remember seeing the dragon bones and teeth?"

"Oh yeah. They were huge! There were so many cool things there, Dad. Can we go back?" his son spoke excitedly.

"Of course, we can. So, you see, we have natural records from bones and teeth of dragons. That's how we know they're real. We don't have any proof of mermaids and oighear-ean. Make sense?"

"Yea, I guess. But, Dad, who will stop the dragons if there aren't any oighear-ean to stop them?"

"I don't think we'll have to worry about that. All the dragons have gone extinct."

"What's that?" his son inquired.

"It means all the dragons in the world have died and no longer live amongst us," he explained.

"All of them?" Abe's voice rose in his question.

"So it seems."

"But what if they're not? What then, Dad?"

"Then it's up to you, Abe."

"No man can beat a dragon, Dad." Robert knelt down to see his son's eyes at his level.

"Why do you think we have fairy tales and fables and things of make believe?" Robert asked his son.

"I don't know," Absolume replied.

"We have these stories to show us that man can do anything. No matter how scary the monster or how difficult the fight, the power that is inside you is far more fearsome and far more powerful than that of any evil creature. These stories of darkness are there to remind us that we are the light for the world, and we must never be vanquished." Robert spoke with conviction. He put his ear on his son's chest. "You hear that?" he asked.

"Hear what?" Absolume questioned back.

"The call of your heart. It's strong, it says, and brave, too." He looked back up at Absolume. "Take good care of it. You might have to slay a dragon one day, and only your heart will give you the power to do so."

"I will, Dad," Abe smiled.

"Strap your gun back on your shoulder. We're nearly there," Robert instructed.

With guns in hand, they walked a mile in the country woods, where pine needles littered the ground they walked on. They got to a tree that overlooked a small field, 100 yards across and 200 yards wide.

"We're here, Abe." Absolume rested his rifle at the base of the tree. "We're here, but not done, bud." He pointed up to a blind in the tree that would hide them from the animals.

"We have to climb it?" Absolume sounded tired just thinking of the act. Robert handed him two sharp picks.

"I'll take your gun, and I'll see you up there," he said, taking the rifle from his son. He noticed Absolume looked nervous.

Abe struck the sickle into the tree and then the other, climbing all of two feet and falling on his caboose.

"You alright, Abe?"

"Ow. That hurt." Absolume spoke as if he felt pain, but his tone said otherwise.

"Here, try again," Robert said, handing him the picks. Absolume climbed again. Half way up the tree he went, and his grip slipped from the axe. His footing unbalanced, he came rushing to the earth. Hard he landed, caught by the soft, inflated cushions Robert had placed at the base of the tree. Abe crawled out of the cushions; he was shaken.

"Are you okay, bud?" Robert knelt next to him and grabbed his shaking hands.

"I'm scared," Abe told his father.

"I can see that, and that's okay. It's normal to be scared, and it's okay to fail," Robert comforted him. "What have we learned while climbing this tree?" he asked.

"That it's hard," Abe answered honestly. Robert grinned.

"What happened the first time, Abe?"

"I went too fast," Abe said.

"Good, then the second time you went slow, and what happened?" Robert led him on.

"My arms got tired, and I fell," his son answered.

"Good." Robert reached into his pack he'd been carrying, and pulled out a rope. "Here," he said, tying the rope around his waist, and the other half in between a belay device.

"What's this, Dad?"

"It's a belay device. If you fall again, this will arrest your fall. So, you'll remain up there instead of down here. With each failure, a lesson," he told Abe. His son looked back up the tree. Robert asked him a question before he began his climb. "Do you hear that?"

"Hear what?" Abe questioned back.

"That heart of yours."

"Strong and brave," he heard Absolume say under his breath, and again he climbed, and Robert watched until he reached the top and crawled into the blind in the tree.

"I did it!" Abe shouted down.

"Great job, bud!" Robert hollered back. He then went behind the pine and into a hidden door, and gullied himself up. Out Robert came into the hunting blind. The look on Absolume's face was priceless, utterly confused.

"There was an elevator this whole time?" Absolume was flabbergasted.

"We must know how to do things the hard way before we take the easy route. It is what builds character. It's what keeps that heart of yours brave and strong. So, when there is no easy route to take, you know you can do what is hard."

"Still, there was an elevator." Abe pointed out the obvious.

"Next time you can use it," Robert chuckled. "Let's rest a bit and get ready." He gave his son a breakfast bar and apple juice he had in his pack, and after they ate, they set up for the wait.

Slowly, the sun rose, as if pulled by a string. It climbed higher into the sky. An hour, nearly two had gone by, and out in the field, 300 yards away, deer came in to graze. Robert was surprise by Absolume's patience. Abe looked back at his dad with wide eyes.

"They're here," he whispered. Robert helped him get ready for the shot.

"Remember what I taught you?" Robert asked in a hush. Abe nodded.

"Firm grip, butt to shoulder, eye at distance of scope. Deep breath, hold, pull, confirm." Absolume spoke his memorized steps quietly to his father. Robert gave him the okay and watched his son as he attempted a complicated shot from quite a distance.

Boom! The shot went off. The barrel of the gun sizzled in the autumn air. Birds nearby panicked in flight, cawing and tweeting as they hustled away. The forest became quiet. Robert looked out from the hunting blind with his binoculars.

"Great shot, Abe." He looked at his boy. "Ready to go down?"

"No," Absolume replied.

"No?"

"I'm afraid to see it dead," his son admitted to him.

"Here, Abe. Let's go down. I need to tell you something." Through the pully system in the trunk of the tree, they went down to the forest floor and walked to the open field.

"The deer we walk to may be dead, but it will bring about life. Its flesh will be eaten when we cook and serve it to the poor. Its fur will be used as a blanket to keep the poor warm, its antlers used for making weapons and tools. With its life, it gives life to us. Though this deer we travel to is gone, we have helped balance the ecosystem. If there are too many deer, they could destroy the balance of nature. They would eat too much grass, and the grass wouldn't grow, and if the grass doesn't grow, then all the deer will die or invade other lands. If the grass and the deer die, then so will the wolf and its pups. So, though you have killed this deer, you have given life to so many. Do you understand?" He explained and asked Absolume as they looked upon the kill.

"I do," Abe answered. "It's still sad, though."

Robert knelt down by him once more. He looked him in his blue eyes. "Death is always sad, Abe. But we must not dwell on death and sadness. Rather we should think of the life and the happiness it has given to others," he elucidated. "Would you like to say a prayer?"

Absolume nodded. Together they thanked the deer for the life it gave and thanked the Lord for its life to give. "I'm proud of you, bud."

"Thanks, Dad." Abe smiled. "How about that shot? Pretty amazing, huh?"

"More amazing than you know." Robert wrapped his arm around Absolume, and his memory faded, and his eyes and mind were back to the present, inside the castle office, looking out the windowpane.

Out his office and through the halls and rooms of Solascnoc, he found his path took him past his children's rooms, and in that hall, his son walked out of his bedroom.

"Abe," called Robert.

"Hey, Dad," Abe responded, dressed in his morning pajamas.

"I was just thinking about ya, laddie." Robert threw his left arm over his son's shoulder.

"Oh yeah, what about?"

"Memories of our first hunting trip."

"Good memories. A lot of meaningful talks. I'll cherish them forever, Dad," Absolume told his father as they walked toward the dining room.

"Me too, laddie, me too." Robert inhaled and could smell the breakfast scents, and the smell was like a guiding force, a guide to lead him and his son to the feast, and Robert listened, and he heard. He heard the sweet sound of his wife's voice and the honeyed chatter of his children talking with one another. He was happy and so very thankful for what he had in his life, and though tough times lay ahead, filled with conflict and peril not even he could imagine, he was overwhelmed with grace. At the entryway to the dining room, food was still rolling in from the runners who were serving, and Aedus was walking toward them.

"Hey, Pops. Morning, Abe."

"Where you off to?" Absolume asked.

"Welcoming Hanns home."

"He's here?" Abe questioned.

"At the gates now," Aedus said, walking by his father and brother.

"Hurry, let's eat all the food before he comes back," Robert joked, and as if Aedus heard him, his son yelled back to them.

"Don't eat everything!"

"Only the good stuff!" Absolume hollered back.

"That's everything!" Aedus clamored as he picked up the pace to meet his cousin at the door. Robert and Absolume shared a belly aching laugh at the dialog.

Upon Hanns arrival, they talked to him of his journey and his stay in Holle. Of what he saw and experienced, he told in detail, but in his telling, the joyous breakfast took a slight turn in un-comfortability. His description of Alamgeer was frightening, but the fear was quickly eased away by a resounding, unladylike belch from Lorena.

Eyes grew wide and mouths dropped, but with full-hearted laughter, the room became wholesome and restored with vibes of good cheer. Lorena blushed yet seemed proud of her unorthodox ways for easing what had been an uneasy discussion. Though the eerie details were over, Robert pondered the words of Hanns and his characterization of Alamgeer. He thought of his words and how Alamgeer could move a room of thousands with just a mere appearance and how he could lead with the sound of his voice and how impressive and sharp his mind in strategy and war. With fresh thoughts in his cerebrum and breakfast complete, Robert pushed back his chair from the table.

"Aye, I'm full." He patted his belly.

"You and me both," his wife chimed in, patting his belly as well and with a grin about her face. One by one, those at the table excused themselves.

"Ready, Hanns?" Robert asked his nephew. Hanns nodded, and together, they walked slowly with rounded stomachs filled with savory goods. They conversed and made their way to Robert's office. They talked of statues of the kings and queens of Saoirse and his frequency in visiting them. They talked of Robert's father, Abraham, and pondered the idea of Robert in the midst of the statues in the hall of kings and queens. It was something Robert did not want to think about but did, nonetheless.

They arrived at Robert's office. The small room was heavenly luminous. Its clash of eras and its design were entirely unique. Robert gestured for his nephew to sit. He sat his behind in an arching chair of columned bricks. Drink he offered to Hanns and which Hanns declined. Robert gave him a glass of water anyway, knowing the conversation would be one to dry the mouth. Robert opened up a leatherbound journal and removed the cap atop the fountain pen he grasped. Turning to a blank page, he looked at Hanns.

"Ready?" he asked. Hanns confirmed with a nod. "Shoot. I'm all ears." With his tongue, Hanns shot out words that whizzed by Robert's ears like bullets from a gun, caught by the kevlar of his cerebellum. Of Avstrija and Danija and the commanding generals of those nations he spoke, and also of their allegiance to Holle. Hanns noted that their allegiance seemed binding, unbent; their treaty with Holle would not be broken.

Onto Möngke of Mongnolerium, a topic which grabbed Robert's ear with a hard tug and brought him to attention. Betrayal, Robert thought, a loose end, a potential chink in the armor of the war game they were now in. Robert needed confirmation that Mongnolerium was neutral. Hanns sought to mentioned that Möngke Khagan's plans were to aid in infrastructure and food of the people of Holle in exchange for property and igneous stones. A small spark struck Robert's mind as Hanns relayed the information to him. *Could Khan's strategy be to buy Holle when they are no longer financially stable? Clever*, he thought to himself.

Of Yuskita, Hanns mentioned very little. Robert tried to search for truth in everything Hanns provided him—something he'd need to mull over and quickly.

The movement of men Hanns mentioned next, noting the people in the castle, detailed notes regarding the castle grounds from its insides to its outside. Hanns provided him descriptions of the city, and of all the things Hanns gave to him, the thing that horrified Robert the most was Alamgeer's way of grabbing people at their souls, when they were weakest, and giving them fuel to commit great acts, both good and evil, for the people loved him though his heart was wretched. As Hanns divulged all he knew, he paused and seemed to wonder deeply.

"Uncle," said Hanns, his voice serious. "The Führer seemed adamant that you be dethroned. He kept talking of your health and how the Hammer from the rock from which you pulled upon the Hill of Hoba was poisoning you—how the hammer made you mad, how it was the weapon of the devil, and you held its curse." Robert bowed his head, stroked his face with his hand, and let out a soft sigh. He made certain to lock eyes with Hanns.

"There is truth within these words," he answered his nephew. "You mustn't tell anyone of this, Hanns." He made sure Hanns knew the severity of the truths and what could happen should they leak to the enemy, or worse, his friends, his allies, and his family. Robert told him everything, and he watched as his nephew wept.

"Don't weep now, lad. Save those tears for another time, for it has not happened yet." He smiled at Hanns. Robert stood from his chair and walked over to Hanns, who stood when he did. He held his nephew with great strength in an embrace that was loving and fatherly. "Do me a favor when you get home?"

"Anything," Hanns replied.

"Read the letter."

"I will, Uncle," Hanns replied. "But how? I had tried using the fireplace but was afraid I'd burn the paper."

"A lighter is easiest."

"Silly me, then." Hanns whipped away the tears that had fallen.

"I love you, Hanns."

"I love you, too, Uncle Rob." They released their embrace and departed from their meeting. As Hanns left through the office doorway, he looked back at his king. His eyes were filled with sadness.

"Brighten those eyes, Hanns. Our lives are the sun, and we must always shine," Robert said to him. Hanns smiled. "There we are, lad."

"Goodbye, uncle."

"Goodbye, Hanns," Robert said softly back. He sat back down into his seat as Hanns closed the door, leaving Robert alone to his thoughts.

He did not think of all the words his nephew said to him. Instead, he thought about the ending conversation and how very precious life is. Despite all life's heartaches, its mountainous struggles, its ever battling ways, it was a truly outstanding miracle and a beautiful blessing. For with life, there is an endless amount of pathways through which to find happiness, an intricate web to discover the mysteries of the world and oneself, and an endless skein of truth and love. As he thought on the value of life, he considered how fortunate he was to find Aedus alone in the world, a babe hidden in the woods, and how only Providence brought Robert to him. What memories he had with Aedus. Robert couldn't imagine life without him. Ever caring and kind, brave and honorable, and though he did not share his blood, Aedus was still his son. Robert reminisced of the long drives he had with Aedus and how each road trip led to a ruined castle, an old fort, or grand cathedral. Aedus loved the history of the structures. He admired what they came from and what they stood for. He would consume knowledge of each destination like sap of a tree crystalizes all it consumes and strengthens over time.

Of all the pictured moments in his mind with Aedus, the lens focused on the day Robert told Aedus he was adopted. It was in the grating core of winter; snow was falling heavily as they stood in the spire of a church. Gothic and medieval was its design, and they stood at the back of the cathedral in view of the enormous and colorful rose window that rained daylight into the space inside. Opposite was a view of the historic city known as Prionsa, a name given by a tale of a prince who set out to rescue his princess. The city was made of art and everlasting style, and so, too, was the cathedral they stood in. Alone they were, just father and son in the noiseless fall of snow inside the spire. Robert knelt down and told Aedus something he'd been regretting since he decided to take Aedus as his own.

"Aed, my sweet boy, Aed."

"Yea, Pops?" Aedus looked at his father. He was but a boy of twelve, slender but strong and with eyes like the blackness of space, eternal with mystery and beauty.

"I need to tell you something—something that will change your life forever."

"What is it?"

"Do you know how much your mother and I love you?"

"With all your heart."

"With all our heart and more. If I could stretch my heart out to infinity, my love for you would fill it," Robert expressed to his son. "Know that we will never abandon you and that we will always be here for you."

"I know, Pops," Aedus told him innocently.

"Did I ever tell you about the first time I laid eyes on you?" Robert asked, knowing he hadn't, and continuing with his thought. "It was a dark and wicked night. The snow fell from the heavens in copious amounts. The menacing clouds struck bolts of lightning in the cimmerian sky. No voice could be heard but that of the wind." Robert could see his story grabbed his son's attention and continued.

"I walked tirelessly through the storm. There was something calling me, a voice, rather a cry. I trekked through the darkness in the deep of the forest, and the more I walked, the louder the cry that filled my ears. Bolts of fire cut through the sky, striking the same location, and after the bolts hit the earth, the snow died, the clouds parted, and the moon shined dazzlingly, like a pearl, pure and resplendent. I walked some more, and I came upon a clearing," Robert explained.

"Were you trying to find your way out of the woods to head to the hospital?" Aedus asked the obvious question without knowing the story.

"No, Aed, I wasn't," Robert answered. Aedus looked confused. "You were not at the hospital, my boy. When I exited the trees, I came upon a small field, and there in the center of the clearing, surrounded by crisped pines and scorched earth, were you," Robert said to him. "I picked you up and held you in my arms, calling for your parents." Robert started to explain before he was interrupted by Aedus.

"You can stop there." His son's voice sounded almost disheartened. "I may be just a child, but I know this. We may not share the same blood, but we share something deeper, a special bond that God has made to link us. It is unbreakable, unbendable, and unmatched in all things. It's our spirits, Dad. They are forever bound together."

Robert pulled his son into his chest and embraced him. "When did you get so wise?"

"When I started listening more to you and Mom. She told me that once, of our special bond, and I never forgot it," Aedus told his father. Robert, still kneeling, met his eyes.

"I don't think you're a boy anymore, Aed. You're growing up to be quite the man, and I'm so very proud of you." He smiled at his son.

"Thanks, Pops. I love you."

"I love you, too, Aed."

Once more, Robert's mind and eyes came to the forefront, back to the present. An exchange of details from foreign lands was to be had with his brother, but there was still time to fill the gap before his meeting with Iscariot. He rose to leave his office, and as he opened the door to enter the hallway, his wife was there, fist shaped, ready to knock on the wood.

"Is that a fist for me or the door?" He spoke tongue in cheek.

"Depends on your behavior." Lagertha grinned. Under her left arm was a cowhide-wrapped present.

"Is that it?"

"It is. It took a while to make the bonds, but the shield is done. I'm curious of the color when she uses it," his wife remarked.

"I can't wait to give it to her. She's wanted it since she was little." Robert spoke with excitement.

"When are you giving the shield to her?"

"I was thinking now if she's still here."

"I believe she is down in the armory with Aedus."

"Practicing again?" Robert wondered.

"I think she is trying to spend as much time with Aed before he goes back to base."

"He'll be good training for her. I'd be surprised if she puts a scratch on him." Robert voiced his opinion.

"I think he's training her in new weaponry."

"Oh." Robert was glad to hear it.

"My thought as well. I think she mentioned a throwing knife and an axe."

"I hope they're still going at it. I'd love to see Lorena using the kunai. Both are completely foreign to her and will help with close combat," Robert spoke excitedly.

"Simmer down, old man. You'll hurt yourself." Lagertha laughed at his boyish way of things.

Steadily tiptoeing down the halls and stairways, they walked— amongst the statues and the paintings, of things past and present, saying hello to the servants and those who helped them daily. They came upon the tings, tacks, and clacks of metal to metal. Robert's ear could hear their battle as he walked closer to the artillery room. The shuffling of feet, the heavy panting of energy exerted—all was an effort to better themselves, but more importantly, to better understand each other and form stronger bonds between brother and sister.

Robert put his arm out in front of Lagertha to stop her from moving forward. He desired to watch in secret, to see how they fought when no one was watching, when there was no one to impress or to criticize—where there was no judgment but self-judgment. He wanted to see the harshness of self-criticism and how they persevered through it. His eyes watched, and his heart told his mind to be pleased, for their actions were the apogee of achievement. He observed Aedus give instructions on a series of moves, and he surveyed Lorena's practicing in light of his instructions, and after she performed the steps flawlessly, Aedus made a very serious comment of praise and warning.

"Your form is flawless, and your speed will progress as you progress. But a word of caution and a recommendation: though you performed this series of movements to perfection, know that battle is not scripted, and when you're this close to the enemy, more than just the blade is your weapon. Here, your fists, your elbows, your head, and your feet and knees are all in play, even your teeth. The knife is just a small extension to the weapons of your body. Never forget this."

"I won't," she answered. Aedus walked up to her and embraced her.

"Good work, today. You learn quickly."

"It's like a dance. I grasp it easily," Lorena told him.

"Lucky you," Aedus grinned. Robert found the moment to interrupt.

"Dare I say, I'm envious of you two."

"Hey Dad, Momma," Lorena greeted them.

"Hey Pops, Ma," said Aedus.

"Hey kiddos." Lagertha smiled at her children.

"A deal is a deal, Lo," Robert started.

"What do you mean?" Lorena was a bit confused. Lagertha pulled from under her arm the wrapped gift.

"Is this what I think it is?" Lorena's voice rose in glee. Lagertha handed her the present. Lorena removed the cowhide covering, and her eyes glowed with joy, and in the bright sky of her eyes, brilliant stars streaked down and fell onto her cheeks. Robert could truly see how much this gift meant to her, but he didn't know exactly why. Lorena lunged into her father's arms and thanked him, soaking his shirt with the starry tears she shed.

"Thank you, Dad."

"You're welcome, Lo." She released her embrace from her father to give the same affection to her mother.

"Lo, I know you've wanted this shield for a while now, but can I ask you why?" Aedus asked his sister. Lorena paused to gather herself and then replied.

"This shield has countless meanings to many people, and every time I hear someone mention this shield, the story that leaves their mouths is beautiful. Westmore sees the shield as hope. He told me of the first time he met Dad and how he saved him from certain death. He told me how the shield struck him as it radiated from Dad's hands, and with every foe he took down, the hope in his heart grew, and fear washed away from him.

"For the people of Saoirse, no matter where I travel, Dad's hammer is mentioned, but the people are always more impressed by his shield. The ultimate defense some call it. Others say it's the shield of liberty, but everyone knows it as the Saoirse Shield. It's become a symbol for our people, but the reason why I've wanted this shield is because, to me, it's a shield of selflessness and love.

"The power of the shield comes from the love of Mom and Dad. Without their love, this shield is nothing, and its meaning would be lost if Mom never sacrificed her internal light to build the shield. When I go off to battle, I want our troops to know Dad is with us in every fight, and if the war grows ever darker, Mom and Dad are there to shield us from the evils that are before us. In Dad's hands, the shield glows white and purple. It is purity and power. It coincides with the image of the shield. The shamrock is of purity, and the triangle it rests in, the power," she explained and continued.

"This is the light of our love, not only the love of Mom and Dad, but the love between God and our people. When soldiers see the shield alight, it will burn bright for them to fight and push them through the darkness of the night."

Robert beamed at his daughter and her thoughts of what the shield signified to her and others. "I'm glad you like it, my tiny dancer. Put it on, and see how it feels in your hands." She locked the braces of the back of the shield onto her forearm, and the armament reacted to the bearer. Like for her father, the shield radiated a stunning white of innocence, but its secondary hue could not be more different. Heat to cold air, the steam appeared and flared a ravishing crimson.

"The red must be from the blood of your enemies. You can start with me," Aedus jested with his sister. Robert laughed at the siblings' rivalry, but underneath his facade, he was curious about what the colors meant. Robert looked over at his wife.

"You worry too much. It's just the chemical compounds that make the colors: the stone used, the intensity of the light, the heat of the flame, the minerals in the metal. It's been reworked dear. The hues wouldn't be the same as yours," Lagertha explained to her husband.

"I know." Robert pulled his wife into him. "My stressful mind conjures up crazy things from time to time."

"Don't fret, my love. I'll ease your mind tonight," she told Robert as they looked on at their two children.

"Use the kunai with the shield. It would be the combination you've been looking for. It's very close combat but should be highly effective," Robert recommended to his daughter. The bout between the brother and sister began, only to be ended in five moves by Aedus.

"Are you okay?" Aedus asked Lorena.

"Yeah, I'm fine. Ready for round two?" she replied to her brother, and again, in five moves, her brother beat her. Lagertha departed from Robert's arms and walked toward her daughter.

"Want some advice?" Lagertha asked Lorena, pulling her up by grabbing her arm inside the shield.

"Please."

"You're using the shield as if it were a standard metal bulwark. Use the light, my dear."

Lorena stood for the third bout, and when she was set, Aedus rushed toward her. In his first strike, she repelled him with the light of the shield. She made the rays a physical matter, and the light exploded from her armament. Aedus looked over at his mother.

"Some good advice you gave her, Mom."

"There is something else I gave her, too. You'll know it when she discovers it," Lagertha told her son. Robert looked on as Aedus changed his approach to battle his sister, yet he was unable to strike her. It seemed his tactic was to wear her down, causing fatigue. The siblings' fight continued. No matter the intensity or difficulty of movement Aedus attacked with, Lorena would not falter. Robert gazed upon theirs faces and saw a grin leave his daughter's face, and then something unexpected happened.

Lorena tossed her shield at Aedus, which he swatted as if it were a lethargic fly. He charged her. Lorena grinned again, and the shield struck Aedus in the center of his back, and he fell to the floor.

"Are you okay, little brother?" Lorena teased him.

"Clever move." He smiled at his sister. "How'd you do that?"

"Seems Mom attached a light capture orb that is synced to the shield. Should I lose it, it will come back to me with a flick of my wrist."

"Dad, I think she's already better with this weapon than you were," Aedus remarked.

"We're the unlucky ones in the family, I'm afraid. I always envied that about your mother." Robert chuckled at their misfortunes as neither could manipulate the light around them.

"You and me both, Pops," Aedus agreed.

"Alright kiddos, I've got some things I need to do. Lo, I want to talk to you later," Robert told his children.

"Okay, Dad. I'll see you later," Lorena said to him.

"Bye, Pops. Bye, Ma," Aedus said. Robert grabbed his wife's hand, and they walked together out of the armory, through the halls of the castle, and out its doors to the paths of the gardens. Together, they reminisced about their lives from before they met and to where they stood now. Not a single regret left Robert's mouth, for he was truly happy. Slowly, they walked out of the freshly blooming garden of flowers yellow, red, blue, and pink, and into the paths of dirt that traveled where the trees of evergreen surrounded Solascnoc.

Romantically alone on the trail, surrounded by the beauty of nature, the lovers kissed. Her arms locked around his neck and his around her waist—they gazed into each other's eyes.

"I love you," he told his wife. "There has not been a day with you where I was not happy. Even in our heated arguments or times of sadness, I was happy because you were the person I was with, and I knew, regardless of the outcome of our fight and no matter how depressing the mood, that you would be with me and I with you. So, when I lay my head to sleep at night, though we may not have been talking, I was happy because I still slept with the woman who was the mother to my children: my bride, and my lover, and my closest friend."

Lagertha shined a face of bliss at her husband. "Unlucky we're in the woods." She kissed his lips. "I'd jump your bones and love you till the sun came up," she teased.

"Well, I'm certainly not going to stop you," he coyly played. Lagertha elbowed him in the ribs.

"Behave yourself," she grinned, and he laughed.

"You started it." He still chuckled, rubbing his ribs from her strike.

"Hurt ya?"

"A little bit," Robert grimaced.

"Good." Lagertha smirked, changing the subject, and asked him of his plans for the remainder of the day. "When do you meet with your brother?"

"In a few hours. I need to go to Westmore's and Myrddin's before I meet with Iscariot." Lagertha seemed to ponder his answer. As man and wife walked back to the castle, he asked of her day, and she answered with a list a mile long, and the list ended with a kiss in bed from the man she loved, him, her husband. "I like the sound of that." Robert smiled, and his eyes looked into hers.

"Me too." The lover's lips locked, lingering lightly, letting the moment last before they parted.

"See you tonight, my love." Robert said goodbye.

"Goodbye, my king." Lagertha beamed at him before she turned and walked away.

Alone again, he made his way to the castle's garage. Silently he walked, sneaking by without being noticed by anyone in Solascnoc. A vehicle was before him. The top of the convertible was down, the forest green gloss of the car shone without imperfection. The white walled tires looked pure and unused. Robert sat in his vehicle, but he did not start the engine. A trigger on the left side of his car door he pulled, and slowly, the car descended underground. It rested on a hidden platform, which was a doorway to tunnels that led out of the castle grounds, and in the tunnels were four routes that led out of the city. Robert and his wife were the only souls that knew of the underground. It was knowledge that was passed down from his father in a letter written long ago by the kings before them.

The elevator platform stopped its descent, and he was in darkness. He brought the car to life in the unseen world before him. The bug-eyed lights struck beams to drive away the shadows, and Robert drove off. As he drove in the underground, he passed signs of street names and landmarks to indicate where he was, but there was nothing else in the great dark void he traveled in. In this tunnel, his mind wandered, not on things eerie or ominous like the road he drove upon, but something of great light in his heart. His daughter electrified his mind in a luminescent glow of his favorite memory of her.

'Twas early in his kinghood inside Solascnoc, a game he and Lorena played, one of a hider and a seeker. Clues he gave of where he would be. Riddles and puzzles she had to decipher in order to find her father. In his memory, he thought of his favorite moment, which included a riddle that led to the location of two items. Those items were counterparts, and if used correctly, would lead to Robert. He recalled his wife's telling of the story as she watched their daughter play the game of wit.

Lorena was a child of five years in age. Her hair already at the base of her spine, and she wore a blue shirt dress, which bowed at the waist. It was white-striped and with red flowers adorned upon it. On her tiny feet were white slippered shoes. She tiptoed on them to the starting point her father told her of, which was a great hallway that ran 300 feet. The room shone with glorious light from the heavens, and in this massive hall was a small table, and sitting on the table was a stone that weighed down a piece of paper. She read it aloud.

"Find the arrows and follow them." She looked around herself in search of the first arrow before realizing it was etched into the stone, and so she walked in its guiding direction. Well hidden in four different rooms, she found them all. The arrows led her to another piece of paper, and on it was a riddle. She spoke its words.

"A picture I make within your mind. Tales fact or fiction, my words are in bind. I'm not smart, but I make you wise. Come find me in my storied guise." Lorena thought a moment. "A book?" she questioned to herself and dashed off to the castle's library. Inside the room of tales, she glanced at an arrow that pointed at a napkin with a number and a book that weighted it down. She turned to page five, seeming utterly confused, at least that's what her mother thought as she spied on her daughter. Bemused, she walked up to her.

"What are you doing, little lady?"

"Hi, Mom. Dad and I are playing hide and seeker," Lorena answered.

"Have you found him yet?"

"No—I think I'm close, though."

"Oh," said Lagertha as she watched her daughter's mind work.

"Five—five—mhmmm," her daughter thought aloud.

"What is five?" Lagertha questioned her.

"The key. I turned to page five, but I don't see anything."

"Well, what else have you tried?" Lagertha pressed Lorena to challenge herself. Lagertha began pointing at the words and then counting.

"Every fifth word?" Lorena quickly jotted it down, but no sense was made of the words.

"What about the fifth letter of every fifth word?" Lorena asked herself and her mother.

"Try and see, my angel," Lagertha urged her on.

"Eureka, Momma. Eureka!" Lorena spoke with satisfaction and pride. Each letter she jotted down from every fifth letter of every fifth word formed the answer she sought. *Car Garage.*

"Thank you, Mom. Love you!" she yelled as she bolted from the room to find her father. She ran as fast as her little feet could move. Through every hall, every shortcut, through every passageway that was the quickest route. Outside she was in the open air with skies blue and white. Out of breath she became with a sly grin dressed upon her face. She saw her father, who was working on his car. Lorena cleared her throat.

"Dad," she said, and a ding she heard as her father hit his head on the bottom of the forest-green machine.

"Ouch." Robert laughed off the pain. "It seems you've found me," he said with a smile. "A smart lass you are, indeed." Lorena blushed and seemed curious as to what her father was doing.

"Is the car broken?" she wondered.

"Oh, no. The car is fine. I've just added something to it," Robert answered vaguely. "Ready for your prize, kiddo?" He quickly changed the topic.

"What did you get me?"

"Hop in." Happiness enveloped her. She jumped into the passenger seat and clicked the seatbelt.

"Where are we going?"

"The Rabbit Foot for tea and coffee and sweets," Robert told her. He closed the driver door, and before he could fasten himself in, the car descended. Lorena yelled in shock and fear. "Oops." Robert clicked the lever he had just installed. "A little faulty," he said to himself.

"Dad. What was that? Are you trying to scare me?" Lorena asked innocently afraid.

"Well, that was supposed to be a secret," he said and then looked at her. "Promise me, Lo, that you will never tell anyone about this elevator. It's a secret only to be known by your mother and me. This tunnel is for our safety should anything bad happen." Lorena shook her head yes.

"I understand, Dad. I promise I won't tell anyone." She crossed her heart as she told him.

"An extra sweet for you, my lady," Robert smirked, and together they drove off with the top of the car down and the cool breeze streaming through their lengthy locks.

The memory he had taken from the safe of his mind, he put safely back in place. In the underground, there was a sign that read Arc. He slowed the green machine he drove, and then turned off the engine. From his glove compartment, he grabbed a lamprog. Robert flicked his wrist to activate his communicator and synced it with the lamprog light. The wings unwrapped from the small golden ball and its body expanded slowly, letting out the glimmer until it filled the space around him, and he was covered in brightness.

Nearly hidden to the eye, blending in with the concrete walls, was a hidden concrete button that met his hand as he glided it across the wall. Robert pushed down on it, and a secret doorway opened. Robert walked through the door, and the lamprog followed him, lighting the way for him to see. The passageway was narrow and short, leading to a stone spiral staircase, which was just snug enough for him to fit through. Robert climbed what he thought were a thousand steps, until it finally plateaued. There was a lever to his left. He pulled it, and another secret door opened, this one above him. He climbed up and appeared outside in an alley of an alley—only three feet wide and barricaded so none would enter.

Out the narrow passage, he walked down the side walkway until he reached Arc Street. Brick-clad and marble buildings lined the road, and dancing on top of every building was a Saoirse flag. Marvelous were the aged structures. He stood in front of a building with a bronze statue of a man named Alexander, who clutched a sword in his right hand, and rode on the back of a lion. Under Robert's feet, etched in stone, read, "Upon the conduct of each depends the fate of all." Robert walked inside the building, and waiting for him was his dear friend, whose voice boomed like thunder—Victor Westmore.

"Victor." Robert spoke his name with a warm welcome heart.

"My king," Westmore replied in soft and friendly tones.

"Sorry I made you travel all this way just for a fifteen-minute meeting."

"No need for I'm sorries. To see my friend is reason enough to be here, but I know this goes even beyond our friendship."

"Nonetheless, thank you," Robert said once more to him, and the two sat down in the room across from the entrance, filled with war-time images of brave men and women. "Once more, heroes will come to the surface of the world. Beacons of light scattered across the country to guide us, to lead us into peace we lost in the darkness."

"A shame it takes such extreme events to see their light shine brightest," Westmore replied.

"I don't think their light gets brighter. It's just that we lost sight of it along the way somewhere only to be found again when all the lights of those good men and women are bound together."

"I suppose you're right. Sad we ever look away from it and fall into the depths of our sins."

"Sad, indeed, my friend."

"So, what calls us here at this solemn hour?"

"Details of what Uriel has been working on and to see your face once more before the war. It may not look so youthful after it," Robert jested.

"If this face were to get any older, I'm afraid I'd be a dead man, and you'd be talking to a ghost," Victor joked along.

"I wanted to also tell you that I've recently discovered a spy ring, but I wasn't entirely sure how accurate my analysis was. I believe it to be led by my brother's good friend, Antony. Keep watch of him during the war. Communicate with Andre. I fear a coup sometime during the war. My nephew gave me some interesting information when he was in Holle, and Alamgeer seems to hold some weight here in Saoirse. We've seen this in all the riots lately. Lastly, note the message at the end of the letter I've given you. Seven-two-two is imperative should the spy ring be as strong as I think it might be," Robert cautioned and informed.

"I'll read through it when I arrive back west. Thank you, Robert, for everything. You are my greatest friend." The meeting was brief and when it ended the two rose from their seats and embraced one another, both saying goodbye to travel in different paths of the same war-torn road that was knocking on their door. Robert didn't show his emotions, but his heart was tight, bound by ropes of thorns. The clouded eyes brewed but did not rain. Instead, he held his head high as he walked back to the bleakness of the underground.

Engine on, wheels rolled, and he was on his way to his next destination. He stopped to visit a man whose eyes could see a candle burn where the sky meets the ocean as he stood along the shore—a magician with a gun and Absolume's laerer. Robert relayed to him the same information he gave to Westmore with one variant in detail. A three-digit number he gave Myrddin, a code on how to reach Westmore during war time. Robert thanked him for all that he did for his family, especially Absolume. Before they left, they prayed together in a small clearing where twenty standing boulders circled a shamrock. He prayed for wisdom. He prayed for guidance should he lose his way in the maze of war, and he prayed for patience should eagerness consume him. They ended their prayer, "Germa," of great thanks.

Robert saw the time upon his wrist and rushed back to the city's castle from the country's green fields. He sought to give himself time before meeting Iscariot. Home he now was in Solascnoc. He saw nothing and heard nothing as he took himself away inside his brick- and wood-clad office. He eased his mind, and blank it became. No memory nor dream he created seeded its way into his brain. His mind was empty as he sat inside his chair with closed eyes. Robert did not open them until there was a knock upon his door, and once more his mind became full.

Iscariot came into the room. Filled with warning and doubt, he divulged all he knew to his king. Opinionated and rotted with discontent, the brothers remarked on not just the Hollen visit, but their judgments on what led them to the moment they were in. Robert could see they differed. He saw how they had, on most matters, been splitting apart like paper torn. His eyes saw the cut growing wider between them. He was saddened and worried deeply for Iscariot, who seemed by every passing moment to lose himself further down the void of unknown. Robert wanted so badly to pull him up, to see the better sides in life and not the misery he had grown accustomed to.

It pained Robert to his core. Such fond and cherished memories he had with him. Iscariot was not only his brother but also his best friend. He was someone whose heart was sown with his, and if the thread should fray or break, his heart would surely feel its torment. He feared the day their hearts would part in two, for he would have lost a bond of friendship, a brotherhood, but also a part of himself. Robert felt that if their bond should sever, a part of him, if not all of him, would surely die.

Iscariot left the room with a parting gift, a jet stone carved bear. He placed it on the windowsill behind Robert's desk before he vanished behind the door, leaving Robert out of sight. Robert turned to the gift and held it in his hands. He clenched his heart, and a stray droplet that hid from behind the vessel of his eyes fell from the lid onto the hard floor. He wiped his eyes to stop any more tears from falling.

The hour glass flipped two times, and in those fallen grains of sand, Robert was in solitude. His mind was overwhelmed of thoughts past, present, and future. The war had not yet begun, but he was already wounded. Could his heart withstand such pain? Could it bear the agony of the death of his brother? Could it beat at the news of the death of his sons? What man could live through the loss of ones loved? Robert became afraid of the questions he asked himself. His heart beat at presto, and with every second passed, his heart struck three beats.

A knock on his office door, his heart still pacing, it slowed, at lento, for what was more calming than his child's face.

"Come in, my tiny dancer," he said to his daughter. His heart adagio.

"Hey, Dad," she smiled.

"Hey, Lo. What brings you up here?"

"The boys are fighting and wanted you to come watch. Abe took your hammer and wanted to show off with it." Lorena rolled her eyes.

"I guess I'll have to show him who's king of the hammer," Robert fooled. He walked with Lorena out of the office door and into the halls of the castle. His ears heard every word she spoke, his eyes took in all her beauty, and his spirit felt the spirit of his child. They stopped briefly in the hall of kings and queens at his father's statue. Robert thought quickly of a million memories with his dad. He looked over at Lorena. His heart overflowed with fatherly affection. He pulled her in and held her fiercely. His embrace was warm and bright. The love for his child could be felt by mere sight with no words to describe such a pure and unbreakable bond.

Taken aback, his daughter asked, "What was that for?"

"Just seeing my father and knowing his love for me. I was compelled to tell you how much I love you, my child, and how I'll always be here for you." Embarrassed, she too expressed her affection.

"I love you, too, Dad, and I know you're always here for me. It's because we have such ties. I can come to you for anything." She was proud of their relationship. Robert smirked with pride and changed the subject.

"The shield looks good on you."

"Thanks, Dad," she beamed.

The two started walking again, but before they could reach the end of the hall, Iscariot, his son, and two guards walked before them. Iscariot's face was of grave concern; worry was upon it.

"Iscariot, what is the matter?" Robert spoke hastily. He could see Hanns was shaking.

"It's begun Robert. We're under attack," his brother answered.

"Where was the first strike, and how did they strike? Lorena, go and get your brothers," he asked and instructed. Lorena started her departure to retrieve Absolume and Aedus. Iscariot came closer to Robert, so too the guards on his left and right, and from Robert's back, the sting of cold metal.

"Here, with a dagger," Iscariot answered his brother. Another blade he felt, this one from the front. Blood ran up his throat and spilled from Robert's mouth. Another bite from both sides—he fell to the ground and onto his knees.

"So, this is your choice?" Robert looked at Hanns whose hands were still shaking.

"Dad!" He heard his name called like he'd never heard it before, and with every ounce of strength he had left within his body, he called out to his daughter.

"Run!" he commanded Lorena. His eyes beheld her crying eyes. His last sight before his closed. *So beautiful*, he thought. His mind struck light to see the face of his wife. *I love you*, said his murmuring mind.

Robert's world became dark, his breath ceased, and the beat in his chest was no more.

Hanns Chapter Two

The world outside Hanns's home was dark and bleak. For a spring night, it was unusually quiet, but he paid it no mind. It was the furthest thing in his well of thoughts. Floating on the surface of his cerebellum were the words of his uncle. He could not fathom what he had spoken to him. He struggled to understand why he didn't seek help and why he told no one. A gunshot thought, Hanns rose from the comfort of his bed and pulled from the drawer of his dresser the blank piece of paper his uncle, Robert, had given him. Hanns snagged a lighter from atop his dresser, remembering what Absolume and Lorena had told him. He held up the parchment and lit the lighter from a distance. Nothing happened, so he brought the flame closer. Suddenly, the paper with nothing on its surface revealed what was hidden within it.

The letter began with love for and pride in him and transitioned into the struggles that lay ahead and how to use his powers of love and his power in the skills he had so diligently worked for. The letter talked about how his love could change the war and how his selflessness could tighten bonds and tie together bonds once lost. As he continued reading and neared the end, Robert wrote something which ignited Hanns's emotions.

Hanns wept. His uncle's words at the end made him feel alone, afraid, choleric, and full of grief. The war had yet begun, and he could already feel its stresses. He folded the paper and placed it in the pocket of his jacket that hung over an accent chair in the corner of his room. He went back to his bed, resting his head on the fluted pillows. His heart was shattered glass, its fragments in flames, and the tears that fell from his eyes could feel its heat.

While he laid upon his bed, filled with an ocean of emotion, there came two knocks on his door. Hanns quickly wiped his eyes to dry them, and he kept his feelings hidden.

"Come in," he said, and the door opened. "Dad?" Iscariot's face showed both worry and anger. "What's the matter?"

"It's your uncle, Hanns. The hammer has truly made him mad," Iscariot told him. "In two days' time, thousands will die at his command. We must stop him, Hanns."

"But, Dad. I saw Uncle Robert today," Hanns began.

"Hanns! Think about what he told you today. I told you that you would have to make a choice, my son. Will you forsake me?"

Hanns thought about what Robert said to him. He reflected on when he told him of the rumors of the hammer and how it was making him crazy and his response that some of the things Alamgeer said of him were true. He then brought back the memory of the promise he made to his father and that he'd always be there for him. Hanns rose from his bed and grabbed his jacket.

"I will never abandon you, Father."

"Thank you, my son. Be ready. We leave in ten minutes." Hanns shook his head, signaling that he understood.

Hanns put on his military slacks and threw his coat that hung on the chair over his shoulders. He donned the Leon cap upon his head and strapped the dagger his father gave him around his waist. He walked out the door and headed to the front of his home where he, Iscariot, awaited him.

"Are you ready, Hanns?" his father asked, and Hanns nodded his head that he was. "Do you know what you must do?"

"We are to arrest King Robert for treason," Hanns answered.

"No, my son," Iscariot began. Hanns's face expressed confusion. "Your uncle has become too dangerous. If we arrest him, people will fight to free him."

"What do we do then?" Hanns was at a loss for words.

"Use the dagger on your hip, my son. It is the only way."

"But, Dad," Hanns started. Iscariot quickly grabbed him by the collar.

"Are you with me or not, Hanns? If you are with me, you must do this. I know you can see what Alamgeer said of your uncle to be true," his father reminded him.

Hanns's mind spun like thread in the mill. The spindle spun, but he was not in control. He could not see what he was sewing. His heart beat faster than his mind wheeled. He could not think farther than the moment before him. When his father mentioned Alamgeer and his words about his uncle, he knew them to be true, but he did not want to believe it. Hanns was panicking internally, wanting more time, wanting this moment to somehow turn or slow the spindle enough for him to think, to see what it was that he was making in the choices in front of him.

Composed on the outside, he looked at his father with his two-toned eyes, who held him by the cuff of his collar.

"His words are true, and I will do my duty," Hanns said to his father, who released him at his word. He walked out the door with Iscariot, and in his mind, he asked himself who was the crazy one. Was it the king? Was it his father, or was it he? Hanns hated this day; every moment of it held something terrible. He could feel his heart consumed by hatred; he could feel it getting darker. Out the door, waiting for him, were two guards. "Who are they?"

"Help," Iscariot responded in one word with no detail. Hanns quickly snared his father's shoulder, turning his father to face him.

"Explain, or I will not go through with this," he told his father. Iscariot swatted his son's hand away.

"Get in the hover," Iscariot commanded. Walking to the passenger side back door while Hanns stood his ground, Iscariot looked back at his son. "I'll explain on the ride over." Hanns strode forward and opened the side door. He sat and turned to Iscariot.

"Tell me everything," Hanns demanded, and Iscariot started from the beginning.

"We have seen a change in your uncle for some time now, Hanns. Robert used to hate war. He always sought an alternative, but it wasn't long after he became king that we noticed his change in ideas. Even his speech, when he pulled the hammer from Hoba—he told the people to be ready to fight. We had just gotten out of the Great War. Who would expect another? There came rumors that he had been hallucinating of horrid creatures, that the hammer was pulling him to seek war, and that the phantoms were the messengers of those words." Iscariot paused. Hanns was still attentive.

"After our dad died is when he made some very interesting decisions. He was so hung up on this war that it is the reason why Absolume, Lorena, and Aedus were taught in weaponry. When I asked him why, he told me that "they needed to be ready for when the day comes," Iscariot told his son.

"What about me, Dad? I've trained my whole life, too. I'm here with you right now in uniform. How am I different?"

"A father's mistake. War is the only thing I know, Hanns. I didn't really know how to raise you. As much as I didn't want you to be in the military, I know nothing else."

"So, what else?" Hanns urged his father to continue.

"His hallucinations got worse, and in the past year or two, his call to war has gotten louder, and Yefimovich has convinced him that Alamgeer means to attack Yisra."

"But, Dad, Alamgeer does want to attack Yisra," Hanns interjected.

"Hanns, Alamgeer evacuated people of the Ivdeyskiy because Yisra attacked them in the dead of night and labeled those Ivdeyskiy, who lived in Holle, as traitors. Yefimovich is another lost soul who only affirms Robert's idea of war.

"It was only about a year ago when Robert's transformation had become complete. It was in the gathering of nations and his urging to them of the Hollen threat. This is when I knew that he had become lost. During this time, Antony and I developed an internal plan to stop your uncle. We got together with the leader of the Leon Coalition."

"General Andre?" Hanns was bewildered to hear this.

"Yes, and our plan was to arrest your uncle and charge him for high treason. That changed after my meeting with him tonight. Arrest is no longer an option." Iscariot was stern.

Hanns was nervous. He didn't want to do what his father was asking of him. He fumbled with his hands, trying to process all that he heard. He loved his uncle. To kill someone he loved was something he could not grasp. His muscles flexed from the tension inside him. He felt warm, flushed, and imbalanced within himself.

Hanns loved his father, too. He was so troubled, so very helpless that Hanns could not leave him. He could not betray his father.

Hanns's mind triggered a memory with his uncle, Robert. It was a moment he was not meant to see or hear, but he witnessed it, nonetheless. His mind drew a picture of the scene. Hanns had just turned seventeen, and he stood outside the hall of Robert's office and heard something that struck his ear.

"He's going to betray me, Lagertha. He's slipped too far down his whirlpool of torment, and time and time again, I have reached out to save him, and every time I reach out, he does not extend his hand to reach for mine," Hanns heard his uncle say.

"Don't give up on him, Robert. He is your brother, your nephew's father. Can you imagine that boy without both his mother and his father? All the pain that Hanns holds, he would surely fall like Iscariot is now." Lagertha guided her husband in words. It was silent; neither said anything. Hanns peeked from around the corner and could see his uncle was readying a reply.

"I'm not so sure, Lagertha. I think Hanns is stronger than you think. To see his father struggle daily and to be the man he is today takes a pure heart and a mighty strong spirit. He also has more than one man who would go to pull him up should he fall like Isc. I have no doubt our children would help him to the surface should he start to drown in despair. Their light is far brighter than mine could ever be."

"I hope you're right. What are you going to do, then?" Lagertha asked.

"I will leave my hand at my chest and cease my aid to him. He must now rise on his own or fall into the sorrow of the sea. The choice has always been his, Lagertha. All I can do now is pray that he finds the current he's been searching for, that brings him back to the surface."

"And I will pray with you and for you and for Hanns," Lagertha added. "Come on, my love, or we'll be late."

Hanns was stuck. His feet could not move from where he stood. Glued, immobile, speechless he became as he saw his aunt walk out the office doorway.

"Hanns, what are you doing here?" she asked with a pleasant smile.

"I—I—" Hanns uttered.

"Hannsie, you looking for Abe and the others?" Robert walked out into the hall where Hanns stood. His mind finally unlocked for him to gather words to speak.

"No—I—I was looking for you, actually."

"Oh."

"I came over to thank you both for my birthday gift," he explained. His aunt grabbed him in a loving embrace.

"You're welcome, Hanns. You mean the world to us." She expressed her love to him.

"Don't mention it, kiddo. You're like our fourth child," Robert remarked. "Where you off to now?" Hanns didn't have an answer, still processing the conversation his aunt and uncle had.

"Hanns, are you okay?" Lagertha wondered aloud to him. He finally managed to say something: "Yeah, I was just wondering where the others were."

"I believe Aed is in the armory, and I think Lo and Abe are out shopping. Give them a call. I'm sure they'll answer," Robert informed his nephew.

"Thanks, Uncle. I'll go downstairs and see what Aed is doing," Hanns answered. He parted from his aunt and uncle, and as they split, Lagertha yelled out to him. "We love you, Hanns." Hanns turned to smile and waved to them as he turned the corner.

Hanns came to, no longer in his mind viewing the past. He saw they were at Solascnoc. The guards had just opened the gate to let them through. His knees were shaking as if they had a mind of their own, wanting to run away. He looked over at his father whose face was cold as steel and stiff as stone. There seemed to be no doubt in him, no fear in his mind. He meant to follow through with what he told Hanns.

The door of the hovercraft opened, and his father stepped out. Rattled Hanns was. He barely managed to pull the handle of the door to the vehicle. He struggled to get himself out of the hovercraft, his mind still wavering on what was right. He walked with his father and the two Leon soldiers they traveled with, through the room of seasons and into the living area, where they saw his aunt.

"Lagertha." Iscariot spoke with haste. "Where is Robert?"

"He's in his office. Is something the matter?" She seemed to know instantly that something was unusual.

"I'll explain shortly," said Iscariot as they paced off to Robert's office. Hanns saw his aunt head toward the armory but said nothing.

Through every hall they passed, Hanns was ever more uncertain of the choice he had to make. They approached the hall of kings and opened its doorway to enter. He stopped for what seemed eternity. He was dumbstruck, and the air he held within his lungs vanished from them. He could not breathe. His eyes beheld his uncle and his cousin Lorena. His mind yelled for them to run, but Hanns's tongue did not move, nor his lips to shape the words he screamed within his mind.

He did not know how, but his feet moved forward with his father. Hanns could see that Robert's eyes only looked at him.

"Iscariot, what is the matter?" Robert asked with worry. Hanns's hands were once again shaking.

"It's begun Robert. We're under attack," Iscariot told his brother.

"Where was the first strike?" Robert looked intently at Hanns and then to his daughter. "Lorena, go get your brothers," Robert instructed her. Hanns reached out to her, his hand briefly grazed her hooded shirt's pocket, trying to stop her and tell her everything, but she moved too quickly and had skirted past him.

Hanns felt a push forward; his father stepped closer to Robert. *This is it*, he thought. *What am I supposed to do?* he asked himself. *PLEASE, SOMEBODY HELP ME!* Hanns's mind went black. He saw nothing. He heard nothing. He felt nothing. He knew not where he was or even if he was. Hanns felt a deep pain in his back that seemed to travel through his heart, and then a stab he felt in the belly, in the center of his gut. The blackness he was in became red.

"So, this is your choice?" he heard a voice, not his own, ask.

"Dad!" cried another soul. It sounded of immense torment. It was a cry so heartrending, so devastatingly tragic, that it felt like a thousand knives had pierced his very spirit. With such a horrid blow, his mind came to see what his eyes and ears were telling him.

"Run!" Hanns thought the command was for him, and he turned back to where he came from and started to run.

"Hanns!" He heard his father's voice yell to him, and he stopped dead in his tracks. "Let her go," his father told him. He did not know what he meant. Hanns was lost. He was afraid and horribly confused in his trauma. He turned back to his father, and he finally saw what had transpired. His uncle lay bloody on the marble floor. He saw his dagger glistening in his uncle's back. Hanns wanted to vomit. He watched as one of the guards bent down to retrieve his blade from Robert's back. He pulled it out of his flesh and then jammed it back into his body.

"No!" Hanns lamented. He strode forward and shoved the soldier away. "Do not touch this dagger. Do not touch this man," he scolded the guard. "I'll handle this, Father."

"Finish what it is you must do," Iscariot said to him. Hanns hardened his heart. Titanium it became. He wiped his uncle's blood on the guard next to him. "Go!" he screamed at them.

"You did well, Hanns. Thank you for staying by me," his father praised him. Hanns's heart burned, inflamed, enraged—it was of great fury consumed in the fire of ire.

He was alone with his uncle. "What a terrible life to live, Uncle. It is one dreadful event after another. I was born into a world of pain and suffering, and I fear that you were wrong. No one can pull me from the darkness I fall into now. I'm not strong, Uncle. I'm weak. There is only so much agony one man can take, and this has surely pushed me past the brink. There is no return for me. Not even the light of your children can guide my ship to shore. Like my father, I will wallow in this life of sorrow. I'm sorry, Uncle. I failed you. I'm so sorry." Hanns wept over Robert's body. He sobbed until his tears ran dry. Like the pool of blood next to him, he shed a pool of tears. He was certain he'd never be able to weep again. Hanns locked his steel heart, and he dammed his eyes. He chose his path. He knew what he must do from this point forward, and he became determined to never stray from it.

Hanns turned his uncle over. He searched his pockets for any clues about the war. The only thing he found was a blank crumpled up piece of paper. He did not open it but put it in his own. He took the wedding band from Robert's finger and placed it on his own. In his solitude, it was soundless while he searched his uncle, and then without warning, shrill screams ran down his spine, and explosions concussed and set his nerves on end.

Has the war truly started? Were we too late? he asked himself. Hanns ran to the open hall that overlooked the town. He could see flames flowing all around. He could hear the sounds of guns popping bullets from their barrels. *Is this the coup? Why are people dying? Why are there bombs and gunfire?* He asked these questions, but he knew the answers. The old world must burn for the new world to flower. Even the things and people he loved must go to clear the way for better things. His mind traced back to his aunt and cousins and let his mind burn away their faces from his memory. "Goodbye," he whispered and watched the terror of the fire night bring way to a new age.

Yefimovich Chapter Five

The Yisra spring desert air swirled in the wind, and the perfumed scents of a thousand blooming flowers from the Rossija desert consumed the senses. Of hummingbird mint, blue frog sage, lemon marigold, and a bounty of others, the blooms gave the capitol city a greater essence of magical attraction as the aromas seemed to match the candied look of the buildings in Erbil. Though the smells in the air were pleasant, Yefimovich could not decipher their wonder, for every morning when he awoke, the woman who laid next him was no longer beside him, and so every morning, he would begin his day with a broken heart, and his senses had become dull.

In his bed with the shine of the sun's light bathing him, he grabbed his wife's pillow and held on to it before he rose for the day. The smell of her had vanished, but he was certain her body's scent was still there. He grieved every morning for her until he convinced himself that his moping would not be what she wanted of him. Yefimovich would remember the words she would frequently tell him of duty, of honor, to listen to the will of his heart. In her death, as in life, she willed Yefimovich to be a better man, to rid himself of self pity, to look at himself fully, and to see how utterly amazing he was, even if it was only from her eyes.

Yefimovich released the pillow he gripped and looked up toward the ceiling. He wondered how his daughter was doing. Did she struggle every morning like he did, or was her resolve stronger than his? Yefimovich assumed the latter, knowing the heart and might of his daughter. Yekaterina was his pride and joy. He feared for her, as the battle of the second Great War was about to begin. He so desperately did not want her to join the war effort but knew how selfish and silly the thought. As she was the Tulku, it was her obligation, ordained by the Maker himself. Not even he, her father, or he, the prime minister could stop her from her holy actions.

After digging through his thoughts and emotions, Yefimovich forced himself to rise. His body was consumed by water, as he let the showerhead rain upon him. He lathered in soap from head to toe and was purified. Dried, he dressed himself in Adamah attire of black boots and slacks, a green officer's jacket with gold buttons and trim, a black belt around his waist, a half cape that hung off his left shoulder with pins of honor and valor decorated upon it. Atop his head was a green cap and, on his hands, black gloves. Dressed for war, he walked out his room, and before him was Rivka.

Yefimovich was a bit startled, not expecting anyone right outside his bedroom door.

"Rivka, what is it, dear?" he asked, seeing the concerned expression on her face.

"You have a visitor, sir. He's downstairs in the tea room," Rivka told him.

"Who is it?"

"It's Doctor Drogee. He said his message is urgent."

"Thank you, Rivka," Yefimovich said as they started walking to the tea room together. "Is Kat awake?"

"No, not as of yet."

"Could you wake her for me? Whatever the news Drogee has, she should know, too," Yefimovich instructed her, and the two separated.

Down the halls and stairs, through the countless rooms, Yefimovich made his way to the tea-room. He entered, and Drogee stood to greet him with steaming tea in one hand and a tea plate in the other. Doctor Drogee realized his hands were full and placed his tea setting on the table next to him.

"Prime Minister." The doctor bowed.

"No need for ff-formalities, Drogee. Please sit back down," Yefimovich said to him. Yefimovich poured himself a cup of tea and buttered a croissant. He could see the doctor was impatient but waited respectfully for Yefimovich until he couldn't any longer.

"Sir, the news I have is urgent."

"Then tell it. Like I said, no need for ff-formalities," Yefimovich stuttered, never able to fully stop his impediment when the same characters followed in sequence with one another.

"Well, as you'd probably expect, it's about Viktoriya, sir," the doctor began. Yefimovich took his seat across from him. "As I told you a few months ago, we believed her death to be of foul play. After exhausting all tests, we confirmed your wife was poisoned." Yefimovich leaned forward, highly interested. He heard nothing around him but the words that left the doctor's mouth.

"The poison comes from an extremely rare plant. Its properties, when used as a poison, are practically untraceable, and given your wife's illnesses over the past year, it made this diagnosis even more difficult. It actually isn't the plant itself but the parasite that can live on the plant. The plant is called Eielah Unkahgah, meaning the dead devil." The doctor was detailed in his description. Yefimovich was paralyzed by the news. His mind went back to his trip to the Heavohen Islands. He envisioned every meal they had on every island they traveled on. The doctor continued as Yefimovich searched his brain.

"It acts slowly over a week or two with flu- and cold-like symptoms," the doctor began again, but was interrupted by the voice of Yekaterina.

"They killed her. Didn't they, Papa?" Yefimovich did not answer, for he did not hear his daughter. "Papa." Katerina was kneeling at his side. "That night, with the fox. I've been thinking about it every night before I go to sleep. The wine, Papa. Mom was the only one to drink it."

Yefimovich peered into his daughter's brown eyes, *It was true*, he thought, *How could I have missed it?* Yefimovich turned to face Drogee.

"You're certain. I-If what you say it true," Yefimovich started.

"It means the Islands lied and could be aiding Holle." Katerina finished her father's thought.

"What time is it?" Yefimovich asked.

"Seven in the morning," Katerina replied.

"The dead of night in Saoirse. We must contact Robert and let him know," Yefimovich informed the room.

"What about Tokugawa?" his daughter questioned him.

"I'll contact him when I-I land in Arpa. Robert's troops are set to travel as we speak," he explained. "Kat, go and ready for the day. I need to talk to you b-before I leave."

"Yes, Papa," she responded and left the tea room with Rivka.

"Doctor. Thank you again for everything." Yefimovich expressed his gratitude.

"I'm only sorry I couldn't do more."

"You've done plenty. I'll walk you out." Yefimovich guided him to the exit and waved goodbye to Drogee.

Yefimovich quickly headed to his office to contact Robert. He dialed out, and an aide received the call. He informed the aide with minor details that an audience with Robert was paramount.

"I understand, sir, but the king is unavailable at the moment. I promise I'll let him know as soon as he is free." The aide countered Yefimovich's urgency.

"Damn it, child. If I don't hear back with-within the hour, I promise, you'll be sorry." Yefimovich ended the call with a threat. He then tried calling Robert directly on his personal line. However, he did not answer the call. He hesitated a moment to call Lagertha, but quickly concluded that the matter was of utmost importance, but like Robert's call, she did not answer. "Damn it!" he yelled in frustration. He paced with the three stones now floating in his hands, as he tried to decide on what to do, only to conclude that he had to continue his course and go on with what was planned.

A soft knock tapped the doorframe of the office. "What did King Robert say?" Katerina asked.

"I could not reach him. I-I only got his pain in the ass aide." He spoke furiously.

"Let's hope we hear something soon."

"I think we'll need a lot of hope in the days and months ahead."

He walked up to his daughter. *So smart and beautiful and filled with talent*, he thought as he looked upon her. "When I leave Sesom Palace today, you are in charge. You, my sweet child, are the commander-in-chief."

"But, Papa. I'm not the prima," Yekaterina invoked.

"Kat. The council members and I, we, we had a private meeting and secretly voted on this. Should anything happen to me, you would be the nation's leader," he disclosed to her.

"Papa." She seemed not to know what to say.

"The people trust you, Kat. The people love you, my dear. Whether you wanted it or not, you are b-born a leader. I know the weight of it is heavy, but you are strong, and I know you are so very brave." He spoke with strong emotions and could see his daughter wanted to cry, for she knew he headed towards danger. "I wrote this long ago and waited for the moment to give this to you." Yefimovich handed her a letter. "And here, I want you to have this as well."

"I can't take this, Papa. It was from Heilagr to you. You'll need it where you're going," she refused. "Please, Papa. Keep it. I have all I need. You made sure of that since the day I was born."

"On my return, then." Yefimovich smiled at his daughter.

"I love you, Papa." She clutched him mightily as if she never intended to let go.

"I love you so very much—my dear, Kat." Yefimovich struggled to let her go, just as she did him, until a small voice rang in the room.

"Excuse me, sir," said Rivka. "Aero is here for you. He says the Orbital One is ready." She looked embarrassed. Yefimovich released his hold, as did his daughter, and he embraced Rivka.

"Thank you, Rivka. Look after my daughter."

"Yes, sir," she replied. Yefimovich tuned back to his daughter and smiled, and her beam returned to him.

"Goodbye, Kat."

"Goodbye, Papa," she spoke, holding back tears, and Yefimovich left the room.

As he walked to the front of the palace, he was stopped abruptly. Nearly startled, Commander Zash spoke with haste and utmost intent. The look on his face was calm but gave clues of tremendous concern.

"Commander, what is the matter? You don't look yourself," Yefimovich asked sincerely.

"Yef," The commander began, and immediately Yefimovich found something off as Zash never called him by that name. "Holle, sir. They are on the move."

"Has General Iri been contacted? Has Polsha called for aid?" Yefimovich asked, cursing them and their neutrality stance.

"The information comes from Iri's men, sir," Zash notified his prime minister.

"Tell him I'm on my way and to be ready to take offensive."

"Godspeed, sir." Zash saluted him.

"Shalom, Commander." Yefimovich departed from his friend, twirling the stones that floated around his hand even faster, and as he approached the palace doors, he formed them into a staff and slammed it onto the floor, gripping the handle tightly, causing a boom to echo throughout the halls.

Aero stood before him. "Prime Minister," the airman greeted him.

"Ready, old sport?"

"Ready and waiting."

"Wait no more, then. Let's go," Yefimovich commanded, moving forward toward the Orbital One. He began to think of the last time he was on this craft. He hated taking orbital flights. As beautiful as it was to see the curvature of the earth, he always felt uneasy. It was the silence that bothered him. He recalled in his memory bank his last flight. It was with his wife, coming back home from Saoirse. He had been reading a book by Thomas Wolfe. He always fancied his magic with a pen, and he remembered the soft hand of his wife. Whenever they flew together, her soothing delicate hand made him feel at ease, and the gaze into her eyes made him feel at home. He always thought them more beautiful than the view of the earth from space. In his reminiscing, he felt melancholic and desperately missed the sight of his wife.

He boarded the orbital craft and strapped himself in. "Are you sure you don't want to take the vetervykl?" Aero asked at the last minute.

"T-time is of the essence. I-I don't think my nerves be of concern," Yefimovich responded, molding the stone staff like clay in his hand, holding it with great strength. "Let's get this over with—shall we?"

"You said it, sir."

The sand of the desert floated unnaturally in the air around the space vehicle, a deep bass that transmogrified to a shallow frequency, and a mechanized sound filled his ears. It quickly became deafeningly silent, and in an instant, the vehicle lashed the air around it, ascending to the heavens, shattering the sound barrier mere feet from the surface of the earth. Yefimovich closed his eyes and tried to control his breathing, squeezing the stone in his hand as ferocious as ever, until finally, the craft floated in the vacuum of space. His reprieve was short-lived as he opened his eyes to take in the earth one last time. He made sure to capture in his mind the browns and greens and blues of God's great work before the only shade became of reds. Yefimovich closed his eyes again, feeling the descent of the craft about to begin.

The Orbital One whirred like running cold water from a faucet at full speed, crashing onto a burning hot plate. The resistance to the air meeting the shuttle was like a rapid drumroll of bedsheets being whipped and laid across the bed. Yefimovich tightened his eyes, as if it would somehow help. The ship decelerated, and the cabin pressure released, but, as always, the speed of Yefimovich's heart beat with rapid tenacity, tapping his ribs like a stick across a xylophone. Perspiration secreted from the hairline of Yefimovich. His hand still gripped tightly the stone he molded in his hand, and he told himself to calm and relax his muscles. "Steady your heart," he whispered to himself. Yefimovich finally opened his eyes and looked at the hand that held the stones, and he laughed, for he formed the rocks into a hand, one he held countless times, and of which he seemed to have memorized every detail.

"Still holding your wife's hand, I see." Aero poked fun at him.

"I-it would appear so, wouldn't it?" He laughed from nerves of the flight or jitters of battle or just his own silliness. He could not tell.

Yefimovich waited for his heart to slow before he unfastened himself from the seat he sat in. The door of the Orbital One opened to the world. Two of the three pilots exited the vehicle; only Aero stayed behind. He knelt down by Yefimovich.

"Ready sir?" he asked. "General Iri is waiting outside." Yefimovich inhaled deeply.

"I'm ready," he confirmed, standing from his seat. "Let's go." He let Aero lead the way and walked out into the early rays of the sun in the country of Arpa.

"Prime Minister." Iri looked eager to speak.

"General. Have Holle started their attack?" Yefimovich asked in his greeting.

"They have, sir. Polsha has requested our aid," Iri briefed him.

"Those fools. Have we supplied them?"

"I have men engaging now."

"What city? I'm going to assist."

"Aid is needed at the town of Plock along the river. Lodz, I have men going to, now. Radom is well fortified. Polsha leaders are sending some men to Pulawy River for aid," Iri detailed.

"You have a hundred Ada troops for me—on standby?" Yefimovich asked.

"Yes, sir."

"T-tell them to get ready. We leave in ten minutes."

"Yes, sir." Iri gave a quick salute and went to his men to give them their orders.

The sun began to bake the sands of Arpa, though the hour was still early. Yefimovich waited for his men to arrive in the desert's heat, and quickly, they were upon him. A hundred Adamah soldiers stood before him, all willing to fight, all willing to die. All together for the same purpose, under the umbrella of God and country, brave men and women awaited Yefimovich's word.

They formed themselves in an orderly fashion in ten rows of ten, each according to their rank within their group. It was quiet. There was no desert wind, no annoying insect crying in the heat, no buzzers buzzing from high in the sky. Yefimovich looked at the troops before him.

"Let us pray," he finally spoke. His words set the tense battalion at repose. Yefimovich spoke in a cadence so as not to stutter.

"Our Holy God, / please / forgive our trespasses / for we call / upon your ear / to ask a troublesome favor. / Our Lord, / before you / are one hundred courageous men / and women / who call upon you / and ask for your protection. / They call for / the glory of your shield. / They call for / the might of your sword. / They call for your courage / in the face of evil. / They call for your resolve / in the face of adversity, / and they call for your love / in this life / and the next. /

"Father, / today we go to war. / Today, we fight an enemy / that has soiled your name, / that has terrorized our nation, / that seeks to bring evil to the world. / Almighty, help us fight an enemy today / so that we can find a friend in them / tomorrow. / Let this truly be / the war to end all wars / so that peace and prosperity / reign upon your people. / In your name we pray! Amen!" Yefimovich raised his head to the sky and whispered in the wind to carry his words to God.

"Protect my child, oh Lord. I-I shall surely miss her all the days that I am gone." He looked back at the soldiers in front of him and spoke to them.

"Let us wander the desert. / Let us storm the capitol. / Let us rain terror into their hearts. / Let us make them wish / that they never spoke war with Yisra. / Let us show them our might, / even when our hands are blistered, / when our feet are sore, / when our minds are tired, / through the darkness of night / and in the shine of day. / Let us fight / until peace is attained. / And when this war is over, / either by death / or by victory, / we can go home / with heads held high / and bear fruit for our Lord forever after!" Yefimovich gave an impassioned roar, and the men who looked to him roared back tremendously.

Yefimovich raised himself up by pushing the sand beneath his feet skyward. "To Polsha!" he exclaimed, and with the power of his mind and body, he pushed the sand to propel him forward. It was as if he surfed on water. He moved with haste, and his men followed.

Yefimovich and his men moved at great speed. They were a sandstorm ready to stop the threat of the enemy, prepared to blot out the wicked, to clear away the troubles of the land and settle the fight until their storm was vanquished.

The time was a quarter after seven in the city of Plock, and Yefimovich could finally see the tragedy before him. It was what he feared all those times he was in the sky looking down onto the planet. Red was the color of the land; black was the color of the air. It was a vision where hope was hard to find, where brutality and cruelty conquered, and the worst of man's deeds surfaced from the depths of their sinful souls. The scene drew him back to the Great War, nearly twenty years ago. Much younger he was then, the war the same. He remembered his first battle of the Great War. Scared he was, as he was now, but just as the war of the past, he had everything to fight for. The only difference between then and now was that, then, he was fighting for a country to call his home, and today, he fought for the country that was his home. All the feelings of the past war came rushing back to him—the buzzing nerves, the doubt of hope, the sickness of the smell of death.

He blew away the thoughts and feelings of his past and let faith employ him. His jitters halted, and hope crawled back into his heart. Yefimovich found the major in charge of the Polsha squadron. They quickly formulated a counterattack to push themselves in front of the river and drive the enemy back, so come tomorrow, they would have a tactical advantage.

Thirty minutes lost, but the major and Yefimovich built a plan to fight the Hollen force. He would split his Adamah men on the right and left of the encroaching force and pincer them toward the Polsha Army, until one by one, they perished or surrendered. There would be no escape for the Hollen troops.

Yefimovich gave the order to his men, and they quickly acted to combat the enemy. Skating on the rocks and the dirt of the earth, they blitzed forward. The first battle of the second great war was about to begin, and Yefimovich led the charge. A steal spine, an armored heart, an unprotected body—he pushed forward gallantly so that when his men turned to him in the anguish of battle, they could see, if only the slightest amount, sanguinity, when all seemed lost.

Yefimovich gave the signal to halt. They had reached their destination. He reiterated what needed to be done and how to move forward. His men waited for his command to fight. Yefimovich checked once more his surroundings. They were just outside the city in a forest of trees. A bridge lay to his right, and the river was in front of him about a mile out. Directly east, past the bridge, was castle Zamek, and he knew the second squad was near the castle's eastern wall. His communicator confirmed their position. The Hollen Army lay between the two squadrons. Some of the enemy soldiers still crossed the bridge. He looked out over his men again.

"Ready?" he asked them, and all fifty gave the okay signal, touching index finger to thumb to form the letter O, and the three outstanding fingers to signify the K. Yefimovich raised his hand with his index and middle finger pointing skyward, and then directed it forward. He and his men rushed the Hollen Army.

Yefimovich could see the enemy was taken by surprise. He coasted toward them, shifting the earth about his feet. He rocketed himself toward the sky, and with him a boulder he cultivated from the ground, fifteen feet tall and twenty feet wide, lingered over his head. Both hands were over his head, his arms extended. It was as if the boulder were held by a pull-string, ready to be released. Yefimovich brought his clutched hands down as if swinging an axe, and the boulder hurtled to the ground. Of the thousand Hollen foes, he extinguished fifteen in one fell swoop.

Yefimovich was now arm's distance with the enemy, and hand-to-hand combat ensued. Surrounded by five men, he took them on at once. With the stomp of his right foot, he summoned a column of dirt from the earth, launching the men he faced twenty feet into the air while simultaneously taking the three stones he frequently played with and formed them into a spear. He turned to his backside and heaved it at the enemy's head, striking his skull. Three men left, two charged at him from opposite directions, prepared to skewer him with their blades. As the two men began to strike, Yefimovich let the earth consume him, sinking into the ground. The two Hollen soldiers pierced one another, ending their lives. One remained, and from the dirt and clay and stone, Yefimovich reached out from the underground, grabbing the enemy's leg, pulling him down and burying his body, letting the earth crush his bones.

War is not beautiful nor poetic. There is no romance when trying to preserve one's own life. There is only the moment of battle when one struggles to cling on to life, to keep bearing its fruits. The only love in war is when one can look back after fighting and be grateful for the ones that saved him in the harshness of battle. To look back and be humbled by those who would risk their own lives for the sake of another, not out of duty, but out of the boldness of one's heart, so consumed with love for their comrade that they seek to put themselves in harm's way for the person they call their brother in arms. This act is the definition of selflessness, and is bred from love. People have deemed this action with such regard, with the highest standard for the greatness of the human condition, that man created a word for such a noble action. Heroism, his eyes beheld. In every man and woman he saw fighting next to him there was not one who did not deserve its title.

The feud of armies continued, and slowly, Yefimovich and the Polshan Army pushed the Hollen force back until they signaled a full retreat. Alas, a reprieve—a break from the illness of war and the pain it brings. However, a new battle ensued—the calm after combat, a contest to keep one's sanity after reflecting on what actions they took and what sights they saw. The struggle of one's emotions in the steadiness of inaction was just as difficult as the fight itself. Faces of childhood friends and fierce bonds through training now lay still and without life, some without limbs or flesh. The pain of seeing a comrade you loved now gone from the world—it is the wound that is hardest to heal. Sometimes time itself fails to remedy the cuts of the human spirit.

The spring season sprung the sun ever higher. The trees and flowers blossomed as they took in the nutrients of its rays and the sustenance of the earth's soil and the air that men breathed. Refortified the base became. The castle stood strong behind Yefimovich. Twenty of his men and a hundred Polshan soldiers now occupied the stronghold. While he and seventy other Adamah soldiers, along with fifty Polshan troops, stood steadfast in front of the river and prepared for the next attack.

In the lull, Yefimovich activated his communicator to contact General Iri. He dialed out and was received.

"Iri—" he greeted him.

"Prime Minister." Iri greeted him back, his tone slightly rattled.

"What is it?" Yefimovich asked, sensing something was off with the general.

"Sir, I have some grave news. It is not easy to tell you this."

"Tell me."

"King Robert, sir." Yefimovich's eyes widened. "He's passed, sir." Flabbergasted, his chest tightened, overcome with immense heartache.

Surely my ears must deceive me, he thought. *A dream this must be*, he tried to trick himself.

"What co-co-confirmation do we have? H-How do we know this? Is th-th-this misinformation from the enemy?" His stutter grew worse as he spoke.

"There has been a coup, sir. Confirmed by Lorena Darroch herself," Iri informed him. *That poor child.* Yefimovich's heart had sunken deep in dolor.

"Do we know how? Who-who lead the coup?"

"It was his brother, sir."

"Do his men still travel toward Holle?" he asked with a suffering heart, distressed from the news. His stutter vanished in his melancholy.

"We do not know. I'm so very sorry, Prime Minister." Iri expressed his heartfelt condolences.

"Excuse me, Prime Minister." A voice from behind him called out.

"Thank you, Iri. I'll talk to you soon." Yefimovich ended the call with his general and turned to the voice behind him. It was the major that stood in front of him.

"Yes, Major."

"The second wave, sir. They approach. The force is tripled." His expression was that of panic.

"Prepare your men. I'll call for reinforcements," Yefimovich instructed. He flipped the communicator and called upon General Iri once more.

"Prime Minister." Iri spoke with a bit of shock.

"Th-three thousand men approach us. This will be my last transmission to you."

"Sir," Iri started to interrupt, only for Yefimovich to keep him from doing so. "Iri," he said with force. "The call is yours. To send reinforcements or to fight another day. Should I die, and this be my last stand, tell my daughter, I love her."

"I will, sir."

"I'm sending one of our soldiers to you with an item. It-it is a ring for my daughter. Goodbye, Iri," he said as he ended the call.

"Goodbye, sir," Iri uttered back. Yefimovich walked out in front of his soldiers and the soldiers of Polsha, and he began to speak.

"Men!" he shouted. "Ready your hearts, for the foe approaches. Reinforcements are on the way. When the enemy comes, we will not retreat! Here, we stand! Here, we fight! Fill your heart with the Lord. Trust in your comrade, and together, we will see a new day." Yefimovich roused the men and women that fought with him.

No quicker did he end his last word, then the first shots of the second battle ensued. Steadily, his men and the men of the Polshan army dwindled. They stood for an hour, and the 240 men fell to fifty. Yefimovich and the forty-nine others fell back to the castle on the other side of the river. He now knew no reinforcements were coming. He looked on at the battered and beaten men. There was no resolve left, and he knew he needed to uplift them should this be their final moments. Before he could beckon a word, a shriek of spine tingling malice overtook the body in a dreadful fear.

Yefimovich looked up to the sky and bore witness to a monster. 'Twas red and brown and black with wings that covered the sun. Its eyes were as if they held all of men's hatred, and it was the bearer to unleash it. The creature's teeth were frightful tangled swords, its claws jet black and that of splintered agony should man dare to touch them.

Sitting on the back of the beast was an armored Hollen man who matched the horror of the animal he rode. His armor was of metal thorns—from bootstrap to helm he was guarded in it. The opening of his helmet looked like the splitting of branches from a tree, and its opening was devoid of color, a haunting blackness. Clutched in his hand was a double bladed scythe that was taller than he.

Yefimovich looked back at the men and women that fought alongside him. He knew no words could bring them to action in the face of such trembling evil. 'Twas only action that could surface their light.

With tremendous strength and will, he created a tsunami of rocks and dirt and all the minerals of the earth and hurled it at the enemy, drowning 500 Hollen souls to their death. Exhausted, he willed himself to find strength to face the heathen that searched the sky in flames. Yefimovich waited for the dragon to fly closer to where he stood. He inhaled deeply, and like a bullet in a gun, he shot himself to the bands of the earth to meet the devil in the clouds. A colonnade of earth was the hammer that launched him to greet his enemy.

Using the stones he always had at his side, he formed a sickle and hooked himself onto the scaled beast. His adversary turned to face him, and as Yefimovich stood to meet the challenge, he was tackled by the rider, and they plummeted to the earth. Bonded they were like a bundle of branches; they fell from the sky like a comet burning down to earth from the vast unknown space of the universe. Their impact cratered the landscape. It trembled the planet. It shocked the air, which gave a resounding concussion in its exclamatory explosion.

Yefimovich could not move, though his mind called his muscles to do so.

"This is the end for you, Hero of the Great War." His voice was haunting behind the frightfulness of his mask.

"Who are you?" Yefimovich spoke with blood oozing from his mouth.

"I am Almaut Bin Hidler, Reaper of the Heavens, son of Alamgeer, and your enemy," he answered in a low petrifying tone.

"And that, that you ride?"

"A gorlab, the Great Shadow."

"A dragon!" Yefimovich said the words in disbelief.

"Of sorts, but nothing you need worry of any longer. A shame you were not at your strongest. I so longed to fight you. Though you are my enemy, your name holds high regard. You fought well, Yefimovich." Almaut held high his scythe, and cast it down unto Yefimovich's body.

The air of God's breath that filled his lungs was no more. His soul escaped him as his blood fell into the earth, and his spirit flew home to the heaven that awaited him above.